BARBARA DELINSKY

A COLLECTION

Born and raised in suburban Boston, **Barbara Delinsky** worked as a researcher, photographer and reporter before turning to writing full time in 1980. Now, with more than 50 novels to her name and over 16 million copies in print, she is one of today's quintessential authors of contemporary romance fiction. This talented author has received numerous awards and honours and her name frequently appears on bestseller lists around the world. Her string of successful novels include *Finger Prints*, *Within Reach*, *Twilight Whispers*, *More Than Friends* and *Suddenly*.

Worldwide Books are proud to bring back three of this outstanding author's previous books with *A Collection*. Vintage Delinsky, this special volume offers fans a unique chance to sample some of her earlier works.

CONTENTS:

The Real Thing

Twelve Across

A Single Rose

THE REAL THING

BY

BARBARA DELINSKY

WORLDWIDE BOOKS

LONDON • SYDNEY • TORONTO

All the characters in this book have no existence outside the imagination of the Author, and have no relation whatsoever to anyone bearing the same name or names. They are not even distantly inspired by any individual known or unknown to the Author, and all the incidents are pure invention.

First published in Great Britain in 1987
Reprinted in Great Britain in 1994
by Worldwide Books, Eton House,
18-24 Paradise Road, Richmond, Surrey TW9 1SR

ISBN 0 373 59316 3

99-9409

Printed in Great Britain by
BPC Paperbacks Ltd

1

IT WASN'T EARTH-SHATTERING in the overall scheme of things. Nor was it unexpected. Yet coming as it did topping six weeks worth of unpleasantness, it was the final straw.

Neil Hersey glared out the window of his office. He saw neither Constitution Plaza below him, nor anything else of downtown Hartford. The anger that blinded him would have spilled into his voice had not frustration already staked its claim there.

"Okay, Bob. Let me have it. We've been friends for too long to beat around the bush." He kept his fists anchored in the pockets of his tailored slacks. "It's not just a question of preferring someone else. We both know I'm as qualified for the job as any man. And we both know that Ryoden's been courting me for the past year. For some reason there's been an eleventh-hour reversal." Very slowly he turned. "I have my suspicions. Confirm them."

Robert Balkan, executive vice president of the Ryoden Manufacturing conglomerate, eyed the ramrod-straight figure across from him. He and Neil Hersey went back a long way. Their friendship was based on mutual admiration and genuine affection, and Bob respected Neil far too much to lie.

"Word came directly from Wittnauer-Douglass," he stated defeatedly. "Your release as corporate counsel there was a compassionate move. It was either let you go or bring you to trial."

Neil swore softly and bowed his head. "Go on."

"They alleged you were responsible for some transactions that were unethical, some that were downright illegal. For your own protection, the details remain private. The corporation is taking internal measures to counter the damage."

"I'll bet."

"What can I say, Neil? The charge was totally unsubstantiated, but it was enough to get the chairman of our board up in arms. One word in the old coot's ear and it became a crusade with him. Someone at Wittnauer-Douglass knew exactly what he was doing when he made that call. Then Ned Fallenworth got in on the act and that was that."

Fallenworth was the president of Ryoden. Bob had had reason to regret that fact in the past, but never as vehemently as he did now. "I've been spitting bullets since Ned gave me his decision. Ned's always been a coward, and what he's doing is a sad reflection on Ryoden. I gave it all I had, but his mind was closed. Narrow minds, Neil. That's what we're dealing with. Narrow minds."

Neil deliberately unclenched his jaw. "Narrow minds with a hell of a lot of power" was his own bleak assessment of the situation.

Leaving the window, he prowled the room, moving from parquet floor to Oriental rug and back, continuing the circle until he reached his gleaming mahogany desk. He leaned against the edge, his long legs extended and crossed at the ankles. His arms were folded over his chest. The pose might have been one of casual confidence under other circumstances. "Six weeks, Bob," he gritted. "This hell's being going on for six weeks. I'm being blackballed and it's touched every blessed aspect of my life. Something's got to give!"

"Do you need money? If it's a question of finances, I'd be glad to—"

"No, no." Neil waved aside the suggestion, then gentled his expression into a half smile of thanks. "Money's no problem. Not for now, at least." With the measured breath he took, the remnants of his half smile vanished. "The way things stand, though," he resumed, unable to stem his irritation, "my future as a lawyer in this town is just about nil, which is exactly what Wittnauer-Douglass intended."

"I think you should sue."

"Are you kidding?" Straightening his arms, he gripped the edge of the desk on either side of his lean hips. "Listen, I appreciate your vote of confidence, but you don't know that company as I do. A, they'd cover everything up. B, they'd drag the proceedings on so long that I would run out of money. C, *regardless* of the outcome, they'd make such a public issue of a suit that what little is left of my reputation would be shot to hell in the process. We're talking piranhas here, Bob."

"So why did you represent them?"

"Because I didn't *know*, damn it!" His shoulders slumped. "And that's the worst of it, I think. I just . . . didn't . . . know." His gaze skittered to the floor, dark brows lowered to hide his expression of deep self-dismay.

"You're human. Like the rest of us."

"Not much by way of encouragement."

Bob rose. "I wish I could do more."

"But you've done what you came to do and it's time to leave." Neil heard the bitterness in his voice; and while he detested it, he couldn't bring himself to apologize.

"I have an appointment at three." Bob's tone verged on apologetic, and Neil was quickly wary. He'd witnessed six weeks of defections, of so-called friends falling by the wayside.

Testing the waters, he extended his hand. "I haven't seen Julie in months. Let's meet for dinner sometime soon?"

"Sure thing," Bob said, smiling a little too broadly as the two shook hands.

Bob was relieved, Neil mused. The dirty work was done. And a "sure thing" for dinner was as noncommittal as Neil had feared it might be.

Moments later he was alone with an anger that approached explosive levels. Slumping into the mate of the chair Bob had just left, he pressed a finger to the crease in the center of his forehead and rubbed up and down. His head was splitting; he had to keep it together somehow. But how to remain sane when everything else was falling apart . . . Where was justice? Where in the hell was the justice in life?

Okay, he could understand why his working relationship with Wittnauer-Douglass would be severed after the abysmal scene six weeks ago. There had been, and was a difference of opinion. A rather drastic difference of opinion. He wouldn't have wanted to continue serving as counsel for the corporation any more than they'd wanted him to. But should he be punished this way?

His entire life was twisted. Damn it, it wasn't right!

Okay, so he'd lost Ryoden. He could have lived with that if it hadn't been for the fact that he'd also lost three other major clients in as many weeks. He was being blackballed within the corporate community. How the hell could he counter it, when the enemy was so much larger, so much more powerful?

He took several slow, measured breaths, opened his eyes and looked around the office. Ceiling-high mahogany bookshelves filled with legal tomes; an impressive collection of diplomas and brass-framed citations; a state-of-the-art telephone system linking him to his secretary and the world beyond; a credenza filled with important forms and personal papers—all worthless. What counted was in his head. But if he couldn't practice law his mind was worthless, too; it was hammering at his skull now, hammering mercilessly.

Neil Hersey had never felt so furious, so bitter—so utterly helpless—in his entire life. He knew that something had to be done, and that he was the one who was going to have to do it. For the life of him, though, he didn't know what action to take. His thoughts were mired in that fury and bitterness. He couldn't think clearly.

Muttering a dark oath, he bolted from his seat. He needed a break, a change of scenery. More than anything at the moment, he needed out.

Rounding the desk, he snatched his personal phone book from the top right-hand drawer and flipped to the *Ls*. Landry. Lazuk. Lee. Lesser. He set the book down, marking the place with his finger. Lesser. Victoria Lesser. Within seconds he'd punched out the number that would connect him with the stylish Park Avenue co-op high above the hustle of Manhattan.

A very proper maid answered. "Lesser residence."

"This is Neil Hersey. Is Mrs. Lesser in?"

"Please hold the phone."

Neil waited, tapping his foot impatiently. He massaged the throbbing spot on his forehead. He squeezed his eyes shut. Only when he pictured Victoria breezing toward the phone—wending her way through the most elegant of furnishings while, very likely, wearing jeans and an oversized work shirt—did he give a small smile.

Victoria Lesser was a character. Thanks to the husband she'd worshipped until his death six years earlier, she was extremely wealthy and influential. She was also a nonconformist, which was what Neil adored about her. Though never outrageous, she did what she wanted, thumbing her nose at the concept of a staid and proper fifty-two-year-old widow. She traveled. She entertained. She took up ballet dancing. She fantasized herself a painter. She was interesting and refreshing and generous to the core.

It was that generosity Neil was counting on.

"Neil Hersey... fine friend you are!" A good-natured tirade burst from the other end of the line. "Do you know how long it's been since I've heard from you? It's been months! *Months!*"

"I know, Victoria. And I'm sorry. How are you?"

"How I am is beside the point," Victoria said more softly. "The question is, how are *you*?"

Neil hadn't been sure how far word had spread, but he should have realized Victoria would have heard. The mutual friend through which they'd originally met was an executive at Wittnauer-Douglass.

"You're speaking to me," he answered cautiously, "which makes me feel better already."

"Of course I'm speaking to you. I know what happened there, Neil. I know that board of directors. That is, I know how to recognize snakes. I also know what kind of lawyer you are—I haven't forgotten what you did for my niece—and I know the bind you're in right now."

"Then you know I need to get away." He broached the topic quickly. He was in no mood, even with Victoria, to pussyfoot around. "I can't think here. I'm too angry. I need peace and quiet. And seclusion."

"Something like a remote and uninhabited island off the coast of Maine?"

Neil's mouth lifted slightly at the corners. "Something like that."

"It's yours."

"No one's there?"

"In October?" She snorted. "People nowadays are sissies. Once Labor Day's passed, you'd think going north to an island was tantamount to exploring the Arctic. It's yours, Neil, for as long as you want it."

"Two weeks should do it. If I can't come up with some solutions by then . . ." There wasn't much more he could say.

"You haven't called me before, and knowing you, you'll want to work this out for yourself. But if there's anything I can do, will you let me know?"

Neil found solace in her words. She had the courage that others lacked. Not only was she unswayed by smear tactics, she would root for the underdog any day. "Use of the island is more than enough," he said gratefully.

"When were you thinking of going?"

"As soon as possible. Tomorrow, I guess. But you'll have to tell me how to get there."

Victoria did so. "Once you get to Spruce Head, ask for Thomas Nye. Big fellow. Bushy red beard. He lobsters from there. I'll call ahead and alert him. He'll take you out to the island."

With brief but heartfelt thanks, plus a promise to call her when he returned, Neil hung up the phone. He spent the rest of the afternoon working with his secretary to clear his calendar for the next two weeks. It was a relatively easy feat, given the amount of work he'd recently lost. He met in turn with each of his two young associates, giving them enough direction to keep them marginally occupied during his absence.

For the first time in his memory, when he left the office his briefcase remained behind. He carried nothing more than a handful of Havana cigars.

If he was going to escape it all, he decided belligerently, he'd go all the way.

DEIRDRE JOYCE glowered at the thick white cast that sheathed her left leg from thigh to toe. It was a diversionary tactic. If she looked into the urgent faces that circled her hospital bed, she was sure she'd explode.

"It was an act of fate, Deirdre," her mother was saying. "A message. I've been trying to get it across for months now, but you've refused to listen, so someone higher up is spelling it out. Your place is in the business with your sister, not teaching aerobics."

"My teaching aerobics had nothing to do with this, Mother," Deirdre declared. "I tripped on the stairs in my own town house. I fell. I broke my leg. I don't see any message there, except that I was careless. I left a magazine where it shouldn't have been and slipped on it. It could as easily have been *Forbes* as *Runner's World*."

"The message," Maria Joyce went on, undaunted, "is that physical fitness will only get you so far. For heaven's sake, Deirdre, you'll be sidelined for weeks. You can't teach your precious dance even if you want to. What better time is there to help Sandra out?"

Deirdre looked at her sister then. Once upon a time she'd have felt compassion for her, but that was before six months of nonstop pressure had taken its toll. "I'm sorry, Sandra. I can't."

"Why not, Dee?" Tall and dark-haired, Sandra took after their mother, while Deirdre was more fair and petite. She had been different from the start. "You have the same education I do, the same qualifications," Sandra pressed.

"I don't have the temperament. I never did."

Maria was scowling. "Temperament has nothing to do with it. You decided early on that you preferred to take the easy way out. Well, you have, and look where it's gotten you."

"Mother..." Deirdre closed her eyes and sank deeper into the pillows. Four days of confinement in a bed had left her weak, and that annoyed her. It had also left her craving a hot shower, but that was out of the question. To say that she was testy was putting it mildly.

Her voice was quiet, but there was clear conviction in her words. "We've been through this a hundred times. You and Dad may have shared the dream of a family corporation, but it's your dream, not mine. I don't want it. I'm not suited for it. It's too structured, too demanding. I gave it a try once and it was a disaster."

"Eight months," Maria argued, "years ago."

"Your mother's right, Deirdre." The deep, slightly gravelly voice belonged to Deirdre's uncle. He had been standing, silent and innocuous up to that point, at the foot of the bed. "You'd only just graduated from college, but even then you showed potential. You're a doer, like your father, but you were young and you let things overwhelm you. You left too soon. You didn't give it a fair shot."

Deirdre shook her head. "I knew myself then," she insisted, scrunching folds of the coarse white sheet between tense fingers, "and I know myself now. I'm not cut out for the business world. Having a technical aptitude for business is one thing. Maybe I do have that. But emotionally—what with board meetings, conferences, three-martini lunches, client dinners, being constantly *on*—I'd go stark raving mad!"

"You're being melodramatic," her mother scoffed.

"Right. That's the way I am, and there's no place for melodrama in Joyce Enterprises. So please," she begged, "please leave me out of it."

Sandra took a step closer. "We need you, Dee. *I* need you. Do you think I'm any more suited to heading a corporation than you are?"

"At least you want to do it."

"Whether I do or not is irrelevant. Things have been a mess since Dad died."

Since Dad died. That was the crux of it. Six months before, Allan Joyce had died in his sleep, never knowing that what he'd done so peacefully had created utter havoc.

Deirdre closed her eyes. "I think this conversation's going nowhere," she stated quietly. "The only reason things have been a mess since Dad died is that not one of you—of us—has the overall vision necessary to head a corporation. What Joyce Enterprises needs is outside help. It's as simple as that."

"We're a family-run company—" her mother began, only to stop short when Deirdre's eyes flew open, flashing.

"And we've run out of family. You can't run a business, Mother. Apparently neither can Sandra. Uncle Peter is as helpless as Uncle Max, and I'm the only one who's willing to acknowledge that the time has come for a change." She gave an exasperated sigh. "What astounds me most is that the corporation is still functioning. It's been running itself, coasting along on Dad's momentum. But without direction it's only a matter of time before it grinds to a halt. *Sell it,* Mother. And if you won't do that, hire a president and several vice presidents and—"

"We have a president and several vice presidents," Maria informed her unnecessarily. "What we lack is someone to coordinate things. You're the organizer. You're what we need. You're the one who's put together all kinds of functions."

"Charity functions, Mother. One, maybe two, a year. Benefit road races and sports days," she replied wearily. "We're not talking heavy business here."

"You're your father's daughter."

"I'm not my father."

"But still—"

"Mother, I have a wicked headache and you're not helping. Uncle Peter, will you please take Mother home?"

Maria held her ground. "Now just a minute, Deirdre. I won't be dismissed. You're being selfish. You've always put your own needs first. Don't you have any sense of responsibility toward this family?"

The guilt trip. It had been inevitable. "I'm not up to this," Deirdre moaned.

"Fine." Maria straightened. "Then we'll discuss it tomorrow. You're being discharged in the morning. We'll be here to pick you up and drive you to the house—"

"I'm not going to the house. I'm going to my place."

"With a broken leg? Don't be absurd, Deirdre. You can't climb those stairs."

"If I can't handle a flight of stairs, how can I possibly run a multimillion-dollar corporation from a seventeenth-floor office?"

"There are elevators."

"That's not the point, Mother!" Deirdre threw an arm over her eyes. She felt tired and unbelievably frustrated. It was nothing new. Just worse. "All I know," she managed stiffly, "is that I'm checking out of here tomorrow morning and going to my own town house. Where I go from there is anyone's guess, but it won't be to Joyce Enterprises."

"We'll discuss it tomorrow."

"There's nothing to discuss. It's settled."

Maria's chin gave a little twitch. It was a nervous gesture, one that appeared when she wasn't getting her way. Deirdre had caused it more times than either of them could count. "You're upset. It's understandable, given what you've been through." She patted her daughter's cheek. "Tomorrow. We'll talk tomorrow."

Deirdre said nothing. Lips set in a grim line, she watched her visitors pass one by one through the door. Alone at last, she pressed her finger hard on the call button.

Her head throbbed. Her leg throbbed. She needed aspirin. She also needed a magic carpet to sweep her up, up and away.

This time when she glowered at her cast, there was no diversion intended. How could she have been so careless as to slip on that magazine? Why hadn't she caught herself, grabbed the banister? Why hadn't she just sat down and bumped her way to the bottom of the stairs?

But that would have been too simple. Deirdre the athlete had had to tumble head over heels. She'd had to catch her ankle in the banister, breaking her leg in three places.

Given the picture of coordination she'd projected day in day out for the past five years, it was downright embarrassing. Given the physical exertion her body was used to, her body craved, her present state was downright stifling.

It was also depressing. Her future was a huge question mark. Rather than a simple break, what she'd done to her leg had required intricate surgery to repair. She'd been trussed up in the hospital for four days. She'd be in the cast for six weeks more. She'd have to work her way through several weeks of physical therapy after that, and only *then* would she learn whether she'd be able to teach again.

As if her own problems weren't enough to bear, there was the matter of her family. . . and Joyce Enterprises. That provoked anger. Ever since her initial eight-month fiasco of a professional introduction to the company, she'd insisted that she wanted no part of it.

While he'd been alive, her father had put in repeated plugs. *Try it again, Deirdre. You'll grow to like it, Deirdre. If the business isn't for my children, who is it for, Deirdre?* After his death, her mother had picked up the gauntlet. Her sister and her uncles in turn had joined in later. And as the company had begun to fray at the edges, the pressure had increased.

Deirdre loved her own career. It was an outlet—demanding, creative and rewarding. She took pride in the fact that she was a good teacher, that she'd developed a loyal following, that her classes were packed to overflowing and that she'd become known as the queen of aerobics at the health club.

Her career had also been a convenient excuse, and now she was without.

A pair of aspirin eased the pain in her leg and, to some extent, her headache. Unfortunately, it did nothing to ease her dilemma. The prospect of leaving the hospital in the morning, and by doing so putting herself at the mercy of her family, was dismal. She could see it now—the phone calls, the drop-in visits, the ongoing and relentless campaign to draft her. Dismal. Unfair. *Unbearable.* If only there were someplace quiet, distant, secluded . . .

Sparked by a sudden determination, she grabbed the phone, dealing first with the hospital operator, then New York City information, then the hospital operator once more. At last her call went through.

A very proper maid answered. "Lesser residence."

"This is Deirdre Joyce. Is Mrs. Lesser in?"

"Please hold the phone."

Deirdre waited, tapping her finger impatiently against the plastic receiver. She shifted her weight from one bed-weary hip to the other. She squeezed her eyes shut, relieving herself of the sight of the sickroom. And she pictured Victoria, dressed no doubt in an oversized shirt and jeans, wending her way through the most elegant of surroundings to pick up the phone. Would she be coming from the music room, having just set down her cello? Or from tending African violets in her rooftop greenhouse?

Victoria was neither a musician nor a gardener, if skill was the measure. But whatever she did she loved, which was more than enough measure for Deirdre. Of all the family friends Deirdre had come to know in her twenty-nine years, Victoria Lesser was the one she most admired. Victoria was a freethinker, an individual. Rather than withering when the husband she'd loved had died, she'd blossomed and grown. She shunned parochialism and put protocol in its place. She did what she wanted, yet was always within the boundaries of good taste.

Deirdre enjoyed and respected her. It had been far too long since they'd seen each other.

"Hey, stranger," came the ebullient voice from the other end of the line, "where *have* you been?"

Deirdre gave a wan half smile. "Providence, as always, Victoria. How are you?"

"Not bad, if I do say so myself."

"What were you doing just now? I've been trying to imagine. Was it music? Gardening? Tell me. Make me smile."

"Oh-oh. Something's wrong."

For an instant Deirdre's throat grew tight. She hadn't spoken with Victoria in months, yet they could pick up a conversation as though it had been left off the day before. Despite the more than twenty years separating them, their relationship was honest.

Deirdre swallowed the knot. "What were you doing?"

"Stenciling the bathroom ceiling... Are you smiling?"

"A little."

"What's wrong, Dee?"

"I've always hated that nickname. Did you know? The only people who use it are members of my family... and you. When they do it, I feel like a child. When you do it, I feel like... a friend."

"You are," Victoria said softly, "which is why I want you to tell me what's wrong. Are they at it again?"

Deirdre sighed and threw an arm across the mop of sandy hair on her forehead. "With a vengeance. Only this time I'm operating from a position of weakness. I broke my leg. Can you believe it? Super athlete hits the dust."

Silence.

Deirdre's voice dropped an octave. "If you're laughing at me, Victoria, so help me..."

"I'm not laughing, sweetheart. I'm not laughing."

"You're smiling. I can hear it."

"It's either that or cry. The irony of it is too much. Of all the people to break a leg, you can stand it the least... no pun intended. Are you going stir-crazy?"

"I can see it coming fast. It's bad enough that I can't work out. Lord only knows when—or if—I'll be able to teach again. But they're closing in on me, and they're not about to let up until I either give in and go to the office or flip out completely." She took an uneven breath. "I need to get away, Victoria. There'll be no peace here and I have to think about what I'm going to do if... if I can't..." She didn't need to finish; Victoria felt her fear.

There was a pause. "You're thinking of Maine."

"If it'd be all right with you. You've mentioned it so often, but the timing's never been right. It might be just what I need now—distant enough, quiet, undemanding."

"And there's no phone."

"You do understand."

"Uh-huh." There was another pause, then a pensive, "Mmmm. Maine might be just what you need. When were you thinking of going?"

For the first time since her fall down the stairs, Deirdre felt a glimmer of spirit. "As soon as I can." Definitely. "Tomorrow, I guess." Why not! "But you'll have to tell me how to get there."

Victoria did so, giving her route and exit numbers. "Can you get someone to drive you?"

"I'll drive myself."

"What about your broken leg?"

"It's my left one."

"Ahhh. Be grateful for small favors."

"Believe me, I am. Okay, once I get to Spruce Head, what do I do?"

"Look for Thomas Nye. Big fellow. Bushy red beard. He lobsters from there. I'll call ahead and alert him. He'll take you out to the island."

Deirdre managed a smile then. "You are a true friend, Victoria. A lifesaver."

"I hope so," Victoria replied cautiously. "Will you give me a call when you get back to let me know how things went?"

Deirdre agreed, adding heartfelt thanks before she finally hung up the phone and lay back on the bed.

Victoria, on the other hand, merely pressed the disconnect button. When the line was clear, she put through her second call in as many hours to Thomas Nye. She wore a distinct look of satisfaction when she finally returned the receiver to its cradle.

IT WAS STILL RAINING. Strike that, Neil amended sourly. It was pouring.

He scowled past his streaming windshield to the rain-spattered road ahead. The storm had followed him north, he decided. Just his luck. From Connecticut, through Massachusetts, to New Hampshire, then Maine—four-plus hours of nonstop rain. Leaden skies promised more of the same.

His windshield wipers flicked from left to right and back in double time, yet the passing landscape blurred. He hadn't minded the lack of visibility when he'd been on the superhighway—there hadn't been much to see. But he was well off the turnpike now, following Route 1 through towns such as Bath, Wiscasset and Damariscotta. He would have welcomed the diversion of an occasional "down east" sight.

But all he saw was the dappling and redappling sweep of grays and browns, in the middle of which—demanding his constant attention—was the road. The only sounds he heard were the steady beat of rain on the roof of the car and the more rhythmic, if frantic, pulse of the wipers. The world smelled wet. He was tired of sitting. And his mind... His mind persisted in rummaging through the baggage it had brought along on the trip.

Shortly before three in the afternoon, his mood as dark as the clouds overhead, Neil pulled his black LeBaron to a stop alongside the weathered wharf at Spruce Head. He should have been relieved that the arduous drive was over. He should have felt uplifted, filled with anticipation, eager to be nearing his destination.

What he felt was dismay. The docks were mucky. Visibility beyond the moored but wildly bobbing boats was practically nil. And the stench in the air, seeping steadily into the car, was nearly overpowering.

Distastefully he studied the large lobster tanks lined up on the wharf, then the nearby vats filled with dead fish, rotting for use as lobster bait. His own fondness for lobster meat in no way made the smell easier to take.

A gust of wind buffeted the car, driving the rain against it with renewed fury. Neil sat back in the seat and swore softly. What he needed, he decided, were a fisherman's oilskins. As far as he could see, though, not even the fishermen were venturing outside.

Unfortunately he had to venture. He had to find Thomas Nye.

Retrieving his Windbreaker from the back seat, he struggled into it. Then, on a single sucked-in breath, he opened the car door, bolted out, slammed the door behind him and raced to the nearest building.

The first door he came to opened with a groan. Three men sat inside what appeared to be a crude office, though Neil doubted he'd interrupted serious work. Each man held a mug filled with something steaming. Two of the chairs were tipped back on their hind legs; the third was being straddled backside-to.

All three men looked up at his entrance, and Neil was almost grateful for his disheveled appearance. His hair was damp and mussed; a day's worth of stubble darkened his cheeks. His Windbreaker and worn jeans were rain spattered, his running shoes mud spattered, as well. He felt right at home.

"I'm looking for Thomas Nye," he announced straightaway. Fishermen were laconic; that suited him fine. He was in no mood for polite chitchat. "Big fellow with a bushy red beard?"

One chair and one chair only hit the floor. Its occupant propped his elbows on his knees and gestured with a single hand. "Down a block . . . feust left . . . second house on y'or right."

Nodding, Neil left. Head ducked low against the torrent, he dashed back to the car and threw himself inside. Rain dripped from his Windbreaker onto the leather seats, but he paid no heed. In the short minutes since he'd arrived at Spruce Head, his focus had narrowed. Reaching Victoria's island and shutting himself inside her house to avail himself of that highly acclaimed master bedroom with its walls of glass, its huge stone fireplace and its quilt-covered king-size bed seemed all-important.

Taking a minute to decide which way was "down" the block, he started the car and set off. One left later he turned, then pulled up at the second house on the right. It was one of several in a row on the street, and he might have said it had charm had he been in a better mood. It was small, white with gray shutters and, with its paint peeling sadly, looked as aged as he felt.

Loath to waste time, he ran from the car and up the short front walk. Seeing no doorbell, he knocked loudly enough to make himself heard above the storm. Shortly the door was opened by a big fellow with a bushy red beard.

Neil sighed. "Thomas Nye."

The man nodded, held the door wide and cocked his head toward the inside of the house. Neil accepted his invitation instantly.

LESS THAN AN HOUR LATER, Deirdre pulled up at the same house. She looked in turn at the humble structure, then at the sporty black car parked in front of her. Even had she not seen the Connecticut license plate she would have bet it wasn't the car of a lobsterman.

Thomas Nye apparently had guests and the thought didn't thrill her. She wasn't exactly at her best—an assessment, she realized, that was decidedly kind.

She'd been lucky. A passerby at the wharf had given her directions, sparing her a dash from the car. Not that she could dash. Or even walk. Hobble was more like it.

But her luck had run out. She was at Thomas Nye's house and there was no way she could speak to the man without leaving the haven of her car. That meant hauling out her crutches, extricating her casted leg from the hollow to the left of the brake and maneuvering herself to a standing position. It also meant getting wet.

Well, why not! she snapped to herself. The day had been a nightmare from the start. What was a little more grief?

Tugging her hip-length Goretex parka from the back seat, she struggled into it. Then, taking a minute to work out the logistics of dealing with cast, crutches and rain, she opened the car door and set to it.

By the time she reached Thomas Nye's front door, she was gritting her teeth in frustration. What might have taken ten seconds, had she been operating on two strong legs, had taken nearly two minutes—long enough for the storm to drench her. Her hair was plastered to her head and dripping in her eyes. Her sweatpants were noticeably heavier. Her wet grip on the crutches was precarious. And her armpits ached.

Tamping down her irritation as best she could, she shifted her weight to one crutch and knocked. As the small porch overhang offered some protection from the gusting rain, she wedged herself closer to the door.

She twitched her nose. The rank odor that had hit her full force at the wharf was less pungent here, diluted by the fresh salty air and the rain.

She tugged at her collar. She was cold. Impatient, she knocked again, louder this time. Within seconds, the door was opened by a big fellow with a bushy red beard.

Deirdre sighed. "Thomas Nye."

Eyes skittering away, he nodded, held the door wide and cocked his head toward the inside of the house. She hitched her way into the narrow front hall, and at another silent gesture from the large man, into the small living room.

The first thing she saw was a low table spread with papers, charts and what looked to be bills. The second was the television set, broadcasting *Wheel of Fortune* in living color. The third was the dark, brooding figure of a man slouched in a chair in the far corner of the room.

The fourth thing she noticed, unfortunately, was that Thomas Nye had calmly settled into a seat by the table, returning to the work her knock had apparently interrupted.

She cleared her throat. "You were expecting me."

"That's right," he said. He had already lifted several papers, and didn't look up. "Want to sit?"

"Uh . . . are we . . . going?"

"Not now."

She ingested that information with as much aplomb as she could, given that the last thing she wanted was a delay. "It's the weather, I take it?" The possibility had been niggling at the back of her mind for the past hour. She'd done her best to ignore it.

The man in the corner grunted.

Thomas Nye nodded.

"Do you have any idea when we *will* be able to go?" she asked, discouraged; it seemed like forever since she'd awoken that morning. She now had to admit that making the trip on the same day as her discharge from the hospital may have been taking too much upon herself. But it was done. The best she could hope for was that the delay would be minimal.

In answer to her question, the bearded man shrugged. "As soon as it lets up."

"But it could rain for days," she returned. When a second grunt came from the man in the corner, she darted him a scowl. At the moment all she wanted was to be dry and warm beneath a heavy quilt on that king-size bed in the house on Victoria's island. Alone. With no one to stare at the sorry sight she made and no one to make her feel guilty about anything.

She willed her concentration on Nye. "I thought you went lobstering rain or no rain."

"The wind's the problem." At precisely that moment a gust howled around the house.

Deirdre shuddered. "I see." She paused. "Is there a forecast? Do you have any idea when it will let up?"

Nye shrugged. "An hour, maybe two, maybe twelve."

She leaned heavily on the crutches. An hour or two she could live with. But twelve? She doubted she could last twelve hours without that warm, dry bed and heavy quilt. And where would she be waiting out the time?

She glanced again at the man in the corner. He sat low in his chair, one leg stretched out, the other ankle crossed over his knee. His elbows were propped on the arms of the chair, his mouth pressed flush against knuckle-to-knuckle fists. His eyebrows were dark, the eyes beneath them even darker. He, too, was waiting. She could sense his frustration as clearly as she felt her own.

"Uh, Mr. Nye," she began, "I really have to get out there soon. If I don't get off this leg, I'm apt to be in trouble."

Nye was jotting something on the top of one of the papers that lay before him. He lifted his gaze to the game show and gestured with his pencil toward a faded sofa. "Please. Sit."

Deirdre watched as he resumed his work. She contemplated arguing further but sensed the futility of it. He looked calm, satisfied...and utterly immovable. With a grimace she plodded to the sofa. Jerking off her wet parka, she thrust it over the back of the worn cushion, coupled her crutches to one side of her and eased her way down.

When she lifted her eyes once more, she found the man in the corner staring at her. Irritated, she glared back. "Is something wrong?"

He arched a brow, lowered his fists and pursed his lips. "That's quite an outfit." It wasn't a compliment.

"Thank you," she said sweetly. "I rather like it myself." Actually, when they were dry, the roomy pink sweatpants were the most comfortable ones she owned, and comfort was a high priority, what with a cast the size of hers. Unfortunately, while dressing, she'd also been fighting with her mother, and consequently she'd pulled on the first sweatshirt that came to hand. It was teal colored, oversized and as comfortable as the pants, though it did clash slightly. And if the man had an argument with her orange leg warmers, that was his problem. The left one, stretched out and tucked into itself beyond her foot, had kept her toes warm and her cast dry. Her lone sneaker on the other foot, was pitifully wet.

So she didn't look like Jaclyn Smith advertising makeup. Deirdre didn't care. In the immediate future, she was going to be all alone on an island. No one would see her. No one would care what she wore. Practicality and comfort were the two considerations she'd made when deciding what to bring with her. The man with the dark, brooding eyes could thank his lucky stars he wouldn't have to see her beyond this day.

Muted pandemonium broke loose on the television screen as a player won a shiny red Mercedes. Looking up, Thomas grinned at the victory, but Deirdre merely lowered her head and pressed chilled fingers to the bridge of her nose. She hated game shows almost as much as she hated soap operas. On occasion when she passed through the lounge of the health club, the set would be tuned to one or the other. Invariably she'd speed on by.

Now she was speeding nowhere. That fact was even more grating than the sound of the show. Disgruntled, she shoved aside the wet strands of hair on her brow and focused on Thomas Nye.

Head tucked low once again, he was engrossed in his paperwork. He looked almost preppy, she reflected, appraising his corduroy pants, the shirt and sweater. A man of few words, and those spoken with a New York accent, he was apparently a transplant. Deirdre wondered about that. Was he antiestablishment? Antisocial? Or simply...shy? He seemed unable to meet her gaze for more than a minute, and though he was pleasant enough, he made no attempt at conversation. Nor had he introduced her to the man in the corner.

Just as well, she decided as she shifted her gaze. The man in the corner didn't appear to be anyone she'd care to meet. He was frowning toward the window now, his fist propped back against his cheek. The furrow between his brows was marked. His lips held a sullen slant. And if those signs of discontent weren't off-putting enough, the heavy shadow of a beard on his lower face gave him an even less inviting appearance.

Just then he looked her way. Their eyes met and held, until at last she turned her head. No, he wasn't anyone she'd care to meet, because he looked just as troubled as she was, and there was precious little room in her life for compassion at the moment.

At the moment, Neil Hersey was thinking similar thoughts. It had been a long time since he'd seen anyone as pathetic-looking as the woman across the room. Oh, yes, the weather had taken its toll, soaking her clothes and matting her short, brown hair in damp strands that grazed her eyelids. But it was more than that. The weather had nothing to do with the fact that she had one fat leg and an overall shapeless figure. Or that she was pale. Or that her crossness seemed to border on orneriness. He assumed Nye was shuttling her to one of the many islands in the Gulf of Maine. But he had woes enough to keep him occupied without bothering about someone else's.

His immediate woe was being landlocked. Time was passing. He wanted to be moving out. But Thomas Nye was calling the shots, a situation that only exacerbated Neil's dour mood.

He shifted restlessly and absently rubbed his hand over the rough rag wool of his sweater. Was that heartburn he felt? Maybe an incipient ulcer? He took a disgusted breath, shifted again and was about to glance at his watch, when he saw the woman do it.

"Mr. Nye?" she asked.

"Thomas," Nye answered without looking up.

"Thomas. How long will the crossing take?"

"Two hours, give or take some."

She studied her watch again, making the same disheartening calculations Neil did. "But if we're held up much longer, we won't make it before dark." It would be bad enough negotiating rugged terrain in daylight with her crutches, but at night? "That . . . could be difficult."

"Better difficult than deadly," Thomas replied gently. "As soon as the wind dies down, we'll go. We may have to wait till morning."

"Morning! But I don't have anywhere to stay," she protested.

Thomas tossed his head toward the ceiling. "I've got room."

She gave an exaggerated nod, which said *that* solved everything, when in fact it didn't. It wasn't what she wanted at all! She wanted to be on Victoria's island, comfortably settled in that spectacular master bedroom she'd heard so much about. She pictured it now—huge windows, an elegant brass bed, dust ruffles, quilt and pillows of a country-sophisticate motif. Silence. Solitude. Privacy. Oh, how she wanted that.

The awful fatigue she was fighting now she did not want. Or the ache in her leg that no amount of shifting could relieve. Or the fact that she was in a room with two strangers and she couldn't throw back her head and scream . . .

Neil had returned his attention to the window. What he saw there wasn't pleasing; the thought of spending the night in this tiny fisherman's house was even less so. *I've got room.* It was a generous enough offer, but hell, he didn't want to be here! He wanted to be on the island!

He was exhausted. The day's drive through the rain had been a tedious cap to six tedious weeks. He wanted to be alone. He wanted privacy. He wanted to stretch out on that king-size bed and know that his feet wouldn't hang over the edge. Lord only knew most everything else had gone wrong with his life lately.

"Does the boat have radar?" he asked on impulse.

"Yes."

"So we're not limited to daylight."

"No."

"Then there's still a chance of getting out today?"

"Of course there's a chance," Deirdre snapped, testy in her weariness. "There's always a chance."

Neil shot her a quelling look. "Then let's put it in terms of probability," he stated stubbornly, returning his attention to Thomas. "On a scale of one to ten, where would you put the chances of our making it out today?"

Deirdre scowled. "How can he possibly answer that?"

"He's a fisherman," Neil muttered tersely. "I'm asking for his professional estimate based on however many number of years he's worked on the sea."

"Three," Thomas said.

Deirdre's eyes were round with dismay. "On a scale of one to ten, we only get a *three*?"

Neil eyed her as though she were daft. "He's only been lobstering for three years."

"Oh." She then focused on Thomas. "What *are* the chances?

Thomas straightened a pile of papers and stood. "Right now I'd give it a two."

"A two," she wailed. "That's even worse!"

Neil glowered toward the window. Thomas stood. The Wheel of Fortune spun, gradually slowing, finally stopping on "bankrupt." The groans from the set reflected Deirdre's feelings exactly.

But she wouldn't give up. "How do you decide if we can leave?"

"The marine report."

"How often does that change?"

"Whenever the weather does."

The man in the corner snickered. Deirdre ignored him. "I mean, are there periodic updates you tune in to? How can you possibly tell, sitting here in the house, whether the wind is dying down on the water?"

Thomas was heading from the room. "I'll be back."

She looked at the man. "Where's he going?" He stared back mutely. "You're waiting to get out of here, too. Aren't you curious?"

Neil sighed. "He's getting the forecast."

"How can you tell?"

"Can't you hear the crackle of the radio?"

"I can't hear a thing over this inane show!" Awkwardly she pushed herself up, hopped to the television and turned the volume down, then hopped back. She was too tired to care if she looked like a waterlogged rabbit. Sinking into a corner of the sofa, she lifted her casted leg onto the cushions, laid her head back and closed her eyes.

Moments later Thomas returned. "Raise that to a seven. The wind's dying."

Neil and Deirdre both grew alert, but it was Neil who spoke. "Then we may make it?"

"I'll check the report in another half-hour." The lobsterman said no more, immersing himself back in his work.

The next half-hour seemed endless to Deirdre. Her mind replayed the events of the day, from her hospital discharge through the cab ride to her town house, then on to the unpleasant scene with her mother, who had been positively incensed that Deirdre would even think of leaving Providence. Deirdre would have liked to believe it was maternal concern for her health, but she knew otherwise. Her refusal to tell Maria where she was headed had resulted in even stronger reprisals, but Deirdre couldn't bear the thought that somehow her mother would get through to her on the island.

She needed this escape. She needed it badly. The way she felt, she doubted she'd get out of bed for days . . . when she finally reached the island.

Neil didn't weather the half-hour any better. Accustomed to being constantly on the move, he felt physically confined and mentally constrained. At times he thought he'd scream if something didn't happen. Everything grated—the lobsterman's nonchalance, the flicker of the television, the sight of the woman across the room, the sound of the rain. Too much of his life seemed dependent on external forces; he craved full control. Misery was private. He wanted to be alone.

At long last Thomas left the room again. Deirdre raised her head and held her breath. Neil waited tensely.

From the look on the fisherman's face when he returned, it seemed nothing had changed. Yet the first thing he did was flip off the television, then he gathered up his papers.

Aware that the man in the corner was holding himself straighter, Deirdre did the same. "Thomas?"

He said nothing, simply gestured broadly with his arms. Deirdre and Neil needed no more invitation. Within seconds, they were up and reaching for their jackets.

2

THE STORM MIGHT HAVE ABATED over the water, but Deirdre saw no letup on shore. The rain soaked her as she limped on her crutches to her car, which, at Thomas's direction, she moved to the deepest point in the driveway. Transferring her large duffle bag to the pickup was a minor ordeal, eased at the last minute by Thomas, who tossed her bag in, then returned to stowing boxes of fresh produce in the back of the truck. The other man was preoccupied, parking his own car, then loading his bag.

Gritting her teeth, she struggled into the cab of the truck. No sooner was she seated than the two men—the dark one, to her chagrin, had turned out to be every bit as large as the lobsterman—boxed her in, making the ensuing ride to the wharf damp and uncomfortable. By the time she was aboard Thomas's boat, propped on a wood bench in the enclosed pilothouse, she felt stiff and achy. Her sneaker was soggy. Her jacket and sweatpants were wet. She was chilled all over.

The nightmare continued, she mused, but at least its end was in sight. She'd be at Victoria's island, alone and in peace, by nightfall. It was this knowledge that kept her going.

The engine chugged to life and maintained an even growl as the boat left the wharf and headed seaward. Deirdre peered out the open back of the pilothouse for a time, watching Spruce Head recede and finally disappear in the mist. Burrowing deeper into her jacket, she faced forward then and determinedly focused on her destination. She pictured the island forested with pines, carpeted with moss, smelling of earth, sea and sky, kissed by the sun. She envisioned her own recovery there, the regaining of her strength, the rebirth of her spirit. And serenity. She conjured images of serenity.

Just as Neil did. Serenity...solitude... Soon, he told himself, soon. He'd wedged himself into a corner of the pilothouse, not so much to keep a distance from Nye's other passenger as to keep his body upright. It had been a long day, a long night before that. He'd grown accustomed to sleeplessness over the past weeks, but never had its effects hit him as they did now.

Though his fatigue was in large part physical, there was an emotional element as well. He was away from the office, relieved of his duties, distanced from his profession. This wasn't a vacation; it was a suspension. Brief, perhaps, but a letdown. And more than a little depressing.

A tiny voice inside accused him of running away; his abrupt departure from Hartford was sure to be seen by some as just that. Maybe he had run away. Maybe he was conceding defeat. Maybe . . . maybe . . . It was very depressing.

His pulse was steadily accelerating, as it always did when he pursued that particular line of thought. He wondered if he had high blood pressure yet. It wouldn't have surprised him, given the kind of nervous tension he'd been living with for days on end. He needed an outlet. Any outlet.

His gaze settled on the woman just down the bench. "Don't you think it's a little stupid going out in all this like that?" He jerked his chin toward the fat leg she'd painstakingly hauled up beside her on the hard bench.

Deirdre had been wondering apprehensively if the rhythmic plunge of the boat, noticeable now that they'd left the harbor behind, was going to get worse. She looked at him in disbelief. "Excuse me?"

"I said, don't you think it's a little stupid going out in all this like that?" He found perverse satisfaction in the verbatim repetition.

"That's what I thought you said, but I couldn't believe you'd be so rude." She had no patience. Not now. Not here. "Didn't your mother ever teach you manners?"

"Oh, yes. But she's not here right now, so I can say exactly what I want." Ah, the pleasure in blurting words out at will. He couldn't remember the last time he'd done it as freely. "You haven't answered my question."

"It's not worth answering." She turned her head away and looked at Thomas, who stood at the controls, holding the wheel steady. His body swayed easily with the movement of the boat. Deirdre wished she could go with the flow that way, but her own body seemed to buck the movement. She was glad she hadn't eaten recently.

In an attempt to divert her thoughts from various unpleasant possibilities, she homed in on the baseball hat Thomas had been wearing since they'd left the house. It had fared unbelievably well in the rain. "Are you a Yankees' fan, Thomas?" she called above the rumble of the motor.

Thomas didn't turn. "When they win."

"That's honest enough," she murmured under her breath, then raised her voice again. "You're originally from New York?"

"That's right."

"What part?"

"Queens."

"Do you still have family there?"

"Some."

"What were you doing before you became a lobsterman?"

A grumble came from the corner. "Leave the man alone. He's hardly encouraging conversation. Don't you think there's a message in that?"

Deirdre stared back at him. "He's a Maine fisherman. They're all tight-lipped."

"But he's not originally from Maine, which means that he *chooses* not to speak."

"I wish *you* would," she snapped. "I've never met anyone as disagreeable in my life." She swung back to the lobsterman. "How'd you get saddled with this one, Thomas? He's a peach."

Thomas didn't answer, but continued his study of the white-capped waves ahead.

Neil propped his elbow on the back of the bench, rested his cheek in his palm and closed his eyes.

Deirdre focused on a peeling panel of wood opposite her and prayed that her stomach would settle.

Time passed. The boat had the ocean to itself as it plowed steadily through the waves amid an eerie air of isolation. The smell of fish mingled with a decidedly musty odor, whether from wet clothing, wet skin or aged wood Deirdre didn't know, but it did nothing for the condition of her insides. She took to doing yoga breathing, clearing her mind, concentrating on relaxation. She wasn't terribly successful.

At length she spoke again, clearly addressing herself to Thomas. "Two hours, more or less, you said. Will it be more, in weather like this?" The rain hadn't let up and the sea was choppy, but, to her untrained eye, they were making progress.

"We're in luck. The wind's at our back."

She nodded, grateful for the small word of encouragement. Then she shifted, bending her good knee up and wrapping her arms around it.

"You look green," came an unbidden assessment from the corner.

She sighed. "Thank you."

"Are you seasick?"

"I'm fine."

"I think you're seasick."

Lips thinned, she swiveled around. "You'd like that, wouldn't you? You'd like to see me sick. What's the matter? Are *you* feeling queasy?"

"I'm a seasoned sailor."

"So am I," she lied, and turned away. Straightening her leg, she sat forward on the bench. Then, fingers clenched on its edge, she pushed herself up and hopped toward Thomas.

"How much longer?" she asked as softly as she could. She didn't want the man in the corner to hear the anxiety in her words. Unfortunately Thomas didn't hear the words at all. When he tipped his head toward her, she had to repeat herself.

"We're about halfway there," he replied eventually. On the one hand it was reassuring; halfway there was better than nothing. On the other hand, it was depressing; another full hour to endure.

"His island's near Matinicus, too?" The slight emphasis on the "his" told Thomas who she meant.

"There are several small islands in the area."

She moved closer and spoke more softly again. "Will you drop me first? I'm not sure I can take much more of this."

"I'm heading straight for Victoria's island."

She managed a wan smile and a grateful "Thank you" before maneuvering back to her seat. She avoided looking at the man in the corner. He raised her hackles. She didn't need the added aggravation, when so much of the past week had been filled with it.

Neil was brooding, thinking of the last time he'd been on a boat. A seasoned sailor? He guessed it was true. Nancy had had a boat. She loved boats. Supposedly she'd loved him, too, but that had been when he'd had the world on a string. At the first sign of trouble she'd recoiled. Granted, her brother was on the board at Wittnauer-Douglass, so she'd been in an awkward position when Neil had been summarily dismissed. Still . . . love was love . . . Or was it?

He hadn't loved Nancy. He'd known it for months, and had felt guilty every time she'd said the words. Now he had a particularly sour taste in his mouth. Her words had been empty. She hadn't loved him—she'd loved what he was. She'd been enthralled by the image of a successful corporate attorney, the affluence and prestige. With all that now in doubt, she was playing it safe. And it was just as well, he knew, a blessing in disguise, perhaps. A fair-weather lover was the last thing he needed.

He looked over at the woman on the bench. She was another can of worms entirely. Small and shapeless, unpolished, unsociable, unfeminine—quite a switch from Nancy. "What did you do to your leg?" he heard himself ask.

Deirdre raised her head. "Are you talking to me?"

He glanced around the pilothouse. "I don't see anyone else with crutches around here. Did you break it?"

"Obviously."

"Not 'obviously.' You could have had corrective surgery for a congenital defect, or for a sports injury."

A sports injury. If only. There might have been dignity in that. But falling down a flight of stairs? "I broke it," she stated curtly.

"How?"

"It doesn't matter."

"When?"

Deirdre scowled. "It doesn't *matter*."

"My Lord, and you called *me* disagreeable!"

She sighed wearily. "I'm not in the mood for talking. That's all."

"You still look green." He gave a snide grin. "Stomach churning?"

"My stomach is fine!" she snapped. "And I'm not green...just pale. It's the kind of color you catch when you've been surrounded by hospital whites for days."

"You mean you were just released?" he asked with genuine surprise.

"This morning."

"And you're off racing through the rain to get to a remote island?" Surprise gave way to sarcasm once more.

"It's only a broken leg! The rest of me is working fine." Not quite true, but an understandable fib. "And, in case you're wondering, I didn't personally request the rain. It just came!"

"You were crazy to come out. Didn't your mother try to stop you?"

She heard the ridicule in his tone and was reminded of her earlier shot at him. Hers had been offered facetiously, as had his, yet he'd unwittingly hit a raw nerve. "She certainly did, but I'm an adult, so I don't have to listen to her!" She turned her head away, but it did no good.

"You don't look like an adult. You look like a pouting child."

Her eyes shot back to him reproachfully. "Better a pouting child than a scruffy pest! Look, why don't you mind your own business? You don't know me, and I don't know you, and before long, thank goodness, this ride will be over. You don't need to take out your bad mood on me. Just stay in your corner and brood to yourself, okay?"

"But I enjoy picking on you. You rise to the occasion."

That was the problem. She was letting him get to her. The way to deal with a man of his ilk was to ignore him, which she proceeded to do. Whether it worked or not she wasn't sure, because she suspected he had freely chosen not to speak further.

But he continued to look at her. She could feel his eyes boring into her back, and she steadfastly refused to turn. The man had gall; she had to hand it to him. He wasn't spineless, as Seth had been....

Seth. Sweet Seth. Parasitic Seth. He'd slipped into her world, taken advantage of her home, her job, her affections, and then turned tail and run when the family pressure had begun. Seth hadn't wanted ties. He hadn't wanted responsibility. And the last thing he'd wanted was a woman whose career demands and family responsibilities took precedence over his own needs.

The irony of it, Deirdre reflected, was that he'd had such little understanding of her. She'd never wanted Joyce Enterprises, and she'd told him so repeatedly. But he'd still felt threatened, so he'd left. In hindsight, she was better off without him.

She was drawn from her reverie when the man in the corner rose from the bench, crossed the pilothouse and positioned himself close by Thomas. He spoke in a low murmur, which, try as she might, Deirdre couldn't hear over the guttural drone of the engine.

"How much longer?" Neil asked.

Thomas glanced at one of his dials. "Half an hour."

"Where's she going?" He put a slight emphasis on the "she."

"Near Matinicus."

"Lots of islands, are there?"

"Some."

"Who gets dropped off first?"

"I'm heading straight for Victoria's island."

Neil considered that. "Look, it's okay with me if you drop her off first. She's really pretty pathetic."

Thomas's eyes remained on the sea. "I thought you didn't like her."

"I don't. She bugs the hell out of me. Then again—" he ran a hand across his aching neck "—just about anyone would bug the hell out of me right about now. She just happens to be here." He was feeling guilty, but was torn even about that. On the one hand, arguing with the woman was thoroughly satisfying. He needed to let off steam, and she was a perfect patsy. On the other hand, she was right. He'd been rude. It wasn't his normal way.

Head down, he started back toward his corner.

Deirdre, who'd been thinking just then about how badly she wanted, *needed* a bath, and what an unbelievable hassle it was going to be trying to keep her cast out of the water, stopped him mid-way. She was feeling particularly peevish. "If you think you can con Thomas into dropping you off first, don't hold your breath. He's already set a course and it happens that *my* island's up there at the top of the list."

"Shows how much *you* know," Neil mumbled under his breath. He passed her by, slid down into his corner of the bench, crossed his arms over his chest and stared straight ahead.

Deirdre passed his comment off as a simple case of sour grapes. He was an ill-humored man. Soon enough she'd be free of his company. Soon enough she'd be at the island.

"There it is," Thomas called over his shoulder a little while later. "Victoria's island."

Deirdre pushed herself to her good knee and peered through the front windshield. "I can't see a thing."

Neil, too, had risen. "No harm," he muttered.

"Do you see anything?"

"Sure. There's a dark bump out there."

"There's a world of dark bumps out there. How do you tell which one's a wave and which one's an island?"

"The island has trees."

The logic was irrefutable. "Swell," she said, sinking back into her seat. When they reached the island they'd reach the island. She'd have plenty of time to see it, time when she wouldn't be tired and uncomfortable and thoroughly out of sorts.

Neil stood by Thomas, watching the dark bump swell and rise and materialize into an honest-to-goodness land mass. It wasn't large, perhaps half a mile square, but it was surprisingly lush. Neither the rain, nor the clouds, nor the approach of dusk could disguise the deep green splendor of the pines. And the house was there, a rambling cape-style structure of weathered gray clapboard, nestling in a clearing overlooking the dock.

Deirdre was on her knee again. "That . . . is . . . beautiful," she breathed.

Neil, who was feeling rather smug at the perfection of his destination, darted her an indulgent glance. "I agree."

"For once. I was beginning to wonder if you had any taste at all."

His indulgence ended. "Oh, I've got taste, all right. Problem is that I haven't seen a thing today that even remotely appealed to it." His eyes didn't stray from her face, making his meaning clear.

It was an insult Deirdre simply couldn't let pass. "The feeling is mutual. In fact—"

"Excuse me," Thomas interrupted loudly, "I'll need everyone's help here. And it's still pouring, so we'd better work quickly." He was already cutting the engine and guiding the boat alongside the short wooden dock. "Neil, you go outside and throw the lines onto the dock, one at the bow, one at the stern. Then hop ashore and tie us up on those pilings. I'll pass supplies to you and Deirdre. Watch yourself on the dock, Deirdre. It'll be slippery."

Deirdre nodded and worked at the wet zipper of her parka, thinking what a waste it was to give a nice name like Neil to such an obnoxious man. But at least he was helping. She'd half expected him to insist on staying dry while Thomas got her set up on shore.

Neil zipped up his jacket and headed for the open pit of the boat's stern, thinking how ironic it was that a woman with as flowing a name as Deirdre should prove to be so thorny. But at least she'd agreed to help. That surprised him. Of course, Thomas hadn't exactly given her a choice.

"The line, Neil. We're here." Thomas's call ended all silent musings.

Head ducked against the rain, Neil raced to tie up the boat, bow and stern.

Biting her lip against a clumsiness foreign to her, Deirdre managed to lumber onto the dock with only a helping hand from Thomas. When she would have thanked him, he'd already turned away to begin off-loading. He handed things, first to her, then to Neil when he reached her side.

"I'll be back in a week with fresh supplies," instructed the lobsterman hurriedly. "These should be more than enough until then. Keys to the front door are in an envelope tucked in with the eggs. If you run into a problem, any kind of emergency, you can reach me on the ship-to-shore radio in the den. The directions are right beside it."

Deirdre nodded, but she was too busy concentrating on keeping her balance to answer. When her large duffel bag came over the side of the boat, she rearranged her crutches and somehow managed to hook the wide strap of the bag over her shoulder, then return the crutches to their prescribed position without falling.

Neil, busy piling boxes of supplies atop one another to keep them as dry as possible, looked up briefly when Thomas handed over his canvas cargo bag. He set it down on the dock, finished up with the supplies, put a box in one arm and the cargo bag's broad strap over his other shoulder, then turned back to thank Thomas.

The boat was already drifting away from the dock, which didn't surprise Neil. Thomas had said they'd work quickly. But there was something that did surprise him....

Deirdre, whose eyes had gone wide in alarm, cleared her throat. "Uh, Thomas?" When the boat slipped farther away, she tried again, louder this time. "Thomas?"

The engine coughed, then started.

This time it was Neil who yelled. "Nye! You've forgotten someone! Get back here!"

The boat backed around the tip of the dock, then turned seaward.

"Thomas!"

"Nye!"

"There's been a mistake!" Deirdre shrieked, shoving her dripping hair from her eyes, then pointing to Neil. "*He*'s still here!"

Neil rounded on her. His face was soaked, but his eyes were hard as steel. "Of course I'm still here! This is my friend's island!"

"It's *Victoria's* island, and Victoria is *my* friend."

"*My* friend, and she didn't mention you. She said I'd have the place all to myself!"

"Which was exactly what she told me!"

They glared at each other amid the pouring rain. "Victoria who?" Neil demanded.

"Victoria Lesser. Who's your Victoria?"

"The same."

"I don't believe you. Tell me where she lives."

"Manhattan. Park Avenue."

"She is Mrs. Arthur Lesser. Tell me about Arthur."

"He's dead. She's a widow, a wonderful... wacky..."

"Conniving..."

Scowling at each other amid encroaching darkness on that windswept dock in the rain, Deirdre and Neil reached the same conclusion at once.

"We've been had," he stated, then repeated in anger, "we've been had!"

"I don't believe it," Deirdre murmured, heart pounding as she looked out to sea. "Oh, damn," she breathed. "He's going!"

Simultaneously they began to yell.

"Thomas! Come back here!"

"Nye! Turn around!"

"Thomas! Don't do this to me, Thomas! Thomas!" But Thomas was well beyond earshot and moving steadily toward the mainland.

"That creep!" Neil bellowed. "He was in on it! Victoria must have known precisely what she was doing, and he went along with it!"

Deirdre didn't remember ever being as miserable in her life. All that she'd faced at home, all that she'd escaped was nothing compared to this having been manipulated. Her frustration was almost paralyzing. She took a ragged breath and tried to think clearly. "I've come all this way, gone through hell . . ." She brushed the rain from her cheek and looked at Neil. "You can't stay! That's all there is to it!"

Neil, who felt rain trickling down his neck, was livid. "What do you mean, I can't stay? I don't know what brought you here, but whatever it was, I need this island more, and I have no intention of sharing it with a sharp-tongued, physically disabled . . . urchin!"

She shook her head, sure she was imagining it all. "I don't have to take this," she spat. Turning, she set her crutches before her and started along the murky dock toward the even murkier path.

Neil was beside her. "You're right. You *don't* have to take it. I'll put through a call to Thomas and get him to come back tomorrow to pick you up."

Deirdre kept her eyes on the wet boarding, then the muddy dirt path. "I have no intention of being picked up, not until I'm good and ready to leave! You can put through that call to Thomas and have him pick *you* up!"

"No way! I came here for peace and quiet, and that's exactly what I'm going to get."

"You can get peace and quiet somewhere else. You sure can't get it with me around, and I sure can't get it with you around, and I don't know how you know Victoria, but she's been a friend of my family's for years and I'm sure she'll give me the right to this place—"

"*Right* to this place? Look at you! You can barely make it to the door!"

He wasn't far off the mark. The path was wet and slippery, slowing her progress considerably. It was sheer grit that kept her going. "I'll make it," she fumed, struggling to keep her footing on the slick incline. "And once I'm inside I'm not budging."

They reached the front steps. Deirdre hobbled up, then crossed the porch to the door. Neil, who'd taken the steps by twos, was standing there, swearing. "Tucked in beside the eggs . . ." He dropped his bag under the eaves, out of the rain, set down the box he'd carried and began to rummage through it. He swore again, then turned and retraced his steps at a run.

Weakly Deirdre leaned against the damp clapboard by the door. Pressing her forehead to the wood, she welcomed its chill against her surprisingly hot temple. The rest of her felt cold and clammy. She was shaking and perilously close to tears. How could the perfect solution have gone so wrong?

And there was nothing to be done about it, at least not until tomorrow. That was the worst of it.

Then again, perhaps it wasn't so bad. Once inside the house, she intended to go straight to bed. She didn't care if it was barely seven o'clock. She was beat and cold, perhaps feverish. Neil whoever-he-was could do whatever he wanted; she was going to sleep through the night. By the time she got up tomorrow, she'd be able to think clearly.

Neil dashed up the steps, his arms laden with boxes.

"I can't believe you did that," she cried. "You've got every last one of them piled up. It's a miracle you didn't drop them on the path, and then where would I be?"

He tossed his head back, getting his hair out of his eyes and the rain out of his hair. "Be grateful I did it myself. I could have asked you to help."

She wasn't in the mood to be grateful. "The key. Can you find the key?"

He'd set the bundles down and was pushing their contents around. "I'm looking. I'm looking." Moments later he fished out an envelope, opened it, removed the key and unlocked the door.

Deirdre, who feared that if she waited much longer she'd collapse on the spot, limped immediately inside. It was dark. She fumbled for a light switch and quickly flipped it on. In one sweeping glance she took in a large living room and an open kitchen off that. To the left was a short hall, to the right a longer one. Calculating that the hall to the right would lead to bedrooms, she single-mindedly headed that way.

There were three open doors. She passed the first, then the second, correctly surmising that they were the smaller guest bedrooms. The third... She flipped another light switch. Ah, she'd been right. It was much as she'd imagined it—a sight for sore eyes.

Swinging inside, she slammed the door shut with her crutch and made straight for the bed. She'd no sooner reached it than her knees buckled and she sank down, letting her crutches slip unheeded to the floor. Hanging her head, she took several deep, shaky breaths. Her limbs were quivering from weakness, exhaustion or chill, or all three. She was wet, and remedying that situation had to take first priority. Though the room was cold, she simply didn't have the wherewithal to confront that problem yet.

With unsteady fingers, she worked down the zipper of her jacket, struggled out of the soggy mass and dropped it on the rag rug by the side of the bed. She began to apologize silently to Victoria for making a mess, then caught herself. After what Victoria had done, she didn't owe her a thing!

She kicked off her sodden sneaker and tugged the wet leg warmer off her cast. The plaster was intact. Gingerly she touched the part that covered her foot. Damp? Or simply cold? Certainly hard enough. So far, so good.

Bending sharply from the waist, she unzipped her duffel bag and began pushing things around in search of her pajamas. Normally the neatest of packers, she'd been in the midst of the argument with her mother that morning when she'd thrown things into the bag. She'd been angry and tired. Fortunately everything she'd brought was squishable.

She'd finally located the pajamas, when the door to the bedroom flew open and Neil burst in. He'd already taken off his jacket, shoes and socks, but his jeans were soaked up to the thigh. Tossing his cargo bag onto the foot of the bed, he planted his hands on his hips.

"What are you doing in here? This is my room."

Deirdre clutched the pajamas to her chest, more startled than anything by his sudden appearance. "I didn't see your name on the door," she argued quietly.

"This is the largest bedroom." He pointed at the bed. "That is the largest bed." He jabbed his chest with his thumb. "And I happen to be the largest person in this house."

Deirdre let her hands, pajamas and all, fall to her lap. She adopted a blank expression, which wasn't hard, given her state of emotional overload. "So?"

"So . . . I want this room."

"But it's already taken."

"Then you can untake it. The two other rooms are perfectly lovely."

"I'm glad you feel that way. Choose whichever you want."

"I want this one."

For the first time since she'd entered the room, Deirdre really looked around. Nearly two complete walls were of thick, multi-paned glass, affording a view that would no doubt be spectacular in daylight. The large, brass-framed bed stood against a third wall; out of the fourth was cut the door, flanked by low, Colonial-style matching dressers, and, at one end, the pièce de résistance; a large raised hearth. Over it all was a warm glow cast by the bedside lamp.

Deirdre looked Neil straight in the eye. "So do I."

Neil, who'd never been in quite this situation before, was thrown off balance by her quiet determination. It had been different when she'd been yelling. This was, strangely, more threatening. Deirdre whoever-she-was was a woman who knew what she wanted. Unfortunately he wanted the same thng.

"Look," he began, carefully guarding his temper, "it doesn't make sense. I need this bed for its length alone. I'm six-three to your, what, five-one, five-two? I'll be physically uncomfortable in any of the other rooms. They all have twin beds."

"I'm five-three, but that's beside the point. I have a broken leg. I need extra space, too...not to mention a bathtub. From what I've been told, the master bath is the only one with a tub. I can't take a shower. It'll be enough of a challenge taking a bath."

"Try," Neil snapped.

"Excuse me?"

"I said, try."

"Try what?"

"To take a bath."

"And what is that supposed to mean?"

"What do you think it means?" he asked rhetorically. "You're filthy." He hadn't been able to resist. When he'd tried logic on her, she'd turned it around to suit herself. He didn't like that, particularly when he had no intention of giving in when it came to the master bedroom.

She looked down at her mud-spattered orange leg warmer and plucked at the odious wet wool. "Of course I'm filthy. It's muddy outside, and that boat was none too clean." She raised her head, eyes flashing. "But I don't have to apologize. Look at you. You're no prize, yourself!"

Neil didn't have to look at himself to know she was right. He'd worn his oldest, most comfortable jeans and heavy sweater, and if she could see the T-shirt under the sweater.... The stormy trip had taken its toll on him, too. "I don't give a damn how I look," he growled. "That was the whole purpose in coming here. For once in my life I'm going to do what I want, when I want, where I want. And that starts with this bed."

Jaw set, Deirdre reached for her crutches. "Over my dead body," she muttered, but much of the fight had gone out of her. Whatever energy she'd summoned to trade barbs with Neil had been drained. Draping the pajamas over her shoulder, she stood. "I have to use the bathroom. It's been a long day."

Neil watched her hobble into the bathroom and close the door. Again he found himself wishing she'd yell. When she spoke quietly, wearily, he actually felt sorry for her. She looked positively exhausted.

But damn it, so was he!

Taking his cargo bag from the foot of the bed, he put it where Deirdre had been sitting. He then lifted her soaked jacket by its collar, grabbed her duffel bag by its strap and carried them down the hall to the more feminine of the two guest bedrooms.

She'd get the hint. With luck, she'd be too tired to argue. Either that, or she'd come after him once she left the bathroom, and they could fight it out some more.

He sighed, closed his eyes and rubbed that throbbing spot on his forehead. Aspirin. He needed aspirin. No. He needed a drink. No. What he really needed was food. Breakfast had been a long time ago, and lunch had been a Whopper, eaten in sixty seconds flat at a Burger King on the turnpike.

Stopping briefly in the front hall to adjust the thermostat, he returned to the kitchen, where he'd left the boxes of food piled up. Plenty for two, he mused dryly. He should have been suspicious when Thomas had continued to hand out supplies. But it had been rainy and dim, and he hadn't thought. They'd been rushing. He'd simply assumed the girl would get back on the boat when the work was done.

He'd assumed wrong. Thrusting splayed fingers through his hair, he stared at the boxes, then set about unloading them. Soon he had a can of soup on to heat and was busy making a huge ham-and-cheese sandwich.

The kitchen was comfortable. Though small, it was modern, with all the amenities he enjoyed at home. He hadn't expected any less of Victoria. At least, not when it came to facilities. What he hadn't expected was that she'd foist company on him, not when he'd specifically said that he needed to be alone.

What in the devil had possessed her to pull a prank like this? But he knew. He knew. She'd been trying to fix him up for years.

Why now, Victoria? Why now, when my life is such a goddamned mess?

The house was quiet. He wondered about that as he finished eating and cleaned up. Surely Deirdre would be finished using the bathroom. He hadn't heard a bath running. Nor had he heard the dull thud of crutches in the hall.

Not liking the possible implications of the silence, he headed for the smaller bedroom where he'd left her things.

It was empty.

Nostrils flaring, he strode down the hall to the master bedroom. *"Damn it,"* he cursed, coming to a sudden halt on the threshold. She was in bed, albeit on the opposite side from his bag. She was in his bed!

His feet slapped the wood floor as he crossed the room and came to stand on the rug by that other side of the bed. "Hey, you! What do you think you're doing?"

She was little more than a series of small lumps under the quilt. None of the lumps moved. The bedding was pulled to her forehead. Only her hair showed, mousy brown against the pillow.

"You can't sleep here! I told you that!"

He waited. She gave a tiny moan and moved what he assumed to be her good leg.

"You'll have to get up, Deirdre," he growled. "I've moved your things to the other bedroom."

"I can't," came the weak and muffled reply. "I'm... too tired and . . . too . . . cold."

Neil glanced helplessly at the ceiling. *Why me? Why here and now?* He lowered his gaze to the huddle of lumps. "I can't sleep in any of the other beds. We've been through this before."

"Mmm."

"Then you'll move?"

There was a long pause. He wondered if she'd fallen asleep. At last, a barely audible sound came from beneath the covers.

"No."

He swore again and shoved another agitated hand through his hair as he stared at the bundle in the bed. He could move her. He could bodily pick her up and cart her to the next bedroom.

"Don't try to move me," the bundle warned. "I'll cry rape."

"There'll be no one to hear."

"I'll call Thomas. I'll make more noise than you've ever heard."

Rape. Of all the stupid threats. Or was it? There were just the two of them in the house. It would be her word against his, and "date rape" had become the in thing. If she was cruel enough to go through with it, she could really make a scene. And a scene of that type was the last thing he needed at this point in his life.

Furious and frustrated, he wheeled around and stormed from the room. When he reached the living room, he threw himself into the nearest chair and brooded. He threw every name in the book at Victoria, threw many of the same names at Thomas, then at the woman lying in *his* bed. Unfortunately, all the name-calling in the world didn't change his immediate circumstances.

He was bone tired, yet there was enough adrenaline flowing through him to keep him awake for hours. Needing to do something, he bolted from the chair and put a match to the kindling that had so carefully been placed beneath logs in the fireplace. Within minutes, the fire was roaring. It was some comfort. Even greater comfort came from the bottle of Chivas Regal he fished from the bar. Several healthy swallows, and he was feeling better; several more, and his anger abated enough to permit him to think.

After two hours he was feeling far more mellow than he would have imagined. He wandered into the den off the shorter of the two halls and studied the directions taped beside the ship-to-shore radio. *Piece of cake.*

Unfortunately no one responded from Thomas's house. *Bastard.*

Okay, Hersey. Maybe he's not back yet. After all, it was still raining, and the man was working in total darkness. No sweat. He'll be there tomorrow. And in the meantime...

Neil banked the fire, nonchalantly walked back to the master bedroom and began to strip. *Let her cry rape,* declared his muzzy brain.

Wearing nothing but his briefs—a concession that later he'd marvel he'd been sober enough to make—he turned off the light, climbed into his side of the bed and stretched out.

"Ah..." The bed was firm, the sheets fresh. He might have imagined himself in his own bed at home had it not been for the faint aroma of wood smoke that lent an outdoorsy flavor to the air. Rain beat steadily against the roof, but it, too, was pleasant, and beyond was a sweet, sweet silence.

He was on a remote island, away from the city and its hassles. Taking a deep breath, he smiled, then let his head fall sideways on the pillow and was soon sound asleep.

3

SEVERAL HOURS LATER Neil's sleep was disturbed. Brow puckering, he turned his head. The mattress shifted, but he hadn't been the one to move. He struggled to open an eye. The room was pitch-black.

When the mattress shifted again, he opened the other eye. Was it Nancy? No, Nancy never stayed the night, and he wasn't seeing Nancy anymore. Then . . .

It took him a minute to get his bearings, and by the time he did, a dull pounding had started at the back of his head. He rolled to his side, tucked his chin down and pulled his knees up. He'd fall back to sleep, he told himself. He'd keep his eyes closed, breathe deeply and steadily, and fall back to sleep.

A soft moan came from the far side of the bed, followed by another shift in the mattress.

Eyes flying open, Neil swore silently. Then, gritting his teeth, he moved nearer his edge of the bed and closed his eyes again.

For a time there was silence. He was nearly asleep, when another moan came. It was a closed-mouth moan, more of a grunt, and, as before, was followed by the rustle of bedding and the shimmy of the mattress.

His head throbbed. Cursing, he threw back the covers and stalked into the bathroom. The sudden light was glaring; he squinted against it as he shoved the medicine chest open. Insect repellent . . . Caladryl lotion . . . antihistamine . . .

aspirin. Aspirin. He fought with the child-proof cap for a minute and was on the verge of breaking the bottle, when it finally opened. Shaking three tablets into his palm, he tossed them into his mouth, threw his head back and swallowed, then bent over and drank directly from the tap. Hitting the light switch with a blind palm, he returned to bed.

The aspirin had barely had time to take effect, when Deirdre moaned and turned again. Neil bolted upright in bed and scowled in her direction, then groped for the lamp. Its soft glow was revealing. She was still buried beneath the covers, but her side of the quilt was pulled up and around every which way. Even as he watched, she twisted, lay still for several seconds, then twisted again.

"Deirdre!" He grasped what he calculated to be a handful of her shoulder and shook her. "Wake up, damn it! I can't sleep with that tossing and turning."

There was movement, independent of his shaking, from the lumps beneath the quilt. One hand emerged, slim fingers clutching the quilt, lowering it until a pair of heavily shadowed and distinctly disoriented brown eyes met his.

"Hmm?"

"You'll have to settle down," he informed her gruffly. "It's bad enough that I have to share this bed, but I refuse to do it with a woman who can't lie still."

Her eyes had suddenly widened at the "share this bed" part; they fell briefly to the shadowed expanse of his naked chest, then flew back up. Slowly, slowly they fluttered shut.

"I'm sorry," she whispered with a sincerity that momentarily took the wind from his sails.

"Were you having a nightmare?"

"No. My leg kills."

He studied the thick wedge that had to be her cast. "Is there something you're supposed to do for it? Didn't the doctor give you any instructions? Shouldn't you elevate it or something?"

Deirdre felt groggy and exceedingly uncomfortable. "They kept it hitched up in the hospital—to minimize swelling—but I thought that was over."

"Great." Neil threw off the covers and headed for the door. "I'm stuck here with a dimwit whose leg may swell to twice its normal size." His voice was loud enough to carry clearly back to her from the hall. "And if that happens your circulation may be cut off by the cast, and if *that* happens, gangrene may set in. Terrific." He stomped back into the master bedroom, carrying two pillows under each arm, went straight to her side of the bed and unceremoniously hauled back the quilt.

"What are you doing?" she cried, blinking in confusion.

"Elevating your leg." He had two of the pillows on the bed and was trying to sort out the legs of her pajamas. "There's so much damned material here . . . Can you move your good leg? There, I've got it." With surprising gentleness, he raised her casted leg just enough to slip the pillows underneath.

"Gangrene won't set in," she argued meekly. "You don't know what you're talking about."

"At least I know enough to prop up your leg." With a flick of his wrist, he tossed the quilt back over her as he rounded the bed to reach his side. "That feels better, doesn't it?"

"It feels the same."

"Give it a minute or two. It'll feel better." He turned off the light and climbed back into bed, dropped his head to the pillow and massaged his temple. Seconds later he was up again, this time heading back to the bathroom. When he returned, he carried a glass of water and two pills. "Can you sit up?"

"Why?"

"Because I think you should take these."

The only light in the room was the sliver that spilled from the bathroom. The dimness made Deirdre feel at a marked disadvantage to the man who loomed above her. "What are they?"

"Aspirin."

He was so large . . . shadowed . . . ominous. He wasn't wearing much. What did he intend? "I don't take pills."

"These are harmless."

"If they're harmless, why should I bother to take them?"

"Because they may just help the ache in your leg, and if that happens you'll lie quietly, and then maybe I'll be able to sleep."

"You can always try another bedroom."

"No way, but that's beside the point. Right now we're discussing your taking two innocent aspirin."

"How do I know they're innocent? How do I know they're aspirin at all? I don't know you. Why should I trust anything you give me?"

Amazed that Deirdre whoever-she-was could be as perverse in the middle of the night as she was during the day, he gave an exasperated sigh. "Because, A, I took these pills from a bottle marked Aspirin, which I found in Victoria's medicine chest. B, I took three of them myself a little while ago, and I'm not up, down or dead yet. And C, I'm Victoria's friend, and that's about as good a character reference as you're going to get." He sucked in a breath. "Besides, it works both ways, you know."

"What does?"

"Character references. I have to trust that you're clean—"

"What do you mean, clean?"

"That you don't have any perversions, or addictions, or contagious diseases . . ."

"Of course I don't!"

"How can I be sure?"

"Because I'm Victoria's friend—"

"And Victoria knowingly stuck us together, so we have to trust that neither of us is an unsavory character, because we both do trust Victoria. At least I do. Or did." He threw his clenched fist in the air. "I don't believe I'm standing here arguing. Do you, or do you not, want the damn aspirin?" His fist dropped and opened, cradling the tablets.

"I want them."

Neil let out an exaggerated breath. "Then we're back where we started. Can you sit up?" He spoke the last very slowly, as though she might not understand him otherwise.

Deirdre was beyond taking offense. "If I can't, I have no business doing what I do," she muttered to herself, and began to elbow her way up. With her leg elevated, the maneuvering was difficult. Still, she was supposedly agile, an athlete, an expert at bending and twisting . . .

Neil didn't wait to watch her fall. He came down on a knee on the bed, curved his arm beneath her back and propped her up. "The pills are in my right hand. Can you reach them?"

His right hand was by her waist; his left held the glass. She took the tablets, pressed them into her mouth and washed them down with the water he offered.

Neither of them spoke.

Neil lowered her to the sheets, removed his knee from the bed and walked back to the bathroom. Quietly he set the glass by the sink, switched off the light and returned to bed.

Deirdre lay silent, unmoving, strangely peaceful. Her leg felt better; her entire body felt better. She closed her eyes, took a long, slow breath and drifted into a deep, healing sleep.

When she awoke it was daylight—overcast still, raining still, but daylight nonetheless. She lay quietly, gradually assimilating where she was and what she was doing there. As the facts crystallized, she realized that she wasn't alone in the bed. From its far side came a quiet breathing; she turned her head slowly, saw the large quilt-covered shape of Victoria's other friend, turned her head back. Then the crux of her dilemma hit her.

She'd fled Rhode Island, driven for hours in the pouring rain, been drenched, mud spattered, nearly seasick—all to be alone. But she wasn't. She was marooned on an island, some twenty miles from shore, with a grump of a man. Now what was she going to do?

Neil was asking himself the same question. He lay on his side with his eyes wide open, listening to the sounds of Deirdre's breathing, growing more annoyed by the minute. He did believe what he'd said the night before. If she was Victoria's friend—and she knew a convincing amount about Victoria—she couldn't be all bad. Still, she was disagreeable, and he wanted to be alone.

Pushing back the quilt, he swung his legs to the floor, then paused to give his head a chance to adjust to the shift in position. His head ached, though he was as ready to blame it on Deirdre as on the amount of Scotch he'd drunk the evening before.

"Don't you have something decent to wear?" came a perturbed voice from beneath the quilt.

His head shot around. Mistake. He put the heels of his hands on his temples and inch by inch faced forward. "There's nothing indecent about my skin," he gritted.

"Don't you have pajamas?"

"Like yours?"

"What's wrong with mine? They're perfectly good pajamas."

"They're men's pajamas." Even as he said it his arm tingled. It was his right arm, the one he'd used to prop her up. Sure, she'd been wearing men's pajamas, but beneath all the fabric was a slender back, a slim waist and the faintest curve of a hip.

"They're comfortable, and warm."

"I don't need warmth," he growled roughly.

"It's freezing in here. Isn't there any heat?"

"I like my bedroom cold."

"Great." It was an argument to be continued later. For the moment, there was something more pressing. Vividly she recalled the sight of his chest, the corded muscles, the dark swirls of hair. "It might have been considerate of you to put *something* on when you decided to crawl into bed with me."

"Be grateful for the consideration I did make. I usually sleep in the buff."

She clenched a fistful of quilt by her cheek. "So macho."

"What's the matter?" he shot back. "Can't handle it?"

"There's nothing to handle. Macho has never turned me on."

"Not enough woman for it?"

The low blow hit hard, causing her to lash out in self-defense. "Too much of a woman. I hate to disillusion you, but machismo is pretty shallow."

"Ah, the expert."

"No. Simply a modern woman."

Muttering a pithy curse, Neil pushed himself from bed. "Save it for Thomas when he comes back for you later. Right now, I need a shower."

She started to look up, but caught herself. "I need a bath."

"You had your chance last night and you blew it. Now it's my turn."

"Use one of the other bathrooms. They've got showers."

"I like this one."

"But it's the only one with a tub!"

"You can have it as soon as I'm done."

"What happened to chivalry?"

"Talk of chivalry from a modern woman?" he chided, and soundly closed the bathroom door behind him.

Deirdre did look up then. He'd had the last word . . . so he thought. Rolling to her side, she grabbed her crutches from the floor and hobbled from the bedroom. Off the short hall on the other side of the living room was a den, and in the den was the ship-to-shore radio.

She checked her watch. Ten-forty-five. *Ten-forty-five*? She couldn't believe she'd slept round the clock and then some! But she'd needed it. She'd been exhausted. And she'd slept soundly once she'd been settled with her leg propped up and aspirin dispersing through her system.

Ten-forty-five. Had she missed Thomas? Would he be home or out on the boat? It was rainy, true, but windy?

She studied the directions beside the radio and, after several unsuccessful attempts, managed to put through the call. A young man responded, clearly not the lobsterman.

"It's urgent that I reach Thomas," she said.

"Is there an emergency?" the young man asked.

"Not exactly an emergency in the critical sense of the word, but—"

"Are you well?"

"Yes, I'm well—"

"And Mr. Hersey?"

Hersey. "Neil? He's well, too, but it really is important that I speak with Thomas."

"I'll have him call you as soon as he can."

She tightened her fingers on the coiled cord of the speaker. "When do you think that will be?"

"I don't know."

"Is he on the boat?"

"He's in Augusta on business."

"Oh. Is he due back today?"

"I believe so."

Frustration. She sighed. "Well, please give him the message."

After the young man assured her he would, Deirdre replaced the speaker and turned off the set. In Augusta on business. She wondered. Thomas would know precisely why she was calling; he'd known precisely what he was doing yesterday when he left both of his unsuspecting passengers on Victoria's island together.

She thought back to the things he'd said. He'd been smooth. She had to hand it to him. He'd been general enough, vague enough. He'd never lied, simply given clever, well-worded answers to her questions.

She wasn't at all sure she could trust him to call back.

Scowling, she turned at the sound of footsteps in the hall. So Neil had finished his shower, had he? And what was he planning to do now? She listened. The footsteps receded, replaced by the sound of the refrigerator door opening, then closing. He was in the kitchen. Good. Now she'd take her bath, and she'd take her sweet time about it.

In truth, she couldn't have rushed if she'd wanted to. Maneuvering herself into the tub was every bit the hassle she'd expected. Particularly awkward—and annoying—was the fact that the tub was flush against one wall, and in order to drape her casted leg over its lip she had to put her back to the faucets. Her decision to climb in before she ran the water resulted in a considerable amount of contortion, not to mention the fact that when she tried to lie back, the spigot pressed into her head. She finally managed to wedge herself into a corner, which meant that she was lying almost diagonally in the tub.

It was better than nothing, or so she told herself when she gave up the idea of relaxing to concentrate on getting clean. That, too, was a trial. With both hands occupied soaping and scrubbing, she slid perilously low in the water. Just as well, she reasoned. Her hair needed washing as badly, if not more than the rest of her. How long had it been since she'd had a proper shampoo? A week?

"Yuk."

Tipping her head back, she immersed her hair, doused it with shampoo and scrubbed. Unfortunately she'd used too much shampoo. No amount of dipping her head in the water removed it completely, and by then the water was dirty. She was thoroughly disgusted. In the end she drained the tub, turned on fresh warm water, sharply arched her back to put her head in the stream and hoped for the best.

By the time she'd awkwardly made her way out of the tub, she was tense all over. So much for a refreshing bath, she mused. But at least she was clean. There was some satisfaction in that. There was also satisfaction in rubbing moisturizing lotion over her body, a daily ritual that had been temporarily abandoned during her stay in the hospital. The scent of it was faint but familiar. When she closed her eyes she could imagine that she was back home, in one piece, looking forward to the day.

She couldn't keep her eyes closed forever, though, and when she opened them, the truth hit. She was neither home, nor in one piece, nor looking forward to the day. Rather, she was in self-imposed exile on Victoria's island. Her left leg was in a heavy cast, her face was decidedly pale and she was pathetically weak. And she was not looking forward to the day, because *he* was here.

Angrily she tugged on her underwear, then the mint green warm-up suit she'd brought. It was loose, oversized and stylish, and the top matched the bottom. He couldn't complain about her clothes today.

Propping herself on the toilet seat, she worked a pair of white wool leg warmers over her cast, then her good leg, put a single white crew sock on the good foot, then a single white sneaker. She towel-dried her hair with as much energy as she could muster, then, leaning against the sink, brushed it until it shone.

She studied her face. A lost cause. Squeaky clean, but a lost cause nonetheless. It was pale, bland, childlike. She'd always looked younger than her years. When she'd been in her late teens and early twenties, she'd hated it. Now, with women her age doing their best to look younger, she had her moments of self-appreciation. This wasn't one of them. She looked awful.

A pouting child? Perhaps, but only because of *him*. With a deep breath, she turned from the mirror and began to neaten the bathroom. *Him.* What an unpleasant man, an unpleasant situation. And a remedy? There was none, until she reached Thomas, until she convinced him that, for her sanity alone, Neil Hersey should be removed from the island.

A few minutes later, she entered the kitchen to find the remnants of bacon smoke in the air, two dirty pans on the stove, the counter littered with open cartons of juice and milk, a bowl of eggs, a tub of margarine, an open package of English muffins and miscellaneous crumbs. Neil Hersey was nonchalantly finishing his breakfast.

"You're quite a cook," she remarked wryly. "Does your skill extend to cleaning up after yourself, or were you expecting the maid to come in and do it?"

Neil set down his fork, rocked back in his chair and studied her. "So that's why Victoria sent you along. I knew there had to be a reason."

Deirdre snickered. "If you think I'm going to touch this disaster area, you're crazy. You made the mess, you clean it up."

"And if I don't?"

"Then you'll have spoiled juice and milk, stale muffins and dirty dishes to use next time." She stared at the greasy pans. "What did you make, anyway?"

"Bacon and eggs. Sound tempting?"

Her mouth was watering. "It might if you didn't use so much fat. I'd think that at your age you'd be concerned about that, not to mention the cholesterol in however many eggs you ate."

"Four. I was hungry. Aren't you? You didn't have supper."

"I had other things on my mind last night." She sent him a look of mock apology and spoke in her sweetest tone. "I'm sorry. Were you waiting for me to join you for dinner?"

His lips twisted. "Not quite. I had better company than you could ever be."

"A bottle of Scotch?" At his raised brows, she elaborated. "It's sitting right there in the living room with a half-empty glass beside it. Now that was brilliant. Do you always drown your sorrows in booze?"

The front legs of his chair hit the floor with a thud. "I don't drink," he stated baldly.

"Then we must have a little gremlin here who just happened to get into the liquor cabinet."

Faint color rose on Neil's neck. "I had a couple of drinks last night, but I'm not a drinker." He scowled. "And what's it to you? I came here to do what I want, and if that means getting drunk every night, amen."

He was being defensive, and Deirdre found she liked that. Not just because she was momentarily on top. There was something else, something related to that hint of a blush on his neck. "You know, you're really not all that bad-looking." Her gaze fell to take in his large, maroon-and-white rugby shirt and slimmer fitting jeans. "Aside from a receding hairline and all that crap you've got on your face—"

Neil reacted instantly. His eyes narrowed and his jaw grew tight. "My hairline is not receding. It's the same one I've had for years, only I don't choose to hide it like some men do. And as for 'all that crap' on my face, they're whiskers, in case you didn't know."

"You could have shaved."

"Why should I?"

"Because I'm here, for one thing."

"Through no choice of mine. This is my vacation you're intruding on, and the way I see it, you don't have any say as to what I do or how I look. Got that?"

Deirdre stared mutely back at him.

"Got that?" he repeated.

"I'm not hard of hearing," she said quietly.

He rolled his eyes. "Thank goodness for that, at least."

"But you've got it wrong. You're the one who's intruding on my time here, and I'll thank you to make yourself as invisible as possible until Thomas comes to pick you up."

Neil stood then, drew himself up and slowly approached her. "Make myself invisible, huh? Just how do you suggest I do that?"

He came closer and closer. Even barefoot he towered over her. Deirdre tipped back her head, stubbornly maintaining eye contact, refusing to be cowed. "You can clean up the kitchen when you're done, for one thing."

"I would have done that, anyway. . . when I was done."

"For another, you can busy yourself exploring the island."

"In the rain?"

"For a third, you can take yourself and your things to one of the other bedrooms."

His voice suddenly softened. "You didn't like my taking care of you last night?"

His question hung in the air. It wasn't that the words were shocking, or even particularly suggestive, but something about his nearness made Deirdre's breath catch in her throat. Yes, he was large, but that wasn't it. Yes, he looked roguish, but that wasn't it, either. He looked . . . he looked . . . warm . . . gentle . . . deep?

Neil, too, was momentarily stunned. When he'd come up so close, he hadn't quite expected—what? That she should smell so fresh, so feminine? That the faint, nearly transparent smattering of freckles on the bridge of her nose should intrigue him? That she should have dusty brown eyes, the eyes of a woman?

Swallowing once, he stepped back and tore his gaze from hers. It landed on the littered counter. With but a moment's pause, he began to close containers and return them to the refrigerator. "How does your leg feel?"

"Okay," Deirdre answered cautiously.

"Any worse than yesterday?"

"No."

He nodded and continued with his work.

Deirdre took a breath, surprised to find herself slightly shaky. "I, uh, I tried to call Thomas. He wasn't in."

"I know."

So he'd tried, too. She should have figured as much. Hobbling on her crutches to the stool by the counter peninsula, she propped herself on its edge. "We have to find a solution."

"Right."

"Any thoughts on it?"

His head was in the refrigerator, but his words carried clearly. "You know them."

She certainly did. "Then we're stalemated."

"Looks that way."

"I guess the only thing to do is to dump the problem in Victoria's lap. She caused it. Let her find a solution."

The refrigerator door swung shut. Neil straightened and thrust a hand on his hip. "That's great. But if we can't reach Thomas, how in the hell are we going to reach Victoria?"

"We'll just have to keep trying."

"And in the meantime?"

She grinned. "We'll just have to keep fighting."

Neil stared at her. It was the first time he'd seen her crack a smile. Her teeth were small, white and even; her lips were soft, generous. "You like fighting."

"I never have before, but, yeah, I kinda like it." She tilted her head to the side, tipped her chin up in defiance. "It feels good."

"You are strange, lady," he muttered as he transferred the dirty pans to the sink with more force than necessary. "Strange."

"Any more so than you?"

"There's nothing strange about me."

"Are you kidding? I haven't been arguing in a vacuum, you know. You even admitted that you enjoy picking on me. I dare you to tell me how that's any different from my saying I like fighting."

He sent a leisurely stream of liquid soap onto a sponge. "Give me a break, will you?"

"Give *me* a break, and hurry up, will you? I'm waiting to use the kitchen, or have you forgotten? It's been twenty-four hours since I've eaten—"

"And whose fault is that? If you'd stayed home where you belonged, you wouldn't have missed any meals."

"Maybe not, but if I'd stayed home, I'd have gone crazy!"

Neil stared at her over his shoulder; Deirdre stared back. The question was there; he was on the verge of asking it. She dared him to, knowing she'd take pleasure in refusing him.

In the end he didn't ask. He wasn't sure he wanted to know what she'd left that was so awful. He wasn't sure he wanted to think of someone else's problems. He wasn't sure he wanted to feel sympathy for this strange woman-child.

Perversely disappointed, Deirdre levered herself from the stool, fit her crutches under her arms and swung into the living room. Though it was the largest room in the house, it had a feel of coziness. Pine, dark stained and rich, dominated the decor—wall paneling; rafters and pillars; a large, low hub of a coffee table, and the surrounding, sturdy frames of a cushioned sofa and chairs. The center of one entire wall was bricked into a huge fireplace. Deirdre thought she'd very much like to see the fire lit.

Propping her hip against the side of one of the chairs, she gave the room a sweeping overview. No doubt about it, she mused sadly. The room, the house, the island—all had high potential for romance. Miles from nowhere . . . an isolated, insulated retreat . . . fire crackling mingled with the steady patter of rain. At the right time, with the right man, it would be wonderful. She could understand why so many of Victoria's friends had raved about the place.

"It's all yours," Neil said. Momentarily confused, Deirdre frowned at him. "The kitchen. I thought you were dying of hunger."

The kitchen. "I am."

"Then it's yours."

"Thank you."

He stepped back, allowing more than ample room for her to pass. "There's hot coffee in the pot. Help yourself."

"Thank you."

Just as she was moving by, he leaned forward. "I make it thick. Any objections?"

She paused, head down. "What do you think?"

"I think yes."

"You're right. I like mine thin."

"Add water."

"It tastes vile that way."

"Then make a fresh pot."

"I will." She looked up at him. His face was inches away. Dangerous. "If you don't mind . . ."

Taking the hint, he straightened. She swung past him and entered the kitchen, where she set about preparing a meal for the first time in a week.

It was a challenge. She began to remove things from the refrigerator, only to find that she couldn't possibly handle her crutches and much else at the same time. So she stood at the open refrigerator, balancing herself against the door, taking out one item, then another, lining each up on the counter. When she'd removed what she needed, she balanced herself against the counter and, one by one, moved each item in line toward the stove. A crutch fell. Painstakingly she worked her way down to pick it up, only to have it fall again when she raised her arm a second time.

For a woman who'd always prided herself on economy of movement, such a production was frustrating. She finally gave up on the crutches entirely, resorting alternately to leaning against counters and hopping. Each step of the preparation was an ordeal, made all the worse when she thought of how quickly and effortlessly she'd normally do it. By the time she'd finally poured the makings of a cheese omelet into the pan, she was close to tears.

Lounging comfortably on the sofa in the living room, Neil listened to her struggles. It served her right, he mused smugly. She should have stayed at home—wherever that was. Where was it? He wondered what would have driven her crazy had she not left, then he chided himself for wondering when he had worries aplenty of his own.

He thought of those worries and his mood darkened. Nothing had changed with his coming here; the situation would remain the same in Hartford regardless of how long he stayed away. He had to think. He had to analyze his career, his accomplishments and aspirations. He had to decide on a positive course of action.

So far he was without a clue.

The sound of shattering glass brought his head up. "What the hell . . ." He was on his feet and into the kitchen within seconds.

Deirdre was gripping the stove with one hand, her forehead with another. She was staring at the glass that lay broken in a puddle of orange juice on the floor. "What in the devil's the matter with you?" he yelled. "Can't you manage the simplest little thing?"

Tear-filled eyes flew to his. "No, I can't! And I'm not terribly thrilled about it!" Angrily she grabbed the sponge from the sink and knelt on her good knee.

"Let me do that," Neil growled, but she had a hand up, warding him off.

"No! I'll do it myself!" Piece by piece, she began gathering up the shards of broken glass.

He straightened slowly. She was stubborn. And independent. And slightly dumb. With her cast hooked precariously to the side, her balance was iffy at best. He imagined her losing it, falling forward, catching herself on a palm, which in turn would catch its share of glass slivers.

Grabbing several pieces of paper towel, he knelt, pushed her hands aside and set to work cleaning the mess. "There's no need to cry over spilled milk," he said gently.

"It's spilled orange juice, and I'm not crying." Using that same good leg, she raised herself. Her thigh muscles labored, and she cringed to think how out of shape she'd become in a mere week. "You don't have to do that."

"If I don't, you're apt to do even worse damage."

"I can take care of myself!" she vowed, then turned to the stove. The omelet was burning. "Damn!" Snatching up a spatula, she quickly folded the egg mixture in half and turned off the heat. "A crusty omelet. Just what I need!" Balling her hands against the edge of the stove, she threw her head back. "Damn it to hell. Why me?"

Neil dumped the sodden paper towels in the wastebasket and reached for fresh ones. "Swearing won't help."

"Wanna bet!" Her eyes flashed as she glared at him. "It makes me feel better, and since that's the case, I'll do it as much as I damn well please!"

He looked up from his mopping. "My, my, aren't we in a mood."

"Yes, we are, and you're not doing anything to help it."

"I'm cleaning up."

"You're making me feel like a helpless cripple. I told you I'd do it. I'm not totally incapacitated, damn it!"

He sighed. "Didn't anyone ever tell you that a lady shouldn't swear?"

Her lips twisted. "Oh-ho, yes. My mother, my father, my sister, my uncles—for years I've had to listen to complaints." She launched into a whiny mimic and tipped her head from one side to the other. "'Don't say that, Deirdre,' or 'Don't do that Deirdre,' or 'Deirdre, smile and be pleasant,' or 'Behave like a lady, Deirdre.'" Her voice returned to its normal pitch, but it held anger. "Well, if what I do isn't ladylike, that's tough!" She took a quick breath and added as an afterthought, "And if I want to swear, I'll do it!"

With that, she hopped to the counter stool and plopped down on it with her back to Neil.

Silently he finished cleaning the floor. He poured a fresh glass of juice, toasted the bread she'd taken out, lightly spread it with jam and set the glass and plate before her. "Do you want the eggs?" he asked softly.

She shook her head and sat for several minutes before slowly lifting one of the slices of toast and munching on it.

Neil, who was leaning against the counter with his ankles crossed and his arms folded over his chest, studied her defeated form. "Do you live with your family?"

She carefully chewed what was in her mouth, then swallowed. "Thank God, no."

"But you live nearby."

"A giant mistake. I should have moved away years ago. Even California sounds too close. Alaska might be better—northern Alaska."

"That bad, huh?"

"That bad." She took a long, slow drink of juice, concentrating on the cooling effect it had on her raspy throat. Maybe she was coming down with a cold. It wouldn't surprise her, given the soaking she'd taken the day before. Then again, maybe she'd picked up something at the hospital. That was more likely. Hospitals were chock-full of germs, and it would be just her luck to pick one up. Just her luck. "Why are you being so nice?"

"Maybe I'm a nice guy at heart."

She couldn't bear the thought of that, not when she was in such a foul mood herself. "You're an ill-tempered, scruffy-faced man."

Pushing himself from the counter, he muttered, "If you say so," and returned to the living room, where he sat staring sullenly at the cold hearth while Deirdre finished the small breakfast he'd made for her. He heard her cleaning up, noted the absence of both audible mishaps and swearing and found himself speculating on the kind of person she was at heart. He knew about himself. He wasn't really ill-tempered, only a victim of circumstance. Was she the same?

He wondered how old she was.

By the time Deirdre finished in the kitchen, she was feeling a little better. Her body had responded to nourishment; despite her sulky refusal, she'd even eaten part of the omelet. It was more overcooked than burned and was barely lukewarm by the time she got to it, but it was protein. Her voice of reason said she needed that.

Turning toward the living room, she saw Neil sprawled in the chair. She didn't like him. More accurately, she didn't want him here. He was a witness to her clumsiness. That, on top of everything else, embarrassed her.

In the back of her mind was the niggling suspicion that at heart he might well be a nice guy. He'd helped her the night before. He'd helped her this morning. Still, he had his own problems; when they filled his mind, he was as moody, as curt, as churlish as she was. Was he as much of a misfit as she sometimes felt?

She wondered what he did for a living.

With a firm grip on her crutches, she made her way into the living room, going first to the picture window, then retreating until she was propped against the sofa back. From this vantage point she could look at the world beyond the house. The island was gray and wet; its verdancy made a valiant attempt at livening the scene, but failed.

"Lousy day," Neil remarked.

"Mmm."

"Any plans?"

"Actually," she said with a grand intake of breath, "I was thinking of getting dressed and going to the theater."

He shook his head. "The show's sold out, standing room only. You'd never make it, one-legged."

"Thanks."

"Don't feel bad. The show isn't worth seeing."

"Not much is nowadays," she answered. If she was going to be sour, she mused, she might as well do it right. By nature she was an optimist, choosing to gloss over the negatives in life. But all along she'd known the negatives were there. For a change, she wanted to look at them and complain. It seemed to her she'd earned the right.

"I can't remember the last time I saw a good show, or, for that matter, a movie," she began with spirited venom. "Most of them stink. The stories are either so pat and contrived that you're bored to tears, or so bizarre that you can't figure out what's happening. The settings are phony, the music is blah and the acting is pathetic. Or maybe it's the casting that's pathetic. I mean, Travolta was wonderful in *Saturday Night Fever*. He took Barbarino one step further—just suave enough, just sweet enough, just sensitive enough and born to dance. But a newspaper reporter in *Perfect*? Oh, please. The one scene that might have been good was shot in the exercise class, but the camera lingered so long on Travolta's pelvis it was disgusting!"

Neil was staring at her, one finger resting against his lips. "Uh, I'm not really an expert on Travolta's pelvis, disgusting or otherwise."

"Have *you* seen anything good lately?"

"In the way of a pelvis?"

"In the way of a movie."

"I don't have time to go to the movies."

"Neither do I, but if there's something I want to see—a movie, an art exhibit, a concert—I make time. You never do that?"

"For basketball I do."

She wondered if he himself had ever played. He had both the height and the build. "What team?"

"The Celtics."

"You're from Boston?"

"No. But I got hooked when I went to school there. Now I just drive up whenever I can get my hands on tickets. I also make time for lectures."

"What kind of lectures?"

"Current affairs-type talks. You know, by politicians or business superstars—Kissinger, Iacocca."

Her eyes narrowed. "I'll bet you'd go to hear John Dean speak."

Neil shrugged. "I haven't. But I might. He was intimately involved in a fascinating period of our history."

"He was a criminal! He spent time in prison!"

"He paid the price."

"He named his price—books, a TV miniseries, the lecture circuit—doesn't it gall you to think that crime can be so profitable?"

Moments before, the conversation had been purely incidental; suddenly it hit home. "Yes," he said stiffly, "it galls me."

"Yet you'd pay money to go hear someone talk about his experiences on the wrong side of the law?"

Yes, he would have, and he'd have rationalized it by saying that the speaker was providing a greater service by telling all. Now, though, he thought of his experience at Wittnauer-Douglass and felt a rising anger. "You talk too much," he snapped.

Deirdre was momentarily taken aback. She'd expected him to argue, either for her or against her. But he was cutting the debate short. "What did I say?"

"Nothing," he mumbled, sitting farther back in his seat. "Nothing important."

"Mmm. As soon as the little lady hits a raw nerve, you put her down as 'nothing important.'"

"Not 'nothing important,' as in you. As in what you said."

"I don't see much difference. That's really macho of you. Macho, as in coward."

Neil surged from his chair and glared at her. "Ah, hell, give me a little peace, will ya? All I wanted to do was to sit here quietly, minding my own business."

"You were the one who talked first."

"That's right. I was trying to be civil."

"Obviously it didn't work."

"It would have if you hadn't been spoiling for a fight."

"Me spoiling for a fight? We were having a simple discussion about the ethics involved in giving financial support to convicted political criminals, when you went off the handle. I asked you a simple question. All you had to do was to give me a simple answer."

"But I don't have the answer!" he bellowed. A vein throbbed at his temple. "I don't have answers for lots of things lately, and it's driving me out of my mind!"

Lips pressed tightly together, he stared at her, then whirled around and stormed off toward the den.

4

WITH NEIL'S EXIT, the room became suddenly quiet. Deirdre listened, knowing that he'd be trying to reach Thomas again. She prayed he'd get through, for his sake as well as hers. She and Neil were like oil and water; they didn't mix well.

Taking advantage of the fact that she had the living room to herself, she stretched out on the sofa, closed her eyes and pretended she was alone in the house. It was quiet, so quiet. Neither the gentle patter of rain nor the soft hum of heat blowing through the vents disturbed the peaceful aura. She imagined she'd made breakfast without a problem in the world, and that the day before she'd transferred everything from Thomas's boat without a hitch. In her dream world she hadn't needed help, because her broken leg was good as new.

But that was her dream world. In reality, she had needed help, and Neil Hersey had been there. She wondered what it would be like if he were a more even-tempered sort. He was good-looking; she gave that to him, albeit begrudgingly. He was strong; she recalled the arm that had supported her when he'd brought her aspirin, remembered the broad chest she'd leaned against. He was independent and capable, cooking for himself, cleaning up both his mess and hers without a fuss.

He had potential, all right. He also had his dark moments. At those times, given her own mood swings, she wanted to be as far from him as possible.

As she lay thinking, wondering, imagining, her eyelids slowly lowered, and without intending to, she dozed off. A full hour later she awoke with a start. She'd been dreaming.

Of Neil. A lovely dream. An annoying dream. The fact that she'd slept at all annoyed her, because it pointed to a physical weakness she detested. She'd slept for fourteen hours the night before. Surely that had been enough. And to dream of *Neil*?

She'd been right in her early assessment of him; he was as troubled as she was. She found herself pondering the specifics of his problem, then pushed those ponderings from her mind. She had her own problems. She didn't need his.

What she needed, she decided, was a cup of coffee. After the breakfast fiasco, she hadn't had either the courage or the desire to tackle coffee grounds, baskets and filters. Now, though, the thought of drinking something hot and aromatic appealed to her.

Levering herself awkwardly to her feet, she went into the kitchen and shook the coffeepot. He'd said there was some left but that it was thick. She didn't like thick coffee. Still, it was a shame to throw it out.

Determinedly she lit the gas and set the coffee on to heat.

Meanwhile, Neil was in the den, staring out the window at the rain, trying to understand himself. Deirdre Joyce—the young man who'd answered at Thomas's house had supplied her last name—was a thorn in his side. He wanted to be alone, yet she was here. It was midafternoon. He still hadn't spoken with Thomas, which meant that Deirdre was going to be around for another night at least.

What annoyed him most were the fleeting images that played tauntingly in the corners of his mind. A smooth, lithe back...a slim waist...the suggestion of a curve at the hip...a fresh, sweet scent...hair the color of wheat, not mousy brown as he'd originally thought, but thick, shining wheat. Her face, too, haunted him. She had the prettiest light-brown eyes, a small, almost delicate nose, lips that held promise when she smiled.

Of course, she rarely smiled. She had problems. And the fact of the matter was that he really did want to be alone. So why was he thinking of her in a way that would suggest that he found her attractive?

From the door came the clearing of a throat. "Uh, excuse me?"

He turned his head. Damn, but the mint-green of her warm-up suit was cheerful. Of course, she still looked lumpy as hell. "Yes?"

"I heated up the last of the coffee, but it really is too strong for me. I thought you might like it." Securing her right crutch with the muscles of her upper arm, she held out the cup.

Neil grew instantly wary. It was the first attempt she'd made at being friendly. Coming after nonstop termagancy, there had to be a reason. She had to want something. "Why?" he asked bluntly.

"Why what?"

"Why did you heat it up?"

She frowned. "I told you. I thought you might like it."

"You haven't been terribly concerned with my likes before."

"And I'm not now," she replied defensively. "It just seemed a shame to throw it out."

"Ah. You're making a fresh pot, so you heated the dregs for me."

"I don't believe you," she breathed. She hadn't expected such instant enmity, and coming in the face of her attempted pleasantness, it set her off. "You would have had me drink the dregs, but suddenly they're not good enough for you?"

"I didn't say they weren't good enough." His voice was smooth, with an undercurrent of steel. "I reheat coffee all the time because it saves time, and yes, it is a shame to throw it out. What I'm wondering is why the gesture of goodwill from you. You must have something up your sleeve."

"Boy," she remarked with a wry twist of her lips, "have *you* been burned."

His eyes darkened. "And just what do you mean by that?"

"For a man to be as suspicious of a woman, he'd have to have been used by one, and used badly."

Neil thought about that for a minute. Funny, it had never occurred to him before, but he had been used. Nancy had been crafty—subtle enough so the fact had registered only subliminally in his brain—but crafty nonetheless. Only now did he realize that often she'd done small things for him when she'd wanted something for herself. It fit in with the nature of her love, yet he hadn't seen it then. Just as he hadn't seen the potential for treachery at Wittnauer-Douglass.

"My history is none of your damned business," he ground out angrily.

"Fine," she spat. "I just want you to know that it's taken a monumental effort on my part to get the dumb coffee in here without spilling it. And if you want to know the truth, my major motivation was to find out where you were so I'd know what room to avoid." She set the mug on a nearby bookshelf with a thud. "You can have this or not. I don't care." She turned to leave, but not fast enough to hide the hint of hurt in her expression.

"Wait."

She stopped, but didn't turn back. "What for?" she asked. "So you can hurl more insults at me?"

He moved from the window. "I didn't mean to do that. You're right. I've been burned. And it was unfair of me to take it out on you."

"Seems to me you've been taking an awful lot out on me."

"And vice versa," he said quietly, satisfied when she looked over her shoulder at him. "You have to admit that you haven't been the most congenial of housemates yourself."

"I've had . . . other things on my mind."

He took a leisurely step closer. "So have I. I've needed to let off steam. Yelling at you feels good. It may not be right, but it feels good."

"Tell me about it," she muttered rhetorically, but he took her at face value.

"It seems that my entire life has been ruled by reason and restraint. I've never spouted off quite this way about things that are really pretty petty."

She eyed him askance. "Like my using the master bedroom?"

"Now that's not petty. That's a practical issue."

"Then what about heat? The bedroom is freezing, while the rest of the house is toasty warm. You purposely kept the thermostat low in that room, didn't you?"

"I told you. I like a cool bedroom."

"Well, I like a warm one, and don't tell me to use one of the other bedrooms, because I won't. You'll be leaving—"

"You'll be leaving." His voice had risen to match the vehemence of hers, but it suddenly dropped again. "Only problem is that Thomas still isn't in, so it looks like it won't be today."

"He's avoiding us."

"That occurred to you, too, hmm?"

"Which means that we're stranded here." Glumly she looked around. "I mean, the house is wonderful. Look." She gestured toward one wall, then another. "Hundreds of books to choose from, a stereo, a VCR, a television—"

"The TV reception stinks. I tried it."

"No loss. I hate television."

"Like you hate movies?"

"I didn't say I hated movies, just that lately they've been awful. The same is true of television. If it isn't a corny sit-com, it's a blood-and-guts adventure show, or worse, a prime-time soap opera."

"Opinionated urchin, aren't you?"

Her eyes flashed and she gripped her crutches tighter. "Yes, I'm opinionated, and I'm in the mood to express every one of those opinions." Silently she dared him to stop her.

Neil had no intention of doing that. He was almost curious as to what she'd say next. Reaching for the mug she'd set down, he leaned against the bookshelf, close enough to catch the fresh scent that emanated from her. "Go on. I'm listening."

Deirdre, too, was aware of the closeness, aware of the breadth of his shoulders and the length of his legs, aware of the fact that he was more man than she'd been near for a very long time. Her cheeks began to feel warm, and there was a strange tickle in the pit of her stomach.

Confused, she glanced around, saw the long leather couch nearby, and inched back until she could sink into it. She raked her lip with her teeth, then looked up at him. "What was I saying?"

"You were giving me your opinion of the state of modern television."

"Oh." She took a breath and thought, finally saying, "I hate miniseries."

"Why?"

"They do awful things to the books they're adapted from."

"Not always."

"Often enough. And they're twice as long as they need to be. Take the opening part of each installment. They kill nearly fifteen minutes listing the cast, then reviewing what went before. I mean, the bulk of the viewers know what went before, and it's a waste of their time to rehash it. And as for the cast listings, the last thing those actors and actresses need is more adulation. Most of them are swellheaded as it is!" She was warming to the subject, enjoying her own perversity. "But the worst part of television has to be the news."

"I like the news," Neil protested.

"I do, too, when it is news, but when stations have two hours to fill each night, a good half of what they deliver simply isn't news. At least, not what I'd consider to be news. And as for the weather report, by the time they've finished with their elaborate electronic maps and radar screens, I've tuned out, so I miss the very forecast I wanted to hear."

"Maybe you ought to stick to newspapers."

"I usually do."

"What paper do you read?"

"The *Times*."

"New York?" He was wondering about her connection to Victoria. "Then you live there?"

"No. I live in Providence."

"Ah, Providence. Thriving little metropolis."

"What's wrong with Providence?"

"Nothing that a massive earthquake wouldn't fix." It was an exaggeration that gave him pleasure.

She stared hard at him. "You probably know nothing about Providence, much less Rhode Island, yet you'd stand there and condemn the entire area."

"Oh, I know something about Providence. I represented a client there two years ago, in the middle of summer, and the air conditioning in his office didn't work. Since it was a skyscraper, we couldn't even open a window, so we went to what was supposed to be the in restaurant. The service was lousy, the food worse, and to top it all off, some bastard sideswiped my car in the parking lot, so I ended up paying for that, too, and *then* my client waited a full six months before settling my bill."

Deirdre was curious. "What kind of client?"

"I'm a lawyer."

"A lawyer!" She pushed herself to the edge of the seat. "No wonder you're not averse to criminals on the lecture circuit. The proceeds could well be paying your fee!"

"I am not a criminal attorney," Neil stated. The crease between his brows grew pronounced. "I work with corporations."

"That's even worse! I hate corporations!"

"You hate most everything."

Deirdre's gaze remained locked with his for a moment. He seemed to be issuing a challenge, asking a question about her basic personality and daring her to tell the truth. "No," she said in a quieter tone. "I'm just airing certain pet peeves. I don't—I can't do it very often."

He, too, had quieted. "What do you do?"

"Hold it in."

"No. Work-wise. You do work, don't you? All modern women work."

Deirdre dipped one brow. "There's no need for sarcasm."

He made no apology. "You pride yourself on being a modern woman. So tell me. What do you do for a living?"

Slowly she gathered her crutches together. She couldn't tell him what she did; he'd have a field day with it. "That—" she rose "—is none of your business."

"Whoa. I told you what I do."

"And I told you where I live. So we're even." Leaning into the crutches, she headed for the door.

"But I want to know what kind of work you do."

"Tough."

"I'll bet you don't work," he taunted, staying close by her side. "I'll bet you're a very spoiled relative of one of Victoria's very well-to-do friends."

"Believe what you want."

"I'll bet you're here because you really wanted to be in Monte Carlo, but Daddy cut off your expense account. You're freeloading off Victoria for a while."

"Expense account?" She paused midway through the living room and gave a brittle laugh. "Do fathers actually put their twenty-nine-year-old daughters on expense accounts?"

Neil's jaw dropped. "Twenty-nine. You're pulling my leg."

"I wouldn't pull your leg if it were attached to Mel Gibson!" she vowed, and continued on into the kitchen.

"Twenty-nine? I would have given you twenty-three, maybe twenty-four. But twenty-nine?" He stroked the stubble on his face and spoke pensively. "Old enough to have been married at least once." He started after her. "Tell me you're running away from a husband who beats you. Did he cause the broken leg?"

"No."

"But there is a husband?"

She sent him an impatient look. "You obviously don't know Victoria very well. She'd never have thrown us together if one of us were already married."

He did know Victoria, and Deirdre was right. "Okay. Have you ever been married?"

"No."

"Are you living with someone?" When she sent him a second, even more impatient look, he defended himself. "It's possible. I wouldn't put it past Victoria to try to get you to forget him if he were a creep.... Okay, okay. So you're not living with someone. You've just broken up with him, and you've come here to lick your wounds."

"Wrong again." Seth had left four months before, and there had been no wounds to lick. Propping her crutches in a corner, she hopped to the cupboard. She was determined to make herself a cup of coffee. "This is sounding like *Twenty Questions*, which reminds me of what I *really* hate, and it's game shows like the one Thomas was watching yesterday. I mean, I know why people watch them. They play along, getting a rush when they correctly guess an answer before the contestant does. But the contestants—jumping all over the place, clapping their hands with glee when they win, kissing an emcee they don't know from Adam . . ." She shook her head. "Sad. Very sad."

Neil was standing close, watching her spoon coffee into the basket. Her hands were slender, well formed, graceful. There was something about the way she tipped the spoon that was almost lyrical. His gaze crept up her arm, over one rather nondescript shoulder to a neck that was anything but nondescript. It, too, was graceful. Strange, he hadn't noticed before. . . .

Momentarily suspending her work, Deirdre stared at him. Her eyes were wider than normal; her pulse had quickened. It occurred to her that she'd never seen so many textures on a man—from the thick gloss of his hair and the smooth slope of his nose to the furrowing of his brow and the bristle of his beard. She almost wanted to touch him . . . almost wanted to touch . . .

She tightened her fingers around the spoon. "Neil?"

He met her gaze, vaguely startled.

"I need room. I'm, uh, I'm not used to having someone around at home."

His frown deepened. "Uh, sure." He took a step back. "I think I'll . . . go take a walk or something."

Deirdre waited until he'd left, then slowly set back to work. *Take a walk. In the rain?* She listened, but there was no sound of the door opening and closing. So he was walking around the house. As good an activity as any to do on such a dismal day. She wondered when the rain would end. The island would be beautiful in sunshine. She'd love to go outside, find a high rock to sit on, and relax.

Surprisingly, when she thought of it, she wasn't all that tense, at least not in the way she'd been when she'd left Providence. In spite of the hassles of getting here, even in spite of the rain, the change of scenery was good for her. Of course, nothing had changed; Providence would be there when she returned. Her mother would be there, as would Sandra and the uncles. They'd be on her back again, unless she thought of some way to get them off.

She hadn't thought that far yet.

Carefully taking the coffee and a single crutch, she made her way into the den. She could put some weight on the cast without discomfort, which was a reassuring discovery. Carrying things such as coffee became a lot easier. Of course, it was a slow trip, and that still annoyed her, but it was better than being stuck in bed.

Leisurely sipping the coffee, she sat back on the leather sofa. Her duffel bag held several books, yarn and knitting needles, plus her cassette player and numerous tapes. None of these diversions appealed to her at the moment. She felt in limbo, as though she wouldn't completely settle down until Neil left.

But would he leave? Realistically? No. Not willingly. Not unless Victoria specifically instructed him to. Which she wouldn't.

Victoria had been clever. She'd known she was dealing with two stubborn people. She'd also known that once on the island, Neil and Deirdre would be virtually marooned. Thomas Nye was their only link with the mainland, and Thomas, while alert to any legitimate physical emergency, appeared to be turning a deaf ear to their strictly emotional pleas.

It was Neil and Deirdre versus the bad guys. An interesting prospect.

On impulse, she set down her cup and limped from the den. The house was quiet. She wondered what Neil was doing and decided that it was in her own best interest to find out. He hadn't returned to the living room while she'd been in the den, and he wasn't in the kitchen.

He was in the bedroom. The master bedroom. Deirdre stopped on the threshold and studied him. He lay on his back on the bed, one knee bent. His arm was thrown over his eyes.

Grateful she hadn't yet been detected, she was about to leave, when the whisper of a sound reached her ears. It was a little louder than normal breathing, a little softer than snoring. Neil was very definitely asleep.

Unable to help herself, she moved quietly forward until she stood by his side of the bed. His chest rose and fell in slow rhythm; his lips were faintly parted. As she watched, his fingers twitched, then stilled, and correspondingly something tugged at her heart.

He was human. When they'd been in the heat of battle, she might have tried to deny that fact, but seeing him now, defenseless in sleep, it struck her deeply. He was tired, perhaps emotionally as well as physically.

She found herself once again wondering what awful things he'd left behind. He was a lawyer; it was a good profession. Had something gone wrong with his career? Or perhaps his troubles related to his having been burned by a woman. Maybe he was suffering the effects of a bad divorce, perhaps worrying about children the marriage may have produced.

She actually knew very little about him. They'd been thrown together the moment she'd arrived at Spruce Head, and he'd simply provided a convenient punching bag on which to vent her frustrations. When she was arguing with him, she wasn't thinking of her leg, or aerobics, or Joyce Enterprises. Perhaps there was merit to his presence, after all.

He really wasn't so bad; at times she almost liked him. Moreover, at times she was physically drawn to him. She'd never before had her breath taken away by a man's nearness, but it had happened several times with Neil. For someone who'd always been relatively in control of her emotions, the experience was frightening. It was also exciting in a way....

Not trusting that Neil wouldn't awaken and lash out at her for disturbing him, she silently left the room and returned to the den. Her gaze fell on the ship-to-shore radio. She approached it, eyed the speaker, scanned the instructions for its use, then turned her back on both and sank down to the sofa. Adjusting one of the woven pillows beneath her head, she yawned and closed her eyes.

It was a lazy day. The sound of the rain was hypnotic, lulling, inducing the sweetest of lethargies. She wondered at her fatigue and knew that it was due only in part to her physical debilitation. The tension she'd been under in Providence was also to blame.

She needed the rest, she told herself. It was good for her. Wasn't that what a remote island was for? Soon enough she'd feel stronger, and then she'd read, knit, listen to music, even exercise. Soon enough the sun would come out, and she'd be able to avail herself of the island's fresh air.

But for now, doing nothing suited her just fine.

She was sleeping soundly when, some time later, Neil came to an abrupt halt at the door to the den. He was feeling groggy, having awoken only moments before. He wasn't used to sleeping during the day. He wasn't used to doing nothing. Oh, he'd brought along some books, and there were tapes here and a vast collection of old movies to watch, but he wasn't up to any of that just yet. If the weather were nice, he could spend time outdoors, but it wasn't, so he slept, instead.

Rationally he'd known that it was going to take him several days to unwind and that he badly needed the relaxation. He'd known that solutions to his problems weren't going to suddenly hit him in the face the moment he reached the island. Nevertheless, the problems were never far from consciousness.

Ironically Deirdre was his greatest diversion.

Deirdre. Looking down at her, he sucked in his upper lip, then slowly released it. Twenty-nine years old. He thought back to when he was that age. Four years out of law school, he'd been paying his dues as an associate in a large Hartford law firm. The hours had been long, the work boring. Frustrated by the hierarchy that relegated him to doing busywork for the partners, he'd set out on his own the following year. Though the hours had been equally long, the work had been far more rewarding.

Now, ten years later, he was approaching forty, sadly disillusioned. He knew where he'd been, saw his mistakes with vivid clarity... but he couldn't picture the future.

If Deirdre was disillusioned about something at the age of twenty-nine, where would she be when she reached his age? What did she want from life? For that matter, what had she had?

Lying there on her side, with her hands tucked between her thighs and her cheek fallen against the pillow, she was the image of innocence. She was also strangely sexy-looking.

He wondered how that could be, when there was nothing alluring about her in the traditional sense. She wore no make-up. Her hair was long in front, short at the sides and back, unsophisticated as hell. Her warm-up suit was a far cry from the clinging things he'd seen women wearing at the racquet club. The bulky fabric was bunched up in front, camouflaging whatever she had by the way of breasts, and yet... and yet... the material rested on a nicely rounded bottom—he could see that now—and she looked warm and vaguely cuddly. He almost envied her hands.

With a quick headshake, he walked over to the ship-to-shore radio, picked up the speaker, shifted it in his hand, frowned, then set it back down. Ah, hell, he told himself, Thomas wouldn't be there; he was conspiring with Victoria. Short of a legitimate physical emergency, he wouldn't be back soon. And that being the case, it behooved Neil to find a way to coexist in relative peace with Deirdre.

But what fun would that be?

Deirdre was, for him, a kind of punching bag. He felt better when he argued with her. She provided an outlet and a diversion. Perhaps he should just keep swinging.

Smiling, he sauntered into the living room. His gaze fell on the fireplace; the ashes from last night's fire lay cold. Taking several large logs from the nearby basket, he set them atop kindling on the grate and stuck a match. Within minutes the kindling caught, then the logs. Only when the fire was crackling heatedly did he settle back in a chair to watch it.

Strange, he mused, but he'd never come to the wilderness to relax before. He'd been to the beach—southern Connecticut, Cape Cod, Nantucket—and to the snow-covered mountains of Vermount. He'd been to the Caribbean and to Europe. But he'd never been this isolated from the rest of the world. He'd never been in the only house on an island, dependent solely on himself to see to his needs.

Nancy would die here. She'd want the option of eating out or calling room service. She'd want there to be people to meet for drinks. She'd want laundry service.

And Deirdre? Broken leg and all, she'd come looking for solitude. Perhaps stupidly, with that leg, but she'd come. Was she indeed a spoiled brat who had run away from all that had gone wrong in her life? Or was she truly self-sufficient? It remained to be seen whether she could make a bed. . . .

"Nice fire."

He looked up. Deirdre was leaning against the wall by the hall, looking warm and still sleepy and mellow. He felt a lightening inside, then scowled perversely. "Where's the other crutch?"

Her eyes grew clearer. "In the kitchen."

"What's it doing there?"

She tipped her chin higher. "Holding up the counter."

"It's supposed to be under your arm. You're the one who needs holding up."

"I've found I can do just fine with one."

"If you put too much strain on the leg," he argued, "you'll slow the healing process."

"You sound like an expert."

"I broke my own leg once."

"How?"

"Skiing."

She rolled her eyes. "I should have guessed. I'll bet you sat around the ski lodge with your leg on a pedestal—the wounded hero basking in homage."

"Not quite. But what I did is beside the point. What you're doing is nuts. The doctor didn't okay it, did he?"

"*She* told me to use common sense. And what's it to you, anyway? You're not my keeper."

"No, but it'll be my job to do something if you fall and crack the cast, or worse, break the other leg."

She smiled smugly. "If anything happens to me, your problems will be solved. You'll get through to Thomas, zip, zip, and he'll be out to fetch me before you can blink an eye."

Neil knew she was right. He also knew that she had momentarily one-upped him. That called for a change of tactics. He took a deep breath, sat back in his chair and propped his bare feet on the coffee table. "But I don't want him to come out and fetch you. I've decided to keep you."

Her smile faded. "You've what?"

"I've decided to keep you."

"Given the fact that you don't *have* me, that's quite a decision."

He waved a hand. "Don't argue semantics. You know what I mean."

She nodded slowly. "You've decided to let me stay."

"That's right."

"And if I decide I want to leave?"

"Thomas won't give us the time of day, so it's a moot point."

"Precisely, which means that you're full of hot air, Neil Hersey. You can't decide to keep me, any more than I can decide to keep you, or either of us can decide to leave. We're stuck here together, which means—" Her mind was working along pleasurable lines. The grin she sent him had a cunning edge. "That you're stuck with me, bad temper and all." The way she saw it, he'd given her license to fire at will, not to mention without guilt. Battling with him could prove to be a most satisfying pastime.

"I think I can handle it," he said smugly.

"Good." Limping directly between Neil and the fire, she took the chair opposite his. "So," she said, sitting back, "did you have a good sleep?"

"You spied on me?"

"No. I walked into my bedroom and there you were. Snoring."

He refused to let her get to him. "Is that why you took your nap in the den?"

"You spied on me."

"No. I walked in there intending to call Thomas. Then I decided not to bother. So I came in here and built a fire. It is nice, isn't it?"

"Not bad." She levered herself from the chair and hopped into the kitchen. A bowl of fresh fruit sat on the counter; she reached for an orange, then hopped back to her seat.

"You're a wonderful hopper," Neil said. "Is it your specialty?"

She ignored him. "What this fire needs is a little zip." Tearing off a large wad of orange peel, she tossed it into the flame.

"Don't do that! It'll mess up my fire!"

"It adds a special scent. Just wait." She threw in another piece.

Neil stared into the flames. "I hate the smell of oranges. It reminds me of the packages of fruit my grandparents used to send up from Florida every winter. There was so much of it that my mother worried about it spoiling, so we were all but force-fed the stuff for a week." His voice had gentled, and his lips curved at the reminiscence. "Every year I got hives from eating so many oranges."

She pried off a section and held it ready at her mouth. "You said 'we.' Do you have brothers and sisters?" The orange section disappeared.

"One of each."

"Older or younger?"

"Both older."

"Are you close?"

"Now? Pretty close." He shifted lower in his seat, so that his head rested against its back, and crossed his ankles. "We went our separate ways for a while. John is a teacher in Minneapolis, and Sara works for the government in Washington. They're both married and have kids, and all our lives seemed so hectic that we really didn't push reunions."

"What changed that?" Deirdre asked.

"My mother's death. Something about mortality hit us in the face—you know, life-is-so-short type of thing. That was almost seven years ago. We've been much closer since then."

"Is your father still living?"

"Yes. He's retired."

"Does he live near you?"

"He still lives in the house where we grew up in Westchester. We keep telling him to move because it's large and empty but for him most of the time. He won't sell." Neil was grinning. "He travels. So help me, nine months out of twelve he's galavanting off somewhere. But he says he needs the house. He needs to know it's there for him to come home to. Personally—" He lowered his voice "—I think he just doesn't want to displace the couple who live above the garage. They've been overseeing the grounds for nearly twenty years. They oversee *him* when he's around, and he loves it."

Absently Deirdre pressed another piece of fruit into her mouth. She chewed it, all the while looking at Neil. It was obvious that he felt affection for his family. "That's a lovely story. Your father sounds like a nice man."

"He is."

She took a sudden breath. "So how did he get a son like you? By the way, aren't your feet freezing? I haven't seen you with socks on since we got here, but it's cold."

He wiggled his toes. "I'm warm-blooded."

"You're foolhardy. You'll get splinters."

"Are you kidding? The floor's been sanded and waxed. Only the walls have splinters, and, thank you, I don't walk on walls." He swung his legs down and stood. "So you'll have to find something else to pick on me for."

"I will," she promised. "I will." She watched him escape into the kitchen. "What are you doing?"

"Contemplating dinner."

"We haven't had lunch!"

"Breakfast was lunch." He flipped on a light in the darkening room. "Now it's dinnertime."

She glanced at her watch. It was well after six o'clock. She supposed she was hungry, though the thought of preparing another meal was enough to mute whatever hunger pangs she felt. So she remained where she was, looking at the fire, telling herself that she'd see to her own needs when Neil was done. She didn't want an audience for her clumsiness. Besides, between her hopping and Neil's size, they'd never be able to work in the kitchen at the same time.

She listened to the sounds of his preparations, wondering how he'd come to be so handy. Various possible explanations passed through her mind, but in the end the question remained. Then she heard the sizzle of meat and began to smell tantalizing aromas, and her admiration turned to annoyance. Why *was* he so good in the kitchen? Why wasn't he as clumsy as she? The men she'd known would have been hollering for something long before now—help in finding the butter or sharpening a knife or preparing vegetables for cooking. Why didn't he need her for something?

Pushing herself from the chair, she limped peevishly to the kitchen. What she saw stopped her cold on the threshold. Neil had set two places at the table and was in the process of lowering one brimming plate to each spot.

He looked up. "I was just about to call you." Her expression of shock was ample reward for his efforts, though his motives went deeper. If he helped Deirdre with things he knew she found difficult, he wouldn't feel so badly when he picked on her. Good deeds for not-so-good ones; it seemed a fair exchange. Not to mention the fact that keeping her off balance seemed of prime importance. "Steak, steamed broccoli, dinner rolls." He beamed at the plates. "Not bad, if I do say so myself."

"Not bad," she echoed distractedly. "You'd make someone a wonderful wife."

He ignored the barb and held out her chair. "Ms Joyce?"

At a loss for anything better to do, particularly when her mouth was watering, she came forward and let him seat her. She stared at the attractive plate for a minute, then looked up as he poured two glasses of wine. "Why?" she asked bluntly.

"Why wine? It's here for us to drink, and I thought it'd be a nice touch.

"Why me? I didn't ask you to make my dinner."

"Are you refusing it?"

She glanced longingly at her plate. Hospital food was nearly inedible; it had been days since she'd confronted anything tempting. "No. I'm hungry."

"So I figured."

"But you must have something up your sleeve."

He sat at his place, nonchalantly shook out his napkin and spread it on his lap. "Maybe I'm thinking of Victoria's kitchen. You broke a glass this morning. Another few, and we'll run low."

"It's not the glass, and you know it. What is it, Neil? I don't like it when you're nice."

He arched a brow as he cut into his steak. "Prefer the rough stuff, do you? A little pushing and shoving turns you on?" He put a piece of steak into his mouth, chewed it and closed his eyes. "Mmmm. Perfect." His eyes flew open in mock innocence. "I hope you like it rare."

"I like it medium."

"Then you can eat the edges and leave the middle." He gestured with his fork. "Go ahead. Eat. On second thought—" He set down the fork and reached for his wine "—a toast." When Deirdre continued to stare at him, he dipped his head, coaxing. "Come on. Raise your glass."

Slowly, warily, she lifted it.

He grinned. "To us." The clink of his glass against hers rang through the room.

5

TO US. Deirdre thought about that through the evening as she sat pensively before the fire. She thought about it that night when she lay in bed, trying her best to ignore the presence of a large male body little more than an arm's length away. She thought about it when she awoke in the morning. By that time she was annoyed.

Victoria had fixed them up. Deirdre had always resented fix-ups, had always fervently avoided them. She'd never been so hard up for a man that she'd risk taking pot luck, and she wasn't now. Who was Neil Hersey, anyway? She asked herself that for the umpteenth time. After spending thirty-six hours with the man, she still didn't know. She did know that she'd been aware of him in some form or another for the majority of those thirty-six hours, and that her body was distinctly tense from that awareness.

She turned her head to study him. Sleeping, he was sprawled on his back with his head facing her. His hair was mussed; his beard sported an additional day's growth. Sooty eyelashes fanned above his cheekbones. Dark swirls of hair blanketed his chest to the point where the quilt took over.

One arm was entirely free of the covers. Her gaze traced its length, from a tightly muscled shoulder, over a leanly corded swell to his elbow, down a forearm that was spattered with hair, to a well-formed and thoroughly masculine hand. As though touched by that hand, she felt a quiver shoot through her.

Wrenching her head to the other side, she took a shallow breath, pushed herself up and dropped her legs over the side of the bed. For a minute she simply sat there with her head bowed, begrudging the fact that she found Neil attractive. She wanted to hate the sight of him after what he'd done to her dreams of solitude. But the sight of him turned her on.

She didn't want to be turned on.

Slowly she began to roll her head in a half circle, concentrating on relaxing the taut muscles of her neck. She extended the exercise to her shoulders, alternately rolling one, then the other. Clasping her hands at the back of her head, she stretched her torso, first to the left, then to the right. The music played in her mind, and she let herself move to its sound, only then realizing what she'd missed during the past week, finding true relaxation in imagining herself back at the health club, leading a class.

"What in the hell are you doing?" came a hoarse growl from behind her.

Startled from her reverie, she whirled around, then caught herself and tempered the movement. "Exercising."

"Is that necessary?"

"Yes. My body is tense."

"So is mine, and what you're doing isn't helping it." He'd awoken with the first of her exercises and watched her twist and stretch, watched the gentle shift in her absurdly large pajamas. And he'd begun to imagine things, which had quickly affected his own body. In other circumstances he'd have stormed from bed right then. As things stood—literally—he didn't have the guts.

"Then don't look," she said, turning her back on him and resuming her exercises. It was spite that drove her on, but all petty thoughts vanished when a strong arm seized her waist and whipped her back on the bed. Before she knew what had happened, Neil had her pinned and was looming over her.

"I think we'd better get something straight," he warned in a throaty voice. "I'm a man, and I'm human. If you want to tempt me beyond my limits, you'd better be prepared to take the consequences."

Deirdre's trouble with breathing had nothing to do with exercising. Neil's lunge had dislodged the quilt, leaving his entire upper body bare. The warmth of his chest reached out to her, sending rivulets of heat through her body, while the intensity of his gaze seared her further.

"I didn't know you were tempted," she said in a small voice. "I'm a bundle of lumps to you. That's all." She'd been a bundle of lumps to most men, lumps that were conditioned by steady exercise, lumps that were anything but feminine. She'd always known she couldn't compete with the buxom beauties of the world, and she fully assumed Neil was used to buxom beauties. The way he'd looked at her that first day had left no doubt as to his opinion of her body. Then again, there had been other times when he'd looked at her...

"You are a bundle of lumps," he agreed, dropping his gaze to her pajama front. "That's what's so maddening. I keep wondering what's beneath all this cover." His eyes made a thorough survey of the fabric—she felt every touch point—before lazily meeting hers. "Maybe if I see, I won't be tempted. Maybe what we need here is full disclosure."

Deirdre made a reflexive attempt at drawing in her arms to cover herself, but he had them anchored beneath his and gave no quarter.

"Maybe," he went on, his voice a velvety rasp, "what I ought to do is to unbutton this thing and take a good look at all you're hiding."

"There's not much," she said quickly. Her eyes were round in a pleading that she miraculously managed to keep from her voice. "You'd be disappointed."

"But at least then I wouldn't have to wonder anymore, would I?"

Her heart was hammering, almost visibly so. She was frightened. Strangely and suddenly frightened. "Please. Don't."

"Don't wonder? Or don't look?"

"Either."

"But I can't help the first."

"It's not worth it. Take my word for it. I'm an athletic person. Not at all feminine."

Neil was staring at her in growing puzzlement. He heard the way her breath was coming in short bursts, saw the way her eyes held something akin to fear. He felt the urgency in his body recede, and slowly, gently he released her. Instantly, she turned away from him and sat up.

"I'd never force you," he murmured to her rigid back.

"I didn't say you would."

"You were talking, rationalizing as though you thought I would. I scared you."

She said nothing to that. How could she explain what she didn't understand herself: that her fear had been he'd find fault with her body? She didn't know why it should matter what he thought of her body. . . .

"You didn't scare me."

"You're lying."

"Then that's another fault to add to the list." She fumbled for her crutches and managed to get herself to her feet. "I'm hungry," she grumbled, and started for the door.

"So am I," was his taunting retort.

"Tough!"

DEIRDRE MADE her own breakfast, grateful to find such easy fixings as yogurt and cottage cheese in the refrigerator. She waited in the den until she heard Neil in the kitchen, then retreated to the other end of the house for a bath.

At length she emerged, wearing the same bulky green top she'd worn during the drive up. This time she had gray sweatpants on, and though the outfit didn't clash, it was less shapely than yesterday's warm-up suit had been.

Reluctant to face Neil, she busied herself cleaning up the bedroom. Making a king-size bed by hobbling from one side to the other and back took time, but for once she welcomed the handicap. She went on to unpack her duffel bag. It wasn't that she hadn't planned on staying, simply that she hadn't had the strength to settle in until now. Yes, she did feel stronger, she realized, and found some satisfaction in that. She also found satisfaction in placing her books, cassette player and tapes atop the dresser. Neil had put his things on the other dresser; she was staking her own claim now.

Under the guise of housekeeping, she crossed to that other dresser and cursorily neatened Neil's things. He'd brought several books, a mix of fiction and nonfiction, all tied in some fashion to history. A glass case lay nearby, with the corner of a pair of horn-rimmed spectacles protruding. Horn-rimmed spectacles. She grinned.

Completing the gathering on the dresser was a scattered assembly of small change, a worn leather wallet and a key ring that held numerous keys in addition to those to his car. She wondered what the others unlocked, wondered where his office was and what it was like, wondered where he lived.

Moving quickly into the bathroom, she wiped down the sink and shower, then the mirror above the sink. She'd put her own few things in one side of the medicine chest. Curious, she slid open the other side. Its top shelf held a number of supplies she assumed were Victoria's. Far below, after several empty shelves, were more personal items—a comb, a brush, a tube of toothpaste and a toothbrush.

Neil's things. He traveled light. There was no sign of a razor. He'd very obviously planned to be alone.

Strangely, she felt better. Knowing that Neil was as unprepared for the presence of a woman as she was for the presence of a man was reassuring. On the other hand, what would she have brought if she'd known she'd have company? Makeup? Aside from mascara, blusher and lip gloss, she rarely used it. A blow dryer? She rarely used one. Cologne? Hah!

And what would Neil have brought? She wondered.

Sliding the chest shut with a thud, she returned to the bedroom, where a sweeping glance told her there was little else to clean. She could always stretch out on the bed and read, or sit in the chaise by the window and knit. But that would be tantamount to hiding, and she refused to hide.

Discouraged, she looked toward the window. It was still raining. Gray, gloomy and forbidding. If things were different, she wouldn't have been stopped by the rain; she'd have bundled up and taken a walk. All too clearly, though, she recalled how treacherous it was maneuvering with crutches across the mud and rocks. She wasn't game to try it again soon.

Selecting a book from those she'd brought, she tucked it under her arm alongside the crutch, took a deep breath and headed for the living room. Neil was there, slouched on the sofa, lost in thought. He didn't look up until she'd settled herself in the chair, and then he sent her only the briefest of glances.

Determinedly she ignored him. She opened the book, a piece of contemporary women's fiction and began to read, patiently rereading the first page three times before she felt justified in moving on to the second. She was finally beginning to get involved in the story, when Neil materialized at her shoulder.

Setting the book down, she turned her head, not far enough to see him, just enough to let him know he had her attention. "Something wrong?" she asked in an even tone.

"Just wondering what you were reading," he said just as evenly.

Leaving a finger to mark her place, she closed the cover so he could see it.

"Any good?" he asked.

"I can't tell yet. I've just started."

"If it doesn't grab you within the first few pages, it won't."

"That's not necessarily true," she argued. "Some books take longer to get into."

He grunted and moved off. She heard a clatter, then another grunt, louder this time, and, following it, a curse that brought her head around fast. "Goddamn it. Can't you keep your crutches out of the way?" He had one hand on the corner of her chair, the other wrapped around his big toe.

"If you were wearing shoes, that wouldn't have happened!"

"I shouldn't have to wear shoes in my own home."

"This isn't your own home."

"Home away from home, then."

"Oh, please, Neil, what exactly would you have me do? Leave the crutches in the other room? You were the one who was after me to use them."

He didn't bother to answer. Setting his foot on the floor, he gingerly tested it. Then he straightened and limped across the room to stand at the window. He tucked his hands in the back pockets of his jeans, displacing the long jersey that would have otherwise covered his buttocks. The jersey itself was black and slim cut, fairly broadcasting the strength and breadth of his shoulders, the leanness of his hips. She wondered if he'd chosen to wear it on purpose.

Returning her eyes to her book, she read another two pages before being interrupted again.

"Crummy day" was the information relayed to her from the window.

She set the book down. "I know."

"That's two in a row."

"Three."

"Two full days that we've been here."

She conceded the point. "Fine. Two in a row." She picked up the book again. Several pages later, she raised her head to find Neil staring at her. "Is something wrong?"

"No."

"You look bored."

"I'm not used to inactivity."

"Don't you have anything to do?"

With a shrug he turned back to the window.

"What would you do at home on a rainy day?" she asked.

"Work."

"Even on a weekend?"

"Especially on a weekend. That's when I catch up on everything I've been too busy to do during the week." At least, it had been that way for years, he mused. Of course, when one was losing clients right and left, there was a definite slackening.

"You must have a successful practice," she remarked, then was taken aback when he sent her a glower. "I meant that as a compliment."

He bowed his head and rubbed the back of his neck. "I know. I'm sorry."

Deirdre glanced at her book, and realized she wasn't going to get much reading done with Neil standing there that way. She was grateful he hadn't made reference to what had happened earlier, and wondered if he was sorry for that, too. If so, she reflected, he might be in a conciliatory mood. It was as good a time as any to strike up a conversation.

"How do you know Victoria?" she asked in as casual a tone as she could muster.

"A mutual friend introduced us several years ago."

"Are you from the city?"

"Depends what city you mean."

For the sake of civility, she stifled her impatience. "New York."

"No." He was facing the window again, and for a minute she thought she'd have to prod, when he volunteered the information she'd been seeking. "Hartford."

A corner of her mouth curved up. She couldn't resist. "Ah, Hartford. Thriving little metropolis. I went to a concert there last year with friends. The seats were awful, the lead singer had a cold and I got a flat tire driving home."

Slowly Neil turned. "Okay. I deserved that."

"Yes, you did. Be grateful I didn't condemn the entire city."

He wasn't sure he'd have minded if she had. At the moment he felt the whole of Hartford was against him. "My allegiance to the city isn't blind. I can see her faults."

"Such as . . . ?"

"Parochialism. Provinciality."

"Hartford?"

"Yes, Hartford. Certain circles are pretty closed."

"Isn't that true of any city?"

"I suppose." Casually he left the window and returned to the sofa. Deirdre took it as a sign of his willingness to talk.

"Have you lived there long?"

"Since I began practicing."

"You mentioned going to school in Boston. Was that law school, or undergraduate?"

"Both."

"So you went from Westchester to Boston to Hartford?"

He had taken on an expression of amused indulgence. "I did a stint in San Diego between Boston and Hartford. In the Navy. JAG division."

"Ah. Then you missed Vietnam."

"Right." He had one brow arched, as though waiting for her to criticize the fact that he hadn't seen combat.

"I think that's fine," she said easily. "You did something, which is more than a lot of men did."

"My motive wasn't all that pure. I would have been drafted if I hadn't signed up."

"You could have run to Canada."

"No."

The finality with which he said it spoke volumes. He felt he'd had a responsibility to his country. Deirdre respected that.

"How did you break your leg?" he asked suddenly.

The look on her face turned sour. "Don't ask."

"I am."

She met his gaze and debated silently for a minute. He'd opened up. Perhaps she should, too. Somehow it seemed childish to continue the evasion. She gave him a challenging stare. "I fell down a flight of stairs."

He held up a hand, warding off both her stare and its unspoken challenge. "That's okay. I'm not laughing."

Averting her gaze, she scowled at the floor. "You would if you knew the whole story."

"Try me. What happened?"

She'd set herself up for it, but strangely she wasn't sorry. It occurred to her that she wanted to tell the story. If he laughed, she'd have reason to yell at him. In some ways, arguing with him was safer than . . . than what had happened earlier.

Taking a breath, she faced him again. "I slipped on a magazine, caught my foot in the banister and broke my leg in three places."

He waited expectantly. "And . . . ? There has to be a punch line. I'm not laughing yet."

"You asked what I did for a living." She took a breath. "I teach aerobic dance."

His eyes widened fractionally. "Ah. And now you can't work."

"That's the least of it! I've always been into exercise of one sort or another. I'm supposed to be ultracoordinated. Do you have any idea how humiliating it is to have done this slipping on a magazine?"

"Was the magazine worth it?" he asked, deadpan.

"That's not the point! The point is that I'm not supposed to fall down the stairs! And if I do, I'm supposed to do it gracefully, with only a black-and-blue mark or two to show for it." She glared at her leg. "Not a grotesque cast!"

"How does the leg feel, by the way?"

"Okay."

"The dampness doesn't bother it?"

"My thigh is more sore from lugging the cast around, and my armpits hurt from the crutches."

"That'll get better with time. How long will the cast be on?"

"Another five weeks."

"And after that you'll be good as new?"

Her anger was replaced by discouragement. "I wish I knew. The doctor made no promises. Oh, I'll be able to walk. But teach?" Her shrug was as eloquent as the worry in her eyes.

Neil surprised himself by feeling her pain. Wasn't it somewhat akin to his own? After all, his own future was in limbo, too.

Leaning forward, he propped his elbows on his thighs. "You'll be able to teach, Deirdre. One way or another you will, if you want to badly enough."

"I do! I have to work. I mean, it's not a question of money. It's a question of emotional survival!"

That, too, he understood. "Your work means that much to you."

It was a statement, not a question, and Deirdre chose to let it rest. She wasn't ready to go into the issue of Joyce Enterprises, which was so much more complex and personal. Besides, Neil was a corporate attorney. He'd probably take *their* side.

"Well," she said at last, "I guess there's nothing I can do but wait."

"What will you do in the meantime?"

"Stay here for as long as I can."

"There's nothing else to keep you busy in Providence while your leg mends?"

"Nothing I care to do."

Neil wondered at her mutinous tone, but didn't comment. "What had you planned to do here? Besides read."

Still scowling, she shrugged. "Relax. Knit. Listen to music. Work up some routines. It may be a waste of time if it turns out I can't teach, but I suppose I have to hope."

"You could have done all that in Providence. I'd have thought that with a broken leg and all, you'd be more comfortable there. The drive up couldn't have been easy, and if Thomas had dumped you on that dock alone, you'd have had a hell of a time getting everything to the house."

Her scowl deepened. "Thomas knew what he was doing. *You* were here. Otherwise he'd probably have helped me himself."

"Still, to rush up here the day you left the hospital... What was the rush?"

"The telephone! My family! It was bad enough when I was in the hospital. I had to get away!"

"All that, just because you were embarrassed?"

Deirdre knew that she'd be spilling the entire story in another minute. Who in the devil was Neil Hersey that he should be prying? She hadn't asked *him* why he'd been in such a foul mood from day one. "Let's just say that I have a difficult family," she concluded, and closed her mouth tightly. Between that and the look she gave him, there was no doubt that she was done talking.

Neil took the hint. Oh, he was still curious, but there was time. Time for . . . lots of things.

She opened her book again and picked up where she'd left off, but if her concentration had been tentative before, it was nonexistent now. She was thinking of that difficult family, wondering what was going to change during the time she was in Maine that would make things any better when she returned.

From the corner of her eye she saw Neil get up, walk aimlessly around the room, then sit down. When a minute later he bobbed up again, she sighed.

"Decide what you want to do, please. I can't read with an active yo-yo in the room."

He said nothing, but took off for the bedroom. Moments later he returned, threw himself full length on the sofa and opened a book of his own. He read the first page, turned noisily to the last, then began to flip through those in between.

"Are you going to read or look at the pictures?" Deirdre snapped.

His face was the picture of innocence when he looked up. "I'm trying to decide if it's worth reading."

She was trying to decide if he was purposely distracting her. "You brought it along, didn't you?"

"I was in a rush. I took whatever books I had around the house and threw them in the bag."

"Then you must have decided it was worth reading when you bought it. What's it about?" She wondered which he'd chosen.

"World War I. History fascinates me."

"I know."

His eyes narrowed. "How would you know?"

"Because I saw the books lying on your dresser, and every one of them dealt with history in some form. You know, you really should wear your glasses when you read. Otherwise you'll get eye strain."

"I only wear them when I *have* eye strain, and since I haven't had much to look at for the past two days, my eyes are fine." He turned his head on the sofa arm to study her more fully. "You're pretty nosy. Did you look through my wallet, too?"

"Of course not! I was cleaning, not snooping. I've never liked living in a pigpen."

"Could've fooled me, what with the way you've been dropping clothes around."

"That was only the first night, and I was exhausted." She noticed a strange light in his eyes and suspected he was enjoying the sparring. It occurred to her that she was, too. "What's in your wallet, anyway? Something dark and sinister? Something I shouldn't see?"

He shrugged. "Nothing extraordinary."

"Wads of money?"

"Not quite."

"A membership card to a slinky men's club?"

"Not quite."

"A picture of your sweetheart?"

"Not . . . quite."

"Who is she, anyway—the one who burned you?"

The day before he wouldn't have wanted to talk about Nancy. Now, suddenly, it seemed less threatening. "She's someone I was seeing, whom I'm not seeing now."

"Obviously," Deirdre drawled. "What happened?"

Neil pursed his lips and thought of the best way to answer. He finally settled on the most general explanation. "She decided I didn't have enough potential."

"What was she looking for? An empire builder?"

"Probably."

"You don't sound terribly upset that she's gone."

"I'm getting over it," he said easily.

"Couldn't have been all that strong a relationship, then."

"It wasn't."

Deirdre settled her book against her stomach and tipped her head to the side. "Have you ever been married?"

"Where did that come from?"

"I'm curious. You asked me. Now I'm asking you."

"No. I've never been married."

"Why not?"

He arched a brow. "I never asked you that. It's impolite."

"It's impolite to ask a woman that, because traditionally she's the one who has to wait for the proposal. A man can do the proposing. Why haven't you?"

It occurred to Neil that there was something endearing about the way Deirdre's mind worked. It was quick, unpretentious, oddly refreshing. He smiled. "Would you believe me if I said I've been too busy?"

"No."

"It is true, in a way. I've spent the past fifteen years devoted to my career. She's a very demanding mistress."

"Then she's never had the right competition, which means that the old cliché is more the case. You haven't met the right woman yet."

He didn't need to ponder that to agree. "I have very special needs," he said, grinning. "Only a very special woman can satisfy them."

Deirdre could have sworn she saw mischief in his grin. She tried her best to sound scornful. "That I can believe. Any woman who'd put up with a face full of whiskers has to be special. Do you have any idea how... how grungy that looks?"

The insult fell flat. To her dismay, he simply grinned more broadly as he stroked his jaw. "It does look kinda grungy. Nice, huh?"

"Nice?"

"Yeah. I've never grown a beard in my life. From the time I was fifteen I shaved every blessed morning. And why? So I'd look clean. And neat. And acceptable. Well, hell, it's nice to look grungy for a change, and as for acceptability—" He searched for the words he wanted, finally thrust out his chin in defiance. "Screw it!"

Deirdre considered what he'd said. He didn't look unclean, or unneat, or unacceptable, but rather... dashing. Particularly with that look of triumph on his face. Helpless against it, she smiled. "That felt good, didn't it?"

"Sure did."

"You're much more controlled when you work."

"Always. There's a certain, uh, decorum demanded when you're dealing with corporate clients."

"Tell me about it," she drawled, bending her right leg up and hugging it to her chest.

Once before, he'd taken her up on the offer. This time he let it ride, because he didn't really want to talk about corporate clients. He wanted to talk about Deirdre Joyce.

"What about you, Deirdre? Why have you never married?"

"I've never been asked."

He laughed. "I should have expected you'd answer that way. But it's a cop-out, you know," he chided, then frowned and tucked in his chin. "Why are you looking at me that way?"

"Do you know that that's the first time I've heard you laugh, I mean, laugh, as in relaxed and content?"

His smile mellowed into something very gentle, and his eyes bound hers with sudden warmth. "Do you know that's the first time I've heard such a soft tone from you. Soft tone, as in amiable." As in womanly, he might have added, but he didn't. He'd let down enough defenses for one day.

For a minute Deirdre couldn't speak. Her total awareness centered on Neil and the way he was looking at her. He made her feel feminine in a way she'd never felt before.

Awkward, she dropped her gaze to her lap. "You're trying to butter me up, being nice and all. I think you're looking for someone to do the laundry."

Laundry was the last thing on his mind. "I don't think I've ever seen you blush before."

The blush deepened. She didn't look up. She didn't trust the little tricks her hormones were playing on her. She felt she was being toasted from the inside out. It was a new and unsettling sensation. Why *Neil*?

Lips turning down in a pout, she glared at him.

"Aw, come on," he teased. "I liked you the other way."

"Well, I didn't." It smacked of vulnerability, and Deirdre didn't like to think of herself as vulnerable. "I'm not the submissive type."

His laugh was gruffer this time. "I never thought you were. In fact, submissive is the last word I'd use to describe you. You prickle at the slightest thing. I'd almost think that *you*'d been burned."

The directness of her gaze held warning. "I have. I was used once, and I didn't like the feeling."

"No one does," he said softly. "What happened?"

She debated cutting off the discussion, but sensed he'd only raise it another time. So she crossed her right leg over her cast and slid lower in the chair in a pose meant to be nonchalant.

"I let myself be a doormat for a fellow who had nothing better to do with his life at the time. The minute he sensed a demand on my part, he was gone."

"You demanded marriage?"

"Oh, no. It was nothing like that. Though I suppose he imagined that coming. My family would like to see me married. They don't think much of my... life-style."

"You're a swinger?"

She slanted him a disparaging glance. "Just the opposite. I avoid parties. I can't stand phony relationships. I hate pretense of any kind."

"What does pretense have to do with marriage?"

"If it's marriage for the sake of marriage alone, pretense is a given."

Neil couldn't argue with that. "Do you want to have children?"

"Someday. How about you?"

"Someday."

They looked at each other for a minute longer, then simultaneously returned to their books. Deirdre, for one, was surprised that she was talking about these things with Neil. She asked herself what it was about him that inspired her to speak, and finally concluded that it was the situation, more than the man, that had brought her out. Hadn't she come here to soul-search, to ponder the direction her life was taking?

Neil was brooding about his own life, his own direction, and for the first time that brooding was on a personal bent. Yes, he'd like to be married, but only to the right person. He was as averse to pretense as Deirdre was. Nancy—for that matter, most of the women he'd dated over the years—had epitomized pretense. One part of him very much wanted to put his law practice in its proper perspective, to focus, instead, on a relationship with a woman, a relationship that was intimate, emotionally as well as physically, and rewarding. And yes, he'd like to have children.

Absently he turned a page, then turned it back when he realized he hadn't read a word. He darted a glance at Deirdre and found her curled in the chair, engrossed in her book. She was honest; he admired her for that. She didn't have any more answers than he did, but at least she was honest.

Settling more comfortably on the sofa, Neil refocused on his book and disciplined himself to read. It came easier as the morning passed. The rain beat a steady accompaniment to the quiet activity, and he had to admit that it was almost peaceful.

Setting the book down at last, he stood. "I'm making sandwiches. Want one?"

Deirdre looked up. "What kind?"

His mouth turned down at the corner. "That's gratitude for you, when someone is offering to make you lunch."

"I can make my own," she pointed out, needing to remind him—and herself—that she wasn't helpless.

"Is that what you'd rather?"

"It depends on what kind of sandwiches you know how to make."

"I know how to make most anything. The question is what have we got to work with?" He crossed into the kitchen, opened the refrigerator and rummaged through the supplies. Straightening, he called over his shoulder, "You can have ham and cheese, bologna and cheese, grilled cheese, grilled cheese and tomato, grilled cheese and tuna, a BLT, egg salad, peanut butter and jelly, cream cheese and jelly—" he sucked in a badly needed breath "—or any of the above taken separately."

Any of the above sounded fine to Deirdre, who'd never been a picky eater. She tried not to grin. "That's quite a list. Could you run through it one more time?"

The refrigerator door swung shut and Neil entered her line of vision. His hands were hooked low on his hips and his stance was one of self-assurance. "You heard it the first time, Deirdre."

"But there are so many things to choose from . . . . and it's a big decision." She pressed her lips together, feigning concentration. "A big decision . . ."

"Deirdre . . ."

"I'll have turkey with mustard."

"Turkey wasn't on the list."

"No? I thought for sure it was."

"We don't have any turkey."

"Why not? Thomas should have known to pick some up. Turkey's far better for you than ham or cheese or peanut butter."

Hands falling to his sides, Neil drew himself up, shoulders back. He spoke slowly and clearly. "Do you, or do you not, want a sandwich?"

"I do."

"What kind?"

"Grilled cheese and tuna."

He sighed. "Thank you." He'd no sooner returned to the refrigerator, when he heard her call.

"Can I have it on rye?"

"No, you cannot have it on rye," he called back through gritted teeth.

"How about a roll?"

"If a hamburg roll will do."

"It won't."

"Then it's white bread or nothing. Take it or leave it."

"I'll take it."

He waited a minute longer to see if she had anything else to add. When she remained silent, he tugged open the refrigerator and removed everything he'd need. He'd barely closed the door again, when Deirdre entered the kitchen.

"If you've changed your mind," he warned, "that's tough. Your order's already gone to the cook. It's too late to change."

She was settling herself on the counter stool. "Grilled cheese and tuna's fine." Folding her hands in her lap, she watched him set to work.

He opened a can of tuna, dumped its contents into a bowl and shot her a glance as he reached for the mayonnaise. A glob of the creamy white stuff went the way of the tuna. He was in the process of mixing it all together with a fork, when he darted her another glance. "Anything wrong?"

"No, no. Just watching. You don't mind, do you? I'm fascinated. You're very domestic for a man."

"Men have to eat."

"They usually take every shortcut in the book, but grilled cheese and tuna . . . I'm impressed."

"It's not terribly difficult," he scoffed.

"But it takes more time than peanut butter and jelly."

"Tastes better, too."

"I *love* peanut butter and jelly."

"Then why'd you ask for grilled cheese and tuna?"

She arched a brow, goading him on. "Maybe I wanted to see what you could do."

Neil, who'd been slathering tuna on slices of bread, stopped midstroke, put down the knife and slowly turned. "You mean you purposely picked what you thought was the hardest thing on the menu?"

Deirdre knew when to back off. "I was only teasing. I really do feel like having grilled cheese and tuna."

With deliberate steps, he closed the small distance between them. "I don't believe you. I think you did it on purpose, just like you asked for turkey when you knew damn well we didn't have it."

She would have backed up if there'd been anywhere to go, but the counter was already digging into her ribs. "Really, Neil." She held up a hand. "There's no need to get upset. Unless you're having ego problems with my being in the kitchen this way—"

The last word barely made it from her mouth, when Neil scooped her up from the stool, cast and all, and into his arms.

"What are you doing?" she cried.

He was striding through the living room. "Removing you from my presence. You wanted to get my goat. Well, you got it. Picking the most complicated sandwich. *Ego* problems." They were in the hall and moving steadily. "If you want to talk, you can do it to your heart's content in here." He entered the bedroom and went straight to the bed, his intent abundantly clear to Deirdre, who was clutching the crew neckline of his jersey.

"Don't drop me! My cast!"

Neil held her suspended for a minute, enjoying the fact of his advantage over her. Then, in a single heartbeat, his awareness changed. No longer was he thinking that she'd goaded him once too often. Rather, he was suddenly aware that her thigh was slender and strong beneath one of his hands, and that the fingertips of the other were pressed into an unexpectedly feminine breast. He was thinking that her eyes were luminous, her lips moist, her cheeks a newly acquired pale pink.

Deirdre, too, had caught her breath. She was looking up at Neil, realizing that his eyes, like her hair, weren't black at all, but a shade of charcoal brown, and that his mouth was strong, well formed and very male. She was realizing that he held her with ease, and that he smelled clean, and that the backs of her fingers were touching the hot, hair-shaded surface of his chest and he felt good.

Slowly he lowered her to the bed, but didn't retreat. Instead he planted his hands on either side of her. "I don't know what in the hell is going on here," he breathed thickly. "It must be cabin fever." His gaze fell from her eyes to her lips, declaring his intent even before he lowered his head.

6

HIS MOUTH TOUCHED hers lightly at first, brushing her lips, sampling their shape and texture. Then he intensified the kiss, deepening it by bold degrees until it had become something positively breathtaking.

Deirdre could barely think, much less respond. She'd known Neil was going to kiss her, but she'd never expected such force in the simple communion of mouths. He drank from her like a man who was dying of thirst, stumbling unexpectedly upon an oasis in the desert. From time to time his lips gentled to a whisper, touching hers almost timidly in reassurance that what he'd found wasn't a mirage.

His hands framed her face, moving her inches away when his mouth would have resisted even that much. "Kiss me, Deirdre," he breathed, studying her through lambent eyes.

His hoarse command was enough to free her from the spell she'd been under. When he brought her mouth back to his, her lips were parted, curious, eager, and she returned his kiss with growing fervor. She discovered the firmness of his lips, the evenness of his teeth, the texture of his tongue. She tasted his taste and breathed his breath, and every cell in her that was woman came alive.

"Deirdre," he whispered, once again inching her face from his. He pressed his warm forehead to hers and worked at catching his breath. "Why did you *do* that?"

Deirdre, who was having breathing difficulties of her own, struggled to understand. "What?"

"Why did you do that?"

"Do what?"

"Kiss me!"

The haze in her head began to clear, and she drew farther away. "You told me to kiss you."

His brows were drawn together, his features taut. "Not like that. I expected just a little kiss. Not . . . not that!"

He was angry. She couldn't believe it. "And who was kissing whom first like that?"

His breath came roughly, nostrils flaring. "You didn't have to do it back!" Shoving his large frame from the bed, he stormed from the room, leaving Deirdre unsure and bewildered and, very quickly, angry.

She sat up to glare in the direction he'd gone, then closed her eyes and tried to understand his reaction. Though she'd never, never kissed or been kissed that way, she wasn't so inexperienced that she couldn't see when a man was aroused. Neil Hersey had been aroused, and he'd resented it.

Which meant he didn't want involvement any more than she did.

Which meant they had a problem.

She'd enjoyed his kiss. More than that. It had taken her places she'd never been before. Kissing Neil had been like sampling a rich chocolate with a brandy center, sweet and dissolving—yet potent. He went straight to her head.

She touched her swollen lips, then her tingling chin. Even his beard had excited her, its roughness a contrast to the smoothness of his mouth. Yes, he was smooth. Smooth and virile and stimulating, damn him!

Dropping her chin to her chest, she took several long, steadying breaths. With the fresh intake of oxygen came the strength she needed. Yes, they were stuck under the same roof. They were even stuck, thanks to a matching stubbornness, in the same bed. She was simply going to have to remember that she had problems enough of her own, that *he* had problems enough of his own. And that he could be a very disagreeable man.

Unfortunately Neil chose that moment to return to the bedroom. He carried her crutches and wore an expression of uncertainty. After a moment's hesitation on the threshold, he started slowly toward the bed.

"Here," he said, quietly offering the crutches. "The sandwiches are under the broiler. They'll be ready in a minute."

Deirdre met his gaze, then averted her own, looking to the crutches. She reached for them, wrapped her hands around the rubber handles and studied them for a minute before raising her eyes again.

The corners of his mouth curved into the briefest, most tentative of smiles before he turned and left the room.

Leaning forward, Deirdre rested her head against the crutches. Oh, yes, Neil was a very disagreeable man. He also had his moments of sweetness and understanding, which, ironically, was going to make living with him that much more of a trial.

She sighed. It had to be done. Unless she was prepared to capitulate and leave the island by choice. Which she wasn't.

Struggling to her feet, she secured the crutches under her arms and, resigned, headed for the kitchen.

Lunch was a quiet, somewhat awkward affair. Neil avoided looking at Deirdre, which she had no way of knowing, since she avoided looking at him. She complimented him on the sandwiches. He thanked her. When they were done, he made a fresh pot of coffee—medium thick—and carried a cup to the living room for her. She thanked him. And all the while she was thinking of that kiss, as he was. All the while she was wondering where it might have led, as he was. All the while she was asking herself why, as was he.

Knowing she'd never be able to concentrate on her book, she brought her knitting bag from the bedroom, opened the instruction booklet and forced her attention to the directions.

Neil, who was in a chair drinking his second cup of coffee, was as averse to reading as she was, but could think of nothing else he wanted to do. "What are you making?" he asked in a bored tone.

She didn't look up. "A sweater."

"For you?"

"Hopefully." She reached for a neatly wound skein of yarn, freed its end and pulled out a considerable length. Casting on—that sounded simple enough.

Neil noted the thick lavender strand. "Nice color."

"Thank you." With the book open on her lap, she took one of the needles and lay the strand against it.

"That's a big needle."

She sighed. Concentration was difficult, knowing he was watching. "Big needle for a big sweater."

"For you?"

Her eyes met his. "It's going to be a bulky sweater."

"Ah. As in ski sweater?"

She pressed her lips together in angry restraint. "As in warm sweater, since it looks like I won't be skiing in the near future."

"Do you ski?"

"Yes."

"Are you good?"

She dropped the needle to her lap and stared at him. "I told you I was athletic. I exercise, play tennis, swim, ski . . . At least, I used to do all of those things. Neil, I can't concentrate if you keep talking."

"I thought knitting was an automatic thing."

"Not when you're learning how."

One side of his mouth twitched. "You haven't done it before?"

"No, I haven't."

"Was it the broken leg that inspired you?"

"I bought the yarn several months ago. This is the first chance I've had to work with it."

He nodded. She lifted the needle again, studied the book again, brought the yarn up and wound it properly for the first stitch. It took several attempts before she'd made the second, but once she'd caught on, she moved right ahead. Before long she had enough stitches cast on to experiment with the actual knitting.

When Neil finished his coffee, he returned the cup to the kitchen and started wandering around the house. At last, all else having failed to divert him, he picked up his book again.

By this time Deirdre was painstakingly working one knit stitch after another. The needles were awkward in her hands, and she continually dropped the yarn that was supposed to be wrapped around her forefinger. Periodically she glanced up to make sure Neil wasn't witnessing her clumsiness, and each time she was frowning when she returned to her work. Simply looking at him turned her inside out.

He was stretched full length on the couch . . . so long . . . so lean. The sleeves of his jersey were pushed back to reveal forearms matted with the same dark hair she'd felt on his chest. *Felt*. Soft, but strong and crinkly. The texture was permanently etched in her memory.

From his position on the sofa, Neil was also suffering distractions. His curiosity as to what Deirdre hid beneath her bulky sweatshirt had never been greater. He'd felt the edge of her breast. *Felt*. Strong and pert, but yielding beneath his fingertips. He'd carried her; she was light as thistledown and every bit as warm. He'd tasted her. That was his worst mistake, because there'd been a honeyed sweetness to her that he never would have imagined. Did the rest of his imaginings pale by comparison to the real thing?

From beneath half-lidded eyes he slanted her a look. Her hands gripped the needles, the forefinger of each extended. She was struggling, he saw, but even then the sweep of her fingers was graceful. Athletic? Perhaps. But if so, in a most healthy, most fitting, most feminine way.

Slapping the book shut, he sat bolt upright. Deirdre's questioning eyes shot to him.

"I can't read with that clicking," he grumbled. "Can't you be any quieter?"

"I'm having trouble as it is. Do you want miracles?"

"Not miracles. Just peace and quiet." Dropping the book on the sofa, he began to prowl the room.

"Book didn't grab you?"

"No." He ran a hand through his hair. "How about playing a game? Victoria has a bunch of them in the other room."

The knitting fell to Deirdre's lap. She wasn't sure she was up to playing games with Neil. "What did you have in mind?" she asked warily.

"I don't know. Maybe Monopoly?"

"I hate Monopoly. There's no skill involved."

"What about Trivial Pursuit?"

"I'm no good at history and geography. They make me lose."

"You make you lose," he argued. "The game doesn't do it."

"Whatever. The result's the same."

"Okay. Forget Trivial Pursuit. How about chess?"

"I don't know how."

"Checkers."

She scrunched up her nose in rejection.

"Forget a game," he mumbled.

"How about a movie?" she asked. It was a rainy day; the idea held merit. Her fingers were cramped, anyway.

"Okay."

"What do we have to choose from?"

In answer he started off toward the den. Deirdre levered herself up and followed, finding him bent over a low shelf in contemplation of the video tapes. She came closer, trying not to notice how snugly his jeans molded his buttocks, how they were slightly faded at the spot where he sat.

"*Magnum Force?*" he suggested.

"Too violent."

"*North by Northwest?*"

"Too intense." Leaning over beside him, she studied the lineup. "How about *Against All Odds*?"

"That's a romance."

"So?"

"Forget it."

"Then *The Sting*. Unromantic, but amusing."

"And boring. The best part's the music."

Her gaze moved across the cassettes, eyes suddenly widening. "*Body Heat*. That's a super movie. William Hurt, Kathleen Turner, intrigue and—"

"—Sex." Neil's head was turned, eyes boring into her. "I don't think we need that."

He was right, of course. She couldn't believe she'd been so impulsive as to suggest that particular movie.

"Ah." He drew one box out. "Here we go. *The Eye of the Needle*. Now that was a good flick."

It had action, intrigue, and yes, a bit of sex, but Deirdre felt she could take it. "Okay. Put it on." She set her crutches against the wall and hopped to the leather couch.

Removing the cassette from its box, Neil inserted it in the VCR, pressed several buttons, then took the remote control and sank onto the couch an arm's length from Deirdre. The first of the credits had begun to roll, when he snapped it off and jumped up.

"What's wrong?" she asked.

"We need popcorn. I saw some in the kitchen cabinet."

"But it takes time to make popcorn, and we're all set to watch."

"We've got time. Besides, it doesn't take more than a couple of minutes in the microwave." He rubbed his hands together. "With lots of nice melted butter poured on top—"

"Not butter! It's greasy, and awful for you."

"What's popcorn without butter?" he protested.

"Healthier."

"Then I'll put butter on mine. You can have yours without."

"Fine." She crossed her arms over her chest and sat back while he went to make the popcorn. Gradually her frown softened. It was rather nice being waited on, and Neil wasn't complaining. She supposed that if she'd had to be marooned with a man, she could have done worse. She *knew* she could have done worse. She could have been stuck with a real egomaniac. True, Neil had his moments. It occurred to her that while she'd given him a clue as to what caused her own mood swings, as yet she had no clue to his motivation. She'd have to work on that, she decided, merely for the sake of satisfying her curiosity. Nothing else.

Neil entered the room carrying popcorn still in its cooking bag. He resumed his seat, turned the movie back on and positioned the bag at a spot midway between them.

"Did you add butter?" she asked cautiously.

"No. You're right. I don't need it."

"Ah. Common sense prevails."

"Shh. I want to watch the movie."

She glanced at the screen. "I'm only disturbing the credits."

"You're disturbing me. Now keep still."

Deirdre kept still. She reached for a handful of popcorn and put one piece, then another in her mouth. The movie progressed. She tried to get into it but failed.

"It's not the same watching movies at home," she remarked. "A theater's dark. It's easier to forget your surroundings and become part of the story."

"Shh." Neil was having trouble of his own concentrating. It wasn't the movie, although as he'd seen it before, it held no mystery. What distracted him was Deirdre sitting so close. Only popcorn separated them. Once, when he reached into the bag, his hand met hers. They both retreated. And waited.

"You go first," he said.

She kept her eyes on the small screen. "No. That's okay. I'll wait."

"I've already had more. Go ahead."

"I don't need it. I'll get fat."

"You won't get fat." From what he'd seen, she wasn't a big eater; as for getting fat, from what he'd felt she was slender enough. Still, he couldn't resist a gibe. "On second thought, maybe you're right. You will get fat. You're smaller than I am, and I'm the one who's getting all the exercise around here. I'll wear it off easier."

He reached for the popcorn, but Deirdre already had her hand in the bag. She withdrew a full fist, sent him a smug grin and with deliberate nonchalance popped several pieces into her mouth.

Neil, who'd almost expected she'd do just that, wasn't sure whether to laugh or scream. Deirdre was impetuous in a way that was adorable, and adorable in a way that was bad for his heart. She had only to look at him with those luminous brown eyes and his pulse raced. He never should have kissed her. Damn it, he never should have kissed her!

But he had, and that fact didn't ease his watching of the rest of the movie. He was constantly aware of her—aware when she shifted on the couch, aware when she dropped her head back and watched the screen through half-closed eyes, aware when she began to massage her thigh absently.

"Leg hurt?" he asked.

She looked sharply his way, then shrugged and looked back at the screen.

"Want some aspirin?"

"No."

"Some Ben-Gay?"

"There is no Ben-Gay."

His lips twitched. "I'd run to the island drugstore for some if you'd let me rub it on."

She glared at the movie, but carried on the farce. "The island drugstore's out. I checked."

"Oh. Too bad."

Deirdre clamped her lips tightly, silently cursing Neil for his suggestion. *Let me rub it on.* Her insides tingled with a heat that, unfortunately, didn't do a whit to help her thigh.

Neil, too, cursed the suggestion, because his imagination had picked up from there, and he'd begun to think of rubbing far more than her thigh. He wondered whether her breasts would fit his hand, whether the skin of her belly would be soft....

He shifted away from her on the couch, and made no further comments, suggestive or otherwise. The movie was ruined for him. He was too distracted to follow the dialogue; the intrigue left him cold; the sex left him hot. The only thing that brought him any relief from the build-up of need in his body was the thought of Hartford, of work, of Wittnauer-Douglass. And because that upset him all the more, he was truly between a rock and a very hard place, where he remained throughout the evening.

He and Deirdre ate dinner together. They sat together before the fire. They pretended to read, but from the way Deirdre's eyes were more often on the flames than her book, he suspected that she was accomplishing as little as he was. He also suspected that her thoughts were running along similar lines, if the occasional nervous glances she cast him were any indication.

There was an element of fear in her. He'd seen it before; he could see it now. And it disturbed him. Was she afraid of sex? Was she afraid of feeling feminine and heated and out of control?

Even as he asked himself those questions, his body tightened. What in the hell was *he* afraid of? Certainly not sex. But there was something holding him back, even when every nerve in his body was driving him on.

He sat up by the fire long after Deirdre had taken refuge in bed. When at last he joined her, he was tired enough to fall asleep quickly. By the time the new day dawned, though, he was wondering whether he should relent and sleep in another room. Twice during the night he'd awoken to find their bodies touching—his outstretched arm draped over hers, the sole of her foot nestled against his calf.

What *was* it that made them gravitate toward each other? Each had come to Maine in search of solitude, so he'd have thought they'd have chosen to pass the time in opposite corners of the house. That hadn't been the case. Spitting and arguing—be it in the bedroom, the kitchen, the living room or den—they'd been together. And now . . . still . . . the bed.

He saw Deirdre look over her shoulder at him, then curl up more tightly on her side. Rolling to his back, he stared up at the ceiling, but the image there was of a disorderly mop of wheat-colored hair, soft brown eyes still misty with sleep, soft cheeks bearing a bed-warmed flush and lips that were slightly parted, unsure, questioning.

He had to get out. Though there was still the intermittent patter of rain and the air beyond the window was thick with mist, he had to get out. Without another glance at Deirdre, he flew from the bed, pulled on the dirty clothes he'd been planning to wash that day, laced on the sneakers that still bore a crust of mud from the day of his arrival on the island, threw his Windbreaker over his shoulders and fled the room, then the house.

Surrounded by the silence left in his wake, Deirdre slowly sat up. Being closed in had finally gotten to him, she mused. It had gotten to her, too. Or was it Neil who'd gotten to her? She'd never spent as uncomfortable an evening or night as those immediately past, her senses sharpened, sensitized, focused in on every nuance of Neil's physical presence. He breathed; she heard it. He turned; she felt it. Once, when she'd awoken in the middle of the night to find her hand tucked under his arm, she'd nearly jumped out of her skin, and not from fear of the dark.

Her body was a coiled spring, taut with frustration. She wanted to run six miles, but couldn't run at all. She wanted to swim seventy-two laps, but couldn't set foot in a pool, much less the ocean. She wanted to exercise until she was hot and tired and dripping with sweat, but . . . but . . . Damn it, yes, she could!

Shoving back the covers, she grabbed her crutches, took a tank top and exercise shorts from the dresser drawer and quickly pulled them on. She sat on the bed to put on her one sock and sneaker and both leg warmers, then pushed herself back up, tucked her cassette player and several tapes under one arm and her crutch under the other, and hobbled into one of the spare bedrooms. Within minutes the sounds of Barry Manilow filled the house.

Deirdre took a deep breath and smiled, then closed her eyes and began her familiar flexibility exercises. Her crutches lay on the spare bed; she discovered she could stand perfectly well without them. And the fact that various parts of the routine had to be altered in deference to her leg didn't bother her. She was moving.

In time with the music, she did body twists and side bends. She stretched the calf and ankle muscles of her right leg, and the inner thigh muscles of both legs. It felt good, so good to be feeling her body again. She took her time, relaxed, let the music take her where it would.

After several minutes, she moved into a warm-up, improvising as she went to accommodate her limited mobility. The music changed; the beat picked up, and she ventured into an actual dance routine. Though she couldn't dance in the true sense of the word, her movements were fluid and involved her entire upper torso as well as her good leg. By the time she'd slowed to do a cool-down routine, she'd broken into a healthy sweat and felt better than she had in days.

So immersed was she in the exercise that she didn't hear the open and closing of the front door. Neil, though, heard her music the minute he stepped into the house. He was incensed; it was loud and far heavier than the music he preferred. Without bothering to remove his wet jacket, he strode directly toward the sound, intent on informing Deirdre that as long as they were sharing the house, she had no right to be so thoughtless.

He came to an abrupt halt on the threshold of the spare bedroom, immobilized by the sight that met him. Eyes closed, seeming almost in a trance, Deirdre was moving in time to the music with a grace that was remarkable given her one casted leg. But it wasn't the movement that lodged his breath in his throat. It was her. Her body.

If he'd wondered what she'd been hiding beneath her oversized clothes, he didn't have to wonder any longer. She wore a skimpy tank top that revealed slender arms and well-toned shoulders. Her breasts pushed pertly at the thin fabric, their soft side swells clearly visible when she moved her arms. Her waist was small, snugly molded by the elasticized band of her shorts, and the shorts themselves were brief, offering an exaggerated view of silken thighs.

He gave a convulsive swallow when she bent over, his eyes glued to crescents of pale flesh. Then she straightened and stretched, arms high over her head, dipping low and slow from one side to the other. He swallowed again, transfixed by the firmness of her breasts, which rose with the movement.

Neil realized then that Deirdre's shapelessness had belonged solely to her bulky sweat clothes. Deirdre Joyce was shapely and lithe. With her hair damp around her face, her skin gleaming under a sheen of perspiration, with her arms flexing lyrically, her breasts bobbing, her hips rocking, she looked sultry, sexy and feminine.

He was in agony. His own body was taut, and his breath came raggedly. Turning, he all but ran down the hall, through the master bedroom, directly into the bathroom. He was tugging at his clothes, fumbling in his haste, knowing only that if he didn't hit a cold shower soon he'd explode.

His clothing littered the floor, but he was oblivious to the mess. Stepping into the shower, he turned on the cold tap full force, put his head directly beneath the spray, propped his fists against the tile wall and stood there, trembling, until the chill of the water had taken the edge of fever from his body. He thought of Hartford, of Wittnauer-Douglass, of his uncle who'd died the year before, of basketball—anything to get his mind off Deirdre. Only when he felt he'd gained a modicum of control did he adjust the water temperature to a more comfortable level for bathing.

Deirdre, who was totally unaware of the trial Neil had been through, finished her cool-down exercises and did several final stretches before allowing herself to relax in a nearby chair. Feeling tired but exhilarated, she left the music on; it was familiar, comfortable and reassuring.

At length she sat forward and reached for her crutches, knowing that if she didn't dry off and change clothes, her perspiration-dampened body would soon be chilled.

She turned off the music and listened. The house was still silent, which meant, she reasoned, that Neil was still outside, which meant, she reasoned further, that she could have the bathroom to herself without fear of intrusion. A warm bath sounded very, very appealing.

The smile she wore as she swung her way down the hall was self-congratulatory. She was proud of herself. She'd exercised, and in so doing had not only proved that she could do it, but had worked off the awful tension she'd awoken with that morning. So much for Neil Hersey and his virility, she mused. She could handle it.

Intending to fill the tub while she undressed, she passed straight through the master bedroom to the bathroom. The door was closed. Without a thought, she shouldered it open and let the rhythm of her limp carry her several feet into the room. There she came to a jarring halt.

Neil stood at the sink. His head was bowed and he was bent slightly at the waist, his large hands curving around the edges of the porcelain fixture. He was stark naked.

The breath had left her lungs the instant she'd seen him, and Deirdre could do no more than stare, even when he slowly raised his head and looked at her. He had a more beautifully male body than she'd ever have dreamed. His back was broad and smooth, his flanks lean, his buttocks tight. Seen in profile, his abdomen was flat, his pelvic bones just visible beneath a casement of flesh, his sex heavy and distinct.

"Deirdre?" His voice was husky. Her eyes flew to his when, without apparent modesty, he straightened and turned to face her. Two slow steps brought him close enough to touch. He repeated her name, this time in a whisper.

She was rooted to the spot, barely able to breathe, much less speak. Her eyes were wide and riveted to his.

He brought up a hand to brush the dots of moisture from her nose, then let his thumb trail down her cheek, over her jaw to her neck and on to the quivering flesh that bordered the thin upper hem of her tank top. Her breath was suddenly coming in tiny spurts that grew even tinier when he slipped his hand beneath her shoulder strap and brushed the backs of his fingers lower, then lower. She bit her lip to stifle a cry when he touched the upper swell of her breast, and though she kept her eyes on his, she was aware of the gradual change in his lower body.

"I didn't know you looked like this," he said hoarsely. "You've kept it all hidden."

Deirdre didn't know what to say. She couldn't quite believe he was complimenting her, not when he was so superbly formed himself. Surely the other women who'd seen him this way had been far more desirable than she. And though she knew he was aroused, her insecurities crowded in on her.

The backs of his fingers were gently rubbing her, dipping ever deeper into her bra. "Take off your clothes," he urged in a rough murmur, eyes flaming with restrained heat. "Let me see you."

She shook her head.

"Why not?"

She swallowed hard and managed a shaky whisper. "I'm sweaty."

"Take a shower with me." His baby finger had reached the sensitive skin just above her nipple, coaxing.

Pressing her lips together to hold in a moan, she shook her head again. "I can't take a shower." Her voice was small, pleading.

"Then a bath. Let me bathe you."

She wasn't sure if it was the sensuality of his words, or the fact that his finger had just grazed the hard nub of her nipple, but her good knee buckled, and she would have fallen had not her crutches been under her arms. His finger moved again, then again, sending live currents through her body. This time she couldn't contain the soft moan that slipped from her throat.

"Feel good?" he whispered against her temple, his own breath coming quicker.

"I don't want it to," she cried.

"Neither do I, but it does, doesn't it?"

It felt heavenly—his touching her, his being so near, so naked. She wanted to be naked beside him, too, but she was frightened. He'd be disappointed. She was sure of it. She was an athlete, "boyish" by her family's definition, and that description had haunted her doggedly over the years. She wasn't soft and fragile and willowy.

And even if Neil wasn't disappointed looking at her, he'd be let down by what would come after that. She felt the ache, the emptiness crying out inside of her, and knew she'd want to make love. And then he'd be disappointed, and the illusion would be broken.

She hobbled back a step, dislodging his hand. "I have to go. I have to go, Neil." Without waiting for his reply, she turned and fled from the bathroom, taking refuge in the bedroom where she'd exercised, collapsing in the chair and cursing her failings. *So much for handling Neil's virility.* Hah!

She didn't know how long she sat there, but the sweat had long since dried from her skin and she was feeling chilled when Neil appeared at the door. He wore a fresh pair of jeans and a sweater, and was barefoot, as usual. She wished she could believe that things were back to normal between them, but she knew better.

Neil felt neither anger nor frustration as he looked at her, but rather a tenderness that stunned him. Padding slowly into the room, he took an afghan from the end of the bed, gently draped it over her shoulders, then came down on his haunches beside her chair. "What frightens you, Deirdre?" he asked in a tone that would have melted her if the sight of him hadn't already done so.

It was a minute before she could speak, and then only brokenly. "You. Me. I don't know."

"I'd never hurt you."

"I know."

"Then what is it? You respond to me. I can feel it in your body. Your breath catches, and you begin to tremble. Is that fear, too?"

"Not all of it."

"You do want me."

"Yes."

"Why don't you give in and let go? It'd be good between us."

She looked down at her hands, which were tightly entwined in her lap. "Maybe for me, but I'm not sure for you."

"Why don't you let me be the judge of that?"

"I'm an athlete, not soft and cuddly like some women."

"Just because you're athletic doesn't mean you're not soft and cuddly. Besides, if it was a cushiony round ball I wanted, I'd go to bed with a teddy bear."

As he'd intended, his comment brought a smile to her face. But it was a tentative smile, a nervous one. "Somehow I can't picture that."

"Neither can I, but, then, I can't picture myself being disappointed if you let me hold you . . . touch you . . . make love to you."

His words sent a ripple of excitement through her, and there was clear longing in her gaze as she surveyed his face. "I'm scared" was all she could manage to say.

Neil studied her a minute longer, then leaned forward and kissed her lightly. "I'd never hurt you. Just remember that." Standing, he left the room.

His words were in Deirdre's mind constantly as the day progressed. She believed that he'd meant what he'd said, but she knew that there were different kinds of hurt. Physical hurt was out of the question; Neil was far too gentle for that. But emotional hurt was something else. If their relationship should take the quantum leap that lovemaking would entail...and he should be let down...she'd be hurt. How it had happened, she didn't know, particularly since they'd spent most of their time together fighting, but Neil had come to mean something to her. She wasn't up to analyzing the exact nature of that something; all she knew was that she was terrified of endangering it.

If he'd thought long and hard, Neil couldn't have come up with a better way to goad Deirdre that day than by being kind, soft-spoken and agreeable. Without a word he prepared their meals. Without a word he did the laundry. He was indulgent when she tackled her knitting again, abiding the noise without complaint. He was perfectly amenable to watching her choice of movie on the VCR. He didn't start a single argument, but, then, neither did she. It was the quietest day they'd spent on the island.

Deirdre was as aware as he of that fact. She was also aware that, by denying her any cause to bicker, Neil was allowing her time to think about what he'd said and what she was going to do about it. If the issue had been entirely cerebral, she might have had a chance to resist him. But her senses refused to be reasoned with and were constantly attuned to his presence. That side of her she'd never paid much heed to was suddenly clamoring for attention. Though all was peaceful on the outside, inside she was a mass of cells crying for release from a tension that radiated through her body in ever-undulating waves.

By the time they'd finished dinner and had spent a quiet hour before the fire, she had her answer. Yes, she was frightened and very, very nervous, but she'd decided that if Neil approached her again, she wouldn't refuse him. The sensual side of her nature wouldn't allow her to deny herself.

Head bowed, she quietly got to her feet, secured her crutches under her arms and left the living room. Once in the bedroom, she slowly changed into her pajamas, then sat on the side of the bed and reviewed her decision. She was taking a chance, she knew. A big one. If things didn't go well, the atmosphere in the house would be worse than ever. Then again, maybe not. They might be able to settle into a platonic relationship for the rest of their time here. Then again, Neil might not even come to her....

Even as she pondered that possibility, she sensed his presence in the room. Her head swiveled toward the door, eyes following his silent approach. Every one of her insecurities found expression in her face. Her back was straight. Her hands clutched the rounded edge of the bed.

More than anything at that moment, Neil wanted to alleviate her fear. It tore at him, because he knew he was its cause, just as he knew that her fear was unfounded. If she worried that she wouldn't please him, she worried needlessly. Deirdre turned him on as no other woman had, turned him on physically and in a myriad of other ways he'd only begun to identify.

Hunkering down, he raised his eyes to hers. He wanted to ask, but couldn't find the words. One part of him was frightened, too—frightened of being turned down when the one thing he wanted, the one thing he needed just then, was to be accepted, to be welcomed. So his question was a wordless one, gently and soulfully phrased.

Deirdre's insides were trembling, but she wasn't so wrapped up in apprehension that she didn't hear his silent request. It was a plea that held its share of unsureness, and that fact, more than anything, gave her the courage she needed.

Of its own accord, her hand came up, touching his cheek, inching back until her fingers wove gently into his hair. Tentatively, nervously, she let her lips soften into the beginnings of a smile.

Neil had never seen anything as sweet. He felt relief, and a kind of victory. But more, a well of affection rose inside, spreading warmth through him. Whatever Deirdre's fears were, she was willing to trust him. That knowledge pleased him every bit as much as the prospect of what was to come.

Holding her gaze, he brought his hands up to frame her face. His thumbs stroked her lips for a minute before he came forward and replaced them with his mouth. His kiss was sure and strong, the sealing of a pact, but it was every bit as gentle in promise, and Deirdre was lost in it. It was almost a shock when he set her back and she remembered that there was more to lovemaking than kisses alone. Her expression reflected her qualms, and Neil was quick to reassure her.

"Don't be frightened," he whispered. "We'll take it slow." Sitting back on his haunches, he slid his hands to her neck, then lower to the first button of her pajamas, which he released. He moved on to the second button, working in such a way that some part of his hand constantly touched her flesh. For him, the touch point reflected sheer greed; for Deirdre it was a sensually electric connection that served as a counterpoint to her apprehension.

Only when the last of the buttons was released did Neil lower his gaze. With hands that trembled slightly, he drew back the voluminous pajama fabric, rolling it outward until her breasts were fully exposed. The sight of them, small and high, but well rounded, shook him deeply. He'd been right; imagination did pale against reality. Or maybe it was that he hadn't dared dream....

The cool air of the bedroom hit Deirdre simultaneously with trepidation, but when her arms would have moved inward, he gently held them still.

"You're beautiful, Deirdre," he breathed. "What could ever have made you think that you wouldn't be right for me?"

She didn't answer, because the light in his eyes was so special, so precious, that she was afraid of distracting him lest his fascination fade. So she watched, mesmerized, as he brought both hands to her breasts. Long fingers circled them, tracing only their contours before growing bolder. A soft sigh slipped through her lips when he began to knead her fullness, and the feeling was so right and so good that she momentarily forgot her fears.

When the pads of his fingers brushed her nipples, she stiffened her back, but it was a movement in response to the surge of heat, not a protest. She had to clutch his shoulders then, because he had leaned forward and opened his mouth over one tight nub, and the sensation was jolting her to her core.

His tongue dabbed the pebbled tip. His teeth toyed with it. And all the while his hand occupied her other breast, caressing it with such finesse that she bit her lip to keep from crying out.

At last, when she simply couldn't help herself, she began to whimper. "Neil . . . I don't think I can stand this. . . ."

"If I can, you can," he rasped against her skin.

"I feel like I'm on fire. . . ."

"You are."

"I can't sit still. . . ."

"Sure you can. Let it build."

"It's been building for three days!"

"But it has to be slow, has to be right."

He drew back only long enough to whip the sweater over his head. Then he came up to sit beside her and take her in his arms. That first touch, flesh to flesh, was cataclysmic. Deirdre's entire body shook when her breasts made contact with his chest. Her arms went around him, holding him tightly, as though otherwise she'd simply shatter.

Neil's grip on her was no less definitive. His large body shuddered at the feel of her softness pressing into it. His breath came raggedly by her ear, while his hands hungrily charted every inch of her bare back, from her shoulders, over her ribs, to the dimpled hollows below her waist. Her pajama bottoms hung around her hips; he took advantage of their looseness to explore the creamy smoothness of her belly, the flare of her hips, the conditioned firmness of her bottom.

Deirdre, whose body all but hummed its pleasure, was finding a second heaven touching Neil. She loved the broad sweep of his back, the textured hollows of his collarbone, the sinewed swells of his chest. Slipping her hands between their bodies, she savored his front as she'd done his back. It was hairier, enticingly so, and his nipples were every bit as taut, if smaller, than hers were.

"What you do to me, Deirdre," he murmured dazedly, recapturing her face with his hands and taking her lips in a fevered kiss. "I think I agree with you. I'm not sure how much more I can stand, either."

She'd been right, he realized. Though they hadn't known it at the time, they'd endured three days of foreplay. From the very first there'd been curiosity. And it had grown more intense, despite every argument they'd had, despite every scathing comment they'd exchanged. Later he would wonder how much of the fighting had been caused by that basic attraction between them, but for now all he could think about was that their mutual desire was on the verge of culmination.

Coming up on one knee, he grasped her under the arms and raised her gently to the pillow. He eased the quilt from under her until she was lying on the bare sheet, then, unsnapping her pajama bottoms, he worked them down her legs and over her cast, finally dropping them to the floor.

Deirdre experienced a resurgence of anxiety when he sat back and looked at her, but his gaze was filled with such reverence that those fears receded once again. The hand he skimmed up her leg was worshipful, and when he reached the nest of pale hair at the juncture of her thighs, he touched her with care that bordered on awe.

She felt totally exposed, yet treasured. Looking at Neil, seeing the way his large frame quivered with restrained desire, she marveled that fate had brought him to her.

"Neil...please..." she begged in a shaky whisper. "I want you."

He needed no more urging. Sitting back, he unsnapped his jeans and thrust them down his legs along with his briefs. Within seconds he was sliding over her, finding a place for himself between her thighs, threading his fingers through hers and anchoring them by her shoulders.

Bearing his weight on his elbows, he rubbed his hot body back and forth over hers. He made no attempt to penetrate her, simply sought the pleasure of his new level of touching. But the pleasure was galvanic, causing them both to breathe quickly and unevenly.

Deirdre had never before known such anticipation. She wasn't thinking about her fears, wasn't thinking about what would happen if Neil didn't find her lovemaking adequate. She was only thinking of the burning deep within her, knowing that she needed his possession now.

Eyes closed, she arched upward, hips straining toward his in a silent plea that dashed the last of his resistance. Nudging her legs farther apart, he positioned himself, then tightened his fingers around hers.

"Look at me, Deirdre," he whispered. "Look at me, babe."

Her eyes opened, then grew wider when, ever so slowly, he entered her. She felt him clearly, sliding deeper and deeper; it was as though each individual cell inside her responded to his presence, transmitting one heady message after another to her brain. By the time he filled her completely, she knew that she'd never, never be the same again.

Neil closed his eyes and let out a long and tremulous sigh. Satisfaction was so clearly etched on his features that Deirdre would have breathed a sigh of relief, too, had she been able to. But he'd begun to move inside her, and breathing became increasingly difficult. All she could do was to give herself up to the spiral of passion he created.

The heat built steadily. Neil set a pace that maximized her pleasure, knowing precisely when to slow, precisely when to speed up. She moved to his rhythm, following his lead with a flair of her own that drove him on and up.

Then, when the fire within her became too hot for containment, she arched her back a final time, caught a sudden deep breath and dissolved into a seemingly endless series of spasms. Somewhere in the middle, Neil joined her, holding himself at the very entrance of her womb while his body pulsed and quivered.

It was a long time before either of them could speak, a long time during which the only sounds in the room were the harsh gasping for air and the softer, more gentle patter of the rain. Only when they'd begun to breath more normally did Neil slide to the side, but he brought her with him, settling them face to face on the pillow.

"Well," he asked softly, "what do you think?"

For an instant, Deirdre's old fears crowded in on her. "What do *you* think?" she whispered.

"I think," he said slowly, reining in a smug smile, "that for a lady with a sharp tongue and a questionable disposition, you're one hell of a lover."

7

RELIEF WASHED OVER HER, this time thoroughly wiping away whatever lingering doubts she'd had. A smile lit her face, unwaveringly, even as she raised her voice in mock protest.

"Sharp tongue? Questionable disposition? It was all because of you, Neil Hersey. You were the one who wasn't supposed to be here!"

Neil was undaunted. His own euphoria was too great. "And if I hadn't been," he ventured naughtily, "just think of all we'd have missed."

Deirdre had no suitable answer for that, so she simply continued to smile, and he was content to bask in her sunshine. After a time, he tenderly brushed a damp wisp of hair from her cheek.

"You're looking happy."

"I am . . . happy . . . satisfied . . . relieved."

"Was it that awful—the thought of our making love?" he chided.

"Oh, no, Neil," she answered quickly. "It was exciting. But you knew I was frightened."

"I'm still not sure why. It couldn't have been the athletic thing alone. Did it have something to do with the fellow who burned you once?"

She thought about that. "Indirectly, I suppose." Her gaze dropped. "Things were okay between us . . . sexually. It's just that when he got the urge to leave, he up and left, like there really wasn't anything worth sticking around for. On a subconscious level, I may have taken it more personally than I should have." She lapsed into silence as she considered why that had been. Her fingers moved lightly over the hair on Neil's chest in a reminder of what had just passed between them, and it gave her the courage to go on.

"I think it relates more to my family than Seth. I've always been the black sheep, the one who didn't fit in. My mother is the epitome of good manners, good looks and feminine poise. My sister takes after her. I've always been different, and they've made no secret of their opinion of me."

He cupped her throat in the vee of his hand, while his thumb drew circles on her collarbone. "They don't think you're feminine enough?"

"No."

His laugh was a cocky one. "Shows how much they know."

She rewarded him with a shy smile. "You're talking sex, which is only one part of it, but you're good for my ego, anyway."

"And you're good for mine. I don't think I've ever had a woman want me as much as you did just now. I know damn well that sex was the last thing on your mind when you got here, and that makes your desire so precious. I'd like to think it wasn't just any man who could turn you on like that."

"It wasn't!" she exclaimed, then lowered her voice. "There's only been one man, and that was Seth. I'm not very experienced."

"Experienced women are a dime a dozen. You're worth far more."

"I've never been driven by sexual need. I've never seen myself as a sexual being."

"We're all sexual beings."

"To one degree or another, but those degrees can vary widely." She moved her thigh between his, finding pleasure in the textural contrast of their bodies. "I guess what I'm saying is that I've always assumed myself to be at the lower end of the scale."

"Do you still?" he asked softly.

The look she gave him was every bit as soft. "With you? No."

He ran his hand down her spine, covered her bottom and pressed her hips intimately close. "That's good," he said, and sucked in a loud breath. "Because I think I'm needing you again."

Deirdre couldn't have been more delighted. Not only was he proving once again that her fears had been unfounded, but he was mirroring the state of her own reawakening desire. She followed the progress of her hand as it inched its way down his chest. "I think the needing is mutual."

"Any regrets?" he asked thickly.

"Only that I can't wrap both legs around you."

"It is a challenge with your cast. I didn't hurt you before, did I?"

She was fascinated by the whorl of hair around his navel. "Did I sound like I was in pain?" she asked distractedly.

"Dire pain."

"It had nothing to do with my leg." Her hand crept lower, tangling in the dark curls above his sex.

"Deirdre?" He was having trouble breathing again.

She was too engrossed in her exploration to take pity on him. "You have a beautiful body," she whispered. Her fingers grazed his tumescence. "I didn't have time to touch you before."

"Oh, God," he breathed when she took him fully into her grasp. His hand tightened on her shoulder, and he pressed his lips to her forehead. "Oh..."

"Do you like that?" she asked, cautiously stroking him.

"Oh, yes...harder...you can do it harder." His body was straining for her touch; when she strengthened it, he gave a moan of ecstasy. "Almost heaven—that's what it is."

"Almost?"

He opened his eyes and gazed at her then. "True heaven is when I'm inside." Inserting his leg between hers, he brought her thigh even higher. "You're hot and moist and tight, so tight. The way I slip in—" he put action to words "—shows how perfectly you...ummmmmm...how perfectly you were made... for me."

It was Deirdre's turn to gasp, then moan. He was lodged deeply within her, while his hand was caressing the rest of her with consummate expertise. When he withdrew, then surged back, she thought she'd explode.

The explosion wasn't long in coming. His mouth covered hers and he filled her with his tongue, as his manhood already filled her. One bold thrust echoed the other in a rhythm that repeated itself until all rhythm was suspended in a climactic surge.

This time when they tumbled back from that pyrotechnic plane, they had neither the strength nor the need to talk. Fitting Deirdre snugly into the curve of his body, Neil held her until her breathing was long and even. Soon after, he, too, was asleep.

THE NEXT DAY was the most glorious one Deirdre had ever known. She awoke in Neil's arms with a smile on her face, and if the smile ever faded, it was never for long. He instructed her to stay in bed while he showered, then he returned and carried her in for a bath. By the time he'd washed her to his satisfaction, they were both in need of satisfaction of another sort. So he carried her back to bed, where he proceeded to adore every bare inch of her body.

He taught her things about herself she'd never known, banishing any modesty she might have had and reaping the benefits. With deft fingers, an agile tongue and pulsing sex, he brought her to climax after climax, until she pleaded for mercy.

"A sex fiend!" she cried. "I'm stranded on an island with a sex fiend!"

"Look who's talking!" was all he had to say. Not only had she been as hungry as he, but she'd taken every one of the liberties with his body that he had with hers.

They didn't bother to get dressed that day. It seemed a waste of time and effort. The weather was as ominous as the thought of putting clothing between them. When they left the bedroom, they shared Deirdre's pajamas—the top was hers, the bottom his. He teased her, claiming that she'd brought along men's pajamas with precisely that goal in mind, but he wasn't about to complain when he knew all he had to do—whether in the kitchen, the living room or the den—was to raise her top, lower his bottom, and enter her with a fluid thrust.

Deirdre let his presence fill her, both body and mind. She knew they were living a dream, that reality lurked just beyond, waiting to pounce. But she refused to be distracted by other, more somber thoughts when she was feeling so complete. Neil accepted her. He'd seen her at her worst, yet he accepted her. His attraction to her wasn't based on who she was, what she did for a living, or what she wore; he liked her as the person she was.

Neil was similarly content. The realization that he was avoiding reality did nothing to temper his feelings about Deirdre. He refused to dwell on the fact that she didn't know about the downturn his life in Hartford had taken, because it didn't seem to matter. She was happy; he'd made her happy.

She didn't care about his financial prospects or his reputation. She was satisfied to accept him as he was.

And so they didn't think about the future. One day melded into the next, each filled with relaxation, leisure activity, lovemaking. Deirdre finished one book and started a second. She got the hang of knitting well enough to begin work on the actual sweater, and made commendable headway on it. She exercised each day but made no attempt to devise new routines, loath to do something that might start her brooding on whether she'd be able to teach again.

Neil did his share of reading. He continued to take responsibility for most of the household chores, and it was his pleasure to do so. From time to time Deirdre tried to help, but he saw the frustration she suffered with her cast, and it was enough to tell him that he wasn't being used.

The bickering they'd done during those first three days was, for all intents and purposes, over. This was not to say that they agreed on everything, but compromise became the mode. Neil accepted the loud beat of Deirdre's music, while she accepted the drone of his radio-transmitted Celtics games. She subjected herself to a clobbering at Trivial Pursuit, while he endured the gyrations in *Saturday Night Fever*.

One night, when he was feeling particularly buoyant, he took a Havana cigar from his bag, lit it and sat back on the sofa in bliss. Deirdre, who'd watched in horror his elaborate ceremony of nipping off the end of the cigar, then moistening the tip, simply sat with one finger unobtrusively blocking her nose. It was an example of how far they'd come; as disgusting as she found the smell, she wasn't about to dampen his obvious pleasure.

He'd been smoking for several minutes before he cast her a glance and saw her pose. "Uh-oh. Bad?"

She shrugged. "Are't dose tings illegal in dis country?" she asked, careful to breathe through her mouth.

"It's illegal to import them. But if a foreigner brings them in for his own personal use and shares them with his friends, it's okay."

"Is dat how you got it?"

"I have a client from Jordan who has business interests here. He gave me a box several months ago." Neil eyed the long cigar with reverence. "I'm not usually a smoker, but I have to admit that if you want to smoke a cigar, this is the way to go."

"Da Mercedes of cigars?"

"Yup." Eyes slitted in pleasure, he put the cigar to his mouth, drew on it, then blew out a narrow stream of thick smoke. "Should I put it out?"

"Dot on my accou't. But do't ask me to kiss you later, commie breath."

His lips quirked at the corners. Leaning forward, he carefully placed the cigar in an ashtray, then stood and advanced on her.

She held up a hand. "Do't come closer. I dow what you're goi'g to do."

He propped his hands on the arm of her chair and bent so that his face was inches from hers. He was grinning. "I'll kiss you if I want to, and you'll like it, commie breath and all."

"Deil, I'm warding you—"

Her warning was cut short by his mouth, which took hers in a way that was at once familiar and new. After the initial capture, his lips softened and grew persuasive, coaxing hers into a response she was helpless to withhold.

When at last he ended the kiss, he murmured softly, "You can breathe now."

Deirdre's eyes were closed, and the hand that had protected her nose had long since abandoned that post and moved from the rich texture of his beard up into his thick, brown hair. "How can I do that . . . when you take my breath away...." When she pulled him back to her, he was more than willing to accede to her demands.

As time passed the cigar burned itself out, but neither of them noticed.

EARLY IN THE MORNING of their one-week anniversary on the island, Thomas called them from shore. Neil was the one to talk to him, but Deirdre, standing by, heard every word.

"How're you folks making out?"

Neil grinned, but made sure his voice was suitably sober. "Okay."

"I got your messages, but I've been away most of the week. I figured that you'd keep trying if there was any kind of emergency."

"He feels guilty," Deirdre whispered mischievously. "Serves him right."

Neil collared her with a playful arm as he spoke grimly back into the receiver. "We'll live."

"Deirdre's doing all right with that leg of hers?"

Neil hesitated before answering. Meanwhile, he toyed gently with Deirdre's earlobe. "The house has taken a beating. She's not very good with her crutches."

Deirdre kicked at his shin with her cast. He side-stepped her deftly.

"Oh," Thomas said. "Well, that's Victoria's problem. Are you two getting along?"

"Getting along?" Deirdre whispered. She slid her hand over Neil's ribs and tucked her fingers in the waistband of his jeans.

Neil cleared his throat and pulled a straight face. "We're still alive."

"You'll drive him crazy," she whispered. "He's dying of curiosity."

"Let him die," Neil whispered back, eyes dancing.

During the brief interlude, Thomas had apparently decided that what was happening between Neil and Deirdre was Victoria's problem, too. "Well," came his staticky voice, "I just wanted to let you know that you've got a store of fresh supplies on the dock."

"On the dock?" Neil looked at his watch. It was barely nine. "You must have been up before dawn."

"I left them last night."

"Coward."

"What's that?" came the static. "I didn't get that last word?"

Deirdre snickered noisily. Neil clamped a hand on her mouth. "I said, thank you," he yelled more loudly than necessary into the handset.

"Oh. Okay. I'll be out next week to pick you up, then. If there's any change in plans, give me a call."

For the first time, Neil's hesitation was legitimate. Looking down, he saw that Deirdre's too, was suddenly more serious. His fingers grew tighter on the handset.

"Will do" was all he said before switching off the instrument and replacing it on its stand. He stood silent for a minute with his arm still around Deirdre. Then, with a squeeze of her shoulder, he took a fast breath. "Hey, do you see what I see?"

She was ready for a diversion. Any diversion. Thomas's last comment had been a depressant. "I don't know. What do you see?"

He raised his eyes to the window. "The sun. Well, maybe not the sun itself, but it's brighter out there than it's been in a week, and it hasn't rained since yesterday, which means that the paths will have begun to dry out, which means that I can get the things in from the dock pretty quick, which means—" He gave her shoulder another squeeze. "—that we can take a walk."

Deirdre followed his gaze, then looked back up at him. "I'd like that," she said softly. "I'd like it a lot."

THE BREAK IN THE WEATHER offered new realms of adventure for them. As though determined to restake its claim after a long absence, the sun grew stronger from one day to the next. The air remained cool, and Deirdre's mobility was limited by her crutches, but she and Neil managed to explore most of the small island. When they weren't wandering in one direction or another, they were perched atop high boulders overlooking the sea. They watched the sun rise one morning, watched the sun set one evening, and in between they agreed that neither of them had ever visited as serene a place.

Unfortunately, with greater frequency as the days passed, their serenity was disturbed by the memory of Thomas's parting words. He'd be by to pick them up at the end of a week, and that week seemed far too short. Deirdre began to brood more and more about Providence, Neil about Hartford, and though the making up was always breathtaking, they began to bicker again.

Finally, three days before they were to leave, things came to a head. They'd finished dinner and were seated side by side in the den, ostensibly watching *Raiders of the Lost Ark*, but in truth paying it little heed. With an abruptness that mirrored his mood, Neil switched off the set.

Deirdre shot him a scowl. She'd been thinking about leaving the island, and the prospect left her cold. "What did you do that for?"

"You're picking your fingernail again. The sound drives me crazy!" What really drove him crazy was the thought of returning to Hartford, but Deirdre's nail picking was as good a scapegoat as any.

"But I wanted to watch the movie."

"How can you watch the movie when you're totally engrossed in your nail?"

"Maybe if you weren't rubbing that damned beard of yours, I'd be able to concentrate."

His eyes darkened. "You haven't complained about my beard for days." In fact, she'd complimented him on it. It was filling in well, she'd said, and looked good. He'd agreed with her assessment. "And maybe I'm rubbing it to drown out the sound of your picking! Why do you *do* that?"

"It's a nervous habit, Neil. I can't help it."

"So why are you nervous? I thought you were supposed to be calm and relaxed."

"I am!" she cried, then, hearing herself, dropped both her gaze and her voice. "I'm not."

Silence hung in the air between them. When Deirdre looked up at last, she found Neil studying her with a pained expression on his face.

"We have to talk," he said quietly.

"I know."

"Thomas will be here soon."

"I know."

"You'll go back to Providence. I'll go back to Hartford."

"I *know*."

"So what are we going to do about it?"

She shrugged, then slanted him a pleading glance. "Tell him we're staying for another week?" Even more frightening to her than the prospect of returning to Providence was the prospect of leaving Neil.

He snorted and pushed himself from the sofa, pacing to the far side of the room before turning on his heel. "I can't do that, Deirdre. Much as I wish it, I can't."

"Then what do you suggest?"

He stood with one hand on his hip, the other rubbing the back of his neck. His gaze was unfocused, alternately shifting from the wall to the floor and back. "I don't know, damn it. I've been trying to think of solutions—No, that's wrong. I've avoided thinking about going back since I arrived, and as a result, I have no solutions. Then there's *this* complication."

Deirdre didn't like the sound of his voice. "What complication?"

He looked her in the eye. "Us."

It was like a blow to her stomach. Though she knew he was right, she couldn't bear to think of what they'd shared in negative terms. "Look," she argued, holding up a hand in immediate self-defense. "*We* don't have to be a complication. You can go your way, I can go mine. *Fini.*"

"Is that how you want it?"

"No."

"How do you want it?"

"I don't know," she cried in frustration. "You're not the only one who's avoided thinking about going back. I haven't found any more solutions than you have."

"But we do agree that we want to keep on seeing each other."

"Yes!"

His shoulders sagged in defeat. "Then it is a complication, Deirdre. On top of everything else, what we have is very definitely a complication." He turned to stare out the window.

Deirdre, in turn, stared at him. "Okay, Neil," she began softly. "You're right. We have to talk. About everything." When he didn't move, she continued. "When we first came here, you were as bad-tempered as I was. I know my reasons, but I've never really known yours. At first I didn't want to know, because I have enough problems of my own. Then, when things got...better between us, I didn't want to ask for fear of upsetting the apple cart." She was sitting forward on the couch, a hand spread palm down on each thigh. "But I'm asking now. If we're going to figure anything out, I have to know. What happened, Neil? What happened in Hartford that brought you up here in such a temper? Why did you need to escape?"

Neil dropped his chin to his chest, her questions echoing in his brain. The moment of truth had come. He gnawed on the inside of his cheek, as though even doing something so pointless would be an excuse for not answering. But it wasn't. Deirdre was curious, and intelligent. As much as he wished he didn't have to tell her, she more than anyone deserved to know.

He turned to face her but made no move to close the distance between them. "I have," he said with a resigned sigh, "a major problem back home. It involves one of my principal clients—strike that, one of my prinicipal *ex*-clients, a very large corporation based in Hartford." He hesitated.

"Go on," she urged softly. "I'm with you."

"I've been chief counsel for the corporation for three years, and during that time I've come to be increasingly familiar with various aspects of the business. Last summer, quite inadvertently, I stumbled onto a corruption scheme involving the president of the corporation."

Deirdre held her breath and watched him with growing apprehension. She refused to believe that he'd knowingly condone corruption, yet, as corporate counsel, his job was to side with his client.

"No," he said, reading her fear, "I didn't demand a cut—"

"I never thought you would! But you must have been put in an awful position."

He was relieved by her obvious sincerity, but in some ways that made his task all the more difficult. He would have liked to be able to tell her that his practice was successful and growing even more so. He would have liked to have shone in her eyes. But the facts were against him.

Deirdre didn't deserve this. Hell, *he* didn't deserve it!

"Awful is putting it mildly," he declared. "I could have chosen to look the other way, but it went against every principle I'd ever held. So I took the matter before the board of directors. That was when things fell apart."

"What do you mean?"

"They were involved! All of them! They knew exactly what was going on, and their only regret was that I'd found out!"

Deirdre felt her anger rising on his behalf. "What did you do?"

"I resigned. I had no other choice. There was no way I'd sit back and watch them pad their own pockets at the expense of not on' their stockholders but their employees. Their employees! The last people who could afford to be gypped!"

"But I don't understand, Neil. If you resigned, isn't it all over? You may have lost one client, but you have others, don't you?"

"Oh, yes," he ground out with more than a little sarcasm. "But those others have dwindled with a suddenness that can't possibly be coincidental." His jaw was tight. "It seems that Wittnauer-Douglass wasn't satisfied simply with my resignation. The executive board wanted to make sure I wouldn't do anything to rock a very lucrative boat."

She was appalled. "They blackballed you."

"Worse. They passed word around that I'd been the mastermind behind the corruption scheme. According to the chairman of the board—and I got this from a reliable source—if I hadn't left, they'd have leveled charges against me."

"But they can't say that!"

"They can say anything they damn well please!"

"Then they can't *do* it!"

"I'm not so sure. There's a helluva lot of murky paperwork in the archives of any large corporation. That paperwork can be easily doctored if the right people give the go-ahead."

"But why would the board at Wittnauer-Douglass want to even mention corruption? Wouldn't it spoil their own scheme?"

"Not by a long shot. They simply reorganize, shift outlets, juggle a few more documents. When you've got power, you've got power. It's as simple as that."

"And you can't fight them." It was a statement, a straight follow-up to Neil's. Unfortunately it touched a nerve in him that was all too raw.

"What in the hell can I do?" he exploded, every muscle in his body rigid. "They've spread word so far and so fast that it's become virtually impossible for me to practice law in Hartford! The major corporations won't touch me. The medium-sized ones are leery. And it's gone way beyond my profession. Nancy—the woman I was seeing—quickly opted out, which was okay, because it was only a matter of time before we'd have split, anyway. But before I knew what had happened, I'd been replaced as chairman of the hospital fund-raising drive. That did hurt. Word is that I'm a crook, and even if some people believe in my innocence, there are still appearances to uphold. Hell, I can't even find a squash partner these days. I've become a regular pariah!"

"They can't do that!"

"They've done it," he lashed back. His anger was compounding itself, taking on even greater force than it had held in Hartford, mainly because he detested having to dump this on Deirdre. "I've worked my tail off to build a successful practice, and they've swept it away without a care in the world. And do you know what the worst part is?" He was

livid now, furious with himself. "I didn't see it coming! I was naive . . . stupid!"

Deirdre was on her feet, limping toward him. "It wasn't your fault—"

He interrupted, barely hearing her argument over the internal din of his self-reproach. "How could I have possibly spent so much time working with those people and not have seen them for what they are? I'm too trusting! I've always been too trusting! Good guys finish last, isn't that what they say? Well, it's true!"

She took his arm. "But trusting is a good way to be, Neil," she argued with quiet force. "The alternative is to be an eternal skeptic, or worse, paranoid, and you couldn't live that way."

"My friends. They even got to my *friends*."

"A real friend wouldn't be gotten to."

"Then I've been a poor judge of character on that score, too."

"You're being too harsh on yourself—"

"And it's about time! Someone should have kicked me in the pants years ago. Maybe if they had, I wouldn't have been such a damned optimist. Maybe I would have seen all this coming. Maybe I wouldn't be in such a completely untenable position now."

"You can find new clients," she ventured cautiously.

"Not the kind I want. My expertise is in dealing with large corporations, and those won't come near me now."

"Maybe not in Hartford—"

"Which means relocating. Damn it, I don't want to relocate. At least, not for that reason."

"But things aren't hopeless, Neil. You have a profession that you're skilled in—"

"And look where it's gotten me," he seethed. "I have a great office, two capable associates and a steadily diminishing clientele. I have a condominium, which the people I once called friends won't deign to visit. I have a record for charity work that's come to a dead halt. I have squash gear and no partner."

Deirdre dropped her hand from his stiff arm. "You also think you have a monopoly on self-pity. Well, you don't, Neil. You're not the only one who has problems. You're not the only one who's frustrated."

"Frustrated?" He raked rigid fingers through his hair. "Now *that's* the understatement of the year. And while we're at it, you can add guilt to the list of my transgressions. I came up here and took every one of those frustrations out on you!"

"But you weren't the only one to do it! I used you for that too, Neil, so I'm as guilty as you are."

"Yeah." His voice was calm now. "Only difference is that your problem has a solution in sight. Once the cast is off—"

"It's not only my leg," Deirdre snapped, turning away from him. "I wouldn't have been in such a lousy mood if it was simply a question of my leg. There's a whole other story to my life, and if you think that in its own way my situation isn't as frustrating as yours, you can add egotistical to that list you're drawing up."

There was silence behind her. For the first time since he'd begun his tirade, Neil's thoughts took a tangent. *A whole other story to my life,* she'd said. He was suddenly more nervous than he'd been angry moments before, inexplicably fearful that his world was about to collapse completely.

"What is it—that other story?"

Head down, she hobbled over to rest her hip against the desk. A dry laugh slipped from her throat. "It's ironic. There you are, without a corporation to represent. Here I am, with a corporation I don't want."

"What are you talking about?"

Slowly she raised her head. Almost reluctantly she replied, "Joyce Enterprises. Have you ever heard of it?"

"I've heard of it. It's based in..." The light dawned. "Providence. You're that Joyce? It's yours?"

"Actually, my family's. My father died six months ago, and my sister took over the helm."

Neil frowned. "I didn't make the connection...I never...it doesn't fit."

"With who I am?" She smiled sadly. "You're right. It doesn't fit. I don't fit, and that's the problem. My parents always intended that the business stay in the family. Sandra—my sister—just can't handle it. I have two uncles who are involved, but they're as ill-equipped to run things as my mother is."

Neil had come to stand before her. "So they want you in."

"Right."

"But you don't want in."

"Right again. I tried it once and hated it. I'm just not the type to dress up all day and entertain, which is largely what the head of a business like that has to do. I don't take to diplomatic small talk, and I don't take to being a pretty little thing on display."

"That I can believe," he quipped.

Deirdre responded to his teasing with a scowl. "I wish my family could believe it, but they won't. They keep insisting that I'm their only hope, and maybe I would be able to handle the management end of the business, but the political end would drive me up a tree! For six months now they've been after me, and while I was busy doing my own thing I had an excuse. At least, it was one I could grasp at. I've always known that sooner or later, as I got older, I'd slow down, but I thought I had time to find a substitute. Now I don't. Suddenly I can't do my own thing, and they've started hounding me to do theirs. Even before I left the hospital they were on me." She paused for a breath, then continued.

"They think I'm selfish, and maybe I am, because I want to be happy, and I know I won't be if I'm forced to be involved in the business. It's really a joke—their pushing me this way. I've always been odd in their minds. I'm a failure. They look down their noses at the work I do. And even beyond that, I don't have a husband, or children, which compounds my sin. What good am I? Nothing I do is right, so they say. Yet they stand over me and insist that I help run Joyce." She rubbed a throbbing spot on her forehead, then looked up at Neil.

"The family needs me. The business needs me. Can I stand by and let it all go down the tubes? Because it will, Neil. I keep telling them to bring in outside help, but they refuse, and if they continue to do that, the whole thing is doomed. Oh, it may take a while. The corporation is like a huge piece of machinery. It's showing signs of wear and tear right now, but the gears are still turning. When it comes time to oil them, though, and there's no one capable of doing the job, things will slow down, then eventually grind to a halt."

She gave a quick, little headshake, more of a shiver. "Talk of guilt, I've got it in spades. I have a *responsibility*, my mother keeps reminding me. And that's the worst part, because as much as I can't bear the thought of having anything to do with the business, I do feel the responsibility. I deny it to them. I've denied it to myself. But it's there." She looked down at her fingers and repeated more softly, "It's there."

Neil wrapped his hand around her neck and kneaded it gently. "We're a fine twosome, you and I. Between us, we've got a pack of ills and no medicine."

She gave a meek laugh. "Maybe the island drugstore has something?"

He sighed. "The island drugstore filled the prescription for two souls who needed a break, but I'm afraid it doesn't have anything for curing the ills back home."

"So," she breathed, discouraged. "We're back where we started. What are we going to do?"

He looked at her intently, then dipped his head and took her lips with a sweetness that wrenched at her heart. "We are going to spend the next three days enjoying each other. That is, if you don't mind dallying with a man who has a very dubious future . . ."

It was at that moment, with Neil standing close, looking at her as though her answer were more important to him than anything else in the world, that Deirdre knew she loved him.

She smiled softly. "If you don't mind dallying with a woman who would rather spend the rest of her life on this island than go back to the mainland and face up to her responsibilities . . ."

His answer was a broad smile and another kiss, this one deeper and more soul reaching than anything that had come before. It was followed by a third, then a fourth, and before long, neither Neil nor Deirdre could think of the future.

THEIR FINAL DAYS on the island were spent much as the preceding ones had been, though now there was direction to their thoughts, rather than a random moodiness. For his part, Neil was relieved to have told Deirdre everything, even if the telling hadn't solved a thing. She'd accepted his quandary without criticism, and her affection—yes, he was sure it was that—for him seemed, if anything, to have deepened.

For her part, Deirdre was relieved to have shared her burden with an understanding soul. Neil hadn't jumped on her for her failings; if anything, his affection—yes she was sure it was that—for her seemed stronger than ever.

If that affection took on a frantic quality at times, each attributed it to the fact that the clock was running out.

Thomas had arranged to pick them up at eight o'clock in the morning on that last day. So the night before they found themselves cleaning the house, making sure that everything was as it had been when they'd arrived two weeks before. Tension suddenly surrounded them, reducing them to nearly the same testy state they'd been in when they'd arrived.

Neil did a final round of laundry, inadvertently tossing Deirdre's teal green sweatshirt into the wash with the towels, half of which were an electric blue not far different from her sweatshirt, half of which were pure white. When the white towels emerged with a distinct green tinge, he swore loudly.

"Goddamn it! I thought you'd packed this thing already!"

"I haven't packed anything yet." She'd been putting that particular chore off for as long as possible. Now, studying the once-white towels, she scowled. "Didn't you see the sweatshirt when you put the towels in?"

"How could I see it in with these blue ones?"

"The sweatshirt's green!"

"That's close enough."

"You must be color-blind."

"I am not color-blind."

They were glaring at each other over the washing machine. Deirdre was the first to look away. "Okay," she said, sighing. "We can put the white towels through again, this time with bleach."

"The little tag says not to use bleach."

Fiery eyes met his. "I've used bleach on towels before, and it does the trick. If you don't want to take the risk, you find a solution." Turning, she swung back to her cleaning of the refrigerator, leaving Neil to grudgingly add bleach to a second load.

Not long after, intent on doing the packing she'd put off, Deirdre was headed for the bedroom, when her crutch caught on the edge of the area rug in the living room. She stumbled and fell, crying out in annoyance as well as surprise.

"Who put that stupid rug there?" she screamed.

Neil was quickly by her side, his voice tense. "That 'stupid' rug has been in exactly the same spot since we got here. Weren't you watching where you were going?"

"It's the damned rubber tips on these crutches!" She kicked at them with her good foot. "They catch on everything!"

Rescuing the crutches, he put an arm across her back and helped her up. "They haven't bothered you before. Are you okay?"

"I'm fine," she snarled, rubbing her hip.

"Then you're lucky. Damn it, Deirdre, are you trying to kill yourself? Why don't you watch where you're going next time?"

"Watch where I'm going? I was watching!"

"Then you were going too fast!"

"I wasn't going any faster than I ever go!"

"Which is too fast!"

Deirdre, who had returned the crutches to their rightful place, backed away from him, incensed. "I don't need advice from you! I've taken care of myself for years, and I'll do it again! Just because you've helped me out this week doesn't give you the right to order me around. If you really wanted to help me, you'd offer to take that damned corporation off my back!"

"If you really wanted to help *me*, you'd *give* me the damned corporation!" he roared back.

For long minutes they stood glaring at each other. Both pairs of eyes flashed; both pairs of nostrils flared. Gradually both chests stopped heaving, and their anger dissipated.

"It's yours," Deirdre said quietly, her eyes glued to his.

"I'll take it," he countered, but his voice, too, was quiet.

"It's a bizarre idea."

"Totally off the wall."

"But it could offer an out for both of us."

"That's right."

They stood where they were for another long minute. Then, resting a hand lightly on her back, Neil urged her toward the sofa. When they were both seated, he crossed one leg over his knee, propped his elbow on the arm of the sofa and chafed his lower lip with his thumb.

"I've done a lot of thinking since we talked the other night," he began, hesitating at first, then gaining momentum. "I've been over and over the problem, trying to decide what I want to do. There are times when I get angry, when the only thing that makes any sense to me is revenge. Then the anger fades, and I realize how absurd that is. It's also self-defeating, when what I really want to do is to practice law." He paused, lowered his hand to his lap and looked at her. "You have a corporation that you don't want. I could make good use of it."

Nervously she searched his features. "For revenge?"

"No. Maybe it'd be a sort of reprisal, but that wouldn't be my main objective. I need something, Deirdre. It kills me to have to say that, especially to you. It's hard for a man—for anyone, I suppose—to admit that he's short on options. But I'm trying to face facts, and the sole fact in this case is that Hartford is no longer a viable place for me to work."

"You said you didn't want to relocate."

"I said I didn't want to relocate because of Wittnauer-Douglass. Maybe it's convoluted logic, but I'm beginning to think that Joyce Enterprises would have attracted me regardless of the problems in Hartford. No matter what you see happening now within the company, Joyce has a solid reputation. I wouldn't be afraid to put my stock in it. And it may be the highest form of conceit, but I do think that I have something to offer. I'm a good lawyer. I'm intimately familiar with the workings of large corporations. I may not be an entrepreneur, but I know people who are. And I know of a headhunter who could help me find the best ones to work with.

"Unfortunately—" he took a breath and his eyes widened as he broached the next problem "—that would mean bringing in an outsider. From what you say, your family has been against that from the start, which raises the even more immediate issue of whether or not they'd even accept me."

Deirdre tipped up her chin in a gesture of defiance. "I hold an equal amount of stock to my mother and sister. If you were to enter the corporation alongside me, they wouldn't dare fight."

"But you don't want to enter the corporation. Wasn't that the point?"

"Yes, but if we were . . ." She faltered, struggling to find the least presumptive words. "If we were together. . . . I mean, if I made it clear that we were . . . involved . . ."

"That we were a steady couple, as in lovers?"

"Yes."

He gave his head a quick shake. "Not good enough. It'll have to be marriage."

"*Marriage?*" She'd wanted to think that they'd be tied somehow, but marriage was the ultimate in ties. "Isn't that a little radical?"

Neil shrugged, but nonchalance was the last thing he felt. He'd been searching for a way to bind Deirdre to him. He loved her. Somewhere along the line that realization had dawned, and it had fit him so comfortably that he hadn't thought of questioning it. He couldn't say the words yet; he felt too vulnerable. Marriage might be sudden, but it served his purposes well. "Radical only in that we've known each other for such a short time. We get along, don't we?"

"We fight constantly!" she argued, playing the devil's advocate. If she knew that Neil loved her she wouldn't have had an argument in the world. But he hadn't said those words, and she didn't have the courage to lay herself bare by saying them herself, so she felt obligated to resist.

"Not constantly. Only when we're frustrated by problems that seem beyond our control. We've had our smooth times, haven't we?"

"Yes," she admitted, albeit reluctantly.

"And if this whole plan solves our problems, we won't have cause to fight, will we?"

"Every married couple fights."

"Then we wouldn't be any different. Look at it objectively, Deirdre. We have similar values and interests. We've already proved that we can live with each other. If we survived these past two weeks, being together twenty-four hours a day, we've got one foot up on many other couples who marry."

She didn't want to look at it objectively. Love wasn't objective. "But we've known each other in such a limited sphere. This isn't the real world. It's possible that we could return to Providence and find that we *hate* each other."

"That's your insecurity talking."

"Okay, maybe it is. I don't think I'm cut out to be a corporate wife any more than I'm cut out to head that corporation." She waved a hand back and forth. "I'm not the prissy little hostess. I'm not the adorable little lady who always wears and says the right things."

"I'm not complaining about who you are. And I wouldn't ask you to do anything you're uncomfortable with. If we entertain—and I assume there'd be some of that—you'd look as beautiful as any woman in the room. And rather than having you cook we could take people out or have something catered."

"In my modest town house?" she squeaked.

"In the house I'd buy for us." He sat forward, determination strong in the gaze he sent her. "I'm not a gigolo, Deirdre. I wouldn't go into this if I felt I was getting a free ride. You may not know it yet, but I do have my pride. If we agree to go ahead with this scheme, I'll work my tail off in the business. I'll be the one to support us, and that means providing the kind of home for you that I think you deserve. I guess I'm old-fashioned in that way."

"Does that mean I can't work or do whatever else I want?"

"You can do anything you want. I'm not *that* old-fashioned. And if you think I'm bothered by the thought of your teaching aerobics, think again. I adore your athletic body. Don't you know that by now?"

She simply slanted him a wry glance.

"Exercise is the way to go nowadays," he continued. "I'll be proud to have a wife who keeps her body toned."

"If I can," she muttered. "Whether I teach or not is still a big question."

"You'll teach. I told you that. When the cast comes off, you'll have physical therapy or whatever else it takes to get that leg working right."

"But . . . even if that happens, many of my classes are evening ones. How will you feel when you come home to an empty house after a hard day's work and there isn't even a hot meal ready?"

"I can cook. You know that. I'll be proud of you, Deirdre. My wife will be doing something that's constructive, something she enjoys." He paused for a breath, sobering. "And while we're talking of pride, if you agree to marry me, I'll insist on a prenuptial agreement."

Deirdre couldn't conceal a quick flare of hurt. "I don't want your money!"

"You've got it backside-to. It's you I want to protect. If you agree to marry me, I'll draw up a paper stating that your holdings in Joyce Enterprises—and anything else you now have to your name—will remain solely yours. If you should decide, at any point, that you want out of the marriage, you'll have everything you had when you entered into it. And if, at any point, you decide that I'm a detriment to Joyce Enterprises, you'll have the full right to can me."

She couldn't imagine that ever happening. For that matter, she couldn't imagine ever wanting out of a marriage to Neil. Unless he wanted it. "But what about your interests? They won't be protected if you sign a document like that. You thought you'd been naive regarding Wittnauer-Douglass. Isn't your plan now equally shortsighted?"

"I'd rather think of it as a challenge, one I'm approaching with my eyes wide open. I think I can make a go of running Joyce Enterprises, and if I do that, you won't have any cause to let me go. Like I said before, I'm not looking for a handout. I'm prepared to do the job. Yes, you'd be doing me a favor by giving me the chance, but I'd be doing you every bit as big a favor by relieving you of a responsibility you don't want."

He took her hand and studied the shape of her slender fingers. "You'd have a husband, which would please your family. And don't you think it's about time, anyway? I know it is for me. I'm not getting any younger. I'm more than ready to settle down."

But love? What about love? Deirdre pleaded silently. "Somehow it seems very... calculated."

"Sometimes the best things are."

"You don't have to marry me. We could still work all of this out."

"I'm sure we could, but marriage will be expedient when it comes to your family. They don't have to know about any agreement we sign. As far as they're concerned, what is yours is mine. I'll be a member of your family. The 'family business' will stay intact." He curved his fingers around hers and lowered his voice. "And I *want* to marry you. I wouldn't be suggesting it if that weren't the case."

But why do you want to marry me? she ached to ask, but didn't. He could give her the answer she craved, which would thrill her, or he could repeat the practical reasons he'd listed earlier, which would distress her. Rather than take the risk, she simply accepted his statement without prodding.

"Will you marry me, Deirdre?" he asked softly.

She met his gaze, knowing that love shone in her own with a strength she was helpless to dim. Silently she nodded, and closed her fingers around his.

8

AS HE'D PROMISED, Thomas was at the dock bright and early the next morning to pick them up. His curiosity was evident in the surreptitious glances he cast toward Deirdre, then Neil, at well-spaced intervals. They simply smiled at each other, feeling smug, but more than that, pleased with what lay ahead. If they'd dreaded the day they'd have to leave their island refuge, the knowledge that they were going to be together reduced that dread to a small twinge of sentimentality as the island faded behind them.

Neil had wanted to drive Deirdre back to Providence, but she insisted, with reason, he finally agreed, that it made no sense for her to leave her car in Maine when she'd want to use it at home. So he followed her on the highway, making sure she stopped periodically to stretch, then later, eat lunch.

It was mid-afternoon when they pulled up at Deirdre's mother's house. They'd discussed that, too, agreeing that the sooner they broke the news of their impending marriage to Maria Joyce the better. And, anticipating that the woman might give Deirdre a hard time, given her history of doing just that, Neil was vehement that he be present.

Maria was in the library when Deirdre called out from the front door. She came quickly, exclaiming loudly even before she entered the hall, "Deirdre! It's about time! I've been worried sick about where you were and how you were making out. If I hadn't thought to call Victoria—" She stopped short when she caught sight of her daughter, leaning on her crutches, beside a tall, bearded man in jeans. "Good Lord," she whispered, staring at the pair, "what have you brought home this time?"

Deirdre felt a movement by her elbow and knew that Neil was trying not to laugh. For that matter, so was she. In her eyes, Neil looked positively gorgeous, but she knew that her mother was wondering what the cat had dragged in.

"Mother, I'd like you to meet Neil Hersey. Neil, Maria Joyce."

Neil stepped forward and extended a firm hand, which Maria had no choice but to meet. "It's my pleasure, Mrs. Joyce. Deirdre has told me a lot about you."

Maria didn't take the time to wonder about the nature of that telling. She was too concerned about retrieving her hand from what was a far-too-confident grip. She nodded at Neil, but her focus was quickly on Deirdre.

"Victoria finally admitted that you'd gone to Maine. I can't believe you did that, Deirdre. The place is totally isolated, and in your condition—"

"My condition is fine. And Neil was there with me." Before her mother could pounce on that, she rushed on. "Neil is a friend of Victoria's, too. Now he's a friend of mine. Furthermore—" she looked at Neil "—we're going to be married. We wanted you to be the first to know." She took perverse delight in her mother's stunned expression.

For a minute the older woman was speechless. Then, pressing a hand to her heart, she revived.

"You can't be serious."

"We are. Very."

"Deirdre, you don't know this man!" She gave Neil a once-over that was disapproving at best.

"You'd be surprised, mother. Two weeks on an island, with no one else around—you can get to know a man pretty well."

Neil rolled his eyes at her smug tone and quickly sought to make amends to Maria. "What Deirdre means is that we had a chance to talk more than many people do in months. We shared responsibility for the house and everything to do with our daily lives. We feel that our marriage would be a good one."

Maria, who'd been eyeing him warily during his brief speech, closed her fingers around the single strand of pearls she was wearing with her very proper silk dress. "I think I need a drink," she said, and turned toward the living room.

Deirdre took off after her, with Neil following in her wake. "It's the middle of the afternoon! You don't need a drink in the middle of the afternoon!"

"Oh, yes, I do," came Maria's voice. She was already at the elegant cherrywood bar, fishing ice from a bucket. "When a woman hears that, after years of nagging, her daughter has decided on the spur of the moment to get married—and to a man she thinks she knows, but can't possibly, since she met him a mere two weeks ago—she needs a drink, *regardless* of the time of day!"

Deirdre took a deep breath and sent Neil a helpless glance before lowering herself to a nearby ottoman. "I think you ought to listen to the rest of what I have to tell you before you pass judgment. You may say something you'll later regret."

"I doubt that," Maria stated. She'd poured a healthy dose of bourbon into the glass and was standing stiffly by the bar. "I don't know where I failed with you, Deirdre, but I very definitely have failed. I've tried to instill in you certain values, and you've rejected every one of them. I tried to raise a lady, but you insist on running around in leotards—"

"Not leotards, mother. A tank top and running shorts. Leotards cut off my circulation."

She waved that aside. "Whatever. The point's the same. I tried to raise you with a sense of family, but you've insisted in going your own way. I've tried to make you see that you have an obligation to the business, but you won't hear of that.

And now, when you've got nothing better to do with your time, instead of giving us a hand, you run off, meet up with a passing . . . hippie, and decide to marry him."

Neil, who'd been standing quietly at Deirdre's shoulder, felt that he'd heard enough. He didn't mind the insults to him, but they were a smaller part of insults to Deirdre, and he wouldn't have that. "I don't think you understand the situation, Mrs. Joyce," he said with such authority that Maria was forced to listen. "I am not a hippie, nor am I passing. If you've formed an opinion of me based on the way I look, I think you should remember that I've just come from a two-week vacation. The bulk of my life is spent in tailored suits, suits that would hold their own—" he looked at the bench before the grand piano "—with that Dunhill tapestry." He shifted his gaze to the small painting to the left of the bar. "Or that Modigliani." He dropped his eyes to the marble coffee table by Deirdre's knees. "Or that Baccarat vase."

Deirdre looked up at him. "I'm impressed," she mouthed.

He nudged her hip with his knee, shushing her with a frown.

Maria arched a well-shaped brow, but she wasn't about to be fully appeased. "The slickest of con men pick up a wealth of knowledge about fine accessories, Mr. Hersey. What is it you do for a living?"

"I'm a lawyer. I head my own firm in Hartford, specializing in corporate work. I can give you a full list of my credits, starting with law review at Harvard, but I don't think that's necessary. Suffice it to say that in recent years I've done work for Jennings and Lange, KronTech, and the Holder Foundation, as well as the Faulkner Company here in Providence." He was confident that the corporations he'd named would give him solid recommendations. He was equally confident that Maria Joyce had heard of them. She would have also heard of Wittnauer-Douglass. There was always the possibility that if the woman ran a check on him, she'd come across that problem, but it was a risk he'd have to take. And besides, by the time she learned anything, his marriage to Deirdre would be a fait accompli.

Maria dipped her head in reluctant acknowledgment of his credentials. "All right. I'll admit that my judgment may have been premature, but the fact remains that this marriage is very sudden. When was it going to take place?"

Deirdre opened her mouth, but Neil spoke first. "As soon as the law will allow. I believe there's a three-day waiting period once the license has been taken out and the blood tests done. I know a judge here in Providence who might cut even that down."

Maria studied her bourbon, pressing her lips together as she ingested that information. "Is there a rush?" She sent Deirdre a meaningful glance. "I know that there are home tests on the market that can give instant results—"

"I am not pregnant, mother," Deirdre interrupted. "And even if I were, I'd have thought you'd be pleased. You've been harping on having grandchildren since I was old enough to vote."

"Every woman wants grandchildren," Maria countered in self-defense.

"So you've said many times. And here's your chance. I don't know why you're complaining. Even if I *were* pregnant, Neil and I will be married before anyone is the wiser. At most, the baby would be born two weeks early, so to speak, which no one would think twice about. You wouldn't have any cause for embarrassment."

Maria scowled at her daughter. "All right," she said crossly. "Forget a pregnancy." Her annoyance broadened to include Neil. "You'll get married and take off for Hartford, leaving Joyce Enterprises in the lurch yet again. Honestly, Deirdre, is that fair?"

Neil answered. "We won't be living in Hartford. We'll be living here."

Maria arched a skeptical brow. "You'd walk away from that successful law practice?"

"I can practice law anywhere," he returned, tamping down a moment's discomfort. "Providence is as good a place as any."

"The fact is, Mother," Deirdre spoke up, "that we are going to bail you out, after all. Neil has agreed to help me with Joyce Enterprises."

For the second time in a very short period, Maria Joyce was speechless. She looked from Deirdre to Neil and back, then raised her glass and took a bolstering drink. By the time she'd lowered the glass, she'd regained a small measure of her composure, though not enough to keep the glass from shaking in her hand. She set it carefully on the bar.

"That," she began slowly, "is an unexpected turn."

"So is our wedding," Deirdre pointed out, "but it all makes sense. You've been after me for years to help with the business. I've been convinced that I'm not right for the job, but I'm equally convinced that Neil is." And she was. She had no doubts but that Neil could handle Joyce Enterprises. "You've wanted to keep things in the family. Neil will be in the family. What more could Dad have asked for than a son-in-law who could take over where his daughters left off?"

"But he's a lawyer," Maria argued, though more meekly this time. "He's not trained in this type of work."

"Neither am I—nor Sandra, for that matter."

Neil joined in. "I've worked closely with large corporations like Joyce for years, so I'm starting with a definite advantage. And I've had the benefit of seeing how other corporations function, which means that I can take the best of the systems and strategies I've seen and implement them at Joyce." He paused. "I think it could work out well for all of us, Mrs. Joyce. I assure you that I wouldn't be putting my career on the line if I didn't feel that the odds were in my favor."

Maria appeared to have run out of arguments. She raised both brows and nervously fingered her pearls. "I . . . it looks like you've thought things out."

"We have," Deirdre said.

The older woman shook her head, for the first time seeming almost confused. "I don't know, Deirdre. It's so sudden. . . . I was hoping that when my daughters got married they'd have big weddings, with lots of flowers and music and people."

Deirdre's shoulders rose with the deep breath she took. "I've never wanted that, Mother. I'll be perfectly happy with something small and private."

Maria looked at them both. "You will be happy? This is what you truly want?" They knew she wasn't referring to the wedding, but to the marriage itself.

Neil's hand met Deirdre's at her shoulder. "It is," Deirdre said softly.

Neil echoed the sentiment. "We'll be happy, Mrs. Joyce. You can take my word for it."

FEELING AS THOUGH they'd overcome their first hurdle, they left Maria, stopped for their marriage license and blood tests, then went to Deirdre's town house. Though Neil agreed that it was on the small side, he was charmed with the way she'd decorated it. Whereas old-world elegance had been the word at her mother's house, here everything was light and airy. The furniture was modern, low and cushiony. One room opened into another with barely a break. There were no Dunhill tapestries, no Modiglianis, no pieces of Baccarat crystal, but a small and carefully chosen selection of work by local artists and artisans.

"I feel very much at home here," Neil said to Deirdre as they lay in bed that night.

Chin propped on his chest, she smiled at him. "I'm glad."

"It's pretty and bright, uncluttered and unpretentious. Like you."

She tugged at his beard. "I think you want something. What is it?"

He smiled back and wrapped an arm around her waist. "Just that when we find the right home, you do it like this. I don't want to live in a museum or . . . or in a shrine to a decorator."

Deirdre narrowed her eyes. "Is that what your place is like?"

"A shrine to a decorator? Yes, it is, and I never thought twice about it until now, but I don't want that, Deirdre. There's a sophistication in the simplicity here. That's what I want. Okay?"

"Okay."

"No argument?"

"No argument."

"Good."

THEY HEADED for Hartford the next day. Neil had a long list of things to take care of, the most pressing and difficult of which was informing his associates that he'd be leaving. Both men were talented lawyers, but being young they hadn't yet developed reputations that would attract new business. Neil gave them the choice of joining other firms or taking over his practice themselves. When they opted for the latter, he assured them that he'd do everything he could to help them out, which included drawing up a letter to send his clients, telling them of the change and assuring them that they'd be in good hands if they remained with the firm.

The second order of business was putting his condominium on the market. The real estate agent, who had a list of people waiting for openings in that particular building, was delighted.

"Are you sure you want to sell it?" Deirdre asked timidly.

"Why not? I won't be living here."

"But if you find that you don't like Providence . . . or that things don't go well . . ."

He took her firmly by the shoulders. "I will like Providence, and things will go well. I'm making a commitment, Deirdre. There's no point in doing it halfway."

She didn't argue further, particularly since his confidence buoyed her. So they returned to Providence and went house hunting. Once again luck was on their side. They found a charming colonial on the outskirts of the city, not far from Deirdre's mother's house ironically, but in a younger neighborhood. The property encompassed three acres of land, with a wealth of trees and lush shrubbery, and though the house needed work, the previous owners had vacated several weeks before, and the work could begin immediately.

Three days after they arrived back from Maine, Deirdre and Neil were married in the church Deirdre had attended as a child. Her mother had made the arrangements—Deirdre felt it was as good a consolation prize as any—and there were more people, more flowers, more food than Deirdre might have chosen herself. But she was too happy that day to mind anything.

Neil looked breathtaking in his dark suit, white shirt, striped tie and cordovans. He'd had his beard professionally trimmed, along with his hair, and she decided that he looked far more like a successful businessman than a conservative corporate lawyer.

Deirdre, who'd had a walking cast put on to replace the original, wore a long white dress, the simplicity of which was a perfect foil for her natural good looks. She'd applied a minimum of makeup—touches each of blusher, mascara, eyeliner and shadow—and though never one to lean heavily toward jewelry, she'd taken pride in wearing the pearl earrings and matching necklace that her father had given her for her twenty-first birthday.

The ceremony was short and sweet, and Deirdre was all smiles as she circulated through the luncheon reception on the arm of her new husband. He'd given her a stunning gold wedding band, as simple as her gown, with a tracing of diamond chips forming a central circle, but she would have been happy with something from the five-and-dime, as long as it told her they were married. Though he still hadn't said the words, she was sure she'd seen love in his eyes throughout that day, and it was the proverbial frosting on the cake.

THE NEXT FEW WEEKS were hectic ones. Neil threw himself fully into Joyce Enterprises, determined to familiarize himself with every aspect of the business. Sandra readily accepted him; not only was she relieved to have the brunt of the load taken from her shoulders, but Deirdre suspected that she was enthralled by Neil. And rightly so. He exuded confidence and was charming not only to Sandra, but to the uncles, as well. If he came home exhausted at night, Deirdre was more than willing to understand. She was also more than willing to make a challenge out of reviving him, which she did with notable success.

He kept her abreast with what was happening at work, sharing his observations, discussing his plans. And he was even eager to hear about the progress at the house, the redecorating of which she was orchestrating with an enthusiasm that surprised her. She'd never seen herself as a decorator. When she'd moved into her town house she'd simply papered and carpeted to suit herself. Knowing that

Neil approved of her taste was a major stimulant—that and knowing the house she now decorated was for the two of them.

By the time they moved in three weeks after the wedding, Deirdre was reeling with confidence. A week later her cast came off, and if that confidence faltered when she experienced a fair amount of pain, Neil was the one to offer encouragement. He personally helped her with the exercises the doctor had outlined, and when those exercise sessions ended more often than not in lovemaking, Deirdre wasn't about to complain. In lieu of verbally professing their love for each other, this physical bonding was crucial to her.

Deirdre put off returning to work, knowing that her leg wasn't ready. Strangely, she didn't miss it as much as she'd thought she would, but, then, between setting up the house and joining Neil for those social engagements he'd warned her would be inevitable, she had little time to miss much of anything.

Strangely, she didn't mind the social engagements, either. But, then, she was with Neil. He never failed to compliment her on the way she looked; as a result, she found that dressing up wasn't as odious as it had been in the past. Moreover, he was the perfect host, drawing her into conversations with their guests such that she experienced far less pain on that score than she'd anticipated.

Neil was exceedingly satisfied with the way things had worked out. Deirdre was as wonderful a wife as she'd been a lover, and as they'd left most of the bickering behind in Maine, he found her to be a thoroughly amiable companion. The only thing that bothered him from time to time was his awareness of the agreement they'd struck. He wanted to think that they were together out of love, not simply taking advantage of a mutually beneficial arrangement. Since the latter was what had brought about this marriage, he went through passing periods of doubt regarding Deirdre's feelings for him.

He had no such self-doubt when it came to Joyce Enterprises. The work was interesting and challenging, and he seemed to have a natural affinity for it. As he'd intended, he brought in a highly experienced executive from a Midwest corporation. Together they mapped out a strategy for keeping Joyce Enterprises not only running smoothly but growing, as well. Between them, they provided the vision that had been lacking since Deirdre's father's death.

Deirdre was thrilled. Her faith in Neil had been justified.

Maria Joyce was likewise pleased, though she made sure Deirdre knew of the risks involved. "I checked up on Neil," she informed her daughter when the two were having lunch at a downtown restaurant one day. "Neither of you was fully honest with me about his past."

Deirdre, who'd been savoring her victory, paused. "We were honest."

"You didn't tell me about Wittnauer-Douglass."

"There wasn't anything to tell. He had a bad experience with one client and was forced to terminate that particular relationship, but it was an isolated incident. He did the same kind of quality work for Wittnauer-Douglass that he did for the rest of his clients."

"According to my friend Bess Hamilton, whose husband is on the board at Wittnauer-Douglass, Neil took part in some unethical dealings."

Deirdre's anger was quick to rise. "If Bess Hamilton's husband was on the board, *he* was involved in the unethical dealings. Neil resigned because he wouldn't have anything to do with it!"

"That wasn't what Bess said."

"And who do you choose to believe, your friend or your son-in-law?"

Maria's gaze didn't waver. "I don't have much choice, do I? Neil is firmly entrenched in the running of our business—"

"And he's doing an excellent job. You can't deny it."

"But I have to wonder what his motives are. From what Bess said, he was washed out in Hartford."

"He wasn't *washed out*. His two associates are doing fantastically well with the business he left them, and if it hadn't been for his own urgings, those clients would have left in a minute and gone elsewhere. They had faith in Neil, which is why they followed his recommendation and stayed with the firm."

Maria wasn't about to be fully convinced. "Still, he got a good thing going for him when he married you. It was a shrewd move."

"What are you trying to say, Mother?" Deirdre asked through gritted teeth.

"Just that I think you ought to be careful. I think we all ought to be careful. He may be trying to take over Joyce Enterprises and sweep it away from us."

"Neil wouldn't do that."

"How do you know?"

"Because I'm *married* to him. Because I *know* him."

"You love him, and love sometimes clouds people's judgment."

"Not in this case. I trust him." She also knew of the papers she'd signed before she and Neil had been married, but she didn't feel that was any of her mother's business. "And I'd think that if you can't find it in yourself to trust him, as well, the least you can do is appreciate him. He's taken a load off all our backs, and what he's doing with Joyce Enterprises would have made Dad proud."

Maria had nothing to say on that score, so she changed the subject. Her words, however, lingered for a long time in Deirdre's mind.

Deirdre had meant what she'd said—that she trusted Neil. There were times, though, when she wondered about the energy he was pouring into the business. Rarely did a night pass when he didn't bring a project of some form home from the office with him. The enthusiasm he had for his work seemed boundless. . . .

Perhaps, Deirdre mused, she was simply jealous. She recalled the days they'd spent in Maine, and there were times when she wished for them again. Neil had been totally devoted to her there; here she had to share him with a very demanding job. She recalled his saying that he'd never married before because the law was such a demanding mistress. At the time she'd argued that the right woman had simply never come along.

Now she wondered if *she* was the right woman, and let her insecurities suggest that she might not be. Yes, Neil was warm and affectionate. Yes, he put aside his work when she came to talk with him. Yes, he was patient with her frustration when her leg seemed to take inordinately long in healing.

But he went off to work quite happily each morning. And he never said that he loved her.

Then again, she realized, maybe her unease was reflective of nothing more than the changes her life had undergone in a few short months. The work on the house was now finished. It was furnished to their mutual satisfaction in the style of understated sophistication that Deirdre had never before thought of as a style; it was merely the way she wanted to live. She wasn't one to spend hours simply looking at the finished product or wandering from one room to another, and the demands Neil made on her for evening engagements weren't enough to occupy her time.

As time passed she grew restless.

She started going to the health club. Though she probably could have taught, she didn't want to. She felt tired. Her leg, though better, still bothered her. She began to wonder whether her compulsion to teach had been directly tied to her need to escape Joyce Enterprises. Since that need was no longer there the compulsion had faded.

She sat at home for long hours, missing Neil, wondering what to do with herself. She lunched with friends, but that brought no lasting relief from her malaise. She took part in the planning of a ten-kilometer charity run, but that occupied far too little of her time.

Finally, on impulse one day, she flew down to meet Victoria for lunch. They hadn't seen each other since the wedding, which Victoria had proudly and delightedly attended, and Deirdre was counting on her friend to bolster her morale.

"How long have you know Neil?" Deirdre asked, broaching the topic as soon as the waiter had left with their order.

"Three years," Victoria answered, cocking her head to the side. "Why do you ask?"

"Did you know him well during that time?"

"We didn't see each other often, but if I were to judge from the quality of the time we spent together, I'd say we were close." She pursed her lips. "Something's up, Dee. Spill it."

Deirdre shrugged, absently playing with the moisture on the outside of her water glass. "I don't know. It's just that everything between us happened so fast. I sometimes wonder if we rushed things."

"You have doubts about Neil?"

"No. Well, maybe once in a while. My mother said something a few weeks ago that bothered me, something about Neil—"

"Your mother," Victoria scoffed. "Your mother is a good friend of mine, but that doesn't mean I can't see her faults. She's one of those people who are never satisfied. You take her too seriously, Dee. I've told you that before."

"I know. But I can't help hearing her little 'words of wisdom.'"

"You may have to hear them. You don't have to heed them."

"But it's like they niggle in the back of my mind and they refuse to go away." She raised beseeching eyes to her friend. "Victoria, do you think Neil is ambitious?"

"I should hope so. No one is successful if he isn't ambitious."

"Ruthlessly so? Would you call Neil ruthlessly ambitious?"

Victoria didn't have to think about that. "No. Unequivocably. Neil is not a ruthless person. If anything, the opposite is true. If he had a little more of the bastard in him, he might not have had that problem with Wittnauer-Douglass."

"If he hadn't had that," Deirdre pointed out with a lopsided grin, "he'd never have run off to Maine and I'd never have met him, so I can't be sorry about Wittnauer-Douglass." Her grin faded. "It's just that my mother learned about all that, and she suggested that Neil might be out for himself when it comes to Joyce Enterprises."

"Is that what you think?"

"No. At least, I want to think that it isn't so. But he's taken to his work with such . . . such *glee*, and there are times when I wish he showered more of that glee on me."

"You can't have it both ways, Dee. If he's to turn Joyce Enterprises around, he's going to have to put in the hours. Take my word for it, though. Neil Hersey has nothing but the most upstanding intentions when it comes to your business. I don't think there's a selfish bone in that man's body. Did he ever tell you what he did for my niece?"

Deirdre frowned. "No. He never mentioned your niece."

"He wouldn't. That's his way."

"Well? What did he do?"

"A while ago, my niece got involved in a criminal matter. The girl was only nineteen at the time, and her mother—my sister—was frantic. They live in a small town in western Connecticut and aren't very well off, and they didn't know where to turn for help. I called Neil, knowing that criminal law wasn't his specialty but hoping that he'd be able to refer us to a capable person. Not only did he do that, but he personally involved himself in the case, and then, when the other lawyer would have given him a referral fee, he insisted that the man deduct it from the fee he charged my sister—a fee, mind you, that was on the low side, anyway, considering that my niece got away with nothing but probation. Now—" she tipped up her chin "—if Neil were only out for himself, would he have done all that for my niece?"

Deirdre felt a rush of pride in her husband. "No. And I know that he's always done charity work. It's just that the situation with us is so different. There's so much at stake for him now."

"I doubt he'd consider anything more important than your love."

Deirdre held her breath.

"Dee? You do love him, don't you?"

"Oh, yes!"

"But . . . ?"

"I'm not sure he loves me."

"Are you kidding?"

Deirdre responded defensively. "No, I'm not kidding. He's never told me he loved me. Our marriage was . . . was . . . expedient, and that was his own word."

Victoria pressed a calming hand on her arm. "Look, sweetheart, I know enough about each of your situations to realize that your getting married solved certain problems for you both. But I saw Neil at your wedding, and if that man wasn't in love, I'll turn in my matchmaker badge." She paused. "What does he say when you tell him that you love him?"

Deirdre didn't have to answer. Guilt was written all over her face.

"My Lord, Dee. Why not? You're no wilting pansy!"

"But I don't want to pressure him. Worse, I don't want to say it and not have him say it back. And anyway, when he's home there's so much else we talk about, and then we don't want to talk at all. . . ."

Victoria shot her a knowing grin. "That's more like it." She raised her eyes when the waiter approached with their plates, and waited until he'd deposited the meal and gone. "So, Neil is very busy with work, and you're feeling lonesome."

"Yes."

"Have you told him that?"

"No."

Victoria cast pleading eyes toward the ornate ceiling high overhead. "I know I shouldn't ask this, but why not?"

"Because in the first place, I don't want to sound like a complainer. When we first got to Maine, that was all I did—bitch at him, and everything else in sight. Then our relationship gelled, and I stopped griping. I liked myself a lot more then. I don't want to go back to that other way." She paused for an exaggerated breath. "And in the second place, there's nothing he can do about it."

"He can reassure you, maybe help find something to keep you busy."

Deirdre shook her head sadly. "I don't know, Victoria. I look at you and I'm envious. When you finish one thing you start another. I used to have a million and one things to do with my day, but now I can't seem to find anything that tempts me."

"You want to be with Neil. Everything else is . . . blah. So why don't you work part-time at the office?"

"That'd be tantamount to surrender. I swore I'd never work there."

"And you're so rigid that you can't reconsider, particularly knowing that working there now would be out of choice, rather than need?"

Deirdre didn't respond immediately; she sat absently nudging her cold salmon with a fork. "Put that way, I sound pretty childish."

"If the shoe fits . . ."

"I don't know, Victoria. I'm not sure that's what I want, either."

"Do me a favor, Dee, and talk with Neil? He's a patient man. Really, he is. And he's resourceful. Most important, he's your husband. He wants you to be happy." She speared a firm green bean and held it over her plate. "Will you?"

"I'll try."

"Don't try. *Do* it!"

DEIRDRE WOULD HAVE done it that night, had Neil not offered her a solution before she'd been able to utter a word. He'd come home particularly tired, and they were relaxing in the living room, sharing a glass of wine.

"I need your help, Deirdre," he announced in a businesslike tone.

"There's a problem at the office?"

He nodded. "In personnel. Art Brickner, our man there, is giving us flack about hiring people to fill in certain gaps. He wanted to bring people up from the ranks, and I agree with him in theory, except that in several of these cases there simply is no one to bring up from the ranks. Most of his resistance is to new blood, and I fall prominently in that category. Art was one of your father's original men."

"I know... But how can I help?"

"Work with him. Ease him through the transition. He's a good man—"

"He's stodgy."

Neil chuckled. "Yes, he's stodgy, but his instincts are good, and your presence in his office might just remind him that, contrary to what he fears, all is not going down the tubes at Joyce Enterprises."

"Oh, Neil... what do I know about personnel?"

"You have common sense, and a feel for the company. Art will take care of the mechanics, while you handle the, uh, the spiritual end. What do you think?"

"I think," she said, studying the features she adored so much, "that you look exhausted. You're working too hard, Neil."

Loosening his necktie, he sank deeper into the sofa. "You're right. But it has to be done." His eyes narrowed. "You look exhausted, too. Was it running down to New York to have lunch with Victoria?"

"Uh-uh. I'm tired from having too much time on my hands."

"Then helping Art could be just the thing."

"Neil—"

"You wouldn't have to work full-time, only twenty hours a week or so."

"But I—"

"You could wear whatever you wanted, since you wouldn't be in the limelight."

"But what—"

"I'd even pay you." He grinned broadly. "How does that sound?"

She sighed, stared at him in exasperation for a minute, then took his silent offer and settled under the arm he held out. "When you smile at me like that, Neil Hersey, I'm a goner. But you know that, don't you, which is why you do it! I'm a sucker. That's all. A real sucker."

"Then you will work?"

"Yes, I will work."

"And you'll tell me if it turns out to be too much?"

"It won't turn out to be too much. I'm young. I'm full of energy. I'm brimming with enthusiasm. . . ."

BUT IT DID TURN OUT to be too much—or rather, it put a strain on Deirdre that she hadn't expected. She worked from nine to two every day, and was positively drained. After a week of mornings when she couldn't seem to get going, she began coming in at ten. Even then she was dragging by the time Neil arrived home at night.

Witnessing her struggle, Neil grew more and more tense. He waited for her to come to him, to broach the subject, but she didn't. Finally, after two weeks of helplessness, he took matters into his own hands.

Arriving home early from work, he found Deirdre curled beneath an afghan on their king-size bed, sound asleep. He sat on the bed beside her, leaned down and kissed her cheek.

Her lashes fluttered, then rose. "Neil!" she whispered, pushing herself up. "I'm sorry. I never dreamed you'd be home this early!"

He pulled a bouquet of flowers—actually, three roses and an assortment of greens—from behind him. "For you."

Groggy still, she looked from him to the roses and back, smiling at last. "They're lovely. Any special occasion?"

"Mmm-hmm. Today's the day we admit that you're pregnant."

Deirdre's smile vanished, as did what little color had been on her cheeks. She lay back on the bed, closed her eyes and spoke in a very small voice. "How did you guess?"

Neil was stricken by the unhappiness he saw on Deirdre's face. He'd assumed that she'd been afraid to tell him—though he didn't know why—but apparently there was more than fear involved. He answered her quietly. "We've been married for nearly three months, and during that time you haven't had a single period."

"I'm an athlete," she pointed out. "That can do strange things to a woman's system."

"You're constantly tired. Even the slightest activity exhausts you."

"It's everything that's happened in the past few months. I'm on emotional overload."

"And the greater fullness of your breasts?" he asked, his voice deep and low. "And the slight thickening of your waist? Things that nobody else sees, I do. Come on, Deirdre. Let's face the facts. You're pregnant. Is it so awful?"

She focused tired eyes on him. "I feel so lousy right now that, yes, it's awful."

"Then you agree that it's true?"

"It's true."

"But you haven't been to a doctor."

"No."

"Why, Deirdre? Don't you want to have a baby?"

"I do!" she cried, then lowered her voice. "It's just that, on top of everything else, it's so sudden. . . ."

"We weren't using any birth control. You had to know there was a possibility this would happen."

"How did you know I wasn't using birth control?" she countered, being contrary.

"Deirdre, I was with you constantly. I would have known."

"Not if I'd had an IUD."

"But you didn't have one, and you're pregnant now!"

"Thanks to you. If you knew I wasn't using anything, why didn't *you* use something?"

"Deirdre, I do not pack prophylactics as a matter of habit. The last thing I expected when I went up to Maine was that I'd be with a woman."

"So neither of us was prepared, and both of us knew it, and we did nothing, and look what happened."

"I don't think it's such a horrible situation, Deirdre."

"You don't?"

"Of course not."

"You don't feel that it's just another burden on your shoulders?"

"Have I ever talked of burdens?"

"No. But they're there."

"This one's a nice one. I told you I wanted children."

" 'Someday,' you said."

"Then 'someday' is now. And the more I think about it, the happier I am." Scooping her up, he tucked her against him. "I know you're not feeling great, Deirdre, but once you see a doctor and he gives you vitamins, and once you pass the initial few months, you'll feel better."

To Deirdre's dismay, she began to cry. Her fingers closed around the lapel of his suit jacket, and she buried her face in his shirt.

"I'll be . . . be fat."

"You'll be beautiful."

"You'll . . . you'll be stuck with me."

"I'm not complaining."

"You're being so . . . kind."

"You're being such a ninny." He hugged her, trying his best to absorb whatever pain she was feeling. He knew she'd been through a lot, and that having a baby at a later time would probably have been better for her, but he wasn't sorry. It bound her all the closer to him.

Weeping softly, Deirdre was thinking similar thoughts. Oh, yes, she wanted the baby, but because it was Neil's, more than for any other reason. When she thought of it, having his baby made the tie between them even more permanent than marriage. It was both a reassuring and a frightening thought, because if something went wrong and Neil decided he'd had enough, a wholly innocent child would be affected.

The scent of roses by her nose interrupted her sniffles. She opened her eyes and saw Neil touch each bloom.

"One for you, one for me, one for baby. A nice bunch, don't you think?"

His sweetness brought a helpless smile to Deirdre's wet face. "A very nice bunch."

Later, she told herself, she'd watch for the thorns. For now, she was too tired to do anything but relax in Neil's arms.

9

Once Deirdre accepted the fact of her pregnancy, she was better able to cope. She saw a doctor and began a regimen of vitamins that compensated for what the baby demanded of her body. She continued working with Art Brickner, adjusting her hours to accommodate her need for sleep.

Neil seemed legitimately pleased about the baby, and that relieved her most of all. In turn, she made up her mind to do everything in her power to make their marriage work.

When she was at the office, she dressed accordingly, intent on making Neil proud. When she was at home she planned their meals and coordinated the various cleaning efforts so that the house was always immaculate should Neil decide to bring people home at the last minute. At Neil's insistence, though, they'd hired a maid to help. She resumed her visits to the health club—the doctor had okayed that—and though she didn't teach, she took part in classes. She swam. She diligently kept herself in shape—as much as a woman with a slowly growing belly could.

And she never argued with Neil. She didn't complain when he was delayed for several hours at the office and dinner was held up. She didn't say a word when he had to go away on a business trip. She didn't nag him to take time off from work to play tennis with her. She graciously attended cocktail parties and dinners, and when she and Neil were finally alone at night, she did her very best to satisfy him, both physically and emotionally.

But because she refused to give him any cause for displeasure, the frustration that had built within her had nowhere to go. She wished he didn't work so hard, but she didn't say so. She yearned for time alone with him—even their weekends revolved around business demands—but she didn't say so. She ached, positively ached to hear him say that he loved her, but she didn't say so, and he didn't tell her what she wanted to hear. She felt as if she were walking a tightrope.

The tightrope began to fray when her mother dropped in one morning. Deirdre was getting ready to leave for work.

"Have you heard his latest scheme?" Maria asked with an arrogance Deirdre found all too familiar. They were standing in the front hall; Deirdre knew enough not to invite her mother to sit, or she'd be in for an even longer siege.

"That depends on which scheme it is," Deirdre countered with confidence. "Neil's had a lot of them lately, and they're all very promising."

"This one isn't."

"Which one?"

"He's bidding on a government contract for the electronics division."

Deirdre had known that. "Is there a problem?" she asked blandly.

"We've never bid for government contracts. We've always devoted ourselves to the private sector."

"That doesn't mean we can't change now, if doing so will be good for the company."

"But will it? That's the question. Is Neil bidding for that contract because it will be good for the company or for him?"

"Aren't they one and the same?" Deirdre asked, ignoring her mother's barely veiled reference to the earlier accusation she'd made.

"Not by a long shot. You may not know it, but one of the other bidders is Wittnauer-Douglass."

Deirdre hadn't known it. She ignored the frisson of anxiety that shivered through her. "I'm sure there are many other bidders—"

"None Neil holds a grudge against."

"Neil doesn't hold a grudge against Wittnauer-Douglass," Deirdre insisted. "What happened there is done. He is very successful in what he's doing now. I think you're way off base."

"You've thought that from the start, when I told you to be careful, but this is the evidence I need."

"Evidence? What evidence?"

"Your husband is involving Joyce Enterprises in something solely for the sake of avenging himself. He would never be bidding for a government contract if it weren't for that. Think about it. Isn't it awfully suspicious that the first time we do anything of this sort, a major competitor is the very one Neil has a gripe against?"

Deirdre set her purse down on the table. "Do you know the details, Mother? Who submitted a bid first, Wittnauer-Douglass or Joyce Enterprises?"

Maria fumbled with the collar of her sable coat. "I don't know that. How could I possibly know that!"

"If it's evidence you're looking for, that'd be a place to start. If Neil submitted his bid first, without ever knowing that Wittnauer-Douglass would be a competitor, his innocence would be obvious."

"The rest of the evidence is against him."

Deirdre was losing her patience. "What evidence?"

"Deirdre," her mother said, sighing. "Think. Neil met you at a time when he needed a change of location and occupation."

"He did not need—"

"He latched onto what you had to offer, married you as quickly as possible and set about implementing his plans."

"The plans he implemented were for the resurgence of Joyce Enterprises, and he's done a remarkable job! He's done us a favor!"

"He's done himself a favor. Look at it objectively. He's at the helm of a successful corporation. He's become so well respected in the community that the two of you are in demand at all the parties that matter—"

"If you had any sense of appreciation, Mother, you'd spend your time tallying all he's done for *you*. He's married the more undesirable of your two daughters and is about to give you a grandchild. He's taken responsibility for the family business—and even gotten *me* involved in it. What more do you want?"

"I want Joyce Enterprises to remain in the black."

"And you think that bidding on a government contract will prevent that?" Deirdre asked in disbelief. "He's just bidding."

"If he wants that contract badly enough, he'll bid low enough to undercut Wittnauer-Douglass, and if he does that, he could jeopardize our financial status."

"And if he does that," Deirdre pointed out angrily, "he'll be jeopardizing the very position he's built for himself. It doesn't make sense, Mother. You're being illogical."

"It's a risk—his bidding for that contract."

"There's always a risk if the prize is worth anything. If Neil only stuck with what was safe, the business would be at a standstill."

"He's being rash. I think you should talk with him."

Deirdre had had enough. "I don't have to listen to this." She snatched up her purse, took her coat from the nearby chair and headed for the door. "You can stay if you like. I have to get to work."

Deirdre might have been fine had the conversation she'd had with her mother been the only one of its kind. But several days later, Art Brickner raised the issue, complaining that Neil had spoken with him about hiring an enlarged cadre of workers if the government contract came through. Art questioned both the logistics and the wisdom of what Neil proposed, and all Deirdre could do was to support Neil and insist that his plan was sound.

Several days after that, she was approached by one of the long-standing vice presidents of the company, who, too, had doubts as to the direction in which Joyce was headed. Again Deirdre expressed her support for Neil, sensing that what she was hearing was simply a resistance to change, but she grew increasingly uncomfortable.

She didn't tell Neil about any of the three discussions. She didn't want to anger him by suggesting that she had doubts, when, in fact, she had no qualms about the viability of winning and working through a government contract. What bothered her was the possibility that his motives weren't entirely pure, that, as her mother had suggested, he was being driven by a desire for revenge. She tried to ignore such thoughts, but they wouldn't leave her.

At the root of the matter were the doubts she had regarding their relationship. Oh, they were close. They said all the right things, did all the right things. To the outside world—and to themselves, on one level—they were a loving couple. If she recalled the original reasons for their marriage, though, as she did with increasing frequency, she couldn't help but question what it was that drove Neil. His questionable motives bothered her far more than the prospect of any contract, government or otherwise.

So she walked the tightrope. On one end was what she wanted; on the other what she thought Neil wanted. The rope frayed. It finally snapped when he arrived home unexpectedly one afternoon. She was instantly pleased, delighted by the thought of spending stolen time with him. The sight of him—ruggedly handsome, with his beard offsetting his more formal suit—never failed to excite her, as did the inevitable kiss with which he greeted her.

Threading his arm through hers, he led her into the den. When he held her back, though, the look of tension on his face told her something was amiss.

"I need a favor, Deirdre. I have to run to Washington for a meeting tonight. Do you think you could handle the dinner party on your own?"

They'd long ago invited three couples to join them at a restaurant in town. Deirdre knew the couples. They weren't her favorite people.

Her face fell. "Oh, Neil . . . do you have to go?"

"I do. It's important." He felt like a heel, but there was no way around it.

"But so sudden. You were planning to go down for the presentation tomorrow morning, anyway. Can't you have this meeting then?"

"Not if I want the presentation to be the best it can be."

"It will be. You've been working on it for weeks."

"I want that contract," he stated, then coaxed her more gently. "Come on. You can handle things at the restaurant."

"You know how I hate dinners like that."

"I know that you manage them beautifully." She'd proved it in the past weeks, and he'd been proud of her.

"With you by my side. But you won't be, which makes the whole thing that much more distasteful."

"I'm asking for your help. I can't be two places at once."

Annoyances, past and present, rose within her. She left his side, grabbed a throw pillow from the sofa and began to fluff it with a vengeance. "And you choose to be in Washington. If you wanted to be here, you could send someone else to Washington. Why can't Ben go?" Ben Tillotson was the executive Neil had brought in from the midwest.

"Ben's daughter is visiting from Seattle. He feels badly enough that he has to leave her tomorrow."

"Well, what about me? You have to leave me tomorrow, too." She dropped the first pillow and started on another.

"It's my responsibility before it's Ben's."

"Then if Ben can't make it, why don't you let Thor go?" Thor VanNess headed the electronics division. In Deirdre's mind, he'd be the perfect one to attend the meeting.

"Thor is fantastic at what he does, but he is not a diplomat, and the meeting tonight is going to involve a fair share of diplomacy."

"And you're the only diplomat at Joyce?"

Her sarcasm was a sharp prod, poking holes in Neil's patience. "Deirdre," he said, sighing, "you're making too much out of a single meeting. If you want, I can have my secretary call and cancel the dinner party, but I'd hoped that wouldn't be necessary. Believe me, I've looked for other outs. I've tried to think of someone else who can get the job done tonight in Washington, but there is no one else. It's *my responsibility*."

She tossed the second pillow on the sofa and leaned forward to straighten a small watercolor that hung on the wall. "Then you take too much on your own shoulders. I was under the assumption that delegation was critical to the smooth functioning of a corporation this size." She lowered her voice in an attempt to curb her temper. Yes, she was making too much out of a single meeting, but it had become a matter of principle. She faced him head-on. "Send someone else. Anyone else."

"I can't, Deirdre. It's as simple as that."

"No, it's not," she declared, unable to hold it in any longer. "It's not simple at all. You put your work before every other thing in our lives, which shows where *your* priorities lie."

Neil bowed his head and rubbed the back of his neck. "You're being unfair," he said quietly.

"Unfair? Or selfish? Well, maybe it's about time!" She stalked to the large ship's clock that hung on another wall, took a tool from its side, opened it and angrily began to wind it.

"Take it easy, babe. You're making a mountain out of—"

"I am not!"

"You're getting upset." His gaze fell to the tiny swell just visible in profile beneath her oversized sweater. "It's not good for you *or* the baby."

She turned to glare at him. "That's where you're wrong. It's the *best* thing for me, and therefore for the baby, because I can't pretend anymore. I'm being torn apart inside."

Neil stiffened. "What are you talking about?"

"I can't stand this, Neil. I've tried to be the perfect wife for you. I've done all the things I swore I'd never do, and I've done them without argument because I wanted to please you. I wanted to make this marriage work."

"I thought it was working. Do you mean to tell me you were faking it all?"

She scrunched up her face in frustration. "I wasn't faking it. On one level the marriage does work. But there has to be more. There has to be total communication. You discuss the business with me, but I don't know what you're really thinking or feeling. There are times when I feel totally left out of what's happening."

"You could ask more."

"You could offer more."

"Damn it, Deirdre, how do I know what you want if you don't ask?"

"Don't you know me well enough to know what I want without my having to ask?"

"No!" he exploded, angry now himself. "I thought you wanted me to make a go of your damned business, but it looks like I was wrong. I've been busting my ass in the office racking my brain, dipping into resources I didn't know I had, looking for one way, then another to make Joyce Enterprises stronger."

For an instant she was taken back. "I thought you enjoyed the work."

"I do enjoy the work, but that's because I've been successful. I've felt good knowing that I was carrying out my part of the bargain, knowing that I had the business moving again. Every bit of my satisfaction relates directly or indirectly to you."

Deirdre eyed him skeptically. "Are you sure? Isn't there a little satisfaction that relates solely to you?"

"I suppose," he answered, rubbing his bearded cheek. "If I stand back and look at what I've been able to do in a few short months, yes, I'm proud of myself. I'm a lawyer by training, not a businessman, yet I've taken on entrepreneurial tasks that two, four, six years ago I'd never have dared tackle."

"But you have now. Why?"

Neil was still for a moment, his tone almost puzzled when he spoke. "It was part of the agreement we made."

"No. Go back further." Her hand tightened around the clock tool. "Why did we make that agreement?"

"Because you needed me and I needed you."

"That's right. And I guess it's one of the things that's been eating at me. You needed a means of reestablishing yourself after what happened in Hartford. You came in here, took over the reins, and you've done more with this company than anyone else—including my father—has done in years. You've done everything I expected, and more. Why, Neil? Why so much?"

"That's an absurd question," he snapped. "If there are things to be done, I believe in doing them. Yes, I could have stopped thinking a while ago, and Joyce Enterprises still would have been in far better shape than it had been. But I've seen potential in the company. I'm trying to realize it."

Replacing the clock tool, Deirdre moved to a plant hanging by the window and began to pick dried leaves from it. "Or are you trying to prove to Wittnauer-Douglass that you can beat them at their own game?"

"What?" He tipped his head and narrowed one eye. "What are you talking about?"

"This government contract. You've told me all about your end of it, and I've been in favor of it. What you didn't tell me was that Wittnauer-Douglass is bidding for the same contract." She crushed the dried leaves in her hand. "My *mother* had to tell me that, and at the same time she leveled a pretty harsh accusation."

"Your mother's leveled accusations before, and they've proved unfounded." He was staring hard at Deirdre. When she reached toward the plant again, he bellowed, "Leave the damn plant alone, Deirdre. I want your full attention right now."

Slowly she turned to face him, but she didn't say a word, because his expression was suddenly one of fury, reminiscent of their first days in Maine, but worse.

His lips were thinned; tension radiated from the bridge of his nose. "You think that I'm going for this contract to get even with Wittnauer-Douglass!" he spat, his eyes widening. "You actually think that I'm out for revenge, that everything I've done since we've been married has been with this in mind! I don't believe you, Deirdre! Where have you *been* all these weeks?"

She grew defensive. "I didn't say I thought that. I said my mother thought that."

"But you're raising it with me now, which means that you have your own doubts."

"Yes, I have my doubts! I've stood behind you one hundred percent, defending you before my mother, before Art Brickner, before others of my father's people who've approached me with questions. I've been as strong an advocate as I can possibly be, but after a while all I can think of is that our marriage was *expedient*." She covered her face with one rigid hand and spoke into her palm. "I hate that word. God, do I hate that word."

"Then why do you use it?" he yelled back.

She dropped her hand. "Because *you* used it, and it's stuck in my mind like glue, and I try to shake it off, but it won't let go! We married for the wrong reasons, Neil, and it's about time we faced it. I can't go on this way. It's driving me nuts!"

Neil thrust a hand through his hair. "Driving *you* nuts! Do you think it's any different for me? I've tried my best to make things work, and I thought they were working. Now I find out that every one of my efforts has been in vain. I thought you trusted me, but maybe all you wanted was someone to bail you out. Now that I've done that, I'm expendable. Is that it?"

"No! I never said that!"

"Then what are you saying? What in the hell do you want?"

She was shaking—in anger, in frustration, in heartache. Clenching her fists by her sides, she cried, "I want it *all*! I don't want an expedient marriage! I never did! I want *love*, Neil! Damn it, *I want the real thing*!"

Neil was far from steady himself. Equal parts of tension, fear and anguish thrummed through his body, clouding his mind, robbing him of the thoughts, much less the words to fight her. Feeling more impotent than he'd ever felt in his life, he turned and stormed from the room.

Deirdre wrapped her arms around her middle and tried to control the wild hammering of her heart. She heard the front door slam, then, moments later, the angry rev of the Le-

Baron. It had long since faded into silence before she began to move in small, dazed steps, working her way slowly toward her favorite room, the loft above the garage.

Late-afternoon sun filtered in across the polished wood floor, splashing on bare stucco walls with a cheeriness that eluded her at the moment. Her cassette player and a pile of tapes lay in one corner. She'd often used the room for exercise, though what she'd really hoped was that one day it would be a playroom for their children.

Now all that seemed in doubt.

Carefully easing herself down onto the cushioned sill of the arched window, she tucked her knees up, pressed her forehead to them and began to cry.

Neil didn't love her. If he had, he'd have said so. She'd given him the opening; she'd told him what she wanted. And he'd left her. He didn't love her.

And their future? A big, fat question mark. In some respects they were back where they'd started when they'd first arrived on Victoria's island.

What had she wanted, really wanted then? Love. She hadn't realized it at the time, but in the weeks since, she realized that everything else would have fallen into place if she'd found love. She could teach, or not. She could work at Joyce Enterprises, or not. The one thing that held meaning was love.

NEIL DROVE AROUND for hours. He stopped at a pay phone to call the office, but he had no desire to show up there. He had no desire to go to Washington. He had no desire to bid for, much less win, that government contract he'd sought. He had no desire to do anything . . . but return to Deirdre.

That was the one thing that became eminently clear with the miles he put on his odometer. Deirdre was all that mattered in his life.

He relived their meeting in Maine, their arguments, their eventual coming to terms with each other. He reviewed the months they'd been married and all that had happened, both personally and professionally, during that time. But mostly he replayed the scene he'd had with Deirdre that day. He heard her words, pondered them, analyzed them.

And it occurred to him that he was possibly on the verge of making the biggest mistake of his life.

Stopping the car in the middle of the street, he ignored the honking of horns, made a U-turn and mentally mapped the fastest route back to the house. When he arrived, it was nearly ten o'clock. The house was every bit as dark as the night was, and for a minute he feared he was too late. Then his headlights illumined Deirdre's car, parked as unobtrusively as she'd left it beneath the huge maple tree. Pulling up behind it, he jumped from his own and ran inside.

"Deirdre?" he called, flipping lights on in each of the ground floor rooms. "Deirdre!" There was no anger in his voice, simply worry. With the irrational fear of a man in love, he conjured up every one of the dreadful things that might have happened to her during his absence. She was upset. She was pregnant. Oh, God . . .

Taking the stairs two at a time, he searched their bedroom, then the others. Only when there was still no sign of her did he stop to think. Then, praying that he'd find her there, he headed for the loft.

"Deirdre?" Fearfully he said her name as he switched on the light, then caught his breath when he saw her curled on the window seat, her head having fallen against the windowpane. In the seconds it took him to cross to her, he added even more dreadful things to his list of fears.

Lowering himself by her side, he brushed her cheek with his thumb. Dried tears streaked her skin, but her color was good and she was warm.

"Deirdre?" His voice was soft and shaky. "Wake up, sweetheart. There's something I have to tell you." He smoothed the hair from her forehead, leaned forward to kiss her wheat-hued crown, framed her face with both hands. "Deirdre?"

She took in a hiccuping breath and, frowning, raised heavy lids. Disoriented, she stared at him for a minute, then her eyes opened fully and she pushed herself up against the window frame. "You're back," she whispered.

He smiled gently. "Yes."

"What . . . what happened to Washington?"

"It's not important."

"But the contract—"

"Isn't important."

"But you wanted it—"

"Not as much as I want you." When her eyes filled with confusion and disbelief, he explained. "I've driven around for hours thinking about things, and when I went back over what you said earlier, I realized that I may have got things wrong. I was so convinced that you wanted out of the marriage, that you'd gotten tired of me and it, that I took your words one way, when they could have been taken another." His hands were cupping her head, thumbs stroking the short, smooth strands of hair behind her ears. "I may be wrong again, but I think it's worth the risk."

He took a deep breath. Once there might have been pride involved, but he'd gone well beyond that. Still, he was nervous. His words came out in a rush. "I love you, Deirdre. *That* was why I wanted to marry you in the first place. Anything else that came along with the marriage was nice, but purely secondary. Maybe I've had my guard up, because I never knew for sure why, deep down inside, you agreed to marry me. And I was afraid to ask outright, because I didn't want to know . . . if you'd married me simply because of our bargain. But what you said earlier set me to thinking. What you said, and the anguish in it, would make sense if you love me and fear that I don't love you back." His eyes grew moist, and his voice shook again. "Do you, Deirdre? Do you love me?"

Tears welled on her lower lids, and her chin quivered. "Very much," she whispered, which was all she could manage because emotion clogged her throat, making further sound impossible.

Neil closed his eyes in relief and hauled her against him. "Oh, Deirdre," he rasped, "we've been so foolish." His arms wound fully around her; hers had found their way beneath his jacket and held him every bit as tightly. "So foolish," he whispered against her hair. "We never said the words. The only words that mattered, and we never said them."

Deirdre's heart was near to bursting. "I love you . . . love you so much," she whispered brokenly, and raised her eyes to his. "We had so much going for us, and we nearly blew it."

A shudder passed through him. He took her mouth in a fierce kiss, gentling only when he reminded himself that she wasn't going to leave. "When I think of everything else I've had in my life, things I've risked, things I've lost, they seem so unimportant now. You're what matters. This is where you belong, in my arms. And I belong in yours."

"I know," she said, and buried her face against his neck. The scent of him was familiar and dear; it was an aphrodisiac in times of passion, a soothing balm in times of emotional need. She breathed deeply of it, and her face blossomed into a smile. Then the smile faded, replaced by a look of horror. "Neil!" She pushed back from his arms. "The dinner party! They'll have gone to the restaurant and we've stood them up!"

He chuckled. "Not to worry. I called my secretary and had her cancel on our behalf. We'll make it another time. Together."

Deirdre wrinkled her nose. "I don't like the Emerys. He is an arrogant bore, and she has bad breath." Neil laughed aloud, but she hadn't finished. "And Donald Lutz is always checking out the room, on the lookout for someone important to greet, while that wife of his can't take her hand off the chunky emerald ring she wears. And as for the Spellmans, they're—"

Neil put a hand over her mouth, but he was grinning. "They're important clients. Once in a while we have to sacrifice our own personal preferences for the sake of the corporation."

"Speaking of which . . ." She mumbled into his hand, then spoke more clearly, if softly when he removed it. "I don't distrust you, Neil. Everything you've done at Joyce has been good. And I *am* in favor of the government project if it comes through."

"I didn't do it because of Wittnauer-Douglass, Deirdre. I didn't even know they were bidding for the same project."

"That was what I suggested to my mother," Deirdre said, feeling faintly smug. "She's a troublemaker. Do you know that? The woman is a born troublemaker! I never realized it, because I always assumed that she was right and that everything was my fault, but she's been dead wrong about us from the start. Victoria had her pegged. My mother is one of those people who are never satisfied. It may be a little late, but I actually feel sorry for my father. No wonder he poured so much of his time and energy into the business. He was running away from her!"

Hearing her evaluation of her parents' relationship gave Deirdre a moment's pause. Her confidence wavered. "Were you doing that, Neil? Were you running away from me, spending every minute thinking about the business?"

"A good many of those minutes you thought I was thinking about the business, I was thinking about you," he said with a crooked smile. Then the smile vanished. "I wanted to please you. I felt that if I couldn't win your heart, I'd at least win your respect."

"You've had that from the start. And I admire—no, I stand in awe of—what you've done with the business." She sharpened her gaze on him. "But I meant what I said about delegating authority. I want more of your time, Neil! I want to do things with you. I want to go out to romantic little lunches every so often, or play tennis, or take off for the weekend and go . . . wherever!"

His eyes twinkled. "I think I can manage that."

"And I want to go to Washington with you tomorrow."

"No."

"Why not?"

"Because I'm not going."

She stared at him for a minute. "You're not?"

"No. Ben can handle it."

"But you're the best one for the job! You know it, and I know it."

"But there is a question of conflict of interest."

"I don't believe that! I was angry, or I'd never have even suggested it!"

"Now you're being diplomatic," he teased.

"I am not!"

He grew serious. "I thought a lot about that situation, too, while I was out driving. No, I didn't originally know that we'd be competing against Wittnauer-Douglass for that contract, but I have to admit that when I found out, there was intense satisfaction in it. I mean, we may not get the contract. The bids are sealed, and I have no way of knowing who bid what.

The contract may go to Wittnauer-Douglass, or it may go to one of the other bidders. But I did get an inordinate amount of pleasure knowing that Joyce is right up there in the Wittnauer-Douglass league."

"There's nothing wrong with that—"

"But the point is that I have already avenged myself."

"Yes, but through honest hard work and talent. Not just anyone could have done what you've done, Neil. Joyce Enterprises was marking time. You have it moving forward. If you won't take the credit, then I'll take it for you!"

Her pride in him gave him a thrill. "You will, will you?"

"Uh-huh." She thought for a minute. "But what about practicing law. That was what you really wanted to do. Don't you miss it?"

"I've been practicing law at Joyce, but with lots of other things thrown in. I do think it's time Ben and I switch places, though. I want to maintain a position of power, because I've enjoyed having a say in what we do when, but I don't need a fancy title, and I *don't* need the full burden of responsibility I've been carrying." He paused. "But what about you? You haven't been teaching, and that was what you really wanted to do. Don't you miss it?"

"No," she said firmly, then grew pensive. "Maybe I've outgrown it. Maybe the need just isn't there anymore. It filled a void in my life, but the void is gone. Being a helpmate to you is far more satisfying than teaching ever was."

He hugged her. "The things you mentioned before—things we could do together—I want to do them, too, Deirdre. We never did take a honeymoon."

"We had that before we were married."

"But I want another one. A *real* one. You know, a luxurious cottage someplace warm, champagne at sunset, hours lying on the beach in the sun, maid service and laundry service and room service."

Deirdre slanted him a mischievous grin. "What happened to the man who could do it all himself?"

"He wants to be able to concentrate solely on his wife. Is that a crime?"

"You're the lawyer. You tell me."

He never did. Rather, he kissed her with such sweet conviction that she didn't care if they broke every law in the book.

TWELVE ACROSS

BY
BARBARA DELINSKY

WORLDWIDE BOOKS
LONDON • SYDNEY • TORONTO

All the characters in this book have no existence outside the imagination of the Author, and have no relation whatsoever to anyone bearing the same name or names. They are not even distantly inspired by any individual known or unknown to the Author, and all the incidents are pure invention.

First published in Great Britain in 1987
Reprinted in Great Britain in 1994
by Worldwide Books, Eton House,
18-24 Paradise Road, Richmond, Surrey TW9 1SR

ISBN 0 373 59316 3

99-9409

Made and printed in Great Britain

1

LEAH GATES MADE A FINAL FOLD in the blue foil paper, then studied her creation in dismay. "This does not look like a roadrunner," she whispered to the woman at the table beside her.

Victoria Lesser, who'd been diligently folding a pelican, shifted her attention to her friend's work. "Sure, it does," she whispered back. "It's a roadrunner."

"And I'm a groundhog." Leah raised large, round glasses from the bridge of her nose in the hope that a myopic view would improve the image. It didn't. She dropped the frames back into place.

"It's a roadrunner," Victoria repeated.

"You're squinting."

"It looks like a roadrunner."

"It looks like a conglomeration of pointed paper prongs."

Lifting the fragile item, Victoria turned it from side to side. She had to agree with Leah's assessment, though she was far too tactful to say so. "Did you get the stretched bird base right?"

"I thought so."

"And the book fold and the mountain fold?"

"As far as I know."

"Then there must be some problem with the rabbit-ear fold."

"I think the problem's with me."

"Nuh-uh."

"Then with you," Leah scolded in the same hushed whisper. "It was your idea to take an origami course. How do I let myself get talked into these things?"

"Very easily. You love them as much as I do. Besides, you're a puzzle solver, and what's origami but a puzzle in paper? You've done fine up to now. So today's an off day."

"That's an understatement," Leah muttered.

"Ladies?" came a call from the front of the room. Both Leah and Victoria looked up to find the instructor's reproving stare homing in on them over the heads of the other students. "I believe we're ready to start on the frog base. Are there any final questions on the stretched bird base?"

Leah quickly shook her head, then bit her lip against a moan of despair. The frog base?

Victoria simply sat with a gentle smile on her face. By the time the class had ended, though, the smile had faded. Taking Leah by the arm, she ushered her toward the door. "Come on," she said softly. "Let's get some coffee."

When they were seated in a small coffee shop on Third Avenue, Victoria wasted no time in speaking her mind. "Something's bothering you. Out with it."

Leah set her glasses on the table. They'd fogged up the instant she'd come in from the cold, and long-time experience told her that they'd be useless for several minutes. The oversize fuchsia sweater Victoria wore was more than bright enough to be seen by the weakest of eyes, however, and above the sweater were the gentlest of expressions. It was toward these that Leah sent a sheepish look. "My frog base stunk, too, huh?"

"Your mind wasn't on it. Your attention's been elsewhere all night. Where, if I may be so bold as to ask?"

Leah had to laugh at that. In the year she'd known Victoria Lesser, the woman had on occasion been far bolder. But not once had Leah minded. What might have been considered intrusive in others was caring in Victoria. She was compassionate, down-to-earth and insightful, and had such a remarkably positive view of the world that time spent with her was always uplifting.

"Guess," Leah invited with a wry half grin.

"Well, I know your mind's not on your marriage, because that's been over and done for two years now. And I know it's not on a man, because despite my own considerable—" she drawled the word pointedly "—efforts to fix you up, you refuse to date. And I doubt it's on your work, because crosswords are in as much of a demand as ever, and because just last week you told me that your contract's been renewed. Which leaves your apartment." Victoria knew how much Leah adored the loft she'd lived in since her divorce. "Is your landlord raising the rent?"

"Worse."

"Oh-oh. He's talking condo conversion."

"He's *decided* condo conversion."

"Oh, sweetheart. Mucho?"

"Mucho mucho."

"When's it happening?"

"Too soon." Idly Leah strummed the rim of her glasses, then, as though recalling their purpose, slipped them back onto her nose. "I can look for another place, but I doubt I'll find one half as nice. Waterfront buildings are hot, and most of them have already gone condo. Even if there were a vacancy in one of the few remaining rentals, I doubt I could afford it."

"Thank you, New York."

"Mmmm." Seeking to warm her chilled fingers, Leah wrapped her hands around her coffee cup. "Prices have gone sky-high in the two years since I rented the loft. The only reason I got it at a reasonable rate in the first place was that I was willing to fix it up myself. It was a mess when I first saw it, but the view was . . . ineffable."

"Ineffable?"

"Indescribable. It isn't fair, Victoria. For weeks I scraped walls and ceilings, sanded, painted, and now someone else will reap the fruits of my labor." She gave a frustrated growl. "I had a feeling this was coming, but that doesn't make it any easier to take."

Victoria's heart went out to this woman who'd become such a special friend. They'd met the year before in the public library and had hit it off from the start. Victoria had enjoyed Leah's subtle wit and soft-spoken manner. Though at the age of thirty-three Leah was twenty years younger, they shared an interest in things new and different. They'd gone to the theater together, tried out newly opened restaurants together, taken classes not only in origami but in papier-mâché, conversational Russian and ballet.

Victoria had come to know Leah well. She'd learned that Leah had been badly burned by an unhappy marriage and that behind the urban adventuress was a basically shy woman. She also saw that Leah had constructed a very tidy and self-contained shell for herself, and that within that shell was a world of loneliness and vulnerability. Losing the apartment she loved would feed that vulnerability.

"You know," Victoria ventured, "I'd be more than happy to loan you the down payment on that condo—"

The hand Leah pressed over hers cut off her words. "I can't take your money."

"But I have it. More than enough—"

"It's not my way, Victoria. I wouldn't be comfortable. And it's not as much a matter of principle as it is the amount of money involved. If I had to make loan payments to you on top of mortgage payments to the bank, I'd be house-poor. Another few years... That's all I'd have needed to save for the down payment myself." It might have taken less if she'd been more frugal, but Leah lived comfortably and enjoyed it. She took pleasure in splurging on an exquisite hand-knit sweater, a pair of imported shoes, a piece of original art. She reasoned that she'd earned them. But a bank wouldn't take them as collateral. "Unfortunately I don't have another few years."

"You wouldn't have to pay me back right away."

"That's bad business."

"So? It's my money, my business—"

"And our friendship. I'd feel awkward taking advantage of it."

"I'm the one who's made the offer. There'd be no taking advantage involved."

But Leah was shaking her head. "Thanks, but I can't. I just can't."

Victoria opened her mouth to speak, then paused. She'd been about to suggest that Richard might help. Given the fact that Leah had been married to him once and that she had no other family, it seemed the only other option. He had money. Unfortunately he also had a new wife and a child. Victoria knew that Leah's pride wouldn't allow her to ask him for a thing. "What will you do?"

"Look for another place, I guess. If I have to settle for something less exciting, so be it."

"Are you sure you want to stay in the city? Seems to me you could get a super place somewhere farther out."

Leah considered that idea. "But I like the city."

"You're used to the city. You've lived here all your life. Maybe it's time for a change."

"I don't know—"

"It'd be good for you, sweetheart. New scenery, new people, new stores, new courses—"

"Are you trying to get rid of me?"

"And lose my companion in whimsy? Of course not! But I'd be selfish if I didn't encourage you to spread your wings a little. One part of you loves new experiences. The other part avoids them. But you're young, Leah. You have so much living to do."

"What better place to do it than here? I mean, if New York isn't multifarious—"

"Leah, please."

"Diverse, as in filled with opportunities, okay? If New York isn't that, what place is?"

"Just about any place. Perhaps it'd be a different kind of experience . . ." The wheels in Victoria's mind were beginning to turn. "You know, there's another possibility entirely. If you were willing to shift gears, if you were game . . ." She shook her head. "No. Maybe not."

"What?"

"It'd be too much. Forget I mentioned it."

"You haven't mentioned anything," Leah pointed out in her quiet way. But she was curious, just as she was sure Victoria had intended. "What were you thinking of?"

It was a minute before Victoria answered, and the delay wasn't all for effect. She hated to be devious with someone she adored as much as she did Leah. And yet. . .and yet. . .it could possibly work. Hadn't a little deviousness brought two other good friends of hers together?

"I have a place. It's pretty secluded."

"The island in Maine?"

"There's that, but it wasn't what I had in mind." The island was totally secluded. She didn't want Leah to be alone; that would defeat the purpose. "I have a cabin in New Hampshire. Arthur bought it years ago as a hunting lodge. I've been up several times since he died, but it's a little too quiet for me." She shook her head again. "No. It'd be too quiet for you, too. You're used to the city."

"Tell me more."

"You like the city."

"Tell me, Victoria."

Again Victoria paused, this time entirely for effect. "It's in the middle of the woods, and it's small," she said with caution.

"Go on."

"We're talking mountain retreat here."

"Yes."

"There are two rooms—a living area and a bedroom. The nearest town is three miles away. You'd hate it, Leah."

But Leah wasn't so sure. She was intimidated by the idea of moving to a suburban neighborhood, but something rustic . . . It was a new thought, suddenly worth considering. "I don't know as I could buy it."

"It's not for sale," Victoria said quickly. "But I could easily loan—"

"Rent. It'd have to be a rental."

"Okay. I could easily rent it to you for a little while. That's all you'd need to decide whether you can live outside New York. You could view it as a trial run."

"Are there people nearby?"

"In the town, yes. Not many, mind you, and they're quiet, private types."

So much the better, Leah thought. She didn't care to cope with throngs of new faces. "That's okay. I could do my work at a mountain cabin without any problem, and if I had books and a tape deck—"

"There's a community of artists about fifteen miles from the mountain. You once mentioned wanting to learn how to weave. You'd have the perfect opportunity for that." Victoria considered mentioning Garrick, then ruled against it for the time being. Leah was smiling; she obviously liked what she'd heard so far. It seemed that reverse psychology was the way to go. "It's not New York," she reminded her friend gently.

"I know."

"It'd be a total change."

"I know."

"A few minutes ago you said you didn't want to leave New York."

"But my apartment's being stolen from under me, so some change is inevitable."

"You could still look for another apartment."

"I could."

"Or move to the suburbs."

Leah's firm head shake sent thick black hair shimmering along the crew neckline of her sweater.

"I want you to think about this, Leah. It'd be a pretty drastic step."

"True, but not an irrevocable one. If I'm climbing the walls after a week, I can turn around and come back. I really wouldn't be any worse off than I am now, would I?" She didn't wait for Victoria to answer. She was feeling more enthused than she had since she'd learned she was losing her loft. "Tell me more about the cabin itself. Is it primitive?"

Victoria laughed. "If you'd had a chance to know Arthur, you'd have the answer to that. Arthur Lesser never did anything primitive. For that matter, you know me. I'm not exactly the rough-it-in-the-wild type, am I?"

Leah had spent time in Victoria's Park Avenue co-op. It was spacious, stylish, sumptuous. She'd also seen her plush summer place in the Hamptons. But neither Manhattan nor Long Island was a secluded mountain in New Hampshire, and for all her wealth, Victoria wasn't snobbish. She was just enough of a nonconformist to survive for a stretch on the bare basics.

Leah, who'd never had the kind of wealth that inspired total nonconformity, liked to go into things with her eyes open. "Is the cabin well equipped?"

"When last I saw it, it was," Victoria said with an innocence that concealed a multitude of sins. "Don't make a decision now, sweetheart. Think about it for a bit. If you decide to go up there, you'd have to store your furniture. I don't know how you feel about that."

"It shouldn't be difficult."

"It'd be a pain in the neck."

"Being ousted from my apartment is a pain in the neck. If movers have to come in, what difference does it make where they take my things? Besides, if I hate it in New Hampshire, I won't have to worry about my furniture while I look around back here for a place to live."

"The green room's yours if you want it."

Leah grinned. While she'd never have taken a monetary loan, the use of that beautiful room in Victoria's apartment, where she'd already spent a night or two on occasion, was a security blanket she'd welcome. "I was hoping you'd say that."

"Well, you'd better remember it. I'd never forgive myself if, after I talked you into it, you hated the mountains and then didn't have anywhere to turn." Actually, Victoria was more worried that Leah would be the one without forgiveness. But it was a risk worth taking. Victoria had gone with her instincts where Deirdre and Neil Hersey were concerned, and things couldn't have worked out better. Now here was Leah—tall and slender, adorable with her glossy black page boy and bangs, and her huge round glasses with thin red frames. If Leah could meet Garrick . . .

"I'll take it," Leah was saying.

"The green room? Of course you will."

"No, the cabin. I'll take the cabin." Leah wasn't an impulsive person, but she did know her own mind. When something appealed to her, she saw no point in waffling. Victoria's mountain retreat sounded like a perfect solution to the problem she'd been grappling with for seventy-two hours straight. It would afford her the time to think things through and decide where to go from there. "Just tell me how much you want for rent."

Victoria brushed the matter aside with the graceful wave of one hand. "No rush on that. We can discuss it later."

"I'm paying rent, Victoria. If you don't let me, the deal's off."

"I agreed that you could pay rent, sweetheart. It's just that I have no idea how much to charge. Why don't you see what shape things are in when you get there? Then you can pay me whatever you think the place merits."

"I'd rather pay you in advance."

"And I'd rather wait."

"You're being pertinacious."

Victoria wasn't sure what "pertinacious" meant, but she could guess. "That's right."

"Fine. I'll wait as you've asked, but so help me, Victoria, if you return my check—"

"I won't," Victoria said, fully confident that it wouldn't come to that. "Have faith, Leah. Have faith."

LEAH HAD FAITH. It grew day by day, along with her enthusiasm. She surprised herself at times, because she truly was a died-in-the-wool urbanite. Yet something about an abrupt change in life-style appealed to her for the very first time. She wondered if it had something to do with her age; perhaps the thirties brought boldness. Or desperation. No, she didn't want to think that. Perhaps she was simply staging a belated rebellion against the way of life she'd known from birth.

It had been years since she'd taken a vacation, much less one to a remote spot. She remembered short jaunts to Cape Cod with her parents, when she'd been a child and remote had consisted of isolated sand dunes and sunrise sails. The trips she'd taken with her husband had never been remote in any sense. Inevitably they'd been tied to his work, and she'd found them far from relaxing. Richard had been constantly *on*, which wouldn't have bothered her if he hadn't been so fussy about how she looked and behaved when she was by his side. Not that she'd given him cause for complaint; she'd been born and bred in the urban arena and knew how to play its games when necessary. Unfortunately Richard's games had incorporated rules she hadn't anticipated.

But Leah wasn't thinking about Richard on the day in late March when she left Manhattan. She was thinking of the gut instinct that told her she was doing the right thing. And she was thinking of the farewell dinner Victoria had insisted on treating her to the night before.

They'd spent the better part of the meal chatting about incidentals. Only when they'd reached dessert did they get around to the nitty-gritty. "You're all set to go, then?"

"You bet."

Victoria had had many a qualm in the three weeks since she'd suggested the plan, and in truth, she was feeling a little like a weasel. It was fine and dandy, she knew, to say that she had Leah's best interests at heart. She was still being manipulative, and Leah was bound to be angry when she discovered the fact. "Are you sure you want to go through with this?"

"Uh-huh."

"There isn't any air-conditioning."

"In the mountains? I should hope not."

"Or phone."

"So you've told me," Leah said with a smile. "Twice. I'll give you a call from town once I'm settled."

Victoria wasn't sure whether to look forward to that or not. "Did the storage people get all your furniture?"

"This morning."

"My Lord, that means the bed, too! Where will you sleep tonight?"

"On the floor. And no, I don't want the green room. I've about had it with packing. Everything's ready to go from my place. All I'll have to do in the morning is load up the car and take off."

A night on the bare floor. Victoria felt guiltier than ever, but she knew a stubborn expression when she saw one. "Is the car okay?"

It was a demo Volkswagen Golf that Leah had bought from a dealer three days before. "The car is fine."

"Can you drive it?"

"Sure can."

"You haven't driven in years, Leah."

"It's like riding a bike—you never forget how. Isn't that what you told me two weeks ago? Come on, Victoria. It's not like you to be a worrywart."

She was right. Still, Victoria felt uncomfortable. With Deirdre and Neil, there had been a single phone call from each and they'd been on their way. With Leah it had meant three weeks of deception, which seemed to make the crime that much greater.

But what was done was done. Leah's mind was set. Her arrangements were made. She was going.

Taking a deep breath, Victoria produced first a reassuring smile, then two envelopes from her purse. "Directions to the cabin," she said, handing over the top one. "I had my secretary type them up, and they're quite detailed." Cautiously she watched Leah remove the paper and scan it. She knew the exact moment Leah reached the instructions on the bottom, and responded to her frown by explaining, "Garrick Rodenhiser is a trapper. His cabin is several miles from mine by car, but there's an old logging trail through the woods that will get you there on foot in no time. In case of emergency you're to contact him. He's a good man. He'll help you in any way he can."

"Goodness," Leah murmured distractedly as she reread the directions, "you sound as though you expect trouble."

"Nonsense. But I do trust Garrick. When I'm up there alone myself, it's a comfort knowing he's around."

"Well—" Leah folded the paper and returned it to the envelope "—I'm sure I'll be fine."

"So you will be," Victoria declared, holding out the second envelope. "For Garrick. Deliver it for me?"

Leah took it, then turned it over and over. It was sealed and opaque, with the trapper's name written on the front in Victoria's elegant script. "A love letter?" she teased, tapping the tip of the envelope against her nose. "Somehow I can't imagine you with a craggy old trapper."

"Craggy old trappers can be very nice."

"Are there lots of them up there?"

"A few."

"Don't they smell?"

Victoria laughed. "That's precious, Leah."

"They don't?"

"Not badly."

"Oh. Okay. Well, that's good. Y'know, this trip could well be educational."

That was, in many ways, how Leah thought of it as she worked her way through the midtown traffic. The car was packed to the hilt with clothing and other essentials, boxes of books, a tape deck and three cases of cassettes, plus sundry supplies. She had dozens of plans, projects to keep her busy over and above the crossword puzzles she intended to create.

Filling her mind with these prospects was in part a defense mechanism, she knew, and it was successful only to a point. There remained a certain wistfulness in leaving the loft where she'd been independent for the first time in her life, saying goodbye to the little man at the corner kiosk from whom she'd bought the *Times* each day, bidding a silent farewell to the theaters and restaurants and museums she wouldn't be visiting for a while.

The exhaust fumes that surrounded her were as familiar as the traffic. Not so the sense of nostalgia that assailed her as she navigated the Golf through the streets. She'd loved New York from the time she'd been old enough to appreciate it as a city. Her parents' apartment had been modest by New York standards, but Central Park had been free to all, as had Fifth Avenue, Rockefeller Center and Washington Square.

Memories. A few close friends. The kind of anonymity she liked. Such was New York. But they'd all be there when she returned. Determinedly squaring her shoulders, she thrust off sentimentality in favor of practicality, which at the moment meant avoiding swerving taxis and swarming pedestrians as she headed toward the East River.

Traffic was surprisingly heavy for ten in the morning, and Leah was the kind of driver others either loved or hated. When in doubt she yielded the road, which meant grins on the faces of those who cut her off and impatient honks from those behind her. She was relieved to leave the concrete jungle behind and start north on the thruway.

It was a sunny day, mild for March, a good omen, she decided. Though she'd brought heavier clothes with her, she was glad she'd worn a pair of lightweight knit pants and a loose cashmere sweater for the drive. She was comfortable and increasingly relaxed as she coasted in the limbo between city and country.

By the time she reached the outskirts of Boston, it was two o'clock and she was famished. As eager to stretch as to eat, she pulled into a Burger King on the turnpike and climbed from the car, pausing only to grab for her jacket before heading for the restaurant. The sun was lost behind cloud cover that had gathered since she'd reached the Massachusetts border, and the air had grown chilly. Knowing that she had another three hours of driving before her, and desperately wanting to reach the cabin before dark, she gulped down a burger and a Coke, used the rest rooms, then was quickly on her way again.

The sky darkened progressively. With the New Hampshire border came a light drizzle. So much for good omens, she mused silently as she turned one switch after another until at last she hit paydirt with the windshield wipers. Within half an hour she set them to swishing double time.

It was pouring. Dark, gloomy, cold and wet. Leah thanked her lucky stars that she'd read the directions so many times before she'd left, because she loathed the idea of pulling over to the side of the road even for the briefest of moments. With the typed words neatly etched in her brain, she was able to devote her full concentration to driving.

And driving demanded it. She eased up on the gas, but even then had to struggle to see the road through the torrent. Lane markers were sadly blurred. The back spray from passing cars made the already poor visibility worse. She breathed a sigh of relief when she found her turnoff, then tensed up again when the sudden sparcity of other cars meant the absence of taillights as guides.

But she drove on. She passed a restaurant and briefly considered taking shelter until the storm was spent, but decided that it would be far worse to have to negotiate strange roads—and a lonesome cabin—in the dark later. She passed a dingy motel and toyed with the idea of taking a room for the night, but decided that she really did want to be in the cabin. Having left behind the life she'd always known, she was feeling unsettled; spending the night in a fleabag motel wouldn't help.

What would help, she decided grimly, would be an end to the rain. And a little sun peaking through the clouds. And several extra hours of daylight.

None of those happened. The rain did lessen to a steady downpour, but the sky grew darker and darker as daylight began to wane. The fiddling she'd done earlier in search of the wipers paid off; she knew just what to press to turn on the headlights.

When she passed through the small town Victoria had mentioned, she was elated. Elation faded in an instant, though, when she took the prescribed turn past the post office and saw what lay ahead.

A narrow, twisting road, barely wide enough for two cars. No streetlamps. No center line. No directional signs.

Leah sat ramrod straight at the wheel. Her knuckles were white, her eyes straining to delineate the rain-spattered landscape ahead. Too late she realized that she hadn't checked the odometer when she'd passed the post office. One-point-nine miles to the turnoff, her instructions said. How far had she gone? All but creeping along the uphill grade, she searched for the triangular boulder backed by a stand of twisted birch that would mark the start of Victoria's road.

It was just another puzzle, Leah told herself. She loved puzzles.

She hated this one. If she missed the road... But she didn't want to miss the road. One-point-nine miles at fifteen miles an hour... eight minutes... How long had she been driving since she'd left the town?

Just when she was about to stop and return to the post office to take an odometer reading, she saw a triangular boulder backed by a stand of twisted birch. And a road. Vaguely.

It was with mixed feelings that she made the turn, for not only was she suddenly on rutted dirt, but forested growth closed in on her, slapping the sides of the car. In her anxious state it sounded clearly hostile.

She began to speak to herself, albeit silently. *This is God's land, Leah. The wild and woolly outdoors. Picture it in the bright sunshine. You'll love it.*

The car bumped and jerked along, jolting her up and down and from side to side. One of the tires began to spin and she caught her breath, barely releasing it when the car surged onward and upward. The words she spoke to herself grew more beseechful. *Just a little farther, Leah. You're almost there. Come on, Golf, don't fade on me now.*

Her progress was agonizingly slow, made all the more so by the steepening pitch as the road climbed the hill. The Golf didn't falter, but when it wasn't jouncing, it slid pitifully from one side to the other, even back when she took her foot from the gas to better weather the ruts. She wished she'd had the foresight to rent a jeep, if not a Sherman tank. It was all she could do to hold the steering wheel steady. It was all she could do to see the road.

Leah was frightened. Darkness was closing in from every angle, leaving her high beams as a beacon to nowhere. When they picked up an expanse of water directly in her path, she slammed on the brakes. The car fishtailed in the mud, then came to a stop, its sudden stillness compensated for by the racing of her pulse.

A little voice inside her screamed, *turn back! Turn back!* But she couldn't turn. She was hemmed in on both sides by the woods.

She stared at the water before her. Beneath the pelting rain, it undulated as a living thing. But it was only a puddle, she told herself. Victoria would have mentioned a stream, and there was no sign of a bridge, washed out or otherwise.

Cautiously she stepped on the gas. Yard by yard, the car stole forward. She tried not to think about how high the water might be on the hubcaps. She tried not to think about the prospect of brake damage or stalling. She tried not to think about what creatures of the wild might be lurking beneath the rain-swollen depths. She kept as steady a foot on the gas pedal as possible and released a short sigh of relief when she reached high ground once again.

There were other puddles and ruts and thick beds of mud, but then the road widened. Heart pounding, she squinted through the windshield as she pushed on the accelerator. The cabin had to be ahead. *Please, God, let it be ahead.*

All at once, with terrifying abruptness, the road seemed to disappear. She'd barely had time to jerk her foot to the brake, when the car careened over a rise and began a downward slide. After a harrowing aeon, it came to rest in a deep pocket of sludge.

Shaking all over, Leah closed her eyes for a minute. She took one tremulous breath, then another, then opened her eyes and looked ahead. What she saw took her breath away completely.

For three weeks she'd been picturing a compact and charming log cabin. A chimney would rise from one side;

windows would flank the front door. Nestled in the woods, the cabin would be the epitome of a snug country haven.

Instead it was the epitome of ruin. She blinked, convinced that she was hallucinating. Before her lay the charred remains of what might indeed have once been a snug and charming cabin. Now only the chimney was standing.

"Oh, Lord," she wailed, her cry nearly drowned out by the thunder of rain on the roof of the car, "what *happened*?"

Unfortunately what had happened was obvious. There had been a fire. But when? And why hadn't Victoria been notified?

The moan that followed bore equal parts disappointment, fatigue and anxiety. In the confines of the car it had such an eerie edge that Leah knew she had to get back to civilization and fast. At that moment even the thought of spending the night in a fleabag motel held appeal.

She stepped on the gas and the front wheels spun. She shifted into reverse and hit the gas again, but the car didn't budge. Into drive . . . into reverse . . . she repeated the cycle a dozen times, uselessly. Not only was she not getting back to civilization she wasn't getting *anywhere*, at least, not in the Golf.

Dropping her head to the steering wheel, she took several shuddering breaths. Leah Gates didn't panic. She hadn't done so when her parents had died. She hadn't done so when her babies had died. She hadn't done so when her husband had pronounced her unfit as a wife and left her.

What she had done in each of those situations was cry until her grief was spent, then pick herself up and restructure her dreams. In essence, that was what she had to do now. There wasn't time to give vent to tears, but a definite restructuring of plans was in order.

She couldn't spend the night in the car. She couldn't get back to town. Help wasn't about to come to her, so . . .

Fishing the paper with the typed directions from her purse, she turned on the overhead light and read at the bottom of the page the lines that she'd merely skimmed before. True, she'd promised Victoria that she'd deliver the letter to the trapper, Garrick Rodenhiser, but she'd assumed she'd do it at her leisure. Certainly not in the dark of night—or in the midst of a storm.

But seeking out the trapper seemed her only hope of rescue. It was pouring and very dark. She had neither flashlight, umbrella nor rain poncho handy. She'd just have to make a dash for it. Hadn't she done the same often enough in New York when a sudden downpour soaked the streets?

Diligently she reread the directions to the trapper's cabin. Peering through the windshield, she located the break in the woods behind and to the left of the chimney. Without dwelling on the darkness ahead, she tucked the paper back in her purse, dropped the purse to the floor, turned off the lights, then the engine. After pocketing the keys, she took a deep breath, swung open the door and stepped out into the rain.

Her feet promptly sank six inches into mud. Dumbly she stared down at where her ankles should have been. Equally as dumbly, she tugged at one foot, which emerged minus its shoe. She stuck her foot back into the muck, rooted around until she'd located the shoe and squished her foot inside, then drew the whole thing up toe first.

After tottering for a second, she lunged onto what she hoped was firmer ground. It was, though this time her other foot came up shoeless. Legs wide apart, she repeated the procedure of retrieving her shoe, then scrambled ahead.

She didn't think about the fact that the comfortable leather flats she'd loved were no doubt ruined. She didn't think about her stockings or her pants or, for that matter, the rest of her clothes, which were already drenched. And assuming that it would be a quick trip to the trapper's cabin, then a quick one back with help, she didn't think once about locking the car. As quickly as she could she ran around the ruins of Victoria's cabin and plunged on into the woods.

An old logging trail, Victoria had called it. Leah could believe that. No car could have fit through, for subsequent years of woodland growth had narrowed it greatly. But it was visible, and for that she was grateful.

It was also wet, and in places nearly as muddy as what she'd so precipitously stepped into from her car. As hastily as she could, she slogged through, only to find her feet mired again a few steps later.

As the minutes passed, she found it harder to will away the discomfort she felt. It occurred to her on a slightly hysterical note that dashing across Manhattan in the rain had never been like this. She was cold and wet. Her clothes clung to her body, providing little if any protection. Her hair was soaked; her bangs dripped into her eyes behind glasses whose lenses were streaked. Tension and the effort of wading through mud made her entire body ache.

Worse, there was no sign of a cabin ahead, or of anything else remotely human. For the first time since her car had become stuck she realized exactly how alone and vulnerable she was. Garrick Rodenhiser was a trapper, which meant that there were animals about. The thought that they might hunt humans in the rain sent shivers through her limbs, over and above those caused by the cold night air. Then she slipped in the mud and lost her balance, falling to the ground with a sharp cry. Sheer terror had her on her feet in an instant, and she whimpered as she struggled on.

Several more times Leah lost a shoe and would have left it if the thought of walking in her sheer-stockinged feet hadn't been far worse than the sliminess of the once fine leather. Twice more she fell, crying out in pain the second time when her thigh connected with something sharp. Not caring to consider what it might have been, she limped on. Hopping, sliding, scrambling for a foothold at times, she grew colder, wetter and muddier.

At one point pure exhaustion brought her to a standstill. Her arms and legs were stiff; her insides trembled; her breath came in short, sharp gasps. She had to go on, she told herself, but it was another minute before her limbs would listen. And then it was only because the pain of movement was preferable to the psychological agony of inaction.

When she heard sounds beyond the rain, her panic grew. Glancing blindly behind her, she ricocheted off a tree and spun around, barely saving herself from yet another fall. She was sure she was crying, because she'd never been so frightened in her life, but she couldn't distinguish tears from raindrops.

A world of doubts crowded in on her. How much farther could she push her protesting limbs? How could she be sure that the trapper's cabin still existed? What if Garrick Rodenhiser simply wasn't there? *What would she do then?*

Nearing the point of despair, Leah didn't see the cabin until she was practically on top of it. She stumbled and fell, but on a path of flat stones this time. Shoving up her glasses with the back of one cold, stiff hand, she peered through the rain at the dark structure before her. After a frantic few seconds' search, she spotted the sliver of light that escaped through the shutters. It was the sweetest sight she'd ever seen.

Pushing herself upright, she staggered the final distance and all but crawled up the few short steps to the cabin's door. Beneath the overhang of the porch she was out of the rain, but her teeth were chattering, and her legs abruptly refused to hold her any longer. Sliding down on her bottom close by the door, she mustered the last of her strength to bang her elbow against the wood. Then she wrapped her arms around her middle and tried to hold herself together.

When a minute passed and nothing happened, her misery grew. The cold air of night gusted past her, chilling her wet clothing even more. She tapped more feebly on the wood, but it must have done the trick, for within seconds the door opened. Weakly she raised her eyes. Through wet glasses she could make out a huge form silhouetted in the doorway. Behind it was sanctuary.

"I..." she began, "I..."

The mighty figure didn't move.

"I am...I need..." Her voice was thready, severely impeded by the chill that had reduced her to a shivering mass.

Slowly, cautiously, the giant lowered itself to its haunches. Leah knew it was human. It moved like a human. It had hands like a human. She could only pray that it had the heart of a human.

"Victoria sent me," she whispered. "I'm so cold."

2

GARRICK RODENHISER would have laughed had the huddled figure before him been less pathetic. Victoria wouldn't have sent him a woman; she knew that he valued his privacy too much. And she respected that, which was one of the reasons they'd become friends.

But the figure on his doorstep was indeed pathetic. She was soaking wet, covered with mud and, from the way she was quaking, looked to be chilled to the bone. Of course, the quaking could be from fear, he mused, and if she was handing him a line, she had due cause for fear.

Still, he wasn't an ogre. Regardless of what had brought her here, he couldn't close his door and leave her to the storm.

"Come inside," he said as he closed a hand around her upper arm and started to help her up.

She tried to pull away, whispering a frantic, "I'm filthy!"

The tightening of his fingers was his only response. Leah didn't protest further. Her legs were stiff and sore; she wasn't sure she'd have made it up on her own. His hand fell away, though, the instant she was standing, and he stood back for her to precede him into the cabin.

She took three steps into the warmth, then stopped. Behind her the door closed. Before her the fire blazed. Beneath her was a rapidly spreading puddle of mud.

Removing her glasses, she started to wipe them on her jacket, only to realize after several swipes that it wouldn't help. Glasses dangling, she looked helplessly around.

"Not exactly dressed for the weather, are you?" the trapper asked.

His voice was deep, faintly gravelly. Leah's eyes shot to his face. Though his features were fuzzy, his immense size was not. It had been one thing for him to tower over her when she'd been collapsed on the porch; now she was standing, all five-seven of her. He had to be close to six-four, and was strapping to boot. She wondered if she should fear him.

"Are you Garrick Rodenhiser?" Her voice sounded odd. It was hoarse and as shaky as the rest of her.

He nodded.

She noted that he was dressed darkly and that he was bearded, but if he was who he said, then he was a friend of Victoria's, and she was safe.

"I need help," she croaked, forcing the words out with great effort. "My car got stuck in the mud—"

"You need a shower," Garrick interrupted. He strode to the far side of the room—the large and only room of the cabin—where he opened a closet and drew out several clean towels. Though he didn't know who his guest was, she was not only trembling like a leaf, she was also making a mess on his floor. The sooner she was clean and warm, the sooner she could explain her presence.

Flipping on the bathroom light, he tossed the towels onto the counter by the sink, then gestured for Leah to come. When she didn't move, he gestured again. "There's plenty of hot water. And soap and shampoo."

Leah looked down at her clothes. They were nearly unrecognizable as those she'd put on that morning. "It wasn't like this in the movie," she cried weakly.

Garrick stiffened, wondering if he was being set up. "Excuse me?"

"*Romancing the Stone*. They went through rain and mud, but their clothes came out looking clean."

He hadn't seen a movie in four years, and whether or not her remark was innocent remained to be seen. "You'd better take them off."

"But I don't have any others." Her body shook; her teeth clicked together between words. "They're in my car."

Garrick set off for the side of the room, where a huge bed shared the wall with a low dresser. He opened one drawer after another, finally returning to toss a pile of neatly folded clothes into the bathroom by the towels.

This time when he gestured, Leah moved. Her gait was stilted, though, and before she'd reached the bathroom, she was stopped by a raspy inquiry.

"What happened to your leg?"

She shot a glance at her thigh and swallowed hard. Not even the coating of mud on her pants could hide the fact that they were torn and she was bleeding. "I fell."

"What did you hit?"

"Something sharp." Rooted to the spot by curiosity as much as fatigue, she watched Garrick head for the part of the room that served as a kitchen, open a cabinet and set a large first-aid kit on the counter. He rummaged through and came up with a bottle of disinfectant and bandaging material, which he then added to the gathering pile in the bathroom.

"Take your shower," he instructed. "I'll make coffee."

"Brandy, I need brandy," she blurted out.

"Sorry. No brandy."

"Whiskey?" she asked more meekly. Didn't all woodsmen drink, preferably the potent, homemade stuff?

"Sorry."

"*Anything?*" she whispered.

Garrick shook his head. He almost wished he did have something strong. Despite the warmth of the cabin, the woman before him continued to tremble. If she'd trekked through the forest for any distance—and from the look of her she had—she was probably feeling the aftereffects of shock. But he didn't have anything remotely alcoholic to drink. He hadn't so much as looked at a bottle since he'd left California.

"Then hot coffee would . . . be lovely." She tried to smile, but her face wouldn't work. Nor were her legs eager to function in any trained manner. They protested when she forced them to carry her to the bathroom. She was feeling achier by the minute.

With the tip of one grimy finger, she closed the bathroom door. What she really wanted was a bath, but she quickly saw that there wasn't a tub. The bathroom was large, though, surprisingly modern, bright, clean and well equipped.

"There's a heat lamp," Garrick called from the other side of the door.

She found the switch and turned it on, determinedly avoiding the mirror in the process. Setting her glasses by the sink, she opened the door of the oversize shower stall and turned on the water. The minute it was hot, she stepped in, clothes and all.

It was heaven, sheer heaven. Hot water rained down on her head, spilling over the rest of her in a cascade of instant warmth. She didn't know how long she stood there without moving, nor did she care. Garrick had offered plenty of hot water, and despite the fact that she'd never been one to be selfish or greedy, she planned to take advantage of every drop. These were extenuating circumstances, she reasoned. After the ordeal she'd been through, her body deserved a little pampering.

Moreover, standing under the shower was as much of a limbo as the highway driving had been earlier. She knew that once she emerged, she was going to have to face a future that was as mucked up as her clothes. She wasn't looking forward to it.

Gradually the numbness in her hands and feet wore off. Slowly, and with distaste, she began to strip off her things. When every last item lay in a pile in a corner of the stall, she went to work with soap and shampoo, lathering, rinsing, lathering, rinsing, continuing the process far longer than was necessary, almost obsessive in her need to rid herself of the mud that was synonymous with terror.

By the time she turned off the water, the ache in her limbs had given way to a pervasive tiredness. More than anything at that moment she craved a soft chair, if not a sofa or, better yet, a bed. But there was work to be done first. Emerging from the shower, she wrapped one towel around her hair, then began to dry herself with another. When she inadvertently ran the towel over her thigh, she gasped. Fumbling for her glasses, she rinsed and dried them, then shakily fit them onto her nose.

She almost wished she hadn't. Her outer thigh bore a deep, three-inch gash that was ugly enough to make her stomach turn. Straightening, she closed her eyes, pressed a hand to her middle and took several deep breaths. Then, postponing another look for as long as possible, she reached for the clothes Garrick had left.

Beggars couldn't be choosers, which was why she thought no evil of the gray thermal top she pulled on and the green flannel shirt she layered over it. The thermal top hit her upper thigh; the shirt was even longer. The warmth of both was welcome.

Tucking the tails beneath her, she lowered herself to the closed commode. Working quickly, lest she lose her nerve, she opened the bottle of disinfectant, poured a liberal amount on a corner of the towel and pressed it firmly to the gash.

White-hot pain shot through her leg. Crying aloud, she tore the towel away. At the same time, her other hand went boneless, releasing its grip on the bottle, which fell to the floor and shattered.

Garrick, who'd been standing pensively before the fire, jerked up his head when he heard her cry. Within seconds he'd crossed the floor and burst into the bathroom.

Leah's hands were fisted on her knees, and she was rocking back and forth, waiting for the stinging in her leg to subside. Her gaze flew to his. "I didn't think it would hurt so much," she whispered.

His grip tightened on the doorknob, and for a split second he considered retreating. It had been more than four years since he'd seen legs like those—long and slender, living silk the color of cream. His eyes were riveted to them, while his heart yawed. He told himself to turn and run—until he caught sight of the red gouge marring that silk and knew he wasn't going anywhere.

Squatting before her, he took the towel from where it lay across her lap and dabbed at the area around the cut. The color of the antiseptic was distinct on the corner of the towel she'd used. He reversed the terry cloth and flicked her a glance.

"Hold on."

With a gentle dabbing motion, he applied whatever disinfectant was left on the towel to her cut. She sucked in her breath and splayed one hand tightly over the top of her thigh to hold it still. Even then her leg was shaking badly by the time Garrick reached for the bandages.

"I can do it," she breathed. Beads of sweat had broken out on her nose, causing her glasses to slip. Her fingers trembled when she shoved them up, but she was feeling foolish about the broken bottle and needed desperately to show her grit.

She might as well not have spoken. Garrick proceeded to cover the wound with a large piece of gauze and strap it in place with adhesive tape. When that was done, he carefully collected the largest pieces of broken glass and set them on the counter.

He looked at her then, eyes skimming her pale features before coming to rest on her temple. Taking a fresh piece of gauze, he dipped it into the small amount of liquid left in the bottom quarter of the bottle and, with the same gentle dabbing, disinfected the cluster of scratches he'd found.

Leah hadn't been aware of their existence. She vaguely recalled reeling off a tree, but surface scratches had been the least of her worries when the rest of her had been so cold and sore. Even now the scratches were quickly forgotten, because Garrick had turned his attention to her hand that had remained in a fist throughout the procedure. She held her breath when he reached for it.

Without asking himself why or to what end, he slowly and carefully unclenched her fingers, then stared at the purple crescents her short nails had left on her palm. They were a testament to the kind of self-control he admired; even when he brushed his thumb across them, willing them away, they remained. Cradling her hand in his far larger one, he raised his eyes to hers.

She wasn't prepared for their luminous force. They penetrated her, warmed her, frightened her in ways she didn't understand. Hazel depths spoke of loneliness; silver flecks spoke of need. They reached out and enveloped her, demanding nothing, demanding everything.

It was an incredible moment.

Of all the new experiences she'd had that day, this was the most stunning. For Garrick Rodenhiser wasn't the grizzled old trapper she'd assumed she'd find in a rustic cabin in the woods. He was a man in his prime, and the only scents emanating from him had to do with wood smoke and maleness.

At that most improbable and unexpected time, she was drawn to him.

Unable to cope with the idea of being drawn to anyone, least of all a total stranger, she looked away. But she wasn't the only one stunned by the brief visual interlude. Garrick, too, was pricked by new and unbidden emotions.

Abruptly releasing her hand, he stood. "Don't touch the glass," he ordered gruffly. "I'll take care of it when you're done." Turning on his heel, he left the bathroom and strode back to the hearth. He was still there, bent over the mantel with his forearms on the rough wood and his forehead on his arms, when he heard the sound of the bathroom door opening sometime later.

With measured movements he straightened and turned, fully prepared to commence his inquisition. This woman, whoever she was, was trespassing on his turf. He didn't like uninvited visitors. He didn't like anything remotely resembling a threat to his peace.

He hadn't counted on what he'd see, much less what he'd feel when he saw it. If he'd thought he'd gained control of his senses during those few minutes alone, he'd been mistaken. Now, looking at this woman about whom he knew absolutely nothing, he was shaken by the same desire that had shocked his system earlier.

Strangely, if that desire had been physical, he'd have felt less threatened. Hormonal needs were understandable, acceptable, easily slaked.

But what he felt went beyond the physical. It had first sparked when he'd barged into the bathroom and seen legs that were feminine, ivory, sleek and exposed. There had been nothing seductive about the way they'd trembled, but he'd been disturbed anyway. He had thought of a doe he'd encountered in the woods; the animal had stared at him, motionless save for the faint tremor in her hind legs that betrayed an elemental fear. He'd been frustrated then, unable to assure the doe that he'd never harm her. He was frustrated now because the woman seemed equally as defenseless, and while he might have assured her, he wasn't able to form the words.

The desire he felt had grown during his ministrations, when his fingers had brushed her thigh and found it to be warmed from the shower and smooth, so smooth. Very definitely human and alive. A member of his own species. At that moment, he'd felt an instinctive need for assurance from her that he was every bit as human and alive.

When he'd cupped her hand in his, he'd felt the oddest urge to guard her well. Fragility, the need for protection, a primal plea for closeness . . . he'd been unable to deny the feelings, though they shocked him.

And when he'd searched her eyes, he'd found them as startled as his own must have been.

He wasn't sure if he believed she was genuine; he'd known too many quality actors in his day to take anything at face value. What he couldn't ignore, though, were his own feelings, for they said something about himself that he didn't want to know.

Those feelings hit him full force as he stared at her. It wasn't that she was beautiful. Her black hair, clean now and unturbaned, was damp and straight, falling just shy of her collarbone, save for the bangs that covered her brow. Her features were average, her face dominated by the owl-eyed glasses that perched on her nose. No, she wasn't beautiful, and certainly not sexy wearing his shirt and long johns. But her pallor did something to him, as did the slight forward curve of her shoulders as she wrapped her arms around her waist.

She was the image of vulnerability, and watching her, he felt vulnerable himself. He wanted to hold her, that was all, just to hold her. He couldn't understand it, didn't want to admit it, but it was so.

"I'm not sure what to do with my clothes," she said. Her eyes registered bewilderment, though her voice was calm. "I rinsed them out as best I could. Is there somewhere I can hang them to dry?"

Garrick was grateful for the mundaneness of the question, which allowed him to sidestep those deeper thoughts. "You'd better put them through a real wash first. Over there." He inclined his head toward the kitchen area.

Through clean, dry glasses, Leah saw what she hadn't been physically or emotionally capable of seeing earlier. A washer-dryer combo stood beyond the sink, not far from a dishwasher and a microwave oven. Modern kitchen, modern bathroom—Garrick Rodenhiser, it seemed, roughed it only to a point.

Ducking back into the bathroom, she retrieved her clothes and put them into the washer with a generous amount of detergent. Once the machine was running, she eyed the coffee maker and its fresh, steaming pot.

"Help yourself," Garrick said. Resuming his silence, he watched her open one cabinet after another until she'd found a mug.

"Will you have some?" she asked without turning.

"No."

Her hand trembled as she poured the coffee, and even the small movement had repercussions in the tension-weary muscles of her shoulders. Cup in hand, she padded barefoot across the floor to peer through the small opening between the shutters that served as drapes. She couldn't see much of anything, but the steady beat.of rain on the roof told her what she wanted to know.

Straightening, she turned to face Garrick. "Is there any chance of getting to my car tonight?"

"No."

His single word was a confirmation of what she'd already suspected. There seemed no point in railing against what neither of them could change. "Do you mind if I sit by your fire?"

He stepped aside in silent invitation.

The wide oak planks were warm under her bare feet as she crossed to the hearth. Lowering herself to the small rag rug with more fatigue than finesse, she tucked her legs under her, pressed her arms to her sides and cupped the coffee with both hands.

The flames danced low and gently, and would have been soothing had she been capable of being soothed. But sitting before them, relatively warm and safe for the first time in hours, she saw all too clearly what she faced tonight. She was here for the night; she knew that much. The storm continued. Her car wouldn't move. She was going nowhere until morning. But what then?

Even once her car was freed, she had nowhere to go. Victoria's cabin was gone, and with it the plans she'd spent the past three weeks making. It had all seemed so simple; now nothing was simple. She could look around for another country cabin to rent, but she didn't know where to begin. She could take a room at an inn, but her supply of money was far from endless. She could return to New York, but something about that smacked of defeat—or so she told herself when she found no other excuse for her hesitancy to take that particular option.

If she'd felt unsettled during the drive north, now she felt thoroughly disoriented. Not even at her lowest points in the past had she been without a home.

Behind her, the sofa springs creaked. Garrick. With her glasses on, she'd seen far more than details of the cabin. She'd also seen that Garrick Rodenhiser was extraordinarily handsome. The bulk that had originally impressed her was concentrated in his upper body, in the well-developed shoulders and back defined by a thick black turtleneck. Dark gray corduroys molded a lean pair of hips and long, powerful legs. He was bearded, yes, but twenty-twenty vision revealed that beard to be closely trimmed. And though his hair was on the long side, it, too, was far from unruly and was an attractive dark blond shot through with silver.

His nose was straight, his lips thin and masculine. His skin was stretched over high cheekbones, but his eyes were what held the true force of his being. Silvery hazel, they were alive with questions unasked and thoughts unspoken.

Had Leah been a gambler, she'd have bet that Garrick was a transplant. He simply didn't fit the image of a trapper. There were the amenities in the cabin, for one thing, which spoke of a certain sophistication. There was also his speech; though his words were few and far between, his enunciation was cultured. And his eyes—those eyes—held a worldly look, realistic, cynical, simultaneously knowing and inquisitive.

She wondered where he'd come from and what had brought him here. She wondered what he thought of her arrival and of the fact that she'd be spending the night. She wondered what kind of a man he was where women were concerned, and whether the need she'd sensed in him went as deep as, in that fleeting moment in the bathroom, it had seemed.

Garrick was wondering similar things. In his forty years, he'd had more women than he cared to count. From the age of fourteen he'd been aware of himself as a man. Increasingly his ego and his groin had been rivals in his search for and conquest of woman. As the years had passed, quantity had countermanded quality; he'd laid anything feminine, indiscriminately and often with little care. He'd used and been used, and the sexual skill in which he'd once taken pride had been reduced to a physical act that was shallow and hurtful. It had reflected the rest of his life too well.

All that had ended four years ago. When he'd first come to New Hampshire, he'd stayed celibate. He hadn't yearned, hadn't w ted. He'd lived within well-defined walls, unsure of himself, distrusting his emotions and motivations. During those early months his sole goal had been to forge out an existence as a human being.

Gradually, the day to day course of his life had fallen into place. He'd had the occasional woman since then, though not out of any gut-wrenching desire as much as the simple need to assure himself that he was male and normal. Rarely had he seen the same woman twice. Never had he brought one to his home.

But one was here now. He hadn't asked for her. In fact, he wanted her gone as soon as possible. Yet even as he studied her, as he watched her stare into the fire, take an occasional sip of coffee, flex her arms around herself protectively, he felt an intense need for human contact.

He wondered if the need was indicative of a new stage in his redevelopment, if he'd reached the point of being comfortable with himself and was now ready to share himself with others.

To share. To *learn* to share. He'd always been self-centered, and to an extent, the life he'd built here reinforced that. He did what he wanted when he wanted. He wasn't sure if he was capable of changing that, or if he wanted to change it. He wasn't sure if he was ready to venture into something new.

Still, there was the small voice of need that cried out when he looked at her. . . .

"What's your name?"

His voice came so unexpectedly that Leah jumped. Her head shot around, eyes wide as they met his. "Leah Gates."

"You're a friend of Victoria's?"

"Yes."

He shifted his gaze to the flames. Only when she had absorbed the dismissal and turned back to the fire herself did he look at her again.

Leah Gates. A friend of Victoria's. His mind conjured up several possibilities, none of which was entirely reassuring. She could indeed be a friend of Victoria's, an acquaintance who'd somehow learned of his existence and had decided, for whatever her reasons, to seek him out. On the other hand she could be lying outright, using Victoria's name to get the story that no one else had been able to get. Or she could be telling the truth, which left the monumental question of why Victoria would have sent her to him.

Only two facts were clear. The first was that he was stuck with her; she wasn't going anywhere for a while. The second was that she'd been through a minor ordeal getting here and that, even as she sat before the fire, she'd begun to tremble again.

Pushing himself from the sofa, he went for the spare quilt that lay neatly folded on the end of the bed. He shook it out as he returned to the fire, then draped it lightly over her shoulders. She sent him a brief but silent word of thanks before tugging it closely around her.

This time when he sank onto the sofa it was with a vague sense of satisfaction. He ignored it at first, but it lingered, and at length he deigned to consider it. He'd never been one to give. His life—that life—had been ruled by selfishness and egotism. That as small a gesture as offering a quilt should please him was interesting . . . encouraging . . . puzzling.

As the evening passed, the only sounds in the cabin were the crackle of the fire and the echo of the rain. From time to time Garrick added another log to the grate, and after a bit, Leah curled onto her side beneath the quilt. He knew the very moment she fell asleep, for the fingers that clutched the quilt so tightly relaxed and her breathing grew steady.

Watching her sleep, he felt it again, the need to hold and be held, the need to protect. His fertile mind created a scenario in which Leah was a lost soul with no ties to the past, no plans for the future, no need beyond that of a little human warmth. It was a dream, of course, but it reflected what he hadn't glimpsed about himself until tonight. He didn't think he liked it, because it meant that something was lacking in the life he'd so painstakingly shaped for himself, but it was there, and it had a sudden and odd kind of power.

Rising silently from the sofa this time, he got down on his haunches beside her. Her face was half-hidden, so he eased the quilt down to her chin, studying features lit only by the dying embers in the hearth. She looked totally guileless; he wished he could believe that she was.

Unable to help himself, he touched the back of his fingers to her cheek. Her skin was soft and unblemished, warmed by the fire, faintly flushed. Dry now, her hair was thick. The bangs that covered her brow made her features look all the more delicate. She wasn't beautiful or sexy, but he had to give her pretty. If only he could give her innocent.

It wouldn't hurt to pretend for one night, would it?

Careful not to disturb her, he gently slid his arms beneath her and, quilt and all, carried her to his bed. When she was safely tucked into one side, he crossed to the other, stripped down to his underwear and stretched out beneath the sheets.

Lying flat on his back, he tipped his head her way. The black gloss of her hair was all he could see above the quilt, but the series of lumps beneath it suggested far more. She wasn't curvaceous. Her drenched clothes had clung to a slender body. And she wasn't heavy. He knew; he'd carried her. Still, even when she'd been covered with mud and soaked, he'd known she was a woman.

Eyes rising to the darkened rafters, he shifted once, paused, then shifted again. With each shift, he inched closer to her. He couldn't feel her warmth, couldn't smell her scent. Multiple layers of bedclothes, plus a safe twelve inches of space prevented that. But he knew she was there, and in the dark, where no one could see or know, he smiled.

LEAH AWOKE THE NEXT MORNING to the smell of fresh coffee and the sizzle of bacon. She was frowning even before she'd opened her eyes, because she didn't understand who would be in her apartment, much less making breakfast. Then the events of the day before returned to her, and her eyes flew open. Last she remembered she'd been lying in front of the fire. Now she was in a bed. But there was only one bed in Garrick's cabin.

Garrick. Her head spun around and she saw a blurred form before the stove. Moments later, with her glasses firmly in place, she confirmed the identity of that form.

It took her a minute to free herself from the cocoon of quilts and another minute to push herself up and drop her feet to the floor. In the process she was scolded by every sore muscle in her body. Gritting back a moan, she rose from the bed and limped into the bathroom.

By the time she'd washed up and combed her hair, she was contemplating sneaking back to bed. She ached all over, she looked like hell, and from the sounds of it, the rain hadn't let up. Going out in the storm, even in daylight, was a dismal thought.

But she couldn't sneak back to bed because the bed wasn't hers. And he'd seen her get up. And she had decisions to make.

Garrick had just set two plates of food on the small table, when she hesitantly approached. His keen glance took in her pale skin and the gingerliness of her movements. "Sit," he commanded, refusing to be touched. He'd had his one night of pretending and resented the fact that it had left him wanting. Now morning had come, and he needed some answers.

Leah sat—and proceeded, with no encouragement at all, to consume an indeterminate number of scrambled eggs, four rashers of bacon, two corn muffins, a large glass of orange juice and a cup of coffee. She was working on a second cup, when she realized what she'd done. Peering sheepishly over the rim of the cup, she murmured, "Sorry about that. I guess I was hungry."

"No dinner last night?"

"No dinner." It must have been close to eight o'clock when she'd finally stumbled to his door. Not once had she thought of food, even when she'd passed the stove en route to the washing machine. With an intake of breath at the memory, she started to get up. "I left my clothes in the washer—"

"They're dry." He'd switched them into the dryer after she'd fallen asleep. "All except the sweater. I hung it up. Don't think it should have been washed, being cashmere."

He'd drawled the last with a hint of sarcasm, but Leah was feeling too self-conscious to catch it. She hadn't had anyone tend to her in years. That Garrick should be doing it—a total stranger handling her clothes, her underthings—was disturbing. Even worse, he'd carried her to his bed, and she'd slept there with him. Granted, she'd been oblivious to it all, but in the light of day she was far from oblivious to the air of potent masculinity he projected. He looked unbelievably rugged, yet unconscionably civilized. Fresh from the shower, his hair was damp. In a hunter green turtleneck and tan cords that matched the color of his hair and beard, he was gorgeous.

"It was probably ruined long before I put it in the washer," she murmured breathily, then darted an awkward glance toward the window. "How long do you think the rain will last?"

"Days."

She caught his gaze and forced a laugh. "Thanks." When she saw no sign of a returning smile, her own faded. "You're serious, aren't you." It wasn't a question.

"Very."

"But I need my car."

"Where is it?"

"At Victoria's cabin."

"Why?"

"Why do I need it?" She'd have thought that would be obvious.

"Why is it at Victoria's?"

In a rush, Leah remembered how little she and Garrick had spoken the night before. "Because she was renting the cabin to me, only when I got there, I saw that it was nothing but—" She didn't finish, because Garrick was eyeing her challengingly. That, combined with the way he was sitting—leaning far back in his chair with one hand on his thigh and the other toying with his mug—evoked an illusion of menace. At least, she hoped it was only an illusion.

"You said that Victoria sent you to me," he reminded her tightly.

"That's right."

"In what context?"

The nervousness Leah was feeling caused her words to tumble out with uncharacteristic speed. "She said that if I had a problem, you'd be able to help. And I have a problem. The cabin's burned down, my car is stuck in the mud, I have to find somewhere to stay because my apartment's gone—"

"Victoria sent you to stay in the cabin," he stated, seeming to weigh the words.

Leah didn't like his tone. "Is there a problem with that?"

"Yes."

"What is it?"

He didn't blink an eye. "Victoria's cabin burned three months ago."

For a minute she said nothing. Then she asked very quietly, "What?"

"The cabin burned three months ago."

"That can't be."

"It is."

If it had been three days ago, Leah might have understood. With a stretch of the imagination, she might even have believed three weeks. After all, no one was living at the cabin. To her knowledge Garrick wasn't its caretaker. But three *months*? Surely someone would have been by during that time. "You're telling me that the cabin burned three months ago and that Victoria wasn't told?"

"I'm telling you that the cabin burned three months ago."

"Why wasn't Victoria *told*?" Leah demanded impatiently.

"She was."

Her anger rose. "I don't believe you."

Garrick was staring at her straight and hard. "I called her myself, then gave the insurance people a tour."

"Call her now. We'll see what she knows."

"I don't have a phone."

Given the other modern amenities in the cabin, Leah couldn't believe there was no phone. She looked around a little frantically for an instrument that would connect her with the outside world but saw nothing remotely resembling one. Then she remembered Victoria saying that she didn't have a phone at her cabin, either.

Why would she have said that, if she'd known that she didn't have a *cabin*?

"She didn't know about the fire," Leah insisted.

"She did."

"You're lying."

"I don't lie."

"You have to be lying," she declared, but her voice had risen in pitch. "Because if you're not, the implication is that Victoria sent me up here knowing full well that I wouldn't be able to stay. And that's preposterous."

The coffee cup began to shake in her hand. She set it on the table and wrapped her arms around her waist in a gesture Garrick had seen her make before. It suggested distress, but whether that distress was legitimate remained to be seen.

He said nothing, simply stared at the confusion that clouded her eyes.

"She wouldn't do that," Leah whispered pleadingly, wanting, needing to believe it. "For three weeks she's been listening to me—helping me—make plans. I stored all my furniture, notified the electric company, the phone company, my friends. Victoria personally gave me a set of typed directions and sat by while I read them. She wouldn't have gone to the effort—or let me go to the effort—if she'd known the cabin was useless."

Garrick, too, was finding it hard to believe, but it was Leah's story rather than Victoria's alleged behavior that evoked his skepticism. Yes, Leah looked confused, but perhaps that was part of the act. If she'd set out to find him, she'd done it. She was in his cabin, wearing his clothing, eating his food, drinking his coffee. She'd even spent the night in his bed, albeit innocently. If she wanted a scoop on Greg Reynolds, she'd positioned herself well.

"Who are you?" he asked.

Her head shot up. "I told you. Leah Gates."

"Where are you from?"

"New York."

"I don't suppose you happen to work for a newspaper," he commented, fully expecting an immediate denial. He was momentarily surprised when her eyes lit up.

"How did you know?"

He grunted.

She didn't know what to make of that, any more than she knew what to make of the fact that his lips were set tautly, almost angrily, within the confines of his beard.

"Have you seen my name?" she asked. If he was a crossword addict, as were so many of her fans, her name would have rung a bell.

"I don't read papers."

"Then you've seen one of my books?"

"You write books, too?" he barked.

His question and its tone had her thoroughly perplexed. "I compose crossword puzzles. They appear in a small weekly paper, but I've had several full books of puzzles published."

Crossword puzzles? A likely story. Still, if she was a reporter, she couldn't be an actress—which didn't explain why her words sounded so sincere. "Why were you moving up here?" he asked in a more tempered tone of voice.

"I lost my apartment and wasn't sure where to go, so Victoria suggested I rent her cabin for a while until I decided." She dropped a frowning gaze to the table as she mumbled, "It seemed like a good idea at the time."

Garrick said nothing.

In the ensuing silence, Leah reran the past few minutes of conversation in her mind. Then, slowly, her eyes rose. "You don't believe what I'm saying. Why not?"

He hadn't expected such forthrightness, and when she looked at him that way, all honesty and vulnerability, he was the one confused. He couldn't tell her the truth. After staunchly guarding his identity for four years, he wasn't about to blow it by making an accusation that revealed all.

So he lifted one shoulder in a negligent shrug. "It's not often that a woman chooses to live up here alone. I take it you are alone."

She hesitated before offering a tentative, "Yes."

Good Lord, could she have a photographer stashed somewhere about? "*Are* you?"

"Yes!"

"Then why the pause?"

Leah's eyes flashed. She wasn't used to having her integrity questioned. "When you've spent your entire life in New York, you think twice about giving a man certain information. It's instinct."

"It's distrust."

"Then we're even!"

"But you did answer me."

"Victoria said you were a friend. I trust her judgment. She even gave me a letter to deliver to you."

He extended one large hand, palm up, in invitation. The smug twist of his lips only heightened her defensiveness.

"If it were on me, you'd have had it by now," she cried. "It's in my car, along with my purse and everything else I own in the world."

"Except for your furniture," he remarked, dropping his hand back to his thigh.

She made a little sound of defeat. "Yes."

"And you can't get to your car. You may not be able to get there for days. You're stuck here with me."

Leah shook her head, willing away that prospect. It wasn't that Garrick was repulsive; indeed, the opposite was true. But while there was a side to him that was gentle and considerate, there was another more cynical side, and that frightened her. "I'll get to my car later."

"Unless the rain lets up, you're not going anywhere."

"I have to get to my car."

"How?"

"The same way I got here. If you won't drive me, I'll walk."

"It's not that I *won't* drive you, Leah," he said, using her name for the first time. "It's that I *can't*. You've arrived up here at the onset of mud season, and during mud season, no one moves. The sturdiest of vehicles is useless. The roads are impassable." Arching a brow, he stroked his bearded jaw with his knuckles. "Tell me. What was it like driving the road to Victoria's cabin last night?"

"Hell."

"And walking from Victoria's to mine?"

The look she sent him was eloquent.

"Well, it'll be worse today and even worse tomorrow. At this time of year, snow melts from the upper mountain and drains down over ground that is already thawing and soggy. When the rains come, forget it."

But Leah didn't want to. "Maybe if we walk back to the car and I get behind the wheel and you push—"

"I'm neither a bulldozer nor a tow truck, and let me tell you, I'm not even sure one of those would do the trick. I've seen off-road vehicles get stuck on roads far less steep than the ones on this hill."

"It's worth a try."

"It isn't."

"Victoria said you'd help me."

"I am. I'm offering you a place to stay."

"But I can't stay here!"

"You don't have much choice."

"You can't *want* me to stay here!"

"I don't have much choice."

With a helpless little moan, Leah rose from the table and went to stare bleakly out the window. He was right, she supposed. She didn't have much choice. She could go out in the rain and trek back to her car, but if what he said was true—and he'd certainly be in a position to know—she'd simply find herself back on his doorstep, wet, muddy, exhausted and humiliated.

This wasn't at all what she'd had in mind when she'd left New York!

3

THE CLATTER OF PANS in the sink brought Leah from her self-indulgent funk a short time later. Feeling instantly contrite, she returned to the kitchen. Garrick had already loaded the dishwasher; taking a towel, she began to dry the pans as he washed them.

They worked in silence. When the last skillet had been put away, she folded the towel and placed it neatly on the counter. "I'm sorry," she said quietly. She didn't look at Garrick, who was wiping down the sink. "I must have sounded ungrateful, and I'm not. I appreciate what you're doing." Pausing, she searched for suitably tactful words. "It's just that this isn't quite what I'd planned."

"What had you planned?"

"Sunshine and fresh air. A cabin all to myself. Plenty of time to work and read and walk in the woods. And cook—" She looked up in alarm at the thought. "I have food in the car! It'll spoil if I don't get it refrigerated!"

"It's cold outside."

"Cold enough?"

"Depends on what kind of food you have."

She would have listed off an inventory had there been any point. But there wasn't, so she simply let out a breath of resignation. He'd made it clear that she couldn't get to her car. Whatever spoiled would spoil.

Tugging the lapels of the flannel shirt more tightly around her, she sent him a pleading glance. "This is the first time I've even thought of living outside New York, and to have things go so wrong is upsetting. I still can't understand why Victoria offered me the cabin."

Garrick was beginning to entertain one particularly grating suspicion. Eyes dark, he set the dishrag aside and retreated to the living room. The sofa took his weight with multiple creaks of protest, but the protests in his mind were even louder.

Leah remained where she was for several minutes, waiting for him to speak. He was clearly upset; his brooding slouch was as much a giveaway as the low shelving of his brows. And he had a right to be upset, she told herself. No man who'd chosen to live alone on a secluded mountainside deserved to have that seclusion violated.

Studying him, taking in the power that radiated from even his idle body, she wondered why he'd chosen the life he had. He wasn't an avid conversationalist. But, then, neither was she, yet she'd functioned well in the city. He'd left it—at least, that was what she assumed, though perhaps it was an ingrained snobbishness telling her that the cultured ring to his speech and his fondness for certain luxuries were urban-born. In any case, she couldn't believe that a simple housing problem such as the one she'd faced had sent him into exile. For that matter, he didn't look as though he were in exile at all; he looked as though he were here to stay.

Leah took advantage of his continued distraction to examine the cabin in its entirety. A large, rectangular room with the fireplace and bed on opposite sides, it had a kitchen spread along part of the back wall, leaving space for the bathroom and what looked to be a closet. Large windows flanked the front door. Sandwiched between door, windows, furniture and appliances were bookshelves—a small one here, a larger one there, each and every one brimming with books.

They explained, in part, what Garrick Rodenhiser did with his time. He wasn't reading now, though. He was sitting as he'd been before, staring at the ashes in the hearth. While moments before he'd been brooding, his profile had mellowed to something she couldn't quite define. Loneliness? Sorrow? Confusion?

Or was she simply putting a name to her own feelings?

Unwilling to believe that, despite the clenching of her heart at the sight of Garrick, she looked desperately around for something to do. Her eye fell on the bed, still mussed from the night they'd spent. Crossing the room, she straightened the sheets and quilt, then folded the spare one he'd wrapped around her and set it at the foot of the bed.

What else? She scanned the cabin again, but there was little that needed attention. Everything was neat, clean, organized.

At a loss, she walked quietly to the window. The woods were gray, shrouded in fog, drenched in rain. The bleakness of the scene only emphasized the strange emptiness she felt.

Garrick's deep voice came out of the blue. "What, exactly, is your relationship to Victoria?"

Startled, Leah half turned to find herself the object of his grim scrutiny. "We're friends."

"You've said that. When did you meet?"

"Last year."

"Where?"

"The public library. Victoria was researching the aborigines of New Zealand. We literally bumped into each other."

His expression turned wry, then softened into a reluctant smile. "The aborigines of New Zealand—that does sound like Victoria. Is she going back to school in anthropology?"

"Not exactly," Leah answered, but she had to force herself to think, because his smile—lean lips curving upward between mustache and beard, the flash of even, white teeth—momentarily absorbed her. "She is, uh, she was fascinated by an article she'd read about the Maori, so she decided to visit. She was preparing for the trip when I met her."

"Did she get there?"

"To New Zealand? What do you think?"

Garrick thought yes, and his eyes said as much, but his mind returned quickly to Leah. "Why were you at the library?"

"I often work there—sometimes doing research for puzzles, sometimes just for the change of scenery."

"So you and Victoria became friends. How old are you?"

"Thirty-three."

He pushed out his lips in surprise. "I'd have given you twenty-eight or twenty-nine—" the lips straightened "—but even at thirty-three, there's quite a gap between you."

"But there isn't," Leah returned with quiet vehemence, even wonder. "That's what's so great about Victoria. She's positively. . . positively amaranthine."

"Amaranthine?"

"Unfading, undying, timeless. Her bio may list her as fifty-three, but she has the body of a forty-year-old, the mind of a thirty-year-old, the enthusiasm of a twenty-year-old and the heart of a child."

The description was one Garrick might have made, though he'd never have been able to express it as well. At the height of his career he'd been a master technician, able to deliver lines from a script with precisely the feeling the director wanted. But no amount of arrogance—and he'd had more than his share—could have made him try to write that script himself.

So Leah did know Victoria, and well. That ruled out one possible lie but left open another. Even knowing that she would compromise her friendship with Victoria, Leah might have taken it upon herself to find and interview the man who'd once been the heartthrob of every woman between the ages of sixteen and sixty-five. Every woman who watched television, that is. Did Leah watch television? Even if she'd come here in total innocence, wouldn't she recognize him?

Shifting his gaze back to the hearth, Garrick lapsed into silence once again. He was recalling how worried he'd been when he'd first arrived in New Hampshire. Each time he'd gone into town for supplies, he'd kept his head down, his eyes averted. Each time he'd waited in dread for telling whispers, tiny squeals, the thrust of pen and paper under his nose.

In fact, he'd looked different from the man who'd graced the television screens of America on a weekly basis for seven years running. His hair was longer, less perfectly styled, and he'd stopped rinsing out the sprinkles of silver that once upon a time he'd been sure would detract from his appeal.

The beard had made a difference, too, but in those early months he'd worried that sharp eyes would see through it to the jaw about which critics had raved. He'd dressed without distinction, wearing the oldest clothes he'd had. Above all, he'd prayed that the mere improbability of a onetime megastar living on a mountainside in the middle of nowhere would shield him from discovery.

With the passing of time—during which he wasn't recognized—he'd gained confidence. He made eye contact. He held his head higher.

Body language. A fascinating thing. He wasn't innocent enough to think that the recognition factor alone had determined the set of his head. No, he'd held his head higher because he felt better about himself. He was learning to live with nature, learning to provide for himself, learning to respect himself as a clean-living human being.

Buoyed by that confidence, he turned to Leah. "You've come to know Victoria well in a year. You must have spent a lot of time with her."

Leah, who'd eyed him steadily during his latest bout of silence, was more prepared for its end this time. "I did."

"Socially?"

"If you're asking whether I went to her parties, the answer is no."

"Are you married?"

"No."

"Have you ever been?" It wasn't crucial to the point of his investigation, but he was curious.

"Yes."

"Divorced?"

She nodded.

"Recently?"

"It's been final for two years."

"Do you date?"

"Do you?"

"I'm asking the questions."

"That's obvious, but I'd like to know why. I'm beginning to feel like I'm on a hot seat."

She sounded hurt. She looked hurt. Garrick surprised himself by feeling remorse, but he was too close to the answer he sought to give up. He did make an effort to soften his tone. "Bear with me. There's a point to all this."

"Mmm. To make me turn tail and run. Believe me, I would if I could. I know that you don't like the idea of a stranger invading your home, but you're a stranger to me, too, and I'm not so much an invader as a refugee, and if you think I like feeling like a refugee, you're nuts . . ." Her voice faded as her eyes began to skip around the cabin. "Paper and pencil?"

Garrick was nonplussed. "What—"

"If I don't write it down, I'll forget."

"Write what down?"

"The idea—nuts, nutty, nutty as a fruitcake, having bats in one's belfry. Perfect for a theme puzzle." She was moving her hand, simulating a scribble. "Paper?"

Bemused, Garrick cocked his head toward the kitchen. "Second drawer to the left of the sink."

Within seconds, she was jotting down the phrases she'd spoken aloud, adding several others to the list before she straightened. Tearing off the sheet, she folded it and tucked it into her breast pocket, returned the pad and pen to the drawer, then sent him a winsome smile. "Where were we?"

Garrick didn't try to fight the warm feeling that settled in his chest. "Do you do that a lot?"

"Write down ideas? Uh-huh."

"You really do make crossword puzzles?"

"You didn't believe me about that, either?"

He moved his head in a way that could have been positive, negative or sheepish. "I've never really thought about people doing it."

"Someone has to."

He considered that for a minute, uttered a quiet, "True," then withdrew into his private world again.

Wondering how long he'd be gone this time, Leah walked softly toward the bookshelf nearest her. Its shelves had a wide array of volumes, mostly works of fiction that had been on best-selling lists in recent years. The books were predominantly hardbacked, their paper sheaths worn where they'd been held. Both facts were revealing. Not only did Garrick read everything he bought, but he bought the latest and most expensive, rather than waiting for cheaper mass market editions.

He wasn't a pauper, that was for sure. Leah wondered where he got the money.

"It must be difficult" came his husky voice. "Finding the right words that will fit together, coming up with witty clues."

It took Leah a minute to realize that he was talking about crossword puzzles. She had to smile. He faded in and out, but the train of his thought ran along a continuous track. "It is a challenge," she admitted.

"I'd never be able to do it."

"That's okay. I'd never be able to lay traps, catch animals and gut them." She'd offered the words in innocence and was appalled at how critical they sounded. Turning to qualify them, she lost out to Garrick's quicker tongue.

"Is that what Victoria told you I do?"

"She said you were a trapper," Leah answered with greater deference, then added meekly, "I'm afraid the elaboration was my own."

His expression was guarded. "What else did Victoria say about me?"

"Only what I told you before—that you were a friend and could be trusted. To be honest, I was expecting someone a little—" she shifted a shoulder "—different."

He raised one eyebrow in question.

"Older. Craggier." Blushing, she looked off across the room. "When Victoria handed me that envelope, I asked her if it was a love letter."

"How do you know it wasn't?" Garrick asked evenly.

Come to think of it, Leah didn't know. She recalled Victoria saying something vague about craggy old trappers being nice, but the answer had been far from definitive. Her eyes went wide behind her glasses.

To her surprise, he chuckled. "It wasn't. We're just friends." His expression sobered. Propping his elbow on the sofa arm, he pressed his knuckles to his upper lip and mustache. Leah was preparing for another silent spell, when he murmured a muffled, "Until now."

"What do you mean?"

He dropped his hand and took a breath. "Her sending you here. It's beginning to smack of something deliberate."

Leah searched his face for further thoughts. When he didn't answer immediately, she prodded. "I'm listening."

"You said that you never went to Victoria's parties. Did you see her in other social contexts?"

"We went out to dinner often."

"As a foursome—with men?"

"No."

"Did she ever comment on that?"

"She didn't have to. I know that she has male friends, but she loved Arthur very much and has no desire to remarry. She's never at a loss for an escort when the occasion calls for it."

"How about you? *Do* you date?" he asked, repeating the question that had sparked earlier resistance.

Leah answered in a tone that was firm and final. "Not when I can help it."

He was unfazed by her resolve, because he was getting closer to his goal. "Did Victoria have anything to say about that?"

"Oh, yes. She thought I was . . . working with less than a full deck." Leah grinned at the phrase she had written down moments before, but the grin didn't last. "She was forever trying to fix me up, and I was forever refusing."

Garrick nodded and pressed his lips together, then slid farther down on the sofa, until his thick hair rose against its back. For several more minutes he was lost in thought.

Eventually he took a deep breath and raised disheartened eyes to the rafters. "That," he said, "was what I was afraid of."

Not having been privy to his thoughts, Leah didn't follow. "What do you mean?"

"She's done the same to me more than once."

"Done what?"

"Tried to fix me up." He held up a hand. "Granted, it's more difficult up here, but that didn't stop her. She's convinced that anyone who hasn't experienced what she had with Arthur is missing out on life's bounty." His eyes sought Leah's, and he hesitated for a long moment before speaking. "Do you see what I'm getting at?"

With dawning horror, Leah did see. "She did it on purpose."

"Looks that way."

"She didn't tell me about the fire, but she did tell me about you."

"Right."

Closing her eyes, Leah fought a rising anger. "She was so cavalier about my paying rent, wouldn't accept anything beforehand, told me to send her whatever I thought the place was worth."

"Clever."

"When I asked if the cabin was well equipped, her exact words were, 'When last I saw it, it was.'"

"True enough."

"No wonder she was edgy."

"Victoria? Edgy?"

"Unusual, I know, but she was. I chalked it up to a latent maternal instinct." She rolled her eyes. "Boy, was I wrong. It was guilt, pure guilt. She actually had the gall to remind me that I wouldn't have air-conditioning or a phone, the snake." Muttering the last under her breath, Leah turned her back on Garrick and crossed her arms over her breasts.

That was the moment he came to believe that everything she'd told him was the truth. Had she started to shout and pace the floor in anger, he would have wondered. That would have smelled of a script, a soap-opera reaction, lacking subtlety.

But she wasn't shouting or pacing. Her anger was betrayed only by quickened breathing and the rigidity of her stance. From the little he'd seen of her, he'd judged her to be restrained where her emotions were concerned. Her reaction now was consistent with that impression.

Strangely, Garrick's own anger was less acute than he would have expected. If he'd known beforehand what Victoria had planned, he'd have hit the roof. But he hadn't known, and Leah was already here, and there was something about her self-contained distress that tugged at his heart.

Almost before his eyes, that distress turned to mortification. Cheeks a bright red, she cast a harried glance over her shoulder.

"I'm sorry. She had no right to foist me on you."

"It wasn't your fault—"

"But you shouldn't have to be stuck with me."

"It goes two ways. You're stuck with me, too."

"I could have done worse."

"So could I."

Unsure of what to make of his agreeable tone, Leah turned back to the bookshelf. It was then that the full measure of her predicament hit her. She and Garrick had been thrust together for what Victoria had intended to be a romantic spell. But if Victoria had hoped for love at first sight, she was going to be disappointed. Leah didn't believe in love at first sight. She wasn't even sure if she believed in love, since it had brought her pain once before, but that was neither here nor there. She didn't know Garrick Rodenhiser. Talk of love was totally inappropriate.

Attraction at first sight—that, perhaps, was worth considering. She couldn't deny that she found Garrick physically appealing. Not even his sprawling pose could detract from his long-limbed grace. His face, his beard, the sturdiness of his shoulders spoke of ruggedness; she'd have had to be blind not to see it, and dead not to respond.

And that other attraction—the one spawned by the deep, inner feelings that occasionally escaped from his eyes? It baffled her.

"I didn't want this," she murmured to her knotted hands.

From the silence came a quiet, "I know."

"I feel . . . you must feel . . . humiliated."

"A little awkward. That's all."

"Here I am in your underwear . . ."

"You can get dressed if you want."

It was, of course, the wise thing to do. Perhaps, once she was wearing her own clothes again, she'd feel less vulnerable, less exposed. . . .

Crossing to the dryer, she removed her things and folded them over the crook of her elbow. When she reached for her sweater, though, she found it still damp.

"Here." Garrick stood directly behind her, holding out one of his own sweaters. "Clean and dry."

She accepted it with a quiet thanks and made her escape to the bathroom. He was working at the fireplace when she came out. She suddenly realized that though the fire had gone out during the night, the cabin had stayed warm.

"How do you manage for heat and electricity?" she asked, bracing her hands on the back of the sofa.

He added a final log to the arrangement and reached for a match. "There's a generator out back."

"And food? If you can't get to the store in this weather..."

"I stocked up last week." Sitting back on his heels, he watched the flames take hold. "Anyone who's lived through mud season once knows to be prepared. The freezer is full, and the cabinets. I picked up more fresh stuff a couple of days ago, but I'm afraid the bacon we had for breakfast is the last of it for a while."

He'd have had some left for tomorrow if he hadn't had to share. Leah's feelings of guilt remained unexpressed, though; there was nothing more boring than a person who constantly apologized.

Garrick stood and turned to face her, then wished he hadn't. She was wearing his sweater. It was far too large for her, of course, and she'd rolled the sleeves to a proper length, but the way it fell around her shoulders and breasts was far more suggestive than he'd have dreamed. She looked adorable. And unsure.

He gestured toward the sofa. With a tight smile, she took possession of a corner cushion, drew up her knees and tucked her feet beneath her. That was when he caught sight of the tear in her slacks.

"How's the leg?"

"Okay."

"Did you change the dressing?"

"No."

"Have you looked under it?"

"I'd be able to see if something was oozing through the gauze. Nothing is."

She hadn't looked, he decided. Either she was squeamish, or the gash didn't bother her enough to warrant attention. He wanted to know which it was.

Facing her on the sofa, he eased back the torn knit of her slacks.

"It's fine. Really."

But he was quickly tugging at the adhesive and, less quickly, lifting the gauze. "Doesn't look fine," he muttered. "I'll bet it hurts like hell." With cautious fingertips he probed the angry flesh around the wound. Leah's soft intake of breath confirmed his guess. "It probably should have been stitched, but the nearest hospital's sixty miles away. We wouldn't have made it off the mountain."

"It's not bleeding. It'll be okay."

"You'll have a scar."

"What's one more scar."

He met her eyes. "You have others?"

Oh, yes, but only one was visible to the naked eye. "I had my appendix out when I was twelve."

He imagined the way her stomach would be, smooth and soft, warm, touchable. When the blood that flowed through his veins grew warmer, he tried to imagine an ugly line marring that flesh, but couldn't. Nor, at that moment, could he tear his eyes from hers.

Pain and loneliness. That was what he saw. She blinked once, as though to will the feelings away, but they remained, swelling against her self-restraint.

He saw, heard, felt. He wanted to ask her, to tell her, to share the pain and ease the burden. He wanted to reach out.

But he didn't.

Instead, he rose quickly and strode off, returning moments later with a tube of ointment and fresh bandages. When he'd dressed the injury to his satisfaction, he replaced the first-aid supplies in the cupboard, took a down vest, then a hooded rain jacket from the closet, stepped into a pair of crusty work boots and went out into the storm.

Leah stared after him, belatedly aware that she was trembling. She didn't understand what had happened just then, any more than she'd understood it when it had happened the night before. His eyes had reflected every one of her emotions. Could he know what she felt?

On a more mundane level, she was puzzled by his abrupt departure, mystified as to where he'd be going in the rain. A short time later she had an answer when a distinct and easily recognizable sound joined that of the steady patter on the roof. She went to the window and peered out. He was across the clearing, chopping wood beneath the shelter of a primitive lean-to.

Smiling at the image of the outdoorsman at work, she returned to the sofa. While she directed her eyes to the fire, though, she wasn't as successful with her thoughts. She was wondering how the hands of a woodsman, hands that were callused, fingers that were long and blunt, could be as gentle as they'd been. Richard had never touched her that way, though as her husband, he'd touched her far more intimately.

But there was touching and there was touching, one merely physical, the other emotional, as well. There was something about Garrick . . . something about Garrick . . .

Unsettled by her inability to find answers to the myriad of questions, she sought diversion in one of the books she'd seen on the shelf. Sheer determination had her surprisingly engrossed in the story when Garrick returned sometime later.

Arms piled high with split logs, he blindly kicked off his boots at the door, deposited the wood in a basket by the hearth, threw back his hood and unbuckled his jacket.

Leah didn't have to ask if the rain had let up. The boots he'd left by the door were covered with mud; his jacket dripped as he shrugged it off.

She returned to her book.

He took up one of his own and sat down.

Briefly she felt the chill he'd brought in. It touched her face, her arm, her leg on the side nearest to him. The fire was warm, though, and the chill soon dissipated.

She read on.

"Do you like it?" he asked after a time.

"It's very well written."

He nodded at that and lowered his eyes to his own book.

Leah had turned several pages before realizing that he hadn't turned a one. Yet he was concentrating on something....

Craning her neck, she tried to reach the running head at the top of the page. She was beginning to wonder whether she needed a new eyeglass prescription, when he spoke.

"It's Latin."

She smiled. "You're kidding."

"No."

"Are you a Latin scholar?"

"Not yet."

"You're a novice."

"Uh-huh."

Reluctant to disturb him, she returned to her own corner. Studying Latin? That was odd for a trapper, not so odd for a man with a very different past. She would have liked to ask about that past, but she didn't see how she could. He wasn't encouraging conversation. It was bad enough that she was here. The more unobtrusive she was, the better.

Delving into her own book again, she'd read several chapters, when his voice broke the silence.

"Hungry?"

Now that he'd mentioned it . . . "A little."

"Want some lunch?"

"If I can make it."

"You can't." It was his house, his refrigerator, his food. Given the doubts he'd had about himself since Leah had arrived, he needed to feel in command of something. "Does that mean you won't eat?"

She grimaced. "Got myself into a corner with that one, didn't I?"

"Uh-huh."

"I'll eat."

Trying his best not to smile, Garrick set down his book and went to make lunch. Despite the time he'd spent at the woodshed, he was still annoyed with Victoria. It was difficult, though, to be annoyed with Leah. She was as innocent a pawn in Victoria's game as he was, and, apparently, as uncomfortable about it. But she was a good sport. She conducted herself with dignity. He respected that.

None of the women he'd known in the past would have acceded to as untenable a situation with such grace. Linda Prince would have been livid at the thought of someone isolating her in a secluded cabin. Mona Weston would have been frantic without a direct phone line to her agent. Darcy Hogan would have ransacked his drawers in search of a flattering garment to display her goods. Heather Kane would have screamed at him to stop the rain.

Leah Gates had taken the sweater he offered with gratitude, had found herself a book to read and was keeping to herself.

Which made him all the more curious about her. He wondered what had happened to her marriage and why she didn't date now. He wondered whether she had family, or dreams for the future. He wondered whether the loneliness he saw in her eyes from time to time had to do with the loneliness of this mountainside. Somehow he didn't think so. Somehow he thought the loneliness went deeper. He felt it himself.

Lunch consisted of ham-and-cheese sandwiches on rye. Leah didn't go scurrying for a knife to cut hers in two. She didn't complain about the liberal helping of mayonnaise he'd smeared on out of habit, or about the lettuce and tomato that added bulk and made for a certain sloppiness. She finished every drop of the milk he'd poured without making inane cracks about growing boys and girls or the need for calcium or the marvel of cows. When she'd finished eating, she simply carried both of their plates to the sink, rinsed them and put them in the dishwasher, then returned to the sofa to read.

Midway through a very quiet afternoon, Garrick wasn't concentrating on Latin. He was still thinking of the woman curled in the opposite corner of the sofa. Her legs were tucked beneath her and the book remained open on her lap, but her head had fallen into the crook of the sofa's winged back, and she was sleeping. Silently. Sweetly.

He felt sorry for her. The trip she'd made yesterday—first the drive from New York, then the harrowing hike to his cabin—had exhausted her. He felt a moment's renewed anger toward Victoria for having put her through that ordeal, then realized that Victoria was probably as ignorant of mud season as any other nonnative. Now that he thought of it, she had only been up to the cabin in the best of weather—late spring, summer, early fall.

They'd met for the first time during one of those summer trips, and even then, barely knowing her, he'd asked her why she came at all. She was obviously a city person. She didn't hunt, didn't hike, didn't plant vegetables in a garden behind the cabin. He remembered her response as clearly as if she'd made it yesterday. She had looked him in the eye and told him that the cabin made her feel closer to Arthur. No apology. No bid for sympathy. Just an honest, heartfelt statement of fact that had established the basis of strength and sincerity on which their relationship had bloomed.

Of course, she hadn't been particularly honest in sending Leah to stay in a cabin that didn't exist. He had no doubt, though, that she'd been well-meaning in her desire to get Leah and him together. What puzzled him, irked him, was that she should have known better. He'd fought her in the past. He thought he'd told her enough about himself and his feelings to make himself clear. Why would she think things had changed?

Once upon a time he'd been a city man. He'd lived high and wild. The only things he'd feared in the world had been obscurity and anonymity. Ironically, that very fear had driven him higher and wilder, until he'd destroyed his career and very nearly himself in the process. That was when he'd retreated from the world and sought haven in New Hampshire.

Now he feared everything he'd once prized so dearly. He feared fame because it was fleeting. He feared glory because it was shallow. He feared aggressive crowds because they brought out the worst in human nature, the need for supremacy and domination even on the most mundane of levels.

He'd had it up to his eyeballs with competition. Even after being away from it for four years, he remembered with vile clarity that feeling of itching under the skin, of not being able to sit still and relax for fear someone would overtake him. He couldn't bear the thought of having to be quicker, cruder, more cutthroat than the next. He didn't want to have to worry about how he looked or how he smelled. He didn't want to have to see those younger, more eager actors waiting smugly in the wings for him to falter. And he didn't want the women, clinging like spiders, feeding off him until a sweeter fly came along.

Oh, yes, he knew what he didn't want. He'd made a deliberate intellectual decision when he'd left California. The world of glitz and glamour was behind him, as was the way of life that had had him clawing his way up a swaying ladder. The life he lived here was free of all that. It was simple. It was clean. It was comfortable. It was what he *did* want.

Why, then, did he feel threatened by Leah's presence?

He blinked and realized that she was waking. Rolling slightly, she stretched one leg until the sole of her foot touched his thigh. He felt its warmth and the slight pressure behind it. He saw the way one hand dropped limply to her belly. He watched her turn her head, as though trying to identify the nature of her pillow, then open her eyes with the realization of where she was.

She looked at him. He didn't blink. Slowly, carefully, she drew back her leg and, pushing herself into a seated position, picked up her book and lowered her eyes.

Leah did pose a threat to him, but it wasn't the immediate one of disturbing his peace. She was peaceful herself, quiet, undemanding. No, the threat wasn't a physical one. It was deeply emotional. He looked at her and saw human warmth and companionship—which were the very two things his life lacked. He'd thought he could live without them. Now, for the first time, he wondered.

Leah, too, was pensive. Silently setting her book aside, she went to the window. Rain fell as hard as ever from an endless cloud mass that was heavy and gray. She figured that the rain would last at least through the rest of the day. But even when it stopped—if she'd interpreted Garrick correctly—she wouldn't be immediately on her way. There was the mud to contend with, and if this was mud season, it was possible she'd be here for a while.

Propping her elbows on the window sash, she cupped her chin in her palms and stared out. She could have done worse, she'd told him, and indeed it was so. Garrick Rodenhiser was an easy cabin mate. She was reading, much as she did at home. If she had her dictionaries and thesauruses with her, she could be working much as she did at home. If his pattern of activity on this day was any indication, they could each do their own thing without bothering the other.

The only problem was that he made her think of things she didn't think of when she was at home. He made her think of things she hadn't thought about for years.

Nine years, to be exact. She'd been twenty-four and a graduate student in English when she'd met and married Richard Gates. She'd had dreams then of love and happiness, and she'd been sure that Richard shared them. He was twenty-six when they married and was getting settled in the business world. Or so she'd thought. All too quickly she'd learned that there was nothing "settled" about Richard's view of business. He was on his way to the top, he said, and to get there meant a certain amount of scrambling. It meant temporarily sacrificing a leisurely home life, he said. It meant long days at the office and business trips and parties. Somewhere along the way, love and happiness had been forgotten.

She'd completed her degree but had given up thought of teaching, of course. A working wife hadn't fit into Richard's concept of the corporate life-style. Out of sheer desperation, she'd begun to create crosswords, then had found that she did it well, that she loved it and that there was a ready market for what she composed. Having a career that was part-time and flexible eased some of the frustration she felt.

Perhaps it would have been different if the babies she'd carried had lived. Somehow she doubted it. Richard would have continued on with the work he adored, the business trips and the parties. And why not? He was good at it. There was a charismatic quality to him that drew people right and left. Even aside from the issue of children, she and Richard were in different leagues.

Now, though, she was thinking of love and happiness. She was thinking of the life she'd lived in New York since the divorce. It had seemed fine and comfortable and rewarding . . . until now.

Garrick affected her. He made her think that there had been something wrong with that single life in New York because it was . . . single. Seeing him, sitting with him, being touched by those hazel and silver eyes, she sensed what she'd missed. He made her feel lonely. He made her ache for something more than what she'd had.

Was it because she was in a strange place? Was it because her life had been turned upside down? Was it because she didn't know where she was going from here?

He made her think of the future. Yes, she'd probably go back to New York, search for and find another apartment. She'd work; she'd visit friends; she'd go to restaurants and museums and parks. She'd do what she'd always found so comfortable. Why, then, did there seem a certain emptiness to it?

With a sigh of confusion, she returned to the sofa and her book, though she read precious little in the hours that passed. From time to time she felt Garrick's eyes on her. From time to time she looked at him. His presence was both comfort and torment.

He made her feel less alone because he was there, because he'd help her, she knew, if something happened. He made her feel more alone because he was there, because the power of his quiet presence reminded her of everything she'd once wanted and needed.

Garrick went out again late in the afternoon. This time Leah had no clue to his purpose. She wandered around the cabin while he was gone, feeling a restlessness that she couldn't explain any more than she could those other feelings she'd glimpsed.

When he returned, he started making dinner. Once again he refused her offer of help. They ate in silence, occasionally glancing at each other, always looking away when their eyes met. After they'd finished, they returned to the fire. This time, despite the fact that she was without resource books, Leah worked with pad and pencil, sketching out simple puzzles. Garrick whittled.

She wondered where he'd learned to whittle, how he did it, what he was making—but she didn't ask.

He wondered where she started a puzzle, how she got the words to mesh, what she did at an impasse—but he didn't ask.

By ten o'clock she was feeling tired and frustrated and distinctly out of sorts. Crumpling up a piece of paper, on which she'd created nothing worth saving, she tossed it into the dying fire, then took a shower, put on the long underwear that seemed as good a pair of pajamas as any and climbed onto the same side of the bed where she'd slept the night before.

By ten-thirty, Garrick was feeling tired and frustrated and distinctly out of sorts. Flipping his piece of wood, out of which he'd whittled nothing worth saving, into the nearly dead fire, he turned off the lights, stripped down to his underwear and climbed onto his own side of the bed.

He lay on his back, wide-awake. He thought of L.A. and the day, several months before he'd left, that he'd finally tracked down his agent. Timothy Wilder had been avoiding him. Phone calls had gone unanswered; each time Garrick had shown up at his office, Wilder had been "out." But Garrick had finally located him on the set of a TV movie, where another of Wilder's clients was at work. It hadn't done Garrick any good. Wilder had barely acknowledged him. The director and crew, many of whom he'd worked with in the past, couldn't have been bothered asking how he was. Wilder's client, the star of the show, hadn't given him so much as a glance. And the woman who, six months before, had sworn she adored Garrick, turned her back and walked away. He'd never felt so alone in his life.

Leah, too, lay on her back, wide-awake. She thought of one of the last parties she'd gone to as Richard's wife. It had been a gala charity function, and she'd taken great care to look smashing. Richard hadn't noticed. Nor had any of the others present. For a time, Richard had towed her from group to group, but then he'd left her to exchange inanities with an eighty-year-old matron. She'd never felt so alone in her life.

Garrick shifted his legs, his gaze on the darkened rafters overhead. He thought of the days following his accident, the three long weeks he'd lain in the hospital. No one had visited. No one had sent cards or flowers. No one had called to cheer him up. Though he fully blamed himself for his downfall and knew that he didn't deserve anyone's sympathy, what he would have liked, could have used, was a little solace. A little understanding. A little encouragement. The fact that it never materialized was the final sorrow.

Leah, too, shifted slightly. She thought of the hours she'd lain in the hospital following the loss of her second child. Richard had made the obligatory visits, but she'd come to dread them, for he clearly saw her as a failure. She'd felt like one, too, and though the doctors assured her that there was nothing more she could have possibly done, she'd been distraught. Had her parents been alive, they'd have been by her side. Had she had her own friends, ones who'd cared for her more than they'd cared for appearances, she mightn't have felt so utterly empty. But her parents were dead, and her "friends" were Richard's. Sorrow had been her sole companion.

Garrick took a deep, faintly shuddering breath. He felt Leah beside him, heard the slight irregularity of her own breathing. Slowly, cautiously, he turned his head on the pillow.

The cabin was dark. He couldn't see her. But he heard a soft swish when her head turned toward his.

They lay that way for long moments. Tension strummed between them, a wire of need, vibrating, pulling. Each held back, held back, fought the magnetism drawing them together until, at last, it became too great.

It wasn't a question of one moving first. In a simultaneous turning, their bodies came together as their minds had already done. Their arms wound around each other. Their legs tangled.

And they clung to each other. Silently. Soulfully.

4

LEAH CLOSED HER EYES and greedily immersed herself in Garrick's strength. He was warm and alive, and the way he held her confirmed his own need for the closeness she so badly craved. His face was buried in her hair. His arms trembled as they crushed her to him, but not for a minute did she mind the pressure. Instead her own arms tightened around his neck, and she sighed softly in relief.

And pleasure. His body was a marvel. It was long and firm, accommodating itself to fit her perfectly. Richard had never accommodated himself to fit her either physically or emotionally. The fact that Garrick, who owed her nothing, should do so with such sweetness was a wonder she couldn't begin to analyze.

Not that she tried very hard. She was too busy absorbing the comfort he offered to think of much of anything except prolonging it. One of her legs slid deeper between his. Her fingers wound into his hair and held.

Garrick, too, was inundated with gratifying sensations. He felt Leah from head to toe and drank in her softness as though he'd lived through a drought. In a sense he had. From birth. His parents had been wonderful people, but they'd both been professionals, engrossed in their careers, and they'd had neither time nor warmth to give to their son. Had he been born with the need for physical closeness? Had he been born a toucher? If so, it explained why he'd turned to women from the time he'd had something to offer. Only that hadn't fully satisfied him, either, because even at fourteen he'd been ambitious. He'd been always angling for something bigger and better, never taking stock of what he had, never quite appreciating it.

Until now. Holding Leah Gates in his arms, he felt a measure of fullness that he'd never experienced before. He moved his hands along her spine. He rubbed his thigh against her hip. He inhaled, heightening the pressure of his chest against her breasts.

She needed him. The soft, purring sounds she made from time to time told him so. She needed him, but not because he would be a notch in her belt, or because he could further her career, or because he had money. She didn't know who he was and where he'd been, yet she still needed him. For *him*.

The moan that rumbled from his chest was one of sheer gratitude.

For a long, long time, they lay wrapped in each other's arms. Their closeness was a healing balm, blotting out memories of past pain and sorrow. Nothing existed but the present, and it was so soothing that neither would have thought to disturb it.

Ironically, what disturbed it was the very solace it brought. For with the edge taken off emptiness came a new awareness. It struck Leah gradually—a pleasantly male and musky scent filtering into her nostrils, the thick silk of hair sifting through her fingers, the swell of muscles flexing beneath her arm. On his part, Garrick grew conscious of a clean, womanly fragrance, the gentleness of the curves that his palms rounded, the heat that beckoned daringly close to his loins. . .

He hadn't been thinking of sex when he'd taken Leah in his arms. He'd simply wanted to hold her and be held back. He'd wanted, for however fleeting the moments, to binge on the nearness of another human being. But his body was insistent. His heart had begun to beat louder, his blood to course faster, his muscles to grow tighter. He'd never been hit by anything as unexpectedly—or as desperately.

He might have restrained himself if Leah hadn't begun, in wordless ways, to tell him how she wanted him, too. Her hands had slipped down his back and were furrowing beneath his thermal top, gliding upward along his flesh. Her breathing was more shallow. Her breasts swelled against him. He might have called all that simply an extension of the act of holding had it not been for the faint but definitely perceptible arching of her hips.

Or was the arching his? His lower body, with a will of its own, was pressing into her heat, then undulating slowly, then needing even more. He, too, was exploring beneath thermal, only his hands had forayed below Leah's waist and were clenching the firm flare of her bottom, holding her closer, increasing the friction, adding to a hunger that was already explosive.

He had to have her. He had to bury himself in her depths, because he needed that closeness, too, and he was frightened that he'd lose it if he waited.

With hands that shook, he pushed her bottoms to her knees. She squirmed free of them while he lowered his own. Her thigh was already lifting over his when he began his penetration, and by the time he was fully sheathed, she was digging her fingers into his back and sighing softly against his neck.

It was fast and mutual. He stroked deeply and with growing speed. She matched each stroke in pace and ardor. He gasped and quivered. She gulped and shivered. Then they surged against each other a final time, and their bodies erupted into simultaneous spasms. Totally earth-shattering. Endlessly fulfilling. Warm and wet and wonderful.

Garrick's heart thundered long after. His breath came in ragged pants that would have embarrassed him had not Leah been equally as winded. He thought about withdrawing, then thought again, reluctant to leave her when he felt so incredibly contained and content. So he stayed where he was until he began to fear that he was hurting her. But when he made to move away, she clutched him tighter.

"Don't go!" she whispered.

They were the sweetest after-love words he'd ever heard. Not only did they tell him that she savored the continuing contact, they also said something about her feelings toward what they'd just shared.

They reassured him, too. He hadn't performed in a particularly skillful way. He hadn't coaxed her, caressed her, teased her into a state of arousal. He hadn't spoken. He hadn't even kissed her. But she'd been ready.

Because she'd needed him. Because she hadn't had a man in a long time. Because it had been more than sex. And because she, too, had felt its uniqueness.

He didn't say anything when he felt the tremors in her body and realized that she was crying. He spoke with his hands, curving one around her neck to keep her pressed close, using the other to gently stroke her hair. He knew why she was crying, and he felt it, too. But he felt more—a protectiveness that kept his movements steady and soothing until, at length, she cried herself to sleep. Only then did he close his eyes as well.

CONSCIOUSNESS CAME SLOWLY to Leah the next morning. She was first aware of being delightfully warm. Drawing her knees closer, she snuggled beneath the thick quilt. With a lazy yawn, she discovered that she felt rested. And satisfied. Her limbs were relaxed, almost languid, but there was a fullness inside that hadn't been there before.

Then she realized that she was wearing nothing from the waist down, and her eyes opened.

Garrick was sitting on the side of the bed. On her side. He was fully dressed. And he was watching her.

Not quite sure what to say, she simply looked at him.

Gently and with a slight hesitance, he smoothed a strand of dark hair from her cheek and tucked it behind her ear. "Are you okay?"

She nodded.

His voice dropped to a whisper. "I didn't hurt you?"

She shook her head.

"Any regrets?"

She spoke as softly as he had. "No."

"I'm glad." His hand fell back to the quilt. "Hungry?"

"Famished."

"Could you eat some pancakes?"

"Very easily."

A tiny smile broke out on his face. She would have reached for her glasses to better see and enjoy it, but she didn't want to move an inch.

"How 'bout I make a double batch while you get dressed?"

"Sounds fair."

He squeezed her shoulder lightly through the quilt before leaving to fulfill his half of the bargain. Only when she heard busy sounds coming from the kitchen did she pay heed to her half. Rooting around between the sheets, she found and managed to struggle into her thermal bottoms. Once in the bathroom, she showered and dressed, then returned to the main room, where Garrick was adding the last of the pancakes to high stacks on each of two plates.

"Real syrup," she observed after she'd sat down. "This is a luxury."

He watched her dribble it sparingly atop the pancakes, then ordered quietly, "More."

"But it's too good to waste."

"There's no waste if you enjoy it. Besides, this is last year's batch. The new stuff will be along in another month."

Leah turned the plastic container in her hand. It had no label. "Is this local?"

"Very."

"You made it yourself?"

He shook his head. "I don't have the equipment."

"I thought all you had to do was to stick a little spigot in a tree."

"That's true, in a sense. But if you stick one little spigot in one tree, then take the sap you get and boil it down into syrup, you get just about enough to sprinkle on a single pancake."

"Oh."

"Exactly. What you have to do is tap many trees, preferably have long hoses carrying the sap directly to a sugar house, then boil it all in huge vats. There are many people in the area who do it that way. I get my syrup from a family that lives on the other side of town."

"Do they make syrup for a living?"

"They earn some money from it, but not enough to support them. The season's pretty limited."

She nodded in understanding, but her appreciation wasn't as much for the information as for the fact that he'd offered it willingly. Up until now they'd exchanged few words. She realized that, living alone, he wasn't used to talking. Still, while she'd been showering she'd wondered whether there would be awkward silences between them, given what had happened last night. She'd meant what she'd said; she had no regrets. But she hadn't asked him if he did.

From his relaxed manner, she guessed that he didn't, and it pleased her. Turning her attention to her pancakes, she cut off a healthy forkful. Her fork wavered just above the plate, though, and she stared at it.

"Garrick?"

His mouth was full. "Mmm?"

"I just wanted to say... I wanted to tell you... what happened last night... well, I haven't ever done anything like that before."

He swallowed what was in his mouth. "I know."

Her eyes met his. "You do?"

"You were tight. You haven't made love in a long time. Not since your divorce?"

Cheeks pink, she shook her head in affirmation. "I wanted to make sure you knew. I didn't want you to get the wrong impression. I mean, I don't regret for a minute what we did, but I'm not the kind of woman who just jumps into bed with a man."

"I know—"

"But I wasn't sex starved—"

"I know—"

"And it wasn't just because you were there—"

"I know—"

"Because I don't believe in casual affairs—"

"I know—"

Setting down her fork, she curved her fingers against her bangs. "This is coming out wrong. Now it sounds as though I'm rigidly principled and expect something from you, but that isn't it at all."

"I know. Leah? If you don't eat, the pancakes will get cold."

"I'm not a prude *or* a sex fiend. It's just that last night I needed you—"

"Leah..." He focused pointedly on her plate.

She gave up trying to explain and set to eating. All she could do was hope that he'd understood what she'd been trying to say. She cared what he thought of her, and though part of her was sure he'd known what she'd been feeling last night another part was less confident.

Confidence was something she lacked where relationships with men were concerned. She'd thought she'd known what Richard had wanted, and she'd been wrong. But that was only one of the reasons she'd avoided men since her divorce.

She avoided them because she was independent for the first time in her life and was enjoying it. She avoided them because she always had and always would detest the dating ritual. She avoided them because none of the men she met sparked the slightest romantic interest. And she avoided them because she had a fair idea of what a man had in mind when he asked out a thirty-three-year-old divorcée.

Yes, she cared about what Garrick thought of her, but before that—and more so now than ever—she cared what she thought about herself. She wasn't a tramp. She wasn't out for gratuitous sex. She liked to think of herself as a woman of pride, a selective woman. She liked to think that when she did something, she did it with good reason.

That had been the case in bed last night. From the first she'd felt an affinity for Garrick. Above and beyond what Victoria had said, her instincts had told her much about the kind of man he was. He wasn't a playboy. Just as he'd known she hadn't made love in a while, she knew the same about him. There was nothing in his cabin—no leftover lingerie, no perfume or errant earrings stuck in a corner of the medicine chest—to suggest that he'd had a woman here. The urgency with which he'd entered her and so quickly climaxed was telling.

Indefinite periods of celibacy notwithstanding, he was all man, ruggedness incarnate. From the way his sandy-gray hair fell randomly over his brow, to the way his beard grew, to his pantherlike gait, to his capacity for chopping and carting wood, he was the kind of macho hero too often limited to the silver screen.

Macho ended, though, with his looks and carriage. He was a three-dimensional man, capable of gentleness and consideration. Those qualities were the ones that had gotten to her first. They were, ironically, the ones that had evoked such a tremendous surge of emotion within her—emotion that had, in the final analysis, been the reason she'd made love with him.

It hadn't been simply because he was there. If he'd been cruel or unfeeling, repulsive either physically or emotionally, she'd never have climbed into his bed, much less made love with him, regardless of the depth of her need. No, she'd sought comfort from him because he was Garrick. He was a man she could probably love, given the inclination and time.

Of course, she had neither, and thought of the time brought her back to the present. Swishing the last piece of pancake around in the remaining drops of syrup, she brought it to her mouth and ate it, then put down her fork and looked toward the window.

"It's still raining, isn't it?" She'd gotten so used to the sound on the roof that she practically didn't hear it.

Garrick, who'd finished well before her, had his chair braced back on its rear legs. He was nursing the last of his coffee. "Uh-huh."

"No sign of a letup?"

"Nope."

It occurred to her that she wasn't as disappointed about that as she might have been, and she felt guilty. Despite all that had happened, she was still imposing on Garrick. "No hope of getting to my car?" she forced herself to ask.

He shrugged. The front legs of his chair met the floor with a soft thud, and he stood, gathering the dishes together. "I was thinking of making a try later. You'd probably like some other clothes."

He hadn't said anything about freeing the car or getting rid of her. She smiled and, looking down, plucked at the voluminous folds of his sweater. "I don't know. I'm beginning to get used to this. It's comfortable."

Garrick wasn't sure he'd ever get used to how great she looked. When he'd first seen her in it, he'd thought she looked adorable. Now, having had the intense pleasure of being inside her, he thought she looked sexy. That went for the way she looked in his thermal long johns, too. He hadn't thought so at first, but he'd changed his mind, and his body wasn't about to let him change it back.

Taking refuge at the sink, he began to clean up with more energy than was strictly necessary. It helped. By the time he was done, he had his libido in check. He didn't want to frighten Leah or act as though she should pay for her keep by satisfying his every urge. And it wasn't as if his every urge *was* for sex, though after last night, he had a greater inclination toward it than he had in years.

Last night...last night had been very, very special. It was sex, but it wasn't. It was so much an emotional act, rather than a physical one, that he didn't have the words to describe it. Yes, if there were to be a repeat, the emotional element would be present, but he knew that there'd be more. He knew that this time he'd want to touch her and kiss her. This time he'd want to explore her body and get to know it as completely as, in some ways, he felt he knew her soul. Her mind, ah, that was another matter. He wanted to get to know it, too, but...probably that wasn't wise. When the ground dried up, she'd be leaving. He didn't want to miss her.

Which was why he reverted into the silence with which he'd grown increasingly comfortable over four years' time. He didn't ask her any of the million questions he had. He told himself he didn't want to know the details of what made Leah Gates tick. If he didn't know it would be easier to pretend that she was shallow and boring. Easier to tell himself, when she was gone, that he was better off without her.

Leah spent the morning much as she had her waking hours the day before. She finished one book and started another. She made frequent notes on a pad of paper when she encountered a word or concept in her reading that would translate into a crossword. She doodled out nonsense puzzles, but the puzzle that commanded her real interest was Garrick.

He was an enigma. She knew that they had at least one need in common, and she knew, in general, the type of man he was. The specifics of his day-to-day life, though, were a mystery, as was his past.

Mentally she'd outlined a crossword puzzle. Garrick's name was blocked in, as were certain other facts pertaining to their relationship, but she needed more information if she hoped to find the words to complete the grid.

It was late morning. They were each sitting in what she'd come to think of as their own little corner of the sofa. Garrick had gone outside for a while, though not to the car, he'd told her when she'd asked. He hadn't elaborated further, and she'd been loath to press. It was his home. He was free to come and go as he pleased. She couldn't help but be curious, though, particularly when he returned after no more than thirty minutes.

After letting him dry off and settle in with his book for a while, she ventured to satisfy her curiosity.

"I hope I'm not keeping you from doing things."

"You're not."

"What would you be doing if I weren't here?"

"On a day like this, not much of anything."

Which was precisely what he was doing now, he mused a tad wryly. He'd gone to the back shed, thinking that working with toothpicks and glue, making progress on the model home he'd been commissioned to make, would be therapeutic. But if the therapy had been intended to take his mind off Leah, it had failed. Even the book that lay open on his lap—a novel he'd purchased the week before—failed to capture him.

Leah broke into his thoughts. "And if it weren't raining?"

"I'd be outside."

"Trapping?"

He shrugged.

"Victoria said you were a trapper."

"I am, but the best part of the trapping season's over for the year."

She let that statement sink in, but it raised more questions than it answered. So a while later, she tried again.

"What do you trap?"

He was crouching before the fire, adding another log to the flames. "Fisher, fox, raccoon."

"You sell the furs?"

He hesitated, wondering if Leah was the crusader type who'd lecture him about the evils of killing animals to provide luxury items for rich people. He decided that there was only one way to find out.

"That's right."

"I've never owned a fur coat."

"Why not?" He turned on his haunches, waiting for the lecture.

"They're too expensive, for one thing. Richard—my ex-husband—thought I should have one, but I kept putting him off. If you walk into a restaurant with a fur, either you're afraid to check it in case it gets stolen, or the management refuses to *let* you check it. In either case, you have to spend the evening worrying about whether your *fruits de mer au chardonnay* will spatter. Besides, I've always thought fur coats to be too showy. And they're heavy. I don't want that kind of weight on my shoulders."

It wasn't quite the answer Garrick had feared, but it was a fearful one nonetheless, for it had given him a glimpse of her life—at least, the one she'd had when she'd been married. Her husband had apparently been well-to-do. They'd gone to fine French restaurants and had kept company with women who *did* worry about spattering sauce on their furs. If he could tell himself that Leah was as turned off by that kind of life-style as he was, he'd feel better. He'd also feel worse, because he'd like her even more.

"I see your point" was all he said, returning to the sofa and lowering his eyes to his book in hopes of ending the conversation. Leah took the hint and said nothing more, but *that* bothered him. If she'd pushed, he might have had something to hold against her. He hated pushy women, and Lord, had he known his share.

Lunchtime came. Halfway through her bologna sandwich, Leah set it down gently. "Did I offend you?"

"Excuse me?"

"When I said that I didn't like fur coats?"

He'd been deep in his own musings, which had gone far beyond fur coats. It took him a minute to return. "You didn't offend me. I don't like them, either."

"No?"

He shook his head.

"Doesn't that take some of the pleasure out of your work?"

"How so?"

"Having someone turn the product of your hard work into something you don't like? I know I'd be devastated if someone used my page of the paper to wrap fish."

"Does anyone?"

"I've never witnessed it personally, but I'm sure it's been done more than once."

"If you did see it, what would you do?"

She considered for a minute, then gave a half shrug. "Rationalize, I suppose."

"How?"

"I'd tell myself that I enjoyed creating the puzzle and that I was paid for it, but that . . . that's the end of my involvement. If it gives someone pleasure to wrap fish in my puzzle—" she hesitated, hating to say the next but knowing she had to "—so be it."

He grinned.

She winced, then murmured sheepishly, "If it gives someone pleasure to wear a fur coat, so be it. . . ." She tucked her hair behind her ear. "Do you enjoy trapping?"

"Yes."

"Why?"

"It takes skill."

"You like the challenge."

"Yes."

"Where did you learn how to do it?"

"A trapper taught me." He stood and reached across the table for her plate. "All done?"

She nodded. "A local trapper?"

"He's dead now." Stacking the plates together, balancing glasses and flatware on top, he carried the lot to the sink.

"I thought I'd make a stab at reaching your car. If you tell me what you want, I'll bring back as much as I can."

She rose quickly. "I'll come with you."

"No."

"Two pairs of hands are better than one."

He turned to face her. "Not in this case. If I have to hold you with one arm, I'll have only one left for your things."

"You won't have to hold me."

"Come on, Leah. You've been through that muck once. You know how treacherous it is."

She approached the sink, intent on making her point. "But that was at night. I couldn't see. I didn't know where I was going. My shoes weren't the greatest—"

"What shoes would you wear now?"

"Yours. You must have an old pair of boots lying around."

"Sure. Size twelve."

She was standing directly before him, her face bright with hope. "I could pad them with wool socks."

"You could also pack your feet in cement and try to move, because that's pretty much what it would be like."

"I could do it, Garrick."

"Not fast enough. In case you've forgotten, it's raining out there. The idea is to make the round trip as quickly as possible."

"How long can it take to dash a mile?"

"A mile?" He laughed. "Is that how far you thought you'd gone?"

"It took me forever," she reasoned defensively, then quickly added, "but that was because it was dark and I kept falling."

"Well, it's light now, but you'll fall anyway, because it's slippery as hell out there. I'm used to it." He brushed a forefinger along his mustache. "By the way, Victoria's cabin is just about a third of a mile from here."

"A *third*—" she began in amazement, then turned embarrassment into optimism. "But that's *nothing*. I'll be able to do it."

Garrick looked down at her. Her head was tipped back, her brows arched high in hope. He found himself caught, enchanted by the gentle color on her cheeks, taunted by her moist, slightly parted lips. He wanted to kiss her just then, wanted it so suddenly and so badly that he knew he couldn't do it. He'd bruise her. He'd be settling an argument in the sexist way he'd used in the past but detested now. Worse, he'd be showing a decided lack of control.

Control was what his new life was about. Self-control. No drinking, no smoking, no carousing. No impulsive kisses.

Instead of lowering his mouth to hers, he raised his hands to her shoulders and held them lightly. "I'd rather you stay here, Leah. For your own safety and comfort, if nothing else."

Had he said it any other way or offered any other reason, Leah probably would have continued to argue. But his voice had been like smooth sand in the sun, fine grains of warmth entering her, quieting her, and his expression of concern was new and welcome.

Sucking on her upper lip, she stepped back, then forward again, this time around his large frame. She gave him a gentle nudge at the back of his waist. "Go. I'll clean up."

"You'll have to tell me what you want."

"Let me think for a minute."

While she thought, he built up the fire and pulled on his rain gear. He was just finishing buckling his boots, when she handed him a list of what she'd like and where in her car he could find it. Tucking that list into the pocket of his oilskin slicker, he tugged up the hood, tipped its rim in the facsimile of a salute, then left.

A SHORT TIME LATER, sitting in the driver's seat of the Golf, Garrick drew Victoria's letter from Leah's purse. He held it, turned it, stared at the back flap. He should slit it open, but he didn't want to. He knew that he'd find an enthusiastic recommendation of Leah, and he certainly didn't need that. Leah was doing just fine on her own behalf.

Damn, Victoria!

Stuffing the letter back into the purse, he quickly collected the things Leah had requested. It was an easy task, actually. She was very organized. Her note was even funny.

> Battered Vuitton duffel (a gift, not my style) on top of no-name suitcases behind passenger's seat. Mickey Mouse bookbag, one across and two down from duffel. Large grocery sack behind driver's seat. (If sack reeks, scatter contents for animals and take black canvas tote bag, riding shotgun, instead.)

The sack didn't reek, and he was able to manage the tote, too. He felt a little foolish with a purse slung over his shoulder, but it was well hidden by the rest of the load, and besides, who would see him?

No one did see him, but as he slogged through the rain heading back toward the cabin, he grew more and more annoyed. He was peeved at Leah for being so sweet and alone and comfortable. He was put out with Victoria for having sent her to him in the first place. He was riled by the bundles he carried, for they swung against his sides and made the task of keeping his balance on the slick mud that much harder. He was irritated with the rain, which trickled up his cuffs and which, if it hadn't come at all, would have spared him the larger mess he was in.

Mostly he was angry at life for throwing him a curve when he least expected or needed it. Things had been going so well for him. He had his head straight, his priorities set. Then Leah came along, and suddenly he saw voids where he hadn't seen them before.

He wanted her with a vengeance, and that infuriated him. She was a threat to the way of life he'd worked so hard to establish, because he sensed that nothing would be the same when she left. And she would leave. She was city. She was restaurants and theater and Louis Vuitton luggage—even if it *had* been a gift. She wasn't about to fit into his life-style for long. Oh, sure, she found it a novelty now. The leisurely pace and the quiet were a break from her regular routine. But she'd be bored before long. So she'd leave. And he'd be alone again. Only this time he'd mind it.

By the time he reached the cabin he was in a dark mood. After silently depositing his load, he went out again and hiked farther up the mountain, moving quickly, ignoring the rain and cold. He felt a little more in control of himself when he finally turned and began the descent, but even then he bought extra time by going to the shed to work.

It was late when he entered the cabin. Leah had turned on the lights, and the fire was burning brightly. But it wasn't the smell of wood smoke that met him. Shrugging from his wet outerwear, he sniffed the air, then glowered toward the kitchen.

Leah was at the stove. She'd looked up when he'd stomped in, but her attention had quickly returned to whatever it was she was stirring. He didn't recognize the pan as one of his own, though he hadn't been that long from civilization not to recognize it as a wok.

"Chinese?" he warbled. "You're cooking Chinese?"

She sent him a nervous glance. "I'm trying. I just finished taking a course in it, but I haven't really done it on my own. It was one of the things I was going to play with at Victoria's cabin." What was apparently an instruction book lay open on the counter beside her, but Garrick wasn't up for marveling at Leah's industriousness.

"You mean—I was hauling Chinese groceries in that sack?"

"Among other things." Many of which she'd quickly put in the freezer, others of which were refrigerated, a few of which she'd questioned and thrown out.

"And a *wok*? I thought I was bringing you *essentials*."

She shot him a second, even more nervous glance. He was angry. She had no idea why. "You asked me to tell you what I wanted. These were some of the things."

He looked around for the other bags he'd carried, but they'd apparently been unloaded and stored—somewhere. Planting his hands on his hips, he glared at her. "What else did I cart through the rain?"

His tone was so reminiscent of the imperious one Richard had often used that Leah had to struggle not to cringe. She kept her voice steady, but it was small. "The wok. It was with my books in the Mickey Mouse bag. And some clothes." She spared a fast glance at the faded jeans she'd put on. "I threw out the torn slacks. They were hopeless." She was also wearing a pair of well-worn moccasins that had been in the duffel, but she hadn't changed out of Garrick's sweater. Now she wished she had.

"What was in the black tote? It was heavy as hell."

At that moment, Leah would have given anything to be able to lie. She'd never been good at it; her eyes gave her away. Not that lying would have done any good in this case, since he would learn the truth soon enough.

"A cassette player and tapes," she mumbled.

"A *what*?"

She looked him in the eye and said more clearly, "A cassette player and tapes."

"Oh-ho, no, you don't! You're not going to disturb my peace and quiet with raucous music!"

"It's not raucous."

"Then loud. I didn't come up here to put up with *that*."

Leah knew she should indulge him. After all, it was his cabin and he was doing her a favor by taking her in. But there'd been so much more between them that having him shout at her only raised her hackles. She'd heard enough shouting from Richard. When they divorced, she'd vowed never to be the butt of unreasonable mood swings again.

She'd thought Garrick was different.

"I'll play it softly, or not at all while you're here," she stated firmly, "but if you're gone for hours like you were today, I'll enjoy it any way I want."

"It bothered you that I left you alone, did it?" he demanded.

"It did not! You can go where you want, when you want and for however long you want. But if you're not here, I'll listen to my music. And anyway, in a few days I'll be gone." She took a shaky breath. "I may be invading your privacy, but, don't forget, if it hadn't been for you Victoria would have never sent me up here!"

That took Garrick aback. He hadn't thought of it quite that way, but Leah had a point. For that matter, Leah often had a point and it was usually reasonable. Which made him feel all the more unreasonable.

Wheeling away, he strode off to hang his wet jacket on a hook, then marched back to the dresser by the bed, yanked his turtleneck jersey and heavy wool sweater over his head in one piece, tossed them heedlessly aside and began tugging out drawers in search of a replacement.

Leah's throat went positively dry as she stared after him. All anger was forgotten in the face of his nakedness. Granted, it was only his back, but his cords hung low on his hips, presenting her with a view of skin that was breathtaking. There was nothing burly about his shoulders. They were broad, but every inch was hard flesh over corded sinew. The same was true of his arms and, for that matter, the rest of his torso. There wasn't a spare ounce of fat in sight. His spine bisected symmetrical pockets of muscle that stretched and flexed as he bent over and tore through the drawer. His waist was lean, the skin there smooth. He wasn't tanned, though she guessed that once the spring sun came he would be. He struck her as a man who'd be outside in good weather, shirtless.

Her insides burned, but jerking her eyes back to the contents of the wok, she realized with relief that that was all that had. She set the cover on the shallow pan with a hand that trembled, turned off the propane gas, then lifted the cover from a second pan, one of Garrick's, and checked the rice.

Everything was ready. The food was cooked. The table was set. And Garrick was slouched on the sofa, wearing a battered sweatshirt, taking his sour mood out on the fire.

She debated leaving him alone. She could dish out the food and sit down. Surely he'd see that dinner was on the table and join her. Or would he?

Her approach was quiet and hesitant. "Garrick?"

His mouth rested against a fist. "Mmm?"

"I'm all set. If you're hungry." She pressed her damp palms to her jeans.

"Ydnnvtmakdnnn."

"Excuse me?"

He raised his fist, but his words remained low and begrudging. "You didn't have to make dinner."

"I know."

"What is it, anyway?"

"Braised chicken with black beans."

He didn't take his eyes from the fire. "I haven't had Chinese food in four years. I've always hated it."

Feeling inexplicably hurt, Leah turned away. She wasn't all that hungry herself, all of a sudden, but she had no intention of letting her efforts go to waste. So she prepared a plate for herself, sat down and began to eat.

Out of the corner of her eye she saw Garrick rise from the sofa. He went to the stove, clattered covers and sniffed loudly. She was struggling to swallow a small cube of chicken, when she heard the distinct sounds of food being dished out. The chicken slid down more easily.

Moments later, he took his place across from her. She didn't look up but continued to eat, though she couldn't have described what she was tasting.

"Not bad," Garrick conceded. His normally raspy voice was gruffer than normal. He took another bite, chewed and swallowed. "What's in it?"

"Ginger root, bamboo shoots, scallions, oyster sauce, sherry. . ."

"Not the kind of stuff that comes in cardboard takeout containers."

"No." She took a minute to concentrate on what she was eating and, to her relief, agreed with his assessment. It was good. She had nothing to be ashamed of, and that mattered to her, where Garrick was concerned. It was the first time she'd cooked for him. As a matter of pride, she'd wanted the results to be highly palatable.

They ate in silence. More than once, Leah had to bite her tongue to keep from voicing the questions on her mind. She wanted to know why he'd been so angry, what she'd done to cause it. She wanted to know what he had against music. She wanted to know when he'd eaten Chinese food from takeout containers and why he'd developed such an aversion to it. And she wanted to know where he'd been and what he'd been doing four years ago.

He didn't offer any further conversation, though, and she didn't dare start any for fear of setting him off. She liked the Garrick who was quiet and gentle, not the one who brooded darkly, or worse, growled at her.

She had no way of knowing that, at that moment, Garrick was disliking himself. He was disgusted with the way he'd behaved earlier, though his present behavior was only a marginal improvement. But he couldn't seem to help himself. The more he saw of Leah, the more he liked her, and paradoxically, the more he resented her.

Chinese food. The mere words conjured up images of late nights on the set, where dinner was wolfed out of cartons scattered along an endless table at the rear of the studio. He'd barely known what he was eating. His stomach had inevitably been upset long before, and the best he'd been able to do was to wash whatever it was down with swigs of Scotch.

Chinese food. Another image came to mind, this one of a midnight date with a willowy blonde who'd been good enough to pick up the food on her way over to his place. He wouldn't have bothered to pick *her* up. He'd known what she'd wanted and he'd delivered—crudely and with little feeling. The next morning, more than a little hung over, he'd retched at the smell of the food that remained in the cartons.

Chinese food. One last image. He'd been alone. No work, no friends. He'd been high on something or other, and he'd gone to the takeout counter and ordered enough for twelve, supposedly to look as though he were having a party. As though he were still important, still a star. He'd gone home, sat in his garish living room, stared at the leather sofas and the huge bags of food and had bawled like a baby.

"Garrick?"

Leah's voice brought him back. His head shot up just as she passed an envelope across the table. Victoria's letter. He glared at it for a minute before snatching it from her fingers. The legs of his chair scraped against the floor. He crossed the room quickly, slapped the unopened letter onto the top of the dresser, then dropped back into the sofa and resumed his brooding.

Quietly Leah began to clear the table. Her movements were slow, her shoulders slumped in defeat. It wasn't the meal that caused her discouragement; she knew it had been good and that for a time Garrick had enjoyed what he'd eaten. She couldn't even take offense at his brusque departure, because she knew he was hurting. She'd seen his eyes grow distant, seen the pain they'd held. Oh, yes, she knew he was hurting, but she didn't know what to do about it, and that was the cause of her distress. She wanted to reach out, but she was afraid. She felt totally impotent.

When there was nothing left to do in the kitchen, she picked up a book—one of her own—and as unobtrusively as possible slid into her corner of the sofa. She couldn't read, though. She was too aware of Garrick.

An hour passed. He looked at her. "You said there were clothes in the bags I brought."

She glanced down at her jeans, then her moccasins.

"Besides those," he muttered.

"There are others." She knew he was complaining because she'd left on his sweater. She closed her fingers around a handful of the wool. "I'll wash this and your long johns in the morning."

He grunted and looked away. Another period of silence passed. He moved only to feed the fire. She moved only to turn an unread page.

Then his rough voice jagged into her again. "I can't believe you sent me for books and tapes. You'll need more than one change of clothes."

"There were two in the duffel."

"That's not enough if you're stuck here a while."

"You have a washer. I'll do fine. Besides, I have boots in the duffel. I can always go back to the car—"

"*Boots?* Why in the hell didn't you put them on the other night?"

She drew her elbows in tighter. Strangely, this kind of criticism had been less hurtful coming from Richard. "I didn't think the mud would be so bad."

"You didn't think period. Your car's stuck in pretty good. That took some doing."

"I'm not an expert—with cars *or* mud," she argued, but she was shaking inside. She had no idea why he was harping at her this way. "I was only trying to get out—"

"By grinding the tires in deeper?"

"I was trying my best!"

Again he grunted. Again he looked away. Tension made the air nearly as heavy as her heart.

"You didn't even lock the damn car!" he roared a short time later. "With your purse lying there, and all your supposed worldly possessions, you left the thing open!"

"I was too upset to think about that."

"And you're supposed to be a New Yorker?"

She slammed her book shut. "I've never *had* a car before. What is the *problem*, Garrick? You said yourself that no one moves in this kind of weather. Even if someone could, who in his right mind would be going to a burned out cabin? My things were safe, and if they weren't, they're only *things*."

He snorted. "You'd probably *give* the rest away, now that you've got your precious books and your tapes and your wok—"

"Damn it, Garrick!" she cried, sliding forward on the sofa. "Why are you doing this to me? I don't tell you how to live, do I? If my books mean more to me than clothes, that's *my* choice." Tears sparkled on her lids but she refused to let them fall. "I may not be like other women in that sense, but it's the way I am. Will it really hurt you if I alternate between two outfits? If I'm clean and I don't smell, why should you be concerned? Am I that awful to look at that I need all kinds of fancy things to make my presence bearable?"

She was on her feet, looking at him with hurt-filled eyes. "You don't want me here. I know that, and because of it, I don't want to be here, either. I never asked to be marooned with you. If I'd known what Victoria was planning, I'd never have left New York!" She was breathing hard, trying to control her temper, but without success. "I'm as independent as you are, and I prize that independence. I've earned it. Do you think it's easy for me to be stuck in an isolated cabin with a sharp-tongued, self-indulgent recluse? Well, it isn't! I took enough abuse from my husband. I don't have to take it from you!"

She started to move away, but turned back as quickly. "And since we've taken off the gloves, let me tell you something else. You have the manners of a *boor*! I didn't have to cook dinner tonight. You've made it clear that you're more than happy doing it. But I wanted to do something for *you*, for a change. I wanted to please you. I wanted to show you that I'm not a wimpy female who needs to be waited on. And what did I get for it? Out-and-out rudeness. You took your sweet time deciding whether you'd privilege me with your company at the table. Then after you shoveled food in your mouth, you stormed off as though I'd committed some unpardonable sin. What did I *do*? Can't you at least tell me that? Or is it beyond your capability to share your thoughts once in a while?"

Through her entire tirade, he didn't move a muscle. Throwing her hands up in a gesture of futility, she turned away. Yanking a nightshirt from the duffel she'd stowed under the bed, she fled to the bathroom. A minute later she was out again, throwing her clothes down on top of the duffel, plopping down on the edge of the bed.

Her breath was ragged and her fingers dug into the quilt with fearsome strength. She was angry. She was hurt. But mostly she was dismayed, because she'd taken both her anger and her hurt out on Garrick. It wasn't like her to do that to anyone. She was normally the most composed of women. Yet she'd disintegrated before Garrick. Garrick. After last night.

She didn't see or hear him until he was standing directly before her. Her eyes focused on his legs. She couldn't look up. She didn't know what to say.

Very slowly, he lowered himself to his haunches. She bowed her head even more, but he raised it with a finger beneath her chin. A gentle finger. Her gaze crept upward.

His eyes held the words of apology that his lips wouldn't form, and that gentle finger became five, touching her cheek with soulful hesitance. Callused fingertips moved falteringly, exploring her cheek, her cheekbone, the straight slope of her nose, her lips.

Her breath caught in her throat, because all the while he was touching her, his eyes were speaking, and the words were so sad and humble and heartfelt that she wanted to cry.

He leaned forward, then hesitated.

She touched her fingertips to the thick brush of his beard in encouragement.

This time when he leaned forward he didn't falter, and the words he spoke so silently were the most meaningful of all.

5

GARRICK KISSED HER. It was the first time their lips had touched, and it wasn't so much the touching itself as its manner that shook Leah to the core. His mouth was artful, capturing hers with a gentleness that spoke of caring, a sweetness that spoke of a deep inner need. He brushed his lips back and forth across her softening flesh, then drew back to look at her again.

His eyes caressed each of her features. Setting her glasses aside, he kissed her eyes, the bridge of her nose, her cheekbone, her temple. By the time he returned to her mouth, her lips were parted. She tipped her head to perfect the fit, welcoming him with rapidly flaring desire.

His enthusiasm matched hers. Oh, he'd fought it. All day and all evening he'd been telling himself that he didn't want this or need it, that it would cause more trouble than it was worth. He'd been telling himself that he had the self-control to resist any and all urgings of the flesh. But then Leah had blown up. She'd given him a piece of her mind, and she'd been right in what she'd said. He'd seen and felt her hurt, and he'd known that urgings of the flesh were but a small part of the attraction he felt for her.

He couldn't fight it any longer, because just as his new life was built on control, it was built on honesty. What he felt for Leah, what he needed from her and with her was too raw, too beautiful to be sullied by ugly behavior or lack of communication. He'd talk. He'd tell her about himself. For now, though, he needed to speak with his body.

Calling on everything he'd ever learned about pleasing a woman, he set to pleasing Leah. His mouth was never still, never rough or forceful, demanding only in the most subtle of ways. He stroked her lips, loved them with his own and with his tongue, worshiped the small teeth that lay behind, then the deeper, warmer, moister recesses that beckoned.

There was nothing calculated in what he did. He might have learned and perfected the technique from and on other women, but what he felt as he pleasured Leah came straight from the heart. And he was pleasuring himself, as well, discovering a goodness he'd never known, realizing yet again that what he'd once thought of as purely physical was emotionally uplifting with Leah. In that sense, he was experiencing a rebirth. His past took on meaning, for it was the groundwork from which he could love Leah completely.

She felt it. She felt the wealth of feeling behind the mouth that revered hers, the tongue that flowed around and against hers, the hands that sifted through her hair with such tenderness. She felt things new and different, things that arrowed into her heart and made her tremble.

"Garrick?" she breathed when his lips left hers for a minute.

"Shhhhh—"

"I'm sorry for yelling—"

He was cupping her head, his breath whispering over her. "We'll talk later. I need you too much now." He kissed her once more, lingeringly, then released her to whip his sweatshirt over his head.

Her hands were on him even before the sweatshirt hit the floor. Palms open, fingers splayed, she ran her hands over his chest, covering every inch in greedy possession. He was warm and firm. A fine mat of hair, its tawny hue made golden by the residual light of the fire, wove a manly pattern over his flesh. She explored the broader patch above his breasts and traced its narrowing to his waist, then dragged her hands upward again until they spanned dual swells of muscle and small, tight nipples rasped against her palms.

The breath he expelled was a shuddering one. He had his eyes closed and his head thrown back. His long fingers closed around her wrists, not to stop her voyage but simply because he needed to hold her, to know that he wasn't imagining her touch. His insides were hot; shafts of fire were shooting toward his loins, and a sheen of perspiration had broken out on his skin, adding to the sensual slide of her hands.

When she rounded his shoulders and began to stroke his back in those same, broad sweeps of discovery, he shakily released the buttons of her nightshirt and pushed the soft fabric down her arms. For a minute he could do nothing but look; the perfection before him all but stopped his breathing. Her breasts were round and full, their tips gilded by the firelight. He touched one. Her nipple was already hard, but grew even more so. Sucking in a breath at the sweet pain, Leah closed her fingers on the smooth flesh at his sides and clung for dear life.

His eyes locked with hers, finding a desire there that was echoed in the shallowness of her breathing. "I want to touch you, Leah. I need to. I need to touch and to taste."

She gave a convulsive swallow, then whispered, "Please!"

Unable to help himself, he smiled. She was so adorable, so sexy, so guileless when it came to this. He had to kiss her again, and he did, and while his lips held hers, he touched her breasts. She jerked at the sudden charge of sensation, but he gentled her with his mouth, and his work-roughened hands circled her, covered her, lifted her with care. She never quite got used to his touch, because each time he moved his palm or a finger, new currents of awareness sizzled through her. When the pads of his thumbs scored her nipples, soft sounds of arousal came from deep in her throat, and when forefingers joined thumbs in an erotic rolling, a snowballing need had her squirming restlessly.

Her hands moved with desperation to the waistband of his cords. His met them there, unsnapping and unzipping, before leaving her to her own devices. He wanted to touch her more, this time her knees, which were widespread, allowing him to kneel between them, then her thighs, which were soft and smooth and quivering. When her hands slipped beneath the band of his shorts in search of the point of greatest heat, his surged higher, similarly seeking and finding the heart of her sex.

Leah's head fell forward, mouth open, teeth braced on his shoulder. Her hands surrounded him. They measured his length and width, weighed the heaviness beneath. They caressed satin over steel and were rewarded when he strained harder against her palms. But her mind was only half there, because Garrick had opened her and begun to do such intimately arousing things to her that she could barely breathe, much less think.

She'd never thought of herself as lacking control where sex was concerned, but she'd never been half as hot as she was now. She felt herself floating, rising, and her attempts to rein in were futile. Sandwiching the power of his virility between them, her hands went still.

"Garrick . . . oh . . . oh." She sucked in a breath, let it out in a tremulous whisper. "Please . . . I need . . . wait."

But just then he took her nipple into his mouth, and it was too late. The brush of his mustache and beard and his gentle sucking snapped the fine thread from which she'd been hanging. Her thighs closed on his hands as her insides exploded, and she could only gasp against his shoulder while she rode out a storm of endless spasms. When they subsided at last, she rolled her face to the crook of his neck.

"I'm sorry. . . I couldn't hold back . . ."

Framing her face, he raised it and kissed her. His lips shifted and angled and sucked, never once leaving hers as he bore her gently back on the bed. His hands tugged the nightshirt from her hips, then went to work baring himself. Naked, he lowered his large frame over her.

Leah was ready to take him in, but he had no intention of simply slaking his desire while she lay quiescent and sated. He wanted her hungry again. He wanted her aroused and aching for him, because he knew that if it was so, his own fulfillment would be all the richer.

So he began to touch her anew. Her breasts, her belly, that ultrasensitive spot between her legs—he stimulated and teased, using hands, lips and tongue. And he was doing just fine until she became active herself, finding the places that set him to shaking, stroking them, tormenting them with fingers that were innocent and eager to please.

And Garrick was pleased, though the word seemed a paltry one to describe his feelings. He'd never felt so valued—not just needed, *valued*. Beneath Leah's hands and lips and the sweet waft of her breath, he felt cherished, special and unique. He felt as though she couldn't be doing this with any other man but him.

At that moment, he knew the future would have to take care of itself. He needed her now and for however long she chose to stay with him. If, at the end of that time, he was alone, he knew that he'd have experienced something most men never even approach. He'd have memories of something rare and wonderful, and he'd be a stronger man for it.

Writhing gently beneath him, Leah urged him to her. He grasped her hands, intertwined his fingers with hers and pinned them to the quilt by her shoulders. Poised above her, he watched her face as slowly, slowly he entered her.

Her eyes fell shut and a tiny smile of bliss curved her lips. Then, with a sigh, she lifted her legs and wrapped them tightly around him. "Don't move," she whispered, still smiling in that catlike way that gave him a thrill. "You feel . . . I feel so . . . good . . . full."

"Leah?" he whispered.

Slowly her eyes opened. They were filled with the same love that filled his heart. He knew it was absurd. He and Leah had known each other for only two days, and those under unusual conditions. They hadn't talked much, hadn't shared thoughts of the past or the future, much less the present, but he *did* love her. He'd never felt anything like it before—the driving desire to please a woman, to make her happy in the broadest sense—but he felt that way toward Leah. He felt that he'd willingly sacrifice his quiet to hear her music, his steak and potatoes to eat her Chinese food, his normal efficiency to take her floundering in the mud. He knew that if she asked him to withdraw from her just then, he'd forgo a climax and still feel complete.

She didn't ask him anything of the sort, though. Rather, she began to move her hips and her inner muscles, holding him ever more tightly, taking his breath away. Lifting her head from the pillow, she sought his lips, and he lost track of everything but the intense pleasure of stroking her tongue and drawing it into his mouth. Bowing his back, he withdrew, then thrust forward, withdrew, then thrust forward. With each thrust he went deeper. With each withdrawal, he returned hotter. Finally, with a surge that touched her womb, he stiffened and held, erupting into a release so powerful that he thought he'd die, so glorious that he would have welcomed it.

Only when awareness returned did he realize that Leah, too, was vibrating in the aftermath of climax. Her cheek was pressed to their intertwined hands. Her eyes were shut tightly. Her lips were parted to allow for the soft panting that was sweet music to his ears. He was glad then that he hadn't died, for there was more to come, so much more.

Very gently he slid from her, but before she could protest, he'd nestled her snugly into the crook of his shoulder. One of his arms encircled her back, the other grasped her thigh and drew it over his. His fingers remained in a warm clasp around her knee.

Eyes closed, Leah sighed in contentment. She rubbed her nose against Garrick's chest, inhaling the scent of man and musk and sex that would have been arousing had not she been so thoroughly sated.

"Ahhh, Garrick," she whispered. "So nice . . ."

"It is, isn't it?" he responded as softly. In the past he would have been reaching for a cigarette. Putting distance between himself and the body next to him. Biding the few obligatory minutes before he could clear whatever woman he was with from his bed. Now, though, the only thing he wanted to do was lie holding Leah. And talk.

"You're spectacular," she said. "Maybe I should yell at you more."

That drew a lazy chuckle from his throat. "Maybe you should. It brings me to my senses."

"I'm not usually the yelling type."

"I'm not usually the brooding type."

"What brought it on?"

He cuffed his chin against the top of her head, knowing that his beard would cushion the gentle blow. "You."

"Is it that difficult having me here?"

"Just the opposite. I like having you here."

"Then why—"

"I like it too much. I thought I had my life all worked out. Then you pop in and upset the apple cart."

"Oh." She took a quick breath. "I know what you mean."

"You do?"

"Mmm. I haven't minded living alone—living without a man. I thought it was the safest thing."

"Did your marriage hurt you that much?"

"Yes."

"You said he abused you. Was it physical?"

"He never beat me. It was more an emotional thing."

"Tell me about him. What was he like?"

Leah thought for a minute, seeking to express her feelings with a minimum of bitterness. "He was good-looking and charming. He could sell an icebox to an Eskimo."

"He was a salesman?"

"Indirectly. He was—is—a top executive in an ad agency. If you want to know what charisma is, you don't have to look farther than Richard. People flock to him. He attracts clients like flies. Lord only knows why he married me."

Garrick gave her a sharp squeeze, but she went on.

"I'm serious. I guess it was the stage he was at when we met. He was just getting started. He needed a wife who looked relatively sophisticated, and when I try, I suppose I do look that. He needed someone who knew the ins and outs of New York, and since I'd lived there all my life, I guess I qualified on that score, too. He needed someone he could manipulate, and I fit the bill."

"You don't strike *me* as being terribly manipulatable," Garrick said with feeling.

She laughed. "How can you say that after what Victoria did?"

"That may be the one exception, and since we were both patsies, we won't count it."

"Well, Richard was able to manipulate me. I wanted to please him. I wanted to make the marriage work."

"Why didn't it?"

"Oh, lots of reasons. Mainly because I couldn't be what Richard wanted."

"Couldn't?"

"That, and wouldn't. I got tired of being told when to be where wearing what. I got tired of feeling that regardless how hard I tried, I didn't measure up."

"What did the guy want?" Garrick barked. The sound reverberated in his chest beneath Leah's ear. Knowing that he was on her side, she didn't mind his anger.

"Perfection."

"None of us is perfect."

"Tell that to Richard."

"Thanks, but I'll pass. He sounds like the kind of guy I avoid."

"You're very wise."

"Either that, or very weak. I haven't quite decided which yet."

Leah shifted, turning her head so that she looked up at him. "You, weak? I don't believe that for a minute. Look at the way you live. It takes strength to do what you do."

"Physical strength, yes."

"No, psychological. To live alone on a mountainside, to be comfortable enough with yourself to live alone—many people can't do that."

It was the perfect opening. He knew he should say something about himself and his past, but the words wouldn't come. He wanted Leah's respect. He feared he'd risk it if she knew where he'd been. "I'm not sure I've done it so well, judging from the way I've latched on to you." Hauling her higher on his chest, he gave her a fierce kiss. But the fierceness mellowed quickly. "You taste so good, Leah," he whispered hoarsely. "You *feel* so good." His hands had begun to glide up and down her body. "You feel so good on top of me."

That was precisely where she was. Her breasts were pillowed by the soft furring of his chest hair. Her thighs, straddling his, knew their sinewed strength. He felt so good beneath her that her body began a slow rocking while her mouth inched over his nose, his cheek and down to the warm, bare skin below his beard.

"You smell good," she whispered against his throat.

Garrick grinned in pure delight. He felt redeemed, almost defiant. He smelled earthy, but Leah liked it. So there, L.A.! Take your Brut and stuff it!

"Garrick?" Her voice was muffled against his chest.

"What is it, love?"

She kept her face buried. "I want you again."

He laughed in continued delight.

"What's so funny?"

"You. You're wonderful."

"Does that mean you want me, too?"

He arched his hips against hers. "What do you think?"

"I think yes, but maybe you think I'm only after your body."

He didn't laugh this time. Instead his long fingers caged her head and gently raised it. His expression was soft and filled with wonder. "What I think is that I'm the luckiest man alive." He didn't say anything else, because his mouth covered hers. His hands spread over her hips, lifting, lowering, until she was fully impaled.

Leah had seldom been in the dominant position, but her desire more than compensated for her lack of experience. He guided her at first, moving her up and down in slow, sure strokes, but then he began caressing her breasts and she let instinct be her guide. She heard the quickening of his breathing and increased rhythm. She felt him lower his head and craned upward so he could reach her breasts with his lips. She sensed when he approached his climax and ground herself more tightly against him. And when he cried out in release, she was with him all the way.

When her heartbeat finally slowed she thought she'd be exhausted, but she wasn't. Her body was sated, but her mind had only begun to hunger. She wanted to talk. It was as though a dam had burst, years of holding in thoughts and questions given way now to a steady flow. She was fearing that Garrick would rather sleep, when his voice drifted over her brow.

"I've never had a woman here before."

They'd slipped between the sheets and were snuggled warmly and closely. "I know," she breathed against his chest.

"I've never had much of anyone here before. Another trapper will stop by once in a while. And buyers come for my furs."

"Is that only in the winter?"

"Pretty much so. I can't trap the good stuff after the middle of January."

"The good stuff—fisher, fox and raccoon?"

"Um-hmm."

"Why not after the middle of January?"

"That's the law, and it makes sense. The furs are thickest in winter, and prime fur draws the best price. But that's secondary to the concept of wildlife management."

"Explain."

"The theory is that hunting and trapping shouldn't be done to exploit the wildlife population, but to control it. Raccoon threaten local cornfields. Beaver threaten the free flow of streams."

"You don't have to justify what you do."

"But it's all part of the explanation. Trapping isn't a free-for-all. At the beginning of each season, the Fish and Game Department issues strict guidelines, in some cases limiting the catch of certain species. For example, I can take only three fisher a year. With roughly eight hundred trappers in the state, three fisher per trapper, the number adds up. If limits aren't set, the population will be endangered."

"How are limits set?"

"The department decides based on information it gets from trappers the previous year. Every catch I make has to be tagged. I tell the department where and when I made the catch, what condition the animal was in and what I observed about the overall population while I was running my trapline."

"Then the limits vary by year?"

"Theoretically, yes. But in the past few years the various populations have been stable, which means that the department has been doing its job right. Once in a while there's politicking involved. For example, fisher feed on turkeys and rabbits. The turkey and rabbit hunters lobby for a higher take of fisher, so that there will be more turkeys and rabbits left for them to hunt."

"Do they win?"

"No. At one point, in the early thirties, fisher were hunted nearly to extinction. The department is very protective of them now."

"But why the January deadline?"

"Because come February, the mating season begins. Trapping after that would be a double hazard to the population."

"Then you trap only three months a year?"

"I can take beaver through the end of March and coyote whenever I want. But the first I use mainly for bait, and the second don't interest me other than to keep them away from my traps. They'll eat the best of my catch if I let them. And they're smart, coyotes are. Trap a coyote in one place, and the rest don't go near that spot again."

Leah loved hearing him talk, not only for his low, husky voice, almost a murmur as they lay twined together, but for his knowledge, as well. "It must be an art—successful trapping."

"Part art, part science. It's hard work, even for those few short months."

"A little more complicated than sticking a spigot in a tree, hmm?"

He chuckled. "A little. The work starts well before the trapping season opens. I have to get a license, plus written permission from any private landowners whose land I may be crossing. I have to prepare the traps—season new ones, repair and prime old ones. Once the season opens and I've set my traps, I have to run the line every morning."

"Every morning?"

"Early every morning."

"You don't mind that?"

"Nah. I like it." He never used to like getting up. When he'd worked in L.A., he'd hated early morning calls. More often than not he'd been partying late the night before, and particularly in the later years, he'd awoken hung over. There were no parties here, though, and no drinks. He had no trouble waking up. Indeed, he'd discovered that the post-dawn hours were peaceful and productive.

"Why early in the morning?"

"Because most of the furbearers are nocturnal, which means that they'll be out foraging, hence caught at night. I want to collect them as soon as possible after they step into the trap."

"Why?"

He laughed. It occurred to him that he'd laughed more in the past few hours than he had in weeks.

"What's so funny?"

He hugged her closer. "You. Your curiosity. It never quits."

"But it's interesting, what you do. Do you mind my questions?"

"No. I don't mind your questions." And he meant it, which surprised him almost as much as the sound of his own repeated laughter. The past four years of his life had been dominated by silence. He'd needed it at first, because he hadn't been fit to carry on any conversation, much less one with a woman. He'd spoken only when necessary, and then with locals who'd been blessedly laconic. Even the old man who'd taught him to trap had been a miser where words were concerned, and that had suited Garrick just fine. He welcomed words that held real meaning, rather than shallow platitudes. He'd had his fill of the latter—sweet talk meant to impress, crude talk meant to hurt, idle talk meant to pass the time, patronizing talk meant to buy or win.

He'd never had the kind of gentle, innocently genuine talk that he now shared with Leah, and he wasn't sure he'd ever get his fill. Unusual as it was to discuss trapping in the dark after lovemaking, he was enjoying it.

"Why do I want to collect my catch as soon as possible? Because if I wait, the fox may close in or the fur may be otherwise damaged. Once I've made the catch, I try to concentrate on the art of preparing the fur."

"There's an art to it?"

"Definitely. For example, when it comes to fleshing . . ." He hesitated. "You don't need to hear this."

"Okay," she said so quickly that he chuckled again, but she was immediately off on a related tangent. "So the trapping season is pretty short. What do you do during the rest of the year?"

"Read. Whittle. Go birding in the woods. Grow vegetables."

She popped up over him. "Vegetables? Where?"

"Out back."

"What's out back? There aren't any windows on that wall so I haven't been able to see."

He stroked her cheek with a lazy thumb. "There's a clearing. It's small, but it gets enough sun in the summer months to grow what I need."

"You eat it all?"

"Not all. You can only consume so much lettuce."

"Lettuce. What else?"

"Tomatoes, carrots, zucchini, peas, green beans. I freeze a lot of stuff for the winter months. Whatever is left over, I give away. Or trade. The maple syrup we had with the pancakes came that way."

"Not bad," she said. Her hands were splayed over his chest. Dipping her head, she dropped an impulsive kiss on the hollow of his throat. "Actually, I'm in awe. I have a brown thumb. Plants die on me right and left. I finally gave up trying to grow them, which I suppose is just as well. If I'd been attached to a plant and then had to give it away when I packed up to come here—"

"You could have brought it."

"It's a good thing I didn't. I mean, here I am with most of my stuff still in the car in the cold. Victoria's place is worthless, and I have no idea where I'll be going—"

Garrick cut off the flow of her words by flipping her onto her back and sealing her mouth with his. He didn't want her to talk about going anywhere. He didn't want her to *think* about going anywhere. He wanted her to love him again.

Leah needed little urging. The weight of his body covering her, pressing her to the mattress, branding her with blatant masculinity was enough to spark fires that she'd thought long since banked. They kissed again and again. They began to touch and explore with even greater boldness than before. Lines and curves that should have been familiar by now took on newness from different angles, heightening the fever that rose between them until, once again, they came together in the ultimate stroke of passion.

This time, when it was over and they'd fallen languidly into each others arms, they lay quietly.

After a bit Leah whispered, "Garrick?"

"Hmm?"

"I've never done this before."

"Hmm?"

"Three times in one night. I never thought I had it in me. I never wanted to . . . more than once."

"Know something?" he returned in the same whisper. "Me, neither."

"Really?"

"Really." Strange, but he was proud to say it. How often he'd lied in the past, how many times he'd bragged about nonstop bouts of sex. He'd had an image to uphold, but it had been an empty one. If a woman had asked for more, he'd always had a ready answer; either she'd worn him out, or the woman the night before had worn him out, or he had an early call in the morning. The fact was that once his initial lust had been fed he'd lost interest.

But it wasn't lust he felt for Leah. Well, maybe a little, but there was love in it, too, and that made all the difference.

"How long have you been here, Garrick?"

"Four years."

"And you went places when you felt the need . . . the urge to . . ."

"I haven't felt it much, but there were women I could see."

"Were they nice?"

"They were okay."

"Do you still see any of them?"

"No. One-night stands were about all I could handle."

"Why?"

Again she'd given him an opening. He could easily explain that he'd been going through a rough time, finding himself, but then she'd ask more questions, and he didn't want to have to answer them. Not tonight. So he gave an answer that was honest, if simplified. "None of them made me want anything more."

"Oh."

"What does that mean—oh?"

"Are you gonna kick me out tomorrow?"

"I can't. Remember, the mud?"

She scraped the nail of her big toe against his shin. "If it weren't for the mud, would you kick me out?"

"We've already had more than a one-night stand."

"You're not answering my question."

"How can I kick you out? You have nowhere to go."

"Garrick..."

His elbow tightened around her neck. "No, Leah, I would not kick you out. I will not kick you out. I like having you here. You can stay as long as you want."

"Because I'm good in bed?"

"Yes."

"Garrick!"

"Because I like being *with* you. How's that?"

"Better."

"You want more?"

"Yes."

"Because you do things for my sweater that I never did."

"I thought you wanted it back."

"I want you to keep it. Wear it."

"Okay."

"And you can cook if you want."

"But you hate Chinese food."

"I didn't hate what you made tonight. I was just being difficult." He paused, then ventured more cautiously, "Do you do anything besides Chinese?"

"I've taken courses in French cooking. And Indian. I doubt you have the ingredients for either of those."

"Do you always cook foreign for yourself in New York?"

"Oh, no."

"What do your normally eat?"

"When I'm not pigging out with Victoria?"

"Come to think of it, you do eat a lot. How do you stay so thin?"

"Lean Cuisines."

"Excuse me?"

"Lean Cuisines. They're frozen. I heat them in the microwave."

"You eat *frozen dinners*?"

"Sure. They're good. A little too much sodium, but otherwise they provide a balanced meal."

"Oh. If you say so."

She yawned. "I do."

"Tired?"

"A little. What time is it?"

"I don't know. I don't have a watch."

She held her wrist before his nose. "I don't have my glasses. What time does it say?"

"Twenty past a freckle."

"Oh." She dropped her hand to his chest. "I left my watch in the bathroom."

"That's okay. The fire's gone out, so I wouldn't have been able to read it anyway."

"It has a luminous dial."

"You come prepared."

"Usually." She burrowed closer, stifling another yawn. "I don't want to go to sleep. I like talking with you."

"Me, too."

"Will we talk more in the morning, or are you going to go mute on me with the break of day?"

He chuckled. "We'll talk more."

"Promise?"

"Scout's honor."

"Were you a Scout?"

"Once upon a time."

"I want to hear about it," she murmured, but she was fading fast.

"You will."

"Garrick?"

"Mmm?"

It was a while before she answered and then her words were slurred. "How old are you?"

"Forty." He waited for her to say something more. When she didn't, he whispered her name. She didn't answer. Smiling, he pressed a soft kiss to her rumpled bangs.

6

WHEN LEAH AWOKE the next morning, Garrick was beside her. He was sprawled on his stomach, his head facing away, but one of his ankles was hooked around hers in a warm reminder of the events of the night before. Heart swelling with happiness, she took a deep breath and stretched. Then she rolled against him, slipped a slender arm over his waist and sighed contentedly.

Weak slivers of light filtered through the shutters, dimly illuminating the room. It was still raining, she knew, but the patter on the roof had eased to a gentle tap, and anyway, she didn't care what the weather was. Garrick had said she could stay as long as she wanted. She wasn't going to think about leaving.

When the body against her shifted, she slid her hand forward, up over his middle to his chest. His own covered it, and then he was turning to look at her.

It was the very first time in his life that Garrick had awoken pleased to find a woman in his bed. He smiled. "Hi."

Oh, how she loved his voice, even that lone word, working like fine sandpaper to make her tingle. "Hi."

"How did you sleep?"

"Like a baby."

"You don't look like a baby." His gaze was roaming her face, taking in the luster of mussed hair on her forehead, the luminous gray of her eyes, the softness of lips that had been well kissed not so very long ago. "You look sexy."

She blushed. "So do you."

His eyes skimmed lower, over her neck to her breasts. "I've never seen you in daylight," he said softly.

"You have."

"Not nude." Very gently he eased back the covers, allowing himself a full view of her body. His gaze touched her waist, the visible line of her pelvis and the length of her legs before returning to linger on the shadowed apex of her thighs. "You're lovely."

Leah was trembling, but not only because of the way he was looking and the sensual sound of his voice. When he'd pulled back the covers he'd bared himself, as well, and what she saw was breathtaking. With his tapering torso, his lean hips and tightly muscled legs, he was a great subject for a sculptor. But it was his sex that held her spellbound, for it was perfectly formed, incredibly full and heavy.

"I do want you," he whispered. "I think I've been like this all night, dreaming of you."

"You don't have to dream," she breathed. "I'm here."

"So hard to believe . . ." Shifting so that he crouched over her, he let his hands drift over each part of her in turn. When he reached her belly, he sat back on his haunches, then watched his fingers lower to brush the dark tangle of curls. He stroked her lightly, but even that light touch spread heat like wildfire through her veins.

"Garrick . . ."

"Warm and beautiful."

"I need you . . ."

His eyes met hers, and there was an intensity in them that held more than one form of passion. "I want you too. I want that more than anything."

When she reached for him, he lifted her and crushed her close. They held each other that way for a long time, bodies flush, limbs faintly quivering. Oddly, the desire to make love passed, replaced by the gratification of simply being together. At that moment it seemed much more precious than anything else in the world.

Garrick's arms were the first to slacken. "I need a shower," he said in a voice lingering with emotion. "Want to share?"

"I've never taken a shower with a man before."

"Never?"

"Never."

"Are you game?"

"If you are. It's a large shower."

"I'm a large man."

"Which means—"

"We'll be close."

"I'd like that."

"Me, too." Scooping her into his arms, he rolled to the edge of the bed. "Come on."

"I can walk."

"The floor's cold."

"You're walking."

"Would you rather switch places?"

"You're too heavy."

"Then hush."

When he reached the bathroom, he lowered her feet to the floor, turned to start the water, then knelt before her and very gently removed the bandage from her leg. She'd given up on gauze and adhesive the day before in favor of a Band-Aid, and the only discomfort she still felt was from the black-and-blue area surrounding the cut.

"Looks okay," he decided, then slid his gaze leisurely up her body. "I like the rest better, though."

She finger-combed his hair back from his forehead. "I'm glad."

After pressing a soft kiss on her navel, he stood and led her into the shower. They soaped themselves and then, for the hell of it, each other. And it *was* hell in some ways, because the glide of suds beneath palms over various bodily areas was erotic, but they didn't want to make love. Resisting the temptation was in part a game, in part a way of saying that there was more to their relationship than sex.

Touching was totally acceptable, and they did it constantly. It astounded Leah that two people who'd been alone for so long could adapt so easily to such closeness. Or maybe it was *because* they'd been alone that they were greedy. Either way, they never strayed far from each other. They watched each other dress—chipping in to help here and there with a button or a sock. Likewise, they chipped in making breakfast, then ate with their legs entwined under the table.

And they talked—constantly and about anything that came to mind.

"I love your hair," Garrick said. He'd settled her onto his lap when she'd come around to clear his plate. "Have you always worn it this way?"

"No. I had it cut the day my divorce became final."

"Celebrating?"

"Declaring my independence. When I was little I always wore my hair long. My mother loved combing it and curling it and tying it up with ribbons. Richard liked it long, too. It was part of the image. He thought long hair was alluring. Y'know," she drawled, "waving tresses sweeping over sequined shoulders." Her voice returned to its normal timbre. "Sometimes he'd have me wear it up, sometimes hitched back with a fancy comb. I used to have to spend hours getting it to look just right. I hated it."

"So you cut it."

"Yup."

He stroked the silky strands. "It's so pretty this way."

"It's easy."

"Then pretty *and* easy." He scalloped a gentle thumb through her bangs. "Did you like going out?"

"Where?"

"To parties, restaurants."

"With Richard? No. And I still don't like parties, but maybe that's because I feel awkward."

"Why would you feel awkward?" he asked in the same gravelly voice she found so soothing. It eased her over the embarrassment of expressing particular thoughts.

"I've never been a social butterfly. I was shy."

"Shy? Really?"

Smiling, she wrapped her arms around his neck and nuzzled his hair. "Really."

"Why shy?"

Sitting back, she shrugged. "I don't know. I was an English major, a bookworm, an . . . intellectual. I suppose one of the things that snowed me about Richard was that he was good with people in a way I wasn't. I could go places with him and be part of the crowd in a way I'd never been."

"Did you like that?"

"I thought I would, and I did at first. Then I realized that I wasn't really part of the crowd. *He* was, but I wasn't. I was just along for the ride, but the ride wasn't fun. The people were boring. I didn't have much to say to them. Richard was always after me to be more pleasant, and I could be charming when I tried, but under the circumstances, I hated it. The whole thing came to be uncomfortable."

He eased her to her feet and reached for the plates. "I can understand that."

Leah didn't have to ask him if he agreed, because she knew he did. If he liked crowds and parties and small talk, he'd never have chosen to live alone in the woods. As they began to load the dishwasher, it occurred to her to ask why he'd chosen to live this way. Instead she asked, "Why are you studying Latin?"

"Because it's interesting. So many of our words have Latin derivatives."

"You didn't study it as a kid?"

"Nope. I studied Spanish. My mom was a Spanish professor."

"No kidding!"

"No kidding." The way he said it—part drawl, part resignation—suggested more to the story. This particular chapter didn't threaten Leah.

"Oh-oh. It wasn't great?"

"She was very involved in her work. When she wasn't teaching, she was traveling to one Spanish-speaking area or another, and when she wasn't doing that, she was entertaining students at our house."

"You didn't like that?"

"I would have liked a little of her attention myself."

"What about your father? What did he do?"

"He was a gastroenterologist."

"And very busy."

"Uh-huh."

"You were alone a lot."

"Uh-huh."

"Do you have any brothers or sisters?"

He shook his head and handed her the pan he'd just washed. "How about you?"

"I was an only, too. But my parents doted on me. Isn't it strange that we should have had such different experiences? Perhaps if we'd been able to put our four parents in a barrel and shake them up, we'd each have had a little more of what we needed."

He chuckled, but it was a sad sound. "If only."

When they finished cleaning the kitchen, Garrick made a fire, then sat on the floor with his back against the sofa and pulled Leah between his legs. She nestled into the haven, crossing her arms over those stronger, more manly ones that wound around her middle.

"Have you always worn glasses?" he asked, his breath warm by her ear.

"From the time I was twelve. I wore contacts for Richard, but I never really liked them."

"Why not?"

"It was a pain—putting them in every morning, taking them out and cleaning them every night, enzyming them once a week. Besides, nearsightedness is *me*. On principle alone, I don't see why I should have to hide it."

"You look adorable with glasses."

Smiling, she offered a soft, "Thank you." Her smile lingered for a long time. "This is . . . so . . . nice," she whispered at last. "I feel so peaceful." She tipped her head back to see his face. "Is that what you feel living up here?"

"More so since you've come."

"But before. Is it the peace that appeals to you?"

"It's lots of things. Peace, yes. Lack of hassle. I work hard enough, but at my own speed."

Implicit was the suggestion that he'd known something very different four years before. Again she had an opportunity to probe that past. Again she let it slide. Returning her gaze to the fire, she asked, "Do you ever get bored?"

"No. There's always something to do."

"When did you learn to whittle?"

"Soon after I came."

"Did the trapper teach you?"

"I taught myself. One good instruction book, and I was on my way."

"What do you make?"

"Whatever strikes me. Mostly carvings of animals I see in the woods."

"I don't see any here. Don't you keep them?"

"Some." They were out in the shed, which he'd come to think of as a sort of studio-gallery. "I give some away. I sell some."

"Do you?" she asked, grinning widely. "You must be good."

"Yes to the first, I don't know to the second."

"If people buy them . . ." she said in a tone that made her point. "Have you always been artistic?" Images of the artists Richard employed crossed her mind. There was a high burnout rate in the advertising world. Perhaps that was what had happened to Garrick.

But he was shaking his head, his chin ruffling her hair. "Not particularly. It was only after I came here that I found I liked working with my hands."

"You're very good with your hands," she teased, and was rewarded with a tickle. "Anyway, I think it's great. Do you have to use special kinds of wood when you whittle?"

"Soft wood is best—like white pine. It has few knots and very little grain. I use harder wood—birch or maple—when I carve chessmen."

"You make *chess* sets?"

He nodded. "Do you play?"

"No, but I've always admired beautiful sets in store windows. More than once, I thought of buying one just to use it for decoration on a coffee table, but somehow that seemed pretentious. I play checkers, though. Have you ever carved a checker set?"

"Not yet, but I can. God, I haven't played checkers since I was a kid!"

"It'd be fun," she mused. "What about knives?"

"I never played with them."

"Whittling. Do you have special knives? The thing you were using the other night looked like a regular old jackknife."

"It was."

Again she tipped back her head, this time looking up at him in surprise. "A regular old jackknife?"

"Carefully sharpened. It has three blades. I use the largest for rough cutting and the two smaller ones for close work."

She was staring at him, fascinated. "You have beautiful eyes. I don't think I've ever seen hazel shot with silver like that."

The suddenness of the comment took Garrick off guard. It was the type of observation he was used to from his past, yet now it was different. As it sank in, he felt a warming all over. He liked it when Leah complimented him, didn't even mind that she'd been distracted from what he'd been saying. Strange that she didn't recognize him . . .

"Do you ever watch television?" he asked.

"Rarely. Why?"

"I was just wondering. . . whether you missed it up here."

"No," she answered, turning her head forward, "and I don't miss a phone, either."

"Didn't use it much at home?"

"Yes."

"Then why don't you miss it now?"

"Because in New York it's a necessity. You have to call to find out whether the book you ordered arrived or to make a reservation at a restaurant. You have to call a friend in advance to make a date for lunch. Up here you don't."

"Did you leave many friends in New York?"

"A few. It's only since my divorce that I've been able to cultivate friendships. Richard wasn't interested in the people I liked."

"Why not?"

"He didn't think they were useful enough."

"Ahh, he's the user type."

"He didn't step on people. He simply avoided those with whom he couldn't clearly identify. He had to feel that there was a purpose in any and every social contact. Getting together with someone simply because you liked him or her didn't qualify as purposeful in Richard's mind."

Garrick was about to say something critical, when he caught himself. He'd been guilty of the same thing once, only it sounded as though Richard had weathered it better. So who was he to throw stones?

Shifting Leah so that she was cradled sideways on his lap, he asked softly, "What are your friends like?"

Arms looped loosely around his neck, she brushed her thumb against his beard. "Victoria you know. Then there's Greta. We met at a cooking class. She has a phenomenal mathematical mind."

"What does she do?"

"She's an accountant."

"Do you see each other often?"

"Once every few weeks."

"What do you do together?"

"Shop."

"*Shop?* That's the last thing I'd expect an accountant to want to do."

"She doesn't want to. She *has* to. She's in a large firm that makes certain demands, one of which is that she look reasonably well put together. Poor Greta is the first to admit she has no taste at all when it comes to clothes. When we go shopping, I help her choose things, soup to nuts." She grinned. "I'm great at spending other people's money."

"That's naughty."

"Not when it's at their own request and for their own good."

"Is Greta pleased with the results?"

"Definitely."

"Then I guess it's okay. Who are some of your other friends?"

"There's Arlen."

"Is that a he or a she?"

"A she. I don't have any male friends. Except you." She plopped a wet kiss on his cheek. "You're a nice man."

"That's what you say now," he teased. "Wait till you know me better." He'd been thinking about cabin fever, about what could happen to two people, however compatible, when they were stuck with each other day after day. He knew it wouldn't bother him; he was used to the mountain, and he loved Leah. But suddenly he wasn't even thinking about whether Leah loved him back. He was thinking about all he hadn't told her about himself. What he'd said had to have been a Freudian slip.

"I am a nice man," he said seriously. "I wasn't always. But those days are done." He took a quick breath. "Tell me about Arlen."

Leah studied his face a minute longer, unaware of the fear in her eyes. *I wasn't always*, he'd said. What had he been before? Oh, Lord, she didn't want anything to pop her bubble of happiness. Not when she'd waited all her life to find it!

"Arlen." She cleared her throat. "Arlen and I met in the waiting room of the dentist's office. Three years ago, actually." They'd both been pregnant at the time. "We struck up a friendship and kept in touch, then started getting together after Richard and I split. She helped me through some rough times."

"The divorce?"

That, too. "Yes."

"Does she work?"

"Like a dog. She has five kids under the age of eight."

"Whew. She isn't a single mother, is she?"

"No, and her husband's as lovely as she is. They live in Port Washington. I've been to their home several times. She barbecues a mean hot dog."

He grinned. "You like hot dogs?"

"Yeah, but y'know which ones I like best?"

"No. Which ones?"

"You'll think I'm crazy."

"Which ones?"

"The ones you buy at the stands on the edge of Central Park. There's something about the atmosphere—"

"Diesel fumes, horse dung and pigeon shit."

She jabbed at his chest with a playful fist. "You're polluting the image! Think gorgeous spring day when the leaves are just coming into bloom, or hot summer day when the park is an oasis in the middle of the city. Brisk fall day when the leaves flutter to the ground. There's something about visiting the park on days like those and eating a hot dog that may very well kill you that's . . . that's sybaritic."

"Sybaritic?"

"Well, maybe not sybaritic. How about frivolous?"

"I can live with that." He could also come close to duplicating a sybaritic kind of atmosphere for her here on the mountain. "What else do you like about New York?"

"The anonymity. I feel threatened by large groups that know me and expect certain things that I may or may not be able to deliver. I don't like to have to conform to other people's standards."

He knew that what she was voicing related in part to the shyness she'd mentioned, but that it was a legacy of her marriage to Richard, as well. He was also stunned because the threat was one he himself felt.

"I'm a total unknown on the streets of New York," she went on. "I can pick and choose my friends and do my own thing without being censured. I think I'd die in a small suburban community. I don't want to have to keep up with the Joneses."

"If anyone's doing the keeping up, it should be the Joneses with you."

"God forbid. I don't want any *part* of people who compete their way through life."

"Amen," he said softly, then, "What else?"

"What else, what?"

"What else do you like about New York?"

She didn't have to think long. "The cultural opportunities. And the courses. I love taking courses, learning new things. Victoria said that there was an artists' community not far from here where I'd be able to learn to weave."

"I know just the one. You want to weave?"

"The process fascinates me. I'd like to be able to create my own patterns and make scarves and rugs and beautiful wall hangings." She lowered suddenly sheepish eyes to her fingers, which toyed idly with the cables on his sweater. "At least, I'd like to try."

"You'll do it." He'd build her a loom himself. The thought of seeing her working it, of listening to the rhythmic shift of harnesses, filled him with a mellowness that spelled home.

Home. Surprising. He hadn't spent much time thinking of having a home. What he'd known as a child had been far from ideal, and when he'd gone off to put his name up in lights, he hadn't had the time to think of it. His world had been the public eye. His interests had revolved around things that would make him more famous. A home didn't do those things. A home was personal, private. It was something for a man and his family.

"Garrick?" Leah whispered.

He blinked, only then realizing that his eyes had grown moist.

"What is it?" Her voice was laden with concern, her eyes with fear. During moments like these, when he looked so sad and faraway, she felt her bubble begin to quiver. He had a past, and for whatever his reasons, he wasn't telling her about it. She didn't have the courage to ask.

He forced a tremulous smile, then drew her in and held her close. "I get to dreaming sometimes," he murmured into her hair. "It's scary."

"Can you share the dream?"

"Not yet."

"Maybe someday soon?"

"Maybe."

They sat that way for a while, holding each other quietly. When the fire gave a loud crack and hiss, they both looked around, startled.

"Is it trying to tell us something?" Leah whispered.

"Nah. It's just being insolent."

"Maybe we'd better feed it."

"I have a better idea. Why don't we get dressed and go out?"

Her eyes lit up. "Me, too?"

"You, too." He tipped his head. "Going stir-crazy being inside?"

"No. I just don't want you going out alone. I want to be with you."

"God, you have all the right answers," he breathed.

Her voice held a touch of sadness. "No. Not yet. Maybe soon."

SO THEY WENT OUT IN THE RAIN, which, mercifully, was more like a drizzle. Garrick led her up the mountain, pointing out various signs of wildlife along the way. The going was sloppy, but in broad daylight and with as indulgent a guide as he was, Leah managed remarkably well. She wasn't quite sure how it happened, but the mountain that had seemed so hostile to her once was now, even in the wet mist, a place of fascination. Garrick belonged, and she was his welcome guest; it was almost as though the landscape had accepted her presence.

After they'd returned to the lower altitude, they trekked to Leah's car and came back carrying more of her things, which he enthusiastically made room for in the cabin and helped her stow.

Later in the day, they succumbed to their urges and made long, sweet love before the fire. In its aftermath, wrapped in each other and a quilt, Leah smiled. "I wonder if Victoria has ESP."

"If so, no doubt she's happy."

"Are you?"

"Very."

She tipped up her face and whispered, "I love you, Garrick."

His eyes went soft and moist. Taking a tremulous breath, he tightened his arms around her. "I love you, too. I've never said that to another living soul, but I do love you, Leah. God, do I love you!" His lips took hers with a fierceness that had never been there before, but Leah didn't mind, because she shared the feeling behind them. The love that flooded her was so powerful that it demanded no less ardent a release.

IN THE DAYS THAT FOLLOWED, their love grew even stronger. They spent every minute together, and never once did they tire of each other's company. There was always something to say, usually in soft, intimate tones, but there were times when they were silent, communicating simply with a look, a touch or a smile.

Garrick showed her his shed and the whittled figures that sat on a long shelf. Not only did he carve them, she found, but many he painted in colors that were true to life. She particularly adored a pair of Canada geese and cajoled him into letting her take them back to the cabin.

He also showed her the toothpick models he built, explaining how he'd started making them for his own amusement. But one of his fur buyers had mentioned them to a couple from Boston, who then wanted a model made of their own stately home. The commission had launched Garrick into a leisurely business.

Leah thought his models were exquisite, particularly those dramatic designs he'd made for himself, on which he'd let his imagination go wild. "You could be an architect," she said, awed by the scope of that imagination and the detail he'd achieved with as unlikely materials as toothpicks.

He was pleased with her comment, but said nothing. He couldn't be an architect. He didn't have the training, for one thing, and for another, to get either that training or employment, he'd have to return to the city. The city—any city—was a threat to him. He'd be recognized. He'd be approached. He'd be tempted.

But he didn't tell Leah that. The words wouldn't seem to come. She loved him for who and what he was right now. He didn't want to disillusion her. He didn't want her to know what a mess he'd made of his earlier life. He feared that she'd think less of him, and the thought of losing her respect or, worse, her love, was more terrifying than anything.

But it bothered him that he didn't tell her the truth. Oh, he'd never lied. He'd simply ignored those seventeen years of his life as though they'd never been. That Leah hadn't asked puzzled him in some ways. They shared so many other thoughts and feelings. He suspected that she knew he harbored a dark secret and that she was afraid to ask for the same reason he was afraid to reveal it.

Perhaps because of that, neither spoke of the future. They took life one day at a time, treating their love as a precious gift that neither of them had expected to receive.

With her dictionary and thesauruses, an atlas and a world almanac on hand, Leah began to work. The peaceful setting was conducive to production, even in spite of the spate of questions Garrick bombarded her with at first.

"Where do you start?"

"On a puzzle? Wherever I want. If it's a theme puzzle—"

"Define theme puzzle."

"One in which the longer entries have to do with a specific topic."

"Like phrases depicting madness—having bats in one's belfry, etc.?"

She grinned, remembering that particular inspiration as he did. "Or names of baseball teams, or automobile models, or parts of the body."

"Oh?"

"Nothing naughty, of course. Once I did a puzzle using phrases like 'keep an eye on the ball,' 'put one's best foot forward,' 'give a hand to a friend'—that of type thing would be part of a theme puzzle."

"So you start with the theme?"

"Uh-huh, and I work from there."

He sat for a few minutes, silently watching her add words to her puzzle before he spoke again. "Do you follow a special formula regarding numbers of black and white spaces?"

She shook her head. "It can vary. The same holds true for checked and unchecked letters."

"Checked and unchecked?"

"Checked letters are ones that contribute to both an across and a down word, unchecked to only one or the other. In the earliest puzzles every letter was checked. If you got all the across clues, you had the puzzle completed."

"Too easy."

"Right. Nowadays, as a general rule of thumb, only fifty-five to seventy-five percent of the letters should be checked."

He digested that, then a bit later asked, "How about clues? Do you spend a lot of time finding them and revising them?"

"You bet. Again times have changed. It used to be that primary definitions were used. For example, the clue for 'nest' would be 'a bird's home.' In recent years, I've seen clues ranging from 'a place to feather' to 'grackle shack.' Actually," she added sheepishly, "my editor is a wonder when it comes to clever clues. I have no problem with her revisions."

"Do you ever have problems with deadlines?" Garrick asked, somewhat sheepish himself now. "I'm not letting you get much work done."

"I don't mind," she said, and meant every word.

In truth, as the days passed, Leah wondered if she was dreaming. Garrick was everything she'd ever wanted in a man. He was patient when she was working, attentive when she wasn't. He was interesting, always ready to discuss whatever topic crossed either of their minds. Even in cases of disagreement, the discussion was intelligent and ended with smiles. He was perceptive, suggesting they go out or make dinner or play checkers with the set he'd carved, just when she needed a break. He was positively gorgeous, tall and rangy, rugged with his full head of hair and his trimmed beard, compelling with his hazel-and-silver eyes. And he was sexy. So sexy. He turned her on with a look, a word, a move, and made love to her with passion, sometimes gently, sometimes fiercely, always with devotion.

The only thing to mar her happiness was the frown that crossed his face at odd moments, moments that became more frequent as the days passed.

Five days became a week, then ten days, twelve, two weeks. Garrick knew he had to tell her who he was. His fear remained, but the need for confession grew greater. He wanted her to know everything and to love him anyway. He wanted her to respect him for the way he'd rebuilt his life. He wanted—needed—to share past pain and present fear, wanted her understanding and support and strength.

Once, when the rain had stopped, he took her for a walk, intending to bare his soul while they were on the mountain. Then they caught sight of a doe and her fawn, and he didn't have the heart to spoil the scene.

Another time he led her off the mountain and they hitched a ride into town. He planned to confess all while they were splurging on lunch at the small restaurant there, but Leah was so enchanted by the charm of the place that he lost his nerve.

And then she insisted on calling Victoria. "I told her I'd give her a ring when I was settled. She may be worrying."

"Yeah, about whether you'll speak to her again after what she did."

"It didn't end up so terribly, did it?"

He grinned. "Nope. But maybe we ought to keep Victoria in suspense."

That was exactly what Leah did. From a pay phone inside the small general store, she dialed Victoria's number.

A very proper maid answered. "Lesser residence."

"This is Leah Gates. Is Mrs. Lesser in?"

"Please hold the phone."

Leah covered the mouthpiece and grinned at Garrick, who was practically on top of her, boxing her into the booth. "Can't you just picture Victoria? She's probably wearing an oversize work shirt and jeans, looking like a waif as she breezes round and about her elegant furnishings to reach the phone. I wonder what she's been doing. Playing the lute? Preparing sushi?" She removed her hand from the mouthpiece when Victoria's excited voice came on the other end.

"Where have you been?"

"Hi, Victoria."

"Leah Gates! I've been worried sick!"

Leah's eyes sparkled toward Garrick. "You shouldn't have worried. I told you I wouldn't have any problem. The cabin is wonderful. I can understand why Arthur loved it up here."

"Leah . . ."

"It's been a little rainy. That's why I didn't get around to calling sooner. My car is still mud-bound."

There was a pause. "Where are you calling from?"

"The general store."

Another pause. "How did you get there if your car is mud bound?"

"Hitched a ride."

"Leah!"

Garrick stole the receiver from Leah's hand. "Victoria?"

There was another brief silence on the other end of the line, then a cautious, "Garrick?"

"You play dirty pool."

"Ahh." A sigh. "Thank God. She's with you."

"As you intended."

"Do you hate me?"

"Not now."

"But you did at first. Please, Garrick, I only wanted the best for you both. You were alone. She was alone. I'm sure my letter explained—"

"I haven't read your letter." His eyes held Leah's, while the arm around her waist held her close.

"Why not?"

"I didn't want to."

"You were that angry? I didn't tell her anything about you, Garrick," she rounded defensively, then paused and lowered her voice. "Have you?"

"Some."

"But not . . . that?"

"No."

"She is staying with you?"

"I couldn't very well turn her out into the rain with nowhere to go," he said, a wink for Leah softening his gruff tone. Of course, Victoria didn't see the wink.

"Oh, Garrick, I'm sorry. I thought for sure you two would get along. You're so *right* for each other."

Garrick covered the mouthpiece and whispered to Leah, "She says we're so right for each other."

"Wise busybody," Leah whispered back, then grabbed the phone. "I won't be sending any rent money, Victoria Lesser."

"But you called. You can't be totally angry."

"I have more of a conscience than you do," Leah said, but she was smiling and Victoria knew it.

"Should I ready the green room for you?"

"Not just yet."

"You'll be staying there awhile?"

Leah didn't bother to cover the phone this time when she spoke to Garrick. Her free hand was drawing lazy circles on the firm muscles of his back. "She wants to know if I'll be staying here for a while."

He took the phone. "She'll be staying. I've discovered that I like having a live-in maid."

"I am *not* his maid," Leah shouted toward the mouthpiece, while Victoria added her own comment.

"Garrick, you are not to use Leah—"

"And a cook," Garrick injected. "She makes super egg foo yong."

"I do not make egg foo yong!" Leah protested, snatching the phone. "He's pulling your leg, Victoria."

Garrick grinned. "Another body phrase. Write it down, Leah."

"Leah, what is he talking about?"

"He's making fun of my cooking and my crossword puzzles. The man is impossible! See what you got me into?"

"Let me speak with Garrick, Leah."

Rather smugly, Leah handed over the phone.

"Garrick?"

"Yes, Victoria."

"Are we alone?"

"Yes."

"I don't want her hurt, Garrick."

"I know that."

"She's been through a lot. It's fine for you both to rib me—I deserve it. But I want you to treat her well, and that means using your judgment. If you'd read my letter, you'd know that she's totally trustworthy—"

"I didn't have to read your letter to learn that."

"If the two of you don't get along, I want her back here."

"We get along."

"Get along well?" Victoria asked hopefully.

"Yes."

"Well enough for a future?"

"I . . . maybe."

"Then you'll have to tell her, you know."

"I know."

"Will you?"

"Yes."

"If you wait too long, she'll be hurt."

"I know that, Victoria," he said soberly.

"I trust you to do the right thing."

"Yes," he said, then added, "Here's Leah. She wants to say goodbye. Say goodbye, Leah," he teased as he handed her the phone, but inside he was dying.

The right thing. The right thing. He had to tell her. But when?

7

As it happened, the truth spilled without any preplanning on Garrick's part, its disclosure as spontaneous as the rest of their relationship.

Leah had been with him for better than two weeks. On that particular morning they'd slogged through the mud to check on the progress of the beaver dam that had been growing steadily broader over a nearby stream. Later, returning to the cabin, they'd changed into clean, dry clothes and settled before the fire.

Garrick was reading one of the books Leah had brought with her from New York; they'd found they enjoyed discussing books they'd both read. Leah was close beside him on the sofa, her back braced against his arm, the soles of her feet flat against the armrest. She was listening to music, wearing the headset he'd salvaged from his nonfunctional CB and adapted for her cassette. On pure impulse, he set down his book and removed the earphones from her ears.

"Unplug it," he said over her forehead. "Let me hear."

She tipped back her head and met his gaze. "Ah, Garrick, you don't want to do that."

"Sure, I do."

"But you like the quiet."

"I want to hear your music. And besides, I don't like feeling cut off from you."

Turning, she came up on a knee and draped her arms around his neck. "You're not cut off. I keep the music low. I'd be able to hear you if you spoke."

"I want to hear your music," he insisted, wrapping an arm around her hips. "If you like it, I might like it, too. We have similar tastes."

"You hated the new Ludlum book that I loved."

"But we both agreed that Le Carré's was great."

"You hated the curried chicken we had the other night."

"Because I added too much curry. And don't say you didn't find it hot, because I saw you gulping down water."

"You hated the roadrunner I folded for you."

"I didn't hate it. I just didn't know what it was." He closed his fingers on a handful of her bottom and gritted his teeth in a pretense of anger. "Leah, I want to listen to music. Will you unplug the headset and let me hear?"

"You're sure?"

"I'm *sure*."

Inwardly pleased, she removed the plug to the earphones. As the gentle sounds of guitar and vocalist filled the room, she sat back and watched Garrick's face.

He was smiling softly. "Cat Stevens. This is an old one."

"Seventy-four."

Sinking lower in the sofa, he stretched out his legs before him and listened quietly. He wore an increasingly pensive look, one that seemed to fade in and out, to travel great distances, return, then leave again. Leah knew the songs brought back memories, and when the tape was done, she would have been more than happy to put the machine away. But he asked her to put on another tape. Again he recognized the song and its artists. "Simon and Garfunkel," he murmured shortly after the first bars had been sung.

"Do you like it?"

He listened a while longer before answering. "I like it. I've never paid much heed to the words before. I always associated songs like this with background music in restaurants."

"Where?" she asked, surprised at how easily the question came out.

"L.A.," he answered, surprised at the ease of his answer. It was time, he realized.

"Were you working there?"

"Yes."

"For long?"

"Seventeen years."

Leah said nothing more, but watched him steadily. When he swiveled his head to look at her, her heart began to thud. His eyes were dark, simultaneously sad, challenging and beseechful.

"I was an actor."

She was sure she'd heard him wrong. "Excuse me?"

"I was an actor."

She swallowed hard. "An actor."

"Yes." His eyes never left hers.

"Movies?" she asked in a small voice.

"Television."

"I . . . your name doesn't ring a bell."

"I used a stage name."

An actor? Garrick, the man she loved for his private lifestyle, an *actor*? Surely just occasionally. Perhaps as an extra. "Were you on often?"

"Every week for nine years. Less often before and after."

She swallowed again and twined her arms around her middle as though to catch her plummeting heart. "You had a major part."

He nodded.

"What's your name?"

"You know it. It's the one I was christened with."

"Your stage name."

"Greg Reynolds."

Leah paled. There wasn't a sound in the cabin; she felt more than heard her bubble of happiness pop. She'd never been a television fan, but she did have eyes. Even had she not had an excellent memory, she'd have been hard-pressed not to recall the name. It had often been splashed across the headlines of tabloids and magazines, glaring up from the stand at the grocery store checkout counter, impossible to miss even in passing.

"It can't be," she said, shaking her head.

"It is."

"I don't recognize you."

"You said you didn't watch television."

"I saw headlines. There must have been pictures."

"I look different now."

She tried to analyze his features, but they seemed to waver. There was the Garrick she knew and . . . and then the other man. A stranger. Known to the rest of the world, not to her. She loved Garrick. Or was he . . . "You should have told me sooner."

"I couldn't."

"But . . . Greg Reynolds?" she cried in horror. "You're a star!"

"Was, Leah. Was a star."

She lowered her head and rubbed her forehead, trying to think, finding it difficult. "The show was . . ."

"*Pagen's Law.* Cops and robbers. Macho stuff—"

"That millions of people watched every week." She withered back into her corner of the sofa and murmured dumbly, "An actor. A successful actor."

Garrick was before her in an instant, prying her hands from her waist and enveloping them in his. "I *was* an actor, but that's all over. Now I'm Garrick Rodenhiser—trapper, Latin student, whittler, model maker—the man you love."

She raised stricken eyes to his. "I can't love an actor. I can't survive in the limelight."

He tightened his hold on her hands. "Neither can I, Leah. Greg Reynolds is dead. He doesn't exist anymore. That's why I'm here. Me. Garrick. This is my life—what you see, what you've seen since you've been here."

If anything, she sank deeper into herself. She said nothing, looked blankly to the floor.

"No!" he ordered, lifting her chin with one hand. "I won't let you retreat back into that shell of yours. Talk to me, Leah. Tell me what you're thinking and feeling."

"You were a phenomenal success," she breathed brokenly. "A superstar."

"*Was*. It's over!"

"It can't be!" she cried. "You can't stay away from it forever. They won't *let* you!"

"They don't want me, and even if they did, they don't have any say. It's my choice."

"But you'll *want* to go back—"

"No! It's over, Leah! I will not go back!"

The force of his words startled her, breaking into the momentum of her argument. Her eyes were large gray orbs of anguish behind the lenses of her glasses, but they held an inkling of uncertainty.

"I won't go back," Garrick said more quietly. His hand gentled on her chin, stroking it lightly. "I blew it, Leah. I can't go back."

The anguish wasn't hers alone. She saw in his eyes the pain she'd glimpsed before. It reached out to her, as it had always done, only now she had to ask, "What happened?"

For Garrick, this was the hard part. It was one thing telling her he'd been a success, another telling her how he'd taken success, twisted it, spoiled it, lost it. But he'd come this far. He owed it to Leah—and to himself—to tell it all.

Backing away from her, he stood and crossed stiffly to the window. The sun was shining, but the bleakness inside him blotted out any cheer that might have offered. Tucking his hands into the back of his waistband, he began to speak.

"I went out to the coast soon after I graduated from high school. It seemed the most obvious thing to do at the time. The one thing I wanted more than anything was to be noticed. I think you know why," he added more softly, but refrained from going into further self-analysis. "I had the goods. I was tall and attractive. I had the smarts that some others out there didn't have, and the determination. I just hung around for a while, getting a feel for the place, watching everything, learning who held the power and how to go about tapping it. Then I went to work. First, I talked a top agent into taking me on, then I willingly did whatever he asked me to do. Most of it was garbage—bit parts—but I did them well, and I made sure I was seen by the right people.

"By the time I'd been there three years, I was consistently landing reasonable secondary roles. But I wanted top billing. So I worked harder. I learned pretty quick that it wasn't only how you looked or acted that counted. Politics counted, too. Dirty politics. And I played the game better than the next guy. I kissed ass when I had to, slept around when I had to. I rationalized it all by saying that it was a means to an end, and I suppose it was.

"Five years after I arrived, I was picked to play Pagen." He lifted one shoulder in a negligent shrug. "Don't ask me why the show took off the way it did. Looking back on it, I can't see that it was spectacular. But it hit a vein with the public, and that meant money for the sponsors, the network, the producers, the directors and me. So we kept going and going, and in time I believed my own press. I convinced myself that the show was phenomenal and that it was phenomenal because of me."

He hung his head and took a shuddering breath. "That was my first mistake. No, I take that back. My first mistake was in ever going to Hollywood, because it wasn't my kind of place at all. Oh, I told myself it was, and that was my second mistake. My third mistake was in believing that I'd earned and deserved the success. After that the mistakes piled up, one after another, until I was so mired I didn't know which side was up."

He paused for a minute and risked a glance over his shoulder. Leah was in the corner of the sofa, her knees drawn up, her arms hugging her body. Her face seemed frozen in a stricken expression. He wanted to go down on his knees before her and beg forgiveness for who he'd been, but he knew that there was more he had to say first.

He turned to face her fully, but he didn't move from the window. "The show ran for nine years, and during that time I flared progressively out of control. I grew more and more arrogant, more difficult to deal with." His tone grew derisive. "I was the star, better than any of the others. I was the hottest thing to hit Hollywood in decades. What I touched turned to gold. My name alone could make the show—any show—a success.

"And there were other shows. After five years in the top ten with *Pagen*, I started making movies during the series' filming break. I fought it at first. I didn't know why at the time. Now I realize that something inside me was telling me that it was too much, that I needed a break from the rat race for a couple of months a year. That I needed to touch base for a short time with who I really was. But then I got greedy. I wanted to be more famous, and *more* famous. I wanted to become an indelible fixture in the entertainment world. I wanted to be a legend."

He sighed and bent his head, rubbing his neck with harsh fingers in an anger directed at himself. "I was running scared. That's really what it was all about. I was terrified that if I didn't grab it all while I had the chance, someone would come along and take it from me. But I wasn't all that good. Oh, I was Pagen, all right. I could play that part because it didn't take a hell of a lot of acting. Some of the other stuff—the movies—did, and I couldn't cut the mustard. None of them were box office hits, and that made me more nervous. Only instead of being sensible, taking stock and plotting a viable future for myself, I fought it. I berated the critics in public. I announced that the taste of the average moviegoer sucked. I got worse and worse on the set."

He looked at her then. "I was paranoid. I became convinced that everyone was waiting for me to fail, that they were stalking me, waiting to pounce and pick the flesh from my bones. I was miserable, so I began to drink. When that didn't help, I snorted coke, took whatever drugs I could get my hands on—anything that would blot out the unhappiness. All I succeeded in blotting out was reality, and in the entertainment world, reality means extraordinary highs and excruciating lows."

Taking a shuddering breath, he sighed. "*Pagen's Law* was canceled after a nine-year run, mostly because I'd become so erratic. The producers couldn't find directors willing to deal with me. They even had trouble gathering crews, because I was so impatient and demanding and critical that it just wasn't worth it. More often than not I'd show up on the set drunk or hung over, or I'd be so high on something else that I couldn't focus on the script. When that happened, I'd blame everyone in sight."

Very slowly he began to walk toward the sofa. His hands hung by his sides and his broad shoulders were slumped, but the desolation he felt was such that he simply needed to be near Leah. "It was downhill all the way from there. There were small parts after the series ended, but they came fewer and farther between. No one wanted to work with me, and I can't blame them. New shows took over where *Pagen* left off. New stars. The king was dead. Long live the king."

Very carefully he lowered himself to the sofa. His hands fell open, palms up in defeat, perhaps supplication, on his thighs. "In the end, I had no friends, no work. I was a pariah, and I had no one to blame but myself." He looked down at his hands and pushed his lips out. "I'd gotten so obsessed with the idea of being a star that I couldn't see any future if I didn't have that. So one day when I was totally stoned, I took my Ferrari and drove madly through the hills. I lost control on a turn and went over an embankment. The last thing I remember thinking was thank God it's over."

Leah's sharp intake of breath brought his gaze to hers. Her hands were pressed to her lips and her eyes were brimming with tears. He started to reach out, then drew back his hand. He needed to touch her, but he didn't know if he had the right. He was feeling as low, as worthless, as he'd felt when he'd awoken in that hospital after the accident.

"But it wasn't over," he said brokenly. "For some reason, I was spared. The doctors said that if I hadn't been so out of it, I'd have been more seriously hurt. I was loose as a goose when I was thrown from the car and ended up with only contusions and a couple of broken bones." His expression grew tight. "Someone had sent me a message, Leah. Someone was telling me that I hadn't spent thirty-six years of my life preparing for suicide, that there was more to me than that. I didn't hear it at first, because I was so wrapped up in self-pity that I couldn't think beyond it. But I had plenty of time. Weeks lying in that hospital bed. And eventually I came to accept what that someone was saying."

His voice lowered and his gaze softened on hers. "As soon as I could drive, I left L.A. I didn't know where I was going, only that I needed to get as far away from that world as possible. I kept driving, knowing that when I hit a comfortable place, I'd feel it. By the time I hit New Hampshire, I'd just about reached the end of the line.

"Then I saw this place. Victoria's husband had owned it—he used it for hunting parties—and Victoria kept it for a while after his death. Shortly before I came, she put it on the market through a local broker. From the first it appealed to me, so I bought it." He looked away. "It's odd how ignorant you can be of your own actions sometimes. Through all those years of success—of excess—the one thing I did right was to hire a financial adviser. He managed to invest the money I didn't squander, and he invested it wisely. I can live more than comfortably on the income from those investments without ever having to touch the capital."

He reached the end of his story, at least as far as the past was concerned. "I've made a life for myself here, Leah. I've been clean for four years. I don't touch alcohol or drugs, and I've sworn off indiscriminate sex." He looked at his hands, rubbed one set of long fingers with the other. "That other life wasn't me. If it had been, I wouldn't have botched it so badly. This is the kind of life I feel comfortable with. I can't—I won't—go back to the other."

Hesitantly his eyes met hers. "You're right. I should have told you all this sooner. But I couldn't. I was afraid. I still am."

Leah's cheeks were wet with tears, and her hands remained pressed to her lips. "So am I," she whispered against them.

Garrick did touch her then, almost timidly cupping her head. "You don't have to be afraid. Not of me. You know me better than any other person ever has."

"But that other man—"

"Doesn't exist. He never really did. He was a phony, an image, like everything else in Hollywood. An image with no foundation, so it was inevitable that it collapse. I don't want that kind of life anymore. You have to believe that, Leah. The only life I want is what I have here, what we've had here for the past two weeks. It's real. It's totally fulfilling—"

"But what about the need for public recognition? Doesn't that get in your blood?"

"It got in mine and nearly killed me. It was like a disease. And the cure was almost lethal, but it worked." He took a quick breath. "Don't let the mistakes I've made in the past turn you off. I've learned from them. Dear God, I've learned."

Leah wanted to believe everything he said. She wanted to believe it so badly that she began to shake, and her hands shot out to clutch his shoulders. "Greg Reynolds wouldn't be attracted to me—"

"Garrick Rodenhiser is."

"I'd be nothing in Greg Reynolds' world."

"You're everything in mine."

"I couldn't play games like that. I couldn't even play them for Richard."

"I don't want games. I want life. This life. And you."

Unable to remain apart from her a minute longer, he captured her mouth in a kiss that went beyond words in expressing his need. It was possessive and desperate and demanding, but Leah's was no less so.

"Don't ever be that other man," she begged against his mouth. "I think I'd want to die if you were."

"I won't, I won't," he murmured, then, while his hands held her head, took her mouth again and devoured it with a passion born of the love he felt. His lips opened wide, slanted and sucked, and he was breathing hard when he released her. "Let me love you," he whispered hoarsely, fingers working on the buttons of her shirt. "Let me give you everything I have... everything I've saved for you... everything that's come alive since you came into my life." Her shirt was open and his hands were greedily covering her breasts. "You're so good. All I've ever wanted."

Leah gave an urgent little cry and began to tug at his sweater. This was the Garrick she knew, the one who turned her on as no man ever had, the one who thought her beautiful and smart, the one who loved her. She felt as though she'd traveled from one end of the galaxy to the other since Garrick had begun his story. On a distant planet was the actor, but on progressively nearer ones was the man who'd suffered fear, then disillusionment, then pain. Even closer was the man who'd hit rock bottom and had begun to build himself up again. And here, with her, was the one who'd made it.

"I love you so," she whispered as his sweater went over his head. He brought her to his chest and held her there, rotating her breasts against the light matting of hair, then wrapping his arms around her and crushing her even closer.

He sighed into her hair, but that wasn't enough, so he kissed her again and again, then eased her back on the sofa and began to tug at her jeans. When her body was bare, he worshiped it with his mouth, dragging his tongue over her breasts and her navel, taking love bites from her thighs, burying his lips in the heart of her.

Leah's knuckles were white around the worn upholstery, her eyes closed tight against the sweet torment of his tongue against that ultrasensitive part of her. The world began to spin—this galaxy, another one, she didn't know—and her thighs tensed on either side of his head.

"Garrick!" she cried.

"Let it come, love," he whispered, his warm breath as erotic as his thrusting tongue.

Wave after wave of electrical sensation shook her, and she was still in the throes of glory when he opened the fly of his cords, stretched over her and thrust forward. She cried out again. Her knees came up higher. And it was like nothing she'd ever dreamed possible. Her climax went on and on—a second, then a third—while Garrick pumped deeply, reaching and achieving his own spectacular release.

He didn't leave her, but brought her up from the sofa until she was straddling his lap. And he began again, stroking more slowly this time, kissing her, dipping his head to lave her taut nipples with his tongue, using his hands to add extra sensation to the similarly taut nub between her legs, until it happened again and again and again.

Only when they were dripping with sweat and their bodies were totally drained did they surrender to the quiet after-storm where emotions raged. Leah cried. Damp-eyed himself, Garrick rocked her gently. Then, when she'd quieted, he pressed his lips to her cheek.

"I want to marry you, Leah, but I won't ask you now. Too much has happened today. It wouldn't be fair. But I'll be thinking it constantly, because it's the one thing that I want in life that I don't have right now."

Leah nodded against him, but she didn't breathe a word. She was sated, exhausted and happy. Yes, too much had happened today. But there was something else, something that went hand in hand with marriage that she hadn't told him. She had her secrets, too, and the burden of disclosure was now hers.

BUT BURDENS HAD A WAY of falling from shoulders when one least expected them to. Such had been the case with Garrick's soul baring. Such was the case with Leah's.

A month had passed since she'd arrived at the cabin, one day blending into the next in a continual span of happiness. With the ebbing of mud season, Garrick's Cherokee was functional again. They drove into town for supplies, drove to the artists' colony, where Leah inquired about weaving lessons, drove to Victoria's cabin and freed the Golf, which Leah drove back to Garrick's and parked behind the cabin. They took long walks in the woods, often at daybreak when Garrick checked the few traps he'd set for coyotes, and picnicked in groves surrounded by the sweet smell of spring's rebirth.

Then, one morning, Leah awoke feeling distinctly muzzy. The muzziness passed, and she pushed it from mind, but the next morning it was back, this time accompanied by sharp pangs of nausea. When Garrick, who'd been fixing breakfast, saw her dash for the bathroom, he grew concerned. He followed her and found her hanging over the commode.

"What is it, sweetheart?" he asked, pressing a cool cloth to her beaded forehead.

"Garrick . . . oh . . ."

He supported her while she lost the contents of her stomach, then, very gently, closed the commode and eased her down. "What is it?" he repeated as he bathed her face. Her skin was ashen. His own hands shook.

"I didn't think it would happen . . . could happen . . ."

"What, love?"

She looked bewildered. "And I was never sick like this . . ."

"Leah?"

"Oh, God." She covered her face with her hands, then removed them to collapse against Garrick. "Hold me," she whispered tremulously. "Just hold me."

His arms were around her in an instant. "You're frightening me, Leah."

"I know...I'm sorry.... I think I'm going to have a baby."

For a minute he went very still. Then he began to tremble. Framing her face with his hands, he held her away from him and searched her eyes. "I thought," he began, "I guess I assumed that you . . . I shouldn't have . . . are you sure?"

"No."

"But you think so?"

"The nausea. I felt a little yesterday, too. And I haven't had a period." She was as bewildered as ever. "I didn't think . . . it was never like this."

"You weren't using birth control . . . an IUD?"

Her eyes were brimming with tears. "I've never had to worry about it. I always had trouble conceiving."

"Not now," Garrick said, pride and excitement surging within him. But something about what she'd said, and her expression, tempered his joy. "Have you conceived before?"

She nodded, then dissolved into tears.

Pressing her face into the warmth of his shoulder, he soothingly stroked her back. "What happened?" he whispered.

It was a while before she could answer, and when she did it was in a voice rife with pain. "Stillborn. I carried for nine months, but the babies were born dead."

"Babies?"

"Two. Two separate pregnancies. Both babies stillborn."

"Ahhhh, Leah," he moaned, holding her closer. "I'm sorry."

She was crying freely, but her words somehow found exit through her sobs. "I wanted . . . them so badly . . . and Richard did. He blamed me . . . even when the doctors said . . . I did nothing wrong."

"Of course you didn't do anything wrong. What did the doctors say caused it?"

"That was the . . . worst of it. They didn't know!"

"Shhhh. It's okay. Everything's going to be okay." As he held her and rocked her, a slow smile formed on his lips. A baby. Leah was going to have a baby. His baby. "Our baby," he whispered.

"I don't . . . know for sure."

"Well, we'll just have to find the nearest doctor and have him tell us for sure."

"It may be too early."

"He'll know."

"Oh, Garrick," she wailed, and started crying all over again. "I'm . . . so . . . frightened!"

He held her back and dipped his head so that they were on eye level with each other. His thumbs were braced high on her cheekbones, catching her tears. "There's nothing to be frightened of. I'm here. We'll be together through it all."

"You don't understand! I want your b-baby. I *want* your baby, and if something happens to it I don't known wh-what I'll do!"

"Nothing's going to happen. I won't let it."

"You can't *stop* it. No one could last time, or the time before that."

"Then this time will be different," he said with conviction. Scooping her into his arms, he carried her from the bathroom and set her gently back on the bed. "I want you to rest now. Later today we're going out to get a marriage license."

"No, Garrick."

"What do you mean, no?"

"I can't marry you yet."

"Because you're not sure if you're pregnant? I want to marry you anyway. You love me, don't you?"

"Yes."

"And I love you. So if you're pregnant, that'll be the frosting on the cake."

"But I don't want to get married yet."

"Why not?"

"Because I don't know if I can give birth to a living child. And if I can't, I'll always worry that you married me too soon and are stuck with me."

"That's the craziest thing I've ever heard. I *love* you, Leah. I told you two weeks ago that I wanted to marry you, and that was before there was any *mention* of a child."

"Don't you want children?"

"Yes, but I've never counted on them. Up until a month ago, I'd pretty much reconciled myself to the idea of living out my life alone. Then you came along and changed all that. Don't you see? Baby or no baby, having you with me is so much more than I've ever dreamed of—"

"Please," she begged. "Please, wait. For me." She pressed a fist to her heart. "*I* need to wait to get married. I need to know what's going to happen. If...if something goes wrong with the baby and you still want me, then I'll marry you. But I wouldn't be comfortable doing it now. If I am pregnant, the next eight-plus months are going to be difficult enough for me. If, on top of that, I have to worry about having my marriage destroyed..." Her voice dropped to an aching whisper. "I don't think I could take that again."

Garrick closed his eyes against the pain of sudden understanding. He dropped his head back, inhaled through flaring nostrils, then righted his head and very slowly opened his eyes. "That's what happened with Richard."

"Yes," she whispered.

"You mentioned other things—"

"There were. And maybe the marriage would have fallen apart anyway. But the baby—the babies—they were the final straw. Richard expected me to bear him fine children. They were part of the image—the wife, the home, the kids. The first time it happened we called it a fluke. But the second time, after all the waiting and praying and worrying—well, there was no hope left for us as a couple."

"Then he was a bastard," Garrick growled. "You could have adopted— No, forget I said that. If you'd done it, you'd probably still be married to him and then I wouldn't have you. I want you, Leah. If the babies come, I'll love it. If they don't and we decide we want children, we'll adopt. But we can't adopt a child unless we're married."

Leah closed her eyes. She was feeling exhausted, more so emotionally than physically. "I hadn't planned on getting pregnant."

"Some of the best things happen that way."

"I would rather have waited and had a chance to enjoy you more."

"You'll have that chance. Marry me, Leah."

Opening her eyes, Leah reached for his hand and slowly carried it to her lips. She kissed each one of his fingers in turn, then pressed them to her cheek. "I love you so much it hurts, Garrick, but I want to wait. Please. If you love me, bear with me. A piece of paper doesn't mean anything to me, as long as I know you're here. But that same piece of paper will put more pressure on me, and if I am pregnant, added pressure is the last thing I'll need."

Garrick didn't agree with her. He didn't see where their marrying would cause her stress, not given what he'd told her about his feelings. But he knew that she believed what she said, and since that was what counted, he had no choice but to accede.

"My offer still stands. If you're not pregnant, will you consider it?"

Feeling a wave of relief, she nodded.

"And if you are pregnant, if at any time over the next few months you change your mind, will you tell me?"

Again she nodded.

"If you are pregnant, I want to take a marriage license out before you're due to deliver. When that baby comes screaming and squalling into the world, it's going to have to wait for its first dinner until a judge pronounces us man and wife."

"In a hospital room?" Leah asked with a wobbly smile.

"Yes, ma'am."

She moved forward into his arms and coiled her own tightly around his neck. She loved the thought of that—a new husband, a healthy baby. She didn't dare put much stock in it, because she'd been let down on the baby part twice before, but it was a lovely thought. A very lovely thought.

8

LOVELY THOUGHTS HAD A WAY of falling by the wayside when other thoughts took precedence. That was what happened to Leah once the local doctor confirmed that she was pregnant. Her initial reaction was excitement, and it was shared with, even magnified by, Garrick's. Then the fear set in—and the concern, and the practical matter of how to deal with a new pregnancy after two had gone so awry.

"I'd like to speak to my doctor in New York," she said one night while she and Garrick were sitting thigh to thigh on the cabin steps. It had been a beautiful May day, marred only by Leah's preoccupation.

"No problem," Garrick said easily. "We can drive into town tomorrow to make the call. In fact, I've been thinking I'd like to have a phone installed here." It was something he'd never have dreamed of doing before, but now that Leah was pregnant, concerns lurked behind his optimistic front. Having a phone would mean that help could be summoned in case of emergency.

Timidly she looked up at him. "I'd like to go back to New York." When he eyed her in alarm, she hurried on. "Just to see John Reiner."

"Weren't you comfortable with the doctor you saw here?"

"It's not that. It's just that John knows my medical history. If anyone can shed some light on what happened before and how to prevent it from happening again, it's him."

"Couldn't we just have Henderson call him?"

"I'd rather see John in person."

Garrick felt a compression around his heart, but it wasn't a totally new feeling. He'd been aware of it a lot lately, particularly when Leah's eyes clouded and she grew silent. "You're not thinking of having the baby in New York, are you?" he asked quietly.

"Oh, no," she answered quickly. "But for my peace of mind, I'd like to see John. Just for an initial checkup. He may be able to suggest something that I can do—diet, exercise, rest, vitamins—anything that will enhance the baby's chances."

Put that way, Garrick could hardly refuse. He wanted the baby as much as Leah did—more, perhaps, because he knew how much it meant to her. Still, he didn't like the idea of her leaving him, even for a few days. He didn't like the idea of her traveling to New York.

And he couldn't go with her.

"I don't want you driving down," he said. "You can take a plane from Concord. I'll have Victoria meet you at LaGuardia."

"You won't come?" she asked very softly. She had a feeling he wouldn't. Garrick didn't seem to dislike the city as much as he feared it. Even here she would have preferred seeing a doctor at a hospital, but that would have meant entering a city, and Garrick shunned even the New Hampshire variety. He'd insisted that she see a local man, though the closest one was a forty minute drive from the cabin. He hadn't even wanted to stop for dinner until they'd reached the perimeter of the small area in which he felt safe.

His eyes focused on the landscape, but his expression was one of torment. "No," he finally said. "I can't come."

Nodding, she looked down at her lap. "Can't" was something she'd have to work on. It was a condition in Garrick's mind and represented a fear that she could understand but not agree with. On the other hand, who was she to argue?

Hadn't she been firm in putting off marriage? Hadn't Garrick disagreed, but understood and conceded?

"I'll have to call to make an appointment, but I'm sure he'll see me within the next week or so. I can make it a day trip."

That Garrick wouldn't concede to. "That's not wise, Leah. Lord only knows I don't want you gone overnight, but for you to rush would defeat the purpose. I don't want anything happening. If you have the pressure of flights and appointments, you'll be running all day. You'll end up tense and exhausted."

"Then I'll sleep when I get back," she protested. She didn't want to be away from Garrick any longer than was necessary. "The baby is fine at this stage. Even the fact that I've been sick is a good sign. Dr. Henderson said so. I didn't have any morning sickness with the other two."

But he was insistent. "Spend the night with Victoria. At least that way I won't worry quite as much."

SO THE FOLLOWING WEEK she flew to New York, saw John Reiner, then spent the night at Victoria's. It should have been a happy reunion, and in many ways it was. Victoria was overjoyed that Leah and Garrick were in love, and she was beside herself when, promptly upon landing and in part to explain her doctor's appointment, Leah told her about the baby.

But some of the things that the doctor said put a damper on Leah's own excitement. She was feeling a distinct sense of dread when Garrick met her plane back in Concord the next afternoon.

"How do you feel?" he asked, leading her to the car. He'd called Victoria's on his newly installed phone the night before and knew that the doctor had pronounced Leah well, and definitely pregnant.

"Tired. You were right. It was a hassle. Hard to believe I used to live in that . . . and like it."

He had a firm arm around her shoulder. "Come on. Let's get you home."

She was quiet during most of the drive. With her head back and her eyes closed, she was trying to decide the best way to say what she had to. She didn't find an answer that night, because when they arrived back at the cabin, Garrick presented her with a small table loom and several instruction books on how to weave belts and other simple strips of cloth. She was so touched by his thoughtfulness that she didn't want to do anything to spoil the moment. Then, later, he made very careful, very sweet love to her, and she could think of nothing but him.

The next morning, though, she knew she had to talk. It didn't matter that she was dying inside. What mattered was that their baby, hers and Garrick's, be born alive.

"Tell me, love," Garrick said softly.

Startled, she caught in her breath. She'd been lying on her back in bed, but at the sound of his voice her head flew around and her eyes met his.

He came up on an elbow. "You've been awake for an hour. I've been lying here watching you. Something's wrong."

She moistened her lips, then bent up an arm and shaped her fingers to his jaw. His beard was a brush-soft cushion; she took warmth from it and strength from the jaw beneath.

"John made a suggestion that I'm not sure you'll like."

"Oh-oh. He doesn't want us making love."

She gave a sad little grin and tugged at his beard. "Not that."

"Then what?"

She took a deep breath. "He thought that it would be better if I stay close to a hospital from the middle of my pregnancy on."

"'Stay close.' What does that mean?"

"It means live in the city. He gave me the name of a colleague of his, a man who left New York several years ago to head the obstetrics department at a hospital in Concord. John has total faith in him. He wants him to be in charge of the case."

"I see," Garrick said. He sank quietly back to the pillow and trained his gaze on the rafters. "How do you feel about it?"

Withdrawing her displaced hand, yet missing the contact, Leah said, "I want what's best for the baby."

"Do you want to move to the city?"

"Personally? No."

"Then don't."

"It's not as simple as that. My personal feelings come second to what's best for this baby's chances."

"What, exactly, did your doctor think that his man in Concord would be able to do?"

"Perform certain tests, more sophisticated ones than a local doctor is equipped to do. Closely monitor the condition of the baby. Detect any potential problem before it proves fatal."

Garrick had to admit, albeit begrudgingly, that that made sense. It was his baby, too. He didn't want anything to go wrong. "Didn't they do all that before?"

"Not as well as they can now. Nearly three years have passed. Medical science has advanced in that time."

"Well," he said, sighing, "we don't have to make a decision on it now, do we?"

"Not right away, I suppose. But John suggested that I see his man soon. They'll be in touch on the phone, and John will forward any records he thinks may be of help. Usually. . ." She hesitated, then pushed on. "Usually there'd be monthly appointments at this stage, but John wants me to be checked every two weeks."

Garrick shut his eyes tight. "That means tackling Concord every two weeks."

"Concord isn't so bad."

He said nothing.

"And besides, we're getting into good weather. It's not such a long drive." But she knew that it wasn't the drive, or the weather, or any conflicting time demand that was the problem. "Will you drive me down twice a month?" she asked. She could easily drive herself, but she desperately wanted Garrick to be with her.

He didn't answer at first. In fact, he didn't answer at all. Instead he rolled toward her and took her into his arms. She felt the pulsing steel of his strength, smelled the musky, wood scent that was his and his alone, and when their lips met, she tasted his fear and worry. . . and love.

GARRICK DID DRIVE HER to Concord twice a month, but he was tense the whole way, and the instant each appointment was done, he quickly tucked her into the car and drove her home. Only on familiar turf was he fully at ease, but even that ease ebbed somewhat as late spring became early summer.

Outwardly life was wonderful. They shed sweaters and long pants for T-shirts and shorts, and more often than not, when he worked in the clearing around the cabin, Garrick was bare chested. Leah could have spent entire days just watching him. Sweat poured freely from his body. The muscles of his upper back and arms rippled with the thrust of a shovel or the swing of an ax. His skin turned a rugged bronze, while the sandy hue of his hair lightened. He was positively gorgeous and she told him so, which, to her surprise and delight, brought a deeper shade of red to his cheeks.

He put in his garden and spent long hours cultivating it. During those times Leah sat near him, either watching, weaving, basking in the sun or working on puzzles. She was regularly shipping parcels off to New York, and the fact that there was now a phone at the cabin facilitated communications with her editor. The queasiness and fatigue that had initially slowed her down had passed by the end of June; come July, she was feeling fine and beginning to show.

They were as deeply in love as ever. Leah made a point of protesting when Garrick doted on her, but she drank in his attention and affection. In turn, she did whatever she could to make his days special, but she had a selfish motive, as well. The busier she was, the more dedicated to his happiness, the less she thought about the child growing inside her.

She didn't want to think about it. She was frightened to pin hopes and dreams on something that might never be. In mid-July she underwent amniocentesis, and though she was relieved to learn that, at that point at least, the baby was healthy, she didn't want to know its sex.

Neither did Garrick. There were times when he was working the soil or whittling or listening to Leah's music when his mind would wander. At those odd moments he had mixed feelings about the baby. Oh, he wanted it; but he resented it, too, for in his gut he knew Leah was going to leave. She didn't say so. They deliberately avoided discussion of what was to come in August, when she reached the midway point of her pregnancy. But he knew what she was thinking when her eyes lowered and her brow furrowed, and he dreaded the day when she'd finally broach the subject.

More than anything he would have liked to stop time. He'd have Leah. He'd have the baby thriving inside her. He'd have the bright summer sunshine, the good, rich earth, the endless bounty of the mountain. He didn't want things to change; he liked them as they were. He felt safe and secure, productive and well loved.

But he couldn't stop time. The heat of each day turned to the chill of evening. The sun set; darkness fell. The baby inside Leah grew until her abdomen was as round as the cabbage he'd planted in the garden. And when Leah approached him in the middle of August, he knew that his time of total satisfaction was over.

"We have to talk," she said, sitting down beside him on the porch swing he'd hung. She'd gone inside for a sweater to ward off the cool night air; it was draped over the T-shirt—Garrick's T-shirt—that covered the gentle bubble of her stomach.

"I know."

"Dr. Walsh wants me closer to the hospital."

He nodded.

"Will you come?"

Looking off toward the woods, Garrick took a deep breath. When he spoke, his voice was gritty. "I can't."

"You can if you want."

"I can't."

"Why not?"

"Because this is my home. I can't live in the city again."

"You can if you want."

"No."

"I'm not asking you to move there for good. It would be for four months at most. Dr. Walsh is planning to take the baby by section in the middle of December."

Garrick swallowed. "I'll be with you then."

"But I want you with me now."

He looked at her sharply. "I can't, Leah. I just can't."

Leah was trying to be understanding, but she had little to work with. "Please. Tell me why."

He bolted up from the swing, and in a single stride was leaning against the porch railing with his back to her. "There's too much to do here. Fall is my busy time. Trapping season opens at the end of October. There's a whole lot to do before then."

"You could live with me part-time in Concord. It'd be better than nothing."

"I don't see why you have to live in Concord. I drive. The Cherokee is dependable. If there's a problem, I could have you at the hospital in no time."

"Garrick, it takes *two hours* to get there. Both times before, things went wrong after I'd gone into labor. Those two hours could be critical."

"We have a phone. We could call an ambulance... or... or call for a police escort if there's a need."

"Ambulance attendants don't have the know-how to handle problem deliveries. Neither do police."

"Okay," he said, turning to face her. "Then we can go to Concord in November. Why September?"

"Dr. Walsh wanted August, but I put him off."

"Put him off for another few months."

Tugging the sweater closer around her, Leah studied the planked floor of the porch. "Do you want this baby, Garrick?"

"That's a foolish question. You know I do."

"Do you love me?"

"Of course!"

She looked up. "Then why can't you do this for me—for the baby—for all three of us?"

With a low growl of frustration, he turned away again. "You don't understand."

"I think I do," she cried, pushing off from the swing and coming up to where he stood. "I think you're frightened—of people, of the city, of being recognized. But that's ridiculous, Garrick! You've made a good life for yourself. You have *nothing* to be ashamed of."

"Wrong. I spent seventeen years of my life behaving like a jackass."

"But you paid the price, and you've rebuilt your life. So what if someone recognizes you? Are you ashamed of who you are now?"

The pale light of the moon glittered off the flaring silver flecks in his eyes. "No!"

"Why can't you go out there and hold your head high?"

"It's got nothing to do with pride. What I have now is much finer than anything I had then. *You're* much finer than any woman I knew then."

"What is it, then? What is it that makes you nervous each and every time we approach civilization? I've seen it, Garrick. Your shoulders get tense. You keep your head down. You avoid making eye contact with strangers. You refuse to go into restaurants. You want to get out of wherever we are as quickly as possible."

"It bothers you not going out on the town?"

"Of course not! What bothers me is that you're uncomfortable. I love you. I'm proud of you. It hurts me to see you slinking around corners as though there's—" she faltered, searching for an analogy "—as though there's a trap set around the next one."

"I know all about traps. Sometimes you don't see them until you're good and caught."

"Then there's the case of the coyote, who won't be caught in the same place twice."

"The coyote's an animal. I'm human."

"That's right. You're smart and fine and strong—"

"Strong? Not quite." He turned to face her. The faint glow spilling from inside the cabin side-lit his features, adding to the harshness of his expression. "What I had for seventeen years was a disease, Leah. It was an addiction. And the one thing a former addict doesn't do is to let the forbidden be waved before his nose. I won't go into restaurants with bars because I'd have to walk by all those bottles to get to a seat. I won't look people in the eye because if they were to recognize me I'd see their star lust. I don't watch television. I don't go to movies. And the last thing I wanted when you came here was heavy sex." He snorted. "Guess I blew it on that one."

"You don't trust yourself," she said, at last comprehending the extent of his fear.

"Damn right, I don't. When you first showed up, I thought you were a reporter. I wanted to get rid of you as soon as possible, and you want to know why? If a reporter—especially a pretty one—were to interview me, I'd feel pretty important. And then I'd get to thinking that I'd done my penance for screwing up once, and maybe I should try for the big time again."

"But you don't *want* that anymore."

"When I'm here I don't. When I'm thinking rationally, I don't. But I spent a good many years thinking irrationally. Who's to say that I wouldn't start doing it again?"

"You wouldn't. Not after all you've been through."

"That's what I tell myself," he said in a weary tone, "but it's not a hundred percent convincing." He thrust a handful of fingers through his hair, which fell back to his forehead anyway. "I don't know how I'd react face to face with temptation."

She slipped her hand under the sleeve of his T-shirt to his shoulder. "Don't you think it's time you tried? You can't go through the rest of your life living under a shadow." She gave him a little shake. "You've been happy here. You feel good about your life. Wouldn't it be nice to prove to yourself, once and for all, that you have the strength that *I* know you have?"

"You love me. You see me through rose-colored glasses."

Leah's hand fell away as she tamped down a spurt of anger. "My glasses are untinted, thank you, and even if they weren't, that's a lousy thing to say. Yes, I love you. But I've been through love once before, and I'm a realist. I entered this relationship with my eyes wide open—"

"You're nearsighted."

"Not where feelings and emotions are concerned. Oh, I can see your faults. We all have them, Garrick. That's what being human is about. But you took on your weaknesses once before and came out a winner. Why can't you take on this last one?"

"Because I might fail, damn it! I might face temptation and succumb, and where would that leave me, or you, or the baby?"

"It won't happen," she declared quietly.

"Is that an ironclad guarantee?"

"Life doesn't come with guarantees."

"Right."

"But you have so much more going for you now than you had before," she argued. "You have the life you've made, and it's one you love. And you have me. I wouldn't sit idly back and watch you fall into a pattern of self-destruction. I don't want that other life any more than you do. And I don't want you hurt. I *love* you, Garrick. Doesn't that mean anything?"

He bowed his head and, in the shadows, groped blindly for her hand. "It means more than you could ever imagine," he said hoarsely, weaving his fingers through hers, holding them tightly.

"Come with me," she pleaded. "I know it's asking a lot, because it cuts into the trapping season, but you don't need the money. You said so yourself. And these are extenuating circumstances. It won't happen every year. It may never happen again."

"God, Leah . . ."

"I need you."

"Maybe you need something I don't have to give."

"But you're a survivor. Look at what you've been through. It isn't every man who can land in a canyon, half-broken in body and more than that in spirit, and rise again to be the kind of person who can—" again she floundered for words "—can take in a bedraggled mess of mud from your doorstep half suspecting that she was planning to stab you in the back with a poison pen story."

He made a noise that, in other circumstances and with a stretch of the imagination, might have been a laugh. "You were a little pathetic."

"The point is," she went on, "that your heart's in the right place. You want the best—for you, for me, for the baby. You can do anything you set your mind to. You can *give* anything you want."

Closing his eyes, Garrick put a hand to the tense muscles at the back of his neck. He dropped his head to the side, then slowly eased it back and around. "Ahhh, Leah. You make it sound so simple. Perhaps I could do it if I had you by my side every minute, whispering in my ear like a Jiminy Cricket. But I can't do that. I won't. I need to stand on my own two feet. Here I can do it."

"You asked me to marry you. Are you saying that we'd never take a vacation, never go somewhere different?"

"If it bores you to be here—"

"It doesn't, and you know it! But everyone needs a change of scenery sometimes. Suppose, just suppose this baby lives—"

"It *will* live," he barked.

"See, you can be optimistic, because you haven't been through the hell I have once, let alone twice. But I'm willing to try again—"

"It happened. We didn't plan it."

"I could have had an abortion."

"You're not that kind of person."

"Just as you're not the kind of person who gave up on life when you came to in that hospital. You could have, y'know. You could have gone right back to drinking and taking whatever else you were taking, but you didn't. You were willing to make a stab at a new life. Some people wouldn't have the courage to do that, but you did. All I'm asking now is that you take it one step further." She gave a frustrated shake of her head. "But that wasn't what I wanted to say. I wanted to say that if the baby lives, and grows and gets more active and demanding, there may be times when I'll want to go off with my husband somewhere, alone, just the two of us. Maybe to somewhere warm in winter, or somewhere cool in summer. Or maybe I'll want to go somewhere adventurous—like Madrid or Peking or Cairo. It would have nothing to do with being bored here, or not loving our child, but simply a desire to learn about other things and places. Would you refuse?"

He was silent for a minute. "I haven't thought that far."

"Maybe you should."

He eyed her levelly. "Before I mention marriage again?"

"That's right."

"Are you issuing an ultimatum, Leah?"

She turned her head aside in disgust. "An ultimatum? Me? I've used the word dozens of times in puzzles, but I wouldn't know how to apply it in real life if I had to." Removing her glasses, she rubbed the bridge of her nose. "No ultimatum," she murmured. "Just something to think about, I guess."

When she didn't raise her head, Garrick did it for her. The tears that had gathered in her eyes wrenched his insides, but he said what he had to say. "I love you, Leah. That won't change, whether you're here or in Concord. But I can't go with you. Not now. Not yet. There are still too many things I have to work out in my mind. I want to marry you, and that won't change, either, but maybe it would be good if we were separated for a time. If you're in Concord, under Walsh's eye, I'll know you're well cared for. While you're there, you'll be able to think about whether I *am* the kind of man you want. Except for two days, we've been together constantly for nearly five months. If it were fifty months or years, I'd still feel the same about you. But you have to accept me for what I am. Baby or no baby, you have a right to happiness. If my shortcomings are going to prevent that down the road, then... maybe you should do some rethinking."

Leah didn't know what to say, which was just as well, because her throat was so clogged she wouldn't have been able to utter a word. There were things she wanted to say, but she'd already said them, and they hadn't done much toward changing Garrick's mind. She'd never been one to nag or harp, and she refused to resort to that now. So she simply closed her eyes and let herself be enfolded in his arms, where she etched everything she loved about him into memory for the lonely period ahead.

SHE LEFT THE NEXT DAY while Garrick was out on the mountain. It didn't take her long to pack, since she had a limited supply of maternity clothes. The things she wanted most were her resource books, her music and her loom, and these she carried to the car in separate trips. She worked as quickly as she could, pausing at the end to leave a short note.

"Dear Garrick," she wrote, "We all have our moments of cowardice, and I guess this is mine. I'm on my way to Concord. I'll call you tonight to let you know where I'll be staying. Please don't be angry. It's not that I'm choosing the baby over you, but that I want you both. You've said that you'll love me no matter where I am, and I'm counting on that, because I feel the same. But I want a chance to love a child of ours, and I want you to have that chance, too. That's why I have to go." She signed it simply, "Leah."

THOUGH SHE DIDN'T HAVE an appointment set up for that particular day, Gregory Walsh saw her shortly after she arrived.

"Aren't you feeling well?" he asked as soon as she was seated.

She forced a small smile. "I'm feeling fine, but I . . . need a little help. I've just driven in. All my things are still in the car. I'm . . . afraid I haven't planned for this very well. It seems—" she grimaced "—that I don't have a place to stay. You're familiar with the area around the hospital. I was hoping you could suggest an apartment or a duplex, something furnished that I could rent."

Walsh was quiet for several minutes, his kindly eyes gentle, putting her at ease as they had from the start. "You're alone," he said at last, softly and without condemnation.

Her gaze fell to her twisting thumbs. "Yes."

"Where's Garrick?"

"Back at the cabin."

"Is there a problem?"

"Not really. He just didn't feel that he could...be here for such a long stretch."

"How do you feel about that?"

"Okay."

"Really?"

"I guess."

Again the doctor was silent, this time steepling his fingers beneath his chin and pursing his lips. His eyes remained on her bowed head. When he spoke at last, his voice was exquisitely gentle. "People often assume that my job is purely physical, examining one pregnant lady after another, prescribing vitamins, delivering babies. There's much more to it than that, Leah. Pregnancy is a time of change, and it brings with it a wide range of emotional issues. It's my job– nd wish—to deal with some of those issues. From a medical standpoint, a more relaxed mother-to-be is a healthier one, and her baby is healthier." He lowered his hands. "Given your medical history, you have more than your share of worries. Having you close by the hospital gives me a medical edge, but I was also hoping that it would serve to ease your fears."

She raised her head. "It will. That's why I'm here."

"But you've always been with Garrick before. It'd take a blind man not to see how close you two are. It'd take an insensitive one not to guess that it bothers you he's not with you now. I'd like to think I'm neither blind nor insensitive. I'd also like to think that you feel comfortable enough with me to tell me, honestly, what you're feeling."

"I do," she said softly. She didn't know how one could *not* feel comfortable with a man life Gregory Walsh. In his early fifties, he was pleasant to look at and talk with. He seemed to have a sensor fine-tuned to his patients' needs; he knew when to speak and when to listen. She'd never once sensed any condescension on his part, quite a feat given his position.

"Then tell me what you really feel about Garrick's staying behind at the cabin."

She thought for a minute, and when she spoke, her voice was unsteady. "I feel . . . lots of things."

"Tell me one."

"Sadness. I miss him. It's only been a few hours, but I miss him. Not only that, but I picture him alone back at the cabin and I hurt for him. I know it's stupid. It was his choice to stay there, and besides, he's a big boy. He lived there alone for a long time before I arrived. He's more than capable of taking care of himself. Still, I . . . it bothers me."

"Because you love him."

"Yes."

He nodded in encouragement. "What else are you feeling?"

She grew pensive and frowned. "Dismay. I've lived alone, too. I've taken care of myself. Yet here I am, all but crying on your doorstep, not knowing where I'm going to spend the night. I feel . . . handicapped."

"You're pregnant. That has to make any woman feel a little more vulnerable than usual."

"That's it. Vulnerable. I do feel that."

"What else?"

She lifted one shoulder and tipped her head to the side, her eyes dropping back to her hands. "Anger. Resentment. Garrick has his reasons for doing what he is, and I'm trying to understand them, but right about now it's hard."

"Because you're feeling alone?"

"Yes."

"And a little betrayed?"

"Maybe. But I don't have a right to feel that. Garrick never said he'd come. In all the time I've know him, he's never promised anything he hasn't delivered."

"You can still feel betrayed, Leah. It's normal."

"He was the one who wanted to get married."

"Has he changed his mind?"

"No. But even if we were married, I doubt he'd be here. He has a certain . . . hang-up. I can't explain it."

"You can, but you won't, because that would be betraying him," Walsh suggested with an insight that drew her grateful gaze to his. "I respect you for that, Leah. And anyway, I don't pretend to be a psychiatrist. All I want to do is help you out where I can. Will you be in touch with Garrick while you're here?"

"I told him I'd call tonight. He'll worry otherwise."

"Will he be down to visit?"

"I don't know. He said he'd be here when the baby's due."

"Well, then, that's something to look forward to. The anger, the resentment, the sense of betrayal—those are things you and Garrick will have to work out. All I can say is that you shouldn't deny them or feel guilty for feeling them." He held up a hand. "I'm not criticizing Garrick, mind you. I haven't heard his side of the story, and I wouldn't deign to imagine what's going on in his mind."

"He probably feels betrayed himself, because I chose to come here instead of staying with him. I do feel guilty about that, but I had no choice!"

"You did what you felt you had to do. That's your justification, Leah. It doesn't mean that you have to like the situation. But if you were to drive back to him right now, you'd probably show up on my doorstep again tomorrow. In your heart, you feel that what you're doing is best for the baby. Am I right?"

She answered in a whisper. "Yes."

"So. I want you to keep telling yourself that." He grinned unexpectedly. "As for feeling alone and having nowhere to stay, I think I have a perfect solution. My place."

"Dr. Walsh!"

He laughed. "I love it when gorgeous young women take me the wrong way. Let me explain. My wife and I moved up here when the last of our boys—we have four—graduated from college. They were all out doing their own thing, and we felt it was time we did ours. We liked New York, but progressively it was getting more difficult for Susan—that's my wife—to handle. She has crippling arthritis and is confined to a wheelchair."

Leah gasped. "I'm sorry."

"So am I. But, God bless her, she's a good sport about it. She never complained in New York, but I knew that she'd love to be in a place where she could go in and out more freely. When the offer came from this hospital, I grabbed it. We bought a house about ten minutes from here." He chuckled. "In New York that would still be city. Here it's a quiet, tree-shaded acre. One of the things we loved about the house was that there was an apartment in what used to be a garage. Separate from the house. Set kind of back in the trees. We thought it would be ideal for when the boys came to visit. And they do come, but never for more than a night here or there, and then they usually sleep on the living room couch." He sat forward. "So, the apartment's yours if you want it. You'd be close to the hospital but away from the traffic. And Susan would love the company."

Leah was dumbfounded. "I couldn't impose—"

"You wouldn't be imposing. You'd be in your own self-contained unit, and I'd know you were comfortable."

"Is it wise for a doctor to be doing this for a patient?"

"Wise? Let me tell you, Leah. There's another reason I left New York, and that was because I was tired of the internal politics at a large city hospital. Here I do what I want. I decide what's wise. And yes, I think my offer is wise, just as I think you'd be wise to take me up on it."

"I'd want to pay rent," she said, then winced. "The last time I said that, I got to where I was going and found it demolished."

"This place isn't demolished, and you can pay rent if it will make you feel better."

"It will," she said, smiling. "Thank you, Dr. Walsh."

"Thank *you*. You've just made my day." At her questioning look, he explained. "When I can make a patient smile, particularly one who walked in here looking as sober as you did, I know I've done something right."

"You have." Her smile grew even wider. "Oh, you have."

9

THE APARTMENT WAS as perfect as Gregory Walsh had said it would be. With walls dividing the space into living room, bedroom and kitchenette, it seemed smaller than the cabin, but it was cozy. The furnishings were of rattan, and where appropriate, there were cushions in pale blue and white, with draperies to match, giving a cheerful, yet soothing effect. Leah had free access to the yard, which was lush in the wild sort of way that reminded her of the woods by the cabin and made her feel more at home.

Susan Walsh was an inspiration. "Good sport" was a mild expression to describe her attitude toward life; her disposition was so sunny that Leah couldn't help but smile whenever they were together, and that was often.

But there were lonely times, times when Leah lay in bed at night feeling empty despite the growing life in her belly. Or times when she sat in the backyard, trying to work and being unable to concentrate because her mind was on Garrick. He called every few days, but the conversation was stilted, and more often than not she'd hang up the phone feeling worse than ever.

The desolation she felt stunned her. She'd never minded when, during each of her previous pregnancies, Richard had gone off on business trips. She tried to tell herself that her separation from Garrick was a sort of business trip, but it didn't help. Garrick wasn't Richard. Garrick had found a place in her heart and life that Richard had never glimpsed.

She missed Garrick with a passion that six months before she wouldn't have believed possible.

Physically, she did well. She saw Gregory at the hospital for biweekly appointments. His examinations grew more thorough and were often accompanied by one test or another. She didn't mind them, for the results were reassuring, as was the fact that the hospital was close should she feel any páng or pressure that hinted at something amiss. She didn't feel anything like that, only the sporadic movements of the baby, movements that became stronger and more frequent as one week merged into the next.

She wanted Garrick to feel those sweet little kicks and nudges. She wanted him to hear the baby's heartbeat, as she had. But she knew she couldn't have it all. In her way, she had made a choice. The problem was learning to live with it.

Then, shortly before dawn one morning, after she'd been in Concord for nearly a month, she awoke to an eerie sensation. Without opening her eyes, she pressed a hand to her stomach. Her pulse had automatically begun to race, but she couldn't feel anything wrong. No aches or pains. No premature contractions. She was barely breathing, waiting to identify what it was that had awoken her, when light fingers touched her face.

Eyes flying wide, she bolted back and screamed.

"Shhhhh." Gentle hands clasped her shoulders. "It's just me."

All Leah could make out was a blurred form in the pale predawn light. "Garrick?" she whispered as she clutched frantically at the wrists by her shoulders. He felt strong like Garrick. He smelled good like Garrick.

"I'm sorry I frightened you," said the gravelly voice that was very definitely Garrick's.

She threw her arms around his neck and held him for a minute, then, unable to believe he was really squatting by her bedside, pushed back and peered at him. She needed neither her glasses nor a light to distinguish each of the features she'd missed so in the past weeks.

"Frightened? You *terrified* me," she exclaimed in a hoarse whisper. "What are . . . why are you . . . at this hour?"

He shrugged and gave a sheepish smile. "It took me longer than I thought to get everything packed."

"Packed?" Her fingers clenched the muscles at the back of his neck. "Are you—"

"Moving in with you? Yes. I figured you owed me."

Softly crying his name, she launched herself at him again. This time she hung on so relentlessly that he had to climb into bed with her to keep from being choked to death.

He didn't mind. Any of it. "I've been in agony, Leah," he confessed in a ragged whisper. "You've ruined the cabin for me. I'm miserable there without you. And those phone calls suck."

She couldn't restrain an emotional laugh. "Ditto for me. To all of it."

"You weren't at the cabin. You don't know how empty it was."

"I know how empty *I've* been." Her mouth was against his throat. "But what about . . . you were so adamant about not coming . . ."

"You said the word in the note you left. Cowardice. It nagged at me and nagged at me until I couldn't take it anymore. I don't know what's going to happen to me here, but I have to take the chance. I don't have any other choice. Being with you means too much."

With a soft moan of heavenly thanks, she began to kiss him—his neck, his beard, his cheekbones, eyes and nose. By the time she'd reached his mouth, she was bunching up his jersey, dragging it from the waistband of his jeans. Her progress was impeded briefly by his hands, which were all over her body, then homing in on those places that had altered most during their separation.

"I want you badly," he groaned. "Can we?"

"Yes, but—"

"Let me make love to you."

"You already have by coming here," she whispered, her breath hot against his skin. She was kissing his chest, moving from one muscled swell to the next, one tight nipple to the other. "Now it's my turn."

Garrick couldn't stop touching her, but he closed his eyes and lay back. He raised his hips when she unzipped his jeans and kicked his legs free after she'd peeled them down.

Leah loved him as she'd never done before. Her appetite was voracious, and the small sounds of pleasure that came from his throat made her all the more bold. His hands were restless in her hair, on her shoulders and back, and while she touched him everywhere, kissed him everywhere, he squeezed his eyes shut against the agony of ecstasy. When she took him into her mouth, he bucked, but her hands were firm on his hips, holding him steady for the milking of lips and tongue. The release he found that way was so intense, so shattering for them both, that the first rays of the sun were poking through the drapes before either of them could speak.

"You make me feel so loved," he whispered against her forehead.

"You are," she returned as softly. "I hadn't realized how much of my time at the cabin was spent showing you that—until I got here and didn't know what to do with myself."

He moved over her then, fingers splayed on either side of her head, eyes wide and brilliant. "You . . . have . . . no idea how much I love you."

"I think I do," she said with a soft smile. "You're here, aren't you?"

"Yes. And I intend to make it. For you."

"No, for *you*."

"And for you."

"Okay, for me."

"And for baby," he said, lowering a hand to properly greet his child.

LEAH LET GARRICK FIND his own pace in Concord. She would have been happy if he just sat with her in the yard or the apartment and accompanied her to the hospital for her appointments. But he did more than that. Within days of his arrival, he signed up to take several courses at the local university. She knew that the first few trips he made there were taxing for him, because he returned to her pale and tired. But he stuck with it, and in time he felt less threatened.

Likewise, he insisted on taking her for walks each day. Gregory had recommended the exercise, and though they began with simple neighborhood trips, Leah's eagerness and Garrick's growing confidence soon had them covering greater distances. Often Garrick wheeled Susan in her chair while Leah held lightly to his elbow; other times Leah and Garrick went alone.

"How do you feel?" Leah asked on one of those private outings.

"Not bad."

"Nervous?"

"Not really. No one seems to recognize me. No one's looking twice." He snorted. "If I had any brains, I suppose I'd be offended."

"It's because you do have brains that you're not. How about at school? Have there been any double takes there?"

"No." He didn't tell her about the anxiety he'd felt when, during one of those very tense first days of classes, he'd stood for five minutes outside a local tavern, aching for a drink, just one to calm him down. Nor did he tell her of the flyers he'd seen posted around the university, advertising dramatic productions in the works; he'd stared at those, too, for a very long time.

But he was with her, and he was doing all right, and *she* was doing all right, which was what really mattered.

MID-OCTOBER BROUGHT the turning of the leaves. Garrick would have liked to show Leah the brilliance of the autumnal spectacle from the cabin, but he didn't dare make even a day trip back to the mountain. The baby was growing bigger and Leah's body more unwieldy; in terms of both comfort and safety, he knew that she was better off staying in Concord.

November brought a marked downshift in the temperature, as well as Garrick's insistence that he and Leah file for a marriage license. It also brought orders from Gregory, soon after, that Leah was to stay in bed. She wasn't thrilled with the prospect, for it meant an end to her outings with Garrick. And that she'd have more time on her hands to worry about the baby.

She'd had every test imaginable. Gregory had made detailed comparisons between the results of those tests and the information gleaned from less frequent and less detailed tests done during her last pregnancy in New York. All signs were good, he declared. The baby appeared to be larger, the heartbeat stronger than ever.

"I think you've planted a monster in me," she complained to Garrick one afternoon when she felt particularly uncomfortable.

"Like father, like son," he teased.

"Ah, but we don't know that. What if we get an amazon of a daughter?"

"She can be a Cyclops, for all I care, as long as she's healthy."

Which was the password. Healthy. Boy or girl, they didn't care, as long as the child was born alive.

Increasingly, though she warned herself not to, Leah did think about the child—what sex it was, what they would name it, whether it would have Garrick's eyes or her hair, whether it would like to read. And the more she day-dreamed, the more nervous she became, for the critical time was fast approaching.

Garrick, too, was growing nervous, and only part of it had to do with the coming delivery. When he was on campus, he found himself drawn more and more often to the building that housed the small theater. Any number of times he simply stood outside and stared at it. Then one day, with his hands balled into fists in the pocket of his high-collared jacket, he ventured inside.

The theater was dim, with rows and rows of vacant seats, one of which he slipped into while he trained his eyes on the lit stage. Though he'd never acted in a classic himself, he knew Chekov when he saw it. The set was distinct, as were the lines. Slouching lower, he propped his chin on a fist and watched the fledgling actors and actresses do their thing.

They were impressive, he decided after a time. Not quite there yet, but on their way. They were interrupted from time to time by the director, a woman whose voice he could hear, though he couldn't see her. The students were attentive, listening quietly to her criticism, then attempting to follow her suggestions. Sometimes they succeeded; sometimes they didn't. But they tried.

Garrick wondered what would have happened if *he'd* tried the way they did. He wondered whether, if he'd listened to directors, perhaps taken formal acting instruction, he would have been able to evolve into a truly good actor. He'd never really given it a shot. *Pagen* had come along and made him a star, so he hadn't had to.

Watching the young performers, he wondered if any of them dreamed of being stars. More aptly, he wondered if any of them *didn't*. He focused on one young man whose voice wasn't quite forceful enough but whose interpretation was a bit more compelling than that of the others. What would he do after college? Go to New York? Work off-Broadway for a while? Make it to Broadway itself? Or think beyond all that and hightail it to the coast, as he'd done?

His eyes skimmed the stage again, this time alighting on a girl, blond haired and petite of build. As she moved the faint bobbing of her breasts was visible beneath an oversize sweatshirt that tucked snugly under her bottom. He wondered whether she was having an affair with one of the boys—perhaps the good-looking one standing off by the wings? If so, it probably wouldn't last. If her career surpassed his, she'd leave him behind and move on. To what? Male leads? Directors? Producers?

He wondered what she'd think if she knew that Greg Reynolds was sitting at the back of the theater, watching her. Then he snorted softly. She was too young. She probably didn't know who in the hell Greg Reynolds was! And besides, he reminded himself, it wasn't Greg Reynolds who sat unnoticed. It was Garrick Rodenhiser, and unnoticed was precisely what he wanted to be.

Shoving himself up from his chair, he strode quickly out of the theater.

But he was back several days later, sitting in the same seat, watching a rehearsal that had benefited from those several days' practice and become more refined. The best of the performers were clearly emerging—the strong ones distinguishing themselves from the weak as the director focused her coaching more and more on the latter. He watched for a while longer, not quite sure why he stayed, knowing that he didn't need the knot in his belly, that there were other things he'd rather be doing, but unable to move. At last he did move, and when he reached the fresh air, he felt a distinct sense of relief. Theaters were confining things, he decided.

Yet he went back again. A week later this time, and still not quite knowing why. But he was there. And this time he stayed in his seat until the rehearsal had ended and the performers, one by one, filed past him. The director was the last to leave, but while the others hadn't given him a glance as they'd passed, she stopped.

She was a pretty woman, Garrick noticed, viewing her up close for the first time. Tall and willowy, she had long brown hair that was pulled into a high clasp at her crown, only to tumble smoothly down from there. She wore jeans and a heavy jacket and was clutching an armload of papers to her chest. She was younger than he'd expected, perhaps in her mid-twenties; he guessed her to be either a teaching assistant or a graduate student.

"I've seen you here before," she said, cocking her head.

Garrick remained sprawled in his seat. "I've stopped by a few times."

"We'll be doing the show next weekend. I'd think you'd rather see it then."

"Rehearsals are more interesting. They allow you to see what really goes into the production."

"Are you a student of the theater?"

He took in a breath and pushed himself straighter. "Not exactly."

"A connoisseur?"

He shrugged, then hoisted himself to his feet. He didn't miss the slight widening of the woman's eyes at his height. "Not exactly. What about you?"

"A grad student. We often direct undergraduate productions." When she turned and started walking toward the door, he followed. His heart was pounding in protest, but his legs seemed not to hear.

"Doing Chekov is an ambitious endeavor," he remarked.

"Isn't that what learning is about—challenge?"

He didn't answer that. He'd never associated the acting he'd done with learning, and his major challenge had been in topping the Nielsens for the week. "Do you get much of a crowd at your shows?" he asked.

"Sometimes yes, sometimes no. This one probably won't be as well attended, since it's more serious and heavy. We'll get some of the university types, but the local crowd is drawn to lighter things." They'd passed through the lobby and reached the door, which Garrick held open with a rigid hand. As she stepped into the daylight, she looked up at him. "Do you live locally?"

"For now."

"Are you affiliated with the university?"

"I'm taking a few courses."

They'd stopped at the top of the stone steps. She was staring at him. "Studying anything special?"

"Latin."

She laughed. "That's an odd one." But her laughter died quickly. Her eyes were fixed on his. She frowned for an instant.

"Is something wrong?"

"Uh, no. You look vaguely familiar. I, uh, I don't think I know any Latin students."

He didn't know if it was a come-on. Yes, he thought her attractive, but it was an objective judgment. She didn't turn him on in any way, shape or fashion. Still, he didn't leave.

"Is this your first year here?" she asked as she continued to study him closely.

"Yes." Feeling inexplicably bold despite the damp palms he pressed to the insides of his pockets, he returned her gaze unwaveringly.

"Are you a professional student?"

"Nope."

"What did you do before you came here?"

"Work."

"Doing . . . ?"

"I work up north."

Again she frowned. Her gaze fell to his beard, then returned to his eyes. "I'm really sorry, but you do look familiar."

"Maybe I just look like someone else," he suggested with an outer calm that was far from matched inside.

She started to shake her head, but paused. "That may be it." Her eyes sharpened; Garrick noticed that they were brown, rather nondescript, nowhere near as warm or interesting as Leah's gray ones. Then she grinned. "That *is* it. Has anyone ever told you that you look like Pagen?"

"Pagen?"

"You know, the guy on television a few years back? Actually, his name was Greg Reynolds. I was a teenager when Pagen was in his heyday. He was one beautiful man." She blushed, then frowned again. "He disappeared from the scene pretty quickly after the series ended. I wonder what happened to him."

"Maybe he left the business and went to live in the woods," Garrick heard himself say.

"Maybe," she mused, then her look grew skeptical. "Are you sure you're not him?"

Of course I'm not, Garrick could have said, or *Are you kidding?* or *No way!* Instead, and for reasons unknown to him, he shrugged.

"You are," she said, an inkling of excitement in her voice. "You are Greg Reynolds. I can see it now. Your hair's a little different and you have a beard, but the eyes are the same...and the mouth." She was looking at the last in a way that made him press it closed.

"You're not talking," she announced with a sage nod, then held up one hand. "And your secret's safe with me. I promise." Then, suddenly, all pretense of maturity crumbled. "I don't believe it's you," she singsonged, eyes aglitter. "What was it like in Hollywood? It must have been so exciting doing the series! I thought you were wonderful! I'd like to be there for one day—one week—one month! You really *made* it. What have you done since then? Have you ever considered doing something here? You can't have retired from acting completely, not after... all that!"

"I've retired," he said quietly, but the statement was ineffective in staunching her enthusiasm.

"I had no idea we had a celebrity in our midst. No one else did, either, or word would have spread. My students would *love* to meet you. You'd be an inspiration!"

He shook his head. "I think not." He took a step to leave, but she put a hand on his sleeve.

"Maybe you'd speak before the theater group. I know the other grad students and the professors would be as excited as I am—"

"Thank you, but I really can't."

When he started off, she fell into step beside him. "Just me, then. Would you let me take you to lunch some day? You have no idea how much I'd like to hear about your experiences. God, they'd make a fantastic book. Have you ever thought of writing about your years as Pagen?"

"No," he said, and quickened his step.

"How about it? Just lunch, or... or dinner? I know a fantastic little place that's dark and quiet. No one would have to know we were there—"

"I'm really not free." He strode on.

The young woman stopped, but she couldn't resist calling after him. "Mr. Reynolds?"

He didn't answer. He wasn't Mr. Reynolds. Not anymore.

THAT NIGHT, WHILE HE AND LEAH were finishing off the last of the stew he'd made, Garrick told her what had happened.

"You told her who you were?" Leah asked in astonishment. It was the last thing she'd have expected him to do.

"She guessed, and I didn't deny it." He was reclining in his chair, one arm hooked over its back, the other fiddling absently with the spoon he hadn't used. He looked nearly as confused as Leah. "It was strange. I think I wanted her to know, but for the life of me I can't understand why. You know how I feel about my anonymity." He looked up, those wonderful hazel-and-silver eyes clouded. "Why did I do that, Leah?"

"I'm not sure," she answered quietly. "Did you feel anything... sitting there in the theater?"

"It was interesting. The kids were pretty good. But did I feel envious? No."

"Did you get the urge to jump up there?"

"God, no."

"You didn't miss being on center stage?"

"I didn't miss being on stage period. I was very happy to be sitting in the dark."

She breathed a tiny sigh of relief.

"I heard that," Garrick chided, narrowing one eye. "You were worried."

"I don't want you to miss anything about that life," she said a little evasively, then added, "What about the woman?"

"What about her?"

"Do you think that somehow, maybe subconsciously, you wanted to impress her?"

He shook his head. "No. She was pretty and all, but not like you."

"But she's a thespian."

"Good word, but it has no relevance."

"Sure, it does. She's involved in the same kind of life you came from. A person like that might not go gaga over trapping, but she would about acting, particularly big-time acting."

"What I used to do was small time compared to the people who do Chekov or Williams or—even more so—Shakespeare. No, I wasn't trying to impress her."

"Maybe you just got tired of the waiting."

"What do you mean?"

Leah searched for an example to illustrate her point. The only one was the most obvious, and since it filled so much of her thoughts, she went with it. "There are times," she began quietly, "when I just want this baby to be born—one way or the other. It's the waiting and worrying and not knowing that's so bad. Even if the worst happens, at least I'll know, so I can go on with my life."

"Leah..."

"I'm sorry, but it's the only thing I can think of, and it makes my point. I would assume that for you, it must be nearly as bad wandering around Concord, waiting for someone to recognize you, worrying about what will happen when someone does. Maybe you wanted to get it over with. Maybe one part of you wanted that woman to know who you were."

He opened his mouth to protest, then clamped it shut and was silent for a minute. "Maybe."

"How did you feel when the truth came out?"

His tawny brows knit as he tried to verbalize his thoughts. "Weird. A little proud, but a little like an imposter, too. I felt distanced . . . like she was talking about someone else entirely when she started bombarding me with questions. I felt like I was playing a game, letting her *believe* I was Greg Reynolds, superstar, when I knew that I wasn't."

"Did she bring back memories of how the fans used to be?"

"Yes and no. She went all wide-eyed and high-voiced like a typical fan, but I didn't like it the way I used to. To tell you the truth, it was disgusting. Up to that point, she'd seemed dignified." He gave a lopsided grin. "I have to admit that I felt damn good walking away from her."

"Do you think she was offended?"

"Lord, I hope so," he answered without remorse. "With luck, she'll dismiss me as a fraud. If she starts blabbing about who I am, things might get a little hairy."

"She doesn't know your real name."

He scowled. "No, but she knows I'm studying Latin. It wouldn't be hard for her to track me down. Maybe I'll cut the next class or two and stay here with you."

"Chicken."

"Nuh-uh." He covered her hand with his and began a gentle massage. "I do want to be here with you. It's getting close."

"Three weeks."

"How do you feel?"

"Tired."

"Emotionally?"

"Tired. I meant what I said before. The waiting's getting to me."

"Everything's been fine so far."

"It was the other two times, too."

"You've never had a ceasarean section before. It'll minimize stress on the baby during delivery."

"I hope."

He squeezed her hand. "It will. Things will work out fine, love. You'll see. A month from now, we'll have a squirming little thing on our hands."

"That's just what I told myself eight months into two other pregnancies."

"But this time is different. That's *my* baby you're carrying."

She sighed, then smiled sadly. "Which is precisely why I want it so badly."

THE NEXT WEEK WAS an uneventful one for Leah, but, then, she'd known it would be. Aside from when she was eating or using the bathroom, she remained in bed. She didn't do much reading because she couldn't seem to concentrate. She didn't do much weaving because, with the bulk of the loom and that of her stomach, she couldn't get comfortable. She listened to music, which was fine for a time, particularly since Garrick kept her supplied with new tapes that they both enjoyed. Susan came to visit often, usually—and deliberately, Leah suspected, to keep an eye on her—while Garrick was in school.

She didn't do much work of the official puzzle-making variety because she'd declared herself on a temporary leave of absence. But she found herself working on that private puzzle, the one involving words that related to what she'd fondly come to think of as the life and times of Garrick and

Leah. It was a whimsical endeavor and it helped keep her occupied.

Garrick's week wasn't quite as uneventful. He went back to school without missing a class, and though he was edgy during the first two days, he saw no sign of the young woman from the theater. On the third day, just when he was beginning to relax again, she accosted him as he was leaving his class.

"I have to talk to you for a minute, Mr. Reynolds," she said quickly and a little nervously as she fell into step beside him. "I was serious about what I said the other day. It would mean the world to all of us if you would agree to speak."

He kept walking at the same even pace. "I have nothing to say."

"But you do. You've had experiences we've only dreamed of having."

"I'm not who you think I am."

"You are. After we talked the other day, I went to the library and pored through the microfilms. The last anyone heard from or saw of Greg Reynolds was shortly before an automobile accident. The accident was reported in the papers. Greg Reynolds survived it, then disappeared. With your face and body, it would be too much of a coincidence to think that you're not him."

He sliced her a glance, but she went on, clearly proud of herself.

"I researched further. Greg Reynolds's real name is Garrick Rodenhiser. That's the name you've enrolled under here."

Garrick stopped then. "I'm a private citizen, Miss—"

"Schumacher. Liza Schumacher."

"I don't give talks, Miss Schumacher—"

"Liza. We could keep it to a small group, if that's what you'd prefer."

"I'd prefer," he said quietly, almost beseechingly, "to have my privacy respected."

"We'd pay you—"

"No, thanks." He started off again.

"An hour. A *half*-hour. That's all we'd ask—"

But he simply shook his head and kept going. Fortunately she didn't follow.

Again he told Leah about the encounter. Again she explored his feelings about it. "Are you sure you don't want to do it?"

"Speak? Are you kidding?"

"She's right, in a way. You have had the kind of experience that many of them want. It's not unusual for representatives of different careers to talk to groups of students."

"Whose side are you on, Leah?"

"Yours. You know that."

Thrusting his legs from the bed, he landed on his feet and stalked off to the window. "Well, I don't want to speak—before students or any other group. For one thing, I don't think much of the kind of experience I had. For another, I don't relish the idea of confessing my sins to an audience."

"There was a positive side to what you did."

"Mmm. Somewhere. I can't seem to see it, though. I suppose I could make up a good story. . . ."

"Garrick . . ."

He continued to stare out the window.

"Why—really—won't you speak?"

He was silent for several more minutes, but he knew that Leah suspected the truth. It remained to be seen whether he had the courage to confirm it.

"Ah, hell," he muttered at last. "The truth of it is that deep down inside, I'm afraid I'll like the feeling of power that comes when you've got an audience in your thrall—the rapt faces, the adulation, the applause. If I do it once, I may want to do it again, and if I do it a second time, a third could follow, and by that time I could be hooked on how wonderful I am."

"You are wonderful."

He bent his head and smiled, then turned and retraced his steps to the bed. Stretching out on his stomach before Leah, he grabbed her hand and pressed it to his lips. "You're the only one I want to hear saying that, because you're the only one who knows the real me. I've never talked to anyone the way I have to you. You're better than an analyst any day."

Leah wasn't sure if she liked the idea of being an analyst, because knowing another person's thoughts meant knowing his fears, and Garrick still had many. She thought he'd made progress since he'd been in Concord, and perhaps, to some extent, he had—but he still didn't trust himself. And that frightened her. She knew that she'd need his strength in the coming weeks and she didn't want anything to dilute it.

"I'll settle for being your soul mate," she said, and offered her lips for a kiss.

THE SUDDEN SNOWSTORM THAT HIT during the first week of December did nothing for Leah's peace of mind. True, Garrick's classes were canceled, so he stayed home with her. But she had visions of going into premature labor while they were snowbound, in which case everything they'd gone through might have been in vain.

They weren't truly snowbound, as it happened. Nor did she go into premature labor. Day by day, though, she felt the baby move lower, and though Gregory had made arrangements to do the section on the fifteenth of December, she wondered if Garrick's monster would wait that long.

It was harder to see Garrick off to class now. She was physically uncomfortable and emotionally strung out. Only when he was with her could she begin to relax, knowing that he'd take over if something happened. But she did send him off. She felt he needed it, in more respects than the obvious one of taking his mind off the baby and her.

On the eleventh of December she wished she'd been more selfish.

10

GARRICK LEFT CLASS and walked to his car, but he'd barely reached for the door, when a loud call echoed across the parking lot.

"Mr. Reynolds!"

His grip tightened on the handle. Only one person would call him that, and the last thing he wanted to do was to talk with her now. He wanted to be home with Leah.

"Mr. Reynolds! Wait! Please!"

He opened the door and fleetingly contemplated jumping inside, slamming down the locks and wheeling off. But he wasn't a coward. Not anymore.

Propping one arm above the window, he turned his head toward the young woman approaching. "Yes, Miss Schumacher?"

Breathing hard from the run, she skidded to a halt by his side. "Thank you for waiting . . . I wanted to get here earlier . . . my class ran late."

"I'm running late myself. Was there something you wanted?" His breath was a white cloud in the cold air, though not quite large enough for him to vanish into as he wished he could do.

"Since you didn't feel comfortable speaking, I had another idea." She darted a quick glance behind her. To Garrick's dismay, a young man was trotting up to join them. "Darryl's with the town newspaper. I thought—we thought—that it would be super to have an article. . . ."

Garrick frowned. "I thought you said this would be our secret."

"I did. But then I started thinking." She was slowly catching her breath. "It didn't seem fair to be selfish—"

"About what?"

"About knowing who you are. It seemed unfair that I should keep everything to myself—"

"Unfair to *you*?"

"No, no. To the people around here who would find your story interesting."

Garrick studied her steadily. "What about me? What about what's fair and unfair where *I'm* concerned?"

If anything, she grew bolder. "You're a star, Mr. Reynolds. Doesn't that bring with it certain responsibilities?"

"I'm not a star anymore," he stated unequivocably and with an odd kind of pride. "I'm a private citizen. I have many responsibilities, but as far as I can see, none of them have to do with you, or your fellow students, or your professors, or your friends." He cocked his head toward the reporter. "Is he your boyfriend?"

She exchanged an awkward look with Darryl. "We've gone out a few times, but that doesn't have anything—"

"Are you lovers?"

"That's not—"

"Is she good?" Garrick asked Darryl.

Liza went red in the face. "That's none of your business. I don't see what my private life has to do with—"

"*My* private life?" Garrick finished. "Nothing, Miss Schumacher. My questions are as much an invasion of your privacy as anything you—or Darryl—would ask *me*. I've already told you that I'm not interested in appearing publicly. That goes for big talks, small talks, newspaper articles and whatever *else* you come up with."

While he'd been speaking, Liza's expression had gone from embarrassment to dismay. In the silent minute that followed, it moved to anger. "The papers I read were right," she decided, abandoning all pretense of deference. "You are arrogant."

"Not really," Garrick said, surprised by the feeling of peace that was settling over him. "I'm simply trying to explain my feelings." And not only to her. Suddenly things were falling into place. His vision of who he was and what he wanted in life was becoming crystal clear.

Liza drew herself straighter. "I think you're a has-been. You disappeared from the acting scene. I think it was because you couldn't land any good parts after *Pagen*. I think you're afraid to stand before a group, knowing that."

She was tall, but Garrick was taller. Setting his shoulders back, he took a deep breath. "You know something, Miss Schumacher? I don't care what you think. The fact of the matter is that I'm not afraid to stand before anyone. I'm simply... not... interested. I chose to give up acting because it did nothing good for my life. You could offer me top billing in your next production and I'd refuse. You could offer to let me direct and I'd refuse. You could offer me headlines in the paper and I'd refuse. I live quietly now. I have a life that is much richer than anything I've known before. If you'd like to do an article, I'd be happy to tell you about trapping, or studying Latin, or whittling chess sets. As for acting, it's not *me* anymore. I've been away from it for nearly five years now, and I don't miss it."

"I find that hard to believe," Liza said.

"I'm sorry."

"You're satisfied being a... a trapper?"

"That's only one of the things I do, but, yes, I'm satisfied. Very satisfied."

"But the publicity—"

"Means nothing to me. I don't need it, and I don't want it." His tone was a mellow one, but it held undisputable conviction, just as the glance he sent Darryl held more sympathy than apology. "I'm sorry you won't get your story, but I really have nothing more to say."

"Mr. Rodenhiser? Mr. Rodenhiser!"

His head shot up in response to the alarmed cry, eyes flying in the direction of the voice. It came from a woman he recognized as being a secretary in the language department. She was clutching a coat around her with one hand, waving a small piece of paper in the other as she speed-walked toward the car.

"Thank goodness you haven't left," she panted.

The sense of peace Garrick had experienced earlier was gone. His blood ran cold.

"You just received a call from a Susan Walsh. She said that you were to meet Leah at the hospital."

"Oh, God," he whispered hoarsely, but the words hadn't left his mouth before he was in the car, leaving Liza Schumacher to jump out of the way of the slamming door. She and her boyfriend, the secretary, the school, the newspaper—all were forgotten. The only things he could think of were Leah and their baby. *What had happened?*

Over and over he asked the question, sometimes silently, sometimes aloud. He drove as fast as he could, swerving after what seemed an eternity into a space outside the hospital's emergency entrance. After being directed from one desk to the next, he finally connected with Gregory, who quickly put a reassuring arm around his shoulder.

"Her water broke. We're prepping her now. Come on. We'll both scrub up."

"How is she?"

"Terrified."

"And the baby?"

"So far, so good. I want to take it as quickly as possible."

Garrick didn't ask any more questions. He was too busy praying. Besides, he knew that Gregory didn't have the answer to the one question he most wanted to ask. Only time would give that, and time was precious. He matched his step to the doctor's as they hurried down the hall.

Leah's eyes were on the door when Garrick entered the delivery room. She held out a shaking hand and clutched his fingers fiercely. "They said you were on your way. Thank God you're here."

"What happened?"

"My water broke. I was lying in bed and it just broke. I hadn't moved, I hadn't done anything—"

"Shhhh." He was bending over her, pressing his mouth to her matted bangs. "You've done everything right, Leah. You've followed doctor's orders to the letter. Tell me, how did you get here?"

"I called Susan. Wasn't that stupid? I should have called Gregory directly, but I remember thinking that Susan was closer and that I was glad we had a phone so I wouldn't have to walk from the apartment to the house."

"It was smart of you to call Susan. She's cool under fire."

"She called Gregory, and Gregory called the ambulance while I just sat there, *trembling*."

"It's okay, honey." He had a hand on her hair but was looking around the room in bewilderment, trying to interpret every nuance of the bustling activity. "Everything's going to be okay." A cloth barrier was being lifted into place to shield the operation from their view. He knew that it was standard procedure for a cesarean section, but then it struck him that, since her water had broken, she had to be in labor. His eyes shot to hers. "Are you in pain?"

She gave a rapid little shake of her head. "I felt a few contractions before, but the spinal's taken effect. I don't feel a thing." Her eyes widened and her fingers tightened around his. "I don't feel anything, Garrick. Maybe something's happened—"

Gregory came up at that moment. "The baby's fine, Leah. We're monitoring the heartbeat, and it's fine." His gaze swung from her face to Garrick's, then back. "All set to go?"

Their nods were identically jerky. Gregory moved off. The anesthetist came to sit by Leah's head, while a nurse slid a stool beneath Garrick.

"Please, let it live," Leah whispered to no one in the room.

"It will," Garrick whispered back, but his eyes were worried as they sought out Gregory.

"We're all thinking positive," was Gregory's response. He wasn't making promises, but he appeared fully confident, which was as much as Leah could have asked.

"Garrick?" she murmured.

"Yes, love?"

"How did everything go at school today?"

He was momentarily startled. His thoughts weren't on school. It was an unlikely subject to discuss given the time, place and circumstance. But he quickly understood what Leah was doing, so he forced himself to shift gears. "Not bad. I aced the exam."

"No kidding?"

His smile was wobbly. "Would I kid you at a time like this? I got a ninety-seven."

"They say that older students do better."

"And I aced something else today."

"What?"

"Liza Schumacher."

They were talking in hushed tones, eyes locked into each other's with an urgency that acknowledged something momentous was taking place.

"What happened with Liza Schumacher?" Leah asked.

"She approached me with a local journalist in tow."

"Journalist!"

"They wanted an interview."

"Oh, no." Her fingers tightened around Garrick's, but it didn't have to do with the interview as much as the quiet talk coming from beyond the cloth barrier. She wanted to ask what was happening but didn't dare.

Garrick seemed in a similar quandary. He darted frantic eyes toward Gregory, who was concentrating on his work, his lower face covered by a mask. Garrick quickly calmed his expression when he looked down at Leah again.

"I said that I wasn't interested and it struck me that I wasn't. I really wasn't."

"Temptation—"

"Isn't temptation. I don't want what's being offered. There's nothing to threaten me."

"But if she's already told one reporter who you are—"

"It doesn't matter. She can tell ten reporters, and it still won't matter."

"And if this one reporter writes something—"

"That's fine. He can write about how I've found a better life. It's not the kind of story that will sell papers, so one installment will be enough. He'll lose interest. Other reporters will, too. And it won't bother me at all."

"I'm glad," she whispered, then added quickly, "What are they doing?"

"Baby's doing well, Leah," came Gregory's call. "You two keep talking. It sounds like a fascinating discussion."

"I want the baby, Garrick," she whimpered.

"Me, too, love. Me, too. Are you feeling anything?"

"No."

"Any pain?"

"No."

All too aware of the emotional pain she was undergoing, he sent a panicky glance toward the anesthesiologist. "Maybe you should have knocked her out."

"No!" Leah cried. "I want to know."

"We're getting there, Leah," came Gregory's utterly calm voice.

It settled Leah momentarily. Tipping her head farther toward Garrick, she pressed their twined hands to her warm cheek. "When . . . when are finals?" she asked in the same small whisper she'd used before.

"Another week. I may skip them."

"Oh, no—after all the work you've done?"

"I'm only taking the courses for fun."

"Then take the exams for fun."

"Exams aren't fun."

"I'll help you study."

"That might be fun. But then you might be—"

A tiny cry cut off his words. His heart began to slam against his ribs, and he jerked up his head.

Leah's breath was catching in her throat. "Garrick?" She raised her voice. "Gregory?"

Another, stronger cry echoed through the room, followed by Gregory's satisfied, "Ahhh, she's a lusty one."

"She," Leah breathed, tear-filled eyes clinging to Garrick's face.

He was rising from the stool, tearing his gaze from Leah to focus on the small bundle Gregory held. A tiny arm flailed the air. Grinning through unchecked tears, he returned to Leah.

"She waved."

"She's moving?"

"See for yourself," said Gregory as he held the baby high.

Leah saw. Arms and legs batted the air to the tune of a sturdy pair of lungs. Leah started to cry, too. "She's . . . alive . . . beautiful . . . Garrick . . . do you . . . see?"

He had an arm curved around Leah's head. "I see," he managed to croak, then pressed his wet cheek to her forehead.

"Show's over," came the decree from the pediatric specialist who'd been assisting in the proceedings. He gently took the infant from Gregory. "Sorry, folks. She's mine for a few minutes."

It was just as well. Leah's arms were around Garrick's neck, and they were burying their faces against each other, muffling soft sobs of gratitude and joy.

"AMANDA BETH. IT'S AS BEAUTIFUL as she is." Leah was lying flat in bed, per doctor's orders, but Garrick was sitting by her side, so she didn't mind the temporary restriction.

Garrick's face was alight with pride. "The pediatrician can't find a thing wrong with her. They'll keep a close watch on her for a few days, but they don't foresee any problem."

"Seven pounds, five ounces."

"Not bad for an early baby."

"Oh, Garrick, I'm so happy!" She was smiling broadly, as was Garrick, neither of them able—or caring—to stop.

"We did it. *You* did it. Thank you, Leah. Thank you for giving me a beautiful daughter, and for giving me self-confidence, and for loving me."

Grabbing his ear, she tugged him down for a kiss. "Thank *you*. I feel so complete."

"That's good," he said, raising his head a trifle. "Because we're expecting visitors in a few minutes, and I want you at your best."

"Victoria?" she asked in excitement.

"Nope. She'll be here later in the week. Insists on helping you out when we take baby home."

Her smile grew dreamy. "Take baby home. I never thought we'd be saying those words." For the first time her smile faltered. Her eyes went wide behind her glasses. "Garrick! Clothes, diapers, a crib—we haven't got *anything*!" After two pregnancies when she'd been fully equipped, only to find herself without a baby, she'd been superstitious.

Garrick was unfazed. "No sweat. I'll pick up a crib—I think maybe a cradle—tomorrow. Victoria's buying the rest."

"Victoria? But she can't—"

He arched a brow. "Victoria?"

"Well, she can, but we can't let her!"

"I'm afraid we can't stop her. She was in a rush to get off the phone so that she could get to the stores before they closed."

Leah was smiling again. "That does sound like Victoria."

"She feels responsible for the baby," he said, eyes twinkling.

"Maybe we should let her think she is. We couldn't very well make her interrupt her shopping to research the facts of life, could we?"

He kissed her nose. "Certainly not."

"Garrick?"

But it wasn't Garrick who answered. "Hello, hello" came Susan's singsong voice from the door. Gregory was wheeling her in, followed closely by a man Leah had never seen before.

"Ah. Our visitors." Garrick stood up quickly, kissing Susan, shaking hands with Gregory, then with the other man, whom he brought forward. "Leah, say hello to Judge Hopkins. He's agreed to marry us."

"Marry us?" Leah cried. "But . . . but I can't get married now!"

"Why not?"

"I . . . because I look a mess! My hair's tangled and I'm sweaty—"

"But you are wearing white," Garrick pointed out in a mischievous tone.

"A hospital gown," Leah returned in dismay. "They won't even let me sit up to change!"

"No problem," said Susan as she tugged a box from where it had been stowed between her hip and the chair. She turned to the men as a group. "Out." Then to her husband. "Be a sweet and send a nurse in here to give us a hand." Then to the judge. "We'll only be a minute, Andrew." Then to Garrick. "Think you can control yourself that long?"

None of them answered, because Gregory was busy pushing them toward the door.

LEAH WAS MARRIED in the gown and matching robe that Susan had somehow known to buy in pale pink. Garrick, wearing the same sweater and cords he'd worn to school that day, stood by her bedside, holding her hand, while the judge conducted the brief ceremony. When, at its conclusion, Gregory produced a bottle of champagne, Leah threw an apprehensive look at Garrick, who leaned low and spoke for her ears alone.

"You can't have any for another few hours, but then we'll share a little. Just a sip in token celebration. I don't need any more of a high than the one I'm on now. I don't think I ever will."

Five days later, Garrick and Leah brought Amanda Beth back to the small garage apartment. Leah was healing well, and the baby was as strong and healthy as they'd prayed she would be.

Victoria, who was staying in the Walsh's main house, was in her element. Declaring that Amanda was more interesting than the Maori any day, she fought Garrick for the honor of bathing, diapering and dressing her.

Since Leah was nursing, the feeding chores were hers alone. She loved those times when Amanda was suckling and the rest of the world became a warm, fuzzy periphery. Even more, though, she loved the times at night when Garrick would stretch out beside her and watch.

"What does it feel like?"

"When she nurses?"

"Mmm. Does it hurt?"

"Oh, no! It's a delightful kind of gentle tugging."

"Like when I kiss you there?" He drew a light forefinger across the upper swell of her breast.

"A little. There's a sense of depth. I feel like there are strings inside me that she's pulling on. Sometimes I feel contractions. But it's different, too."

"How?"

"When she does it, it's satisfying in and of itself. When you do it, it makes me want more." She blushed. "Different kinds of sensations."

Garrick moaned and shifted his legs, making no attempt to hide his problem. The light in the eyes he raised to hers wasn't one of uncontrollable desire, though, as much as love. "I can't conceive of life without you, Leah. You...Amanda...when I think of the sterile existence I had before..."

"Don't look back," she urged in a whisper as she bent forward and brushed his lips with hers. "We've conquered the past. We have a wonderful present. Let's look forward to the future for a change."

They did just that. After long discussions with Leah, Garrick decided that he rather liked the idea of working toward the college degree he'd never earned. Baby and all, he managed to study for and do well in his finals, paving the way for his acceptance at Dartmouth, which had an excellent Latin department.

"You'll love Hanover," he told Leah. "It's got charm."

"I know I'll love it, but what about you? Don't you miss the cabin?"

"To tell you the truth, no." He seemed as surprised as she that the answer came so quickly. "I love it up there, but my life now is so full that I rarely think of it. I'd like to get a house in Hanover and use the cabin as a vacation retreat."

That was exactly what they did. With Amanda strapped into a carrier against Garrick's chest, they looked at every possible home in Hanover, finally falling in love with and buying a small Victorian within walking distance of Garrick's classes. During school vacations, weather permitting, they returned to the cabin. Come June, shortly before they were to retreat there for the summer, Garrick approached Leah with a proposal.

"How about a trip to New York?"

Her eyes lit up. "New York?"

"Yeah. I know you hated it last time you went—"

"I was pregnant and tired and worried, and you weren't with me." Her voice lowered. "Will you go this time?"

"I won't let you and Amanda go alone, and Victoria has been begging us for months to visit."

She wrapped an arm around his waist. "I'd love to go, Garrick, but only if you're sure."

"I'm sure." He winked down at her. "We may even be able to get some time to ourselves."

Their visit to New York was enlightening in several respects. Garrick found that he was relaxed and at ease. Leah found that though they had a wonderful time, she was ready to leave again when the time came.

Equally as gratifying was Victoria's news. She'd heard through the grapevine that Richard and his wife had had a second baby—this one stillborn. And while Leah's heart went out to them, she couldn't help but close her eyes in relief. It seemed that Richard's wife, not about to take the tragedy sitting down, had done some research. Richard had been adopted at birth, but she'd managed to work through the courts to determine his biological parents—and had discovered that infant mortality had been documented over two generations on his father's side.

"All our worrying was for nothing," Leah breathed, but Garrick was quick to disagree.

"No, love. The worry may have been unnecessary, but it served a purpose. If you hadn't been worried, you'd never have left me and moved to Concord. And if you hadn't done that, I would have stayed at the cabin, where I would be to this day. Think of all we'd have missed."

She knew that he was right. His self-confidence had been fully restored, and his self-respect had taken on new dimensions. He'd survived the auto accident and found a fresh basis for life, but only since Leah had come had he begun to really grow.

Which was what she wanted to do...again. "This means we can have another baby—"

"Without worry."

"But not just yet."

"Maybe when Amanda's two."

"We'll go for a boy this time."

"How're we gonna arrange that?"

"There are ways. I was reading an article recently that said—"

"Since when do you read articles about planning a baby's sex?"

"Since the world has opened up to me and I've begun to dream again."

THROUGH THE YEARS TO COME, Leah and Garrick both did their share of dreaming, each time setting out to make those dreams come true. But during that first summer at the cabin with Amanda, they were too content to do much dreaming. The sun was warm, the air fresh, the forest as magnificent and lush as they'd ever seen it. Garrick worked in his garden, often with Amanda babbling in sweet baby talk beside him. Leah was always nearby, often constructing puzzles to send off to her editor. The crossword from which she took the most pleasure, though, was the one that chronicled the life and times of Leah and Garrick. Now there was Amanda to fit into the grid, but doing so was simple.

"Aha," Garrick teased. "So *that's* why you wanted to name her Amanda. Three a's. You need them."

"I named her Amanda because I love the name and you love the name and because, obviously, *she* loves the name."

"She'd love *any* name, as long as there's banana ice cream after we call her."

"I love banana ice cream."

"So do I. But I love you and Amanda more. Hey—" he studied her puzzle "—have you got it here?"

"What?"

"Love."

"Sure. It's all over the place—in every noun, every adjective, every—"

"Four letters. L-O-V-E."

"It's there."

"I can't find it."

"Look closer."

"I can't find it."

"Look higher."

"I can't find it."

"To the right."

"I can't—I can. Ahhhh. There it is. Twelve across. L-O-V-E. Very simple and straight to the point. Now that's my kind of word."

A SINGLE ROSE

BY

BARBARA DELINSKY

WORLDWIDE BOOKS
LONDON • SYDNEY • TORONTO

All the characters in this book have no existence outside the imagination of the Author, and have no relation whatsoever to anyone bearing the same name or names. They are not even distantly inspired by any individual known or unknown to the Author, and all the incidents are pure invention.

First published in Great Britain in 1988
Reprinted in Great Britain in 1994
by Worldwide Books, Eton House,
18-24 Paradise Road, Richmond, Surrey TW9 1SR

ISBN 0 373 59316 3

99-9409

Made and printed in Great Britain

1

VICTORIA LESSER TOOK A BREAK from the conversation to sit back and silently enjoy the two couples with her. They were a striking foursome. Neil Hersey, with his dark hair and close-cropped beard, was a perfect foil for his fair and petite wife, Deirdre, but the perfection of the match didn't stop at their looks. Deirdre's quick spirit complimented Neil's more studied approach to life. In the nineteen months of their marriage, they'd both grown personally and professionally.

As had the Rodenhisers. Though married a mere six months, they'd been together for nearly fifteen. Leah, with her glossy raven pageboy and bangs and the large round glasses perched on her nose, had found the ideal mate in Garrick, who gave her the confidence to live out her dreams. Garrick, sandy-haired, tall, and bearded like Neil, had finally tasted the richness of life that he'd previously assumed existed only in a scriptwriter's happy ending.

Glancing from one face to the next as the conversation flowed around her, Victoria congratulated herself on bringing the four together. It had been less of a brainstorm, of course, than her original matchmaking endeavors, but it was making for a lively and lovely evening.

Feeling momentarily superfluous, she let her gaze meander among the elegantly dressed patrons of the restaurant. She spotted several familiar faces on the far side of the room, and when her attention returned to her own party, she met Deirdre's eye. "Recognize them, Dee?"

Deirdre nodded and spoke in a hushed voice to her husband. "The Fitzpatricks and the Grants. They were at the lawn party Mother gave last fall."

Neil's wry grin was a flash of white cutting through his beard. His voice was low and smooth. "I'm not sure I remember the Fitzpatricks or the Grants, but I do remember that party. We were leaving Benji with a baby-sitter, and almost didn't get away. He was three months old and in one hell of a mood." He sent a lopsided grin across the table. "He takes after his mother in that respect."

Deirdre rolled her eyes. "Don't believe a word he says."

"Just tell me it gets better," Leah Rodenhiser begged. "You heard what Amanda gave us tonight."

Victoria, who had never had a child of her own and adored even the baby's wail, answered with the gentle voice of authority. "Of course it gets better. Amanda was just frightened. My apartment is strange and new to her. So is the babysitter. I left this number, but we haven't gotten a frantic call yet, have we?"

"I think you're about to get a frantic call from across the room," came a gravelly warning from Garrick. "They've spotted you, Victoria."

"Oh dear."

"Go on over," Deirdre urged softly. "If you don't, they'll come here. Spare us that joy. We'll talk babies until you get back."

Victoria, who knew all too well Deirdre's aversion to many of her mother's friends, shot her a chiding glance. But the glance quickly mellowed, and touched each of her guests in turn. "You don't mind?"

Leah grinned and answered for them all. "Go. We're traveling sub rosa."

"Sub rosa?"

"Incognito." Beneath the table she felt Garrick squeeze her hand. Once a well-known television star, he cherished his privacy. Basically shy herself, Leah protected it well.

"Are you sure you can manage without me?" Victoria quipped, standing when Neil drew out her chair. "Talk babies. I dare you." Her mischievous tone faded away as she headed off to greet her friends.

Four pairs of eyes watched her go, each pair as affectionate as the next. Victoria held a special place in their hearts, and they weren't about to talk babies when there were more immediate things to be said.

"She is a wonder," Leah sighed. "Little did I know what a gem I'd encountered when I ran into her that day in the library."

Neil was more facetious. "We didn't think she was such a gem when she stranded us on her island up in Maine. I don't think I've ever been as furious with anyone before."

"You were pretty furious with *me* before that day was out," Deirdre reminded him.

His grin grew devilish. "You asked for it. Lord, I wasn't prepared for you." He shifted his gaze to Leah and Garrick. "She was unbelievably bitchy. Had her leg in a cast and a mouth—"

Deirdre hissed him into silence, but couldn't resist reminiscing on her own. "It was just as well there weren't any neighbors. We'd have driven them crazy. We yelled at each other for days."

"While Leah and I were silent," Garrick said. "We were isolated in my cabin together, barely talking. I'm not sure which way is worse."

"Amazing how both worked out," Leah mused.

Deirdre nodded. "I'll second that."

"We owe Victoria one," Neil said.

"Two," Garrick amended.

Deirdre twirled the swizzle stick in her spritzer. "It's a tall order. The woman has just about everything she wants and needs."

Leah frowned. "There has to be something we can do in return for all she's given us."

"She needs a man."

Deirdre was quick to refute her husband's contention. "Come on, Neil. She has all the men she wants. And you know she'll never remarry. Arthur was the one and only love of her life."

Garrick exchanged a glance with Neil. "That doesn't mean we can't treat her to some fun."

Leah studied her husband. "I'm not sure I care for that mischievous gleam in your eye. Victoria is my friend. I won't have you—"

"She's my friend, too," he interrupted innocently. "Would I do anything to harm her?"

Neil was on Garrick's wavelength all the way. "The idea is to do something for her that she wouldn't dream up by herself."

"But she does just about everything she wants to," Deirdre pointed out. "She lives in luxury, dabbles in ballet, ceramics, the cello. She travels. She has the house in Southampton...." Her eyes brightened. "We could rent a yacht, hire a crew and put them at her disposal for a week. She'd be able to go off alone or invite friends along."

Garrick absently chafed his mustache with a finger. "Too conventional."

"How about a stint with Outward Bound?" Leah suggested. "There are groups formed specifically for women over forty."

Neil shot Garrick a look. "Not quite what I had in mind."

Deirdre had caught and correctly interpreted the look. "You have a one-track mind. Believe me, we'd be hard put to find a man with enough spunk for Victoria. Can you think of anyone suitable at Joyce?" Joyce Enterprises was Deirdre's family's corporation. Upon their marriage, Neil had taken it over and brought it from stagnation to productivity to expansion. Of the many new people he'd hired—or clients and associates of the company—Deirdre couldn't think of a single male who would be challenge enough for Victoria.

Neil's silence was ample show of agreement.

"It would be fun," Leah declared, "to turn the tables on Victoria."

"Someone good-looking," Deirdre said, warming to the idea.

Leah nodded. "And bright. We want a match here."

Neil rubbed his bearded jaw. "He'll have to be financially comfortable if he can afford to go in for adventure."

"Adventure," Garrick murmured. "That's the key."

Deirdre's brows lifted toward Neil. "Flash?" Flash Jensen was a neighbor of theirs in the central Connecticut suburb where they lived. A venture capitalist and a divorcé, he was always on the lookout for novel ways to spend his time.

Neil shook his head. "Flash is a little *too* much."

Leah chuckled. "We could always fix her up with one of Garrick's trapper friends. She'd die."

Garrick nodded, but he was considering another possibility. "There's a fellow I've met. One of my professors." Earlier he'd explained to the Herseys that he was working toward a Latin degree at Dartmouth. "Samson may well...fit the bill."

"Samson?" Leah echoed in mild puzzlement. She knew who he was, but nothing of what Garrick had told her in the past put the man forward as a viable candidate.

"He's a widower, and he's the right age."

Deirdre sat straighter. "Samson. From the name alone, I love him."

"That's because you've always had this thing about full heads of hair," Neil muttered in her ear. He'd never quite forgotten their earliest days together, when, among other things, she'd made fun of his widow's peak.

Deirdre hadn't forgotten either. As self-confident as Neil was, he had his sensitivities, and his hairline was one of them. "Forget hair," she whispered back. "Think strength. You have it even without the hair."

"You're putting your foot in deeper," he grumbled.

"I think you're right." Hastily she turned to Garrick, who'd been having a quiet discussion with Leah during the Herseys' private sparring. "Tell us about Samson."

Garrick was more than willing. "His name is Samson VanBaar. Leah thinks he's too conservative, but that's because s' doesn't know him the way I do."

"He smokes a pipe," Leah informed them dryly.

"But that's all part of the image, love. Tweed jacket, pipe, tattered briefcase—he does it for effect. Tongue-in-cheek. A private joke."

"Weird private joke," was Leah's retort, but her tone had softened. "Do you really think he'd be right for Victoria?"

"If we're talking adventure, yes. He's good-looking and bright. He's independently wealthy. And he loves doing the unconventional." When Leah remained skeptical, he elaborated. "He's a private person, shy in some ways. He takes his little trips for his own pleasure, and they have nothing to do with the university. I had to coax him to talk, but once he got going, his stories were fascinating."

Deirdre sat forward, propping her chin in her hand. "We're listening."

"How does dog-sledding across the Yukon sound?"

"Challenging."

"How about a stint as a snake charmer in Bombay?"

"Not bad, if you're into snakes."

"Try living with the Wabians in Papua New Guinea."

"That does sound a little like Victoria," Leah had to admit. "When I first met her, she was boning up on the Maori of New Zealand."

Neil rubbed his hands together. "Okay. Let's see what we've got. A, the guy is okay in terms of age and marital status. B, he's good-looking and reasonably well-off. C, he's a respected member of the academic community." At the slight question in his voice, Garrick nodded. "And D, he's an adventurer." He took a slow breath. "So how do we go about arranging an adventure that Victoria could join him in?"

"I believe," Garrick said with a smug gleam in his eye, "it's already arranged. Samson VanBaar will be leaving next month for Colombia, from which point he'll sail across the Caribbean to Costa Rica in search of buried treasure."

"Buried treasure!"

"Gold?"

"He has a map," Garrick went on, his voice lower, almost secretive. "It's old and faded—"

"You've seen it?"

"You bet, and it looked authentic enough to me. Samson is convinced that it leads to a cache on the Costa Rican coast."

"It's so absurd, it's exciting!"

"Could be a wild goose chase. On the other hand—"

"Victoria would love it!"

"She very well might," Garrick concluded.

Neil was weighing the pros and cons. "Even if nothing comes of it in terms of a treasure, it'd certainly be a fun—how long?"

"I think he's allowed himself two weeks."

"Two weeks." Deirdre mulled it over. "Could be disastrous if they can't stand each other."

"She threw *us* together for two weeks, and we couldn't stand each other."

"It wasn't that we couldn't stand each other, Neil. We just had other things on our minds."

"We couldn't stand each other."

"Well, maybe at the beginning, but even then we couldn't keep our hands off each other."

Garrick coughed.

Leah rushed in to fill the momentary silence. "She threw us together for an *indefinite* period of time."

"Not that she planned it that way. She didn't count on mud season."

"That's beside the point. She sat by while I gave up my loft and put my furniture into storage. Then she sent me off to live in a cabin that had burned to the ground three months before. She knew I wouldn't have anywhere to go but your place, and those first few days were pretty tense...." Her words trailed off. Remembering the nights, she shot Garrick a shy glance and blushed.

Deirdre came to her aid. "There's one significant difference here, I believe. Victoria got us together in Maine; she got you two together in New Hampshire. Costa Rica—that's a little farther afield, and definitely foreign soil."

"It's a democratic country," Garrick pointed out, "and a peaceful one."

"Right next door to Nicaragua?" Leah asked in dismay, pushing her glasses higher on her nose as she turned to Neil. "Do you know anything about Costa Rica?"

"She *is* peaceful. Garrick's right about that. She's managed to stay out of her neighbors' turmoil. And she happens to be the wealthiest country in Central America."

"Then Victoria would be relatively safe?"

Garrick nodded.

"From Samson?" Deirdre asked. "Is he an honest sort of man?"

"Completely."

"Gentle?"

"Infinitely."

"Law abiding?"

"A Latin professor on tenure at one of the Ivies?" was Garrick's answer-by-way-of-a-question.

Neil stopped chewing on the inside of his cheek. "Is he, in any way, shape or manner, a lecher?"

"I've never heard any complaints," Garrick said. "Victoria can handle him. She's one together lady."

Having no argument there, Neil put the matter to an impromptu vote. "Are we in agreement that two weeks with Samson VanBaar won't kill her?"

Three heads nodded in unison.

"I'll speak with Samson and make the arrangements," Garrick offered. "I can't see that he'd have any objection to bringing one more person along on the trip, but we'd better not say anything to Victoria until I've checked it out."

"It'll be a surprise."

"She won't be able to refuse."

"She'll never know what hit her."

Garrick's lips twitched. "That'd be poetic justice, don't you think? After what she did to us—" His voice rose and he broke into his best show-stopping smile as the object of their discussion returned. "Hel-lo, Victoria!"

FIVE DAYS AFTER THAT DINNER in New York, Victoria received a bulky registered letter from New Hampshire. Opening it, she unfolded the first piece of paper she encountered.

"Dear Victoria," she read in Garrick's classic scrawl. "A simple thank you couldn't possibly convey our gratitude for all you've done. Hence, the enclosures. You'll find a round-trip ticket to Colombia, plus detailed instruction on where to go once you're there. You'll be taking part in a hunt for buried treasure led by one of my professors, a fascinating gentleman named Samson VanBaar. We happen to know you have no other plans for the last two weeks in July, and if you try to call us to weasel your way out, we won't be in. Samson is expecting you on the fourteenth. Have a wonderful time! All our love, Garrick and Leah and Deirdre and Neil."

Bemused, Victoria sank into the Louis XVI chair just inside the living-room arch. A treasure hunt? She set aside the plane tickets and read through the instructions and itinerary Garrick had seen fit to send.

New York to Miami to Barranquilla by plane. Accommodations in Barranquilla at El Prado, where Samson VanBaar would make contact. Brief drive from Barranquilla to Puerto Colombia. Puerto Colombia to Costa Rica—*Costa Rica*—by sail. Exploration of the Caribbean coast of Costa Rica as designated by Samson VanBaar's treasure map. Return by sail to Colombia and by plane to New York. Expect much sun, occasional rain. Dress accordingly.

The instructions joined the letter and tickets on her lap. She couldn't believe it! She'd known they had something up their sleeves when she'd returned to the table that night and seen smugness in their eyes.

They'd been sly; she had to hand it to them. They'd waited until the arrangements were made before presenting her with the fait accompli. Oh, yes, she could graciously refuse, but they knew she wouldn't. *She* knew she wouldn't. She'd never gone in search of buried treasure before, and though she certainly had no need for treasure, the prospect of the search was too much to resist!

Other things had been swirling around in those scheming minds of theirs as well. She knew because she'd been there herself. And because she'd been there, she knew it had something to do with Samson VanBaar. Were they actually fixing her up?

She'd sent Deirdre and Neil to the island in Maine after receiving separate, desperate calls begging for a place of solitude. She'd sent Leah to New Hampshire, to a cabin that didn't exist, knowing Leah would have no recourse but to seek out Garrick, her nearest neighbor on the mountain. What would Victoria find when she arrived in Colombia?

If Samson VanBaar was one of Garrick's professors, he had to be responsible. He might be wonderful. Or he might be forty years old and too young for her, or old and stuffy and too dry for her. One of Garrick's professors. A Latin professor. Definitely old and stuffy and dry. Perhaps simply the organizer of the expedition. In which case the Herseys and the Rodenhisers had someone else in mind. Someone else in the group?

There were many questions and far too few answers, but Victoria did know one thing. She had already blocked out the last two weeks in July for a treasure hunt. It was an opportunity, a challenge, an adventure. Regardless of her friends' wily intentions, she knew she could handle herself.

AS THAT DAY ZIPPED BY and the next began, Victoria couldn't help but think more and more about the trip. She had to admit that there was something irresistibly romantic about a sail through the Caribbean and a treasure hunt. Perhaps this Samson VanBaar would turn out to be a pirate at heart. Or perhaps one of the other group members would be the pirate.

That night, unable to shake a particularly whimsical thought, she settled in the chintz-covered chaise in the sitting area of her bedroom and put through a call to her niece.

"Hi there, Shaye!"

"Victoria?" Shaye Burke hadn't called Victoria "aunt" in years. Victoria was a dear friend with whom she'd weathered many a storm. "It's so good to hear your voice!"

"Yours, sweetheart, is sounding foreign. Do you have something against dialing the phone?"

Duly chastised, Shaye sank onto the tall stool by the kitchen phone and spoke with a fair amount of contrition. "I'm sorry, Victoria. Work's been hectic. By the time I get home my mind is addled."

"Did you just get in?"

"Mmm. We're in the process of installing a new system. It's time consuming, not to mention energy consuming." Shaye headed the computer department of a law firm in Philadelphia that specialized in corporate work. Victoria was familiar enough with such firms to know that computerization had become critical to their productivity.

"And the bulk of the responsibility is on your shoulders, I'd guess."

Shaye nodded, too tired to realize that Victoria couldn't see the gesture. "Not that I'm complaining. The new machines are incredible. Once we're fully on-line, we'll be able to do that much more that much more quickly."

"When will that be?"

"Hopefully by the end of next week. I'll have to work this weekend, but that's nothing new."

"Ahh, Shaye, where's your private life?"

"What's a private life?" Shaye returned with mock innocence.

Victoria saw nothing remotely amusing in the matter. "Private life is that time you spend away from work. It's critical, sweetheart. If you're not careful, you'll burn out before you're thirty."

"Then I'd better get on the stick. Four more months and I'll be there."

"I'm serious, Shaye. You work too hard and play too little."

Suddenly Shaye was serious, too. "I've played, Victoria. You know that better than anyone. I had six years of playing and the results were dreadful."

"You were a child then."

"I was twenty-three when I finally woke up. It was a pretty prolonged childhood, if you ask me."

"I'm not asking you, I'm telling you. What you did then was an irresponsible kind of playing. We've discussed this before, so I'm not breaking any new ground. When I use the word 'playing' now, I'm talking about something quite different. I'm talking about reading a good book, or going shopping just for the fun of it, or watching a fluff movie. I'm talking about spending time with friends."

Shaye knew what she was getting at. "I date."

"Oh yes. You've told me about those exciting times. Three hours talking shop with a lawyer from another firm. Another firm—that is daring. Of course, the fellow was nearly my age and probably arthritic."

Shaye chuckled. "We can't all reach fifty-three and be as agile as you."

"But you *can*. It's all in the mind. That lawyer's mind was no doubt ready for retirement five years ago. And your stockbroker friend doesn't sound much better. Does he give you good leads, at least?"

"It'd be illegal for me to act on an inside tip. You know that."

Victoria did know it. She also knew that her niece gave wide berth to anything vaguely questionable, let alone illegal. Shaye Burke had become a disgustingly respectable pillar of society. "Okay. Forget about stock tips. Let's talk fun. Do you have fun with him?"

"He's pleasant."

"So is the dentist. Have you been with anyone lately who's fun?"

"Uh-huh. Shannon."

"Shannon's your sister!" Victoria knew how close the two were; they'd always been so. Shaye, the elder by four years, felt personally responsible for Shannon. "She doesn't count. Who else?"

"Judy."

Victoria gave an inward groan. Judy Webber was a lawyer in Shaye's firm. The two women had become friends. If occasional weekend barbecues with Judy, her husband and their two teenaged daughters comprised Shaye's attempts at relaxation, she was in pretty bad shape.

"How is Judy?" Victoria asked politely.

"Fine. She and Bob are heading for Nova Scotia next week. She's looking forward to it."

"That does sound nice. In fact, that's one of the reasons I called."

"To hear about Judy and Bob and Nova Scotia?"

"To talk to you about *your* vacation plans. I need two weeks of your time, sweetheart. The last two weeks in July."

"Two weeks? Victoria, I can't take off in July."

"Why not?"

"Because I'm scheduled for vacation in August."

"Schedules can be changed."

"But I've already made reservations."

"Where?"

"In the Berkshires. I've rented a cottage."

"Alone?"

"Of course alone. How else will I manage to do the reading and shopping and whatever else you claim I've been missing?"

"Knowing the way you've worked yourself to the bone, you'll probably spend the two weeks sleeping."

"And what more peaceful a place to sleep than in the country?"

"Sleeping is boring. You don't accomplish anything when you sleep."

"We're not all like you," Shaye pointed out gently. "You may be able to get by on five hours of sleep a night, but I need eight."

"And you don't usually get them because you work every night, then get up with the sun the next day to return to the office."

Shaye didn't even try to refute her aunt's claim. All she could do was rationalize. "I have six people under me—six people I'm responsible for. The hours are worth it because the results are good. I take pride in my work. And I'm paid well for my time."

"You must be building up quite some kitty in the bank, because I don't see you spending much of that money on yourself."

"I do. I live well."

"You're about to live better," Victoria stated firmly. "Two weeks in July. As my companion."

Shaye laughed. "Your companion? That's a new one."

"This trip is."

"What trip?"

"We're going to Colombia, you and I, and then on to Costa Rica."

"You aren't serious."

"Very. We're going on a treasure hunt."

Shaye stared at the receiver before returning it to her ear. "Want to run that by me again?"

"A treasure hunt, Shaye. We'll fly to Barranquilla, spend the night in a luxury hotel, drive to Puerto Colombia and then sail in style across the Caribbean. You can do all the sleeping you want on the boat. By the time we reach Costa Rica you'll be refreshed and ready to dig for pirates' gold."

Shaye made no attempt to muffle her moan. "Oh, Victoria, where did you dream this one up?"

"I didn't dream it up. It was handed to me on a silver platter. The expedition is being led by a friend of a friend, a professor from Dartmouth who even has a map."

"Pirates' gold?" Shaye echoed skeptically.

Victoria waved a negligent hand in the air. "Well, I don't actually know what the treasure consists of, but it sounds like a fun time, don't you think?"

"I think it sounds—"

"Absurd. I knew you would, but believe me, sweetheart, this is a guaranteed adventure."

"For you. But why *me*?"

"Because I need you along for protection."

"Come again?"

"I need you for protection."

Shaye's laugh was even fuller this time. "The day you need protection will be the day they put you in the ground, and even then, I suspect they'll be preparing for outrageous happenings at the pearly gates. Try another one."

Anticipating resistance, Victoria had thought of every possible argument. This one was her most powerful, so she repeated it a third time, adding a note of desperation to her voice. "I need your protection, Shaye. This trip was arranged for me by some friends, and I'm sure they have mischief in mind."

"And you'd drag me along to suffer their mischief? No way, Victoria. I'm not in the market for mischief."

"They're trying to fix me up. I know they are. Their hearts are in the right place, but I don't need fixing up. I don't want it." She lowered her voice. "You, of all people, ought to understand."

Shaye understood all too well. Closing her eyes, she tried to recall the many times people had tried—the many times

Victoria herself had tried—to fix her up with men who were sure to be the answer to her prayers. What they failed to realize was that Shaye's prayers were different from most other people's.

"All I'm asking," Victoria went on in the same deliberately urgent tone, "is that you act as a buffer. If I have you with me, I won't be quite so available to some aging lothario."

"What if they're fixing you up with a younger guy? It's done all the time."

Then he's all yours, sweetheart. "No. My friends wouldn't do that. At least," she added after sincere pause, "I don't think they would."

Shaye began, one by one, to remove the pins that had held her thick auburn hair in a twist since dawn. "I can't believe you're asking this of me," she said.

Victoria wasn't about to be touched by the weariness in her voice. "Have I ever asked much else?"

"No."

"And think of what you'll be getting out of the trip yourself. A luxurious sail through the Caribbean. Plenty of sun and clean air. We can spend a couple of extra days in Barranquilla if you want."

"Victoria, I don't even know if I can arrange for those two weeks, let alone a couple of extra days."

"You can arrange it. I have faith."

"You always have faith. That's the trouble. Now your faith is directed at some pirate stash. For years and years people have been digging for pirate treasure. Do you honestly believe anything's left to be found?"

"The point of the trip isn't the treasure, it's the hunt. And for you it will be the rest and the sun and—"

"The clean air. I know."

"Then you'll come?"

"I don't know if I can."

"You have to. I've already made the arrangements." It was a little white lie, but Victoria felt it was justified. She'd simply call Samson VanBaar and tell him one more person would be joining them. What was another person? Shaye ate like a bird, and if there was a shortage of sleeping space, Victoria herself would scrunch up on the floor.

"You're forcing me into this," Shaye accused, but her voice held an inkling of surrender.

"That's right."

"If I say no, you'll probably call the senior partner of my firm first thing tomorrow."

"I hadn't thought of that, but it's not a bad idea."

Shaye screwed up her face. "Isn't there *anyone* else you can bring along in my place?"

"No one I'd rather be with."

"That's emotional blackmail."

"So be it."

"Oh, Victoria . . ."

"Is that a yes?"

For several minutes, Shaye said nothing. She didn't want to traipse off in search of treasure. She didn't want to take two weeks in July, rather than the two weeks she'd planned on in August. She didn't want to have to spend her vacation acting as a buffer, when so much of her time at work was spent doing that.

But Victoria was near and dear to her. Victoria had stood by her, compassionate and forgiving when she'd nearly made a mess of her life. Victoria understood her, as precious few others did.

"Are we on?" came the gentle voice from New York.

From Philadelphia came a sigh, then a soft-spoken, if resigned, "We're on."

Later that night, as Shaye worked a brush through the thick fall of her hair, she realized that she'd given in for two basic reasons. The first was the she adored Victoria. Time spent with her never failed to be uplifting.

The second was that, in spite of all she might say to the contrary, the thought of spending two weeks in a rented cottage in the Berkshires had a vague air of loneliness to it.

VICTORIA, MEANWHILE, basked in her triumph without the slightest twinge of guilt. Shaye needed rest, and she'd get it. She needed a change of scenery, and she'd get that too. Adventure was built into the itinerary, and along the way if a man materialized who could make her niece laugh the way she'd done once upon a time, so much the better.

A spunky doctoral candidate would do the trick. Or a fun-loving assistant professor. Samson VanBaar had to be bringing a few interesting people along on the trip, didn't he?

She glanced at the temple clock atop a nearby chest. Was ten too late to call? Definitely not. One could learn a lot about a man by phoning him at night.

Without another thought, she contacted information for Hanover, New Hampshire, then punched out his home number. The phone rang twice before a rather bland, not terribly young female voice came on the line. "Hello," it said. "You have reached the residence of Samson VanBaar. The professor is not in at the moment. If you'd care to leave a message, he will be glad to return your call. Please wait for the sound of the tone."

Victoria thought quickly as she waited. Nothing learned here; the man could be asleep or he could be out. But perhaps it was for the best that she was dealing with a machine. She could leave her message without giving him a chance to refuse her request on the spot.

The tone sounded.

"This is Victoria Lesser calling from New York. Garrick Rodenhiser has arranged for me to join your expedition to

Costa Rica, but there has been a minor change in my plans. My niece, Shaye Burke, will be accompanying me. She is twenty-nine, attractive, intelligent and hardworking. I'll personally arrange for her flight to and from Colombia, and, of course, I'll pay all additional costs. Assuming you have no problem with this plan, Shaye and I will see you in Barranquilla on the fourteenth of July."

Pleased with herself, she hung up the phone.

Four days later, she received a cryptic note typed on a plain postcard. The postmark read, "Hanover, NH," and the note read, very simply, "Received your message and have made appropriate arrangements. Until the fourteenth—VanBaar."

Though it held no clue to the man himself, at least he hadn't banned Shaye from the trip, and for that she was grateful. Shaye had called the night before to say she'd managed to clear the two weeks with her firm, and Victoria had already contacted both the Costa Rican Embassy in New York regarding visas and her travel agent regarding a second set of airline tickets.

They were going on a treasure hunt. No matter what resulted in the realm of romance, Victoria was sure of one thing: come hell or high water, she and Shaye were going to have a time to remember.

2

THE FOURTEENTH OF JULY was not one of Shaye's better days. Having worked late at the office the night before to clear her desk, then rushing home to pack for the trip, she'd gotten only four hours' sleep before rising to shower, dress and catch an early train into New York to meet Victoria. Their plane was forty-five minutes late leaving Kennedy and the flight was a turbulent one, though Shaye suspected that a certain amount of the turbulence she experienced was internal. She had a headache and her stomach wouldn't settle. It didn't help that they nearly missed their transfer in Miami, and when they finally landed in Barranquilla, their luggage took forever to appear. She was cursing the Colombian heat by the time they reached their hotel, and after waiting an additional uncomfortable hour for their room to be ready, she discovered that she'd gotten her period.

"Why me?" she moaned softly as she curled into a chair.

Victoria came to the rescue with aspirin and water. "Here, sweetheart. Swallow these down, then take a nap. You'll feel better after you've had some sleep."

Not about to argue, when all she wanted was an escape from her misery, Shaye dutifully swallowed the aspirin, then undressed, sponged off the heat of the trip, drew back the covers of one of the two double beds in the room and slid between the sheets. She was asleep within minutes.

It was evening when a gentle touch on her shoulder awakened her. Momentarily disoriented, she peered around the room, then up at Victoria.

"You missed the zoo."

"Huh?"

"And you didn't even know I'd gone. Shame on you. But I'm back, and I thought I'd get a bite to eat. Want anything?"

Shaye began to struggle up, but Victoria easily pressed her back to the bed.

"No, no, sweetheart. I'll bring it here. You need rest far more than you need to sit in a restaurant."

Shaye was finally getting her bearings. "But . . . your professor. Aren't we supposed to meet him?"

Settling on the edge of the bed, Victoria shook her head. "He sent a message saying he'll be tied up stocking the boat for a good part of the night. We're to meet him there tomorrow morning at nine."

"Where's there?"

"A small marina in Puerto Colombia, about fifteen miles east of here. The boat is called the *Golden Echo*."

"The *Golden Echo*. Appropriate."

Victoria gave an impish grin. "I thought so, too. Pirates' gold. Echoes of the past. It's probably just a coincidence, since I assume the boat is rented."

"Don't assume it. If VanBaar does this sort of thing often, he could well own the boat." She hesitated, then ventured cautiously, "He does do this sort of thing often, doesn't he?"

"I really don't know."

"How large is the boat?"

"I don't know that either."

"How large is our group?"

Victoria raised both brows, pressed her lips together in a sheepish kind of way and shrugged.

"Victoria," Shaye wailed, fully awake now and wishing she weren't, "don't you ask questions before you jump into things?"

"What do I need to ask? I know that Samson VanBaar is Garrick's friend, and I trust Garrick."

"You dragged me along because you *didn't* trust him."

"I didn't trust that he wouldn't try to foist me off on some unsuspecting man, but that's a lesser issue here. The greater issue is the trip itself. Garrick would never pull any punches in the overall scheme of things."

Shaye tugged at a hairpin that was digging into her scalp. "Exactly what *do* you know about this trip?"

"Just what I've told you."

"Which is precious little."

"Come on, sweetheart. The details will come. They'll unfold like a lovely surprise."

"I hate surprises."

"Mmm. You like to know what's happening before it happens. That's the computerized you." Her gaze dropped briefly to the tiny mark at the top of Shaye's breast, a small shadow beneath the lace edging of her bra. "But there's another side, Shaye, and this trip's going to bring it out. You'll learn to accept it and control it. It's really not such a bad thing when taken in moderation."

"Victoria . . ."

"Look at it this way. You're with me. I'll be your protector, just as you'll be mine."

"How can you protect me from something you can't anticipate?"

"Oh, I can anticipate." She tipped up her head and fixed a dreamy gaze on the wall. "I'm anticipating that boat. It'll be a beauty. Long and sleek, with polished brass fittings and crisp white sails. We'll have a lovely stateroom to share. The food will be superb, the martinis nice and dry. . ."

"You hope."

"And why not? Look around. I wouldn't exactly call this room a hovel."

"No, but it could well be the equivalent of a last meal for the condemned."

Victoria clucked her tongue. "Such pessimism in one so young."

Shaye shifted onto her side. She was achy all over. "Right about now, I feel ninety years old."

"When you're ninety, you won't have to worry about monthly cramps. When you're fifty, for that matter." She grinned. "I rather like my age."

"What's not to like about sixteen?"

"Now, now, do I sound that irresponsible?"

"Carefree may be a better word, or starry-eyed, or naive. Victoria, for all you know the *Golden Echo* may be a leaky tub and Samson VanBaar a blundering idiot."

Victoria schooled her expression to one of total maturity. "I've thought a lot about that. Samson won't be an idiot. Maybe an absentminded professor, or a man bent on living out his childhood dreams." She took a quick breath. "He could be fun."

"He could be impossible."

"But there will be others aboard."

"Mmm. A bunch of his students, all around twenty and so full of themselves that they'll be obnoxious."

"You were pretty full of yourself at that age," she reminded her niece, smoothing a stray wisp of hair from Shaye's pale cheek.

"And obnoxious."

"You didn't think so at the time."

"Neither will they."

But Victoria's eyes had grown thoughtful again. "I don't think there'll be many students. Garrick wouldn't have signed me on as a dorm mother. No, I'd guess that we'll be encountering adults, people very much like us looking for a break from routine."

"Since when do you have a routine you need a break from?"

"Not me. You. You need the break. I don't need anything, but my friends wanted to give me a good time, and that's exactly what I intend to have." She pushed herself gracefully from the bed. "Starting now. I'm famished. What'll it be—a doggie bag from the restaurant or room service later?"

Shaye tucked up her knees and closed her eyes. "Sleep. Tomorrow will be soon enough for superb food and nice dry martinis."

THE TWO WOMEN HAD NO TROUBLE finding the *Golden Echo* the next morning. She was berthed at the end of the pier and very definitely stood apart from the other craft they'd passed.

"Oh Lord," Shaye muttered.

Victoria was as wide-eyed as her niece. "Maybe we have the wrong one."

"The name board says *Golden Echo*."

"Maybe I got the name wrong."

"Maybe you got the trip wrong."

They stood with their elbows linked and their heads close together as, eyes transfixed on the boat before them, they whispered back and forth.

"She isn't exactly a tub," Victoria offered meekly.

"She's a pirate ship—"

"In miniature."

"Looks like she's been through one too many battles. Or one too few. She should have sunk long ago."

"Maybe not," Victoria argued, desperately searching for something positive to say. "She looks sturdy enough."

"Like a white elephant."

"But she's clean."

"Mmm. The chipped paint's been neatly scraped away. Lord, I don't believe I've seen anything as boxy since the Tall Ships passed through during the Bicentennial."

"They were impressive."

"*They* were."

"So's this—"

"If you close your eyes and pretend you're living in the eighteenth century."

Victoria didn't close her eyes, but she was squinting hard. "You have to admit that she has a certain . . . character."

"Mmm. Decrepit."

"She takes three sails. That should be pretty."

Her enthusiasm was lost on Shaye, who was eyeing in dismay the ragged bundles of canvas lashed to the rigging. "Three crisp . . . white . . . sails."

"Okay, they may not be crisp and white. What does it matter, if they're strong?"

"Are they?"

"If Samson VanBaar is any kind of friend to Garrick—and if Garrick is any kind of friend to me—they are."

Shaye moaned. "And to think that I could have been in the Berkshires, lazing around without a care in the world."

"You'll be able to laze around here."

"I don't see any deck chairs."

"But it's a nice broad deck."

"It looks splintery."

"So we'll lie on towels."

"Did you bring some?"

"Of course not. They'll have towels aboard."

"Like they have polished brass fittings?" Shaye sighed. "Well, you were right in a way."

"What way was that?" Victoria asked, at a momentary loss.

"We are going in style. Of course, it's not exactly *our* style—for that matter, I'm not sure whose style it is." Her voice hardened. "You may be crazy enough to give it a try, but I'm not."

She started to pivot away, intending to take the first cab back to Barranquilla, but Victoria clamped her elbow tighter and dragged her forward. "Excuse me," she was calling, shading her eyes from the sun with her free hand. "We're looking for Samson VanBaar."

Keeping step with her aunt through no will of her own, Shaye forced herself to focus on the figure that had just emerged from the bowels of the boat. "It gets worse," she moaned, then whispered a hoarse, "What *is* he?"

"I'm VanBaar," came the returning call. "Mrs. Lesser, Miss Burke?" With a sweep of his arm, he motioned them forward. "We've been expecting you."

Nothing they'd imagined had prepared either Shaye or Victoria for Samson VanBaar. In his mid to late fifties, he was remarkably tall and solid. His well-trimmed salt-and-pepper hair, very possibly combed in a dignified manner short days before, tumbled carelessly around his head, forming a reckless frame for a face that was faintly sunburned, though inarguably sweet.

What was arguable was his costume, and it could only be called that. He wore a billowy white shirt tucked into a pair of narrow black pants, which were tucked into knee-high leather boots. A wide black belt slanted low across his hips, and if it lacked the scabbard for a dagger or a sword, the effect was the same.

"He forgot the eye patch," Shaye warbled hysterically.

"Shh! He's darling!" Victoria whispered under her breath. Smiling broadly—and never once releasing Shaye, who, she knew, would head in the opposite direction given the first opportunity—she started up the gangplank. At the top, she put her free hand in the one Samson offered and stepped onto the deck. "It's a delight to meet you at last, Professor VanBaar. I'm Victoria Lesser, and this is my niece, Shaye Burke."

Shaye was too busy silently cursing her relationship with Victoria to say much of anything, but she managed a feeble smile in return for the open one the professor gave her.

"Welcome to the *Golden Echo*," he said, quietly now that they were close. "I trust you had no problem finding us."

"No, no," Victoria answered brightly. "None at all." She made a grand visual sweep of the boat, trying to see as little as possible while still conveying her point. "This is charming!"

Shaye nearly choked. When Victoria gave a tight, warning squeeze to her elbow before abruptly releasing it, she tipped back her head, closed her eyes and drew in an exaggerated lungful of Caribbean air. It was certainly better than having to look at the boat, and though Samson VanBaar was attractive enough, the insides of her eyelids were more reassuring than his getup.

"I felt that the *Golden Echo* would be more in keeping with the spirit of this trip than a modern yacht would be," he explained. "She's a little on the aged side, but I've been told she's trusty."

Shaye opened one eye. "You haven't sailed her yet?"

Almost imperceptibly he ducked his head, but the tiny movement was enough to suggest guilt. "I've sailed ones like her, but I just flew in yesterday myself, and the bulk of my time between then and now had been spent buying supplies. I hope you understood why I couldn't properly welcome you in Barranquilla last night."

"Of course," Victoria reassured him gently. "It worked out just as well, actually. We were both tired after the flight."

"You slept well?"

"Very well."

"Good." He ran a forefinger along the corner of his mouth, as though unsure of what to say next. Then his eyes brightened. "Your bags." He quickly spotted them on the pier. "Let me bring them aboard, then I'll give you the Cook's tour."

He'd no sooner descended the gangplank when Shaye whirled on Victoria. "The Cook's tour?" she whispered wildly. "Is he the cook or are we?"

"Don't fret," Victoria whispered back with confidence, "there's a cook."

"Like there's a lovely stateroom for us to share? Do you have any idea what's down there?"

"Nope. That's what the Cook's tour is for."

"Aren't you worried?"

"Of course not. This is an adventure."

"The boat is a wreck!"

"She's trusty."

"So says the professor who's staging Halloween three months early."

Victoria's eyes followed Samson's progress. "And I thought he'd be stuffy. He's precious!"

"Good. Since you like him so well, you won't need my protection after all. I'll just take my bag and head back—"

"You will not! You're staying!"

"Victoria, there'll be lots of other people..." The words died on her lips. Her head remained still while her eyes moved from one end of the empty deck to the other. She listened. "Where are they? It's too quiet. We were ten minutes late, ourselves. Where are the others?"

Victoria was asking herself the same question. Her plan was contingent on there being other treasure seekers, specifically of the young and good-looking male variety. True, in terms of rest alone, the trip would be good for Shaye, and Victoria always enjoyed her niece's company. But matching her up with a man—it had worked so well with Deirdre, then Leah . . . Where *were* the men?

Concealing her concern behind a gracious smile, she turned to VanBaar, who had rejoined them with a suitcase in either hand. "We don't expect you wait on us. Please. Just tell us what to do." She reached for her bag, but Samson drew it out of her reach.

"Chivalry is a dying art. You'll have plenty to do as time goes on, but for now, I think I can manage two bags."

Chivalry? Shaye thought, amused. *Plenty to do?* she thought, appalled.

Victoria was thinking about the good-looking young men she didn't see. "Is this standard service given to all the members of your group?" she ventured, half teasing, half chiding, and subtly fishing for information.

"No, ma'am. We men fend for ourselves. You and your niece are the only women along."

Swell, Shaye groused silently, *just swell.*

Victoria couldn't have been more delighted. "How many others are there, Professor VanBaar?"

He blushed. "Samson, please."

She smiled. "Samson, then. How many of us will there be in all?"

"Four."

"Four?" the women echoed in unison.

"That's right." Setting the bags by his booted feet, he scratched the back of his head. "Didn't Garrick explain the situation?"

Victoria gave a delicate little cough. "I'm afraid he didn't go quite that far."

"That was negligent of him," Samson said, but he didn't seem upset, and Victoria saw a tiny twinkle in his eye. "Let me explain. Originally there were to be just two of us, myself and an old college buddy with whom I often travel in the summer. When Garrick called me about your joining us, I saw no problem. Unfortunately, my friend had to cancel at the last minute, so I hoodwinked my nephew into taking up the slack." He stole a glance at Shaye's dismayed expression. "It takes two to comfortably man the boat, and since I didn't know whether either of you were sailors—"

"We're not," Shaye burst out. "I don't know about my aunt, but I get seasick."

"Ignore her, Samson. She's only teasing."

"*Violently* seasick."

"Not to worry," Samson assured her in the same kind tone that made it hard to hold a grudge. "I have medicine for seasickness, though I doubt you'll need it. We shouldn't run into heavy seas."

At that moment, Shaye would have paid a pirate's ransom to be by her lonesome in the Berkshires. A foursome—Victoria and Samson, Samson's nephew and her. It was too cozy, too convenient. Suddenly something smacked of a setup. Could Samson have done it? Or Garrick? Or... She skewered her aunt with an accusatory glare.

Victoria had her eyes glued to Samson. "I'm sure we'll be fine." She took a deep breath and straightened her shoulders. "Now then, I believe you said something about a tour?"

NOAH VANBAAR WAS nearly as disgusted as Shaye. Arms crossed over his chest and one knee bent up as he lounged on a hardwood bench within earshot of the three above, he struggled in vain to contain his frustration. He'd had other plans for his summer vacation, but when his uncle had called, claiming that Barney was sick and there was no one else who could help him sail, he'd been indulgent.

Samson and he were the only two surviving members of the VanBaar family, but even if sentimentality hadn't been a factor, Noah was fond enough of his uncle to take pity. He knew how much Samson looked forward to his little jaunts. He also knew that Samson was an expert sailor and more than capable of handling the boat himself, but that for safety's sake he needed another pair of hands along. If Noah's refusal meant that Samson had to cancel his trip, there was no real choice to be made.

Naturally, his uncle had waited until last night to inform him that they wouldn't be sailing alone. Naturally, he had waited until this morning to inform him that the pair joining them would be female.

Noah didn't want one woman along, much less two. Not that he had anything against women in general, but on this trip, they would be in the way. He'd planned to relax, to take a break from the tension that was part and parcel of his work. He'd planned to have one of the two cabins on the boat to himself, to sleep to his heart's content, to dress as he pleased, shave when and if he pleased, swim in the buff, and, in short, let it all hang out.

The presence of women didn't figure into his personal game plan. They were bound to screw things up. A widow and her niece. Charming. Samson was already carrying their bags. If they thought *he* was going to wait on them, they had another think coming!

Actually, he mused, the aunt didn't sound so bad. She had a pleasant voice, sounded lively without being obnoxious, and to her further credit, had protested Samson's playing bellboy. He wondered what she looked like and whether Samson would be enthralled. He hoped not, because then he'd be stuck with the niece, who sounded far less lively and more obnoxious than her aunt.

It was obvious that the niece wasn't thrilled with the looks of the sloop. What had she expected? The *Brittania*? If so, he decided as his eyes skimmed the gloomy interior of the

Golden Echo, she was in for an even ruder awakening than she'd already had.

Not that the boat bothered him; he'd sailed in far worse. This time around, though, he could have asked for more space. This time around he'd have preferred the *Brittania*, himself. At least then he'd have been able to steer clear of the women.

Though he didn't move an inch, he grew instinctively alert when he heard footsteps approaching the gangway. Samson was in the lead, his booted feet appearing several seconds before the two suitcases. "The *Golden Echo* was refurbished ten years ago," he was saying, his voice growing louder as his head came into view. "The galley is quite modern and the cabins comfortable—ah, Noah, right where I left you." Stepping aside, he set down the bags to give an assisting hand to each of the women in turn.

Noah didn't have to marvel at his uncle's style. Though a bit eccentric at times, Samson was a gentleman through and through, which was fine as long as he didn't expect the same standard from his nephew. Noah spent his working life straddling the lines between gentleman, diplomat and czar; he intended to spend his vacation answering to no one but himself.

"Noah, I'd like you to meet Victoria Lesser," Samson said. He knew better than to ask his nephew to rise. Noah was intimidating enough when seated; standing he was formidable. Given the dark mood he was in at the moment, intimidation was the lesser of the evils.

Noah nodded toward Victoria, careful to conceal the slight surprise he felt. Victoria had not only sounded lively, she looked lively. What had Samson said—that she was in her early fifties? She didn't look a day over forty. She wore a bright yellow, oversize shirt, a pair of white slacks with the cuffs rolled to mid-calf, and sneakers, and her features were every bit as youthful. Her hair was an attractive walnut shade and thick, loosely arranged into a high, short ponytail that left gentle wisps to frame the delicate structure of her face. Her skin was flawless, firm-toned and lightly made up, if at all. Her eyes twinkled, and her smile was genuine.

"It's a pleasure to meet you, Noah," she said every bit as sincerely. "Thank you for letting us join you on this trip. I've done many things in my day, but I've never been on a treasure hunt before. It sounds as though it'll be fun."

Lured by the subtle melody of her voice, Noah almost believed her. Then he shifted his gaze to the young woman who'd followed her down the steps and took back the thought.

"Shaye Burke," Samson was saying by way of introduction, "Noah VanBaar."

Again Noah nodded his head, this time a trifle more stiffly. Shaye Burke was a looker; he had to give her that. Slightly taller than her aunt, she was every bit as slender. Her white jeans were pencil thin, her blousy, peach-colored T-shirt rolled at the sleeves and knotted chicly at the waist. Her skin, too, was flawless, but it was pale; she'd skillfully applied makeup to cover shadows beneath her eyes and add faint color to her cheeks.

Any similarities to her aunt had already ended. Shaye's deep auburn hair was anchored at the nape of her neck in a sedate twist from which not a strand escaped. The younger woman's lips were set, her nose marked with tension, and the eyes that met his held a shadow of rebellion.

She didn't want to be here. It was written all over her face. Adding that to the comments he'd overheard earlier, he begrudged her presence more than ever. If Shaye Burke did anything to spoil his uncle's adventure, he vowed, he would personally even the score.

Samson, who'd sensed the instant animosity between Noah and Shaye, spoke up quickly. "If you ladies will come this way, I'll show you to your cabin. Once we've deposited your things there, we can walk around more freely."

Short of turning and fleeing, Shaye had no choice but to follow Victoria, who followed Samson through the narrow passageway. Her shoulders were ramrod straight, held that way by the force of a certain man's gaze piercing her back.

Noah. Noah and Samson. The VanBaar family, she decided, had a thing about biblical names. But her image of *that* Noah was one of kindness; *this* Noah struck her as being quite different. Sitting in the shadows as he'd been, she hadn't been able to see much beyond gloom and a glower. She knew one thing, though: She hadn't expected to have to protect her aunt, but if Noah VanBaar so much as dared do anything to dampen Victoria's spirits, he'd have to answer to her.

SAMSON LED VICTORIA AND SHAYE to the cabin they'd be sharing, then backtracked to show them the salon, the galley and the captain's quarters in turn. Noah was nowhere in sight during the backtracking, and Shaye was grateful for that. There was precious little else to be grateful for.

"We do have our own bathroom," Victoria pointed out when they'd returned to their cabin to unpack. She lowered herself to Shaye's side of the double bed that occupied three quarters of the small cabin's space. "I know that it's not quite what we expected, but if we clear our minds of those other expectations, we'll do fine."

Shaye's lips twisted wryly. "Grin and bear it?"

"Make the most of it." She jabbed at the bedding with a delicate fist. "The mattress feels solid enough." Her eye roamed the trapezoid-shaped room. "And we could have been stuck with a V-berth."

"This bed is bolted to the wall. I thought Samson said it'd be a calm trip."

"This one will be, but we have no idea what other waters the *Golden Echo* has sailed."

"If only she were somewhere else—without us."

"Shaye . . ."

"And where do we go to relax?"

"The salon."

"For privacy?" She was thinking of the dagger-edged gaze that had followed her earlier, and wasn't sure whether she'd be able to endure it as a constant.

Victoria's mind was still on the salon. "There are comfortable chairs, a sofa—"

"And a distinctly musty smell."

"That's the smell of the sea. It adds atmosphere."

Shaye snorted. "That kind of atmosphere I can do without." She knew she was being unfair; after all, the cottage she'd booked in the Berkshires very probably had its own musty smell, and she normally wasn't that fussy. But her bad mood seemed to feed on itself and on every tiny fault she could find with the boat.

"Come on, sweetheart," Victoria coaxed as she rose to open her suitcase. "We'll have fun. I promise."

Shaye's discouraged gaze wandered around the cabin, finally alighting on the row of evenly spaced, slit-like windows. "At least there are portholes. Clever, actually. They're built into the carving of the hull. I didn't notice them from the dock."

"And they're open. The air's circulating. And it's relatively bright."

"All the better to see the simplicity of the decor," Shaye added tongue-in-cheek. She watched her aunt unpack in silence for several minutes before tipping her head to the side and venturing a wary, "Victoria?"

"Uh-huh?"

"How much did you really know about all this?"

Victoria stacked several pairs of shorts in a pile, then straightened. "About all what?"

"This trip."

"Haven't we discussed this before?"

"But something's beginning to smell."

"I told you," Victoria responded innocently. "It's the sea."

"Not smell as in brine. Smell as in rat. Did you have any idea at all that there'd be just four of us?"

"Of course not."

"It never occurred to you that Samson would be 'precious' and that I'd be left with his nephew?"

Victoria gave a negligent shrug and set the shorts in the nearby locker. "You heard what Samson said. Noah's joining us was a last-minute decision. I mentioned this trip to you nearly a month ago."

But Shaye remained skeptical. "Samson didn't say exactly how 'last-minute' the decision was. Are you sure you're not trying to pair me up with Noah?"

"Would I do that—"

"She asks a little too innocently. You did it with Deirdre Joyce."

"I thought you approved."

"In that case I did—do. Neil Hersey is a wonderful man." Shaye had never forgotten that it was Neil, with his legal ability and compassion, who had come to the rescue when Shannon had been arrested.

Victoria was grateful that Shaye knew nothing of her role in bringing Garrick and Leah together. The less credence given the word *matchmaker*, the better, she decided. "Noah VanBaar may be every bit as wonderful."

Shaye coughed comically. "Try again."

"He may be!"

"Then you did do it on purpose?"

Victoria felt only a smidgen of guilt as she propped her hands on her hips in a stance of exasperation. "Really, Shaye. How could I have done it on purpose when I had no idea Noah would be along?"

"Then you intended to fix me up with Samson's old-fart friend?"

"I did not! I truly, truly expected that we'd be only two more members of a larger group."

Sensing a certain truth to that part of Victoria's story at least, Shaye sighed. "If only there *were* a larger group—"

"So you could fade into the woodwork? I wouldn't have let you do that even if there were fifty others on board this boat." She lifted a pair of slacks and nonchalantly shook them out. "What did you think of Noah, by the way?"

"I thought he was rude, by the way. He could have stood up when we were introduced. He could have said something. Do you realize the man didn't utter a single word?"

"Neither did you at that point."

"That's because I chose silence over saying something unpleasant."

"Maybe that's what he was doing. Maybe he's as tired as you are. Maybe he, too, had other plans before Samson called him."

"I wish he'd stuck to his guns."

"Like you did?"

Bowing her head, Shaye pressed the throbbing spot between her eyes. "I gave in because you're my aunt and my friend and because I love you."

Draping an arm around Shaye's shoulders, Victoria hugged her close. "You know how much that means to me, sweetheart. And it may be that Noah feels the same about Samson. Cheer up. He won't be so bad. How can he be, with an uncle like that?"

WHEN VICTORIA LEFT to go on deck, Shaye stayed behind to unpack. But there was only so much unpacking to do, and only so much to look at within the close cabin walls. She realized she was stalling, and that annoyed her, then hardened her. If Noah VanBaar thought he could cower her with his dark and brooding looks, he was in for a surprise.

Emboldened, she made her way topside to find Samson drawing up the gangplank. A powerboat hovered at the bow of the *Golden Echo*, prepared to tow her clear of the pier. At Samson's call, Noah cast off the lines, the powerboat accelerated and they were off.

When the other three gathered at the bow, Shaye took refuge at the stern. Mounting the few steps to the ancient version of a cockpit, she bypassed the large wooden wheel to rest against the transom and watch the shore slowly but steadily recede.

It was actually a fine day for a sail, she had to admit. The breeze feathered her face, cooling what might otherwise have been heated rays of the sun. But she felt a wistfulness as her gaze encompassed more and more of the Colombian shore. Given her druthers, she'd have stayed in Barranquilla and waited for Victoria's return. No, she insisted, given her druthers, she'd be working in Philadelphia, patiently waiting for her August break.

But that was neither here nor there. She was on the *Golden Echo*, soon to be well into the Caribbean, and there was no point bemoaning her fate. She had to see the bright side, as Victoria was doing. She'd brought books along, and she'd spotted cushions in the salon that could be used as padding in lieu of a deck chair. And if she worked to keep her presence as inconspicuous as possible, she knew she'd do all right.

"Having second thoughts?"

The low, taunting baritone came from behind her. She didn't have the slightest doubt as to whose voice it was.

"What's to have second thoughts about?" she asked quietly. "This is my vacation. I'm looking forward to it."

"Are you always uptight when you're looking forward to something?"

"I'm not uptight."

He moved forward until he, too, leaned against the wood. "No?"

Shaye was peripherally aware of his largeness and did her best to ignore it. "No."

"Then why are your knuckles white on that rail?"

"Because if the boat lurches, I don't want to be thrown."

"She's called a sloop, and she doesn't lurch."

"Sway, tilt, heel—whatever the term is."

"Not a sailor, I take it?"

"I've sailed."

"Sunfish? Catboat?"

"Actually, I've spent time on twelve-meters, but as a guest, not a student of nautical terminology."

"A twelve-meter is a far cry from the *Golden Echo*."

"Do tell."

"You're not pleased with her?"

"She's fine," Shaye answered diplomatically.

"But not up to your usual standards?"

"I didn't say that."

"You're thinking it. Tell me, if you're used to something faster and sleeker, what are you doing here?"

Shaye bit off the sharp retort that was on the tip of her tongue and instead answered calmly, "As I said, I'm on vacation."

"Why here?"

"Because my aunt invited me to join her."

"And you were thrilled to accept?"

She did turn to him then and immediately wished she hadn't. He towered over her, a good six-four to her own five-six, and there was an air of menace about him. She took a deep breath to regain her poise, then spoke slowly and as evenly as possible.

"No, I was not thrilled to accept. Sailing off in the facsimile of a pirate ship on a wild goose chase for a treasure that probably doesn't exist is not high on my list of ways I'd like to spend my vacation."

Noah's gaze was hard as he studied her face. She was a beauty, but cool, very cool. Her features were set in rigid lines, her hazel eyes cutting. Had he seen any warmth, any softening, he would have eased off. But he was annoyed as hell that she was along, and to have her match his stare with such boldness was just what he needed to goad him on.

"That was what I figured." His eyes narrowed. "Now listen here, and listen good. If you repeat any of those pithy comments within earshot of my uncle, you'll regret it."

The blatant threat took Shaye by surprise. She'd assumed Noah to be rude; she hadn't expected him to be openly hostile. "Excuse me?"

"You heard."

"Heard, but don't believe. What makes you think I'd say anything to your uncle?"

"I know your type."

"How could you possibly—"

"You expected a luxury yacht, not a wreck of a boat. You expected a lovely stateroom, not a small, plain cabin. You expected a captain and a cook, not a professor who's staging Halloween three months early."

Shaye's blood began a slow boil. "You were eavesdropping!"

His eyes remained steady, a chilling gray, and the dark spikes of hair that fell over his brow, seeming to defy the wind, added to the aura of threat that was belied by the complacency of his voice. "I was sitting below while you and your aunt chatted on deck."

"So you listened."

"The temptation was too great. In case you haven't realized it yet, we'll be practically on top of each other for the next two weeks. I wanted to know what I was in for." His gaze dropped to her hands. "I'd ease up if I were you. Those nails of yours will leave marks on the wood."

Shaye's fingernails weren't overly long, though they were neatly filed and wore a coat of clear polish. Instead of arguing, she took yet another deep breath and squared her shoulders. "Thank you for making your feelings clear."

"Just issuing a friendly little warning."

"Friendly?"

"We-e-e-" maybe that is stretching it a little. You're too stiff-backed and fussy for my tastes."

Shaye's temper flared. "You have to be one of the most arrogant individuals I've ever had the misfortune to meet. You don't know me at all. You have no idea what I do, what I like or what I want. But I'll tell you one thing, I don't take to little warnings the likes of which you just issued."

"Consider it offered nonetheless."

"And you can consider it rejected." Eyes blazing, she made a slow and deliberate sweep from his thick, dark hair over his faded black T-shirt and worn khaki shorts, down long, hair-roughened legs to his solid bare feet. "I don't need you telling me what to do. I can handle myself and in good taste, which is a sight more than I can say for you." Every bit as deliberately as she'd raked his form, and with as much indifference to his presence as she could muster, she returned her gaze to the shrinking port.

"I'd watch it, if I were you. I'm not in the mood to be crossed."

"Another threat?" she asked, keeping her eyes fixed on the shore. "And what will you do if I choose to ignore it?"

"I'll be your shadow for the next two weeks. I could make things unpleasant, you know."

"I have the distinct feeling you'll do that anyway." Turning, she set off smoothly for the bow.

3

VICTORIA SQUINTED UP at Samson. "How much farther will we be towed?"

"Not much. We're nearly clear of the smaller boats, and the wind is picking up nicely."

Shaye joined them in time to catch his answer. "What happens if it dies once we're free?"

Samson grinned. "Then we'll lie on the deck and bask in the sun until it decides to come back to life."

She had visions of lying in the sun and basking for days, and the visions weren't enticing. Still smarting from her set-to with Noah, she feared that if they were becalmed she'd go stark, raving mad. "Given a reasonable wind, how long will it take to reach Costa Rica?"

"Given a reasonable wind, four days. The *Golden Echo* wasn't built for speed."

"What was she built for?" Shaye asked, her curiosity offset by a hint of aspersion.

"Effect," came Noah's tight reply as he took up a position beside her.

Her shadow. Was it starting already? Tipping up her head, she challenged him with a stare. "Explain, please."

Noah directed raised brows toward his uncle, who in his own shy way was a storyteller. But Samson shook his head, pivoted on his heel and headed aft, calling over his shoulder, "It's all yours. I have to see to the sails."

Noah would have offered his assistance if it hadn't been for two things. First, Samson would have refused: he took pride in his sailing skill and preferred, whenever possible, to do things himself. Second, Noah wanted to stay by Shaye. He knew that he annoyed her, and he intended to take advantage of that fact. It was some solace, albeit perverse, to have her aboard.

"The *Golden Echo* was modeled after an early eighteenth century Colonial sloop," he began, broadening his gaze to include Victoria in the tale. "She was built in the 1920s by a man named Horgan, a sailor and a patriot, who saw in her lines a classic beauty that was being lost in the sleeker, more modern craft. Horgan wanted to enjoy her, but he also wanted to make a statement."

"He did that," Shaye retorted, then asked on impulse, "Where did he sail her?"

"Up and down the East Coast at first."

"For pleasure?"

Noah's eyes bore into her. "Some people do it that way."

Victoria, who'd been watching the two as she leaned back against the rail, asked gently, "Did he parade her?"

"I'm sure he did," Noah answered, softening faintly with the shift of his gaze, "though I doubt there was as much general interest in a vessel like this then as there is today. From what Samson learned, Horgan made several Atlantic crossings before he finally berthed the *Golden Echo* in Bermuda. When his own family lost interest and he grew too ill to sail her alone, he began renting her out. She was sold as part of his estate in the mid-sixties."

"That leaves twenty years unaccounted for," Shaye prompted.

"I'm getting there." But he took his time, leisurely looking amidship to check on his uncle's progress. By the time he resumed, Shaye was glaring out to sea. "The new owners, a couple by the name of Payne, expanded on the charter business. For a time, they worked summers out of Boston, where the *Golden Echo* was in demand for private parties and small charity functions. Eventually they decided that the season was too limited, so they moved south."

"Why aren't they with us now?" Shaye asked without turning her head.

"Because there isn't room. Besides, they have a number of other boats to manage. The business is headquartered in Jamaica."

"Why are we in Colombia?"

"Because that's where the last charter ended. It's a little like Hertz—"

"Noah!" came Samson's buoyant shout. "Set us free!"

With a steadying hand on the bowsprit, Noah folded himself over the prow, reaching low to release the heavy steel clip that had held the powerboat's line to the *Golden Echo*.

The powerboat instantly surged ahead, then swung into a broad U-turn. Its driver, a Colombian with swarthy skin and a mile-wide white grin, saluted as he passed. A grinning Victoria waved back, moving aft to maintain the contact.

Shaye was unaware of her departure. She hadn't even seen the Colombian. Rather, her eyes were glued to the spot where Noah had released the clip. The large, rusty ring spoke for itself, but what evoked an odd blend of astonishment and amusement was the fact that it protruded from the navel of a scantily clad lady. That the lady was time-worn and peeling served only to accentuate her partial nudity.

"That's the figurehead," Noah informed her, crossing his arms over his chest.

"I know what it is," she answered, instantly losing grasp of whatever amusement she'd felt. "I just hadn't seen her earlier."

"Does her state of undress embarrass you?"

"I've seen breasts before."

Insolent eyes scanned the front of her T-shirt. "I should hope so."

Shaye kept her arms at her sides when they desperately wanted to cover her chest. She was far from the prude that Noah had apparently decided she was, but while she'd learned to control her desires, there was something about the way he was looking at her that set off little sparks inside. She felt nearly as bare-breasted as the lady on the bow and not nearly as wooden—which was something she sought to remedy by turning the tables on Noah.

"Does she excite you?"

"Who?"

Shaye tossed her head toward the bow, then watched as he bent sideways.

"She's not bad," he decided, straightening. "A little stern-faced for my tastes. Like you."

"Your tastes are probably as pathetic as old Horgan's. If he were building a boat like this today and dared to put a thing like that at the bow, he'd have women's groups picketing the pier."

Noah drew himself to his full height and glared down at her. "If there's one thing I can't stand it's a militant feminist."

She glared right back. "And if there's one thing *I* can't stand, it's a presumptuous male. You're just itching for a fight, aren't you?"

"Damn right."

"Why?"

"Why not?"

"The way I see it," she said, taking a deep breath for patience, "either you're annoyed that I've come along or you didn't want to be here in the first place."

His hair was blowing freely now. "Oh, I would have been happy enough sailing off with Samson. He's undemanding. I'd have gotten the R and R I need."

"Then it's me. Why do I annoy you?"

"You're a woman, and you're prissy."

Unable to help herself, Shaye laughed. *"Prissy?"* Then some vague instinct told her that prissy was precisely the way to be with this man. "Prissy." She cleared her throat. "Yes, well, I do believe in exercising a certain decorum."

"I'm sure you give new meaning to the word."

Shaye was about to say that Noah probably didn't know the *first* meaning of the word when the sound of unfurling canvas caught her ear. She looked up in time to see the mainsail fill with wind, then down to see Samson securing the lines.

"Shouldn't you give him a hand?"

"He doesn't need it."

"Then why are you here at all?"

Noah's smile might have held humor but didn't. "To give you a hard time. Why else?" With that, he sauntered off.

Aware that he'd had the last word this time around, Shaye watched him until he disappeared into the companionway. Then she turned back to the bow and closed her eyes. His image remained, a vivid echo in her mind of tousled dark hair, a broad chest, lean hips and endless legs. He was attractive; she had to give him that. But the attraction ended with the physical. He was unremittingly disagreeable.

And exhausting. It had been a long time since she'd sparred with anyone as she was sparring with him. Not that she didn't have occasional differences with people at work, but that was something else, something professional. In her private life she'd grown to love peace. She avoided abrasive people and chose friends who were conventional and comfortable. She dated the least threatening of men, indulging their occasional need to assert themselves over choice of restaurants or theaters because, through it all, she was in control. Not even her parents, with their parochial views, could rile her.

But Noah VanBaar had done just that. She wasn't sure how they'd become enemies so quickly. Was it his fault? Hers? Had she really seemed prissy?

A helpless smile broke across her face. Prissy. Wouldn't André and the guys from the garret—wherever they were today—die laughing if they heard that! Her parents, on the other hand, wouldn't die laughing. They'd choke a little, then breathe sighs of relief, then launch into a discourse on her age and the merits of marriage.

Prissy. It wasn't such a bad thing to be around Noah. If he hated prissiness so much, he'd leave her alone, which was all she really wanted, wasn't it?

Buoyed by her private pep talk, she sought out Victoria, who was chatting with Samson as he hauled up the first of two jibs. Indeed, it was Samson she addressed. "Would you like any help?"

Deftly lashing the line to its cleat, he stood back to watch the sail catch the wind. "Nope. All's under control." He darted them a quick glance. "Have you ladies had breakfast yet?"

"Victoria, has, but I, uh, slept a little later."

"You'll find fresh eggs and bacon in the icebox. Better eat and enjoy before they spoil."

Fresh eggs and bacon sounded just fine to Shaye, even if the word *icebox* was a little antiquated. Somehow, though, coming from Samson it didn't seem strange. Without pausing to reflect on the improvement in her attitude toward him, she asked, "How about you? Can I bring you something?"

"Ah no," he sighed, patting his belt. "I had a full breakfast earlier."

"How about coffee?"

"Now that's a thought. If you make it strong and add cream and two sugars, I could be sorely tempted."

Shaye smiled and turned to her aunt. "Anything for you?"

"Thanks, sweetheart, but I'm fine."

"See you in a bit, then." Still smiling, she entered the companionway, trotted down the steps and turned into the galley. There her smile faded. Noah was sprawled on the built-in settee that formed a shallow U behind the small table. He'd been alerted by the pad of her sneakers and was waiting, fork in hand, chewing thoughtfully.

"Well, well," he drawled as soon as he'd swallowed, "if it isn't the iron maiden."

"I though you'd already eaten."

"Samson has, but I don't make a habit of getting up at dawn like he does."

She was looking at his plate, which still held healthy portions of scrambled eggs and bacon, plus a muffin and a half, and a huge wedge of melon. "Think you have enough?"

"I hope so. I'm going to need all the strength I can get."

"To sit back and watch Samson sail?"

"To fight with you."

Determined not to let him irk her—or to let him interfere with her breakfast—she went to the refrigerator. "It's not really worth the effort, you know."

"I'll be the judge of that."

She shrugged and reached for two eggs and the packet of bacon. After setting them on the stove, she opened one cabinet, then the second in search of a pan.

"In the sink," Noah informed her.

She took in the contents of the sink at a disdainful glance. "And filthy. Thanks."

"You're welcome."

Automatically she reached for the tap, only to find there was none.

"Try the foot pump. You won't get water any other way. Not that you really need it. Why not just wipe out the pan with a paper towel and use it again?"

"That's disgusting."

"Not really. You're having the same thing I had."

"But there's an inch of bacon fat in this pan."

"Drain it."

There was a subtle command in his voice that drew her head around. "I take it we're conserving water."

"You take it right."

She pressed her lips together, then nodded slowly as she considered her options. She could pump up the water in a show of defiance, but if water was indeed in short supply, she'd be biting off her nose to spite her face. Bathing was going to be enough of a challenge; a little water spared now would make her feel less guilty for any she used later.

Very carefully she drained the pan, then swabbed it out with a paper towel and set it on the stove to heat.

"Need any help?" he taunted.

"I can crack an egg."

"Better put on the bacon first. It takes longer."

"I know that."

"Then you'd better start separating the bacon. The pan will be hot and you'll be wasting propane."

"Are you always a tightwad?"

"Only when I'm with a spendthrift."

"You don't know what you're talking about."

"So educate me."

But Shaye wasn't about to do any such thing. It suited her purpose to keep Noah in the dark, just as it suited her purpose to leisurely place one rasher of bacon, then another in the pan. While they cooked, she rummaged through the supplies until she located the coffee, then set a pot on to perk.

"I'm impressed," Noah said around a mouthful of food. "I didn't think you had it in you."

She'd been acutely aware of his eyes at her back, and despite good intentions, her temper was rising. "Shows how much you know," she snapped.

"Then you don't have a cook back in wherever?"

"I don't have a cook."

"How about a husband?"

Without turning, she raised her left hand, fingers rigidly splayed and decidedly bare.

"The absence of a ring doesn't mean anything. Militant feminists often—"

"I am not a militant feminist!" Gripping the handle of the frying pan, she forked the bacon onto its uncooked side. Slowly and silently she counted to ten. With measured movements, she reached for an egg.

It came down hard on the edge of the pan. The yoke broke. The white spilled over the rim.

Repairing the damage as best she could, she more carefully cracked the second egg, then stood, spatula in hand, waiting for both to cook.

"I thought you said you could crack an egg."

She didn't respond to the jibe.

"Got anything planned for an encore?"

She clamped her lips together.

"You could always flip an egg onto the floor."

"Why don't you shut up and eat?"

"I'm done."

Eyes wide, she turned to see that his plate, piled high short moments before, was now empty. "You're incredible."

He grinned broadly. "I know."

Her gaze climbed to his face, lured there by a strange force, one that refused to release her. Even after the slash of white teeth had disappeared, she stared, seeing a boyishness that was totally at odds with the man.

Unable to rationalize the discrepancy, she tore herself away and whirled back to the stove. The tiny whispers deep in her stomach could be put down to hunger, and the faint tremor in her hands as she transferred the eggs and bacon to a dish could be fatigue. But *boyishness*, in *Noah*?

A warning rang in her mind at the same moment she felt a pervasive warmth stretch from the crown of her head to her heels.

"Like I said," Noah murmured in her ear, "I'll need all my strength."

One arm reached to her left and deposited his dish, utensils clattering, in the sink. The other reached to her right and shifted the frying pan to the cold burner. The overall effect was one of imprisonment.

"Do you mind?" she muttered as she held herself stiffly against the stove.

He didn't move. Only his nose shifted, brushing the upper curve of her ear. "You smell good. Don't you sweat like the rest of us?"

Shaye felt a paradoxical dampness in the palms of her hands, at the backs of her knees, in the gentle hollow between her breasts, and was infinitely grateful that he couldn't possibly know. "Would you please move back?" she asked as evenly as she could.

"Have you ever been married?"

"I'd like to eat my eggs before they dry up."

"Got a boyfriend?"

"If you're looking for something to do, you could take a cup of coffee to your uncle."

"You never get those sweet little urges the rest of us get?"

Swinging back her elbow, she made sharp contact with his ribs. In the next instant she was free.

"That was dirty," he accused, rubbing the injured spot as she spun around.

"That was just for starters." Her hands were balled at her sides, and she was shaking. "I don't like to be crowded. Do you think you can get that simple fact through your skull, or is it too much to take in on a full stomach?"

Noah's hand stilled against his lean middle, and he studied her for a long minute. "I think I make you nervous."

"Angry. You make me angry."

"And nervous." He was back to taunting. "You're flushed."

"Anger."

Silkily he lowered his eyes to her left breast. "That, too?"

She refused to believe that he could see the quick quiver of her heart, though she couldn't deny the rapidity of her breathing. Even more adamantly she refused to believe that the tiny ripples of heat surging through her represented anything but fury. "That, too."

His gaze dropped lower, charting her midriff, caressing the bunching of jersey at her waist, arriving at last at her hips. His brow furrowed. He seemed confused yet oddly spellbound. Then, as though suddenly regaining the direction he'd lost, he snapped his eyes back to her face. "Too bad," he said, his lips hardening. "You've got the goods. It's a shame you can't put them to better use."

Shaye opened her mouth to protest his insolence, but he had already turned and was stalking away. "You left your dirty things in the sink!" she yelled.

He didn't answer. His tall frame blended with the shadow of the companionway, then disappeared into the blinding light above.

SOME TIME LATER, bearing cups of coffee for Samson and herself, Shaye returned to the deck. Samson stood at the helm, looking utterly content. He accepted the coffee with a smile, but Shaye didn't stay to talk. He was in his own world. He didn't need company.

Besides, Noah sat nearby. His long legs formed an open circle around a coil of rope and, while his hands were busily occupied, he watched her every move.

So she proceeded on toward the bow, where Victoria leaned against the bulwark gazing out to sea.

"Pretty, isn't it?"

Shaye nodded. The Colombian coast was a dark ridge on the horizon behind. Ahead was open sea. Far in the distance a cargo ship headed for Barranquilla or Cartagena. Less far a trawler chugged along, no doubt from one of the fishing villages along the coast.

Her fancy was caught, though, by a third, smaller craft, a yacht winging through the waters like a slender white dove. Peaceful, Shaye thought. Ahh, what she'd give for a little of that peace.

"Everything okay?" Victoria asked.

"Just fine."

"You look a little piqued."

"I'm tired."

"Not feeling seasick?"

Shaye shot her the wry twist of a grin. "Not quite."

"Have you ever been seasick?"

"Nope."

"Mmm." Victoria shook back her head and tipped it up to the sky. "In spite of everything, you have to admit that this is nice." When Shaye didn't respond, she went on. "It doesn't really matter what boat you're on, the air is the same, the sky, the waves." She slitted one eye toward Shaye. "Still want to go back?"

"It's a little late for that, don't you think?"

"But if you could, would you?"

Shaye dragged in a long, deep breath, then released it in a sigh. "No, Victoria, I wouldn't go back. But that doesn't mean this is going to be easy."

"What happened in the galley?"

Shaye took a deliberately lengthy sip of her coffee. "Nothing."

"Are you sure?"

"I'm sure."

"You sound a little tense."

"Blame that on fatigue, too." Or on anger. Or on frustration. Or, in a nutshell, on Noah VanBaar.

"But it's not even noon."

"It feels like midnight to me. I may go to bed pretty soon."

"But we've just begun to sail!"

"And we'll be sailing for the next four days straight, so there'll be plenty of time for me to take it all in."

"Oh, Shaye . . ."

"If I were in the Berkshires, I'd still be in bed."

"Bo-ring."

"Maybe so, but this is my vacation, isn't it? If I don't catch up on my sleep now, I never will. Weren't you the one who said I could do it on the boat?"

Victoria yielded with grace. "Okay. Sleep. Why don't you drag some cushions up here and do it in the sun?"

Because Noah is on deck and there's no way *I could sleep knowing that*. "That much sun I don't need."

"Then, the shade. You can sleep in the shade of the sails."

But Shaye was shaking her head. "No, I think I'll try that bed of ours." Her lips twisted. "Give it a test run." She took another swallow of coffee.

Victoria leaned closer. "Running away from him won't help, y'know. You have to let him know that he doesn't scare you."

"He doesn't scare me."

"He can't take his eyes off you."

"Uh-huh."

"It's true. He's been watching you since you came on deck."

"He's worried that I'm going to spoil Samson's trip by saying something ugly."

"He said that?"

"In no uncertain terms."

"What else did he say?" Victoria said, and Shaye realized she'd fallen into the trap. But it wasn't too late to extricate herself. She didn't want to discuss Noah with Victoria, who would, no doubt, play the devil's advocate. Shaye wasn't ready to believe *anything* good about Noah.

So she offered a cryptic, "Not much."

Victoria had turned around so that her back was to the bulwark. Quite conveniently, she had a view of the rest of the boat. "He's very good-looking."

"If you say so," Shaye answered indifferently.

"He appears to be good with his hands."

"I wouldn't know about that."

"Do you have any idea what he does for a living?"

"Nope."

"Aren't you curious?"

"Nope."

"Then you're hopeless," Victoria decided, tossing her hands in the air and walking away.

"Traitor," Shaye muttered under her breath. "I'm only here because of you, and are you grateful? Of course not. You won't be satisfied until I'm falling all over that man, but I can assure you that won't happen. He and I have nothing in common. Nothing at all."

THEY DID, as it turned out. Noah was as tired as Shaye. He'd flown in the day before from New York via Atlanta, where he'd had a brief business meeting, and rather than going to a hotel in Barranquilla, he'd come directly to the *Golden Echo* to help Samson prepare for the trip.

Though he'd never have admitted it aloud, Shaye hadn't been far off the mark when she'd called the boat a wreck. Oh, she was seaworthy; he'd checked for signs of leakage when he'd first come aboard and had found none. The little things were what needed attention—lines to be spliced, water pumps to be primed, hurricane lamps to be cleaned—all of which should by rights have been done before the *Golden Echo* left Jamaica on her previous charter. But that was water over the dam. He didn't mind the work. What he needed now, though, was rest.

"I'm turning in for a while," he told Samson, who was quite happily guarding the helm. "If you need me for anything, give a yell."

The older man kept his eyes on the sea. "Do me a favor and check on Shaye? She went below a little while ago. I hope she's not sick."

Noah knew perfectly well that she'd gone below. He wouldn't have said that she'd looked particularly sick, since she'd seemed pale to him from the start.

"I'd ask Victoria to do it," Samson was saying, "but I hate to disturb her." She was relaxing on the foredeck, taking obvious pleasure in both the sun and the breeze. "Since you're going below anyway..."

"I'll check."

But only because Samson had asked. Left to his own devices, Noah would have let Shaye suffer on her own. His encounter with her in the galley had left him feeling at odds with himself, and though that had been several hours before, he hadn't been able to completely shake the feeling. All he wanted was to strip down and go to sleep without thought of the woman. But Samson had asked...

She wasn't in the galley or the salon, and since she certainly wouldn't be in the captain's quarters, he made for her cabin. The door was shut. He stood for a minute, head bowed, hands on his hips. Then he knocked very lightly on the wood. When there was no answer, he eased open the door.

The sight before him took him totally by surprise. Shaye had pulled back the covers and was lying on her side on the bare sheets, sound asleep. She wore a huge white T-shirt that barely grazed her upper thighs. Her legs were slightly bent, long and slender. But what stunned him most was her hair. It fanned behind her on the pillow, a thick, wavy train of auburn that caught the light off the portholes and glowed.

Fascinated, he took one step closer, then another. She seemed like another woman entirely when she was relaxed. There was gentleness in her loosely resting fingers, softness in her curving body, vulnerability in the slight part of her lips and in the faint sheen of perspiration that made her skin gleam. And in her hair? Spirit. Oh, yes. There it was—promise of the same fire he'd caught from time to time in her eyes.

Unable to resist, he hunkered down by the side of the bed. Her lashes were like dark flames above her cheekbones. Free now of tension, her nose looked small and pert. Her cheeks were the lightest shade of a very natural pink that should have clashed with her hair but didn't. And that hair—he wondered if it were as soft as it looked, or as hot. His fingers curled into his palms, resisting the urge to touch, and he forced his eyes away.

It was a major mistake. The thin T-shirt, while gathered loosely in front, clung to her slender side and the gentle flare of her hip, leaving just enough to the imagination to make him ache. And edging beneath the hem of the shirt was a slash of the softest, sweetest apricot-colored silk. His gaze jumped convulsively to the far side of the bed, where she'd left the clothes she'd discarded. There, lying atop the slacks and T-shirt she'd been wearing earlier, was a lacy bra of the same apricot hue.

With a hard swallow, he flicked his gaze back to her face. Stern, stiff-backed and fussy—was that the image she chose to convey to the world? Her underthings told a different story, one that was enhanced by her sleeping form. It was interesting, he mused, interesting and puzzling.

Image making was his business. He enjoyed it, was good at it. Moreover, knowing precisely what went into the shaping of public images, he prided himself on being able to see through them. He hadn't managed to this time, though, and he wondered why. Was Shaye that good, or had his perceptiveness been muddled?

He suspected it was a little of both, and there was meager comfort in the thought. If Shaye was that good, she was far stronger and more complex than he'd imagined. If his perceptiveness had been muddled, it was either because he was tired . . . or because she did something to his mind.

He feared it was the latter. He'd been ornery because he hadn't wanted her along, but that orneriness had been out of proportion. He didn't normally goad people the way he had her. But Shaye—she brought out the rawest of his instincts.

In every respect. Looking at her now, all soft and enticing, he felt the heat rise in his body as it hadn't done in years. How could he possibly be attracted to as prickly a woman? Was it her softness his body sensed and responded to? Or her hidden fire?

His insides tensed in a different way when her lashes fluttered, then it was too late to escape. Not that he would have, he told himself. He'd never run from a woman, and he wasn't about to now. But he'd be damned if he'd let her know how she affected him. Retrieving his mask of insolence, he met her startled gaze.

Shaye didn't move a muscle. She simply stared at him. "What are you doing here?"

"Checking on you. Samson thought you might be sick."

"I'm not."

"Not *violently* seasick?"

"... No."

His gaze idly scored her body. "Did you lie about anything else?"

Why, she asked herself, did he sound as though he knew something he shouldn't? Victoria would never have betrayed her. And there was no way he could see through her T-shirt, though she almost imagined he had. She'd have given anything to reach for the sheet and cover herself, but she refused to give him the satisfaction of knowing that his wandering eye made her nervous. "No," she finally answered.

"Mmm."

"What is that supposed to mean?"

"That you're a contradiction," he said without hesitation.

He'd obviously been thinking about her—or crouching here, watching her—for some time. The last thought made her doubly nervous, and the explanation he offered didn't help.

"Cactus-prickly when you're awake, sweet woman when you're asleep. It makes me wonder which is the real you."

"You'll never know," she informed him. Her poise was fragile; there was something debilitating about lying on a bed near Noah, wearing not much more than an old T-shirt.

His gray eyes glittered. "It'd be a challenge for me to find out. Mmm, maybe I'll make it my goal. I'll have two full weeks with not much else to do."

Shaye didn't like the sound of that at all. "And what about the treasure you're supposedly seeking?" she demanded.

"Samson's doing the seeking. As far as I'm concerned, there are many different kinds of treasure." He surveyed her body more lazily. "Could be that the one you're hiding is worth more than the one my uncle seeks."

"As though I could hide anything this way," she mumbled.

"Precisely."

"Look, I was sleeping. I happen to be exhausted. Do you think you could find a tiny bit of compassion within that stone-hard soul of yours to leave me be?"

He grinned, wondering what she'd have said if she'd known something else had been close to stone-hard moments before. No doubt she'd have used far more potent words to describe his character. Come to think of it, he wondered how many of those potent words she knew.

"You're really very appealing like this," he said softly. "Much more approachable than before. I like your hair."

"Go away."

"I hadn't realized it was so long. Or so thick. The color comes alive when you let it down like that. Why do you bother to tack it up?"

"To avoid comments like the ones you just made."

"I'd think you'd be flattered."

"I'm not."

"You don't like me," he said with a pout.

"Now you're getting there."

"Is it something I said, something I did?"

She squeezed her eyes shut for a minute, then, unable to bear the feeling of exposure any longer, bolted up and reached for the sheet.

Noah looked as though he'd lost his best friend. "What did you do that for? I wouldn't have touched you."

There was touching and there was touching. He could touch her with his hands, or with his eyes. Or he could touch her with the innocent little expressions he sent her way from time to time. She knew not to trust those little expressions, but, still, they did something to her. Far better that he should be growling and scowling.

"It's your eyes," she accused as she pressed her back to the wall. "I don't like them."

This time his innocence seemed more genuine. "What's wrong with my eyes?"

"They creep."

"They explore," he corrected, "and when they find something they like, they take a closer look." He shrugged. "Can you blame them? Your legs are stunning."

She quickly tucked her legs under her. "Please. Just leave and let me sleep."

Since the path had been cleared for him, he hopped up and sat on the bed.

"Noah . . ." she warned.

"That's the first time you've called me by name. I like it when you say it, though you could soften the tone a little."

"Leave this cabin now!"

He made himself more comfortable, extending an arm, propping his weight on his palm. "You never answered me when I asked about boyfriends. Do you have any back home? Where is home, by the way?"

"Philadelphia," she growled. "There, you've gotten some information. Now you can leave."

"A little more. I want a little more. Is there a boyfriend?"

In a bid for dignity, she drew herself up as straight as she could. Unfortunately he was sitting on the sheet, which ended up stretched taut. And even with the extra inches she felt dwarfed. Why did he have to be so *big*? Why couldn't he be of average height like her lawyer friend, or the stockbroker? For that matter, why couldn't he be malleable, like they were? They'd have left the instant she'd asked *if* they ever made it to her room at all.

"Boyfriends?" he prompted.

"That's none of your business."

"I'll tell you about me if you tell me about you," he cajoled.

"I don't want to know about you."

Bemused, he tipped his dark head to the side. "Wouldn't it be easier if you knew what you faced?"

"I'm not facing anything," she argued, but there was a note of desperation in her voice.

"Two weeks, Shaye. We're going to be together for two long weeks."

"Miss Burke, to you."

For a split second he looked chastised, then spoiled it with a helpless spurt of laughter.

"All right," she grumbled quickly. "Call me Shaye."

"Shaye." He tempered his grin. "Do you have any boyfriends?"

She knew she'd lost a little ground on the Miss Burke bit, which even to her own ears had sounded inane. But she was supposed to be prissy. And as far as boyfriends were concerned, a few white lies wouldn't hurt.

"I don't date."

His eyes widened. "You've got to be kidding."

"No."

"With a body like yours?"

"For your information, there's more to life than sex." She wondered if she was sounding *too* prissy. She didn't want to overdo it.

"Really?"

"I'm too busy to date. I have a very demanding job, and I love it. My life is complete."

He shook his head. "Whew! You're something else." He didn't believe her for a minute, but if she wanted to play games, he could match her. "I have a demanding job myself, but I couldn't make it through life without steady helpings of sex. Women's liberation has its up side, in that sense."

"Then what are you doing on this trip?" she asked through gritted teeth. "How could you drag yourself away from all those warm beds and passionate arms?"

"And legs," he added quickly. "Don't forget legs. I'm a leg man, remember?"

She was getting nowhere, she realized. He looked as though he had no intention of budging, and she didn't think she had the physical strength to make him. "Please," she said, deliberately wilting a little, "I really am tired. I don't want to fight you, and I don't want to be on guard every minute of this trip. If you just leave me alone, I'll stay out of your way."

"Please, Noah."

"Please, Noah."

Her meekness was too much, he decided. When she was meek, there was no fire in her eyes, and he rather liked that fire. "Well, I have learned something new about you."

"What's that?"

His eyes slid over the moistness of her skin. "You sweat."

"Of course I sweat! It's damn hot in here!"

He grinned. So much for meekness. "The question," he ventured in a deep, smooth voice, "is whether you smell as good like this as you did before." He leaned closer.

Shaye put up here hands to hold him off, losing her grip on the sheet in the process. But she'd been right; she was no match for his strength. Her palms were ineffective levers against his chest, and despite her efforts, she felt his face against her neck.

His nose nuzzled her. His lips slid to the underside of her jaw. He opened his mouth and dragged it across her cheek to her ear.

And all the while, Shaye was dying a thousand little deaths because she liked the feel of his mouth on her, she liked it!

"Even . . . better," he whispered hoarsely. His lips nipped at her earlobe, and the hoarse whisper came again. "You smell . . . even better."

Her eyes were shut and her breathing had grown erratic. "Please, stop," she gasped brokenly. "Please, Noah . . ."

He was dizzy with pleasure at the contact, and would have gone on nuzzling her forever had he not caught the trace of fear in her voice. He hadn't heard that before, not fear, and he knew instinctively that there was nothing put on about it. Slowly and with a certain amount of puzzlement, he drew back and searched her eyes. They were wide with fear, yes, but with other things as well. And he knew then, without a doubt, what he was going to do.

He'd leave her now, but he'd be true to his word. He'd spend the next two weeks shadowing her, learning what made her tick. She might in fact be the prissy lady she wanted him to believe she was. Or she might be the woman of passion he suspected she was. In either case, he stirred her. That was what he read in her eyes, and though he wasn't sure why, it was what he wanted.

"Go back to sleep," he said gently as he rose from the bed. He was halfway to the door when he heard her snort.

"Fat chance of that! Can I really believe you won't invade my privacy again? And if I were to fall asleep, I'd have nightmares. Hmph. So much for a lovely vacation. Stuck on a stinking pirate ship with a man who thinks he's God's gift to women—"

Noah closed the door on the last of her tirade and, smiling, sauntered off through the salon.

4

*"A*HH*, mes belles amies. Notre dîner nous attend sur le pont. Suivez-moi, s'il vous plaît."*

Shaye, who'd been curled in an easy chair in the salon, darted a disbelieving glance at Victoria before refocusing her eyes on Samson. She'd known he'd been busily working in the galley and that he'd refused their offers of help. But she hadn't expected to be called to the table in flawless French—he was a professor of *Latin*, wasn't he?—much less by a man sporting a bright red, side-knotted silk scarf and a cockily set black beret.

Victoria thought he was precious; eccentric was the word Shaye would choose. But he was harmless, certainly more so than his nephew, she mused, and at the moment she was in need of a little comic relief.

It had been a long afternoon. She hadn't been able to fall back to sleep after Noah had left her cabin, though she'd tried her best. After cursing the sheets, the mattress, the heat and everything else in the room, she'd dressed, reknotted her hair and gone on deck.

Noah hadn't been there—he was sleeping, Samson told her, which had irritated her no end. *He* was sleeping, after he'd ruined her own! She'd seethed for a while, then been gently, gradually, helplessly lulled by the rocking of the boat into a better frame of mind.

And now Samson had called them to dinner. The table, it turned out, was a low, folding one covered by a checkered cloth, and the seats were cushions they carried up from the salon. Noah had lowered the jibs and secured the wheel, dashing Shaye's hope that he'd be too busy sailing to join them. To make matters worse, he crossed his long legs and fluidly lowered himself to the cushion immediately on her left.

The meal consisted of a hearty bouillabaisse, served with a Muscadet wine, crusty French bread and, for dessert, a raspberry tart topped with thick whipped cream. Other than complimenting the chef on his work, Shaye mostly stayed out of the conversation, which involved Samson and Victoria and the other unlikely trips each had taken.

Noah, too, was quiet, but his eyes were like living things reaching out, touching her, daring her to reveal something of herself as Victoria and Samson were doing. Since she had no intention of conforming, she remained quiet and ignored his gaze as best she could.

Samson, bless him, was more than willing to accept help with the cleanup, and Shaye was grateful for the escape. By the time she finished in the galley, she was feeling better.

Armed with a cup of coffee and a book, she settled in the salon. Hurricane lamps provided the light, casting a warm golden glow that she had to admit was atmospheric. In fact, she had to admit that the *Golden Echo* wasn't all that bad. Sails unfurled and full once again, the sloop sliced gently through the waves. A crosswind whispered from porthole to porthole, comfortably ventilating the salon. The mustiness that had bothered Shaye earlier seemed to have disappeared, though perhaps, she reflected, she'd simply grown accustomed to it.

She was well fed. She was comfortable. She was peacefully reading her book. Would a vacation in the Berkshires have been any different? *It's all in the mind, Shaye.* Isn't that what Victoria would say? *He can only be a threat if you allow it, whereas if you put him from mind, he doesn't exist.*

For a time it worked. She flew through the first hundred pages of her book, finally putting it down when her lids began to droop. Victoria was still on deck. Samson had turned in some time before, intending to sleep until two, when he would relieve Noah at the helm.

Intending to sleep far longer than that, Shaye went to bed herself. When she awoke, though, it wasn't ten in the morning as she'd planned. It was three and very dark, and she was feeling incredibly warm all over.

A fever? Not quite. She'd awakened from a dream of Noah. A nightmare? she asked herself, as she lay flat on her back taking slow, easy breaths to calm her quivering body. Only in hindsight. At the time, it had been an excitingly erotic dream. Even now her skin was damp in response.

It isn't fair, she railed, silently. She could push him from her thoughts when she was awake, but how could she control the demon inside while she slept? And what breed of demon was it that caused her to dream erotic dreams about *any* man? She'd lived wildly and passionately for a time, and the lifestyle left much to be desired. She'd sworn off it. She'd outgrown it. She was perfectly content with what she had now.

Could that demon be telling her something?

Uncomfortable with the direction of her thoughts, she carefully rose from the bed so as not to awaken Victoria, dragged a knee-length sweatshirt over her T-shirt and padded silently to the door.

All was quiet save the slap of the waves against the hull and the sough of the breeze. She passed through the salon and the narrow passageway, sending a disdainful glance toward the door of the captain's cabin, where Noah would no doubt be sleeping by now, and carefully climbed the companionway.

On deck she dropped her head back and let the breeze take her unfettered hair as it would. The sea air felt good against her skin, and the sweatshirt was just loose enough, just warm enough to keep her comfortable. Almost reluctantly she straightened her head and opened her eyes, intending to tell Samson that she would be standing at the bow for a bit.

Only it wasn't Samson at the helm. Though the transom's hanging lamp left his face in shadows, the large frame rakishly planted behind the wheel could belong to no one but Noah.

The image struck her, then, with devastating force. He didn't need a billowing shirt, tight pants, boots and a cross belt. He didn't need anything beyond gently clinging shorts and a windbreaker that was barely zipped. He had the rest—thick hair blowing, broad shoulders set, strong hands on the wheel, bare feet widespread and rooted to the deck. Looking more like a descendant of Fletcher Christian than the nephew of Samson VanBaar, he was a rebel if ever there was one. And his prize? Her peace of mind . . . for starters.

"Welcome," he said with unexpected civility. "You wouldn't by chance care to take the helm for a minute while I go get a cup of coffee?"

She certainly wouldn't have allowed herself to turn tail and run once he'd seen her, but she felt impelled to explain her presence. The last thing she wanted was for him to think she was seeking him out. "I thought this was Samson's shift."

"He's exhausted. I decided to let him sleep a while longer."

"You seem tired yourself," she heard herself say. He certainly didn't *sound* like a rebel just then.

He shrugged. "I'll sleep later."

Nodding, she looked away. Something had happened. It was as though the intimacy they'd shared in her dream had softened her. Or was it his fatigue, which softened *him*? Or the gently gusting night air? Or the hypnotic motion of the sloop? Or the fact that starlit nights in the Caribbean were made, in the broadest sense, for love, not war?

Whatever, she turned and started back down the companionway.

"Don't go," he said quickly.

"I'll bring up some coffee."

It was an easy task to reheat what was in the pot. When she returned a few minutes later carrying two mugs, Noah accepted his with a quiet, "Thank you."

Nodding, Shaye stepped back to lean against the transom. For a time, neither spoke. Noah's eyes were ahead, Shaye's were directed northward.

Philadelphia seemed very far away, and it occurred to her that she didn't miss it. Nor, she realized, did she regret the fact that she wasn't heading for the Berkshires. Come light of day, she might miss both, but right now, she felt peaceful. Sated. As though . . . as though her dream had filled some need that she'd repressed. She felt as though she'd just made love with Noah, as though they were now enjoying the companionable afterglow.

"Couldn't sleep?" he asked quietly.

"I, uh, it must have been the rest I had earlier."

"That'll do it sometimes."

They relapsed into silence. Shaye sipped her coffee. Noah did the same, then set the mug down and consulted his compass.

"I was wondering about that," she ventured. "I didn't see any navigational equipment when Samson showed us around."

"I'm not sure what was available when Horgan built the sloop in the twenties, but I assume he felt—and the Paynes must have agreed—that fancy dials would have been sacrilegious." He made a slight adjustment to the wheel, then beckoned to her. "Hold it for a second?"

Setting the mug by her feet, she grasped the wooden wheel with both hands while he moved forward to adjust the sails.

When he returned, though, it was to take the place she'd left at the transom, slightly behind her, slightly to the right.

"So you use a compass?"

"And a sextant. My uncle's the expert with that."

"Is there a specific point we're aiming at?"

Noah took a healthy swallow of his coffee. "He has coordinates, if that's what you mean."

"For the treasure?"

"Uh-huh."

She was looking ahead, holding the wheel steady, assuming that Noah would correct her if she did something wrong. "He hasn't said much about that."

"He's a great one for prioritizing. First, the sail. Then the treasure."

She felt a nudge at her elbow and turned to find him holding out her mug. She took it and lifted it, but rather than drinking, she brushed her lips back and forth against the rim. "It's strange . . ."

"What?"

"That Samson should be a Latin professor and yet have such a proclivity for adventure. Not that I'm being critical. I just find it . . . curious."

"Not really," Noah said. He paused for a minute, deciding how best to explain. "It's a matter of having balance in one's life. Samson has his teaching, which is stable, and his adventures, which are a little more risqué. But there's a link between the two. For example, he sees the same beauty in Latin that he sees in this sloop. They're both ancient—forefathers of other languages, other boats. They both have an innate beauty, a romanticism. Samson is a romantic."

"I hadn't noticed," Shaye teased.

Belatedly, Noah chuckled. "Mmm. He must seem a little bizarre to you."

"No. He's really very sweet."

"He stages Halloween year-round."

She wondered if she'd ever live down that particular comment, but since Noah didn't seem to be angry anymore, there was no point in defending herself. "So I gather," she said with a little grin.

Noah was content with that. "Samson has always believed in doing what he loves. He loves teaching." Reaching out, he rescued a blowing strand of her hair from her mouth and tucked it behind her ear. "He takes delight in making the language come alive for his students. And he does it. I've sat in on some of his classes. In his own quiet way, he is hilarious."

Shaye could believe it. "His stories are something else."

"You were listening?"

She shot him a quick glance. "Tonight? Of course I was."

"I wasn't sure. You were very quiet."

She wasn't about to say that listening hard to Samson had kept her mind off *him*. "Why interrupt something good when you have nothing better to add? It's really a shame that Samson doesn't write about his adventures. They'd make wonderful reading."

"They do."

"Magazine articles?" she asked with some excitement, immediately conjuring up images of a beautiful *National Geographic* spread.

"Books."

"No kidding!"

"How do you think he pays for these little adventures?"

"I really hadn't thought about it." She frowned. "He didn't say anything tonight about writing."

"He's an understated man. He downplays it."

"Can he do that? Isn't there a certain amount of notoriety that comes with being a published author?"

Noah leaned forward and lowered his voice to a conspiratorial level. "Not if you publish under another name." He leaned back again.

"Ahh. So that's how he does it."

"Mmm." He took another drink. "But don't tell him I told you."

She grinned. "Can I ask him where he learned to cook?"

"Cooking he'll discuss any day. It's one of his passions."

Passions. The word stuck in Shaye's mind, turning slowly, a many-faceted diamond with sides of brilliance, darkness, joy and grief.

She shook her hair back, freeing it for the caress of the wind. "You and he seem to be very close. Do you live in Hanover?"

It was a minute before Noah heard the question. He was fascinated by the little movement she'd made. It had been totally unaffected but beguiling. Bare-legged as she was, and with that gorgeous mane of hair—soft, oh yes, soft—blowing behind her, she didn't look anything like the prissy little lady he'd accused her of being.

He closed his eyes for a second and shook off both images, leaving in their place the same gentle ambiance that had existed before. Did he live near Samson in Hanover? "No. But we see each other regularly. There's just him and me. All the others are gone. We have a mutual-admiration society, so it works out well."

"All the others—you mean, your parents?"

"And Samson's wife. Samson and Gena never had children of their own, and since Samson and my father had no other siblings, I was pretty much shared between them."

She smiled. "That must have been fun."

"It was."

She thought about her own childhood, the time she'd spent with her parents. Fun wasn't a word she'd ever used to describe those days. "Was your father as much of a character as Samson?"

"No. He was more serious. Dividing my time between the two men gave a balance to my life, too."

It was the second time he'd spoken of balance, and she wondered if he'd done it deliberately. Her life was far from balanced. Work was her vocation, her avocation, the sole outlet for her energies. Victoria argued that there was more to life, and Shaye smiled and nodded and gave examples of the men she dated and the friends she saw. But apart from her friendship with her sister, the others were largely token friendships. And she knew why. To maintain a steady keel in her life, she chose to be with people who wouldn't rock the boat. Unfortunately, those people were uninspiring. They left her feeling alone and frustrated. Her only antidote was work.

But Noah couldn't possibly know all that, could he?

Feeling strangely empty, she took a large gulp of her coffee, then set the mug down and grasped the wheel more firmly. But neither the solidity of the hard wood nor the warm brew settling in her stomach could counter the chill she was feeling. Unconsciously, she rubbed one bare foot over the other.

In the next instant a third foot covered hers, a larger, warmer one. And then a human shield slipped behind her, protecting her back, her hips, her legs from elements that came from far beyond the Caribbean.

Noah had surrounded her this way in the galley, but the sense of imprisonment was far different now. It was gentle, protective and welcome.

She closed her eyes when she felt his face in her hair, and whispered, "Why are you being so nice?"

His voice was muffled. "Maybe because I'm too tired to fight."

"Then the secret is keeping you tired?"

"The secret," he said as his lips touched her ear, "is keeping your hair down and your legs bare and your mouth sweet. I think something happens when you screw back your hair and cinch yourself into your clothes. Everything tightens up. Your features stiffen and your tongue goes tart."

"It does not!" she cried, but without conviction. She couldn't believe how wonderful she felt, and she wasn't about to deny it any more than she could think to end it. When his face slid to her neck, she relaxed her head against his shoulder.

"I won't argue," he murmured thickly. "Not now."

"You're too tired."

"Too content."

He was pressing open-mouthed kisses to the side of her neck, inching his way lower to the spot where her sweatshirt began. She felt a trembling start at her toes and spread upward, and she grasped the wheel tighter, though she wasn't about to move.

He shifted behind her, spreading his legs to cradle her at the same time his hands fell to her thighs and began to work their way upward.

"Noah . . ." she whispered.

"So soft . . ." His fingers were splayed, thumbs dragging up along the crease where her thighs met her hips, tracing her pelvic bones, etching a path over her waist and ribs. Then his fingers came together to cup her breasts, and she went wild inside. She arched into his hands, while her head came around, mouth open, tongue trapped against his jaw.

She was melting. Every bone in her body, every muscle, every inch of flesh seemed to lose definition and gather into a single yearning mass. Had she missed this so, this wonderful sense of anticipatory fulfillment? Had she ever experienced it before?

He was roughly caressing her breasts, but it wasn't enough, and her mouth, with hungry nips at his chin, told him so. Then her mouth was being covered, eaten, devoured, and she was taking from him, taste for taste, bite for bite.

Totally oblivious to her role at the helm she wound her arms backward, around Noah. Her hands slid up and down the backs of his thighs, finally clasping his buttocks, urging his masculine heat closer to the spot that suddenly and vividly ached.

"Oh God," he gasped, dragging his mouth from hers. He wrapped quivering arms tightly around her waist and breathed raggedly as his pelvis moved against her. "Ahh . . ."

More hungry than ever, Shaye tried to turn. She wanted to wrap her arms around his neck, to feed again from his mouth, to drape her leg over his and feel his strength where she craved it so. But he wouldn't have it. He squeezed her hard to hold her still, and the movement was enough to restore the first fragments of reason. When he felt that she'd regained a modicum of control, he eased up his hold, but he didn't release her.

With several more gusts of wind, their breathing, their pulse rates, began to slow.

Shaye was stunned. It wasn't so much what had happened but the force with which it had happened that shocked her most. She didn't know what to say.

Noah did, speaking gently and low. "Has it been a long time?"

She'd returned a hand to the wheel, though her fingers were boneless. "Yes," she whispered.

"It took you by surprise?"

Another whispered, "Yes."

"Will you be sorry in the morning?"

"Probably."

He released her then, but without anger. When he reached for the wheel, she stepped aside. "Go below... please?" he asked gruffly.

She knew what he was doing, and she was grateful. He was alerting her to the fact that if she stayed she might have even more to be sorry for in the morning. She'd felt his arousal; she'd actively fed it. She had to accept her share of responsibility for what had happened, just as she had to respect the pleading note in his voice. He was human. He wanted her. And he was asking her not to want him back... at least, not tonight.

Without saying a word, she climbed down the companionway. At the bottom, she gasped, a helpless little cry.

"I frightened you," Samson said. "I'm sorry. You seemed very deep in thought."

She was, but her heart was pounding at thoughts that had taken a sudden turn. *What if Samson had awakened earlier and come up on deck during... during...*

"I should have been up a while ago," he was saying. "Noah must be exhausted. I'm glad he wasn't alone all that time."

Shaye wasn't sure whether to be glad or not. As she made her silent way to the cabin, then stole back into bed, she wasn't sure of much—other than that she'd be furious with herself later.

SHE WAS FURIOUS. She didn't sleep well, but kept waking up to recall what had happened, to toss and turn for a while, then bury her face in the pillow and plead for the escape of sleep. Mercifully, Victoria was gone from the cabin by seven, which meant that Shaye could do her agonizing in peace.

She slept. She awoke. She slept again, then awoke again. The cycle repeated itself until nearly noon, when she gave up one battle to face the next.

Noah was in the galley. All she wanted was a cup of coffee, but even that wasn't going to be easy.

"Sleep well?" he asked in a tone that gave nothing away.

"Not particularly."

"Bad dreams?"

"It was what was *between* the dreams that was bad," she muttered, pouring coffee into a cup with hands that shook.

"Are you always this cheerful in the morning?"

"Always."

"If you'd woken up in bed with me, it might have been different."

Bracing herself against the stove, she squeezed her eyes shut and made it to the count of eight before his next sally came.

"I'll bet you're dynamite in bed."

She went on counting.

"You were dynamite on the deck."

She cringed. "Don't remind me."

"Are you schizophrenic?"

At that, she turned and stared. "Excuse me?"

"Do you have two distinct personalities?"

"Of course not!"

"Then why are you so crabby this morning when you were so sweet last night?" He gave her a thorough once-over, then decided, "It *has* to be the clothes. You're wearing shorts, but they must be binding somewhere." Her T-shirt was big enough for *him* to swim in, so it couldn't be that. "And your hair. Safely secured once again. Does it make you *feel* secure when it's pinned back like that?"

She grabbed her coffee and made for the salon.

He was right behind her. "Careful. You're spilling."

She whirled on him, only to gasp when several drops of coffee hit his shirt.

He jumped back. "Damn it, that's hot!"

She hadn't intended to splatter him. Without thinking, she reached out to repair the damage.

He pushed her hand away. "It's all right."

"Are you burned?" she asked weakly.

"I'll live."

"The coffee will stain if you don't rinse it out."

"This shirt has seen a lot worse."

Eying the T-shirt, Shaye had to agree. She guessed that it had been navy once upon a time, but no longer. It was ragged at the hem and armholes, and it dipped tiredly at the neck, but damn if it didn't make him look roguish!

Sighing unsteadily, she moved more carefully into the salon and sank into a chair. Her head fell back and she closed her eyes. She felt Noah take the seat opposite her.

"Why are you doing this to me?" she whispered.

He didn't have to think about it, when he'd done nothing else for the past few hours. "You intrigue me."

It wasn't the answer she wanted. "I didn't think you were intrigued by cactus prickly women."

"Ahh, but are you really cactus prickly? That's the question."

"I'm prissy."

"Really?"

"You said it yourself."

"Maybe I was wrong."

"You weren't."

"Could've fooled me last night."

Eyes still closed, she scrunched up her face. "Do you think we could forget about last night?"

"Jeeez, I hope not. Last night was really something."

She moaned his name in protest, but he turned even that to his advantage.

"You did that last night and I liked it. You wanted me. Was that so terrible?"

Her eyes shot open and she met his gaze head-on. "I do not want you."

"You did then."

"I was too tired to know what I was doing."

He was sitting forward, fingers loosely linked between spread knees. "That's just the point. Your defenses were down. Maybe that's the real you."

"The real me," she stated as unequivocably as she could, "is what you see here and now." She had to make him believe it. She had to make *herself* believe it. "I live a very sane, very structured, very controlled existence."

"What fun's that?"

"It's what I choose. You may say its boring, but it's what *I* choose!"

"Is that why you burst into flames in my arms?"

She was getting nowhere. She'd known from the moment she'd left the deck so early this morning that she was in trouble, and Noah wasn't helping. But then, she hadn't really expected he would. So she closed her eyes again and tuned him out.

"You were hungry."

She said nothing.

He upped the pressure. "Sex starved."

Still silence.

He pursed his lips. "You can't seduce Samson because he has his eye on your aunt, so that leaves only me."

"I wouldn't know how to seduce a man if I tried," she mumbled. It fit in with the image of prissiness, but it was also the truth. She'd never had to seduce a man. Sex had been free and easy in the circles she'd run in. Perhaps that was why it had held so little meaning for her. Last night—this morning—had been different. She was still trying to understand how.

"I told you. All you have to do is bare those legs, shake out that hair and say something sweet." He shifted and grimaced. "Lord, you're only one-third of the way there, and I'm getting hard."

Her eyes flew open. "You're crude."

He considered that. "Crude connotes a raw condition. Mmm, that's pretty much the same thing as being hard."

She bolted from the chair and stormed toward her cabin.

"You can't hide there all day, y'know!" he called after her.

"I have no intention of hiding here," she yelled back. "I'm getting a book—" she snatched it from her suitcase, which, standing on end, served as a makeshift nightstand "—and I'm going on deck." She slammed past Noah back through the salon, then momentarily reversed direction to grab a cushion from the sofa.

"You can't escape me there," he warned.

"No," she snapped as she marched down the alley toward the companionway, "but with other people around, you might watch your tongue."

He was on her heels. "I'd rather watch yours. I liked what it did to me last night."

"This morning." She stomped up the steps. "It was this morning, and I can guarantee it won't happen again."

"Don't do that," he pleaded, once again the little boy with the man's mind and body. "You really turned me on—"

"Shh!" She whipped her head around to give him a final glare, then with poise emerged topside, smiled and said, "Good morning, Samson."

NOAH STOOD AT THE WHEEL, his legs braced apart, his fingers curled tightly around the handles. Steering the *Golden Echo* didn't take much effort, but it gave him a semblance of control. He needed that. He wasn't sure why, but he did.

Shifting his gaze from the ocean, he homed in on Shaye. She was propped on a cushion against the bulwark in the shade of the sails, reading. Her knees were bent, her eyes never left the page. Not a single, solitary strand of hair escaped its bonds to blow free in the breeze.

Prickly. God, was she prickly! She was the image of primness, but he knew there was another side. *He* knew it. She refused to admit it. And the more he goaded her, the more prickly she became.

He was no stranger to women. Granted, he wasn't quite the roué he'd told Shaye he was, but his work brought him into contact with women all the time. He'd known charming ones, spunky ones, aggressive and ambitious ones. Shaye was as beautiful as any of them—or, he amended, she was when she let go. She'd done it last night, but it had been dark then. He wanted to see her do it now. If she freed her hair from its knot, relaxed her body, tossed back her head and smiled, he knew he'd take her image to his grave.

But she wouldn't do that. She wouldn't give him the satisfaction. He recalled the times when they'd bickered, when she'd bitten back retorts, taken deep breaths, done everything in her power to ignore his taunts. Sometimes she'd lost control and had lashed back in turn, but even then she'd been quick to regain herself.

What had she said—that she lived a structured and controlled existence? Beyond that he didn't know much, other than that she was from Philadelphia and that she had neither a husband nor a cook. He did know that she was aware of him physically. She couldn't deny what had happened right here, on this very spot, less than twelve hours before.

Nor could he deny it. He knew he was asking for trouble tangling with a woman who clearly had a hang-up with sex. But sex wasn't all he wanted. She intrigued him; he hadn't lied about that. He felt a desperate need to understand her, and that meant getting to know her. And *that* meant breaking through the invisible wall she'd built.

As he saw it, there were two ways to go about it. The first, the more civil way, was to simply approach her and strike up conversation. Of course, it would take a while to build her trust, and if she resisted him he might run out of time.

The second, the more underhanded way, was to keep coming at her as he'd been doing. She wouldn't like it, but he might well be able to wear her down. Since she was vulnerable to him on a physical level, he could prey on that—even if it meant prying out one little bit of personal information at a time.

He had to get those bits of information. Without them, he couldn't form a composite of her, and without that, he wouldn't be able to figure out why in the hell he was interested in the first place!

"HOW'S IT GOING, ladies?"

Shaye looked up from her book to see Noah approach. So he'd finally turned the sailing over to Samson. She had to admit, albeit begrudgingly, that he was doing his share.

"I should ask you the same question," Victoria said, smiling up in welcome. "Are we making good progress?"

Noah looked out over the bow toward the western horizon. "Not bad. If the trade winds keep smiling and we continue to make five knots an hour, we'll reach Costa Rica right on schedule."

Shaye was relieved to hear that.

Victoria wasn't so sure. "I'm enjoying the sail," she said, stretching lazily. "I could take this for another month."

Noah chuckled, then turned to Shaye. "How about you? Think you could take it for another month?"

Had it not been for that knowing little glint in his eye, Shaye might have smiled and nodded. Instead, she boldly returned his gaze and said, "Not on your life. I have to be back at work."

He hunkered down before her, balancing on the balls of his feet. "But if you were to stretch your imagination a little and pretend that work wasn't there, could you sail on and on?"

She crinkled her nose. "Nah. I'm a landlubber at heart. Give me a little cottage in the Berkshires and I'd be in heaven."

"Not heaven, sweetheart," Victoria scoffed. "You'd be in solitary confinement."

"Is that what she usually does for her vacations?" Noah asked.

"What I usually do—"

"That's what she would have been doing this year if I hadn't suggested she come with me."

"Suggested! That's—"

"I can understand what she sees in it," Noah interrupted blithely, ignoring both Shaye and her attempts to speak. "I have my own place in southern Vermont. I don't usually make it there for more than a few days at a stretch, but those few days are wonderful. There's nothing like time spent alone in a peaceful setting to replenish one's energies."

Victoria disagreed. "No, no. Time spent with someone special—that's different. But alone?"

"You spent time alone," Shaye argued hurriedly before someone cut her off.

"Naturally. I can't be with people all the time. But to choose to go off alone—just for the sake of being alone—for days at a time isn't healthy. It says something about your life, if you need that kind of escape."

"We all need escapes from habit," Noah reasoned, "don't we, Shaye?"

He'd tagged on the last in an intimate tone, leaving no doubt in Shaye's mind that he was referring to what had happened between them beneath the stars.

"Victoria is right. Certain kinds of escape are unhealthy."

"But, hot damn, they're fun," he countered in that same low tone.

Victoria looked from one to the other. "Am I missing something?"

"You missed it but good," Noah said with a grin. His eyes were fixed on Shaye. "We had quite a time of it last night—"

"Noah—"

"You did? Shaye, you didn't *tell* me."

Shaye couldn't believe what was happening. "What Noah means is that we had a little disagreement—"

"Only after the fact. It wasn't a disagreement at the time."

Turning to Victoria, Shaye affected a confident drawl. "He gets confused. Poor thing, he's so used to being ornery that it doesn't faze him."

"What happened last night?"

"Nothing hap—"

"You stole out while I was asleep, clever girl." She turned to Noah. "I hope she didn't shock you."

"As a matter of fact—"

"Please!" Shaye cried. "Stop it, both of you!" In her torment she shifted her legs, the better to brace herself.

Noah's gaze shifted too.

She snapped her knees together.

With an almost imperceptible sigh of regret, he dipped his head to the side. "Your niece has beautiful hair, Victoria. It's thick and rich like yours, but the color—where did she get the color?"

"Her father is a flaming redhead. When Shaye was a child—"

"That's enough, Victoria."

Victoria ignored her. "When she was a child, hers was nearly as red as his."

"Does she get her temper from him, too?"

"What do *you* think?"

"Victoria, if you—"

"I think she does," Noah decided with a grin that turned wry. "I'm not sure if I should thank him or curse him."

"You should leave him out of this," Shaye cried.

"Now, now, Shaye," Victoria soothed, "no need to get upset."

Noah added, "I want to know about him. You're much too closemouthed, Shaye. In all the talking we've done, you've barely said a word about yourself."

"Shame on you, Shaye," Victoria chided. "You act as though you have something to hide."

It was a challenge, well intended but a challenge nonetheless. If Shaye denied that she had anything to hide, she'd have to answer Noah's questions. If she came right out and said that she *did* have something to hide, he'd be all the more curious. For a long minute she glared at her aunt, then at Noah, but she still didn't know what to do.

At last Noah took pity. At least, he mused mischievously, he was willing to defer the discussion of her parents until later. But he wasn't about to miss out on another golden opportunity.

In a single fluid movement, he was sitting by her side against the bulwark. "What say we go for a swim later?"

She didn't answer at first. Her right side was tingling—her arm, her hip, everywhere his body touched. She cleared her throat and looked straight ahead. "Be my guest."

"I said 'we.'"

"Thanks, but I don't care to be left in the water while the boat sails on ahead." Implied was that she wouldn't mind if *he* was left behind.

He ruled out that possibility. "We'll lower the sails and drift. The *Golden Echo* won't go anywhere, and we can play."

With one finger he blotted the dampness from her upper lip. "It'll be fun."

She was afraid to move. "I'll watch."

"But the water will feel great." He pried his back from the bulwark. "My shirt's sticking. You'd think the breeze would help."

"You're too hot for your own good."

"I don't know about that," he said in a sultry tone, "but I am hot." Without another word, he leaned forward and peeled off his shirt.

Shaye nearly died. She'd never seen a back as strong and as well formed, and when he relaxed against the bulwark again, the sight of his broad, leanly muscled chest was nearly more than she could bear. She swallowed down a moan.

"Did you say something?" he queried innocently.

"No, no."

"Your voice sounds strange. Higher than usual."

"It's the altitude. We must be climbing."

"We're at sea level."

"Oh. Mmm. That's right."

Without warning he stole her hand, linked their fingers together and placed them on his bare thigh. Then he looked at Victoria. "Maybe you'd like to join us for that swim."

Victoria grinned. "I'd like that."

"'Course, if you come, I'll have to behave."

Shaye grunted. "Like you're doing now?" She tried to pull her hand away but only succeeded in getting a better feel of his warm, hair-roughened thigh.

He feigned hurt. "I'm behaving."

"You're half-naked."

"I'm also half-dressed. Would you rather I'd left on my shirt and taken off my shorts?"

Victoria laughed. He was outrageous! And still he went on, this time turning injured eyes her way.

"I beg your pardon, Victoria. Are you suggesting that I have something to be ashamed of?"

Unable to help herself, she was laughing again. "Of course not. I—"

"This is no laughing matter! You wound my pride!"

"No, no, Noah," she managed to gasp. "I didn't intend—"

"But the damage is done," he said with such an aggrieved expression that she burst into another peal of laughter, which only made him square his chin more. "I can guarantee you that I'm fully equipped."

"I'm sure—"

"You don't believe me," he said in a flurry. He looked at Shaye. "You don't believe me either." He dropped his hand. "Well, I'll show you both!" He had the drawstring of his shorts undone and his thumbs tucked under the waistband before Shaye pressed a frantic hand to his belly.

"Don't," she whispered. "Please?"

Never in his life had Noah seen as beseeching a look. Her hand was burning a hole in him, but she seemed not to notice. She was near tears.

In that moment he lost his taste for the game. "I was only teasing," he said gently.

She looked at him for a minute longer, her eyes searching his face, moving from one feature to another. Her lower lip trembled.

Then she was up like a shot, running aft along the deck and disappearing down the companionway.

He started after her, but Victoria caught his hand. "Let her be for a while. She has to work some things out for herself."

"I don't want to hurt her."

"I know that. I trust you. Your uncle is a talker once he gets going. He's proud of you, and with good reason."

Noah frowned. "When did he do all this talking?" His eyes widened. "While we were on deck last night?"

"While *we* were on deck this *morning,*" she answered, grinning mischievously. "You and Shaye sleep late. Samson and I wake up early."

"Ahh," Noah said, but his frown returned. "I'm trying to understand Shaye, but it's tough. She doesn't like to talk about herself."

"She's trained herself to be that way."

He wanted to ask why, just as he wanted to ask Victoria about all those other things Shaye wouldn't talk about. But it wasn't Victoria's place to talk. What was happening here was between Shaye and him. Sweet as she was, Victoria wasn't part of it, and he refused to put her in the position of betraying her niece.

"She'll tell you in time," Victoria said.

"How can you be sure?"

"I know, that's all. Be patient."

Thrusting a hand through his hair, he realized that he had no other choice. With a sigh, he scooped up his shirt and started off.

"Noah?"

He turned.

She dropped a deliberate glance to his shorts, which, without benefit of the drawstring, had fallen precariously low on his hips.

"Oh." He tied the string almost absently, then continued on.

So comfortable with his body, Victoria mused. *So comfortable with his sexuality. If only he could teach Shaye to be that way. . . .*

5

NOAH WAS RIGHT, Shaye knew. She couldn't hide in her cabin forever. It had been childish of her to run off that way, but at the time she'd been unable to cope with the feelings rushing through her. Noah had been so close, so bare, so provocative, and she was so drawn to him on a physical level that it frightened her to tears.

Brash and irreverent, impulsive and uninhibited, he was on the surface everything she tried to avoid. What was beneath the surface, though, was an enigma. She didn't know much about him—what he did for a living, whether he was attached in any manner to a woman, where his deepest needs and innermost values lay. She wanted to label him as all bad, but she couldn't. He was incredibly devoted to Samson and unfailingly kind to Victoria, and that had to account for something.

So. Here she sat—eyes moist, palms clammy, feeling perfectly juvenile. A reluctant smile played along her lips. Was this the adolescence she'd never had? She'd matured with such lightning speed that she'd never had time to feel growing pains—as good a term as any to describe what she was feeling now. She was being forced to reevaluate her wants and needs. And it was painful.

But nothing was accomplished sitting here. She wasn't an adolescent with the luxury of wallowing for hours in self-pity. Her wisest move, it seemed, would be to pull herself together, rejoin the others and try to regain a little of her self-esteem. She would sort things out in time.

Changing into a bathing suit, she unknotted her hair, brushed it out, then caught it up into a ponytail at her crown. After splashing her face with water, she belted on a short terry-cloth robe and left the cabin.

Noah was waiting in the salon, sitting in one of the chairs. She stopped on the threshold and eyed him uncertainly. He didn't comment on her outfit, or on her bare legs, or on her hair. In fact, he seemed almost as uncertain as she, which was just the slightest bit bolstering.

"You said something about going swimming," she reminded him softly.

He sat still for another minute, his face an amalgam of confusion, hesitation and hope. "You want to?" he cautiously asked.

She nodded.

With the blink of an eye, his grin returned, "You're on." He stood and headed for his cabin. "Stay put. I'll just change into trunks and we'll be ready."

"But the sails—"

"Tell Samson to take them in. He'll be game; he loves to swim. And tell Victoria to change, too. She wanted to come."

The door of the aft cabin closed. Shaye watched it for a minute, then walked quietly past and started up the companionway. She wondered about the way he'd been sitting in the salon, about the uncertainty she'd read on his face. That was a side of him she'd never seen, one she hadn't thought existed. It was a far cry from the smugness—or arrogance or annoyance—he usually granted her, and even his returning confidence was somehow different and more manageable. If only she knew what was going on in his head . . .

Noah hung a rope ladder off the port quarter and let Shaye climb down first. She went about halfway before jumping. In the very first instant submerged, she realized by contrast how hot and grubby she'd felt before. Her sense of exhilaration was nearly as great as her sense of refreshment.

Ducking under a second time, she came up with her head back and a smile on her face. She opened her eyes in time to see Noah balance on the transom for an instant before soaring up, out, then down, slicing neatly into the waves. Feeling incredibly light, she treaded water until he appeared by her side.

"Not bad," she said, complimenting his dive.

"Not bad, yourself," he said, complimenting her smile. Then he took off, stroking strongly around the *Golden Echo*'s stern, then along her starboard side. Shaye followed a bit more slowly, but he was waiting for her at the bow before starting down the port side.

Completing the lap, he turned to her with a grin. "You're a good swimmer. It must be that suit you're wearing. It covers up enough of your body. Is it covering up a flotation device, too?"

She rolled her eyes. "Fifteen minutes."

"Fifteen minutes, what?"

"That's how long you made it without a snippy comment. But now you've blown it, and by insulting my suit, no less! There is nothing wrong with this suit." It was, in fact, a designer maillot that she'd paid dearly for.

He sank beneath the surface for a minute, tossing his hair back with a flourish when he came up. "I was hoping to see more of your body. I was hoping for a bikini."

"Sorry," she said, then turned and swam off.

He'd caught up to her in a minute. "You are not sorry. You take perverse pleasure in teasing me."

"Look who's talking!"

"But you're so teasable," he argued, eyes twinkling. "You rise to my taunts."

"No more," she decided and propelled herself backward.

He negated the distance with a single stroke. "Wanna test that out?"

"Sure." She turned sideways and tipped up her nose in an attempt to look imperturbable. It was a little absurd given the steady movement of her arms and legs, but she did her best.

Noah went underwater.

She waited, eventually darting a sidelong glance to where he'd gone down, then waited again, certain that any minute she'd feel a tug at her leg. When she felt so such thing, she glanced to the other side.

No Noah. No bubbles. Nothing but gentle waves.

Vaguely concerned, she made a complete turn. When she saw no sign of him, she submerged for an underwater look.

Nothing!

"Noah?" she called, reaching the surface again. "Noah!"

Samson's head appeared over the side of the boat. "Problem, Shaye?"

Her heart was thudding. "It's Noah! He went under and I can't find him!"

Samson cocked his head toward the opposite side of the boat. "Try over here," he said and disappeared.

Performing a convulsive breast stroke, Shaye sped to the port side, to find Noah riding the waves on his back, eyes closed, basking in the sun.

"You bastard!" she screamed, furiously batting water his way. "You terrified me!"

His serenity ruined by her splashing, he advanced on her, turning his face one way then the other against her wet attack. Then he cinched an arm around her waist and drew her against him, effectively stopping the barrage.

"Y'see?" he gloated. "It worked."

"That was a totally stupid thing to do!" she cried, tightly clutching his shoulders. "And irresponsible! What if something really had happened to you? I'm not a trained lifesaver. I couldn't have helped! And think of *me*. I could have gone under looking for you and stayed there too long. You would never have known I was drowning, because you were out of sight, on the far side of the boat, playing your silly little game."

"Samson was keeping an eye on you."

"That's not the point!" She narrowed her eyes. "Next time I won't even bother to look. You know what happened to the little boy who cried wolf?"

"But I'm not a little boy."

She snorted.

His arm tightened. "Wrap your legs around my waist."

"Are you kidding?"

"I'll keep us afloat."

"I don't trust you."

"You don't trust yourself."

He was right. "You're wrong."

"Nuh-uh." His lips twitched. "You don't want to wrap your legs around me because that would put you flush against my—hey, stop that!"

She'd found that he was ticklish, and in the nick of time. Within seconds they were both underwater, but at least she was free, and when she resurfaced, Noah was waiting. What ensued then was a good, old-fashioned, rollicking water fight that was broken up at length by Samson's, "Children! Children!"

The water settled some around them as they looked up.

"Bath time," he called. He was lowering a small basket that contained soap and shampoo.

Shaye looked at Noah; Noah looked at Shaye.

"Do you think he's trying to tell us something?" he asked.

"Diplomatically," she answered.

He wrinkled his nose. "Was I that bad?"

"Was *I*?"

"Maybe we canceled each other out."

"So we didn't notice?"

"Yeah." He scowled. "Hell, it's only been three days."

"Three? That's disgusting!"

His eyes widened in accusation. "It has to have been just as long for you."

"Two. Only two, and I've been—"

"Are you going to wash or not?" came the call from above. "We're dying to swim, but we don't want to go in until you get out!"

Shaye looked at Noah in horror. "Is it that bad that they don't want to be near us even in water?"

He laughed and swam toward the basket. "For safety, Shaye. One of us should be on the boat at any given time, and since no one should swim alone, it makes sense to divide it up, two and two." He drew a bright yellow container from the basket and squirted liberal jets of its contents on his arms, hands and neck.

"Joy?" she asked, swimming closer.

He tossed her the plastic bottle. "It's one of the few detergents that bubbles in salt water," he explained as he scrubbed his arms, offering proof. "Go on. It does the trick."

She followed his lead and, scissoring steadily with her legs, had soon lathered her arms, shoulders and neck. Noah took the bottle from the basket again and filled his palm, then set to work beneath the waterline. Shaye took her time rinsing her arms.

His eyes grew teasing. "I'm doing my chest. How about you?"

"I'm getting there," she managed, but she was feeling suddenly awkward. She darted a self-conscious glance upward and was relieved to see no sign of Samson.

"You'll need more soap." He tossed his head toward the basket.

She took the bottle, directed a stream of the thick liquid into her hand and replaced the bottle. Then she stared at her palm, wondering how to start.

"Don't turn around," he said. "I want to watch."

"I'm sure."

"Come on. We're in the shadow of the boat. The water's too dark to see anything."

It wasn't what he could see that she feared. It was what he could picture. She knew what *she* was picturing as his shoulders rotated, hands out of sight but very obviously on that broad and virile chest.

"You'd better hurry, Shaye. Samson won't wait forever."

"Okay, okay." With hurried movements, she rubbed her hands together, then thrust them under her suit.

"You could lower the suit. It'd help."

"This is fine." Eyes averted, she soaped her breasts as quickly as she could.

"Look at me while you do that," he commanded softly.

She shot him a glance that was supposed to be quelling, but when her eyes locked with his, she couldn't look away. There was nothing remotely quelling in her gaze then; it mirrored the desire in his. Sudden, startling, explosive. They were separated by a mere arm's length, which, given the expanse of the Caribbean, seemed positively intimate.

Her hands worked over and around her breasts while his hands worked over and around his chest, but it was his fingers she seemed to feel on her sensitive skin, his harder flesh beneath her fingers. When he moved his hands to his lower back, she followed suit and the tingling increased, touching her vertebrae, sizzling down to the base of her spine.

Her lips were parted; her breath rushed past in shallow pants. Her legs continued to scissor, though hypnotically. She was in Noah's thrall, held there by the dark, smoldering charcoal of his eyes and by the force of her own vivid imagination.

The curve of his shoulders indicated that his hands had returned to his front and moved lower. She gulped in a short breath, but her shoulders were also curving, her hands moving forward, then lower.

His eyes held hers, neither mocking nor dropping in an attempt to breach the sea's modest veil. The waves rose and fell around and with them, like a mentor, teaching them the movement, rewarding them with gentle supplementary caresses.

But supplementary caresses were the last things they needed. Shaye felt as though she were vibrating from the inside out, and Noah's muscles were tense, straining for the release that he wouldn't allow himself.

When he closed his eyes for an instant, the spell broke. Two sets of arms joined trembling legs in treading water, and it was a minute more before either of them could speak.

Noah's lips twisted into a self-mocking grin. "You are one hell of a lady to make love with," he said gruffly. "Com'ere."

Shaye gave several rapid shakes of her head.

"I want to do your hair."

"My hair's okay."

He was fishing a bottle of shampoo from the basket when Victoria's voice came over the side. "Aren't you two done *yet*?"

"Be right up," Shaye gasped. She turned to start for the ladder, but a gentle tug on her ponytail brought her right back to Noah. The water worked against her then, denying her the leverage to escape him. And his fingers were already in her hair, easing the thick elastic band from its place. "Please don't, Noah," she begged.

His voice was close to her ear. "Indulge me this, after what you denied me just now."

"Denied you? I didn't deny you a thing!"

"You didn't give me what I *really* wanted. . . ."

She wasn't about to touch that one. So she faced him and held out a hand, palm up. "The shampoo?"

"Right here," he said, pressing his gloppy hand on the top of her head and instantly starting to scrub.

She squeezed her eyes shut. "I'll do it, Noah."

"Too late," he said with an audible grin, then paused. "I've never washed a woman's hair before. Am I doing it right?"

His fingers were everywhere, gathering even the longest strands into the cloud of lather, massaging her scalp, stimulating nerve ends she hadn't known about. Was he doing it right? Was he ever!

She tried to think of something to say, but it was as though his fingers had penetrated her skull and were impeding the workings of her brain. Her eyes were still closed, but in ecstasy now. Her head had fallen back a little as he worked his thumbs along her hairline. She was unaware that her breasts were pushing against his chest, or that her legs had floated around his hips and she was riding him gently in the waves, because those were but small eddies in the overall vortex of pleasure.

His fingers were suddenly still, cupping her head, and his voice was gruff as he pressed his lips to her brow. "Maybe this wasn't such a good idea after all. Better rinse and let me do mine. If our time isn't up, my self-control is."

Shaye opened her eyes then. They widened when she realized how she was holding Noah. "Oh Lord," she whispered and quickly let go. With frantic little movements, she sculled away.

"You're a hussy, Shaye Burke!" Noah taunted. He poured shampoo directly from the bottle onto his head.

She sank underwater and shook her own. When she resurfaced, he was scrubbing his hair, but wore a grin that was naughty.

"A hussy and a tease!"

"You are a corrupter!" she cried back.

"Me? I was washing your hair! You were the one who tried to make something more of it!"

Tipping her head to the right to finger-comb water through her hair, she glared at him. "That's exactly how you're going to look in ten years, Noah—all white-haired and prune-faced." She tipped her head to the left and rinsed the long tresses further. "*No* woman's going to want to look at you then!"

"So I'd better catch someone now, hmm? Take out an insurance policy?" He submerged, raking the soap from his hair with his fingers.

"I dare say the premiums would be too high," she called the minute he'd resurfaced.

"Are you selling?"

"To you? No way!" She headed for the ladder. "You are a sneaky, no-good . . . seducer of innocent women."

Noah caught her on the second rung, encircling her hips with one strong arm. He said nothing until she looked down at him, then asked quietly and without jest, "Are you innocent?"

She could take the question different ways, she knew, but if she were honest the answer would be the same. No, she wasn't innocent in what had just happened, because no one had told her to wrap herself so snugly around him. No, she hadn't been innocent last night. He hadn't asked her to go wild in his arms. And she wasn't innocent in that broadest sense; she'd lost her virginity half a lifetime ago.

Sad eyes conveyed her answer, but she said nothing. Noah held a frightening power over her already. That power would surely increase if she confirmed how truly less than innocent she was.

His gaze dropped over her gleaming shoulders and down her bare back to the edge of her suit. His hand slid lower, over the flare of her bottom to her thigh. When he gave her a gentle boost, she climbed the ladder, then crossed the deck to the bow, knowing Noah would remain at the stern to serve as lifeguard to Samson and Victoria.

She needed to be alone. The past weighed too heavily on her to allow for even the most banal of conversation.

SHAYE HAD BEGUN TO REBEL at the age of thirteen, when her father's fierce temper and her mother's conventionalism first crowded in on her budding adolescence. Life to that point had been placid, a sedate cycle revolving around school and church. But she had suddenly developed from a redheaded little girl into an eye-catching teenager, and even if she hadn't seen the change in herself, it would have been impossible for her to mistake the admiring male looks that came her way.

Those looks promised excitement, something she'd never experienced, and she thrived on them, since they compensated for the more dismissing ones she'd received before. Her father was a factory hand, and though he worked hard, the socio-economic class in which the Burkes were trapped was on the lower end of the scale. Donald Burke had been proud to buy the small, two-bedroom cottage in which they lived, because it was on the right side of the tracks, if barely. Unfortunately, the tracks delineated the school districts, which put Shaye and Shannon in classes with far more privileged children.

Gaining the attention of some of the most attractive boys around was a heady experience for Shaye. For the first time she was able to compete with girls she'd envied, girls whose lives where less structured and more frivolous. For the first time she was able to partake in that frivolity—as the guest of the very boys those girls covetously eyed.

In theory, Anne Burke wouldn't have objected to the attention her daughter received. She idolized her husband and was perfectly comfortable with their life, which was not unlike the one she'd known herself as a child. But she'd seen how well her sister, Victoria, had done in marrying Arthur Lesser, and she had no objection to her daughter aiming high.

What she objected to was the fact that Shaye was only thirteen and that the boys of whom she was enamored were sixteen and seventeen. They were dangerous ages, ages of discovery, and Anne Burke didn't want her daughter used. So she set strict limits on Shaye's social life, and when Shaye argued, as any normal teenager would, Donald Burke was there to enforce the law.

Perhaps, Shaye had often mused later, if they'd been a little more flexible she'd have managed—or if she'd been more manageable, they'd have flexed. But by the time she was fifteen, she felt totally at odds with her parents' conventionality, and her response was to flaunt it in any way she could. She stole out to a party at Jimmy Danforth's house, when she was supposedly studying at the library. She cut classes to go joyriding with Brett Hagen in the Mustang his parents had given him for his eighteenth birthday. She told her parents she was baby-sitting, when the baby in question was a dog that belonged to Alexander Bigelow.

Three days before her sixteenth birthday, she made love with Ben Parker on the floor of his parents' wine cellar. She'd known precisely what she was doing and why. She'd given her innocence to Ben because it was fun and exciting and a little bit dangerous—and because it was the last thing her parents wanted her to do.

She was her own person, she'd decided. If her parents were happy with their lives, that was fine, but she resented the dogma of hard work and self-restraint that they imposed on her. Discovering that she could have a wonderful time—and get away with it—was self-perpetuating.

She played her way through high school. Reasonably bright, she maintained a B average without much effort—a good thing, since she didn't have much time to spare from her social life. Fights with her parents were long and drawn out, until true communication became almost nonexistent. That didn't bother Shaye. She knew what she wanted to do, and she did it. She applied to NYU, was accepted on scholarship, and finally escaped her parents' watchful eyes.

New York was as much fun as she'd hoped. She liked her classes, but she liked even more the freedom she had and the people she met. And she adored Victoria, whom she saw regularly. In hindsight, Shaye knew that keeping in such close touch with her aunt represented a need for family ties. At the time she only knew Victoria understood her as her parents never had.

Victoria was as different from her sister, Anne, as night from day. While Anne chose to take the more traveled highways through life, Victoria took the back roads that led to greater beauty and pleasure. The one thing they shared was their devotion to their husbands, but since each had married a man to suit her tastes, their differences had grown more marked as time went on.

Shaye identified with Victoria. It wasn't that she yearned to be wealthy; wealth, or the lack of it, had never played as prominently in her mind as had adventure. But Victoria *did* things. She acted on her impulses, rather than putting them off for a day far in the future. And if she subtly cautioned Shaye to exercise moderation, Shaye put it down to the loyalty Victoria felt toward Anne.

Despite Victoria's subtle words of caution, Shaye had a ball. In February of her freshman year she hitchhiked with

Graham Hauk to New Orleans for Mardi Gras. That summer she took a house in Provincetown with five friends, all of whom were working, as she was, in local restaurants. Much of her sophomore year was spent at the off-campus apartment of Josh Milgram, her latest love and a graduate student of philosophy, who had a group of ever-present and fascinating, if bizarre, friends.

She spent the summer before her junior year selling computer equipment in Washington. She'd secured the job principally on her interview, during which she'd demonstrated both an aptitude for handling the equipment and an aptitude for selling herself. She loved Washington. Sharing an apartment with two friends from school, she had regular working hours, which left plenty of time for play.

It was during that summer that Shannon joined her, and Shaye couldn't have been more delighted. She'd always felt that Shannon was being stifled at home. More than once she'd urged her sister to break out, but it was only by dint of a summer-school program held at American University for high school students that Shannon made it.

Proud of her sister, Shaye introduced her to all her friends. At summer's end, she sent Shannon back home reasonably assured that she was awakened to the pleasures of life.

Shaye whizzed through her junior year seeing Tom, Peter and Gene, but the real fun came in her senior year when she met André. André—né Andrew, but he'd decided that that name was too plebeian—was a perpetual student of art. He had a small garret in Soho, where Shaye spent most of her time, and a revolving group of friends and followers who offered never-ending novelty. André and Shaye were a couple, but in the loosest sense of the word. André was far from possessive, and Shaye was far from committed. She adored André for his eccentricity; his painting was as eclectic as his lovemaking. But she adored Christopher's brashness and Jamal's wild imagination and Stefan's incredible irreverence.

She was treading a fine line in her personal life, though at the time she didn't see it. Graduating from college, she took a position in the computer department of an insurance company, and if her friends teased her about such a staid job, she merely laughed, took a puff of the nearest pipe and did something totally outrageous to show where her heart lay.

She was one year out of college and living at the garret with André and his friends when the folly of her life-style hit home.

"FRÄULEIN?"

Shaye's head shot up, her thoughts boomeranging back to the present. Her eyes focused on Samson, who was wearing a black tuxedo jacket with tails and, beneath it, a white apron tied at the waist and falling to mid-calf.

"Darf ich Sie bitten, an unserem Dinner *teilzunehmen? Wir sind bereit; bitte sagen Sie nicht nein."*

It was a minute before comprehension came. She didn't speak German, but a pattern was emerging, reinforced by the sight of Victoria and Noah already settling at the table on the other end of the deck.

She didn't know how long she'd been sitting so lost in thought—an hour, perhaps two—but she was grateful for the rescue. Smiling, she took the hand Samson graciously offered, realizing only after she'd risen that she was still wearing her bathing suit.

"Let me change first," she said softly.

"You don't need to."

But she'd be asking for trouble from Noah if she appeared at dinner so minimally covered. "I'll be quick."

Hurrying below, she discarded the suit and drew on a one-piece shorts outfit. She'd reached the companionway before realizing that her hair was still down. Deciding that it was too late to pin it up, she finger-combed it back from her face and continued to the deck.

Dinner was sauerbraten, red cabbage and strudel. It was accompanied by a sturdy red Ingelheimer whose mildly sedative effect helped Shaye handle both the lingering shadow of her reminiscing and Noah's very large, very virile and observant presence.

Actually, he behaved himself admirably, or so he decided. He didn't make any comments about Shaye's free-flowing hair, though he was dying to. Even more, he was dying to touch it. Clean and shining, it seemed thicker than ever, as though its life had been released by the sea and the breeze. Nor did he comment on her smile, which was coming more frequently. He wondered if it was the wine, or whether the afternoon swim had eased a certain tension from her. Somehow he doubted the latter, after the words they'd exchanged in the water. But she'd spent a good long time since then at the bow, and he wondered if what she'd been thinking about was responsible for the softening of her mood.

He'd watched her but she hadn't known it. She'd been lost in a world of her own. Even now, sitting over the last of the wine, she faded in and out from time to time. During those "out" phases her expression was mellow, vaguely sad—as it had been on the rope ladder when he'd asked about her innocence.

He was more curious about her than ever, but he could bide his time. Sunset was upon them. Soon it would be dark. Perhaps if her mellow mood continued, he'd be able to pry some information from her without a fight.

After dinner Shaye returned to her perch at the bow. She took a cushion with her, and though she'd fetched a book, she didn't bother to open it. Instead, she propped herself comfortably and studied the sky.

To the west were the deepening orange colors of the waning day, above that the purples of early night. As she watched, the purples spread and darkened, until the last of the sun's rays had been swallowed up.

She took one deep breath, then another. Her body felt clean and relaxed, and if her mind wasn't in quite that perfect a state, it was close. There were things to be considered, but not now, not when the Caribbean night was so beautiful.

Victoria was with Samson at the helm. They clearly enjoyed each other, and, deep down inside, Shaye was pleased. Samson was an interesting man. He had the style and spirit to make Victoria's trip an adventure even without the treasure no one had spoken of yet.

Shifting herself and the cushion so that she was lying down, she crossed her ankles, folded her hands on her middle and closed her eyes. So different from home, she mused. She couldn't remember the last time she'd lain down like this and just . . . listened. What was there to listen to in her Philadelphia apartment? Traffic? The siren of a police car or an ambulance? Peals of laughter from a party at one of the other apartments?

None of that here. Just the rhythmic thrust of the waves against the hull and the periodic flap of a sail. There was something to be said for going on a treasure hunt after all.

Her brow creased lightly. Noah had said that there were different types of treasures to be sought, and he was right. He seemed to be right about a lot of things. She had to define the treasure *she* was seeking. Was it a job well done in Philadelphia? Career advancement? Perhaps movement to a broader, more prestigious position?

After all she'd thought about that afternoon, she had to smile. Her life now was the antithesis of what it had been seven, eight, nine years before. If someone had told her then what she'd be doing in subsequent years, she'd have thought him mad.

But even back then, without conscious planning, she'd made provisions for a more stable life. She'd completed her education and had established herself in a lucrative field. Had her subconscious known something?

The question was whether the life she now had would stand her in good stead for the next thirty years. If so, if she was as self-contained and complete a being as she'd thought, why did Noah VanBaar make her ache? Did her subconscious know something else?

Eyes still closed, she grew alert. He was here now. She hadn't heard him approach, but she knew he was near. There was something hovering, newly coagulating in her mind...a sense of familiarity, a scent. Noah. Smelling of the sun and the sea, of musk and man.

She opened her eyes and met his curious gaze. He was squatting an arm's length away, a dimly-glowing lantern hanging from his fingers.

"I wasn't sure if you were sleeping."

"I wasn't."

"You've been lying here a long time."

And still she didn't move; she felt too comfortable. "It's peaceful." Was that a hint that he should leave? She was trying to decide if she wanted him to when he reached up, hooked the lantern on the bowsprit, then sat down and stretched out his legs. She'd known he wouldn't ask to join her; that wasn't his style. In a way she was glad he hadn't. She'd been spared having to make the choice.

Resting his head back, he sighed. "We're almost halfway there. From the looks of the clouds in the east, we may get a push."

"Clouds?" She peered eastward. "I don't see a thing."

"Mmm. No moon, no stars."

"Oh, dear. A storm?"

He shrugged. "Who knows? Maybe rain, maybe wind, maybe nothing. Storm clouds can veer off. They can dissipate. Weather at sea is fickle."

Sliding an arm behind her head, she studied him. "You must sail a lot."

"Not so much now. I used to though. Samson got me hooked when I was a kid. I spent several summers crewing on windjammers off the coast of Maine."

"Sounds like fun."

"It was. I love the ocean, especially when it's wild. I could sit for hours and watch the waves thrash about."

"You should have a place on the coast, rather than in Vermont."

"Nah. Watching the ocean in a storm is inspirational, not restful. When I leave the city on weekends, I need rest."

"The city—New York?"

He nodded.

"What do you do?"

"Are you sure you want to know?"

"Why wouldn't I?"

"Because knowing about me will bring us closer, and I had the impression that you wanted to stay as far from me as possible."

"True. But tell me anyway."

"Why?"

"Because I'm curious."

He considered that. "I suppose it's as good a reason as any. Of course," he tilted his head and his voice turned whimsical, "it would be nicer if you'd said that you've changed your mind about staying away, or that you want to know about the man who's swept you off your feet, or—" his voice dropped "—that you're as interested in exploring my mind as you are in exploring my body."

Her skin tingled and she was grateful that the lantern was more a beacon to other ships than an illuminator of theirs. The dark was her protector, when she felt oddly exposed. "Just tell me," she grumbled, then added a taunting, "unless you have something to hide."

That was all Noah needed to hear. "I'm a political pollster."

"A political—"

"Pollster. When a guy decides to make a run for political office, he hires me to keep tabs on his status among the electorate."

"Interesting," she said and meant it.

"I think so. Actually, I started out doing only polling, but the business has evolved into something akin to public relations."

"In what sense?"

Encouraged that she wanted to hear more, Noah explained. "John Doe comes to me and says that he's running for office. I do my research, ferreting out his opponent's strengths and weaknesses, plus the characteristics of the constituency. Between us we determine the image we want to project, the kind of image that will go across with the voters—"

"But isn't that cheating? If you tailor-make the candidate to the voters, what about issues? Isn't John Doe compromising himself?"

"Not at all. He doesn't alter his stand; he merely alters the way that stand is put across. One or another of his positions may be more popular among the voters, so we focus on those and push the others into the background. The key is to get the man elected, at which point he can bring other issues forward."

"Clever, if a little devious."

"That's the way the game is played. His opponent does it; why shouldn't he? It's most useful on matters that have little to do with the issues."

"Such as . . . ?"

"Age. Marital status. Religion, ethnic background, prior political experience. Again, it's a question of playing something up or down, depending on the bias of the voters."

Shaye frowned. "Sounds to me like there's a very fine line between your job and an ad agency's."

"Sure is, and that's who takes over from me. Ad agencies, media consultants—they're the ones who put together the specifics of the campaign itself."

"And your job is done at that point?"

He shook his head. "We keep polling right up to, sometimes beyond, the campaign. Obviously, some candidates have more money to pay for our services than others. By the same token, some political offices require more ongoing work than others."

She could easily guess which offices those would be and was duly impressed. "I suppose that's good for you. Otherwise you'd have a pretty seasonal job."

"Seasonal it isn't," he drawled. "I use the word 'political' in the broadest sense. We do polling for lobbyists, for public interest groups, for hospitals and real estate developers and educational institutions."

"When you say 'we,' who do you mean?"

"I have a full-time staff of ninety people, with several hundred part-timers on call."

"But you're the leader?"

"It's my baby, yes."

"You started it from scratch?"

"Planted the seed and nurtured it," he said with an inflection of intimacy that made her blush. He didn't follow up, though, but leaned forward and rubbed his back before returning to his original position.

"You must feel proud."

"I do."

"There must be a lot of pressure."

He nodded.

"But it's rewarding?"

"Very." He sat forward again and flexed his back muscles, then grumbled crossly, "This boat leaves much to be desired by way of comfort. I've never heard of a boat with a deck this size and no deck chairs."

She was hard put not to laugh, clearly recalling the discussion she'd had with Victoria when they'd first boarded the sloop, a discussion Noah had overheard and mocked. "You don't like the *Golden Echo*?" she asked sweetly.

He heard the jibe in her tone and couldn't let it go unanswered. In the blink of an eye, he'd closed the distance between them, displaced her from the cushion and drawn her to him so that her back was against his chest.

6

SHAYE TRIED TO WIGGLE AWAY, but Noah hooked his legs around hers. When she continued to squirm, he made a low, sexy sound. "Ooh, that feels good. A little more pressure . . . there . . . lower."

Abruptly she went still. "This is not a good idea, Noah."

"My back sure feels a hell of a lot better."

"Mine doesn't."

"That's because you've got a rod up it—" He caught himself and backed off. "Uh, no, that came out the wrong way. What I meant was that you've stiffened up. If you relax and let me cushion you, you'll be as comfortable as you were before."

That was what Shaye feared, but the temptation was great. It was a peaceful night and she'd been interested in what he'd been saying. Would it hurt to relax a little?

"Better," he said with a sigh when he felt her body soften to his. Though his legs fell away, his arms remained loosely around her waist. He'd thrown on a shirt after dinner, but it was unbuttoned. Her hair formed a thick pillow on his chest, with wayward strands teasing his throat and chin.

Having made the decision to stay in his arms, Shaye was surprisingly content. "Have you ever been married?"

"Where did that come from?"

"I was thinking about your work. You said there was pressure, and I assume the hours are long. I was curious."

Curious, again. Okay. "No. I've never been married."

"Do you dislike women?"

"Where did *that* come from?"

"One of the first things you said you didn't like about me was that I was a woman."

"Ah. That was because I hadn't known there were going to be women along on this trip until a few minutes before you and your aunt arrived."

"And it bothered you?"

"At the time."

"Why?"

"Because I wanted to get away from it all. Before Samson drafted me I'd planned to spend two weeks alone in Normandy."

"Normandy." She slid her head sideways and looked up at him. "A château?"

"A small one."

She righted her head. "Small one, big one . . . it sounds lovely."

"It would have been, but this isn't so bad."

"Would you have done anything differently if Victoria and I hadn't been along?"

"A few things."

"Like . . . ?"

"Shaving. I wouldn't have bothered."

"You don't have to shave for our sakes. Be my guest. Grow a beard."

He'd been hoping she'd thank him; after all, stubble looked grubby, and then there was the matter of kissing. But she wouldn't consider that. Not Shaye.

"I don't want to grow a beard," he grumbled. "I just didn't want to have to shave unless I felt like it."

"So don't." She paused. "What else would you have done if we weren't along?"

"Swam in the nude. Sunbathed in the nude. *Sailed* in the nude," he added just for spite.

Forgetting that she was supposed to be prissy, she grinned. "That would be a sight."

"Oh God, are we onto that again? Why is it that everyone's always insulting my manhood?"

She shaped her hands to his wrists and gave a squeeze. "I'm just teasing . . . though I don't believe I've ever seen a naked pirate before."

"This is not a pirate ship," was his arch response.

"Then, a naked patriot."

"Have you ever seen any man naked?"

Her grin was hidden. He should only know. "I saw *American Gigolo*. There were some pretty explicit scenes."

He tightened his arms in mock punishment. "A real man. In the flesh. Have you ever seen one up close and all over?"

"I walked in on my father once when I was little."

He sighed. "I'm not talking about—"

"I've learned to keep my eyes shut since then."

Which told him absolutely nothing. So he put that particular subject on hold and tried one he thought she'd find simpler to answer. "What kind of work do you do?"

She hesitated, then echoed his own earlier question. "Are you sure you want to know?"

"Why wouldn't I?"

"Because you won't like the answer."

"Why not?"

"Because it fits my personality to a tee."

"You're the headmistress of an all-girls school?"

"Nope."

"A warden at a penitentiary?"

She shook her head.

"I give up. What do you do?"

Again she hesitated, then confessed, "I work with computers."

"That figures."

"I told you you wouldn't like it."

"I didn't say I didn't like it, just that it figures. You work with machines. Very structured and controlled." He lowered his voice. "Do they turn you on?"

"Shows how much you know about computers. Noah, you have to turn *them* on or they don't do a thing."

She was teasing, and he loved it. He wasn't quite sure why she was in such good humor, but he wasn't about to upset the applecart by saying something lewd. "Once you turn them on, what do you do with them?"

"Same thing you do. Program them to store information and spit it back up on command."

"Your command?"

"Or one of my assistants'."

"Then you're the one in charge?"

"Of the department, yes."

"Where is the department?"

"In a law firm."

"A law firm in Philadelphia." Her head bobbed against his chest. He loved that, too—the undulating silk of her hair against his bare skin. "So—" he cleared his throat "—what kind of information are we dealing with here?"

"Client files, financial projections, accounts receivable, attorney profitability reports, balance sheets." She reeled them off, pausing only at the end for a breath. "Increasingly we're using the computers for the preparation of documents. And we're plugged into LEXIS."

"What's LEXIS?"

"A national computer program for research. By typing certain codes into the computer, our lawyers can find cases or law review articles that they need for briefs. It saves hours of work in the library."

"I'm impressed."

She swiveled and met his gaze. "By LEXIS?"

"By you. You really know what you're talking about."

"You didn't think I would?"

"It's not that," he said. "But you sound so . . . so on top of the whole thing."

"How do you think I got where I am?"

"I don't know. How did you?" His voice dropped to a teasing drawl. He couldn't resist; she was so damned sexy peering up at him that way. "Did you wow all those computer guys with your body?"

She stared at him for a minute, then faced forward. "Exactly."

"Come on," he soothed, brushing her ear with his mouth. "I know you wouldn't do that. Tell me how you got hooked up with computers."

"I took computer courses in college."

"And that was it? A few courses and, pow, you're the head of a department?"

"Of course not. I worked summers, then worked after graduation, and by the time the opening came at the law firm, I had the credentials and was there."

"How large is the firm?"

"Seventy-five lawyers."

"General practice?"

"Corporate."

"Ahh. Big money-getters."

"Lucky for me. If they weren't, they'd never be able to support a computer department the size of ours, and my job would be neither as interesting nor as challenging."

"Are they nice?"

"The lawyers? Some I like better than others."

"Do they treat you well?"

"I'm not complaining."

"But you do love your work."

"Yes."

"Any long-range ambitions?"

"I don't know. I'm thinking about that. I've risen pretty fast in a field that's steadily changing."

"Personnel-wise?"

"Equipment-wise. Personnel-wise, too, I guess. A lot of people jumped on the bandwagon when computers first got big, but time has weeded out the men from the boys."

"Or the women from the girls."

"Mmm."

He nudged her foot with his. "What about marriage? Or pregnancy? Does that weed out the women from the girls?"

"Not as much as it used to. The firm is generous when it comes to maternity leave. Many of the women, lawyers included, have taken time off, then returned. In my department, word processing is done round the clock. Women can choose their shifts to accommodate child-care arrangements."

"Is that what you'll do?"

"I hadn't thought I was pregnant," she remarked blithely.

"Do you want to be?"

"I like what I'm doing now."

"Cuddling?"

"Heading the computer department."

He bent his knees and brought his legs in closer. "But someday. Do you want to have kids?"

"I haven't really thought about it."

"Come on. Every woman thinks about it."

"I've been too busy."

"To do it?"

"To think about doing it."

He dipped his head, bringing his lips into warm intimacy with her cheek. "I'll give you a baby."

She shifted, turning onto her side so she could better see his expression. "You're crazy, do you know that?"

"Not really."

"Give me a baby—why in the world would you say something like that? In case you don't know it, a baby takes after both its parents. I've been bugging you since I stepped foot on this sloop. How would you like to have a baby that bugged you from the day it was born?"

He shrugged. "There's bugging, and there's bugging." Her hand was using his chest for leverage; he covered it with his own. "You have certain qualities that I'd want in a child of mine."

"Like what?"

It was a minute before he answered. "Beauty."

She shot a quick glance skyward. "Spare me."

"Intelligence."

"That's a given." She tipped up her chin. "What else?" When he was quiet, she gave him a lopsided grin. "Run out of things already?"

It wasn't that he'd run out, just that he was having trouble concentrating. She was so soft in his arms, her face so pert as it tilted toward his, her legs smooth as they tangled with his, her hip firm as it pressed his groin.

"There's . . . there's spunk."

"Spunk?"

"Sure. Seven times out of ten you have answers for my jibes."

"Only seven?"

Almost imperceptibly, he moved her hand on his chest. He closed his eyes for a minute and swallowed hard. "Maybe eight."

"But I'm stern-faced and prissy," she said, shifting slightly. "Is that what you want your children to inherit?"

He'd closed his eyes again, and when he opened them, he was smiling ever so gently, ever so wryly, and his warning came ever so softly. "You're playing with fire."

"I . . . what?"

"Your legs brush mine, your hair torments me." His voice began to sizzle. "You move those hips and I'm on fire, and your hand on my skin gives me such pleasure. . . . Can't you feel what's happening?"

Her stunned eyes dropped to her hand. It was partially covered by his, but her fingers were buried in the soft, curling hairs on his chest. As she watched, they began to tingle, then throb above the beat of his heart.

"A little to your right," he whispered huskily. "Move them."

She swallowed. Her fingers straightened and inched forward until a single digit came to rest atop a clearly erect nipple.

He moaned and moved his hips.

Her eyes flew to his face.

"Shocked?" he asked thickly. "Didn't you know? Am I the only one suffering?"

"I . . . we were talking . . . I was comfortable." The words seemed feeble, but they were the truth. She couldn't remember when she'd ever been with a man this way, just talking, enjoying the physical closeness for something other than sex. "I'm sorry. . . ."

But she didn't move away. Her senses were awakening to him with incredible speed. All the little things that had hovered just beyond sexual awareness—the sole of his foot against her instep, the brush of his hair-spattered legs against her calves and thighs, the solidity of his flesh beneath her hand, his enveloping male scent, the cradle of his body, the swelling virility between his legs—all came into vivid focus. And his voice, his voice, honing her awareness like scintillating sand . . .

"I'd like to make love to you, Shaye. I'd like to open that little thing you're wearing and touch you all over, taste you all over. I think I could bury myself in your body and never miss the world again. Would you let me do that?"

The rising breeze cooled her face, but she could barely breathe, much less think. "I . . . we can't."

"We can." He had one arm across her back in support while his hand caressed her hip. The other hand tipped up her face. "Kiss me, Shaye. Now."

Say no. Push him away. Tell him you don't want this. She had the answers but no motivation, and when his mouth closed over hers, she could do nothing but savor its purposeful movement. Caressing, sucking, stroking—he was a man who kissed long and well. He was also a man who demanded a response.

"Open your mouth," he ordered in an uncompromising growl. "Do it the way I like it."

Shaye wasn't quite sure how he liked it, but the break in his kiss had left her hungry. This time when he seized them, her lips were parted. As they had the night before, they erupted into a fever against his, building the heat so high that she had to use her tongue as a coolant. But that didn't work, either, because Noah's own response increased the friction. Her breath came quickly, and her entire body was trembling by the time he dragged his lips away.

"Ahh, you do it right," he said on a groan.

Gasping softly, she pressed her forehead to his jaw. She felt his hand on her neck, but she was too weak to object, and in a second that hand was inside her blouse, taking the full weight of her breast. Her small cry was lifted and carried away by the wind.

"This is what I want," he whispered. His long fingers kneaded her, then drew a large arc on her engorged flesh. The top snap of her blouse released at the pressure of his wrist, but she barely heard it. His palm was passing over her nipple once, then again, and his fingers settled more broadly when his thumb took command.

"Look at me, Shaye."

Through passion-glazed eyes, she looked.

His voice was a rasping whisper. "This is what I'd do for starters." As he held her gaze, he dragged his thumb directly across her turgid nipple. He repeated the motion. "Do you feel it inside?"

"Oh yes," she whispered back. The thrumming still echoed in her core. Her legs stirred restlessly. "Do it again."

A tiny whimper came from the back of her throat when he did, but then he was whispering again. "I'd touch the other one like that, too. And then I'd take it in my mouth. . . ." Another snap popped and he lowered his head. She took handfuls of his hair and held on when his thumb was replaced by the heat of his mouth, the wetness of his tongue, the gentle but volatile raking of his teeth.

Nothing had ever felt so exciting and so right. Shaye had spent the past six years of her life denying that the two—exciting and right—could be compatible, but she couldn't deny what she felt now. As his mouth drew her swelling breast deeper and deeper into its hot, wet hold, she knew both peace and yearning. She wanted him to tell her what he'd do next, and she wanted him to do it. She ached to do all kinds of wild things in return. And still there was that sense of rightness, and it confused her.

"Noah . . . Noah, Samson . . ."

"Can't see. Shh."

She wanted, but she didn't. The feel of Noah's mouth firmly latched to her burning flesh was a dangerous Eden. She didn't trust herself and her judgement of rightness, and she couldn't trust Noah to understand what she felt. She was in deep water and sinking fast. If she didn't haul herself up soon, she'd be lost.

Tugging at his hair, she pulled him away with a moan. "We have to stop."

"Samson's way back at the stern," Noah argued hoarsely. "The sails are between us and him, and it's dark."

But Shaye was already sliding from his lap. He watched her scramble against the bow, clutching the lapels of her blouse with one hand, holding her middle with the other. His body was throbbing and his breathing unsteady. He hiked his knees up and wrapped his arms around them. "It's not just Samson," he stated.

"No."

"Is it me?"

"No."

"Then it's you."

She said nothing, just continued to look at him. The wind had picked up, blowing her hair around her face. She was almost grateful for the shield.

Her insides were in knots. She felt as though she'd been standing on the brink of either utter glory or total disaster—only she didn't know which. If he took her back in his arms, coaxed the least bit, pushed the least bit, she'd give in. Her nipple was still damp where he'd suckled; both breasts—her entire body—tingled. She'd never in her life felt as strong a craving for more, and she didn't understand why.

But common sense cried for self-control. Self-control! Was it so much to ask? Shaye wondered. When she'd been younger, she'd thought that by doing her own thing when and where she wanted, she was controlling her life. In fact, the opposite had been the case. For years she'd been out of control, acting irresponsibly with little thought for the consequences of her actions.

Now she was older and wiser. Responsibility had closed in on her, weighing her down at times, uplifting her at others. Perhaps it was an obsession, but self-control had been a passion in and of itself.

"What is it, Shaye?" Noah asked. "You're not an eighteen-year-old virgin."

She'd never been an eighteen-year-old virgin, and that was part of the problem. She'd given in too soon, too fast, too far.

"Have you been hurt . . . abused?"

"No!"

"But you're afraid."

"I just want to stop."

"You're afraid."

"Think what you will."

"But it doesn't make sense!" he burst out in frustration. "One minute you want me, the next you don't."

"I know."

"Well? Are you going to explain?" The demands of his body had died. He stretched out his legs in a show of indolence he was far from feeling. The wind was whipping at his shirt, but when he folded his arms over his chest, it was more because he felt exposed to Shaye's whims than to those of the weather. He wasn't used to the feeling of exposure and didn't like it.

"I can't explain. It's just . . . just me."

"Have you ever been involved with a man?"

"I've never been in love."

"That wasn't the question. Have you ever had a relationship with a man?"

"Certainly—just as you have."

"Sexually. Have you ever been involved sexually with a man?"

"You pointed out—" she began, then repeated herself in a voice loud enough to breach the wind "—you pointed out that I'm not an eighteen-year-old virgin."

He sighed, but the sound was instantly whisked away. "Shaye, you know what I'm getting at."

"I've been involved with many men, but never deeply," she blurted out, then wondered why she had. At the time she'd thought herself deeply involved with Josh...or André...or Christopher. But "deep" meant something very different now. It was almost...almost the way she was beginning to think herself involved with Noah, and that stunned her.

"Have you ever lived with a man?"

It was a minute before she could answer. "I, uh, lived in a kind of communal setup for a while," she hedged, and even that was pushing it a little. The garret had been André's; the others had simply crashed there for a time. She'd spent seven months with Josh, who'd eventually run off—with her blessing—to follow the Maharishi. She'd lived with other men for brief periods; she'd quickly gotten restless.

"Communal setups can mean either constant sex or no sex at all. Which was it?"

"I'm prissy. Which do you think?"

"I'm beginning to think this prissy bit is a cop-out. I'm beginning to think you're not one bit prissy. At least, that's what your fiery little body leads me to suspect."

She shrugged.

"Damn it, don't do that," he snapped. The sloop seemed to echo his frustration with a sudden roll. "I'm trying to get information. Shrugging tells me nothing."

"I don't like being the butt of your polling."

He rubbed the tight muscles at the back of his neck. "Was it that obvious?"

"Now that I know what you do for a living, yes."

The flapping of canvas high above suddenly grabbed their attention. Noah sprang to his feet. "It's about to rain. Do you have a slicker?"

Shaye, too, had risen. She'd snapped up her blouse and was holding her hair off her face with both hands. "A poncho." She swayed toward the bulwark when the boat took a lunge.

"Better get it," he said as he started toward the stern. She was right behind him. "Better still, get below. This deck in a storm is no place for a woman."

Shaye was about to make a derisive retort when Noah started shouting to Samson. And at the moment the first large drops of rain hit the deck. Having no desire to get drenched, she made straight for the companionway.

For several hours, she remained in the salon with Victoria while the *Golden Echo* bucked the waves with something less than grace. The men had run below in turns to get rain gear, and Shaye's repeated offers of help had been refused. She noticed that Victoria wasn't offering. In fact, Victoria was very quiet.

"Are you feeling all right?"

"I'm fine," Victoria said softly. "Or I will be once the wind dies down."

"That could be hours from now."

The expression on Victoria's face would have been priceless if she hadn't been so pale. "Don't remind me."

"Why don't you lie down in the cabin?"

"I'm afraid that might be worse." She scowled. "This tub isn't the best thing to be on in weather like this."

"So it's a tub now, is it?" Shaye said with a teasing smile. "You didn't think so before."

"Before I wasn't being jostled. And the portholes were open then." Victoria fanned herself. "It's hot as Hades here."

"Would you rather the waves poured in?"

"No, no. Not that."

"Are you scared?"

"Are you?"

Shaye was, a little. But the storm was a diversion. It gave her something to think about besides Noah and herself. Even now, with little effort, she could feel his arms around her and his tongue on her breast. She felt the same yearning she had then, the same confusion, the same fear. She'd come so close to giving in....

But she couldn't think about that. There was the storm to consider, one danger exchanged for another. She did trust that Samson and Noah knew what they were doing. She wondered if they were frightened—but didn't really want to know.

So she pasted a crooked grin on her face and said to Victoria, "I'm sure we'll pull through fine. Look at the experience as exciting. It's not everyone who gets tossed over the high seas in an ancient colonial sloop."

"Cute," Victoria said, then gingerly pushed herself from the sofa. "On second thought, I will lie down."

Concerned, Shaye started out of her chair. "Can I do anything to help?"

But Victoria pressed her shoulder down as she passed. "If death is imminent, I'll call."

SHAYE DIDN'T WAIT for the call. She checked on Victoria every few minutes, trying to talk her out of her preoccupation with her insides. But with each visit, Victoria felt less like talking. By the third visit, she'd lost the contents of her stomach and was looking like death warmed over.

"Let me get you something."

Victoria moaned. "Leave me be."

"But I feel helpless."

"It'll pass."

"My helplessness?"

"My seasickness."

"What about my guilt?" Shaye asked in a meek stab at humor. "I was the one who joked about getting violently seasick."

"Tss. You're making it worse."

"Samson said he had medicine."

"Don't bother Samson. He has enough on his hands."

Shaye rose from the bed. "I'm getting his medicine."

"They'll think I'm a sissy."

"God forbid."

"Shaye, I'm fine—"

"You will be," she said as she left the cabin. Shimmying into her poncho, she climbed the companionway. She paused only to raise her hood and duck her head in preparation for the rain before pushing open the hatch. The wind instantly whipped the hood back and her hair was soaked before she'd reached the helm, where Samson stood wearing bright yellow oilskins and a sou'wester, looking for all the world like a seasoned Gloucester fisherman.

"Whatcha doin' up heah, geul?" he yelled in an accent to match.

The rain was coming down in sheets while the wind whipped everything in sight, but still Shaye laughed. His role playing conveyed a confidence that was contagious. "You're too much, Samson!"

"Best enjoy ev'ry minute!" he declared in a voice that challenged the storm.

Shaye tugged up her hood to deflect the rain from her face while she looked around. The sea was a mass of whitecaps. The jibs were down, the mainsail reefed. In essence, Samson was doing little more than holding the keel steady while they rode out the storm.

"Has Noah gone overboard?" she yelled.

"Not likely!"

She was about to ask where he was when the boat heaved and veered to port. Steadying herself as best she could, she shouted, "Are we in danger?"

He straightened the wheel and shouted back, "Nope!"

"How long do you think it'll keep up?"

"Mebbe an hour. Mebbe five."

"Victoria won't be terribly pleased to hear that."

"She'll prob'ly be hopin' it las' ten," he roared with an appreciative smile.

"I don't think so, Samson. She's sick!"

While the storm didn't faze him, that bit of news did. For the first time, he seemed concerned. The accent vanished. "Her stomach's acting up?"

Shaye nodded vigorously. "You said something about medicine?"

"In the locker by the galley. Noah may have it, though."

"Where *is* Noah?"

"In bed."

"What's he doing in bed when—oh, no, he's sick?"

"And not pleased about it at all! He wanted to stay on deck, but when he started to reel on his feet, I ordered him down."

Shaye had no way of knowing that the same concern she'd seen on Samson's face moments before now registered on her own. Noah sick? He was so large, so strong. She couldn't picture him being brought down by anything, much less *mal de mer*.

Actually, though, the more she thought about it, the more she saw a touch of humor in it. Or poetic justice.

"I didn't see him come in," she said more to herself than to Samson. "It must have been while I was with Victoria."

At the reminder of her aunt, she turned quickly back to the hatch. Once below, she peeled off the soaking poncho and checked the locker for Samson's medicine. It was there. Either

Noah wasn't all that sick or he was too proud to take anything.

Victoria wasn't too proud. When Shaye lifted her head and pressed the pill between her lips, she sipped enough water to get it down, then sank weakly back to the pillow. Pill bottle in hand, Shaye returned to the locker. She paused before opening it, though, eyes moving helplessly toward the captain's quarters. Then, without asking herself why or to what end, she took the few steps necessary and quietly opened the door.

A trail of sodden clothes led to the bed, and on that bed lay Noah. He was sprawled on his stomach atop the bare sheets, one arm thrown over his head. The faint glow from the lamp showed the sheen of sweat that covered his body. He was naked.

Feeling not humor but a well of compassion that she'd never have dreamed she'd feel for the man, she quietly approached and knelt down by the bed. "Noah?" she asked softly.

He moaned and turned his face away.

"Have you taken something?"

He grunted.

Compassion turned to tenderness. She reached out and stroked his hair. It was wet from the rain, but his neck was clammy. "Victoria's sick. I just gave her some of Samson's medicine. If I get water, will you take some, too?"

He groaned. "Let me die in peace."

"You're not going to die."

He made a throaty sound of agreement. "I won't be so lucky."

"If you die, who'll be left to give me a hard time?"

There was a short silence from Noah, then a terse, "Get the pill."

Shaye brought water and held his head while he managed to swallow the pill. Then she sponged his back with a damp cloth.

"It's not helping," he mumbled. Though his head was turned her way, his eyes remained closed.

"Give it time."

"I haven't got time. I'm already in hell."

"Serves you right for living the life of a sinner."

He moaned, then grumbled, "What would you know about the life of a sinner?"

"You'd be surprised," she answered lightly, continuing to bathe him.

At length he dragged open an eye. "Why aren't *you* sick?"

"I'm just not."

"Are you scared."

"No."

"You should be. We're about to be swallowed by a great white whale."

"Does delirium come with seasickness?"

He gave up the effort of keeping that one eye open, pulled the pillow between his chest and the sheet and moaned again.

"Does that help?" she asked.

"What?"

"Moaning."

"Yes." A minute later he turned onto his side and curled into a ball, with the pillow pressed to his stomach. "God, I feel awful."

He looked it. His face was an ashen contrast to his dark hair, and tight lines rimmed his nose and mouth.

"Are you going to be sick?" she said.

"I *am* sick."

"Are you going to throw up?"

"Already have. Twice."

"That should have helped."

He grunted.

"It's really a shame. After Samson went to such efforts with the sauerbraten—"

"Shut up, Shaye," he gasped, then gave another moan.

"The storm should be over sometime tomorrow."

"If you can't say something nice . . ."

"I thought the storm was pretty exciting. I've never seen waves quite like that."

This time his moan had more feeling. Shaye said nothing more as she smoothed the cloth over his skin a final time. Then, brushing the damp hair from his brow, she asked, "Will you be okay?"

"Fine."

"I should get back to Victoria."

"Go."

"Can I check on you later?"

"Only if you're into autopsies."

She smiled. He was the fallen warrior, but there was something endearing about him. "I'll steel myself," she said, then quietly rose from his bedside and left the cabin.

She didn't steel herself for an autopsy, of course. She checked on Victoria, who'd settled some, then went to sleep to dream dreams of a long-legged, lean-hipped man whose body had to be the most beautiful she'd ever seen in her life.

7

THE STORM HAD DIED by morning. Shaye awoke to find Victoria on deck with Noah, who'd sent Samson below for a well-earned rest.

"Well, well, if it isn't our own Florence Nightingale," Noah remarked as she approached the helm.

The last time he'd said something like that, Shaye mused, he'd called her an iron maiden. She didn't particularly care for either image, but at least she didn't hear sarcasm this time.

She had wondered how he'd greet her after the state she'd last seen him in. Some men would have been embarrassed. Others, particularly those with a macho bent—and Noah did have a touch of that—would have been defensive. But Noah seemed neither defensive nor embarrassed. He'd bounced right back to his confident self. She should have known he would.

"You're both looking chipper," she said.

Victoria smiled. "Thanks to you."

Noah seconded that. "She really is a marvel. Has an unturnable stomach and an unrivaled bedside manner."

"Mmmm. She does have a way of coaxing down medicine."

"And bathing sweaty bodies."

Victoria gaped at him. "She bathed you? I didn't get a bath!"

"I guess she can't resist a naked man."

"Naked?" She turned to Shaye, but the twinkle in her eyes took something from the horror of her expression. "Shaye, how could you?"

Before Shaye could utter a word, Noah was wailing, "There you go again—suggesting that my body's distasteful! What is it with you women?"

"I didn't suggest anything of the sort," Shaye said smoothly, and turned to Victoria. "He actually has a stunning body—a sweet little birthmark on his right hip and the cutest pair of buns you'd ever hope to see."

"I didn't think you noticed," Noah drawled to Shaye, then said to Victoria, "but don't worry. I kept the best parts hidden."

Shaye didn't answer that. She'd seen the "best parts" too, and they'd been as impressive as the rest. But she wasn't about to play the worldly woman so far that she totally cancelled out the prissy one. So she tipped back her head, to find the sky a brilliant blue. "No clouds in sight, and we're making headway again. Did we lose much ground during the storm?"

"A little," Noah answered, indulgently accepting the change in subject, "but we're back on course."

"Good." She rubbed her hands together. "Anyone want breakfast?"

Noah and Victoria exchanged a glance, then answered in unison, "Me."

"You're cooking for all of us?" Noah asked.

"I'm feeling benevolent."

He snagged her around the shoulders and drew her to his side. "Domestic instincts coming to the fore?"

"No. I'm just hungry."

"So am I."

She sent him a withering look.

He didn't wither. "Just think," he murmured for her ears alone, "how nice it would be to have breakfast together in bed."

"I never eat breakfast in bed."

"If I were still sick, would you have brought it to me there?"

"If you were still sick, you wouldn't have wanted it."

"What if my stomach was fine but my knees were so weak that I couldn't get up?"

"That'd be the day."

"You were very gentle last night. No one's taken the time to bathe me like that since I was a child."

She knew he was playing on her soft side, but before she should could come up with suitably repressive words, he spoke again.

"So you liked what you saw?"

"Oh yes. The storm was breathtaking."

"*Me*. My *body*."

"Oh, that. Well, it wasn't quite as exciting as the sea."

"Catch me tonight, and I'll show you exciting."

"Is another storm brewing?" she asked, being purposely obtuse.

Noah wasn't buying. "You bet," he said with a naughty grin.

Shaye quickly escaped from his clutches and went below to fix breakfast. Throughout the morning, though, she thought of Noah, of his body and its potential for excitement. The more she thought, the more agitated she grew.

She tried to understand what it was about him that turned her on. He was cocky and quick-tongued. He could be presumptuous and abrasive. He was, in his own way, a rebel. There were so many things not to like. Still, he turned her on.

Always before she'd been safe, and it wasn't merely a question of dating bland men. She encountered men at work, men in the supermarket, men in the bookstore, the hardware store, the laundry. She'd never given any of them a second glance.

Granted, she'd had no choice with Noah. She was stuck on a boat with him, and in such close quarters second glances were hard to avoid, particularly when the man in question made his presence felt at every turn.

Not only was she looking twice, she was also fantasizing. With vivid clarity she recalled how he'd looked naked. She hadn't been thinking lascivious thoughts at the time, but since then her imagination had worked overtime. Everything about him was manly, with a capital *M*—the bunching muscles of his back, the prominent veins in his forearms, the tapering of his torso, his neat, firm bottom, the sprinkling of dark hair on the backs of his thighs. And in front—she could go on and on, starting with the day's growth of beard on his face and ending with the heaviness of his sex.

If the attraction were purely physical, she could probably hold him off. But increasingly she thought of other things—his sense of humor, his intelligence, his daring, his disregard for convention—and she felt deeply threatened. Last night hadn't helped. What she'd felt when he'd been sick, when he'd needed her and she'd been there for him, came dangerously close to affection. She'd never experienced the overwhelming urge to care for a man before.

So why was it wrong? In principle, she had nothing against involvement. She supposed that some day she'd like to fall in love, just as some day she'd like to have children. She hadn't planned on falling in love now, though, when her career was in full swing. And she hadn't planned on falling in love with a man like Noah.

Not that she was in love with him, she cautioned herself quickly. But still . . .

The problem was that Noah wasn't meek. He wasn't conservative or conventional. She couldn't control him—or herself when she was with him. He was wrong for her.

Had she been in Philadelphia, she'd have run in the opposite direction. But she wasn't in Philadelphia. She was stuck on a boat in the middle of the Caribbean with Noah, and she was vulnerable. In his arms, she was lost—and she fell into his arms easily!

She'd just have to be on her guard, she decided. That was all there was to it.

THE AFTERNOON BROUGHT a torment of its own. Where the night before the wind had picked up, gusted, then positively raged, today it faded, sputtered, then died.

Shaye was sitting on deck reading when the sails began to pucker. She looked up at the mast, then at Victoria, who was sitting in blissful ignorance nearby, then down at her book again. But the sails grew increasingly limp, and at the moment of total deflation, she didn't need the unusual calm of the sea to tell her what had happened.

Noah sauntered by, nonchalantly lowering and lashing the sails.

"How long?" she asked.

He shrugged. "Maybe an hour or two. We'll see."

An hour or two didn't sound so bad. The part she didn't like was the "maybe." If their idle drifting lasted for eight hours, or sixteen, or God forbid, twenty-four...

"You look alarmed," he commented, tossing her a glance as he worked.

"No, no. I'm fine."

"View it as a traffic jam. If you were in the city, chances are you'd be on your way somewhere. But you wouldn't be able to move, so you'd be frustrated, and you'd be sick from exhaust fumes. Here you have none of that." He took a long, loud breath that expanded his chest magnificently. "Fresh air. Bright sun. Clear water. What more could you ask?"

Shaye could have asked for the wind to fill the sails and set them on their way again. The sooner they reached Costa Rica, the sooner they'd return to Colombia and the sooner she'd go home. One virile man with a magnificent chest was pushing her resolve.

"I couldn't ask for anything more," she said.

"Sing it."

"Excuse me?"

"The song. You know—" Noah jumped into a widespread stance, leaned back, extended both arms and did his best Ethel Merman imitation: "I got rhythm, I got music . . ."

She covered her face with a hand. "We did that in junior high. I believe the last line is, '*Who* could ask for anything more?'"

"Close enough."

She peered through her fingers. "Were you in the glee club?"

"Through high school. Then I was in an *a cappella* group in college. We traveled all over the place. It was really fun." His face suddenly dropped.

"What?"

"Well, it was fun for a while."

"What happened?"

He hesitated, then shrugged. "I resigned."

"Why did you do that?"

"I, uh, actually there were three of us. We got into a little trouble."

"What kind of trouble?"

He returned to his work. "It was nothing."

"What kind of trouble?"

He secured the last fold of the mainsail to the boom, then mumbled, "We went on a drinking binge in Munich. The administrators decided we weren't suitable representatives of the school."

"You didn't resign. You were kicked out."

"No, we resigned."

"It was either that or be kicked out."

He ran a hand through his hair. "You don't have to put it so bluntly."

"But that was what it boiled down to, wasn't it? You should be ashamed of yourself, Noah."

Victoria, who'd remained on the periphery of the discussion to that point, felt impelled to join in. "Aren't you being a little hard on the man, Shaye? You were in college once. You know what college kids do. They're young and having fun. They outgrow it."

"Thank you, Victoria," Noah said.

Shaye echoed his very words, but with a different inflection. She picked up her book again.

Having nothing better to do, Noah stretched out on his back in the sun. Within thirty seconds, he bobbed up to remove his shirt. Then he lay back again, folding his arms beneath his head. "I'll bet Shaye never did anything wrong in school. The model student. Hmmmm?"

Shaye didn't answer.

Victoria pressed a single finger to her lips, holding in words that were aching to spill out. Shaye shot her a warning look. The finger stayed where it was, which was both a good sign and a bad sign.

"Did you study all the time?" Noah asked.

"I studied."

"What did you do for fun?"

"Oh, this and that." She glanced toward the stern. "Where's Samson?"

"I believe he's cooking," Victoria answered, dropping her finger at last.

"What's it going to be tonight?"

Noah smirked. "Now, if he told us, it wouldn't be a surprise, and that's half the fun."

"I hate surprises."

"You hate fun. What a boring person."

"Noah," Victoria chided.

But Shaye could stand up for herself. "It's okay. I have a strong back."

"Stiff," Noah corrected in an absent tone. His eyes were closed, his body relaxed. "Stiff back. But not all the time. When I take you in my arms—"

Shaye cut him off. "Does Samson always cook foreign?"

He grinned and answered only after a meaningful pause. "Not always. He does a wicked Southern-fried chicken."

"What does he wear then?"

"I'm not telling."

She glared at him for a minute, but his eyes were still closed so he didn't see. "You wouldn't," she muttered, and returned to her book. She couldn't concentrate, of course. Not with Noah stretched out nearby. The occasional glances she darted his way brought new things to her attention—the pattern of hair swirling over his chest, the bolder tufts beneath his arms, the small indentation of his navel.

She looked back at her book, turned one page, waited several minutes, turned another. Then she set the book down in disgust. "How long have we been sitting?"

"Half an hour."

"And still no wind."

"It'll come."

"Why doesn't this boat have an engine? Nowadays every boat has an engine."

"The *Golden Echo* wasn't built 'nowadays.'"

"But she was refurbished. She has a stove and a refrigerator. Why doesn't she have an engine?"

Noah shrugged. "The Paynes must be purists."

With a snort, she picked up her book, turned several more pages, then sighed and lifted her ponytail from her neck. "Is it ever hot!"

Noah opened a lazy eye and surveyed the shorts and T-shirt she wore. "Feel free to strip."

Sending him a scowl, she pushed herself up, stalked to the companionway and went below.

He looked innocently at Victoria. "Did I say something wrong?"

Victoria didn't know whether to scold or laugh. She compromised by slanting him a chiding grin before she, too, rose.

"Hey," he called as she started off, "don't you leave me, too!"

"I'm going to visit with your uncle. It can't be much hotter down there than it is up here, and at least there's some shade."

Noah lay where he was for several minutes, then sat up and studied the horizon. He gave a voluminous sigh and pasted a jaunty smile on his face. This was what he wanted, wasn't it? Peace and quiet. The deck all to himself. He could relax if he wanted, sing if he wanted, do somersaults if he wanted.

So why did he feel restless?

Because he was hot and bothered and the damn sun wasn't helping. Abruptly dropping the smile, he surged to his feet, reached for the rope ladder, hung it from the starboard quarter, kicked off his shorts and dove into the sea. He'd done two laps around the boat when he overtook Shaye. He was as startled as she was.

"What are you doing here?" she gasped. "I thought I was alone."

"Who do you think put the ladder out?" he snapped. "And if you thought you were alone, why in the hell were you swimming? You're not supposed to swim alone."

"You were."

"That's different."

"How so?"

"I'm a man and I'm stronger."

"What a chauvinistic thing to say!"

"But it's true."

"It's absurd, and, besides, it's a moot point. You don't exactly need strength in a bathtub like this. If there were waves, there'd be a wind, and if there were a wind, we wouldn't be stuck out here floating in the middle of nowhere!"

"Always the logical answer. Y'know, Shaye, you're too rational for your own good. Ease up, will ya?"

She gave him a dirty look and started to swim around him, but he caught her arm and held it. "Let go," she ordered. "I want to swim."

"Need the exercise?"

"Yes."

"Feeling as restless as I am?"

"Yes."

"How about reckless?" he asked, his eyes growing darker.

Shaye recognized that deepening gray. His eyes went like that when he was on the verge of either mischief or passion. She didn't know which it was now, but she did know that with his hair slicked back and his lashes wet, nearly black and unfairly long, he looked positively demonic. Either that or sexy. Was she feeling reckless? "No," she stated firmly.

"Do you *ever* feel reckless?"

She shook her head.

"Not even when I take you in my arms?" He did it then, and she knew better than to try to escape. After all, he was stronger then she. "Why do I frighten you?"

"You don't."

He tipped his head to the side and gave her a reproving look.

"You don't," she repeated, but more quietly. As though to prove it—to them both—she put her hands on his shoulders.

"Are you afraid of sex?"

"I'm not a virgin."

"I know. We've been over that one before. I'm not asking whether you've done it, just whether you're afraid of it."

She was afraid of *him*, at that moment, because his mouth was so close, his lips firm and mobile. She couldn't seem to take her eyes from them. The lower was slightly fuller than its mate and distinctly sensual. Both were wet.

"Shaye?"

She wrenched her gaze to his eyes. "I'm not afraid of sex."

"Are you afraid of commitment?"

"No."

"Then why haven't you married?"

"I thought that was clear. I've been busy."

"If the right man had come along, you'd have married."

"How do you know that?"

"You ooze certain values. There's a softness to you that wouldn't be there if you were a hard-bitten career woman all the way. I have to assume that the right man just hasn't come along."

"I said that I don't date."

"You also said that you'd been involved with many men."

"But not recently. And if I don't date now, how can I possibly meet the right man?"

You don't have to date to meet men, Noah thought. *You could meet one during a vacation in the Caribbean.* "With your looks—come on, baby, with your looks the right man would make sure you dated. Him. Exclusively."

Baby. It was a stereotypically offensive endearment, yet the way he said it made her tingle. "What are you trying to prove, Noah?"

"I'm working on the theory that you turn away from men who threaten your very sane, very structured, very controlled existence. Just like you turn away from me."

"And now that you have me analyzed, you can let me go."

His arms tightened. "Hit a raw cord, did I?"

She slid her hands to his elbows and tried to push. "Not raw, nonexistent." Her teeth were gritted. "Let me go, Noah."

"I can make your body hum, but still you fight me. Why won't you let me make love to you, Shaye?"

"Because—" she was still pushing "—I don't want to."

"It'd be so easy. We could do it right here. Right now."

Her limbs were shaking, but it wasn't from the effort of trying to free herself. His tone was tender, his words electric. The combination was devastating. "Don't do this to me," she begged.

"What would I be doing that's so wrong? Is it wrong to feel drawn to someone? I do feel drawn to you, Shaye, sour moods and all."

She didn't want to hear this. Closing her eyes, she gave a firm shake of her head. "Don't say another word."

"I respect your work and your dedication to it. I respect what you feel for your aunt. I respect and admire your independence, but I want to know more about where it comes from. At the slightest mention of your family or your past, you clam up."

"I have two parents with whom I don't get along and a sister with whom I do. There. Are you satisfied?" She tried to propel herself away from him, but he wasn't letting go. She only succeeded in tangling her legs with his, which were warm, strong and very bare.

"Why don't you get along with your parents?"

"Noah, I'm getting tired. I'd like to go back on the boat."

"I'm not tired. I'll hold you. You know how."

She turned her head to the side and let out an exasperated breath. "Will you let me go?"

"No."

"I'll scream."

"Go ahead. There's no one to hear but Samson and Victoria, and they trust me." He pressed a warm kiss to her cheek, then asked gently, "Why do you do this to yourself? Why do you fight?"

His gentleness was her undoing. Suddenly tired of the whole thing, she dropped her chin to his shoulder. "Oh Lord, sometimes I wonder." Her arms slipped around him, and she felt his hands on the backs of her thighs, spreading them. In as natural a movement as she'd ever made, she wrapped her legs around his waist. "You're not wearing a suit," she murmured. "Why not?"

"I was in a rush to get in the water and there was no one around."

"Oh Noah."

He was nuzzling her ear. "What is it, hon?"

"I really am tired. I'm not used to constant sparring. I'm not good at it."

"Could've fooled me."

"All I wanted was a peaceful vacation in the Berkshires."

"Things don't always work out the way we plan. Good sometimes comes from the unexpected."

The lazy frog kick he was doing kept them bobbing gently on the sea's surface. Beneath the surface the bobbing was more erotic—the tiniest glide of their bodies against one another, a teasing, a soft simulation. Her suit was thin. She clearly felt his sex. But while her body craved the contact, she felt too spent to carry though.

"I'm so tired," she murmured, tightening her arms around him simply for the comfort of his strength.

"Things are warring inside?"

"Yes."

"Maybe if we talk it out you'll feel better."

She sighed sadly against his neck. "I don't know. For so long I've drummed certain things into my head. . . ." Her voice trailed off.

He was stroking her back. "I'm listening."

But she couldn't go on. There were too many thoughts, too much confusion, and as comfortable as she was with him just then, she was deathly afraid of saying something she'd later regret.

"Hey," he breathed. He took her head in his hands and raised it to find her eyes brimming with tears. "Ah-h-h, Shaye," he whispered hoarsely, "don't do that. Don't torment yourself so."

She could only shut her eyes and shake her head, then cling more tightly when he hugged her again.

"I guess I've come on pretty strong."

She nodded against his neck.

"That wasn't very nice of me."

She shook her head.

"I'm really not a bad guy when you get to know me."

She was coming to see that, and it was part of the problem. Brashness she could withstand, as she could irreverence and impulsiveness. But mix any of those with gentleness, and she was in trouble.

"Come on," he said softly. His hands left her back and broke into a broad breast stroke. "Let's go back on board."

She made no effort to help him swim, and when they reached the ladder she was almost sorry to let go of him. It had been so nice holding on and being held without other threats. But she did let go and climbed the ladder, then stood on the deck pressing a towel to her face.

She heard Noah's wet feet on the wood behind her. She heard the swish of material that told her he was pulling on his shorts. For a fleeting instant she wondered whether he ever bothered with underwear, then his voice came quietly.

"Why don't you stretch out in the sun to dry? It looks like we're not going anywhere yet."

Dragging the towel slowly down her face, she nodded. Moments later, she was lying on her stomach in the sun. She cleared her mind of all but her immediate surroundings—the warmth of the sun feeling good now on her wet skin, the utter silence of the air, the gentle sway of the boat as it drifted. Noah sat nearby, but he did nothing to disturb her other than to ask if she wanted a cool drink, then fetch it when she said yes.

She knew that there were other things he could have done and said, such as stretching out beside her, offering to spread lotion on her back, suggesting that she lower the straps of her suit to avoid getting marks. He could have prodded her, pried into her thoughts, forced her to think about those things she was trying so hard to avoid.

But he did none of those things. He seemed to respect the fact that she needed a break from the battle if she was to regain her strength for the skirmishes ahead.

Late in the afternoon, Victoria joined them on deck, followed a few minutes after that by Samson. Conversation was light and for the most part flowed around Shaye. When the others decided to swim, she took her turn and savored the coolness but remained subdued, and after climbing back on board she went below to change for dinner.

When all four had gathered back on deck, Samson declared, "*Nu, yesly vnyesyosh stol, Noah, ee vee pryekrasnie zhenshchina vnyes yote pagooshkee, prig at oveem yest.*"

"*Myehdlyeenyehyeh, pahzhahloostah,*" Victoria requested.

Straightening the red tunic over his shorts and shirt, Samson repeated his instructions, but more slowly this time. He accompanied them with hand motions, for which Victoria was grateful. Her course in conversational Russian had only gone so far, and she was rusty.

By the time she was ready to interpret, the others had gotten the drift of Samson's request. Noah set up the table, while Shaye and Victoria brought cushions from the salon. Samson then proceeded to serve a dinner of *kulebiaka* and salad, and with a free-flowing vodka punch, the meal was lively.

Still, Shaye was more quiet than usual. She listened to the others joke about experiences they'd had, following particularly closely when Noah spoke. She learned that he'd taken Spanish through college, that he'd spent a semester in Madrid, that he'd spent the year following graduation working on a cattle ranch in Argentina. She also learned that, while there, he'd been nicknamed the Playboy of the Pampas, and though he'd been annoyed when Samson had let that little jewel slip, he hadn't denied it.

They lingered for a long time over coffee. With no wind, there was nowhere to go and no work to do. At length Samson went below deck, reappearing moments later wearing a tricorne. Then, with one of the hurricane lamps supplementing the silver light of the moon, he produced his treasure map.

Not even Shaye could resist its lure. She sat forward with the others to study the weathered piece of paper-thin parchment. "Where did you get it?" she asked.

"I was on Montserrat last winter and befriended an old British chap, who'd found it in an old desk in the villa he'd bought there fifteen years before. We'd been discussing the lore of the pirates in these parts when he brought out the map."

Victoria leaned closer to peer at the markings. "When was it supposed to have been drawn?"

"In the mid eighteen hundreds. My friend—Fitzsimmons was his name—theorized that the crew of a pirate ship stashed its booty and left, planning to return at a later, safer time."

"Only they never made it?"

"We don't know that for sure, but it's doubtful, since the map was well hidden and intact. The desk in which Fitzsimmons found it was traced back to a man named Angus Cummins, and Englishman who settled on Montserrat in the 1860s. No one seems to have known much about Cummins other than that he was a shady character, usually drunk and alone. My own research showed him to have been quartermaster on an English vessel that was shadowed by trouble. In 1859, during one of its last voyages to the Caribbean, the captain died at sea. When the boat returned to England, there were rumors of piracy and murder, but the crew stood as one and nothing was ever proven."

Victoria expelled a breath. "Murder!"

Samson shrugged. "We'll never know, but given this," he tapped the map, "there's reason to suspect that the crew was involved in piracy."

"But if that's true, why didn't Cummins—or one of the others—ever return for the treasure?" Shaye asked.

"Cummins may have been the only one with the map. As quartermaster, he was in a position of power second only to the captain. My guess is that he left England under dubious circumstances, stationed himself on Montserrat in the hope of one day crossing the Caribbean to retrieve the treasure, but never quite found the wherewithal to do it."

Assuming the accuracy of Samson's research, Noah agreed with his guess. He was skeptical, though, about the treasure still existing. "People have been searching for gold along the Costa Rican coast since Columbus dubbed the country the 'rich coast,' but the only riches discovered were bananas. If there were anything else hidden there, wouldn't it have been long since plundered?"

Feeling an odd sense of vindication, Shaye glanced at Victoria. She'd expressed a similar sentiment when Victoria had first called her about the trip.

But Samson was undaunted. "They didn't have the map." He held up a hand. "Now, I'm not saying that the treasure's there. I've checked with the Costa Rican authorities and they have no record of anyone reporting a stash being found in the area where we're headed. But that doesn't mean the treasure hasn't been stolen. Cummins may have gone back for it, then lived out his life in frustration when he realized he couldn't return to England a wealthy man. It's possible, too, that only his small portion of the take was hidden. Then again, the map may have been a fraud from the start."

Shaye leaned closer. "It looks authentic enough."

"Oh, it's authentic. At least, it was drawn during the right time period. I had it examined by experts who attested to that."

"Then how could it be fraudulent?" Victoria asked.

"Cummins may have drawn the map on a whim. He may have drawn it to indicate the spot where he'd put a treasure if he ever had one."

"You mean, there may never have been any treasure to begin with?"

"There's always that possibility." He smiled. "For the sake of adventure, though—and until we prove otherwise—we'll assume the treasure's there."

Shaye was grateful that she'd had a few drinks with dinner. Though the coffee had lessened the vodka's effects, her senses were still numbed. Had they not been, she feared she'd have said something blunt, and she didn't want to dampen Samson's enthusiasm any more than she wanted to evoke Noah's ire. "Are we talking gold?" she asked carefully.

"Most likely. Artifacts would be found in an undersea wreckage. I doubt that a man who planted a treasure with the intention of retrieving it in his lifetime would want anything but gold."

Noah was studying the map. "This spot is between Parismina and Limón?"

Samson cleared his throat, pushed the tricorne back on his head and got down to business. "That's right." His finger traced the pen scratchings. "The Costa Rican coast is lowland. Between the Nicaraguan border at the north and Puerto Limón, which lies about midway to Panama at the south, much of that lowland is swampy."

"Swampy?" Shaye cried in dismay.

"Not to worry. We're heading for a sandy spot just north of Puerto Limón, a small bay, almost a lagoon. It should be lovely."

She hoped he was right. "And once we get there . . . ?"

"Once we get there, we look for the rose."

Shaye bit her lip. She shot a glance at Victoria, then lowered her eyes to her lap.

Victoria was as dismayed as Shaye but had the advantage of being the quintessential diplomat. "An orchid I could believe," she began softly. "Orchids are the national flower. Roses, though, are not indigenous to Central America. Is it possible that a rose Cummins planted would still be alive?"

Noah chuckled as he looked from Shaye's face to Victoria's. "Tell them, Samson. They're dying."

Samson, too, was smiling. "The rose is a rock, possibly a boulder. Cummins must have taken one look at it and associated its shape with the flowers he knew from home. The treasure, if it exists, will be found in a series of paces measured from the rock."

Dual sighs of relief came from the women, causing Noah to chuckle again. But while Samson elaborated on the specifics of those paces, Shaye's thoughts lingered on the rock.

The rose. Was it pure coincidence . . . or an omen? She had a rose of her own, and it symbolized all she'd once been and done. She hid it carefully; no more than a handful of people had ever seen it. It was her personal scarlet letter, and she was far from proud of its existence.

She'd never been a superstitious person, but at that moment, she wanted nothing at all to do with the Costa Rican rose.

8

NOAH AWOKE AT EIGHT on the fourth day of the trip and lay in bed for a long time. After spending most of the night on deck, manning the sails when the wind picked up shortly after one, he'd expected to sleep later. But Shaye had invaded his dream world as much as she was invading his thoughts now that he was awake.

A change had come over her in the water yesterday, and it hadn't been a momentary thing. She'd been distracted for most of the afternoon and thoughtful for much of the evening.

Was it surrender? Not quite. She hadn't come to him that night on deck to declare her devotion and beg him to make love to her. But she did seem to have conceded to an inner turmoil. She seemed to have realized that it wouldn't just go away, that it had to be faced.

He wished he knew what was at the root of that inner turmoil, but she guarded it closely. He wasn't dumb; he knew when to push a subject and when to back off. Not that he really thought of her as a "subject." He was too personally involved for that. But his feel for people had gotten him where he was professionally, and he was counting on it now.

She'd opened up a bit before she'd gone to bed. He'd produced a deck of cards and they'd played several games of gin, and during this she'd mentioned that she and her sister, Shannon, had played gin when they'd been kids. It was one of the few things her parents had thought harmless, she'd said wryly, and when he'd teased her, she'd admitted that her parents were strict. She obviously resented that, yet from what he could see she was nearly as strict with herself as they'd been with her.

Wouldn't she have rebelled? That was what often happened to the offspring of strict parents. Or perhaps she had rebelled and been subsequently swamped by guilt. Ingrained values were hard to shake.

She was a passionate woman. He didn't doubt that for a minute. The way she'd come alive to him on those few occasions when she'd stepped out of her self-imposed mold had been telling. She had a fire inside, all right. The question was whether she'd allow it to burn.

He wasn't about to let it go out, though he was biding his time just now. He'd found her weakness and knew that when he played it soft and gentle she was more vulnerable. Yes, he was impatient; soft and gentle hadn't traditionally been strong points in his character. But then, he'd never met a woman quite like Shaye—or felt quite as compulsively drawn to one before.

He had to admit, with some surprise, that behaving softly and gently toward Shaye wasn't as much of a hardship as he might have expected. She responded well to it. Of course, that didn't mean that his loins didn't ache. He felt an utterly primal urge to make her his. But he wanted far more than a meaningless roll in the hay—or on the deck, or in a cabin, as the case might be.

Hell, where could they do it? His cabin was Samson's, too, and Shaye shared hers with Victoria. The deck was neither comfortable nor private. There was always the water, but he wanted leverage, not to mention access to certain parts of her body without fear of drowning. On the other hand, a sandy beach on the Costa Rican coast . . .

Allowing for the time they'd lost during the storm and then being becalmed, they had two days' sailing ahead before they reached their destination. Two days in which to soften her up. He'd have to work on it, he decided as he sprang from the bed and reached for a pair of shorts. He'd have to work on it, starting with a soft and gentle morning talk.

He went on deck to find Victoria and Samson but no sign of Shaye. And since he was reserving all his softness and gentleness for her, his impatience found vent in the demand, "Where is she?"

Samson tried to conceal a grin and didn't quite make it. "I haven't seen her yet this morning."

"I think she's still sleeping," Victoria added innocently. "It was after two before she finally dozed off."

A scowling Noah left them and crossed to the bow.

"Now how would you know that?" Samson drawled softly. "You were asleep yourself by eleven."

Victoria didn't ask him how *he'd* known *that*. While Noah and Shaye had been playing cards on deck, Samson had walked her to her cabin, then sat talking with her until she'd fallen asleep. She was normally a night owl, but knowing Samson relieved Noah at the helm between three and four, she'd wanted to be up soon after. Watching the sunrise with him was a memorable experience.

"Actually," she whispered, "I don't know it for sure, but I could feel her tossing and turning. And it won't do any harm to let Noah know she's losing sleep over him."

"Is that what she's doing?"

"I believe so."

He narrowed one eye. "Are you matchmaking?"

She narrowed an eye right back at him. "No more than you."

He lowered his head in that same subtle gesture of guilt that Victoria and Shaye had seen the first day. "I wasn't matchmaking, exactly," he hedged. "But when you called to say that your niece was coming along and that she was twenty-nine, attractive, intelligent and hardworking—well, I couldn't help but think of Noah."

"So you *did* get him to come after I called."

"Barney was ticked off."

"But other than what I said, you knew nothing about Shaye."

"I knew Noah. He needed a break, and not at an isolated château in Normandy. He needs a woman. He's the proverbial man who has everything...except that. Besides," he added with a roguish smile, "Garrick had told me about you, and I knew that if the niece took after the aunt in any small way..."

Victoria reached up to kiss him lightly. "You're a very sweet man. Have I told you that lately?"

"I don't mind hearing it again."

"You're a very sweet man. Thank you for the compliment...and for bringing Noah along. He and Shaye are right for each other. I just know it."

At that moment, Noah swung by en route to the companionway. "Enjoy yourselves, folks."

"Where are you off to?" Samson asked.

"Breakfast," was all Noah said before he disappeared.

It was a brainstorm, he mused as he quickly whipped up pancake batter. She was still in bed, and she hadn't eaten since dinner, and since he was hungry and she was bound to be hungry... Very innocent, he decided, it would all be very innocent. He'd simply carry in breakfast, wake her gently, and they'd eat.

As he spooned batter onto the griddle, he recalled his initial fear that she'd expect to be waited on. But he wasn't waiting on her, at least not in the sense of pandering to a woman who refused to do for herself. She'd proven more than willing to pitch in. She'd even made him breakfast yesterday.

So now he was returning the favor. Only with a sightly different twist.

A short time later, balancing the tray that Samson always used to cart food to the deck, he went to her cabin. When a light knock at the door produced no response, he quietly opened it and slipped inside. Then he stood there for a minute, stunned as always by the sight of her in bed. She was on her stomach this time, dark red hair spilling around her head, more vivid than ever against the white linens. Where the sheet left off at mid-back, her T-shirt took over in covering her completely. Still she was alluring. All white and red, primness and fire. God, was she alluring!

He quietly set the tray down by the side of the bed and perched on its edge. "Shaye?" he whispered. His hand hovered over her shoulder for a minute before lowering and squeezing lightly. "Shaye?"

She stirred, turning her head his way. Her eyes were still closed. Lock by lock, he stroked her hair back from her face.

She barely opened her mouth, and the words were slurred. "Something smells good."

"Pancakes and apple butter. I thought maybe you'd join me."

She was quiet for such a long time that he wondered if she'd fallen back to sleep. Then she murmured, "I never eat breakfast in bed."

"Are you turning down room service?"

Again a pause. Her eyes remained closed. "No."

He swallowed down a tiny sigh of relief. "Would you rather sleep a little longer?"

She yawned and struggled to open one eye. "What time is it?"

"Nine-thirty."

With a moan, she turned away. "I didn't get to bed until two."

"Get to bed" versus "doze off." Two very different connotations. "Get to bed" meant she could have been reading; he'd been on deck, so he hadn't seen whether she'd stayed in the salon for a while. "Doze off," the phrase Victoria had used, suggested that she'd tried to sleep but that her thoughts had kept her awake. He hoped it was the latter, but he wasn't about to ask. For someone who usually woke up crabby, she was in a relatively civil mood.

"Are you falling asleep on me?" he whispered.

She shook her head against the pillow.

"Just taking it slow?"

She didn't move. At length she said, "I'm trying to decide whether or not to be angry. You woke me up."

The fact that she didn't sound at all angry gave Noah hope. "I'll leave if you want. I'm hungry enough to eat both helpings."

She turned over then, pushed herself up until she was sitting against the wall, straightened the sheet across her hips and patted her lap.

With a smile he reached for the tray.

Few words were exchanged as they ate. She glanced at him from time to time, thinking how considerate it had been of him to bring her breakfast, and how good he looked even before he'd shaved, and how well he wore an unbuttoned shirt. He glanced at her from time to time, thinking how the shadows beneath her eyes had faded, and how becoming her light tan was, and how disheveled and sexy she looked.

From time to time their glances meshed, held for a second or two, broke away.

When Shaye had finished the last of her pancakes she said, "You're nearly as good a cook as Samson."

"Breakfast is my specialty."

"Between you and your uncle, you could run a restaurant."

"I have enough to do already, thank you."

She sat very still for a minute. "We're moving."

"Have been since one this morning."

She hadn't realized that and wondered how she could have been so caught up in her thoughts that she hadn't noticed.

"Want to go on deck?" Noah asked.

"I'll have to get dressed first."

"You do that while I take care of these," he said, indicating the dishes. "I'll meet you up there in, say, ten minutes?"

"Okay," she agreed quietly and watched him leave.

Ten minutes later they were standing side by side at the bow. She raised her face and closed her eyes. "Mmm, that feels good."

Noah didn't comment on the fact that she'd left her hair down, or that it was positively dancing in the breeze, or that it was tempting him nearly beyond reason. Instead he took a deep breath and asked casually, "Where do you live in Philly? An apartment?"

"Condominium. It's in a renovated building not far from the historic area."

"Is your family in Philly, too?"

"Uh-uh. Connecticut."

He turned around to lean back against the bulwark. The sails were full. He studied them, wondering if he dared ask more. Before he had a chance to decide either way, she asked, "How about you? A condo in the city?"

"Yup."

"What's your place like in Vermont?"

"Contemporary rustic."

She laughed softly. "That's honest. Most people would pride themselves on saying rustic, when in fact they have every modern amenity imaginable."

A short time later, after they'd watched a school of fish swim by, she asked, "Do you ski?"

"Sure do. You?"

"I tried a few times in college, but I never really went at it seriously."

He wanted to say that she could use his place anytime, that he'd teach her how to ski, that the most fun was après-ski, with a warm fire, a hot toddy and a bear rug before the hearth. Instead he asked what she'd been reading the day before.

Eventually they brought cushions up and made themselves more comfortable. Their talk was sporadic, never touching on deep issues, but even the trivia that emerged was enlightening.

Shaye learned that Noah was an avid Mets fan, that he want to games whenever he could spare the time, which wasn't often enough, and that he'd even became friends with a few of the players. Once he'd been mistaken for a bona fide member of the team by a small-town reporter, who interviewed him outside the locker room after a game. She learned that when he watched television, it was usually a program of the public information or documentary type. He had certain favorite restaurants he returned to often, the most notable of which was a no-name dive on the Lower East Side that had filthy floors, grumpy waiters and the best guacamole north of Chihuahua. She learned that he hated shopping, loved dressing up on Halloween—which, he assured her, came only once a year at his office—and fantasized about buying a Harley and biking across the country.

Noah learned that Shaye talked to her plants and that she generally hated to cook but could do it well when inspired. He learned that she'd always loved to read and belonged to a book group, that she wanted to take up aerobics but didn't have the time, that she liked Foreigner, Survivor, and Chicago but never went to live rock concerts.

The day passed with surprising speed. Shaye wasn't quite sure whether the new Noah, the one who was companionable rather than seductive, was the real Noah. But since he'd offered her a respite from the torment he'd previously inflected, she wasn't about to raise the issue aloud.

Her subconscious wasn't quite as obedient. No sooner had she gone to bed that night than the sensual Noah popped up in her dreams, only it was worse, now, because the man who excited her physically was the same one she'd begun to respect. She awoke in a frenzy, torn apart and sweaty, and immediately put the blame on the Vietnamese dinner Samson had prepared that night. By the next morning, though, that excuse had worn thin. One look at Noah, freshly shaved and wearing nothing but a low-slung pair of shorts, stirred her blood.

She fought it all day, but to no avail. They were together nearly constantly, and though he didn't fall back on either double entendres or provocative observations, his eyes held the dark sexuality that expressed her own deepest thoughts. She was acutely, viscerally, passionately aware of him.

While they ate breakfast, which he consumed in bulk and with enthusiasm, she was entranced by his mouth. It was mobile and firm, yet sensual. She couldn't help but recall how aggressively it had consumed her own, and when her eyes met his for a fleeting moment, she knew he was remembering the same.

Later she sat with him on deck while he cleaned the hurricane lamps, his long, lean fingers working the cloth over brass. She was mesmerized by those fingers and finally had to tear her eyes away, but the memory of them working her breasts with agile intimacy caused a rush of warmth to spread beneath her skin. Noah didn't comment on the blush or on the sudden shift of her gaze, but when she dared look back at him, she caught a starkly hungry expression.

Later still, when he relieved Samson at the helm, she relaxed against the transom—or she'd intended to relax, until Noah's bold stance commanded her attention. He had a beautiful body and he held it well, shoulders back, head up. Whether standing with his legs spread or with his ankles crossed or with his weight on one hip, he oozed self-confidence. And when he walked, as he did to occasionally adjust the sails, he oozed masculinity. She wondered what it was about tight-hipped men who moved with nothing more than the subtlest shift of their bottoms—whether it was the economy of movement that made a woman greedy, or the pelvic understatement that was overwhelmingly suggestive, or simply the fact that between waist and thigh men were built so differently from women.

Of course, she couldn't remember ever having taken much notice of men's bottoms before, not even in the old days. So it had to be Noah.

Self-confident, sexy, every move natural and spontaneous. He wasn't a preener. Not one of his motions seemed tutored. His body was simply. . . his body. And his very indifference to it made him all the more attractive to Shaye.

And all *that* was before she got down to the details. The roughened skin on his elbows . . . the compact lobes of his ears . . . the symmetry of his upper back, the gleam of sun-bronzed skin over flexing muscles . . . the shallow dip at his hipline just before his shorts cut off the view . . . So many things she wanted to touch, so many things that touched her even without actual physical contact.

Like his chest. Noah's chest inspired wanton behavior. She wanted to feel its varying textures, to touch her finger to a smooth spot, a hairy spot, a firm spot, a soft spot. His nipples were small in that male kind of way, but that didn't mean there was anything less intimate about them. The more she looked, the more intimately she was moved.

In the end, though, it was his eyes, always his eyes that touched her most deeply. To say that his eyes stripped her naked was too physical a description. They delved far deeper, burrowing beneath her skin and touching hidden quarters that no man, *no* man had ever touched. With each look she felt his thoughts, and she knew that he wanted her.

So the sexual tension built. What had rippled in the morning was simmering by noon and smoldering three hours later. The air between them grew positively charged, but they could no more have left each other's sides than they could have denied that the charge existed.

Then, shortly before five, a low shadow materialized on the distant horizon.

"Land, ho!" Noah shouted from the bow, grateful to relieve his tension with the hearty yell.

Shaye was at his elbow. "Costa Rica?"

"It had better be," he said, "or we're in trouble."

She knew he wasn't referring to an accidental landing in another country. They needed a diversion, and they needed one fast.

"What happens now?" Victoria asked, joining them.

Noah and Shaye exchanged a quick, hot look. "Now," he said, "we try to find out exactly where we are."

Samson was already doing that, working with binoculars, a compass, and the charts and notes he'd made. "We're pretty much on target," he finally announced to his waiting audience. "Assuming that the cargo ships we've seen are heading for either Limón or Moin, all we need to do is to sail a little north. Once we're in closer, I'll know more."

It took a while, for the wind lessened the closer they got, but they gradually worked their way in the right direction. Shaye, who'd begun the trip with a minimum of enthusiasm for Costa Rica, couldn't deny the country's tropical beauty. Spectral mountains provided a distant backdrop for the lush jungle growth that grew more delineated as they neared the shore. The graceful fronds of tall palms arched over small stretches of sandy beach. Thicker mangroves and vines populated swampier sections.

They approached a small bay, and three pairs of eyes sought Samson's. But he shook his head. "The configuration is wrong."

"Perhaps it's changed with time?" Shaye asked.

"Not that much," was his answer. So they sailed on.

After a time they neared another sandy area. Low outcroppings of rock lay at either end, curving out to give a lagoon effect. "Could be," Samson said. "It's broad enough in the middle, flat enough from front to back.... Could be," he repeated, this time with enthusiasm. "I won't know for sure until can take a reading with the sextant, and it looks like the stars will be elusive for a while."

Those three pairs of eyes joined him in scanning the cloud cover that was fast moving in.

Recalling how sick she'd been on the second night of the trip, Victoria asked with a touch of horror, "Another storm?"

"Probably nothing more than rain," Noah guessed, then asked Samson, "Should we go in and drop anchor?"

"That's our best bet."

By the time the *Golden Echo* was anchored about two hundred yards from shore, night had fallen. The four gathered in the salon, with an air of great expectancy.

"This is frustrating," Victoria decided. "To be here and not really know whether we are, in fact, here...."

"Patience," Samson urged with a smile. "We'll know soon enough. We've made good time, and I've allowed five days to search for the treasure. That's far more than we should need once we reach the right lagoon. Even if this one isn't it, we can't be far."

Shaye's eyes met Noah's for a minute before slanting away.

Victoria's eyes were on Samson. "How does the Costa Rican government take to treasure hunts like ours?"

"I filed the proper papers and was granted a permit. The government has a right to half of anything we recover."

Victoria knew by this time that Samson had as little need of gold as she did. "What will you do with it?"

"The treasure? Of the half that's left, only a quarter will be mine." His gaze skipped meaningfully from one face to another.

"I don't want any treasure," Shaye said quickly. It had never occurred to her that she'd receive a thing, and picturing the rose-shaped rock, she felt vehement about it.

"Count me out, too," Noah said forcefully. He looked at Shaye, and his eyes grew smoky. *There are many different kinds of treasure....*

"I'm bequeathing my portion to you," Victoria informed Samson. "Lord only knows I pay enough in taxes now." She settled more comfortably onto the sofa. "What will you do with it?"

Samson gave a quick shrug. "Give it to charity—four times as much as I'd originally planned."

Victoria grinned. "I like that idea. What do you think, Shaye?"

Shaye's head popped up. She'd been studying her knotted hands, wishing that they could somehow take the tension from inside her and wring it away. "Excuse me?"

"Charity. Samson plans to give our treasure to charity."

"I like that idea."

Victoria laughed. "That was what I said."

"Oh."

"How about you, Noah?" Samson asked. "Any objections?"

Hearing his name, Noah tore his gaze from Shaye. "To you and Victoria splitting the treasure?"

Samson sighed. "To my giving the entire thing to charity."

"I like that idea," Noah said, then frowned when both Samson and Victoria laughed. He'd obviously missed something, but he didn't know what it was. He did know that he was the brunt of the joke. Then again, Shaye wasn't laughing.

Victoria took pity on him and turned to Samson with what she hoped was a suitably serious expression. "What's for dinner tonight?"

"Bologna sandwiches."

"Bologna sandwiches?"

"That's right."

Neither Noah nor Shaye showed the slightest reaction to his announcement. They were alternately looking at each other, looking at the floor, looking at Samson or Victoria for the sake of politeness. They saw little, heard even less.

"So you finally got tired of cooking," Victoria declared with relief. "You're human, after all."

Arching a brow her way, Samson grabbed her hand, pulled her from the sofa and made a beeline for the galley, muttering under his breath, "I could probably open a can of dog food and neither of them would notice."

He was right. Neither Noah nor Shaye commented on the artlessness of the menu, though both drank their share of the Chianti Samson decanted.

Shaye tried, really she did, to concentrate on the dinner conversation, but her thoughts and senses were too filled with Noah to allow space for much else.

Noah tried every bit as hard to interject a word here or there to suggest he was paying attention, but more often than not the word was inappropriate, several sentences too late or offered in a totally wrong inflection.

They roused a bit when it began to rain and everything had to be carried below deck in a rush, but the alternate arrangements had them sitting close together in the galley. Not only was sane thought all the harder, but the tension between them rose to a fevered pitch.

"Why don't we adjourn to the salon and finish the wine?" Samson suggested at last. "There's no reason why Chianti won't go with Ding-Dongs."

"You didn't bring Ding-Dongs," Victoria chided.

"I certainly did. Next to chocolate mousse, Ding-Dongs are my favorite dessert."

Neither Noah nor Shaye had a word to say about Ding-Dongs, but they came to when Samson and Victoria rose to leave. "I'll clean up," they offered in unison, then eyed each other.

Shaye said, "You go on into the salon with the others. I'll take care of this."

Noah said, "There isn't much. I don't mind. You go relax."

"I've been relaxing all day. I'd like to do something."

"And I feel guilty because my uncle has been the major cook. The least I can do is clean up."

"Noah, I'll do it." She started stacking dirty plates.

He had the four wineglasses gathered, a finger in each. "*I'll* do it."

"We wanted those glasses," Samson remarked.

Noah sent him a confused look. "I thought we were done."

"I had suggested that we finish the wine in the salon."

"Oh." He looked down at the glasses. "But they're mixed up now. I don't know whose is whose."

"Obviously," said Samson, whereupon Noah turned on Shaye.

"If you hadn't been so stubborn, this wouldn't have happened."

"Me, stubborn? You were the one who was being difficult."

"How can you say that someone offering to do the dirty work is being difficult?"

"*I* offered to do the dirty work *first*."

"Then *you* were the one who was difficult, when all I wanted was to relieve you of the chore."

"But I didn't *want* to be relieved—"

Victoria cut her off with a loud declaration. "We'll take clean glasses." She did just that and led Samson from the galley.

Shaye attacked the dishes with a vengeance.

"Take it easy on the water," Noah snapped. "There's no need to run more than you need."

"I need *some*, if you want the plates clean."

"Of course I want the plates clean, but you could be economical."

She thrust a dripping plate his way. "Dry this."

"You're very good at giving orders. Is that what you do all day at work?"

"At least I don't get any back talk there."

"I'm sure they wouldn't dare or you'd boot them out. I assume," he drawled, "that you have the power to hire or fire."

"In my department, I certainly do. Lawyers know nothing about computers or the people who use them."

He held up the plate he'd been drying and asked with cloying sweetness, "Is this shiny enough for Her Highness?"

She simply glared at him and handed him another, then started on the next with a double dose of elbow grease.

"You're gonna break that plate if you're not careful."

She ignored him. "And you're a fine one to talk. You're the head of your own company—a power trip if there ever was one. I'll bet *you* run a tight ship. A regular Captain Bligh."

"I have high standards, as well I should. My name's on top. I get the blame when someone flubs up."

"And the same isn't true for me? Don't you think the lawyers get on *my* back when documents come out screwed up?"

"What I want to know," he snarled, "is if they ever get you *on* your back."

The glass she'd been scrubbing came close to breaking against the sink. "You have the filthiest mind I've ever been exposed to!"

"And who's been fueling it? Little looks here, darting glances there. I'm not made of stone, for Christ's sake!"

She'd rinsed off the glass she'd nearly broken and was onto another. "Could've fooled me. Your eyes are as lecherous as your mind. You sit there making me squirm, and what do you expect me to do—whistle 'Dixie'?"

"You couldn't whistle if you tried. Your lips are too stiff."

"It's a lucky thing they are. Anything but a stiff lip around you would result in a physical attack."

"I have never physically attacked a woman in my life! But I'm beginning to wonder about you and that past you try so hard to hide. It comes out, y'know. I can see it in your eyes. You've had sex, and you've had it but good. What was it—with a married guy? Or a highly visible guy you're determined to protect?"

"You're out in left field, Noah." She thrust a handful of forks and knives at him, then, having run out of things to wash, went at the sink itself.

"I think it was with a married guy. You fell in love, gave him everything and only after the fact learned that he wasn't yours for the taking."

"Dream on." She began to wipe down the table with a fury.

"Either that, or you're totally repressed. Your parents instilled the fear of God in you and you're afraid to do a damn thing. But the urges are there. You live them vicariously through sexy rock ballads, but you don't have the guts to recognize what you need."

"And you know what that is, I suppose?"

"Damn right I do. You need a man and lots of good, old-fashioned loving. You may like to think of yourself as a prim and proper old maid, but I've seen your true colors. They're hot and vibrant and dripping with passion."

She turned to him, hands on her hips, nostrils flaring. "What I need is none of your business. I sure don't need *you*."

"You need a man who's forceful. I fight you, and I'd wager that's a hell of a lot more than any other man has ever done."

"Power trip, ego trip—they're one and the same with you, aren't they?" Throwing the damp rag into the sink, she whirled around and stalked out of the galley. A second later she was back, glowering at Noah while she reached for a clean wineglass.

Snatching up his own, he followed her. He filled it as soon as she'd set down the bottle, then took his place in the same chair he'd had before dinner.

"We were talking about pirates," Victoria said. She and Samson sat on the sofa, hard-pressed to ignore the foul moods the newcomers were in. "Samson's done a lot of reading. He says that many of the stereotypes are wrong."

"In what way?" Shaye demanded.

Noah grunted. "They were frustrated men, stuck on a boat without a willing woman to ease their aches."

"Not every man is fixated on his libido," she snapped, then turned to Samson. "Tell me about pirates."

"Pirates turn you on, huh?"

"Keep quiet, Noah. You were saying, Samson . . ."

"I was saying that when one begins to study the age of piracy, one learns some interesting things. For example, pirates rarely flew the skull and crossbones. They rarely made anyone walk the plank. They rarely marooned a man."

Noah snorted. "And when they did, they left him a pistol so that he could put an end to his misery. That's compassion for you."

"I'm not trying to idealize the buccaneer, simply to point out that he was more than a blood-thirsty ruffian with no respect for life. Pirates had their own kind of code."

"Nonpolitical anarchy," was Noah's wry retort.

"It worked for them," Samson said. "They chose their captains at will and could dismiss them as easily."

"Dismiss or execute?"

"Noah, let the man talk."

Noah slid lower in his chair. His brows formed a dark shelf over his eyes, but he said nothing.

"They did execute their captains on occasion," Samson conceded, "but only when those captains mistreated them. You have to understand that most of the men who crewed on pirate ships had known the brunt of poverty, or religious or political persecution at home. Fair treatment was one of the few benefits of piracy."

"But what about the gold they captured?" Shaye asked. "Didn't they benefit from that?"

Noah looked her in the eye. "They blew it on women in the first port they hit. I hope to hell the doxies were worth it."

"You'll never know, will you?" she asked sweetly.

He glared at her. She glared right back. Then he bolted from his chair and stormed toward the companionway.

"Where are you going?"

"Out."

"But it's raining!"

"Good!"

Shaye dragged her gaze back to the salon. She looked first at Victoria, then at Samson. "He's impossible!"

Samson contemplated that for a minute, then went on in his customary gentle voice, "The popular image is that pirates were irreligious plunderers who had a wonderful time for themselves, but it wasn't so. They were unhappy men. With each voyage, their hopes of returning home dimmed. It didn't matter that home wasn't wonderful. Home was familiar. It had to have been frustrating."

Shaye dropped her gaze to her hands. Victoria took up the slack and continued talking with Samson, but it wasn't until Noah reappeared that Shaye raised her eyes.

He was soaking wet and impatient. "Come on," he said, grabbing her hand.

"What—"

"We'll be back," he called over his shoulder as he led her toward the companionway.

"Hold on a minute." She tugged back on her hand. "I'm not going up there."

But he refused to let go, and he wasn't stopping. "You won't melt." He pushed the hatch open and had pulled her through before she could do anything about it.

9

THE RAIN was a warm, steady shower, drenching Shaye within seconds. "Noah, this is crazy!"

He loomed over her, the outline of his face glistening in the light of the lamp that hung at the stern. "We're going ashore."

"But it's pouring!"

Plowing his fingers into her hair, he took her mouth in a kiss that was as fevered as the tension had been earlier, as hungry as he'd felt all day, as wild as he'd ever been at his boldest moments. By the time he raised his head, Shaye was reeling.

"We're going ashore," he repeated hoarsely.

The night was dark and stormy, but that meager light from the stern clearly illuminated the intent on his face and the desire in his eyes. At that moment, she knew precisely what he had in mind. And she knew at that moment that she wouldn't refuse him. The flame within her was too hot to be denied. It blotted out everything but a basic, driving need.

"How?" she whispered shakily.

"The dingy." Snatching up a huge flashlight, he aimed it over the side of the boat, where the small rubber lifeboat he'd just inflated bobbed in the rain. Then he swung onto the rope ladder and started down. Midway, he waited for Shaye. When she was just above him, he lowered himself into the raft. As soon as she was safely settled, he began to row quickly toward shore.

With a trembling hand, Shaye tossed back her dripping hair. She didn't know whether what she was doing was right, but she knew that she had no choice. The darkness abetted her primal need; it erased reality, leaving only the urgency of the moment. Her entire body shook in anticipation of the intimacy she was about to share with Noah. Her eyes were locked on his large dark form throughout the brief trip, receiving an unbroken message that sizzled through the rainy night.

The dingy touched shore with a quivering bump. Noah jumped out seconds before Shaye, made a brief survey of the beach with the light, then dropped it and, in a single flowing movement, whipped the boat onto the sand and reached for her.

She was made for his arms, fitting them perfectly. Her hands went into his wet hair as her open mouth met his. Tension, hunger, fierceness—the combined effect was galvanic. His tongue plunged deeply. She nipped it, sucked it, played it wildly with her own.

With a groan, Noah set frenzied fingers to work tugging the soaked T-shirt from her body. But he was unwilling to release her mouth for an instant, so he abandoned it at her shoulders and dug his fingers under the waistband of her shorts. She helped him in the tugging, her lips passionate beneath his all the while. As soon as the soggy cotton passed her knees, she kicked free of the shorts and turned her efforts to Noah's. They'd barely hit the sand when he dropped his hands to her thighs and lifted her onto his waiting heat.

At the bold impaling, Shaye cried out.

"It's okay, baby," he soothed, panting. "It's okay."

She gasped his name and clung to his neck. "I feel so full..."

"You're hot and tight around me. Ahh, you feel good!" His fingers dug into her bottom, holding her bonded to him as he sank to his knees. "Have I hurt you?" he asked between nips at her mouth.

"No. Oh, no."

"I was afraid you'd change your mind, and I couldn't last another minute without being inside." His hands had risen to cover her breasts, stroking her through silk, then hastily releasing the front catch of her bra and seeking out her naked flesh.

Again she cried out. His fingers were everywhere, circling her, kneading her, daubing her nipples with raindrops. She was in a lagoon. She couldn't see the lagoon or the jungle, but she knew it was paradise, she just knew it, and with less thought than Eve she gave in to temptation.

Her hands began a greedy exploration under his shirt, over his waist, across his buttocks, up and down his thighs. He wasn't moving inside her, but she could feel every inch of him against her moist sheath, and the solid stimulation was breathtaking. Whispering his name, she tried to move her hips. But he followed the movement with his own, preventing even the slightest withdrawal.

"You're mine now," he said with the tightness of self-restraint. "We'll take it slow."

She raked her teeth against his jaw. "I want to feel you move."

"Soon, baby. Soon."

His mouth plundered hers. His thumbs began a slow, sliding rotation of her nipples. Live currents snapped and sizzled so hotly inside her that she almost feared she'd be electrocuted in the rain. Noah was grounding her, she told herself, yet still she burned. She caught at his hair and kissed him more deeply. She drew her nails across his shoulders, then dug them in and tried to move again, but he wouldn't have it.

"Noah . . ."

He worked her T-shirt over her head and pushed the bra straps from her shoulders, leaving her naked in the night but hot, so hot against him. "Soon," he murmured thickly.

"Soon." The last was breathed against her breast moments before he sucked her in.

For a minute all she could do was hold his head. Her own was thrown back, her eyes were closed, and the rain was as gentle, as persistent and seductive as his ever-moving tongue. With the visual deprivation imposed by the night, her senses grew that much sharper. She felt everything he did with vivid clarity, and the knot of need inside her grew tighter.

Shaye wondered where he got his self-control and vowed to break it. While her mouth grew more seductive, her hands taunted his chest. Short, wet hairs slid between her marauding fingers and his nipples grew hard. She undulated her middle, then, when he clutched her there to hold her still, her hips. She felt him quiver insider her, and, encouraged, repeated the motion.

But through it all there was something more. Instead of simply snapping his control, she wanted to give him a pleasure so hot and intense that he'd be branded every bit as deeply as she was. Bent on that, she reached low and stroked that part of him that hung so heavily between his thighs.

The bold caress was his undoing. Making a low, guttural sound, he tumbled her down to the sand. Bowing his back, he withdrew, then thrust upward with a force that thrilled her. She'd been right to want movement, for the friction, the sliding pressure was exquisite. But Noah had been right, too, for the wait had enhanced both her desire and appreciation.

He set a masterful rhythm that varied with their needs. Faster or slower, she met him and matched him, each arching stroke stretching the heavenly torment into an ever-tautening fine wire.

The tension snapped with a final, agonizingly deep thrust. Implosion and explosion, simultaneous and mind shattering, sent blind cries slicing through the beat of the rain. Soft gasps followed, an occasional whimper from Shaye, a moan from Noah. They clung tightly to each other until they were totally limp, and then the rain began to soothe their bodies, cleansing, cooling and replenishing.

When Noah had regained a modicum of strength, he maneuvered them both into the kneeling position from which they'd fallen. He wasn't ready to leave Shaye, and given the renewed strength of her hold, he suspected he'd have been unable to if he tried. It was gratifying, the perfect denouement to what had been a heartrending experience.

He spread his hands over her bare back, able to savor now the delight of her shape as he hadn't had the patience to do earlier. "I knew it would be like that," he murmured. "We're like tinder, Shaye. All it takes is a single match and we go up." He gave a throaty laugh. "I'm still up."

She could feel that. Oh, she could feel it, and she was astonished to find that corresponding parts of her were similarly alert. "You're a powerful lover," she whispered. It was an understatement, but she didn't think the words existed to adequately describe what she'd felt.

"I could say the same about you," he whispered back. He was thinking that he didn't care how many other lovers she'd had or who had first awakened her to the fiery art of passion, but he didn't say so. It wasn't that he didn't want to know, because that jealous male part of him did, but he didn't want to disturb the precious peace that existed between them. So he asked, "Do you mind the rain?"

"No. There's something erotic about it."

"There's something erotic about this whole setting. I wish to hell I could see it."

Resting her cheek on his shoulder, she chuckled. She knew what he meant. But then, she needed the darkness. She didn't want to see herself, and she didn't want Noah to see her. There was still the matter of the small mark on her breast; she had no idea how she would explain it, whether she wanted to, what the ramifications would be. Too much thought at too sensitive at time . . . she was still into feeling, rather than thinking.

"Take off your shirt," she whispered, then slid her hands to his waist to hold their bodies together while he complied. When he was as naked as she, she wrapped her arms around his neck, bringing her breasts into contact with his chest for the very first time.

The feeling was heavenly. She moved gently against him. He sucked in a shaky breath, and when she felt him swell inside her, her muscles automatically tightened.

"Ohh, baby . . ."

"You can feel that?" She smiled when his groan clearly indicated that he could, but then he was kissing her smile away and touching her in ways that reduced her to quivering jelly. She sighed when he released her mouth, only to gasp when he slid a hand between their bodies and began an ultrasensitive stroking. It wasn't long before she reached a second fierce climax.

She was panting against his shoulder, her hands grasping his chest, thumbs on his nipples, when he went tense, uttered a strangled cry and pushed more deeply into her. She felt the spasms that shook him, felt his warmth flowing into her and knew an incredible joy.

"Ahh, Shaye," he whispered when he could finally speak, "you're amazing."

She basked in the glow of his words. She'd heard similar ones before, but never spoken with quite the same awe, and that meant the world to her. Pressing her face to his neck, she nestled into his arms. It was apparently the right thing to do, for he held her closely and seemed as satisfied as she with the silence.

At length, though, it occurred to her that a rainy Eden had its drawbacks. She wanted a bed. She wanted to lie down beside Noah in the darkness, to breathe in his undiluted scent, to hear the unaccompanied beat of his heart. She wanted to rest in his arms, just rest. She was suddenly very tired.

"I think we'd better go back," he murmured into her hair.

She wondered if he'd read her mind. His voice sounded as tired as she felt. More than that, it contained a note of sadness that she understood; no matter how they looked at it, there wasn't a bed for them to share.

She let him help her to her feet and together they retrieved their clothing. As though afraid of breaking the spell further, Noah didn't turn on the flashlight. He set the dingy in the water, helped Shaye inside, then climbed in and more slowly rowed back to the *Golden Echo*. As had been the case during the trip to shore, her eyes held him the entire way back. This time, though, rather than the heat of desire, she felt something even deeper and more tender. Shaye wasn't about to put a name to it any more than she was ready to face what it entailed. She simply wanted it to go on and on.

After securing the dingy to the stern of the sloop, they climbed back on deck. Holding Shaye's hand firmly in his, Noah cast a despairing glance at the rain that continued to pour. Then he guided her down the companionway and closed the hatch.

"Want to change into dry things and sit in the salon for a little while?" he asked softly.

She nodded, but still she didn't move. Their fingers were interlaced; she tightened hers. She feared that even the briefest parting would allow for an unwelcome intrusion.

Noah raised her hand and gently kissed each of her fingers, then lowered his head and gently kissed her mouth. "Go," he whispered against her lips. "I'll be waiting for you."

Determined to change as quickly as possible, she whirled around and promptly stumbled. She'd have fallen to the floor had not Noah caught her. While he held her to his side, he frowned at the cause of her near-accident. A large bundle and one about half its size were stacked in the passageway by the aft cabin.

"My duffel bags?" he asked softly. His confused gaze shifted to Shaye before returning to the bundles. "Packed?" He stared at them a minute longer, then, with dawning awareness, broke into a lopsided grin. "I'll be damned. . . ."

Shaye left his side long enough to check out the forward cabin. It was empty. "They must both be in your cabin," she whispered, draping an arm around his neck in delight.

"Looks that way."

"But . . . how did they know?"

"Maybe they had the dingy bugged."

"Impossible."

"Then they're simply very wise people."

"Or very selfish."

"Hell, they deserve pleasure, too. On the other hand, maybe they meant this as punishment for the way I behaved earlier."

"You could be right."

He scowled. "That's not what you were supposed to say."

Her eyes turned innocent, while her heart positively brimmed. "What was I supposed to say?"

"That I was only being ornery out of frustration." His whisper grew softer. "Are you going to make me sleep on the couch?"

She gave a quick shake of her head.

"I can share your bed?"

She nodded as quickly.

"Because you feel sorry for me?"

"Because I want you with me."

His smile was so warm then, so filled with satisfaction that she knew a hundred-fold return on her honesty. He didn't make a smug comment on her primness, or lack thereof. He didn't accuse her of being wanton. He just smiled, and another bit of the retaining wall surrounding her defenses fell away.

Without a word, he scooped up his bags and followed her to the forward cabin. Once side, he dropped his things and took her in his arms. He didn't kiss her. He didn't caress her. He simply held her.

"Shall I light the lamp?" he asked quietly.

"No."

"I'd like to get out of these wet things."

"Me, too."

"Got a towel?"

She nodded, and when he released her, went to get it. He'd shed his shorts and shirt by the time she returned with the towel, and by the time she'd wrestled her way out of her own things, he was ready to dry her. There was nothing seductive in his touch; it was infinitely gentle and made her feel more special than she'd ever felt before. The feeling remained when they curled next to each other in bed, and it was so strong and gave her such confidence that she probably would have answered any question he'd asked just then.

He only asked one thing. "Comfortable?"

"Mmm."

He was quiet for a time before he spoke. "There is such pleasure in this. Just lying here. Close."

"I know," she whispered and softly kissed his chest.

"I just want to hold you."

"Me, too."

"I want you with me when I wake up."

"I will be."

"You can kick me if I snore."

She yawned. "Okay."

"If Samson wakes us at five to go digging for his damned treasure, I'll wring his neck."

"I'll help you."

"On the other hand," he added, his voice beginning to slur, "maybe they'll sleep late themselves."

"Or maybe they'll take pity on us."

"Fat chance . . ."

"Mmm . . ."

ALL THINGS WERE relative. The knock on the door didn't come until eight the next morning, but Shaye and Noah weren't ready for it even then. They'd been awake on and off during the night and were dragged out of a sound sleep by Samson's subsequent shout.

"We've been waiting for two hours! Can you give us an ETA?"

"That's Expected Time of Arising," Victoria called.

After bolting upright in alarm, Noah collapsed, burying his face in Shaye's hair. "Make them go away," he whispered.

"Noon!" she shouted to the two beyond the door.

"Noon?" Victoria echoed. "That's obscene!"

Samson agreed. "If you think we're going to wait until noon to go ashore, think again!"

"Go ashore," Shaye suggested, tugging the sheet higher. "I'll just sleep a little longer."

"But I need Noah's help," Samson argued.

"He's on shore. I left him there last night."

"What do you mean, you left him there?"

"He was behaving like a jackass." She twisted over Noah to muffle his snicker. "What choice did I have? And it's a good thing I did leave him there. Exactly where did you expect him to sleep?"

There was silence on the other side of the door, so she went on. "That was a fine stunt you two pulled—behaving like a pair of oversexed teenagers." Noah nuzzled her collarbone.

She slid to her side again and wrapped her arms around his neck. "What kind of an example is that to set? I have to say that I was a little shocked—"

Her words were cut off by the abrupt opening of the door. Victoria stood with one hand on the knob, the other on her hip. Samson was close behind her. Their eyes went from Shaye to the outline of bodies beneath the sheet.

"I am assuming," Victoria said drolly, "that Noah is hidden somewhere under that mane of hair. Either that, or you've grown an extra body, a pair of very long legs and a dark beard."

"Tell her to go away," came Noah's muffled voice.

"Go away," Shaye said.

"ETA?" Samson prodded.

"Noon."

Victoria made a face. "Nine."

"Eleven."

"Ten," said Samson. "Ten, and not a minute later." He raised his voice. "Do you hear me, Noah?"

Noah groaned. "I hear."

"Good. Ten o'clock. Topside." His hand covered Victoria's as he pulled the door shut.

Closing her eyes, Shaye slid lower to lay her head on Noah's chest. He wrapped an arm around her back and murmured, "I'd like to stay here all day."

"Mmm."

"Sleep well?"

"Mmm."

"Shaye?" He began to toy with her hair.

"Mmm?"

"That little mark on your breast. What is it?"

Her eyes came open and for several seconds she barely breathed. "Nothing," she said at last.

"It isn't nothing. It looks like a tattoo."

She was silent.

"Let me see."

She held him tighter.

"Shaye, let me see." Taking her shoulders, he set her to the side. His eyes didn't immediately lower, though, but held hers. "You didn't really hope to hide it forever, did you?" he asked gently. "I've touched and tasted every part of you. There's pleasure to be had from looking, too."

She bit her lip, but she knew that she wouldn't deny him. If he'd sounded smug or lecherous, she'd have been able to put up a fight. But against gentleness she was helpless.

Very carefully he eased the sheet away. He sat up and pushed it lower, then leaned back on his elbow while his eyes began at her toes and worked their way upward. His hand followed, skimming her calves and her thighs, brushing lightly over auburn curls before tracing her hip bones and belly to her waist.

His hand was growing less steady. He swallowed once and took a deep breath. "Your body is lovely," he whispered as his eyes crept higher. He touched her ribs, then slowly, slowly outlined her breasts.

She'd been lying on her left side. Gently rolling her to her back, he brought a single forefinger to touch the small mark that lay just above her pounding heart.

"A rose," he breathed. It was less than half the size of his smallest fingernail, delicately etched in black and red. His gaze was riveted to it. "When did you get it?"

"A lifetime ago," she whispered brokenly.

"Why?"

"It . . . I . . . on a whim. A stupid whim."

"You don't like it?"

She shook her head, close to tears. "But I can't make it go away."

Lowering his head, he kissed it lightly, then dabbed it with the tip of his tongue. "It's you," he whispered.

"No!"

"Yes. Something hidden. A secret side."

She was clenching her fists. "Please cover it up," she begged.

He did, but with his mouth rather than with the sheet, and at the same time he covered the rest of her body with his. "You are beautiful, tattoo and all. You make me burn." Holding the brunt of his weight on his forearms, he moved sensuously over her.

Shaye, too, burned. She'd lost track of the number of times they'd made love during the night, but still she wanted him. There was something about the way she felt when he made love to her—a sense of richness and completion. When he possessed her, she felt whole. When she was with him, she felt alive.

It didn't make sense that she should feel that way, when what she'd found with Noah was a moment out of time, when he was everything she'd sworn she didn't want, when he was everything she feared. But it wasn't the time to try to make sense of things. Not with his lips closing over hers and his hand caressing her breast. Not with their legs tangling and their stomachs rubbing. Not with his sex growing larger by the minute against her thigh.

Raising her knees to better cradle him, she responded ardently to his kisses. She loved the firmness of his lips and their mobility, just as she loved the feel of his skin beneath her fingers. His back was a broad mass of ropy muscles, his hips more narrow and smooth. The heat his body exuded generated an answering heat. His natural male scent was enhanced by that of passion.

Slowly and carefully, he entered her. When their bodies were fully joined, his back arched, his weight on his palms, he looked down at her and searched her eyes. "I want to see this, too," he said hoarsely. His breathing was unsteady. The muscles of his arms trembled. He was working so hard to rein in the same desires that buzzed through her, and he was doing so much better a job of it than she, that she broke into a sheepish smile.

Carefully he brought her up onto his lap, then, hugging her to him, inched his way backward until he'd reached the edge of the bed. When he slid off to kneel on the floor, she tightened the twist of her ankles at the small of his back. Not once was the penetration broken.

Shaye couldn't believe what happened then. Where another man would have simply begun to move while he watched, Noah cupped her face and kissed her deeply. He worshipped her mouth, her cheeks, her chin. He plumped up her breasts with his hands and devoured them as adoringly. And only when she was thinking she'd die from the searing bliss did he lower his gaze. Hers followed.

He withdrew and slowly reentered. A long, low moan slipped from his throat. His head fell back, eyes momentarily closed against the enormity of sensation.

Needing grounding of her own, Shaye looped her arms around his neck and dropped her forehead to his shoulder. She was panting softly. Her insides were on fire. She was stunned by the depth of emotion she felt, the profoundness of what they were doing, the overwhelming sense of rightness.

His cheek came down next to hers. He pulled back his hips, slowly pushed forward, pulled back, pushed forward. Every movement was controlled and deeply, deeply arousing.

When Shaye began to fear that she'd reach her limit before him, she unlocked her ankles and moved her thighs against his hips. Unable to resist, Noah ran his palms the length of her legs. The feel of the smooth, firm silk was too much. He made a low, throaty sound and within seconds surged into a throbbing climax. Only then did she allow herself the same release.

He whispered her name over and over until their bodies had begun to quieten. Then he framed her face with his hands and tipped it up. "I love you, Shaye." He sealed the vow with a long, sweet kiss, and when he held her back again, there were tears in her eyes. "There are more secrets. I know that. But I do love you. Secrets and all. I don't care where you've been or what you've done. I love you."

She didn't return the words, but held him in tight, trembling arms. *Do I love him? Can I love him? Will I be asking for trouble if I love him? I can't control him. I can't control myself when I'm with him. If love is forever, can it possibly work?*

THE ACTIVITY that followed offered Shaye a welcome escape from her thoughts. She and Noah dressed, ate a fast breakfast, then joined Victoria and Samson on deck. Though the rain had stopped, the sky remained heavily overcast. Ever the optimist, Samson said it was for the best, that without the sun, they'd be cooler.

Shaye wondered about that. It was hot and sticky anyway. One glance at Noah told her he felt the same, and she noted that Samson had even passed up his pirate outfit in favor of more practical shorts and T-shirt. He wore his tricorne, though. She couldn't begrudge him that.

Since there had, as yet, been no stars by which to measure their position, Samson was left with making a sight judgment. Having carefully studied the small bay from the deck of the sloop, he'd already decided that it compared favorably with the one on his map. When he questioned Noah and Shaye about what they'd seen when they'd been ashore the night before, they looked at each other sheepishly. He didn't pursue the issue.

Loading the dingy with shovels and a pick, they left the *Golden Echo* securely anchored and rowed to shore. As soon as they'd safely beached the raft, Samson pulled out his map.

"Okay, let's look for the rose."

Shaye winced. Noah sent her a wink that made her feel a little better. Then he, too, turned his attention to the map. "According to this, the rock should be near the center of the back of the lagoon and not too far from shore."

Samson nodded distractedly. His gaze alternated between the map and the beach before them. "That's what the map suggests, though I dare say it wasn't drawn to scale." He refolded and pocketed the fragile paper. "Let's take a look."

The spot where they were headed was a short distance along the beach. After allowing Samson and Victoria a comfortable lead, Noah took Shaye's hand and they set off.

"Excited?" he asked.

"Certainly."

He cast her a sidelong glance. "Is that a little dryness I detect in your tone?"

"Me? Dryness?"

"Mmm. Do you believe we'll find a treasure?"

"Of course we'll find a treasure," she said. Her eyes were on Samson's figure striding confidently ahead.

"Forget about my uncle. What do *you* think?"

"Honestly?" She paused. "I doubt it."

"Are you in a betting mood?"

"You think there is a treasure?"

"Honestly? I doubt it."

"Then why bet?"

"'Cause it's fun. You say no. I say yes. Whoever wins . . . whoever wins . . ."

She was smiling. "Go on. I want to know. What will you bet?"

"How about a pair of Mets tickets?"

"Boo-hiss."

"How about a weekend in the country?"

"Not bad." She pursed her lips. "What country?"

He chuckled. She'd deftly ruled out his place in Vermont. "Say Canada—the Gaspé Peninsula?"

"Getting warm."

"England—Cornwall?"

"Getting warmer."

"France?"

"A small château in Normandy?" At his nod, she grinned. "You're on."

He studied her upturned face. "You look happy. Feeling that confident you'll win?"

"No. But win or lose I get to visit Normandy."

He threw back his head with an exaggerated, "Ahh," and made no mention of the fact that according to the terms of the bet, win or lose, she'd be visiting Normandy with *him*. For a weekend? No way. It'd be a full week or two if he had his say.

Draping an arm around her shoulder, he held her to his side. Their hips bumped as they walked. She suspected he was purposely doing it and, in the spirit of fun, she bumped him right back. They were nearly into an all-out-kick-and-dodge match when Samson's applause cut into their play.

"Bravo! Nice footwork there, Shaye. Noah, your legs are too long. Better quit while you're ahead." Turning his back on them, he propped his hands on his hips and studied the shoreline. "This is our starting point."

"Quit while I'm ahead," Noah muttered under his breath as he looked around. There wasn't a rock in sight. He lowered his head toward Shaye's. "Seaweed, driftwood, sand and palm trees. That's it."

"Ahh, but beyond the palm trees—"

"More palm trees."

"And a wealth of other trees and shrubs—"

"And monkeys and parrots and alligators—"

"Alligators! Are you kidding?"

"Would I kid you about something like that?"

"Victoria," Shaye cried plaintively, "you didn't tell me there'd be alligators!"

"No problem, sweetheart," Victoria said breezily. "Just watch where you step."

Samson started toward the palms and gestured for them to follow. Within ten minutes it was clear that they were going to have to broaden the search. They'd seen quite a few rocks among the foliage, but nothing of significant size and nothing remotely resembling a rose.

"Let's fan out. Shaye, you and Noah head south. Victoria and I will head north. Don't go farther inland then we are now, and head back out to the beach in, say—" he checked his watch "—half an hour. Okay?"

"Okay," Shaye and Noah answered together. They stood watching as Samson and Victoria started off.

Noah raked damp spikes of hair from his forehead. "Man, it's warm in here."

"Do you want to take off your shirt?"

"And get bitten alive?" He swatted something by his ear. "Was there any insect repellent in the dingy?"

"I think Samson had some in his pocket."

"Lots of good it'll do us there," he grumbled, then did an about-face to study the area Samson had assigned them. "Wish we had a machete."

"It's not that dense." She took a quick breath. "Noah, wouldn't alligators prefer a wetter area?"

"There are marshes just a little bit inland." He was studying the jungle growth. "I think if we work back and forth diagonally we'll be able to cover the most space in the least time."

"Is it alligators that bite, or crocodiles?"

"Crocs, I think." He rubbed his hands together, clearly working up enthusiasm. "Okay. L-l-l-l-l-let's hit it!"

Shaye stayed slightly behind Noah on the assumption that he'd scare away anything crawling in their path. She kept a lookout on either side, more than once catching herself when her eyes skimmed right past a rock formation simply because it didn't have a scaly back, a long tail, four squat legs and an ominous snout.

They followed a zigzag pattern, working slowly from jungle to shore and back. Soon after the third shore turn, they stopped short.

"It is a large rock," Shaye said cautiously.

"Would you go so far as to call it a boulder?"

"Depends how you define boulder. But it does have odd markings. Do you think it resembles a rose?"

Noah tipped his head and, squinted. "With a stretch of the imagination."

"Mmm. Let's look around a little more."

They completed that zig and the next zag and found a number of rocks that could, by that same stretch of the imagination, be said to resemble a rose. None were as large, though, and none stood alone as the first had.

"That has to be it," Noah decided.

Against her better judgment, Shaye felt a glimmer of excitement. "Let's tell the others." They started back. When they cleared the palms, they saw Samson and Victoria heading their way.

"We found it!" Shaye cried.

Victoria stopped short. "*We* found it!"

"Oh boy," Noah murmured.

Samson beamed. It looked as though they had a double puzzle on their hands, which was going to make the adventure that much more exciting.

10

THE FOUR TREKKED from one rock to the other. "Either could be it," Victoria decided.

"Or neither," said Shaye.

Noah mopped his face on the sleeve of his T-shirt. "If you ask me, there are half a dozen other rocks here that could fit the bill." He received three dirty looks so quickly that he held up a hand. "Okay. Okay. I'll admit that these two are more distinctive than the others." He frowned at the rock. "What do you think, Samson—could the markings be man-made?"

"They could be, but I don't think they are. Even allowing for lousy artistry and the effects of time, something man-made would be more exact. These are just irregular enough to look authentic."

"Which leaves the major problem of choosing between the two rocks," Shaye reminded them. "Does the map give any clue?"

Samson removed the map from his shirt pocket and extended it to her. She unfolded it and studied it. Victoria peered in from her right side, Noah hung over her left shoulder.

After a short time, Shaye and Victoria looked at each other in dismay. "You were right before," Victoria told Noah. "According to the map, the rose is smack in the middle of the back stretch of beach. But there wasn't any rose-shaped rock there. It has to be one of these two."

"But which one?" Shaye asked.

"Which looks more like a rose?"

"I don't know, so we're back to square one."

Victoria held up a finger. "I want to look at the other rock." Grabbing Shaye's arm, she propelled her through the jungle to the second rock.

Samson and Noah didn't move. They waited until the women returned, then Noah asked, "Okay, ladies, which rock will it be?"

"This one—"

"That one—"

He dug into his shorts pocket. "I'll flip a coin."

"You can't flip a coin on something as crucial," Victoria cried.

Shaye agreed.

"I don't have a coin anyway," Noah said and turned to Samson. "Got a coin?"

Samson produced a jackknife. "We'll let it fall. The slant of the handle will determine which rock we go with."

"A jackknife—"

"Is worse than a coin!"

The women were overruled. Samson flipped the knife. They went with the southern rock, the one Shaye and Noah had found and, coincidentally, the one Shaye thought looked more like a rose.

Putting defeat behind her, Victoria read off instructions from the map. "Seventeen paces due west."

"How long is a 'pace'?" Shaye asked.

"An average stride. Noah, you walk it off."

"Noah's stride can't be average. Samson, you walk it off."

"Samson is nearly as tall as Noah," Victoria pointed out. "Shaye you do it. Just stretch your stride a little."

With the others supervising, Shaye accepted and consulted the compass, marked off fifteen paces due west, then stopped.

"You need two more," Noah said.

"Two more paces will take me into the middle of that bromeliad colony. What do the instructions say from there, Victoria?"

"Twenty paces due south."

"Twenty paces due south," Shaye murmured, making estimates as she positioned herself on the south side of the bromeliads. "Say we're two paces south now. Three... four...five..."

Her progress was broken from time to time by another bit of the forest that was impenetrable, but she finally managed to reach twenty. Victoria, Samson and Noah were by her side.

"What now?" she asked.

"Southeast twenty-one paces," Victoria read.

"This is really pretty inexact—"

"Twenty-one paces," Noah coaxed. "Walk 'em off."

Compass in hand, she started walking. Victoria counted, while Samson followed the progress with an indulgent smile on his face. In the same manner they worked their way through additional twists and turns.

"What next?" Shaye finally asked.

"Nothing," Victoria said. "That's it. A big X on the map. You're standing on the treasure."

Shaye looked at the hard-packed sand beneath her feet. "It could be here, or here." She pointed three feet to the right. "Or even over there. Now, if we had some kind of metal detector, we might be in business."

"No metal detector," Samson said. "That would be cheating."

"But treasure hunters always use metal detectors," Shaye argued.

"We don't have one," Noah said in a tone that settled the matter. If there was no metal detector, there was no metal detector.

Shaye pointed straight down and raised skeptical eyes to Noah, who gave a firm nod.

A quick trip to the dingy produced the digging equipment and a knapsack that Victoria had filled with sandwiches and cans of soda earlier that morning. The soda had gone a little warm, but none of them complained. It was thirst quenching. The sandwiches were energizing. The insect repellent was better late than never.

They started digging in pairs, trading off every few minutes. There were diversions—a trio of spider monkeys swinging through the nearby trees, the chatter of a distant parrot—and the occasional reward of a quick swim in the bay. But by three in the afternoon, they had a large, deep hole and no treasure.

They'd initially dug down three feet, then another, then had widened the hole until it was nearly five feet in diameter. Now Noah stood at its center with his arms propped on the shovel handle. He looked hot and tired.

Shaye, who'd stopped digging several minutes before, sat on the edge of the hole. Victoria was beside her, and Samson stood behind them with a pensive look on his face.

"How much deeper do we go before we give up?" Shaye asked softly. She felt every bit as hot and tired as Noah looked.

"It has to be here," Victoria said. "Maybe we marked it out wrong."

"It *doesn't* have to be here," Shaye reminded her. "We knew there was the possibility the map was a sham."

Noah leaned against their side of the pit. He pushed his hair back with his forearm, smudging grime with the sweat. "I've dug the pick in another foot and hit nothing. I doubt a pirate would have buried anything deeper than this."

"If only we knew what we were looking for," Victoria mused. "Large box, small box, tiny leather pouch . . ."

Shaye sighed. "It's like trying to find a needle in a haystack, and you don't even know which haystack to look in."

"The other rock," said Noah. "It has to be that. We picked the wrong one to start pacing from." He hoisted himself from the hole. "Y'know, whoever drew up this map was either a jokester, a romantic or an imbecile."

Shaye was right beside him, followed by Victoria and Samson, as he strode quickly toward the other rock. "What do you mean?"

"The directions. They were given in paces west, south, southeast, etc., when we would have reached the same spot by one set of paces heading due south. When I first saw the map, I assumed there were natural barriers to go around, but we didn't find any." He'd reached the second rock and was studying the map. Then he closed his eyes and made some mathematical calculations.

"How many paces due south?" Samson asked.

"Let's try sixty-five."

He stood back while Shaye marked sixty-five paces due south. When she finished counting, she was standing directly before the first rock. She looked up at the others.

Victoria was the only one who seemed to share her surprise. "Let's walk it off the original way," she suggested.

So Shaye went back, walked through the directions again, and wound up in the same spot, directly before the second rock. "He was a jokester," she decided in dismay.

Samson scratched the back of his head. "He has made things interesting."

"Interesting?" Victoria echoed, then grinned. "Mmm, I suppose he's done that." She shifted her gaze from Samson to Noah, who was striding off. "Where are you going?"

"To get the shovels."

"We're not going to do this now, are we?"

"Why not?"

Shaye ran after him, looping her elbow through his when she caught up. "Isn't it a little late in the day to start something new?"

"It's only four."

"But we've been digging all day."

"All afternoon," he corrected.

"The treasure's not going anywhere."

His eyes twinkled. "I'm curious to see if it's there."

"But wouldn't it be smarter to start again fresh tomorrow morning?"

Having arrived back at the first hole, he scooped up the pick and shovels. Then he leaned in close to Shaye and whispered, "But if we finish this up tonight, we can do whatever we want tomorrow."

She took in a shaky breath and whispered back, "But aren't you tired?"

"Are you?"

"Yes. And it looks like it might rain any minute."

"Then we'll have to work quickly," he said with a mischievous grin and started back toward the rock.

As it happened, Noah did most of the work. Shaye made a show of assisting, silently reasoning that she was young and strong. But the digging she'd done earlier had taken its toll. She was tired. She had blisters. To make matters worse, the hole was only three feet deep and wide when it started to drizzle.

"Leave it," Shaye urged.

Samson agreed. "She's right, Noah. We can finish in the morning."

"No way," he grunted, setting to work with greater determination. "Another eighteen inches either way." He hoisted a shovelful of wet sand and tossed it aside with another grunt. "That's all we need."

"We can do it tomorrow—"

"And have the rain wash the sand—" another toss, another grunt "—back into this hole during the night? Just a little more now—give me forty-five minutes." Another shovelful hit the pile. "If I haven't struck anything by then, I'll quit."

The rain grew heavier. When Shaye eased into the hole and started to shovel again, Noah set her bodily back up on the edge. Likewise, when Samson tried to give a hand, Noah insisted that he could work more freely on his own.

They were all soaked, but no one complained. The rain offered relief from the heat. Unfortunately, though, it made Noah's work harder. Each shovelful of sand was wetter and heavier than the one before, and, if anything, he seemed bent on making this hole bigger than the last. He was obviously tiring. And neither the shovel nor the pick, which he periodically used, were turning up anything remotely resembling hidden treasure.

Then it happened. Shaye was watching Noah work under the edge of the large rock, wondering what would happen if the rain lessened the stability of the sand, when suddenly that side of the hole began to crumble.

"Noah!" she cried, but the rock was already sliding. Through eyes wide with horror, she saw Noah twist to the side and try to scramble away without success. He gave a deep cry of pain as the lower half of his right leg was pinned beneath the rock. In a second, Shaye had shimmied down into the narrow space left and was pushing against the rock, as were Samson and Victoria from above.

It wouldn't budge.

"Oh God," Shaye whispered. She took a quick look at Noah's ashen face and pushed harder, but the rock had sunk snugly in the hole with precious little space for maneuvering.

Samson, too, was pale, but he kept calm. "Let me take your place, Shaye. You and Victoria scoot up against the side, put your feet flat against the rock and push as hard as you can when I say so."

They hurried into position. He gave the word. They pushed. Nothing happened.

"Again," he ordered. "Now!"

Nothing happened that time or, when they'd slightly altered position, the next. Even Noah tried then, though he wasn't at the best angle—or in the best condition—to help. Despite the varied attempts they made, the rock didn't move.

Samson shook his head. "We can't get leverage. If we could only raise it the tiniest bit, even for a few seconds, you could pull free. A broom handle would snap. We could try a palm—"

Noah gave a rough shake of his head and muttered, "Too thick."

"Not at the top, but it's too weak there. We need metal."

"We don't have metal," Noah said tightly. The lower part of his leg was numb, but pain was shooting through his thigh. In an attempt to ease the pressure, he turned and sank sideways on the sand.

Shaye's heart was pounding. She couldn't take her eyes off him. "There has to be something on the *Golden Echo* we can use," she said frantically, then tacked on an even more frantic, "isn't there?"

Noah groped for her hand, but it was Samson to whom he spoke. "There's nothing on the boat. You'll have to go for help."

Samson had reached the same conclusion and was already on his feet and motioning for Victoria. "We'll make a quick trip to the boat for supplies. You'll stay here, Shaye?"

"Yes!"

With a nod, he was gone.

Shaye turned back to Noah. He was resting his head against the side of the hole. She combed the wet hair from his forehead. "How do you feel?"

He was breathing heavily. "Not great."

"Think it's broken?"

"Yup."

"I should have seen it coming. I should have been able to warn you."

"My fault. I was careless. Too tired." The word broke into a gasp. "I usually do better—"

She put a finger to his lips. "Shh. Save your strength."

He grabbed her hand. "Stay close."

She slid into the narrow space facing him and tucked his hand beneath her chin. For a long time neither of them spoke. The rain continued to fall. Noah closed his eyes against the pain that he could feel more clearly now below his knee.

Shaye alternately watched him and the shore. "Where are they?" she demanded finally in a tight, panicky whisper.

Noah didn't answer. It was fast getting dark. The rain continued to fall.

Samson and Victoria returned at last with a replenished knapsack, rain ponchos and two lanterns. Then Samson knelt with a hand on Noah's shoulder. "We'll be back as soon as we can. There are painkillers in the sack. Don't be a hero, and whatever you do, don't try to tug that leg free now or you'll make the damage worse."

Noah, who'd already figured that out, simply nodded.

"Hurry," Shaye whispered, hugging both Victoria and Samson before they left. "Hurry." Moments later, she watched them push off in the dingy, then she sank down beside Noah and put her hand to his cheek. "Can I get you anything?"

He shook his head.

"Food?"

Again he shook his head.

"Drink?"

"Later."

She didn't bother to ask if he wanted the poncho. She knew that he wouldn't. In spite of the rain, the night was warm. It did occur to her, though, that they'd feel more comfortable if they were leaning against rubber rather than grit. Popping up, she spread the ponchos over the side of the hole. Noah shifted and helped, then sank back against them with his head tipped up to the rain. Very gently, she washed the lingering grime from his face with her fingers, then slid back to his side and watched him silently.

His facial muscles twitched, then rested. His brow furrowed, then relaxed. Then he swore under his breath.

"The leg?"

"God, it hurts."

"Damn the rose. I had a feeling. I knew it would be bad luck."

"No. My own stupid fault. I was so determined to dig, so determined to find that treasure."

"It was the bet—"

"Uh-uh. I just wanted to get it done. But I should have anticipated the problem. Take the ground out from under a rock and it's gonna fall."

"You didn't take much out. I had to have been the rain."

"I should have seen it coming."

"*I* should have. I was the one sitting there watching. If I'd been able to give you a few more seconds' warning . . ."

Noah curved his hand around the back of her neck and brought her face to his throat. "Not your fault." He kissed her temple and left his mouth there. "I'm glad you're with me."

She lifted her face and kissed him. "I just wish there were something I could do to make you more comfortable."

"How about . . . that drink . . ."

She quickly dug into the knapsack, extracted first a can of Coke, then, more satisfactorily, a bottle of wine. Tugging out the cork, she handed it to him. "Want a sandwich with it?"

He tipped the bottle and took several healthy swallows. "And dilute the effects? No way?"

"You want to get smashing drunk?"

He took another drink. "Not smashing. Just mildly." He closed his eyes again, and the expression of pain that crossed his face tore right through Shaye.

"Is it getting worse?" she whispered fearfully.

He said nothing for a minute, but seemed to be gritting his teeth. Then he took a shaky breath and opened his eyes. "Talk to me."

"About what?"

"You."

"Me? There's nothing much to say—"

"I want to hear about the past. I want to hear about all the things you've sidestepped before."

"I haven't—"

"You have."

She searched his eyes, seeing things that went beyond the physical pain he was experiencing. "Why does it matter?"

"Because I love you."

She put her fingertips to his mouth, caressing his lips moments before she leaned forward and kissed them. "I didn't expect you in my life, Noah," she breathed brokenly, then kissed him again.

"Tell me what you feel."

"Frightened. Confused." She sought out his lips again, craving their drugging effect.

He gave himself up to her kiss, but as soon as it ended, the pain was back. "Talk to me."

She carried his hand to her mouth and kissed his knuckles.

"My leg hurts like hell, Shaye. If you want to help, you can give me something to think about beside the fact that it's probably broken in at least three places."

"Don't say that—"

"Not to mention scraped raw."

"Noah—"

"I may well be lame for life."

"Don't even think that!"

"Tell me you wouldn't care."

"If you were lame? Of course, I'd care! The thought of your being in pain—"

"Tell me that you wouldn't care if I were lame, that you'd love me anyway."

"I'd love you if *both* legs were lame! What a stupid thing to ask."

"Not stupid," he said quietly, soberly, almost grimly. "Not stupid at all. Do you love me, Shaye?"

Shocked, she looked at him.

"Do you?" he prodded.

She bit her lip. "Yes."

"You haven't thought about it before now?"

"I've tried not to."

"But you do love me?"

She frowned. "If loving a person means that you like him even when you hate him, that you think about him all the time, that you hurt when he's hurt—" she took a tremulous breath "—the answer is yes."

"Ahh, baby," he said with a groan that held equal parts relief and pain. He drew her in close and held her as tightly as his awkward sideways position would allow.

"I love you," she whispered against his chest, "do love you."

His arms tightened. He winced, then groaned, then mumbled, "Talk to me. Talk to me, Shaye. Please?"

There seemed no point in holding back. With the confession he'd drawn from her, Noah had broken down the last of her defenses. He knew her. He knew what made her tick. He knew what pleased her, hurt her, drove her wild. Revealing the details of her past to him was little more than a formality.

Closing her eyes, Shaye began to talk. She told him about her childhood and the teenage years when she'd grown progressively wild. She told him about going off to college, about being free and irresponsible and believing that she had the world on a string. She told him about the boys and the men, the trips, the adventures, the apartments and the garret. Once started, she spilled it all. She wanted Noah to know everything.

For the most part, he listened quietly. Once or twice he made ceremony of wiping the rain from his face, but she suspected he was covering up a wince. At those times she stopped, offered him aspirin, and finally plied him with more wine, which was all the painkilling he'd accept. And she went on talking.

Only when she was near the end did she falter. She grew still, eyes downcast, hands tightly clenched.

"What happened then?" he prodded in a voice weakened by pain. "You were with André when you got a call from Shannon, and . . . ?"

She raked her teeth over her lower lip.

"Shaye?"

She took a broken breath. "She was in trouble. She'd been hanging around a pal of André's named Geoff, and when he introduced her to another guy, a friend of his, she didn't think anything of it. The friend turned out to be from the vice squad. Poor Shannon. She was nineteen at the time, not nearly sophisticated enough to protect herself from the Geoffs of the world. He was picked up on a dozen charges. She was arrested for possession of cocaine. She never knew what hit her."

"And you blamed yourself."

"I was at fault. I'd introduced her to André, André had introduced her to Geoff. I should have checked Geoff out myself." She waved a hand impatiently. "But it was more than that. The whole *scene* was wrong. Rebellion for the sake of rebellion, adventure of the sake of adventure, sex for the sake of sex—very little that went deeper, and nothing at all that resulted in personal growth. For six years I did that." She was shaking all over. "Blame myself? Not only was I responsible for what happened to Shannon, by rights, I should have been the one arrested!"

"Shh," Noah whispered against her temple. "It's okay."

"It's not!"

"What finally happened to Shannon?"

Shaye took several quick breaths to calm herself. "Victoria came to the rescue. She introduced us to a lawyer friend who introduced us to another lawyer friend, and between the two of them, Shannon got off with a suspended sentence and probation. She went on for a degree in communications and has a terrific job now in Hartford."

He shifted, and swallowed down a moan. The pain in his leg was excruciating. He had to keep his mind off it. "Sounds like she got off lighter than you did," he said tightly.

"Lighter?"

"You sentenced yourself to a lifetime of hard labor."

"No. I just decided to become very sane and sensible."

"Where do I fit into sane and sensible?"

She smoothed wet hair back from her forehead with the flat of her hand. "I don't know."

"Do you see me as being sane and sensible?"

"In some respects, yes. In others, no."

"And the 'no's' frighten you."

She nodded.

"Why?"

"Because I can't control them. Because you can be spontaneous and impulsive and irreverent, and that's everything I once was that nearly ended tragically!"

"But you like it when I'm that way. That's part of the attraction."

"I know," she wailed.

"And it's not bad. Look at it rationally, Shaye. You're nearly thirty now. Your entire outlook on life has matured since the days when you were wild." He caught in a breath, squeezed his eyes shut, finally went on in a raspy voice. "But you haven't found a man to love because the men you allow yourself to see don't excite you. You'd never have allowed yourself to see me if we'd met back in civilization, would you?"

"No."

"But there's nothing wrong with what we share! Okay, so we go nuts together in bed. Is that harmful? If it's just the two of us, and we're consenting adults, and we get up in the morning perfectly sane and sensible. Where's the harm?" His voice had risen steadily in pitch, and he was breathing raggedly by the time he finished.

"Oh God, Noah," she whispered. "What can I do—"

"Talk. Just talk."

She did, trying her best to tune out his pain. "I hear what you're saying. It makes perfect sense. But then I get to worrying and even the sensible seems precarious."

"You trust me?"

"I . . . yes."

"And love me?"

She nodded.

"Nothing is precarious. I'll protect you."

"But I have to be responsible, myself. That was one of the first things I learned from Shannon's fiasco."

"Ahh, Shaye, Shaye . . ." He tightened his arm around her shoulder and pressed his cheek to her wet hair. "You've gone to extremes. You don't have to be on guard every minute. There are times to let go and times not to." He stopped, garnering his strength. "Where's the lightness in your life, the sunshine, the frivolity? We all need that sometimes. Not all the time, just sometimes. There has to be a balance—don't you see?" His words had grown more and more strained. He loosened his hold on her and took a long drink of wine.

Shaye looked up, eyes wide. She stroked the side of his face with the backs of her fingers. "Don't talk so much, Noah. Please. It must be taking something out of you."

"It's the only thing that's helping. No, that's not true. The wine helps. And you. Your being here. Marry me, Shaye. I want you to marry me."

"I—"

"It looks like the trip is going to be cut short. We have to face the future."

"But—"

"I love you, Shaye. I didn't plan to fall in love. I've never really been in love before in my life. But I do love you."

"But these are such...bizarre circumstances. How can you possibly know what your feelings will be back in the real world?"

"I know my feelings," he said with a burst of strength. "I know what's been wrong with my life, what's been missing in the women I've known. You have everything I want. You're dignified and poised and intelligent. You're witty and gentle. You're compassionate and loyal. You're gorgeous. And you're spectacular in my arms. I meant it when I said I wanted you to mother my children. I do want that, Shaye. But I want you first and foremost for *me*." He punctuated the last with a loud, involuntary groan, followed by a pithy oath.

Shaye was on her knees in a minute, cradling his dripping face with both hands. "Let me get the codeine."

He shook his head. "Wine." He lifted the bottle and swallowed as much as he could.

"Where are they?" she cried, looking out to sea.

"They've just left. Won't be back until morning."

"Morning! Why morning?"

"It's a lee coast. We lucked out yesterday. It'll take them a while to reach Limón—"

"Isn't Moin closer?"

"No resources. Samson may try it, but by the time he locates a rescue team—"

"He has to do something before morning. You're in pain."

"Make that agony."

"This is no time for joking, Noah."

"I'm not."

"Oh. Oh God, isn't there anything I can do?"

"Say you'll marry me."

"I'll marry you."

"Ahh. Feels better already." He pried his head from the poncho. "Is there another bottle of wine?"

She reached for the bottle he held and saw that it was nearly empty. With relief, she found two more bottles in the knapsack. Opening one, she gave it to Noah in exchange for the first, the contents of which she proceeded to indulge in herself.

Had she just agreed to marry Noah?

She took another drink.

He drew her against his chest and encircled her with his arms, leaving the wine bottle to dangle against her side. "I need to hold on," he said, his voice husky with pain.

"Hold on," she whispered. "Hold on."

They sat like that for a while. Shaye heard the rain and the lap of the sea on the shore, but mostly she heard Noah's heart, beating erratically beneath her ear.

"I'm well-respected in the community," he muttered out of the blue. "I give to charity. I pay my taxes. Okay, so I do the unexpected from time to time, but I've never done anything illegal or immoral."

Gently, soothingly, she stroked his ribs, working at the tension in the surrounding muscles.

"I'll buy us a place midway between Manhattan and Philly, so you won't have to leave your job."

She kissed his collarbone.

"In fact," he rushed on, "you don't have to work at all if you don't want to. I'm loaded."

She laughed.

"I am," he protested.

"I believe you," she said, still smiling, thinking how incredibly much she did love him.

He took a shuddering breath, then another drink of wine. "I want the whole thing—the house, the kids, the dog, the station wagon."

"You do?"

"Don't you?"

"Yes, but I didn't think you would."

"Too conventional?"

"No, no. Very stable."

He closed a fist around her ponytail, pressed her head to his throat and moaned, "This isn't how it was supposed to be. There's nothing romantic in this. It's *sick*. My damn leg's caught under a rock. I can't move. I can't sweep you off your feet and carry you to bed, or bend you back over my arm and kiss you senseless. I'm not sure I can even get it up—that's how much everything down there hurts!"

Shaye knew he was in severe pain. She knew he was feeling frustrated. She couldn't do anything about either, so she decided to use humor. "The Playboy of the Pampas—impotent?"

"Not impotent—temporarily sidelined. You'll still marry me, won't you?"

"I'll still marry you." She took a deep breath and looked around. "It is a waste, though. We did so well in the rain last night, just think of what we could have done tonight." She moved her lips against his jaw, her voice an intimate whisper. "I'd like to make love in the water. Not deep water—shallow, just a few feet out from shore. Do you remember how it was when we were swimming? Only this time neither of us would have suits on, and there'd be a sandy floor for maneuvering, but the tide would wash around us. I'd wrap my legs around you—"

Noah interrupted her with a feral growl. "Enough. You've made your point."

"I have?"

He tried to shift to a more comfortable position, which was nearly impossible, given the circumstances.

Shaye felt instantly contrite. "Can I help?" she whispered, dropping her hand to his swollen sex.

He covered it and pressed it close for a minute, then raised it to his chest. "I think I'll take a rain check."

He took another drink, then held the bottle to her lips while she did the same. The sounds of the rain and the sea and the jungle night surrounded them, and for a time they sat in silence. Then Shaye asked, "The lanterns will keep the alligators away, won't they?"

He nodded.

"Hungry?"

He shook his head.

"Is there any chance of this hole flooding?"

He shook his head again.

"Do you have Blue Cross-Blue Shield?"

"Through the nose." A little while later, he said, "Maybe you're pregnant."

"No."

"Are you taking the pill?"

"No. But my period just ended. Last night was about as safe a time as any could be."

He considered that, then said, "No wonder you felt so lousy at the start of the trip."

She snorted. "You should have seen me when we first got to the hotel in Barranquilla."

"Don't use anything."

"What?"

"When we make love. I like knowing that there's a chance . . ."

"You really do want children."

"Very much. If you want to wait, though. I'll understand."

But the more she thought about it, the more Shaye liked the idea of growing big with Noah's child. She smiled into the night.

"You are going to marry me, aren't you?" he asked.

"I've said I would."

"What if you change your mind?"

"I won't."

"What if you have second thoughts when we get back home?"

"I won't."

"Why not?"

"I can't answer that now. Ask me again later."

He did, several times during the course of the night, but it wasn't until a pair of helicopters closed noisily in on the beach the following morning that Shaye had an answer for him.

She'd been with Noah throughout the night, had suffered with him and worried for him, had done what little she could to make him comfortable. She'd forced him to eat half a sandwich for the sake of his strength and had limited her own intake of wine to leave more for him. She'd sponged him off when the rain stopped and the air grew thick and heavy. She'd batted mosquitoes from his skin and had held his hand tightly when he'd twisted in pain.

The night had been hell. She never wanted to live through another like it. But she knew she wouldn't have been anywhere else in the world that night, and that was what she told Noah when the sheer relief of his impending rescue loosened her thoughts.

"You have the ability to make me happy, sad, excited, frustrated, angry, aroused and confused—but through it all I feel incredibly alive."

She combed her fingers through his hair. "You have the spirit and the sense of adventure I had before, only you've channeled it right." Affectionately she brushed some sand off his neck. "I want you to help me do that. Make my life full. Be my friend and protector." She kissed his forehead. "And lover. I want all that and more." She shot a glance at the crew bounding from the chopper, then tacked on, "Think you can handle it?"

He was a mess—dirty, sweaty, with one leg crushed beneath a boulder—but the look he sent her was eloquent in promise and love. She knew that she'd never, never forget it.

Epilogue

"TWO HELICOPTERS?" Deirdre asked.

Victoria nodded. "One for the medics, the other for the fellows who raised the rock."

Leah winced. "Noah must have been out of his mind with pain by that time."

"He was out of it with something—whether pain or wine, I'll never know. The doctors in Limón did a preliminary patch-up job while Samson arranged for our transportation home. Noah's had surgery twice in the six weeks we've been back. He's scheduled to go in for a final procedure next week."

"Is the prognosis good?"

"Excellent, thank God. But even if it weren't, Noah's a fighter." She sighed. "He's quite a man."

Deirdre curled her legs beneath her on the chaise. It was the last day in August, a rare cool, dry, sunny summer day in New York, and Victoria's rooftop garden was the place to be. "When did they get married?"

Victoria smiled. "Four days after we got back. It was beautiful. Very simple. A judge, their closest friends and relatives." Her eyes grew misty. "Shaye was radiant. I know they say that about all brides, but she was. She positively glowed. And when Noah...presented her with...that single rose..."

Leah handed her a tissue, which Victoria waved around, as though it didn't occur to her to wipe her tears.

"When he gave her the rose, he said...he said—" her voice dropped to a tremulous whisper "—so softly and gently that I wouldn't have heard if I hadn't been standing right there..."

Both women were waiting wide-eyed. Deirdre leaned forward and asked urgently, "What did he say?"

Victoria sniffled. "He said, 'One rose. Just one. Pure, fresh and new. And it's in our hands.'" She took in a shuddering breath. "It was so . . . beautiful . . ." She pressed the tissue to her trembling lip.

Leah didn't understand the deeper significance of Noah's words any more than Deirdre did, but the romance of it was still there. She sighed loudly, then burst into a helpless smile. "Victoria Lesser strikes again." She was delighted with Victoria's latest story. She'd had no idea what to expect when Victoria had invited her down for a visit, and now she couldn't wait to get back to tell Garrick. But there was still more she wanted to know. "What about you and Samson?"

Victoria took a minute to collect herself. "Yes?"

"I thought you liked him. You said that in spite of the accident the trip was wonderful."

"It was."

"Well?" Deirdre prompted. "Is that all you have to say—just that it was wonderful? Neil will spend the entire night cross-examining me if I don't have anything better to give him when I get home."

Gracefully pushing herself from her chair, Victoria breezed across the garden to pluck a dried petal from a hanging begonia. "It'd serve you right," she said airily, "after what the four of you did."

"It was poetic justice," Deirdre argued.

Leah agreed. "Just deserts."

"A taste of your own medicine."

"Lex talionis." When Victoria turned to arch a brow her way, Leah translated. "The law of retribution. But all with the

best of intentions." She paused. "So. Were our good intentions in vain?"

Victoria hesitated for a long moment. Her gaze skipped from Leah's face to Deirdre's. Then she slanted them both a mischievous grin. "I won't remarry, you know."

"We know," Deirdre said.

"He was . . . very nice."

Leah held her breath. "And . . . ?"

"And we've decided to make a return visit to Costa Rica next summer to find out for sure whether that treasure does exist. Noah and Shaye weren't thrilled with that thought; they're hung up on the idea of going to some château in Normandy. So we'll just have to put together another group. In the meantime, Samson thought he'd do a bicycle tour of the Rhineland and asked if I'd like to go along."

"Where does he get the time?" Deirdre asked. "I thought he taught."

"Vacations, sweetheart. Vacations." Her eyes twinkled and her cheeks grew pink. "And weekends. There are lovely things that can be done on weekends." Turning her back on the two younger women, she busied herself hand pruning a small dogwood. "I was thinking that I'd drive north next month. The foliage is beautiful when it turns. Samson has invited me to stay with him in Hanover, claims he makes a mean apple cider. Now, theoretically, making apple cider should be as boring as sin. But then, theoretically, Latin professors should be as boring as sin, too, and Samson isn't. I guess I'll have to give his apple cider a shot. . . ."

DAILEY